N IN THE

ESS

TAINS

MICKELSSON'S GHOSTS

MICKELSSON'S

GHOSTS

a novel

John Gardner

Illustrated with photographs by Joel Gardner

ALFRED A. KNOPF   NEW YORK   1982

THIS IS A BORZOI BOOK
PUBLISHED BY ALFRED A. KNOPF, INC.

Copyright © 1982 by John Gardner
Photographs Copyright © 1982 by Joel Gardner
All rights reserved under International and
Pan-American Copyright Conventions. Published
in the United States by Alfred A. Knopf, Inc.,
New York, and simultaneously in Canada by
Random House of Canada Limited, Toronto.
Distributed by Random House, Inc., New York.

Library of Congress Cataloging in Publication Data
Gardner, John [date]
Mickelsson's ghosts.
I. Title.
PS3557.A712M5   1982   813'.54   81–48114
ISBN 0–394–50468–2   AACR2

Manufactured in the United States of America
FIRST EDITION

To Liz

ACKNOWLEDGMENTS

One of the songs sung in the fictional recital in this novel is adapted from "Agonies of Heaven," by Hakim Yama Khayyam. For Mickelsson's philosophical broodings I am especially in debt to R. M. Hare and to Daniel C. Maguire, whose writings I frequently quote, usually in altered form. I am indebted, too, to Alasdair MacIntyre (*After Virtue*). I've borrowed ideas and good lines from various other philosophical writers and poets, past and present, notably Martin Luther (and one of his biographers, H. G. Heile), Friedrich Nietzsche, Ludwig Wittgenstein, Norman O. Brown, Martin Heidegger, the late Walter Kaufmann (who would mainly not approve of my treatment of Nietzsche), and from numerous acquaintances, friends, and loved ones, especially my wife, L. M. Rosenberg. The diligent will perhaps discover that I have additional literary sources, more than I know myself, among those sources the fiction of John Updike and Joyce Carol Oates and some of the poems of Carl Dennis. I am also indebted to Jack Wilcox, who helped remove from the story some philosophical improbabilities, suggested books I might read, and so on. Any stupidities which survive must be blamed on the characters. Where this novel touches on historical Mormonism, I am indebted mainly to two books, Fawn M. Brodie's *No Man Knows My History: The Life of Joseph Smith*, and William Wise's *Massacre at Mountain Meadows: An American Legend and a Monumental Crime*. This novel's incursions into the kingdom of the peacetime and wartime nuclear industry, the various industrial-waste depositors, and so on, are based on books and articles too numerous and various to cite. I would like to express special gratitude to Craig and Alice Gilborn, of the Adirondack Museum, who gave me a place to write, as well as friendship and inspiration, and the English Department at SUNY-Binghamton, who gave me time and mechanical assistance, as well as advice and encouragement. My special thanks, too, to Bernard and Evelyn Rosenthal, Pat Wilcox, Burton Weber, Carl Dennis, Susan Strehle, William Spanos, my children Joel and Lucy Gardner, and my wife, Liz, all of whom read the manuscript in various stages and helped me see mistakes—not that there aren't still plenty.

Though based on and named for real places, the settings in this novel are essentially fictitious. I've moved things around (for instance the old Susquehanna depot restaurant and what locals call the Oakland block) to suit plot convenience. So far as I know there are no ghosts in Susquehanna County, but looking at the place one feels there ought to be. If there are witches, I've never run into one.

The town of Susquehanna, Pennsylvania, fictionalized setting of most of this novel's action, is not, in real life, the dire, moribund place my story makes it, though at the time this story was set the town was endangered. It is a town that has more than once come close to extinction. In 1919, at the time of the great railroad strike in Susquehanna, the townspeople took the side of the striking railroad workers, fought the scabs and resisted the railroad executives, with the result that the railroad made a decision to abandon the town. The railroad then employed some two thousand Susquehanna workers and indirectly supported many more. When the railroad broke off all dealings with the town, Susquehanna staggered but somehow remained on its feet. It has similarly resisted more recent strokes of bad luck, mainly thanks to the town's pervasive sense of humor and stubborn independence, and the urgent concern with which people take care of one another. As of this writing the old railroad depot (which was not in fact demolished, though it was badly decayed) is being restored to its former grandeur by a local businessman, Mike Matis. It will be the last Victorian railroad hotel in America, and it was from the beginning one of the most grand and beautiful, an architectural wonder worthy to stand, as it does, not far from the immense and justly famous stone-hewn Starucca Viaduct. And a local park and dam project promises to free Susquehanna from dependence on outsiders for electricity. So this novel, insofar as it treats Susquehanna as a gloomy, dying place, is fiction, or fictionalized recent history. It tells of what might have happened and nearly did, but didn't. The old rusted sign mentioned in this story— VACATION IN THE ENDLESS MOUNTAINS—gives good advice. If any neighbor, having heard me say this, still feels ill-served, let him be angry at Peter Mickelsson, the "hero," so to speak, of this novel. I've done my best with him, but the man's a lunatic. May he get his just deserts hereafter.

PART ONE

1

Sometimes the sordidness of his present existence, not to mention the stifling, clammy heat of the apartment his finances had forced him to take, on the third floor of an ugly old house on Binghamton's West Side—"the nice part of town," everybody said (God have mercy on those who had to live in the bad parts)—made Peter Mickelsson clench his square yellow teeth in anger and once, in a moment of rage and frustration greater than usual, bring down the heel of his fist on the heavy old Goodwill oak table where his typewriter, papers, and books were laid out, or rather strewn. He'd intended to split the thing in two, though perhaps the intent was not quite conscious. In any case, no such luck. He was strong; a weight-lifter, once (in his college days) a frequently written about football player, though no one any longer remembered that; but the ringed and cigarette-scarred table had proved too much for him. For days he'd had to walk with his right hand in his pocket, too sore to lift a pencil. At times like that Mickelsson wished his estranged wife—still living in style, back in Providence—dead. The rest of the time what he felt was not anger but a great, sodden depression.

He could see from one end of the apartment to the other—kitchen and diningroom at one end, livingroom at the other, sloping-roofed bedroom and entryway to one side—but he couldn't see out. Though the apartment had windows at either end, they opened onto branches and lush green leaves of immense old maples, so close that, if he'd wanted, he could have poked through the screen to reach his arm out and pick a few clusters of winged pods. On windy nights the trees brushed the walls and roof above his head. Occasionally as he sat in just his undershorts and sandals, wiping sweat from his forehead, armpits, and back, slapping at flies, moths, Junebugs, or mosquitoes, his eyes would unfocus and drift up slowly from the print before him, and he would brood for a moment on the idea of renting a small, cheap place in the country, maybe getting himself a second-hand air-conditioner. He would sigh, take off his glasses, wipe sweat from his eyelids, and after a while return his attention to his book. Rarely did Mickelsson read anything he did not hate.

It would be pleasant, he thought, not to feel hemmed in by the so-called faculty ghetto: big, boxy houses of brick and wood, drably painted brown, green, yellow, or blue, about a fourth of them partly supported by shabby, tree-crowded apartments like his own—stained ceilings, lumpy cracked linoleum, threadbare rugs, furniture that looked as if, years ago, it had been left out in snow and rain. In the country, if he felt like walking late at night he could be fairly sure of meeting no one he knew, only deer, raccoons, porcupines, maybe owls; and if he felt like working he would not be always listening for an unwelcome too hearty knock. For an unpopular teacher, as he knew he was, Mickelsson got a surprising number of visits from students or young colleagues who just happened to be passing. Presumably it had to do with the fact that he was alone and could generally be counted on to be in—he rarely went to parties, no more than one or two a month—and also with the fact that, for a man of his circumstances, he had a well-stocked liquor cabinet. "We saw your light was on," they would say, "so we said to ourselves . . ." smiling brightly, eagerly, as if afraid of spending a night out there alone, cold sober. Despite his irritation, he sympathized. "Come in, make yourselves at home," he would say, so gloomy of eye it was somewhat surprising that they accepted, though they always did. They would sit chatting earnestly, emptily, for hours—sometimes of the heat, sometimes of politics, sometimes of trash they'd picked up at local auctions—taking refill after refill, helping themselves, drinking and laughing in his kitchen sometimes even after Mickelsson said his good-nights and went to bed.

He resented their coming up and guzzling his liquor, heavy as he was with financial responsibilities—hardly two nickels he could clink in his pocket; college expenses of his son and daughter, the heavy debts and expenses of his wife in Providence—and he resented even more his visitors' invasion of the narrow space his life's errors had left him, though it was true, he would admit, that he took some comfort from their proof that, contrary to what he'd always thought, misery was universal. All the same, with a house in the country he'd be spared such nuisances. He had work to do, all the more urgent for the fact that, of late, his creative juices had dried away to dust. And there would be obvious advantages to living some distance from where his hunchbacked, crazy-eyed department chairman was forever calling meetings, and every other night some fool was invited to read a paper on "Rationality$_1$ and Rationality$_2$" or "Whether," and where Heidegger's parlamblings on "Nothing" and "Not" and "the Nothing that Nothings" were the last supposedly respectable gasp of classical philosophy; where Ethics (Mickelsson's specialty, more or less) was quickly and impatiently snorted away, superseded by the positivist fairytale of "value-free objectivity"; where, worst of all (to tell the bitter, banal truth; and what could be worse than that this, of all things, should be "worst of all"?), people whose names he'd forgotten or never known were forever inviting him—pressuring him to come—to cocktail parties, most of them in honor of people about to retire, of whom he'd never heard.

But the place in the country remained, for the moment, an idle dream.

He had no time for house-hunting, and no energy. He labored on, struggling to read, think, and write—propping windows open, stirring the heavy, sticky air with a gray Monkey Ward's electric fan, taking frequent showers and, when depression weighed on him, trying to sleep, sprawled naked, his legs and arms thrown wide, on top of his musty, Bounce-scented sheets. The table-lamp by which he worked, leaning on one fist—or stared at some wretched girlie mag, strangling the goose—was as warm as an oven and threw a dead yellow light aflicker with shadows of insects. (He rarely changed the flypapers—he disliked touching them—and he distrusted the chemistry of pest-strips.) The whole apartment reeked of old tobacco from Mickelsson's pipe or, sometimes, cigarettes, and often in the morning it had, besides, a country barroom smell of beer or gin. Often, late at night, instead of working, he wrote long letters to his daughter and son, letters he would crumple and discard the next day, because they showed his drunkenness or—his children would think—imbalance.

Mickelsson, once the most orderly of men, a philosopher almost obsessively devoted to precision and neatness (despite his love of Nietzsche), distrustful if not downright disdainful of passion (his pencils always sharpened and formally lined up, from longest to shortest, even in his pocket), a man dispositionally the product of a long line of Lutheran ministers and one incongruous, inarticulately rebellious dairy farmer, Mickelsson's father . . . Who would have thought that he, Peter Mickelsson, could come to this? Sweating, drinking, listening for visitors, sleeping off depressions or hangovers, he wasted so much time (more and more, these days) he began to feel almost constant guilt and panic. His stomach was so sour he was forced to eat Di-Gels like candy. "So this is what it's like to be poor," he would say to himself, cocking one eyebrow or staring, suddenly lost, at the broken plastic soap-dish in his rusty shower stall. Moving with the crowd at the Binghamton July-fest, inching past tables of leatherwork, canned goods, dolls, ceramic ware, or moving in and out of booths displaying paintings and photographs, lacework, cabinetry, and tinwork (none of which Mickelsson could afford), he would find himself brought up short by some whiskey-reeking pan-handler in four-day-old whiskers, with bloodshot milky-blue eyes beginning to fall inward. Quickly, after the first, startled instant, Mickelsson would push his way past the man—merciless, shoving him away—thinking, with a tingle of alarm: "So this is what it leads to!"

Sometimes the feeling that his life was hopeless—and his misery to a large extent undeserved (like everyone else's, he began to fear)—would drive him down to the maple- or oak-lined streets at night, to prowl like a murderer, looking in through strangers' windows with mixed scorn and envy, avoiding those streets where he was likely to meet someone who knew him, from the university, someone who might pity him for living like a starveling graduate student or first-year instructor after all he'd been once, not long ago, a full professor in a prestigious university, with a house that would put all of these to shame; or someone who might want him to stop and chatter about campus politics or the general decline of student ability and educational standards; or some *Gelehrter* riding high on the crest of his career, who would be secretly amused to see Peter J. Mickelsson out walking, muttering to himself, late at night, Mickelsson who'd fooled them for a time, all right, but look at him now, furtively gesturing, lecturing the empty air! (Weren't there rumors that he'd had some kind of breakdown, back at Brown?) No doubt they weren't all of them as villainous as he imagined; one or two in his department seemed decent enough, and there was one professor of sociology, Jessica Stark, who was pleasant to talk to—an original mind and apparently good-hearted, and beautiful, to tell the truth—but on the whole, the less he had to do with these people the better. He knew what they said of him behind his back, knew the narrow margin that had gotten him his appointment and the fuss certain members of the department had made about whether or not he should arrive with tenure—he, who had outpublished the pack of them, one of the only two members of the department who could be said to have a national reputation.

Lately, of course, he'd been publishing practically nothing—as they'd no doubt noticed—and if that damned apartment was not the whole reason, it was certainly part of it: airless, oppressive, so hot that even when it was balmy outside, as it sometimes was on summer nights in Binghamton, sweat washed down his flesh in rivers. One prayed for rainy nights, but then when the rain came gloom came with it, such sharp memories of playing Chinese checkers or chess with his children—rain washing down the leaded windows, ocean-wind groaning through the heavy old trees, his daughter's soft blond hair lighted like hair in a sixteenth-century painting—he could no more work than fly. Often on rainy nights he would fix himself four or five large martinis in a row and go to bed (so much for saintly self-transcendence), where he would lie wide awake, staring at the ceiling or at the branches outside his window.

All this progressed.

Walking down the night or early-morning streets, most of them named for famous poets or composers, usually mispronounced (his own street was, locally, "Beeth-ohven"; but then, the State University of New York, his employer, was called "Sunny"), he would feel a great rage of frustration and general hatred of his complacent, well-off neighbors—though also he felt such terrible loneliness that sometimes he would find himself seeking out and moving slowly past the darkened apartments of unmarried female graduate students or middle-aged, unattached female colleagues. (Indeed, once or twice he even knocked at a door; once or twice he went in.) Sometimes he felt so misused and cheated, passing some large, dark, wide-gabled house, seeing a dim light burning in the bathroom, or the ghostly aura of a television set—two or three expensive bicycles on the porch—it was all he could do to keep from howling like a wolf, or snatching things up out of the gutter and throwing them through windows. What a joy it would be to hear those spotless, innocently staring panes go crash! He kept himself moving, allowed himself no pause, no thoughtful lingering—not that, really, the temptation was more than a brief, waking dream. He walked cocked forward, as if pitched against high wind, a largish, stout man in dark, tight trousers and a darker shirt, around his thick neck (if the night air was cool) an ascot tie, two fingers clamped tightly on the brim of his hat, holding it down firmly—not really to protect it from gusts, one might have thought, but as if, freed of the pressure of his hat, his head might explode—his steps quick and heavy, stamping out small lives, his short, stubby pipe or sometimes cigarette sending up smoke-clouds, flags of his own mortality, in quick, white puffs. His hair was unkempt and red, as his father's had been and as his son's was yet, his own now ominously graying in tight iron curls at the temples and neck. He walked faster and faster, his shadow stretching and shrinking under streetlamps, until he thought he might have a heart attack; and then at last the fit would pass.

He found his well-being, if one could call it that, increasingly dependent on these late-night walks. Not that even his walks were exactly carefree. Sometimes large dogs would come out at him; or the hulking silhouettes of teen-aged boys, gathered on some porch, would suddenly fall silent as he passed. He'd taken to carrying a heavy walking-stick he'd picked up at one of Binghamton's innumerable antique stores. It was intended only for self-defense—or less than self-defense, mere symbolic protection—though it had also aesthetic and social functions useful to Mickelsson just now. It was an article from the age of well-made objects, the age when possessions were adornments of a life presumed-until-proven-otherwise to be noble and worthwhile. That presumption had, for Mickelsson, lost force, though it was, when one came right down to it, the whole basis of his ethical theory, every word he'd written through all those ruinous years. Lately he'd come to be increasingly cynical, increasingly impressed by accident: chance virtue, chance wickedness, at best the magpie gatherings of emotivism. He'd paid too little attention to deep-down meanness—the right wing shaking its Jesus-loving, eager-to-kill, fat fists over "the horror of abortion"—all those hundreds of thousands of poor dead babies—the left wing sweating with pious indignation over all those poor dead mothers. "Atheists! Antichrists!" one side screamed. "Motherfuckers! Assholes! Baptist shit-heads!" the other screamed back. A noble debate. He did not doubt that human beings had the equipment to make relatively unbestial choices, but he doubted more and more that they would ever get around to it or that, in the final analysis, it mattered. If Life had become for him less the grand thing he'd once supposed it, the so-called

Life of the Mind—of which he'd once written so glowingly—now fared even worse with him, seemed to him, in fact, a joke. Mind. God help us! The country was gearing up to make its stupendous intellectual choice between Reagan and Carter, or possibly Ted Kennedy. The newspapers had long since moved their tear-jerker stories of starving Cambodians back to page 22, making room for new horrors. Mainly Iran and the hostages. (Every gas station had its picture of Uncle Sam looking stern, however futilely, and its emptily ferocious legend "Let my people go!") Carter became thinner of voice every day, Reagan—in his dyed hair and make-up —more jokey. In such a world Mickelsson's walking-stick, with its smooth, dark, glowing wood, silver-tipped, and its heavy silver handle in the shape of the head of a lioness, was comforting, a steadying force; or so he would tell himself, holding the cane to the light, admiring it one more time, up in his kitchen, or swinging it jauntily, firmly grasping the head as he walked dark streets, his broad hat cocked.

One night, passing down a narrow, shabby, poorly lit street where he'd seldom walked before—dull houses, each with its enclosed or open or long-ago-screened-in, full-width porch, its light over the door (turned off by this hour), its one large or two small windows, its rusty porch-glider, fridge, potted plants—Mickelsson suddenly froze in his tracks, the hair on the back of his neck rising. Right in front of him on the sidewalk, barring his path, stood a large, pitchdark chunk of shadow—a dog, he realized after an instant: a black Doberman, or perhaps a Great Dane. It simply stood there, head level with Mickelsson's waist, not growling but firmly blocking passage. Seconds fell away. Mickelsson could see no one to call to, no movement anywhere, though from somewhere not far off came the tinny noise of a TV.

Now the dog did begin to growl: a low, uncertain rumble. Carefully, making no sudden movements, Mickelsson shifted the cane to both hands and raised it like a bat. And then, an instant before he knew he would do it, quick as a snake, he brought down the cane with all his might, aiming for the animal's head. To his surprise—then horror—the dog did not leap back with the predictable lightning quickness of its kind, nor did it, as Mickelsson had expected, lunge forward to bite him. It simply went down the way cows had gone down at slaughtering time, when his father hit them between the horns with the eight-pound maul. Perhaps the dog was old, half blind, half deaf. In any case, down it went, almost without a sound—no snarl, just the crack of the canehead striking home, then the *huff* of escaping breath as the body struck the sidewalk. Mickelsson stared, the TV's rootless harmonics suddenly loud in his ears. It was too dark to see well, but he sensed, if he did not see, the death tremor. He turned left and right, looking around in alarm at the nearby porches and windows. Miraculously, no one seemed to have witnessed the thing. He moved the tip of the cane toward the animal, thinking of poking it to make sure it was dead, but then resisted the impulse. He raised the cane, thinking of hurling it away into the shrubbery, but again changed his mind, imagining the dog leaping up at him as soon as he was weaponless. He looked around one last time—still no one—then tucked the cane under his arm and fled.

Back in his apartment, with the door bolted, Mickelsson cleaned the head of the cane under the kitchen faucet with great care, though he could see no sign of hair or blood, then poured himself a drink and sat down with it at the kitchen table, swallowed half of the drink at once, and after that sat with his glasses off, his forehead on his fists, eyes narrowed, almost shut, trying to think what he should do. He would call the police if he were the ethicist he'd all his life claimed to be and thought himself; but that thought had hardly entered his mind before he pushed it away forever. Back in Providence, where he'd been well-to-do and respected, he'd have gone to the police at once; but in Providence he wouldn't have killed the dog.

It began to seem to him that when he'd first stood there, blocked by the thing on the sidewalk in front of him, a car had passed. Surely he was wrong: surely the lights would have shown him what kind of dog it was. No, then; there had definitely been no car. Yet somehow he couldn't convince himself. He remembered distinctly how, then or at some other time, headlights had shown him the rough bark on the tree just ahead of him, right beside the tilting, crumbling sidewalk, then the bark on the next tree and the next. He looked again at the silver cane-handle, dented now, the left eye of the lioness blanked out, as if blinded.

"Jesus," he whispered, almost prayerful, covering his eyes, reliving the moment of the dog's silent fall. Something nagged for his attention, then at last broke through: a siren, not far off. He listened as if his heart had stopped, then at last realized that it was moving away, not coming nearer —and not a police siren anyway; the ascending and sinking wail that meant somebody's house was on fire.

He got up, weak and heavy-limbed, his gorge full of acid, carried the walking-stick to the closet of the bedroom, and hid it in the darkest corner, behind an outgrown suit, the long brown bathrobe he never wore, and a box of old windowshades that had stood there, abandoned, when he'd moved in.

It was nonsense, of course, all this anguish of fear and guilt. No one had seen. And it had been, strictly speaking, an accident—at worst, an act of legitimate self-defense. The city had a leash law. Even if someone had seen him do it, no one could say he'd done anything wrong; the law was on his side. He compressed his lips. He was beginning to sound like Heidegger in the days of the Führer.

The kitchen smelled of old coffee grounds, stale tobacco, must and mould. Again vague alarm rose up in him, the peripheral sense of dread that comes when a dream begins to decay toward nightmare. At last the cause of his unease reached his consciousness: a mouse was stirring in the garbage bag or in one of the junk-filled drawers under the sink.

He looked up in alarm, freezing for an instant, then drawing back his head from the innards of the once-again jammed-up Xerox copying machine, hearing his name called—Geoffrey Tillson, his department chairman, bleating in a voice as thin as a bassoon's: "Professor Mickelsson, could I ask you to step in here a minute when you're free?"

His heart raced, but at once he steadied himself. By the chimpanzee grin old Tillson wore on his gray-bearded face (thrust forward and slung low, level with the rock-solid hump on his back), Mickelsson made out that, almost certainly, it was nothing, just some ordinary nuisance. The chairman, it must be, had a student in there with him, or a disgruntled parent, or someone from the State Education Office, in any case someone to be dealt with gently, petted and stroked, the kind of thing Mickelsson, mainly by virtue of his standing in the department, was thought to be good at. (It was summer vacation. The bastard had no right.) He stole a last look at the snarled-up paper trapped among plastic cams and mysterious metal pins. All day long things had been going wrong for him, as if even inanimate objects were hostile, wary of him. Then he straightened up, took his glasses from the top of the machine, and put them on— bifocal lenses for which everything in the world was slightly too near at hand or far away.

"I guess I'm more or less free now," he said, still blushing, and faked a laugh—two sharp hacks. He saw that the secretary's eye was on him, over behind the desk to the left of Tillson's open door. She seemed to be watching him suspiciously, and he blushed more deeply. He asked, as if to account for the blush, "Charlotte, do you think you could clear this thing for me?"

"Surely," she said, and at once stood up, automatically smoothing her skirt with one hand, giving him one of those pitying, superior smiles. No doubt she was a man-hater, her nice, secretarial smile masking private scorn. All pretty, well-built young women were despisers of men, these days, or all except the born-again Christians. His female students' papers were full of it. They batted their lashes and swung their rear ends, but their hearts seethed. Not that their anger was necessarily ill-advised. Here he was now, hunched over, looking irate and imploring, as domineering males had been doing for centuries, ever since they'd learned it was frequently quicker than hitting those fat little asses with sticks. He thought of saying, sheathing anger in a joke, "I'll pay you of course. Keep track of your time!" But the girl was still covertly eyeing him, and he decided he'd better not. They already had reason enough to believe he was crazy.

He worked on his expression, rolling down and buttoning his cuffs again, then moved toward Tillson's inner sanctum, smiling, holding his hand at half-ready, prepared for the necessary handshake. He entered with his head tipped forward like a bull's, one eyebrow raised, eyes dead serious, the rest of his features assembled to a hearty grin. They could always count on old Mickelsson, he thought; madman Mickelsson, born for better things, maybe for selling used cars. He was aware of Tillson's watchful eye and the queer, no doubt accidental gesture of the right hand raised toward his grizzled chin, two fingers lifted above the rest and aiming outward, like a claw raised to strike, or a papal blessing, or the sly cobra sign of ancient Tibetan art. The young man who turned to shake Mickelsson's hand had such glassy eyes and pallor of skin, color like a dead man's, that Mickelsson was for an instant almost thrown. Careful, he thought, and tightened the screws on his expression, letting no muscle slip.

"Professor Mickelsson," Tillson said, beaming with fake pleasure, "this is Michael Nugent. He's transferring into philosophy from engineering." He continued to beam, head twisted painfully up toward Mickelsson's, as if tickled pink to have the honor of introducing two such marvels. Tillson's black trousers were baggy at the knees. His shapeless black coat hung forlorn on the back of his chair. His tie was wide and wrinkled, not quite clean.

"Glad to meet you, Michael," Mickelsson said. He gave him a nod and put the smile on *energize*. "Good to have you with us! Glad you saw the light!"

The boy mumbled something, accepting Mickelsson's football-coach handshake without returning it—not just responding limply, but actively refusing to respond (or so it seemed)—and his eyes, meeting Mickelsson's, threw a challenge. Clearly something was eating the boy. The leaden skin, the reddened eyelids, the nervous, weak mouth like a child's all gave ominous warning. He wore a blue, pressed workshirt with starch in the collar, and neat, pressed slacks, such clothes as nobody in philosophy had worn since the fifties. His elbows and knuckles and the tip of his nose were red, as if scrubbed with Fels Naptha. Mickelsson drew his hand back.

"Professor Mickelsson, as you may know, is our department's most distinguished philosopher," Tillson said, and he put one hand on Nugent's arm, the other on Mickelsson's, preparing to press them subtly toward the door. Mickelsson smiled on, though he knew pretty well what the praise was worth, and he kept his eyes, with their familiar look of (he knew) intense, crazed interest, on the young man's face. What a world, Mickelsson was thinking. Tillson and himself, arch-enemies, shepherding another poor innocent—fugitive from the clean, honest field of Engineering—into the treacherous, ego-bloated, murder-stained hovel of philosophy. But Mickelsson was a team man, at least when he was set up for public view—

had been one all his life, even here in the Department of Philosophy he none too secretly despised. The show of happy solidarity rose in him instinctively, which was one of the reasons Tillson called on him in delicate cases like this one, whatever the delicacy of the moment might be (he would learn soon enough, he knew).

"What I thought, Pete," Tillson said, "was that maybe you could run over Mr. Nugent's program with him—help him figure out what he'll need, what he might take first, and so on. What he might manage to get out of. Ha ha. Little fatherly guidance." His face took on, briefly, a startled look; then he jerked the smile wider, the edges of his moustache twitching from the strain, and asked Nugent, "Did I remember to give you your papers back?" He looked over at the low table in front of the couch where he liked to take cat-naps—the tabletop was littered with professional magazines and a clumsy stack of student papers—then over at the desk, finally at the young man's left hand, rising now as if of its own accord to show a ragged sheaf of forms and the computerized Fall Schedule of Courses. "Ah, good, good! If my head weren't screwed on—" He raised his smile toward Mickelsson again, gave a little wink, and, as if without knowing he was doing it, began pushing Mickelsson and Nugent gently out of the room.

"Fine! No problem!" Mickelsson said, so heartily that probably not even Tillson understood that nothing could be farther from the truth.

As soon as the three of them were outside his office, Tillson pretended to have a memory flash and, catching Mickelsson's arm again, said, "Oh, there's something I meant to ask you, Pete." He turned to the boy. "Would you excuse us just a moment? It shouldn't take more than a second or two." He laughed. He was already leading Mickelsson back in, drawing the door shut behind him, tossing the boy one last apologetic nod. "Sorry about this, Pete," he said when the door was closed. "I know you don't deal with undergraduate advising—"

"What's up?" Mickelsson asked, hoping to cut past the chit-chat. He shifted his eyes away, forcing himself not to stare at Tillson's hump.

"You do go straight at things, don't you," Tillson said, but smiling, edging away toward his desk. He cranked his head around, rolling his eye back at Mickelsson like a sheep. "I got a call from the dean about Nugent, out there. It seems he's been going through something of a crisis—attempted suicide, apparently depressed about the death of his father. A sad, sad business." He shook his head, involuntarily raising two fingers to his beard. "I don't know all the details, I'm afraid. It seems Blickstein and the boy had a talk, and I understand the boy's dead set on"—Tillson's ironic smile twitched briefly—"'the consolation of philosophy.' " Again he rolled his eyes up at Mickelsson. "I'm sure you'll agree that's more your line than mine. Maybe more your line than anybody else's in this department."

"It's true," Mickelsson said, unable to resist, "I do still try to deal with life-and-death issues from time to time. But it hardly makes me a psychiatrist."

"Yes of course. I realize—"

"It sounds to me as if the young man shouldn't be in school at all," Mickelsson pushed on, slightly reddening. "If we're so hard up for students we've got to rob the state hospitals—"

"Now listen! Take it easy!" Tillson said, surprised, reaching out to touch Mickelsson's forearm. "It's not a question of state hospitals!" He peered into Mickelsson's eyes as if trying to read his peculiar, twisted mind. "I must say," he said—the smile twitched, then vanished—"I have no *idea* whether or not he belongs in school—"

"Yes, I see," Mickelsson broke in. "I'm sorry." Before he could stop himself, he wiped his forehead with his shirtsleeve. "You're right, I'm probably the one who should advise him." He forced a laugh.

"You've been under a strain," Tillson said, somewhat questioningly, as if to see if that were it.

"It's that God damned apartment," Mickelsson said, and laughed again.

"You ought to get out of there," Tillson said. For an instant he looked much older, distinctly smaller. "You oughtta get a really good lawyer, Pete. It's just not right."

Mickelsson looked down, abruptly formal. "We'll see," he said. "Right now I'd better go deal with our angry young friend."

Nugent sat rigid, as if straining every muscle to appear relaxed, nothing moving but his rapidly blinking red eyelids. His red-knuckled hands lay loosely folded, and his knees hung far apart, the outsides of his upper legs jammed against the fronts of the chair-arms. He sat to Mickelsson's right, in the wooden chair Mickelsson privately called his learner's seat. He had a disconcerting way of staring straight at you, or into you, his childish, vulnerable-looking lips slightly parted. His eyelashes were colorless, almost invisible.

He said nothing as Mickelsson—puffing from time to time at his pipe, making furtive, tight gestures—explained the content of the philosophy courses available during the coming semester, the general requirements for the B.A. degree, and, in joking, careful fashion, something of the character of the teachers Nugent would run into. He recommended Garret's survey of modern philosophers, Lawler's Aquinas—"more for Lawler than for Aquinas," he said, and laughed—then, grudgingly, mentioned Tillson's logic course. Almost without knowing he was doing it he avoided mention of the lower-level Plato and Aristotle course he himself would be teaching, nor did he mention the pop courses thrown in to attract non-majors and swell the F.T.E.—The Philosophy of Death and

Dying, Human Sexuality, The Essential Karl Marx. As he spoke he made notes for the boy to take with him—carefully pencilled, succinct phrases that cut deep into the yellow, legal-sized pad he wrote on. Though the world was muggily baking, out beyond the partly drawn venetian blinds, the office was cool, all shade, almost tomblike. A flat smoke-cloud hung above their heads. On most of three sides the room was walled by books.

The boy asked, breaking in on him, "What about the Plato and Aristotle course?"

"Hmm," Mickelsson said, looking down at the schedule, leaning his forehead onto the fingertips of his left hand, elbow on the desk. He laid the pipe on his growing stack of unopened mail. (It could wait. He wasn't supposed to come in to his office anyway during the summer.) "Well, yes, that's open," he said. "Of course the Plato-Aristotle course is basically for freshmen. I'm afraid you might find it—"

"It's unusual, isn't it?" Nugent asked. "Senior professors teaching freshmen? Most departments I don't think they do that. They throw the freshmen to the grad students."

"Well, actually," Mickelsson said, then stalled. The young man's stare was unnerving. At last, heartily, cocking his eyebrow, he said, "Never underestimate the power of conviction, Mr. Nugent! No matter how good he is—no matter how mightily he believed in the beginning—when a man's taught for fifteen, twenty years, he can begin to leak steam at the joints. These graduate students . . . The biggest problem we have with our grad students is they put too much time into their teaching and not enough into their coursework." He grinned.

Nugent raised his arm for a quick, impatient wave, then returned it to artificial rest. An extremely odd gesture, Mickelsson thought, dropping the grin and staring hard at the computer-printed words PLATO/ARISTOTLE, 10 A.M., M.W., RM. 27 F.A. BLDG. (MICKELSSON), NO PREREQ. Before he could make out what to think of Nugent's fierce little wave, the boy was saying, "A friend of mine told me that most of this department does 'analytic,' you're practically the only one that does real philosophy."

"Well, 'real,' " Mickelsson said, picking up the pipe again, allowing himself an ironic half-smile. He glanced at the middle of Nugent's forehead and let the sentence trail off.

"I'm after the real thing, whatever level it is." Something faintly distressing had entered the boy's voice, a sort of catch, as if he were fighting strong emotion.

Mickelsson sat very still for an instant, then put his pencil down, slowly leaned back in his chair, lowered his chin to his chest, and, holding the pipe, interlaced his fingers over his paunch, avoiding the young man's eyes. After a long moment's thought he said, more weary than ironic this time: " 'The real thing.' " He stole a furtive glance at his watch: 2 p.m. Again he raised one eyebrow, sliding his eyes toward the boy. "Mr. Nugent, let me tell you something. If I were you, I wouldn't pin my life's highest hopes on philosophy. It's all right as entertainment—keeps you off the streets—but it's always been better at framing questions that have a chance of making sense than at figuring out answers. In fact there are some philosophers, Ludwig Wittgenstein, for instance, who claim that getting the question right *is* the answer." He'd meant to smile as he said it, but no smile came. He glanced down at his watch again. The hairs curling over the leather strap were silver. "Believe me, I can tell you from bitter experience—" he began soberly.

"Philosophy's the only discipline there is that even cares about figuring things out," Nugent said. He seemed to grow more pale by the minute. "All the others, except maybe chemistry, are just tinkering. History, mathematics, English lit, poly sci—" The very names seemed to stir his indignation. "Don't worry, I've thought it through! It may be that—" He paused, swallowed, then forced himself on, slightly sneering: "It may be that certain individual philosophers are not what they ought to be"—he gave Mickelsson what might or might not be an accusing look—"but philosophy itself *per se* is the highest activity known to man, and *certain* individual philosophers, at least—" He broke off to get back control of his voice, then continued as if angrily, "I don't mean to fawn or anything, but I know how you live, I know how much—" Again he was forced to break off.

Mickelsson sat perfectly still, dreadful revelation spreading through him. Was it worship, then, that made Nugent stare? He said rather sharply, "It sounds to me like what you're looking for is religion. You know how Kant described philosophy? 'One man holding the sieve while the other milks the he-goat.'"

Nugent said nothing, simply went on staring at him, blinking.

Mickelsson's scalp tingled unpleasantly. He cleared his throat and sat forward, laying the pipe aside with finality, shot his cuffs, then picked up his pencil and scowled at the notes on the pad. "I'd definitely recommend that you take Lawler's Aquinas," he said, businesslike, conscious that he was blushing a little, "and Tillson's Introduction to Logic." He underlined them, then put brackets around them. "As for the Plato-Aristotle course—" The hand holding the pencil gave a tight little wave, dismissive.

"Maybe I could get the book and read into it a little, before the semester starts. If you could give me the title—"

Mickelsson scowled harder, every nerve alert, like a diver in the presence of large, groping tentacles, then abruptly gave way and wrote down the title of the course, the time and place, and the two required texts. "It's two titles, actually," he said. He erased the crossed *l* in *Plato* and retouched the loop. Then he said, glancing at Nugent, "I see you haven't taken any Greek." He said it for no honorable reason, simply to throw a small impediment in the way of the young man's devouring earnestness.

"Not yet," Nugent said, and looked uneasy.

"Let's put you down for Greek, then." Neatly, pressing firmly, he wrote down *Greek 101, M.W.F., 4–5 p.m., Rm. 226 Lib. N. (Levin).*

"I want to thank you for this," Nugent said, his voice husky, his body pale and motionless, eyelids rapidly blinking.

"It's nothing, believe me," Mickelsson said, and glanced at his watch.

That afternoon he began his house-hunting.

In the beginning his premise was that buying was impossible, he was looking only for a place to rent. He had nothing, not a penny, with which to make a down payment, and even if he did by some miracle find money, chances were, if he bought a place, the I.R.S. would swoop in on him and snatch it. He'd never made up to them the money his ex-wife had "borrowed" from his tax account three years ago, nor had he paid his taxes for the last two years; in fact, until his lawyer had broken his daze with hell-fire warnings, he'd been too depressed and disorganized to file. But when Mickelsson had looked for houses for a week, finding nothing that would do—tarpaper shacks, falling-down cottages on still, gloomy lakes, low-ceilinged dungeons of cinderblock, one uninsulated, half-converted barn—nothing, nothing, and no prospects ahead (realtors were so uninterested in rental property he could hardly get them to drive out with him and look), he began to have second thoughts.

There was, in fact, one place where he could get a few thousand. He'd started, some years ago, a small account he'd be able to draw on if his mother should need a nursing home. It seemed unlikely that she would, given her spirit and her evident happiness where she was, with relatives in Wisconsin; but one never knew. Now, uncomfortably, disliking himself for it, he began to think about turning to that account. It was not as if his mother were destitute—she was, one might say, better off than he was. And the I.R.S. could as easily snatch his mother's money (as he'd always thought of it) as it could snatch a house. Besides, what would it gain them, snatching a shabby little farmhouse he had practically no money in? Soon he'd settled on flight to a house of his own as if the matter were out of his hands, blind destiny. No use worrying, he told himself; the "examined life" was easily overrated.

Now he began to hunt with considerable intensity, pulling together all his powers of concentration, poring over booklets and brochures, burrowing through newspapers, writing himself notes in his Pocket Calendar and Daily Reminder, then hurrying from one end of the county to the other to poke through damp cellars, bump his head on attic beams, wipe and shake sticky cobwebs from his fingers, blush, apologize, and back away ("Thank you, I'll call you, yes good, good, thank you"—cringing inwardly, with each exaggerated bow, at his moral cowardice), even now finding nothing that would do, nothing but termite-fodder, overpriced trash.

He did not like that increasing tendency to lie to himself and others—"I'll call you, yes good." An existentialist, of course, could defend it without a blink; another kind of thinker could argue its rightness in a community of liars; another might assert its suitability to a stock behavioral mode voluntarily elected; but Mickelsson—glowering with rage turned inward, fists clamped tight on the steeringwheel—had never been friendly to the notion that human beings are free to turn into tomato plants at will, or even to the best utilitarianism, and least of all to R. M. Hare's opinion, Oxonian and therefore unassailable, that morality is life-style. He wouldn't have denied, if anyone other than his psychiatrist had asked him, that his search had all the earmarks of a mad compulsion, though of course one could always manufacture fine theories, delimiting categories, *obs* and *sols*.

"Perhaps," he'd said on the phone to Dr. Rifkin, back in Providence, "where I live is the only thing left that I have any real control of." He blew out smoke, angrily drumming his short, hard fingers on the tabletop, his head down, like a bull's. It had seemed the kind of reason Dr. Rifkin would accept. Dr. Rifkin was a fool, an absurdly sloppy thinker if indeed it could be said that he ever thought at all; but Mickelsson was in the habit of consulting him now and then, touching bases in the fashion of a sandlot ballplayer on a diamond whose bases are yards out of position but familiar.

"Come on now," Rifkin said, his voice adenoidal, as ironic and peevish as a meow. He was always saying "Come on now." A tiresome—tirelessly tiresome—little man, slightly crabby, though good-hearted to a fault, fresh from his internship somewhere in Texas, still stained by the tan, when Mickelsson had first met him. He was painstaking; would've made an excellent dentist. Perhaps, like Martin Luther, he was dizzied by the stink of human breath. It was Mickelsson's ex-wife that had chosen him, or confirmed the choice of the hospital where Mickelsson had been placed.

Rifkin, at the other end of the line, would be sitting with his knees together, protecting his cock—long, if one could judge by his ears, nose, and thumbs—hair parted in the middle, two fingercurls in front, delicately pushing his glasses up his nose with a carefully manicured, spatulate middle finger, his thick lips puckered (moustache poised, uplifted) as if ready to give the receiver a quick little love-peck. His eyebrows would be arched in faintly ironic astonishment—possibly amusement, possibly reprobation; he purposely kept it ambiguous, playing it safe. He played everything safe. He never spoke of "Freud," like a normal human being, always of "Doctor Freud." On the mahogany-panelled wall behind him hung a framed pen-and-ink sketch, probably something his wife had picked out. Again the scratchy, ironic cat's voice: "Come on now, Professor. What's the *real* reason?"

Mickelsson imagined himself saying, "All right; I murdered a dog."

Even before he'd decided whether or not it was funny, or whether or not it could be construed as relevant, he'd decided on discretion. He said, tapping the tabletop again, "I suppose the truth is I'd like to spite my wife, maybe go to jail and shame her."

"That's not impossible," Rifkin said. "Very interesting." He'd be sitting with his eyes closed to chinks, grinning like a fox with indigestion.

"Maybe spite my children too," Mickelsson said, "lose my earning capacity and deprive them of college educations."

"Mmm," Rifkin said, suspicious now, from the sound of it. "It's something you might think about, anyway."

"I will, believe me."

"Is that irony I detect?"

"If you detect it, then it is."

"Come on now, Professor," Rifkin said crossly, whiningly, "let's not logic-chop."

"All right. Sorry," Mickelsson said. He glanced at his watch. "OK, so I'm jealous of my children."

"As I say, you might *think* about it," Rifkin said.

Mickelsson shook his head. What a profession! After he'd gotten rid of Rifkin he'd gone back to looking through the paper for a house, writing himself notes, occasionally giving a little whistle or muttering to himself. " 'Priced to sell.' I'll bet! Right before it vanishes in the quicksand!" It was a habit of long standing, this talking to himself, just above a whisper, often in high-flown orotund phrases, often with close-to-the-chest little gestures. One of the things he liked best about his business was the grand tradition of ornate formulations, the effloriate rhetoric of a Goethe, Santayana, Collingwood, or Russell, not to mention Nietzsche—dimly recalled in the prose of living philosophers like Blanchard or, among the younger crowd, Richard Taylor, Peter Singer. In this as in everything, needless to say, he was hopelessly out of fashion, following the no-longer-believed (dis-cred-ited, from *creed*, Heideggerians would bray); nor did it help when he quoted the ghost of Adam Smith on ethics books that are "dry and disagreeable, abounding in abstruse and metaphysical distinctions, but incapable of exciting in the heart any of those emotions which it is the principal use of books of morality to excite." Rhetoric was of *die Welt*, not *die Erde*, and therefore, in the new, upside-down universe, sin and error. Brahma was *out*; the jigglings and gyrations of Shiva were in.

And so the hunt continued. His books and papers lay strewn on the table as they'd been when he'd given up trying to work on them. The sink was filled with dishes, and rather than wash them he bought paper cups and plates. He no longer went out for walks on hot nights but climbed into his rattletrap car, an old Chevy he'd bought for seventy dollars from a student, and drove out to look at houses he couldn't go through until tomorrow. If the house was empty or there was no one about, he would park in the weeds across the road and sit looking for half an hour, going over in his mind what one might do to save it and dimly imagining what his life might be like if he were to take the place. Mornings, he would dress in the slightly dandified fashion he favored—dark shirt, ascot tie, a light summer suit only slightly frayed, dark blue hankie in the pocket, and on his head—pressing down his erumpent red hair—the vaguely Westernish broad-brimmed hat that signalled his difference from other philosophers (as if any such signal were needed), aligning him more nearly with the Southern or Western poets who came, every week or so, to read their flashy junk to the Department of Anguish.

He pursued the hunt as if doomed to it, locked on his senseless course like a planet. Not quite senseless, perhaps. One might speak of the quiet without which creativity cannot hear itself think; one might mention the example of Wittgenstein, who had come to a whole new vision while designing and building his sister's house. But those were not really Peter Mickelsson's reasons—unless in this too, as in so many things, he was deluded. Never mind, for the moment. (That was the slogan of his crisis: *for the moment.*) It must suffice, for the moment, that, reading in the paper of a house for sale—"Country living, 10 acres . . ." or "Cottage, 2 bedrooms, trout stream, outbuildings"—he felt an urge, almost irresistible, to go look. Whatever the meaning of the compulsion, it kept him moving, kept him just ahead of the shadow at his back, despair.

It also kept his smouldering anger fed. Who would believe the desperation and shamelessness of humanity! He saw so-called farmhouses in the middle of town, chopped-up rooms, shoddy plastering, panelling made of paper, light fixtures too tawdry for the grungiest motel; went out to see something described as "small ranch, top condition," and found a trailer. He saw dry-rot, termites, flood-wrecks, asphalt front yards ("tennis courts"); pleasant little cottages on two hundred acres of swamp (ninety thousand); a decaying stone house on an island, no road or telephone. . . . Maybe it was the not quite predictable nature of the certain outrage that kept his interest up. Or maybe his half-unconscious awareness that wrath was good for him. "Repression is a dangerous habit," Dr. Rifkin said. "Go ahead! Get mad at me!" He said it repeatedly, as if imitating someone who had greatly impressed him, back in Texas. He did not seem to notice his patient's heavy sigh.

Then when Mickelsson had nearly given up, had blown up at almost the last of his realtors, he came upon the Bauer place. (It was late afternoon. He couldn't be sure what day it was. According to the days-of-the-week window on his Japanese watch it was 大.) He approached the place not directly, through the town of Susquehanna, but by a mountainous back route, one that looked relatively easy on the map, though in the driving it proved otherwise.

Perhaps it was the light, some special, seemingly magical tint that he remembered from somewhere long ago; or perhaps it was the way the dappled sunlight flickered on the road or in the glowing-green maple leaves above, some centuries-old neurological trigger, hypnotic, probably dangerous to epileptics. He'd been driving for something like an hour and a half on the high-crowned, pot-holed asphalt roads that wound as if aimlessly through the Pennsylvania mountains—steeply banked curves where the road looped smoothly back on itself like the flightpath of a hawk, sudden dips and rises, short sunlit stretches shaving valley floors— then gentler curves, the roadway following a creekbed for a time, passing small settlements where nothing seemed alive: large, decaying houses and collapsing barns, lawns held in by stone-locked retaining walls and shaded by great, dark sugar maples; passing old graveyards and white wooden churches, crossing stone bridges, skirting small lakes where there were dingy, crooked cottages, trailers, butane tanks, drunkenly listing, bone-gray docks; passing, on higher ground, small, paintless houses with handmade signs nailed to trees in front: NIGHT WALKERS; RABBITS FOR SALE; LOCUST POSTS, $1.00. Increasingly it seemed to him a part of the world time had forgotten, or rather—despite the visible decay—had spared. It stirred in him memories, at first only a general mood—exhilaration, a sense of rejuvenated options—and then, all at once, a specific moment: running naked, as a boy, in his father's overgrown apple orchard, given over, by the time of his memory, to cows—running naked, his clothes and glasses hidden in the shadow of a tree, imagining as he ran the nakedness of his tall older cousin Mary Ann, or some naked female stranger from beyond the marsh. He remembered the astonishing smoothness of cowpaths; then he remembered vividly the glorious sensation, impossible to explain or justify to unfortunates who'd never been granted it, of stepping barefoot (walking now) into a day-old cowplop, sun-warmed cow manure squeezing up between the toes. Strange that it should come back so clearly now— ironically dragging with it (thesis-antithesis) an image of his grandfather in his dark, plain suit, sitting stiffly upright at his desk in the manse, books laid out in front of him, dusty late-afternoon sunlight slanting in, his steel-rimmed spectacles insensibly cutting red wounds into the sides of his peculiar, leftward-aiming nose. (He'd been the dullest man on earth, except for one oddity. In his seventieth year he'd developed second sight.) Nothing in these mountains was the same, really, as the broad, green farm and outdoorsman country—or the stiff, trim villages with their obscurely Vikingish shutters and gables—where Mickelsson had grown up in Wisconsin. Yet here under the changeable sky, moving through pockets of sudden warmth, then sudden cold, he felt himself hovering on the brink of something, as if the stubborn will by means of which he'd survived his troubles were at last getting ready to pay off.

He drove on, plunging between walls of damp shale into the darkness of suddenly sloping woods, the chill of another bright swirl of fog, then up onto a high, clear overgrown meadow where there were lilacs, a solitary chimney, low stone walls that had once been bounded by orchards or pastures. Light, then shadow, flashed on his windshield and glasses.

"If I were you I'd try Pennsylvania," Tom Garret's wife had told him weeks ago. It seemed to him incredible now that he'd dismissed her advice out of hand. But she was a strange woman—creepy, in fact: shy and furtive as a mouse; large, gypsy-black eyes. She was said to be "intuitive," almost psychic. (Mickelsson had his doubts.) At parties she would hide in the corner of the room, hugging herself inside her shawl. "It's the most beautiful country in the world—but very queer, people say." She slid her eyes toward the others, making certain she wasn't overheard, then put her hand on his arm—a bony, small-fingered hand that made him think of a rat's. "Full of witches and heaven knows what." She smiled. "That's where I see you, Peter. Really!" "I'm sure you do," he'd said, edging away. Not the least of her oddities was the smell that came from her, something faintly like wet, burnt wood.

Now the road dropped sharply, like a twisting waterfall—so he would remember that first encounter later, when the descent no longer seemed so frighteningly steep—passed through a cavern of interlocked trees and fog, curved around abruptly, and emerged into strange, charged light. It was not at all the light of Wisconsin. If the light there was unearthly, it had a luminous, strained, Scandinavian unearthliness, so that it seemed no wonder that men like his grandfather (before the coming of his gift) should ponder God—even God's love and grace—in a fashion almost chillingly logical, respectful; and that even common grocers should carry about them an aura of the scholarly, a wintry crispness and clarity that one might mistake—here among the yellows and misty greens of Pennsylvania—for icy-hearted. He slowed, the car's weight laboring against the brakes, pulled the rumbling old Chevy onto the shoulder, and switched off the engine, knowing though not yet quite believing that this was the place he'd discovered in the Snyder Realty brochure ("Beautiful old farmhouse, 4 bedrooms, outbuildings, pond, woods, pasture"). After a moment he got out to stand beside the blue, pitted fender, looking down at his prospect from a quarter-mile away and a hundred yards above. The engine clicked noisily. There were blackberries by the roadside, grown up in profusion as if to hide the broad scar of an abandoned gravel pit with a chain across what remained of the entrance and a sign, NO DUMPING! He picked a handful of berries and absently ate them as he looked. He could now see the realtor's red and white sign.

"Son of a gun," he muttered, and shook his head.

Long blue shadows reached from the woods above down the cant of the mountain—pale, new-mown hay—toward the house and barns. Between the house and the nearest shed, a creek glittered, and directly above the house, startling as a wolf in the late-afternoon light, stood a perfect, white full moon.

Finney, his lawyer, would stage one of his grand-operatic fits when he heard the price. "Listen, pal. Take an old goat-fucker's word for it—" he would say.

Mickelsson wiped his hands on his handkerchief, climbed back into the car, put the gearshift in neutral, and coasted nearer. In front of the house he pushed in the brake, took off his glasses and cleaned them, then fitted them back over his ears.

The lawn was mowed, the barndoors padlocked. The owner was apparently not at home—so he gathered, though he didn't get out of the car, much less go up onto the wide, shaded porch and knock. From beyond the largest of the barns, behind him, across the road from the house, came the roar of a waterfall.

He slid out a cigarette, tamped it on the dashboard, cupped his hands around the end, and lit it.

Everything below the porch roof lay in shadow, and the gables, now that he looked at them more closely, had a knife-cut sharpness of outline that touched him with foreboding. Beyond the gables the wooded mountain was as gray as a chalkboard, rising into mist. He noticed now for the first time—or anyway for the first time consciously registered—the Pennsylvania-Dutch hex signs on the barns.

The design of the spindles on the porch balusters, just visible in the dark, still wedge of shadow, was unusually complex, as if the spindles had been wrought for some old-world mansion, perhaps some grand old Victorian hotel for the very rich when they retreated for a weekend to the mountains. It was a beautiful place, no question about it, but the longer he looked the more ambivalent his sense of it became. Over by the plank bridge spanning the creek, just beyond a startling splash of lighted ferns, lay a shape he thought at first to be a bright clump of heather, until it moved, turning into a cat, gray and white, stalking.

The light changed again. The shadows behind the house and the darkening barns, spilling out across the valley, filling it like a cup, were more blue now, growing darker and bluer by the minute. It was that early span of twilight his father had called "cockshut," back in that lost age when every slightest flicker of reality had a name—birds, grasses, weathers, times of day and season. The moon had grown brighter, as if sneaking in close. He waited on, breathing in the scents of new-mown hay and honeysuckle. His thoughts drifted. A faint chest-pain brought it to his attention that he was thinking of the student Michael Nugent. Already, it was clear, the boy had decided to make demands on him, urged on by Tillson, probably Dean Blickstein too, and whoever it was that had persuaded Nugent that he, Mickelsson, was the only "real" philosopher. *I know how you live. I know how much*— Mickelsson sucked in breath and moved

the palm of his right hand on his chest. Surely the past should be sufficient trouble, his children and ex-wife; but no, the inevitable future must nag him too, pull like quicksand. Mickelsson had nothing but scorn for the so-called Me generation, emotivism at plague proportions; nonetheless it was true that there were times when a man could help no one. Here stood this house, possibility of escape—increasingly sombre in the deepening twilight—and there, all around it, to his imagination, were the stretched-out bony arms of those with legitimate demands.

He forgot what he'd been thinking.

The seeming timelessness was part of it, all right. (The thought welled up into his consciousness abruptly, after a lapse of perhaps minutes.) Dropped out of nowhere into this still shade, one couldn't have known it wasn't 1940—or even 1840, except for the electric and telephone lines, harsh against the sky.

Now the windows of the house were just darker places in the ghostly walls. The steep, stern gables, raised like old shields or defenseworks, dark against the darker mountainside, the darkening sky, had a look both forbidding and forlorn, the look of a stronghold that has outlasted its occupants by centuries. It was now no longer cockshut but purple dusk edging into night.

"Interesting," he said aloud. Quite suddenly, all around him, as if they'd leaped out of nowhere, there were shadows cast by the moon. The same instant that he noticed the shadows, he caught, out of the corner of his eye, some movement on the porch. He definitely saw the thing, he would have said, though he couldn't see it well enough to know what it was—a woman, he would have guessed—but when he looked directly at where the thing ought to be, there was nothing. A pleasurable shiver ran up his back. It had been a long time since he'd imagined things watching him in the dark. (What had it been? A moth, perhaps, much closer to his eye than he'd imagined? A bat?) The place wouldn't seem so eerie, of course, when you were used to it. In any event, eerie or not, it was beautiful.

He ground out his cigarette, let smoke float slowly out through his nostrils, and decided to make an offer.

That night, when he climbed the crooked, dimly lit stairs to his apartment—in his left arm his meagre week's supply of groceries, in his right hand his mail, all of it depressing (bills, two letters marked "Occupant," another computerized stern complaint from the I.R.S.)—he found a note poking out from below his door. He froze, then looked around as if whoever it was that had crept in on him might still be lurking near, in the shadows just beyond the reach of the cheaply shaded bulb. All around his door stood bulky, misshapen cardboard boxes—junk books he'd never bothered to unpack, junk appliances (the portable radio he

had no use for anymore, his iron, probably his toaster, he wasn't certain)—
the shadows of the boxes low on the wall, as if trying to hide behind the
boxes. There was no one there. He unlocked the door, carried the
groceries in and set them down, then went back to stoop over and pick
up the note. It was written in a stiff, old-mannish hand, and signed, with
a sudden dissilient flourish, *Michael Nugent*. He read the first words:
"It is extremely urgent that . . ."

He closed the door and, without reading further, crumpled the note
in his fist.

2

"A what?" Finney wailed, dramatic. It was the omnipresent potential for theater that had gotten him into the law-game, Mickelsson was convinced. It was better than acting; he wasn't impeded by some humdrum playwright's lines.

"House," Mickelsson repeated, reaching toward the pocket where he kept his pipe, then changing his mind, getting out his cigarettes and hunting around under papers and books for matches. No luck.

"House! Well, saints preserve us!" Finney said. He cracked his voice, old-time Irish. Mickelsson could see him: fat and sweat-washed; gold-rimmed glasses; black toupee, gray sideburns below; little blue eyes crossed with anger or, more likely, impatience as he stared for just an instant at the phone. While he talked he'd be reading and signing letters, motioning to his secretary, furtively scratching himself, raising his rear end off the chair to catch a breeze. "That's good, Pete! Cute! Give the feds something solid to aim their pissers at."

"I know," Mickelsson said. "Look—"

"Also makes your generous offer to your wife more interesting." Abruptly solemn.

"Believe me—"

"I can see you're not wild for good advice, Professor, but take it from me, ole pal ole sock, by all the little golden, curly hairs on—"

"It's relatively cheap, Finney. If I can't manage it, then I can't. Are you listening?"

"OK." There was a pause, no doubt while Finney ran his eyes over some paper, then handed it back to his secretary. "OK, cheap. Gotcha. Spare me the details! I don't suppose you could get it in a friend's name? That might be a very good idea, you know. Keep the feds' sticky fingers off the moola—"

"No chance."

Finney laughed. "You oughtta be nicer to people, you know that, Professor? Let 'em see your sweet side! But OK, OK. I dig. I'm glad you touched base on this. If it looks like this is where the cheese starts to bind I'll get back to you." Another pause, then: "OK, I'm prepared—like they say, 'Ahm protected.' What the hell, you only live once, hey, pal? OK,

I hear what you're saying. All right! So good luck to ya for once, you poor bastard!" Even his voice was half elsewhere.

"Thanks. Don't worry, I'll handle it all right."

" 'What, me worry?' " He laughed. "Well, love ya, Professor. Anything else?"

"That's it for now."

"For now." He laughed again. "OK, blood-brother, keep the wick clean, hey?"

"I'll do that."

It would have served no useful purpose to explain to Finney that he was far past keeping his wick clean, in whatever sense Finney might have meant it—though it was true that with the one woman who made his heart race Mickelsson was clean as a whistle.

Jessica Stark said, in the hallway—her office was just a few doors down from his, and it was there, just as she was leaving, that he'd caught her— "It sounds great!" She was wearing jeans and a mannish shirt, and her face had that electric look it sometimes got, supercharged, thunder behind the eyes. He hadn't the faintest idea what it meant—maybe something to do with the death of her husband, a year ago—but it alarmed him. Everything about her alarmed him. She was tall enough to play quarterback to Mickelsson's fullback, and in some ways she was tough enough, he suspected. She was supposed to be a force to be reckoned with, in her field—so someone had told him, possibly his chairman, Tillson—and it was easy to believe. Mickelsson had thought a good deal about Jessica, carefully and futilely, as one thinks about Free Will and Determinism; in fact, after the first time he'd met her, he'd thought about nothing else for weeks. She was so beautiful it made him uncomfortable to be around her—but also, whenever they happened to meet, made him hang around longer than he should, and later mention her too often in conversation. If she was for real, he'd once told Tom Garret jokingly—though he'd been drunk at the time, something had kept him from particularizing: her smile, the absurdly *Playmate* shapeliness of shoulders, breasts and hips, her apparent good-heartedness, the dangerous sharpness of her mind and the unabashed Jewish directness (she asked personal questions no one else would ask, as if nosiness were the highest of civilized virtues, and indeed so she made it seem)—if all those were real, then everything one thought one knew about reality must be scrapped.

At first, passing mention of Jessica Stark—Jessica Tauber, as she signed her articles—stirred Mickelsson to instant erection. Several times he'd drawn the blinds on his office windows and locked the door, and had thus brought the tendency of his reflections to conclusion. But little by little, through mental discipline, he'd been able to place her in the ordinary. She was in early-middle-age, thirty-five or so, he guessed; hence one could be sure, considering the shape she was in, that she was careful about exercise and diet. Every morning at the crack of dawn, someone had told him, she went jogging, three or four miles. Obviously something was wrong with anyone who gave that much care to appearance—or, for that matter, got up that early. Moreover, it was unthinkable that a woman so good-looking should be a first-class scholar. That was not cynicism but realism. All Nature uses only what it needs to thrive, and Jessica, with those murky gray eyes and outward-arching eyebrows, sensual mouth and perfect teeth (Mickelsson was morbidly fascinated by teeth), had no reason to develop deep talents of the heart and mind. At last it had come to him, one afternoon as he was standing in the mailroom staring unseeingly at a mimeographed letter, that Jessica Tauber Stark was a woman to be pitied. The revelation had cleansed him like a new idea; but so far his knowledge hadn't helped him to meet her eyes, much less deal with her rabbinical wit. Only when Mickelsson hadn't seen her for a while could he confidently deny that she frightened him. Her office (behind her now, the door still open) was dark with books and journals, far more crammed than his own —more books than anyone could possibly read, so it was fair to assume that she kept them for the power they lent, though also, to some extent, for reference. She edited a magazine, *Historical Sociology,* alleged to be somewhat right-wing (but it was one of her enemies who'd said that, one of the department's child-faced Marxists: "Slightly to the right of Adolf Hitler" was in fact what he'd said) and she was supposed to be the first woman in her field to have done . . . something or other. It was all very vague in Mickelsson's mind. Secretly he suspected that the whole discipline was a magic trick: snap your fingers and it would turn into a quivering white rabbit or an array of silk flags. Nevertheless, only a maniac would dare raise objections in the flame of that quick, tense smile. She seemed to be always in a hurry, at least when he met her in the hallway (at parties she relaxed somewhat, though even then there was something ready-to-spring about her, at once intensely engaged and wary), so when she stopped to talk with him, usually at his instigation, as now, he felt uncomfortable, dutifully saying whatever she seemed to expect till she dismissed him. She stood with her legs apart, braced, long and lean, her feet in engineer's boots. In his mind her lines were unnaturally firm, for all their softness, like stones in a clear mountain lake.

"Yes, it's really wonderful in Susquehanna," he said. "Remote." When she narrowed her dark-circled eyes, he added guiltily, "I need to get someplace quiet, get some work done. It's like the nineteen forties there. You hardly hear a sound."

"Good," she said. "If that's what you want." Her smile flashed, vanished. Her right hand went furtively to push a lock of silver-streaked dark hair back from her ear. No doubt what he was doing was part of a dangerous national trend. He was suddenly conscious of his paunch, his rumpled trousers; conscious above all of the widowhood she seemed to carry just out of sight, like a dagger. Nothing he could do, nothing anyone could do, would serve.

"Can you afford it?" she asked. "I know things are cheaper down there—"

"No problem," he said, and waved it away.

"With all your tax troubles, and all that money you pay your wife . . ." That was the least of what she'd wormed out of him, yawning behind her hand but leaning forward with interest, the night he'd stayed late after her party. They'd talked till nearly 6 a.m. He frowned now, suddenly startled by the notion that she was hinting at offering him money. At once he dismissed the idea and almost laughed.

She said, "People say there are rattlesnakes in Susquehanna."

"I doubt it. It's possible, I suppose."

"It doesn't bother you?" she asked. When she saw that he didn't intend to tell the truth, she let her smile flash again, not at full voltage. "Well, good luck," she said. She looked down the corridor, then thoughtfully back at his face, only for a moment. Abruptly—untruthfully, he thought— she said, "I'm sorry I can't talk longer, Pete. Gotta run." She reached back and closed her office door. She tried the knob, making sure the door had locked.

"Sure. I'm sorry if—"

"You'll remember to bring me that book?"

"Book?" he asked.

She grinned like a woman ten years younger. "I knew you wouldn't remember. Something by someone named Hare. We talked about it at Bryants'."

"Oh, that!" He smiled, pretending to remember.

She shook her head, giving up on him, and, as Mickelsson stood flat-footed, she went past him, patting his arm. He turned heavily, watching her go, her free arm waving back to him without her turning. She walked quickly, in long, smooth strides. He thought again of what it might be like to be her lover—a thought that always depressed him. He was overweight, wrecked, no doubt half crazy, and Jessica's husband had been, everyone said, "just wonderful!" Whenever the man was mentioned Mickelsson would prick up his ears, secretly hoping to hear that the man had not been wonderful, that he was a dullard, and ugly as death. It never happened. He realized now how ridiculous he must have looked, intensely smiling, fake as a peddler of snake-oil, waving away her near-offer, if it was that. *No problem.* He thought of the long, intense conversation they'd had at Bryants', not a word of which he remembered. Old devil gin.

Mickelsson went back into his office and closed the door.

Almost nothing he'd written on the loan application was strictly true. Strange affair! No one who had known him two years ago, not even his wife, could have anticipated this radical change of character—or rather, loss of character. It was astonishing, in fact: conscious, utterly indefensible falsehood from Mickelsson the moralist, howler in the wilderness of his desiccate age, ranter against sloganers and simplifiers, both Communists and capitalists, liars and lob-wits of every persuasion—Professor Peter Mickelsson, indefatigable shamer of the shallow-minded, fulminator against the frivolous and false, who had written scornfully of both fundamentalist straight-world bigotry and the latest campus fad, homosexual uncloseting—et cetera, et cetera. Yet it was so: his application was (not to put too fine a point on it) a pack of lies. His enemies, if they heard, would whinny with glee. He had a demon in him, his friends would have to say; there was no other reasonable explanation.

But what was he to do? (He sat bent forward, his right hand making small gestures two inches under his chin. The banker went on skimming the papers in front of him, his glasses low. He breathed audibly, steadily, like a man who smoked too much or had trouble with his digestion, or like a large animal asleep.) Mickelsson would never have gotten the loan— it was surely a fact—if he'd mentioned his unpaid taxes and penalties, or the payments he'd doubtless have to make to his wife, if ever he could get her to meet him in court (meanwhile he was sending her monthly checks— odd amounts, now more, now less, as much as he could manage—a generous act, as any reasonable observer would admit)—not, in fact, that he fooled himself for a minute.

Perhaps he really was in the possession of some demon, that is, some daemonic idea. Though all his life he'd trumpeted rationality, circumspect behavior in the deepest, broadest sense, self-mastery, it could hardly be denied that, for all his care, his ship was foundering, had foundered. He was reeling yet from the surprise of his wife's demand that he get out. ("Just beat it, Professor. I'm not interested in debating it. You see that door? Just glide on through it.") His career was on the skids. . . . Yet on the other hand, on the other hand . . . "The *Übermensch* is 'dumb,' his ideas unrestricted by the language of the herd"—F. Nietzsche. "Great truths are felt before they are expressed," says Teilhard de Chardin. "Like great works, deep feelings always mean more than they are conscious of saying," says Camus. Or Ralph Waldo Emerson: "Every man's life is a solution in hieroglyphic to those inquiries he would put. He acts it as life before he apprehends it as truth." (But then again, of course: "Men will find reasons for the harm they intend to do anyway.") It was not as if Mickelsson acted with his own approval.

He sighed and for a moment put his hand over his face.

He looked at the pink that showed through the banker's hair and remembered his father's annual trips to the bank in Wausau—twenty miles away, the nearest big town—for fertilizer and seed money. He remembered how his father would sit, oddly shrunken, by the loan-officer's desk, his straw hat on his knees, on his face white splotches that would later turn out to be skin cancer. Mickelsson, ten or twelve, would be sitting outside the railing, nothing to play with but the worn-smooth chair-arms and his plastic-rimmed glasses. The loan man in Wausau (by now long dead) had been almost an albino. He'd had a large, white jaw and a long, straight nose with prominent, flared pink nostrils. The pale lashes around his bulging eyes were like silk. Mickelsson, in his childhood, had frequently met the man in nightmares.

Well, so Mickelsson had been less than forthcoming, as politicians say. But the president, loan-officer, and sometime head-teller of the small Susquehanna bank, County National, asked no questions or anyway none that would make trouble; he and his committee apparently took Mickelsson's optimistic estimate of wages and "probable additional income" in gentlemanly stride. No doubt they were accustomed, in this depressed, backwoods area, to loan applications more poetic than factual. (Or was it, conceivably, that the man had read Mickelsson's articles for popular magazines—on the arms race, the ethical implications of test-tube babies, et cetera—and had never entertained the possibility that a man of such good sense might throw prudence to the wind?) No matter, no point worrying, for the moment. Look on the bright side: he'd taken the old Kierkegaardian leap. (Needless to say, he would not seriously appeal to the authority of that righteous, crackpot Dane.)

The banker glanced up, and Mickelsson instantly broke off his furtive gesturing. The banker was silver-haired, silver-moustached, a boyish, ruddy man with dimples in his cheeks. On his glass desktop he had a sign in loopy, girlish script, with a flower, *Thank You for Not Smoking*. He pushed a sheaf of papers across the desk for Mickelsson's signature. "Well, everything looks OK," he said; and Mickelsson, taking his word for it, drew off his useless bifocals and hastily signed. He carefully dotted the *i* and crossed the *t*. Then they shook hands, both half rising from their chairs, reaching across the desk, grinning like conspirators. Mickelsson was half tempted to open a checking account, in token of his gratitude, but resisted. Bounced checks would stretch the poetry thin.

"Well, Professor," the banker said, drawing his hand back across the desk and standing up the rest of the way, "welcome to Seskehenna."

"Thank you," Mickelsson said, also standing up, towering above the man, mentally noting the local pronunciation. He toyed with his hat, his smile locked firmly in place.

"Any time we can be of service," the banker said, hanging his fingers from the top of his vest, "just drop by."

"I will." He backed toward the door, grinning and bowing. "*Gratitude is hatred in a mask.*" *F. Nietzsche.* "*Gratitude to a fellow mortal is excrement.*" *Luther.*

"Anybody told you the history of that house?" the banker asked, smiling. When Mickelsson looked blank, pausing in his retreat, his eyebrows raised with exaggerated interest, the banker continued, "Lot of legends about that old house. I'm not up on 'em, myself—if there's two things on earth I can never remember it's history and jokes. But you should talk to the neighbors. You'll find it interesting, I'm sure."

"I'll do that," Mickelsson said. "Well, thanks for everything. It's been a pleasure to do business with you!" He smiled again, bowing one last time, and, after an instant's hesitation, put his hat on, setting it in place with both hands, then cocking it.

The banker smiled a touch too thoughtfully, as if Mickelsson, leaving, had gotten some small detail wrong, had perhaps started with the incorrect foot, or had failed to put his chair back exactly where he'd found it. One sensed, all the same, that the banker would do everything he could to make things easy. Small-town solidarity. Yes-siree-bob. They needed each other. Outside the unwashed glass front door with its black and silver lettering, around behind the pillar where his new friend the silver-haired banker couldn't see him, Mickelsson hunched his shoulders and lit a cigarette. He glanced once at the bench-loungers sizing him up from across the street—four men, two women; they might have been sitting there, observing events around the town's one traffic light, for years. Mickelsson sent them a stiff little salute. No one seemed to notice. Then he moved hurriedly, perhaps a little furtively, to the real-estate office next door.

The salesman was a young man of thirty or so, named Tim Booker, a grinning country boy with a face shaped like an apple, thinning brown hair, big farmboy muscles. Wherever the sun had touched him he was coppery brown. He dressed in a black leather motorcycle jacket, yellow T-shirt (FISHER STOVES, it said), blue jeans, scuffed brown leather boots. From the moment he'd met him Mickelsson had been hard put not to like him. He seemed obviously honest, blessed with the heartiness and dependable gentleness Mickelsson had associated since childhood with dairy farmers—people like his father, whose survival, not to mention their peace of mind, depended on a gift for dealing patiently with big stupid animals inclined to push fences down, hide in the woods at calving time, grow moody around strangers, occasionally butt or kick. He'd of course been predisposed to like the young man. Tim had been his first real introduction to the character of the people who'd be his neighbors if he managed to get the Bauer place. From the outset the signs had been promising. Even Tim's accent was a pleasure, or anyway interesting, a sort of key to the place—a set of clues, if Mickelsson could figure them out, to the ungraspable phantom meaning he'd felt up at the house. The secret of wholeness, perhaps, if he was lucky. His cracked-up life's second chance.

Though he'd seen the world—had been a paramedic in Vietnam, he said—Tim had, in purer form than any of the others Mickelsson had talked to, what Mickelsson was coming to recognize as the standard old-time voice of Susquehanna: the flat, sweet yokel sound of rural New York State, richly shaped *r*'s designed to make up for all the lost *r*'s of New England ("car" was *cah-urr*, by some magic compressed to one syllable), and overlaid on that, the Scots' short *ow* sound and bitten-off *t*'s, the accent that distinguished the northern tier of Pennsylvania, as in (Tim slapping the pockets of his jeans) "If I can find my dahrn keys I'll drive you *owt*."

After Mickelsson's experience with the real-estate people of Binghamton, Tim's directness was like ozone. "She'll come down," he'd said, ritching back happily on his chair. "She needs to get moved owt of it, and you're the best chance she's gaht." He laughed, lifting his dimpled chin. "I'd say a fair price for both of you'd be fifty thowsand dahllers."

Mickelsson leaned forward, startled. Her asking price was seventy. "You think so?"

"Well," Tim said, smiling more widely, throwing his arms out, "it can't hurt to ask." Grinning head tipped, arms reaching wide, he was a startling, happy-child parody of the crucifixion.

As they'd driven up to the farmstead that first time, Tim had talked about his life and pleasures as if no one could help but find them interesting—as indeed Peter Mickelsson did, listening to Tim with a touch of envy, wondering with momentary morbid excitement whether he too ought to have a motorcycle. (He'd had one long ago, in his farmboy and college days; an Indian.) Tim had a blond Harley-Davidson, he said; a hog, fully equipped; more lights than a 747. He didn't ride it much, mostly just pahlished it. Mickelsson grinned and nodded, sucking at his recalcitrant pipe. Though Tim had never had much to do with boats—he couldn't swim, he said—he'd just bought a hardly used trimaran. All these lakes hereabouts, just laying there, it seemed sort of un-American not to pollute them. He lightly hit the steeringwheel as he laughed, head tossed sideways. He also owned a camper in which he'd taken trips to places as far away as Arizona, camping his way across the country with his wife and child. Whether the child was a boy or girl Mickelsson never learned. Tim spoke of him or her as "the kid."

"What do you teach up at the cahllege?" Tim asked. He spoke with his head thrown forward and laid over on the side, like a motorcycle rider glancing back.

"Philosophy," Mickelsson said.

He looked impressed. "Philahsaphy! That's something I never got into too much. Plato's cave and like that?"

"Something like that," Mickelsson said, and gave a nod.

Tim laughed, swung his head, and hit the steeringwheel again. He was looking down into the valley to the left of them now, driving without a glance at the road but driving well. "I took an English course down at

Lehigh Cahllege where we read some philahsaphy. It was hard going, but it was interesting. Aristahtle?"

"That's one of the people we treat." He nodded again, a barely perceptible movement, like a boxer's feint.

"Is that what you mostly do?—study the old-timers? Or do you make up philahsaphy on your own?" Now he turned back, his head still leaning toward the window, to look at Mickelsson.

"We do a little of both, most of us." He was beginning to feel it was time to change the subject.

But Tim was interested. "You write about things like what's really owt there?" He took his left hand from the steeringwheel to wave generally at the world.

"Well, in a sense—" Still with the grin locked on, he got out his cigarettes.

"Boy, that's interesting stuff, that's all *I* can say," Tim said, and shook his head. "You ever work on ghosts, or people that can see into the future and that?"

Mickelsson hesitated. "Some philosophers work on such things," he said at last. "William James, more recently people like C. D. Broad. As for myself . . ."

"The world's a weird place, when you think abowt it," Tim said. Though he was still smiling, he was watching Mickelsson closely. Now Mickelsson had his matches out. He lit the cigarette.

Shale bluffs rose up on each side of them, large locust trees arching across the gap. Then they came out into the hazy sunlight again, and they could see the Bauer place above them, rising sharp-gabled against the mountain. The hexes on the barns, squarely lit, looked oddly grim today, more recently painted than the walls they adorned, yet more ancient nonetheless, archaic as runes.

Mickelsson would hardly remember, later, his inspection of the house that first time he'd gone up with Tim. Everything in it had been better than he'd hoped for—the rooms larger, the views from every window more surprising. If the decor was not to his taste, he'd hardly noticed. In any event, most of it would go when the owner moved. (Pressed-board bookshelves, Swiss-dotted curtains, hospital-style drapes . . .) He would make changes, a number of them, but none of that especially occupied his mind as he walked through the house with Tim and the large, light-voiced woman, Dr. Bauer, the owner. She was pale and even taller than Mickelsson. She seemed to have accepted the fact of her height; she walked as if it were the rest of the world that was peculiar.

He'd pretended to weigh things carefully, nodding, frowning, trying the upstairs faucets (not so good), but his decision had already been 90 per cent made when he'd stepped over the threshold. The inside, he found, struck the same mysterious chord in him. Once when he was seven or eight he'd been taken to the stark frame house in Minnesota where his mother had grown up. This was somehow like that, he thought, not that the houses were the same in color or shape or smell or any other physical detail that he could notice. . . .

Light fell in tinted, dusty beams through the stained-glass panes of the arched door into the entryroom and draped itself over the bottom three stairs and around the newel post. When the owner stepped into the splay of light and her black, homely shoes turned as blue as barnflies, Mickelsson gave a little start and looked suddenly into her eyes. She smiled, no doubt puzzled, and glanced up at the shadows at the top of the stairs.

When he stepped into Tim's office to announce the verdict on his loan application, he found that Tim already knew. "Easy as pie, hay?" Tim said, rising behind his completely bare desk, stretching his muscular arms out wide in welcome, grinning from ear to ear. "O-kay! How *abowt* that!"

"You already heard," Mickelsson said, grinning but accusing.

"Well, you know these small towns," Tim said, and laughed. "I guess all we have to do now is arrange for a meeting with the doc's lawyer in Montrose." He pronounced it Mont-*rose*. "Sign the papers," he explained. "If you want to bring a lawyer of your own, that's fine, or I guess you could both use the doc's lawyer—" His eyes met Mickelsson's, then skidded off.

"That'll be all right," Mickelsson said; and it would be, he knew. It was strange how safe he felt in Tim's hands. Why not one same lawyer, in fact?—though Finney, when he heard, would howl. How long had it been since Mickelsson had been anywhere where trust was standard? He thought of his reviewers—those who disliked him—whining like bandsaws, no more interested in truly representing his thought, not to mention understanding it, than in describing the aesthetics of bingo. Not that Mickelsson brooded often on reviews; more were favorable than not, in any case, though the reviews in the supposedly prestigious journals were always unrelentingly scornful, written by pedantic young men and women from "the best universities," little pricks who intended to go far, come hell or high water. "In this thin yet surprisingly repetitive little tract . . ." "Without mentioning Ayn Rand, though his dependence falls little short of plagiarism . . ."

"Well," Tim said, and grinned again, "all right, I'll arrange it." The barely perceptible cloud over his mood had passed, some doubt removed. "You free Tuesdee?"

Who was ever, in this sad, long-winded universe, free?

"I can manage it, I think," he said, and laughed.

Instead of driving straight back to Binghamton, that afternoon, he drove out past the house again, then farther into the mountains, turning onto whatever road seemed to beckon. He drove lost for hours, breathing the zesty air in deep, passing high, sunlit meadows, lakes, wooded entrances to summer camps with Indian names or noble-hearted names, "Equity Camp," "Camp Sky"—here and there a farm with tall blue silos and fields bounded by stone walls. In the end he accidentally circled back into Susquehanna—or rather, as it seemed, came upon one more pretty little village which suddenly, as he crested a hill, turned into a place much larger than he'd thought it, a town of brick streets plunging hell-bent down a steep mountainside toward a wide, solemn river—now broad, now narrow tree-lined streets following a series of deep, shady ravines with hurrying dark water and ferns in their basins, and above, glum old poverty-battered houses propped up on stilts or slate-gray, water-seeping walls, occasional small stores, steep lawns that old men or old women mowed by playing out and hauling back ropes they'd attached to their lawn-mower handles. He wasn't aware that he was back in Susquehanna till he came upon the traffic light and the bank sign, COUNTY NATIONAL, and, in computer lights, $62°$, then $7:13$. On the watchers' bench tonight there were only two old women, one of them eating an ice-cream cone. He thought of stopping off for supper at the town's one restaurant, or anyway the only one he'd found so far; but inertia and the shabbiness of the place kept him going. He would take in his new world a little at a time. Beside the curbs, up on the sidewalks, and in the Acme Supermarket parking lot, there were big-tired pickup trucks with airbrush flames pouring up, circus-yellow and -red, from the engines and, on the cabs' back windows, sleazy Western landscapes: elk and bear, leaping fish, mountain lakes. He turned in to the rough stone underpass that led onto the long iron bridge, green as algae, spanning the river.

Driving on the crooked road that followed the Susquehanna—not hurrying, getting the feel of the walled-in, shadowy valley, giving himself time to admire the blood-red sunset lighting up the tops of mountains and the undersides of clouds—feeling himself pleasantly alone in the world, everything around him serene, asleep—he came upon a stretch of road where cars were parked bumper to bumper on both shoulders: cars of every description and make—new Cadillacs and Lincolns, neatly kept seven- or eight-year-old Plymouths, Hondas and Saabs, Volkswagens, beat-up campers. (He did not notice until later that the license plates were all from far away.) It seemed to him the strangest thing in the world— here, miles from nowhere, all these cars. He drove for a mile or so between these hedges of tightly parked vehicles, their roofs and windows lighted by the sunset—beyond them, on the left side, the broad, still river moving silently past weighed-down willowtrees and mountains. Then he saw that the road ahead of him was blocked: taillights in the right lane, parking- lights in the left. He pulled up behind the taillights—it turned out to be a paneltruck with several cars ahead of it—and after a moment switched off his engine. At first there seemed no one around. Then he saw the red glow of cigarettes over among the trees beyond the cars on the left-side shoulder. He got out, shut the car-door behind him, pressed his hat on more firmly, and, shoulders hunched, went to find out what was wrong.

In the grove of flowering locusts beside the road there were dark silhouettes of men and women, people standing with their backs to him, now and then saying a word or two, occasionally laughing, looking down, where the trees parted, at the still, burning river. "What's up?" Mickelsson was about to ask, but then drew in a sharp breath instead and, without thinking, took off his hat and bent forward.

In the winding, wide, perfect mirror below, hundreds of people, adults and children, stood sunk to the waist or higher. They didn't seem to be fishing or dredging for a body. . . . To the man at his right he said, "What's going on down there?"

"Mormons," the man said, and reached out, trying to catch something, perhaps a moth. He was young, frazzle-bearded, dressed in mechanic's coveralls. His accent was richly Susquehanna. "Every year abowt this time they come owt here and try to drown each other." He reached out again.

"Drown—" Mickelsson began, then understood that, despite the man's tone, and despite the sombre landscape that made it half credible, it was a joke. "Ah," Mickelsson said, and laughed. He got out his pipe. After a moment he asked, "Why here?"

"Holy land," the young man said, then turned to look up at him, interested to meet a being so ignorant, a city feller in a suitcoat, willing to be instructed. "You ever hear of Joseph Smith?" He cracked a laugh.

Mickelsson nodded, then inclined his head. When he lit the match for his pipe, he saw that the young man's face was round and dimpled, filthy with oil or maybe soot. The woman and the fat man beyond him had faces creased with age, though they were probably not old. Their teeth were sharply outlined.

"He used to live right back there." The young man pointed past Mickelsson into the darkness. "Other side of the graveyahrd. Lived in a lot of diffrint howses arownd here, but that was one of 'em."

"Ah!" Mickelsson said again. "So that's what makes—"

"Sh!"

The woman on the other side of the young man, apparently his wife, gat-toothed and pregnant, jerked her gray face forward and raised her fingers to her lips. The two women beyond her and the fat, sighing man, in a Phillies baseball cap, looked over in Mickelsson's direction with interest. Several feet beyond the fat man stood a small boy in glasses, who never moved or spoke. There were others. Twenty or thirty feet farther on Mickelsson could make out bearded men and women in dark formal clothing—in the darkness that was as much as he could tell. He remembered hearing somewhere, from Jessica Stark, perhaps, that there were Mennonites up in the mountains. A mosquito landed on his neck and he slapped it.

Now a strange sound came from the river—at first impossible to identify, then the next instant so obviously what it was that Mickelsson could hardly believe it had eluded him. They were singing. The bearded young man poked Mickelsson's arm with the back of his hand and, when Mickelsson looked down, held something toward him—a bottle, he thought at first, but when he somewhat tentatively accepted the offer, feeling a quick little flush of distress, the bottle turned into binoculars. "Oh. Oh, thank you," Mickelsson said, still startled by the magical transformation, and raised the binoculars to press them against the lenses of his glasses. At first he could see nothing but a colorful blur. He moved the binoculars from side to side and up and down until large, gawky shapes swung into view, disappeared, then appeared again. He realized for the first time that some of the Mormons were wearing white robelike things, sleeveless. He looked for several seconds. Some of the people looked eighty or more, standing there in the ice-cold water with their mouths open, grimly enduring. Their mouths and eyes were like pits. Fogwisps hovered over the water around them. Then he remembered that the binoculars were on loan and gave them back.

"Is that *robes* they're wearing?" Mickelsson whispered.

"That's that underwear they gaht," the man said.

His wife shot a look at him to hush him.

Ah yes, Mickelsson thought. He'd once spent a week at the University of Utah. Someone there had told him about the underwear they wore, with religious writing on it. According to whoever it was that had told him, they never took it off.

He'd never in his life heard music so unearthly. Perhaps it was the shale of the mountainsides, or the breath of cold fog on the river; whatever the reason, the music, by the time it reached Mickelsson, seemed nothing that human voices could conceivably produce. If stones were to sing, taking their own natural harmonies, or if the restless spirits of dead animals were to cry out, this might be their sound.

Whispering again, Mickelsson asked, "Do you know what they're singing?"

"I'm naht real sher," the man whispered back. "It don't sownd like country and western." He laughed. In spite of herself, the woman beyond him laughed too.

That night, when Mickelsson was trying to get to sleep, he found the image in his mind—all those Mormons in the river—depressing. The water was still and red, glowing; in the span of sky between the lighted-up mountaintops and bellies of clouds, birds arced slowly back and forth, shrilly crying. He didn't need Dr. Rifkin to explain why he was gloomy.

He remembered that one night when he was a boy of eight or nine, heavy, dark-haired strangers—hairy all over, males and females—had come to the swimming-hole where he and his cousins often went after chores, a place they'd always thought of as strictly their own, though in fact it had been on railroad property. The strangers were loud, the kind of people his mother called "coarse," always grabbing each other, splashing water, screaming, throwing pebbles. They had beer with them. Though he himself hadn't seen it, his cousin Erik had whispered into his ear that one of the males had stuck his thing up into one of the females, under-water—she'd helped him, pulling her suit out of the way. From above you'd have thought they were just horsing around, maybe fighting.

When he finally did get to sleep that night, Mickelsson had bad dreams. In the spillway from the pond at the Bauer place, he found a drowned child. Its pale blue eyes were weighted like a doll's, closing and opening as the head moved back and forth.

All the next day he was depressed, morbid. He tried to read a book, *The New Nietzsche*. The title should have warned him. "The," as if there were *one*, and "New," as if . . . Toward evening he washed his mountain of dirty dishes, some of them with mould on them, and mechanically went over the floors with a broom. Once the phone rang, Edie Bryant, whose husband was in English, inviting Mickelsson to a party. "I'll see," he said, and put his hand on his forehead, closing his eyes. *I'll see. I'll see.* He seemed to have lost the ability to tell the truth.

3

Nevertheless—all caution blasted to the moon—he was pleased when the signing of papers in the Montrose lawyer's office went smoothly, and the house became his. He could call back later only a few moments of the ritual, mainly Dr. Bauer smiling and talking, one arm cocked forward in the shade of her enormously wide hat, the pale hand twisted like a cripple's, signing the papers left-handed. She'd come dressed in a suit, as if the ceremony were a serious matter, but for all the formality of her dress—midnight blue, heightening the effect of her bread-dough pallor— she chatted pleasantly. Except for Mickelsson, they were all old friends: the ancient, coughing, chain-smoking lawyer with his thick-lensed glasses, white hair in his ears, gnarled, palsied hands; the fat, blond, chinless, large-bosomed secretary who brought them coffee and showed pictures of her children to Dr. Bauer; Tim's boss, Charley Snyder (Tim wasn't there), whom Mickelsson mistook at first for the Susquehanna banker (he realized later that Snyder was younger, and talked and dressed more like a man of the world, sporty and natty, quick to grin; he was probably good at golf, probably had a farm somewhere with riding horses); and of course Dr. Bauer, at once gigantic and inconspicuous, shy as a wren.

Throughout the whole business, Mickelsson's mind was mostly elsewhere. He'd felt twenty emotions at once, in the beginning, listening to their banter. The lawyer, a Mr. Cook, sat behind an extremely large, cluttered desk elevated on a kind of dais, as if the desk had been intended for use as a judicial bench. He had windows at his back, and all around the rest of the room—the desk took up a third of it—he had high wooden filing cabinets and dully gleaming law books. Mickelsson and the others sat across from him, in forced respect—all but the secretary, who moved back and forth from the outer office to this one, running errands for the lawyer. It was a cunning arrangement: except for the windows, the room was quite dark, and against the sunlight, hazed by cigarette smoke, the lawyer's head was blurry and defeatured, symbolic of the godly power of his position—counsellor, arbiter, guardian of *das Recht*. In all fairness, he wore his mantle lightly, chatting casually, pausing for a coughing fit or to search his enfeebled memory for a name, or a date, or where the sam hill he'd put his ink-pen. Besides being forgetful and half blind, Mr. Cook was very nearly stone deaf.

The talk ebbed and flowed like pure Being; Mickelsson refrained from wading in. He liked these people, liked their comfortable ease with one another, but he was by no means one of them, not yet anyway, and in general, he thought, he wanted no more to do with them than need be. He was moving to the country to get off by himself; one could be amused from a distance—one could feel a sort of neighborly rapport, so to speak—without being sworn into the gang. And so he smiled stiffly, playing with his Western gentleman's hat, rather pleased with himself despite his uneasiness about the lies, the money, allowing his mind to drift to thoughts of how he would fix up the house, someday paint the barns—nodding when by accident he met someone's eyes. "That's right," he would say occasionally, throwing out his look of intense, crazed interest, eyebrows raised, grin eager, hardly aware what he was concurring in.

They were clearly in no hurry, and at times, briefly, their prelapsarian time-sense stirred his irritation. When the fat young woman showed the pictures of her children to Dr. Bauer, who had delivered them (the doctor tilted her large frame forward, nodding under her hat, exclaiming "My! Oh my!"), he felt such a twinge of impatience he had to stop himself and think the feeling out. It came to him at last that his earlier assessment had been entirely wrong. Say what he would about membership in the gang, he was in fact feeling snubbed—and *was* being snubbed, just a little. If he were seven, he thought, he would have burst into tears. Not surprising, of course. In this new life he'd invested so heavily in—risking, in fact, financial and maybe psychological catastrophe—they, with their small-town, narrow minds, were keeping their distance as they'd do with some smiling fat banker from New Jersey. Absurd that he should mind. He knew about small towns. Ah, ah, what a ridiculous creature was the whimpering, snivelling human psyche! (He realized with a start that he was whispering, just perceptibly moving his right hand. He checked himself and glanced around the room. No one had noticed.) Given the slightest encouragement, he knew (unbeknownst to him, his right hand was moving again), the secretary would happily have shown him her snapshots. She'd have shown them to a nut-tree if the tree showed interest. She didn't show her pictures to Charley Snyder either, or the lead-faced, trembling, coughing, wheezing old lawyer; but her smiles and chatter made them part of the conversation. They laughed, tossed her a word now and then like a puppy-treat, but mostly talked with one another. The child of someone they knew had wandered into a cave somewhere and had come across something radioactive. "That sucker came out glowing like a candle," the lawyer cried in his thin piping voice. Charley Snyder shook his head, sympathetic, but asked with interest, "Uranium, was it?" "*Refuse* is what it was," the lawyer yelled, "refuse brought down here from Canada or New Jersey!" Then he doubled over, covering his mouth with his already clenched fist, for a coughing fit. As soon as it was over he pulled again at his cigarette, hollowing his cheeks.

The conversation of the lawyer and Charley Snyder rippled into the conversation of the secretary and the doctor. As if unaware what it was that had altered the tone of their talk, the two women wondered what the world was coming to, briefly troubled about the future of the secretary's children. "So many strangers coming in with their different ideas," the secretary said as if Mickelsson weren't there. "Lot more Mormons these days, not that I gaht anything against the Mormons."

"Course not," Dr. Bauer said.

"And all those people from New York City and so on, buying up the land so's an ordinary person can't afford it anymore—buying it and not even *moving* to it."

"Buying it for retirement, they say," Dr. Bauer said, and briefly closed her eyes.

For all his deafness, the lawyer somehow caught the secretary's last remark and said to Snyder, as if it were he who'd made it, "Buying it to make the whole state of Pennsylvania their God damn garbage dump."

Mickelsson, listening with only half his mind, remembered "Punk" Atcheson, the grinning, freckle-faced, red-headed boy who'd first made friends with him when—timid, knowing no one—he'd transferred to the big highschool in Wausau. One day Mickelsson had been the weird out-sider, the next it was as if he'd lived in Wausau all his life. Punk had been on the football team and a star in the highschool chorus, which Mickelsson had quickly joined. They'd become, as they say, inseparable. Again and again they'd gone into laughing fits—Mickelsson could no longer remem-ber the reason—and had been thrown out of classes. That was what he wanted now, of course: a Punk Atcheson to let him through the door.

Almost the instant he figured out his feelings, Mickelsson began to feel nothing at all, or nothing but the boredom and weariness he felt at faculty meetings. It was of course not that anyone had done anything wrong. His gloom had nothing to do with them—had more to do with his dream of the child in the spillway.

And so, for these reasons and various others, when he looked back later almost the only image he retained was of the blurred silhouette of the lawyer's torso and head against the window and, below, the doctor awkwardly twisted above her stack of gray papers, even her mouth twisted hard to one side (he could not see her eyes), signing her name, wherever there was an *x*, with her curled, long-fingered left hand.

He also remembered, sometime much later, one joke they'd neglected to let him in on. When Mickelsson was introduced to the secretary, when he'd first arrived, the woman smiled warmly and exclaimed, "So you're buying the Sprague place! You must have steady nerves!"

"No," he'd said, then realized that that must be their name for it (his mind went briefly to Sprague the philosopher), then realized there must be something more he was missing. "Steady nerves?" he echoed.

They were all laughing, Charley Snyder calling out, "Shame on you, Martha! You trying to make him change his mind?"

Mickelsson had meant to press her for what she'd meant, though he'd assumed he more or less knew. It was an *odd*-looking house, "Pennsylvania Gothic," as Tim had said, laughing. Mickelsson laughed now with the others, trying to concentrate on the continuing introductions—the lawyer and Charley Snyder; Dr. Bauer he'd met before—and when the introductions were over, something else coming up immediately, the joke he wasn't sure he'd understood had slipped his mind. It was no grave matter; it would be weeks, in fact, before Mickelsson would remember that he'd forgotten.

At the door, as he was leaving, the old lawyer pinched at his sleeve and cried out, "You've been here to Montrose before, Professor?"

"Yes," Mickelsson said, nodding, poking tobacco into his pipe. "I looked at a couple of houses here."

"You oughtta run up and see Lake Avenue before you leave," the old man said. He interrupted himself, coughing, and took out a wadded gray handkerchief to press to his lips. When he'd finished he patted Mickelsson's arm, old-womanish, his fingers like sticks. "Right up toward the courthouse and bear left by the bandstand. Can you see the bandstand? They use to hang people up there, in the old days." He smiled, baring his teeth. "Lake Avenue, as I was saying—" He stepped out onto the concrete stoop so he could point the way.

"I've seen Lake Avenue," Mickelsson said, raising his voice. "You're right, it's a beautiful sight."

"Prettiest place you ever laid eyes on," the old man said. Again he raised the handkerchief to his lips, but no cough came. "Just bear left at the bandstand. Go on, just walk up and have a look at it."

"I've seen it," Mickelsson said, almost shouting now, stiffening.

The old man stood with the handkerchief near his mouth, nodding and waiting, smiling as if pleased that the professor had at last been persuaded. Behind the thick lenses of his glasses, the lawyer's eyes were all gray, swimming iris.

In the end, with what seemed to Mickelsson himself an abrupt and rather crazy laugh—consciously giving himself up to absurdity and feeling, as he did so, suddenly light, as if someone had switched off gravity— Mickelsson turned, pushed his hands into his pockets, and set off for the bandstand, bore left when he came even with it, then stopped for a moment and stood looking, his hat pushed back. "Nice," he said aloud, broadly gesturing with his pipe. He waved at the cupolas, the rose-trellised porches, whatever people might be peeking from behind their lace curtains and heavy drapes. "Beautiful!" He laughed somewhat sharply, then put his hands and pipe into his coatpockets, his expression growing thoughtful.

It was true that the village of Montrose was beautiful—quite remarkable if you came to it from Binghamton, with its vast wrecked-car piles and cluttered freightyards, its four- or six- or eight-lane highways sectioning the town, looking at the scabby backs of poor people's houses; its grim miles of black, decaying factories and failing warehouses, its trucker stops (Texaco, Shell, Sunoco; between them short-order restaurants, bars, and shoddy little rental stores); mighty Binghamton, blasted by the idiocy of Urban Removal, so that the city's once-grand old downtown section was like a beautiful old lady with teeth knocked out . . . though at sunset, in all fairness, Binghamton too could be beautiful in its way, with its thousands of lights reflected in its two wide gentle rivers and sweeping grandly up misty, dark hills, here and there the gleaming golden onion domes, or the paired golden domes, of a Polish church, to the south the brick, glass, and aluminum towers of the State University. After Binghamton, the village of Montrose suggested another reality entirely (neither had it anything at all in common with cracked-voice, puffy-faced, sooty Susquehanna, sister city twenty miles east). Montrose was the mythic American past, westernmost settlement of the Connecticut Land Grant—large white houses set like gleaming palaces or grand old-fashioned inns on broad side-hill lawns or shrubbed, well-cared-for hill-crests, the tallest, darkest evergreens in the world rising along their driveways. Inside each house there were innumerable rooms, occasionally a small, discreet apartment, a side-door physician's office. Sunlight, filtering down through the trees onto the high lawns and green-shuttered houses of Montrose, the rounded, fading red brick of Lake Avenue (Susquehanna's brick streets were asphalt-patched, shabby and lumpy as the skin of a witch), gave an effect that, in a sentimental fifties movie, would call for a background of angels' music. Indeed, music something like that might actually be heard there, in summertime at least, since at the far end of Lake Avenue stood the buildings and grounds of the Montrose Bible Conference.

It was true that Montrose was beautiful; but Mickelsson was unmoved. It was a village of old and dying rich people, superannuated doctors, lawyers, bankers, many of them retired to this place from Philadelphia. Nothing much had changed here in two hundred years, but not because it stood outside time, like the Bauer place (in Mickelsson's admittedly queer opinion): in Montrose one had the feeling that time had been stubbornly resisted, refused lawful entrance, with the result that, somehow, nothing was secret here, nothing more mysterious than a Baptist's sweet smile or a banker's jovial "Good morning." Nothing to be learned.

It was odd, a sympathetic observer might say, that the great white houses stirred in him no emotion. If the house he was buying were ever brought back to its former state, it would be much like one of these. Professor Mickelsson smiled, thinking of the warped, peeling shutters of his house, the dangling eaves, the knotty, slanting floors of native chestnut.

It made him feel a little like a secret agent, standing here—a tall, stout scholar spy, pipe in hand, hat level now—thinking of his battered old shadow-filled monster in the presence of these proud, white, Christian homes.

Well, he was glad Montrose existed. He turned, bowing to Lake Avenue, touching his hatbrim, excusing himself, then walked to where his rusted, dented car was parked, down on the sidewalk in front of the lawyer's office. Charley Snyder, Mr. Cook, and tall, wide-hatted Dr. Bauer all stood looking more or less in Mickelsson's direction, laughing up- roariously—too far away to hear—teetering, hanging on to one another's elbows. He blushed, then on second thought nodded in their direction and touched his hat. There was no reason to believe they were laughing at him. He climbed into the car, switched on the engine, and covered his nose and mouth with his right hand while with his left he hastily rolled up the window against the foul-smelling cloud that exploded all around him, a great shameless blast of yellow-gray luminous pollution from the Chevy's rear end.

Driving back to Binghamton, he noticed for the first time how many slag-heaps there were on the road out of Montrose, how many signs reading FILL WANTED—STONE ONLY, and NO DUMPING!

When he reached his apartment, late that evening, the first thing he saw was the dark, completely unornamented car parked, more or less in shadow, under the trees across the street. For some reason he did not think about it, merely registered its existence, as he pulled the old Chevy up the driveway to the back of the house. He got out, noisily closed the car-door, and crossed the pitchdark back yard to the door opening onto the stairs up to his apartment. He heard a car-door close, like a belated echo, somewhere in front of the house, and then footsteps. Even now he did not quite understand, though some animal part of him came alert. He climbed the stairs more quickly than usual, hunting in his trouser pocket as he did so for the key to his apartment door. Then he knew there was someone on the stairs below him, and his mind came fully awake. He turned, craned his head around, and saw in the stairwell's dimness two men in suits. Fear flashed through him, and he imagined himself running up the stairs for dear life, reaching the boxes of books outside his door and hurling them down at his pursuers, then going in for the silver-headed cane. The same instant, the man in the lead—small and wiry, dark-haired; the other was larger, almost fat—called up to him, "Professor Mickelsson?" They stood frozen as in a movie still, or one of his son's photographs, the smaller man with his hand on the bannister, the larger one just behind him, his hand flat on the opposite wall, both of them looking up at him as if in fear. Both of them wore hats. The one in front was holding something up for Mickelsson to see. Crazily, he thought at first it was something he'd dropped, which they'd come running to give back.

But the man was saying, "We're with Internal Revenue, Professor," and Mickelsson saw that what he held up was an identification card. Now the other man had his out too, holding it up as if Mickelsson might be able to read it in the dim yellow light, from twenty feet away.

"I see," Mickelsson said, and touched his left cheek with the back of his right hand. At last he said, "Come on up."

He did not bother to listen to their names as they introduced themselves, nor did he bother to look carefully at the cards they insisted on showing him up close, standing under the plastic-shaded light outside his door. When they told him their business he said "Fine," obligingly—assuming he had no choice in the matter—cleared his typewriter and books from the table, and sat down beside the smaller man. The larger one stood over by the window in the kitchen, looking out at the wall of leaves, occasionally moving a little, leaning on the sink, walking over to read the calendar on the wall, bending his head to watch carefully as he cleaned his fingernails with a silver nail-clipper.

They had photostats of every check he'd paid or received over the past ten years, and a large, leatherbound notebook full of neatly penned words and numbers. Mickelsson's job was to identify, insofar as he could remember, what each check received had been for and whether the checks he'd written were "business" or "personal." Somehow, though Mickelsson wasn't conscious of panic, his mind substituted "pleasure" for "personal," so that he would say, stupidly, as he went through the photostats, "Pleasure, business, pleasure, pleasure, pleasure . . ." Once he said, "Pleasure—not that paying an electric bill is much pleasure, ha ha!"

"Actually," the man said, unamused, coolly polite, "it's 'personal,' not 'pleasure.' "

"Yes. Yes of course," Mickelsson said, but instantly his mind returned to the mistake. The man did not bother to correct him again.

They sat for hours—he had no idea how long—Mickelsson turning over photostats, the small man, expressionless, taking notes. They did not explain to him, nor did he dare ask, why it was necessary to go through all this, all these years, not just the two he hadn't paid. Neither did they explain why both of them had to come, though one of them did nothing. Once, when they were between stacks of photostats, the man asked, "Would you say you're personally responsible for your unpaid taxes, or were there others involved?"

Something about the way he asked it made Mickelsson feel that they knew about his wife's having "borrowed" the tax-money he'd saved in '77. The same instant he saw the opening he turned his eyes from it. "No, I'm responsible," he said. "Ultimately, anyway."

"Ultimately?"

He reached for his pipe and matches. "I'm responsible," he said.

Without comment, the man slid him the next stack of photostats.

The night was still, unbearably muggy. Both men, like Mickelsson, had taken their coats off, though only Mickelsson's shirt was pasted to his back. Moths bumped against the lamp on the table, occasionally striking the metal shade, softly ringing it. He could feel around him, stretching out infinitely in all directions, the government's silent watchfulness.

Once, between stacks of photostats, the man drew out an envelope, took the folded paper from it, and placed both the paper and the envelope on the table in front of Mickelsson. "You don't need to sign this now," he said. "Talk to your lawyer, if you like." Mickelsson saw, just glancing at it, that it was some kind of medical disclaimer. They knew about his bouts with mental illness. He was hardly surprised. He nodded, put the paper back in the envelope, and laid it to the right of his workspace.

"You think of everything," he said, and smiled.

The man said nothing.

Was it possible that they had wives and children, troubles of their own? He bent over the stack of photostats the man had placed in front of him. "Pleasure, pleasure, pleasure," he said, "business, I think. Pleasure. Business."

All Binghamton was asleep, all but the moths, Mickelsson, and the United States government.

"Would you care for a beer?" he asked.

"No thanks."

"Coffee?"

"No thanks."

Once the man asked, "Is your son still financially dependent on you?"

"I'm not sure, legally," Mickelsson said. "I still send him money."

"He's engaged in anti-nuclear activities. Is that right?"

"He's a student," Mickelsson said, blushing, his muscles subtly tensing. "As for his politics—"

The man said nothing.

"What do you mean? What are you implying?"

The man studied his notes. His right hand moved to the upper corner of the page, closed on it, and turned it. "The question's routine," he said. "We're not interested in his politics." The statement was so flat, so mechanical, that Mickelsson, despite his better judgment, was inclined to believe it. The man looked at the stack of photostats to be identified.

Mickelsson looked down, unable to read for a moment, then said, "Pleasure. Business. Business."

In the night outside a siren went off, police this time. He thought of the black dog.

The leaves outside his windows were stirring. Rain coming on. He got an image, sharp as an image in a dream, of rain and wind whipping the trees in the yard of the Bauer place—or rather, Sprague place.

"Pleasure," he said. Mechanically, the man noted it.

He looked at the next of the photostats.

"Pleasure," he said.

4

Though he would not entirely deny the possibility of the existence of ghosts, or of anything else in this crazy universe, he was skeptical, to say the least; or, to put it more precisely, while he was not quite willing to deny absolutely that Swedenborg or William James' cousin, or Mickelsson's own grandfather, might now and then have communicated with "the other side," or even that certain living psychics, much studied of late, might indeed, as they claimed, get occasional help in their work from spirits, he could not help dismissing as country foolishness the idea that the Bauer place—Sprague place—was haunted. If he felt uneasy, it was not about the ghosts but about the people who'd sold him the house without mentioning—that is, without giving more than delicate hints of—its local reputation. In a sense, of course, there was no reason they should have. If they considered the whole thing superstitious nonsense, as well they might—if none of them actually believed the place haunted—then perhaps it had simply slipped their minds. A man of sense would let it go at that. It was a mark of his paranoia that, despite what he knew to be the sensible course, he felt uneasy.

He could see no evidence, carefully thinking back, of any special eagerness to be rid of the house on Dr. Bauer's part, much less on Tim's. It was true that she'd come down considerably in price, but in all likelihood only for the reason she'd given, that she had to get away soon to Florida. (On the other hand, neither had she seemed at all reluctant to see a house so magnificent go cheaply.) Perhaps—abstracted and gloomy as he was, and eager to get the place—he hadn't been watching very closely.

He'd been rather more depressed than usual, he remembered, the only time he'd really talked to the woman, when he'd gone up to the house to get the keys. The idea that had at first seemed just a madcap notion—a possibility to toy with at cocktail parties or when his apartment got him down—had changed, the minute he was granted that loan, to a sober, dangerous commitment: he'd agreed to buy the thing; now he must pay for it, actually move out to it, cough up money to movers, deal with up-keep and repairs. Sometimes when he thought seriously about his financial situation, his hands became so weak he could hardly keep his grip on a pencil. The words *Out of control* would flash into his mind. *Out of control!* But then he would tighten his jaw, rein in. All the universe was out of control, or at least showed no signs of the kind of control his grandfather's dry, stern sermons on works and grace had read into it, the under-lying order Mickelsson had taken for granted all those years, even after he'd abandoned theism—until suddenly the ground had dropped out from under him and he'd clearly grasped his situation.

He remembered his grandfather in his rose garden—a side of him Mickelsson hadn't thought of for a long, long time. He remembered the old man, like a crooked-nosed black bird, bending over to sniff a flower. Was it possible that he'd simply been testing it by smell for some sick-ness—that he had no more feeling for scents than he had for children, dogs, or sunsets? Had he gotten any pleasure out of conceiving his own children—seven of them, only two of whom (Mickelsson's father was the seventh) had survived?

The weather, when he'd gone up to the Bauer place, had been bright and crisp, much cooler in the mountains than down in Binghamton. The glen below the farmstead was full of restless bird movement and the sombre echo of waterfalls; up above, white luminous clouds hovered. Once the farm had been quite an operation, one could tell by the size of the empty barns; but that had been long ago. Now it came with only thirty acres. Dr. Bauer had lived here fourteen years, she said, and it had already been long past farming, grown up in wildflowers, brush, and woods, when she'd moved in.

She was a likeable person; a large, farmish woman whom everyone affectionately called "the doc." She had the same *owt*'s and *gaht*'s as her neighbors, the same flattened vowels and enriched *r*'s. She worked at the grim, dark-brick local hospital (torn green windowshades on the office windows, in the patients' rooms gray venetian blinds), and nearly every-one he'd met in Susquehanna had at one time or another been helped by her. She was sixty, a dowdy dresser (she'd been wearing that day a light, countryish flowerprint dress of inexpensive material)—her bodily con-struction tall, squarish, heavy, her flesh queerly pale and soft. Something about her made Mickelsson suspect at once that she must be vegetarian. Except for that, the vegetarian look, if he'd met her on the street he'd have set her down as a well-to-do farmer's wife, old-fashioned, no doubt religious. The hex signs on the barns, though more recently painted than the walls themselves—or touched up, perhaps—were so old and weather-worn they had to be the work of a previous owner—except that, he thought fleetingly, that hardly explained the relatively new one on the pleasantly crude Dutch door into the kitchen. What the hex signs meant he had no idea, nor could the doctor enlighten him, apparently. "Interesting, aren't they?" she'd said, smiling. It was as if for her they were simply strange flowers that had one day, through no effort of hers, bloomed there, and seemed to do no harm. Mickelsson had his doubts. Each of them was set inside a circle of black, and Mickelsson knew enough of symbolism to be suspicious. But of course he hadn't pressed her. All over that section of

Pennsylvania, though they began in earnest farther south, there were hexes. He'd felt, if anything, a little pleased with himself for having found a place with special character; and except in those moods when nothing pleased him, he'd enjoyed that specialness more and more as time passed. (He would get up, mornings, after he'd moved in, and go out onto his lawn to watch the swallows lift and swoop, the martins step out of their high, red apartment house and fly heavily off to work, the fat catbird in the branches of the birchtree mewing crossly. Across the glen below his house, shadowy trees slowly darkened into view through their broad, low fogbank like ships drawing nearer. The yellow morning light—hitting the barns broadside, giving the old, faded hexes sharp detail—could fill Mickelsson, when depression wasn't on him, with a wonderful satisfaction.) The doctor had no doubt felt the same when she'd lived here; had no doubt felt pleased, as he did now, when tourists stopped their cars and took pictures of the signs on the barns or the waterfall beyond. (In the large, unheated workroom that jutted out behind the house toward the rise of the mountain and the woods—a room Mickelsson intended to convert, as soon as he could afford it, into a large, formal diningroom, not that he expected to be having much company—he found evidence of the magic the doctor cared most about: a picture of Jesus in a crown of thorns, looking mournfully, with gentle Anglo-Saxon eyes, toward heaven.)

He'd walked up into the woods with her for a look at the old concrete reservoir, his water supply.

"I'm sure you won't be having any trouble, Prahfessor," she'd said. "It doesn't exactly come gushing, but there's only the one of you." Her laugh was girlish, the laugh of someone perfectly at peace with the world.

Mickelsson had nodded, half smiling politely, standing precariously in his leather-soled shoes on the slope of crumbling shale and wet weeds, hatless today (he'd left his hat on the front seat of the Chevy), his red hair streaming as if angrily in all directions, tugged by the wind they'd found up here, the tips of his pink, freckled fingers in his tight trouser pockets. It was probably true that the water system had never given her, as she said, a speck of trouble. She had the look of one of the elect. For Mickelsson things would go otherwise. The two pipes visible above the dark, clear water had orange, cancerous-looking growths of rust; they would disintegrate at a touch. And the overflow pipe, just above the ground-line, was large enough for a rabbit to crawl through. Sooner or later some rabbit would try it, it was a foregone conclusion, and the water would be polluted. But Mickelsson knew from his farm childhood, when rats would occasionally drown in the cistern and swell obscenely, that polluted water did not necessarily mean instant death; it was more likely to mean just a little more unpleasantness in the general run: a taste and smell that would gradually build up until suddenly, before you were quite aware of why, you were seized, sniffing your glass, by an urge to retch. He would get to the reservoir eventually—replace the old pipes, put an iron mesh on the overflow. For now it would do. With luck, he thought . . . and let the thought trail off. He'd managed this much; had risen out of his despair and bought a house. He would manage the rest. What the doctor brought about by faith—the smiling expectation that made mountains tip their cloud-hats and move—Mickelsson would manage by will.

"I beg your pahrdon?" the doctor said, smiling.

"Sorry," he said. "Nothing." He felt his cheeks redden.

"Oh! I didn't mean to interrupt!" She laughed. "I talk to myself all the time. It helps you keep your mind on things, don't you think so?"

When she'd put the reservoir lid back on—lifting it easily with mannish strength, Mickelsson doing almost nothing to help, bending down just an instant too late and grabbing with only one hand at the slimy edge, ineffectually, standing off balance—the doctor said, "Keep an eye out for rattlesnakes when you come up here. They won't bother you, as a rule. But I always like to see them first." She laughed again. Her face was round and bright.

He glanced at her eyes to see if there were any trace of irony behind the laughter. There was not. She was smiling sociably now, gazing over at a burned place on the hillside, as matter-of-fact as when she'd told him the sump pump would have to be replaced. (He noticed now two more gray patches where the grass had been burnt off, maybe the work of ordinary fire, maybe that of lime or acid—perhaps something to do with killing woodchucks or discouraging some troublesome weed.) Standing level with him on the mountain's slope, the doctor was taller than he was by several inches. She stood with her arms folded, her fingers on the soft flesh just above the red, wrinkled elbows. Her hair and eyes were full of sunlight. He looked around at the tall grass, the sun-filled creepers and lacy ferns, the trunks of ash trees, maples, oaks, and one very large old cherry tree, dead, above the reservoir clearing. How one was supposed to see a snake in all this he had no idea, but that too he let pass.

"Yes," he said, and turned to look out across the valley. He would never get over it that he'd stumbled onto such a view—in fact owned it, St. Augustine and his ilk to the contrary: the Susquehanna River wandering grandly, at royal leisure, toward the dark, decayed town out of sight around the bend; beyond the river more mountains, dark green, then blue; in the sky, two hawks. It was all like a richly glazed Romantic painting, luminous and wonderfully old, invaded here and there by shadows and—ah yes—snakes. He'd been told several times now that Susquehanna was famous for rattlesnakes. If August was dry, they came down off the mountain onto the streets of the town, heading for the river. The people simply stepped aside for them, it was said, though some of the snakes could be six feet long. He'd been no more frightened than were the people of the town (if the stories were true), though those who'd told him had intended him to be. Except in zoos, Mickelsson had never seen a rattlesnake. The idea that they were here, all around him in the woods, was interesting, faintly disquieting, nothing more. But no, that was not quite right, he corrected himself. He was pleased that there were snakes. He'd looked at a house, about a month ago, in a town called Jackson, a few miles south of Susquehanna, where a day or two earlier two large trees beside the road had been torn out by the roots by a twister. It was that, he'd realized when he thought about it, that had led him to consider buying the place. He knew the theory—Nietzsche, Sorel, Karl Jaspers when he spoke of "the abysses which lie on each side of the foot-path"—that the human spirit comes alive in the proximity of danger, or perhaps one might better say, with Sartre, the presence of temptation—the temptation to sink back into Nature: bestiality and death. No doubt there was truth in it. If so, rattlesnakes were better than twisters: they were always there, steady-hearted, dependable; unlike wind, they had a certain dim intelligence or, to be precise, had almost no intelligence but were nonetheless alive: struck out from their cover of lacy ferns with murderous volition and no thought of the future. This much was sure: the snakes, like the hexes on the barns, were "something." The fact of their existence, their indifferently deadly otherness, brought on a shudder of consciousness, a spasm of sharp awareness that one was alive. (Fancy talk; he'd readily admit it. Nevertheless, he was pleased that there were rattlesnakes.)

The doctor had turned just after he did to look out across the valley. She stood for a moment, her arms still folded, as if lost in thought, basking in the view—gazing at the railroad far in the distance, the famous stone viaduct built, according to the sign he'd seen beside the road, in 1847—then bent her head as if making some decision, and started down the path. She sang out, not turning, "The first time I saw one, I thought I'd have a stroke!" As she said it, she made a gesture with her right hand: fist clenched, knuckles forward, she moved her arm out slowly to the right of her, so exactly like a snake that his heart skipped.

"Scary things," he said, probably too softly for her to hear. Mickelsson drew his pipe out and patted his pockets for matches, then, finding none—he'd left them, along with his hat, in the car—followed her carefully down the slippery shale path, trying to think what more he ought to ask her. Nothing came to him.

Back in the house, the doctor had walked with him again from room to room, most of them as bare as the insides of empty wooden boxes—she'd used only a little of the house—the doctor taking long, light strides, pointing out once more what wonderful views he had from every window, not another house in sight. He imagined her sweeping through the hospital corridors, coming like sunlight into her patients' rooms, chattering with them of their children while she clamped on the blood-pressure cuff or took a pulse, exclaiming "My! Oh my!" as she'd done with the big-breasted woman in the lawyer's office. No wonder she was liked. Such pleasure in life! It was a great mystery, these powerful, inhumanly vital spirits. In her presence he felt weak.

As they travelled through the rooms she mentioned trivial faults and problems that had slipped her mind when he'd come to look at the house the first time, with Tim. The bedrooms upstairs had no heat except what came up through the registers, it would be best to leave the doors open to pick up what came up the stairs; the livingroom floor was buckled from the moisture of the spring under the house; in the kitchen and one bedroom at the back of the house small fires—defective space-heaters, from the looks—had left smoke damage, a sort of mouldy rottenness. That reminded her that the wiring in the room he would use as his study (as he'd decided at once; it looked out on roses and a birdbath) was a farmer's cobble, in the long run probably not safe. She shook her head sadly and laughed. Mickelsson nodded, troubled but at the same time amused by her belated concern.

When the keys were in his pocket and he was ready to leave, she had stood for a moment at the hexigrammed door that opened from the kitchen onto the livingroom, a long room grubbily panelled, carpeted in drab mustard yellow, like the lobby of a seedy motel (he would change that with wallpaper and a hardwood floor), and she'd gazed, expression-less, at some point beyond the far wall of the room, presumably trying to think what more she ought to warn him of. She was faintly smiling.

"Well, thanks very much," he'd said. "Good luck to you in Florida."

She hadn't seemed to hear, so he'd cleared his throat and said again, soberly, "Well, thank you very much."

She'd started, then turned to him, smiling more brightly, reaching out like a man to shake his hand. "Thank *you*," she said. "Good luck with the house!"

"Thank you," he'd said yet again, and then, awkwardly, turning to-ward the door, "Well, be seeing you."

"Why, maybe so," the doctor said, and laughed.

He felt himself blushing, his right hand fumbling with the keys in his pocket. Accidentally, he'd given his words peculiar emphasis.

That was all. Mickelsson had walked out to the car, backed carefully down the steep driveway onto the high-crowned hardtop road, and nosed down the mountain, presumably never to see her again. It was odd that he should feel so embarrassed about that trifling slip, that stupidly em-phatic "be seeing you." It was not so much that the phrase was childish, more appropriate to one of his freshmen or sophomores than to a philos-ophy professor on the dark side of fifty. It had more to do with the suggestion it carried of indifference to her life, his own as well. Indiffer-ence to the obvious truth of things. Ordinarily not even that ought to have bothered him. One saw every day, no doubt, people one would never again lay eyes on, and one said "be seeing you" and thought nothing about it. Yet the emotion had risen in him strongly, causing him to blush.

It was as if he'd let slip some truth that were better left unmentioned, as if he were warning her that he *would* see her, under circumstances not quite so pleasant. Absurd, of course. But there was no doubt of it, it seemed to him; that was what he'd seemed to say. Not surprising. Mickelsson wasn't himself these days, pursued everywhere he went by the image of his wife, back in Providence with the young man she'd learned to prefer to him. "A cheerful person, warm-*hearted*," she'd said—as if she too were that and her new love therefore suited her. No doubt the most primitive part of his brain still insisted it wouldn't last. Privately, Mickelsson called the young man The Comedian. He had a quick, nervous laugh. Willard was his name. He was forever mugging, making jokes, throwing out curious, clowning gestures. In all fairness, no doubt, it was just the young man's self-consciousness in Mickelsson's presence. Confronted by his enemy, he put on any shape he could think of except of course his own.

"You're a fine one to be talking about weird behavior," Mickelsson's wife had said.

"He hasn't got the brains to go crazy," Mickelsson had snapped. Then he'd turned on his heel, fleeing the conversation. In these battles of wit, he never won. His wife stood too firmly planted, firing too skillfully, too calmly. As for his son, twenty, and his daughter, seventeen, he hadn't spoken to either of them in weeks. It was a difficult period, "a period of redefinition," as Jessica Stark had said, her tone apologetic; she was as annoyed by rhetoric as he was.

"Where was I?" he asked himself aloud; then he remembered. No, the doctor had shown no sign that she was even aware of the stories that her house had ghosts.

He'd first learned that the house was haunted (or anyway that some people thought it to be haunted) from his neighbor from higher on the mountain, beyond the woods. "Seen any sign of them ghosts yet?" the old man asked.

Mickelsson threw a sharp look at him, interested and wary. The man was tall and old—just how old, Mickelsson couldn't guess. He was a farmer, had been one, on that same high rocky piece of land, all his life. His hair and beard were snow-white, his hue leaden, and behind the thick bifocals, his eyes, dark blue as a mountain lake deadened by snowflakes, had that blurred-at-the-edges look of eyes gradually going blind. He stood with his head unnaturally lifted and drawn back, like a watchful ghost. Mickelsson had seen him—it was almost as if he'd been expecting him—the minute he stepped out from under the eaves of the woods above the house: erect, wide-shouldered, angular and unstooped, no fat on him anywhere, though he was not a man with muscles of iron either, Mickelsson had observed as the man drew near. When he reached out to shake Mickelsson's hand, the old man, John Pearson, held his hand horizontal, palm down, like a country politician. It was a style of handshaking Mickelsson hadn't seen in years, not since boyhood, and with part of his mind he thought about it as he turned his own hand palm up, as if in submission, to take the old man's. Pearson had a shotgun on his left arm, and at his side a mongrel dog sat grinning, black and rather small, not a hunter, part collie; that and a few sheep were the only animals he kept anymore, he said. He'd once had cows and a team of horses, but his wife had been poorly, the past two years, and had spent a lot of time at the hospital down in Scranton. (He spoke of it with seeming disapproval, annoyance.) With the dairy it had been hard to get down there to see her, and anyway, these days a herd the size he'd been able to manage, up there among the pines and boulders, had been not worth the keep. He grew a few vegetables, hunted a little, sold firewood—he'd sold to the doctor. Maybe the professor would need some, he suggested, one eyebrow raised. The reason he'd dropped by this morning, he said, was to find out if Mickelsson minded if he shot a few squirrels now and then, up in the wooded stretch between their two properties. "Why, I guess that would be all right," Mickelsson said. From the way the old man nodded and pulled back his angular mouth for a grin, it was clear that the question had been just a formality; whatever answer Mickelsson had given him, Pearson would have done as he pleased.

Though it seemed they had nothing more to say, the old man went on standing there, looking at Mickelsson as if he, Mickelsson, were the visitor, and the reason for the visit had not yet come clear. Mickelsson waited, impatient to get back inside to his unpacking, resisting the temptation to ask some question or volunteer information about his life and work, as the old man was apparently hoping he'd do. He felt the awkwardness of the silence growing, and though he was nearly as tall as Pearson and a good deal heavier, he felt increasingly like a young man under suspicion, an intruder. Then, abruptly, not from embarrassment, it seemed to Mickelsson, but simply because he'd decided to do so— Pearson turned his head and looked over at the large, sharply gabled farmhouse. "Seen any sign of them ghosts yet?"

It did not seem intended as country humor, much less a cruel reference to Mickelsson's bouts with illness. Anyway, there was no way the man could know. Pearson's eyes, swinging back to judge Mickelsson's reaction, showed no sign of teasing—no sign of anything, not even much interest.

"There are supposed to be ghosts?" Mickelsson asked after an instant.

"That's what folks say. They never told you that?"

Mickelsson fished his pipe out of his coatpocket and turned to look at the house. Poking tobacco into the bowl, he said, "No, they didn't mention it."

The old man nodded, eyebrows drawn outward, ends lifted. Though he did not say so, he seemed of the opinion Mickelsson himself was now privately entertaining, that they'd kept the matter secret for fear that if they let out the truth Mickelsson might not buy. Pearson said, his head tilted like a dangerous bird's, "Old brother and sister use to live here, years ago. Odd pair. I remember seeing them a time or two, when I was a boy." He hung his right hand from the bib-strap of his overalls. "Sprague was their name. The brother and sister looked exactly alike, except the man wore a beard and the woman wore long dark dresses. Killed theirselves, or that's what folks say. Or one killed the other and then was hanged."

"Anyone know why?" Mickelsson asked. He lit the pipe, for a moment sending out smoke-puffs one after another, like an engine. Pearson looked at the smoke with interest.

At last he said, "I suppose it's easy enough to speculate." Though he did not go on to speculate, it was somehow clear what his own idea would be: strange goings-on behind those high, harsh windows—incest, most likely; at any rate something that had made them outcasts, no one to turn to in time of trouble. Mickelsson allowed his mind to toy for an instant with the queer idea that he could see someone standing at the upstairs south-east window. Secretly he knew from the beginning that it was only a reflection of the maple in the yard.

"Well, life has strange twists and turns," he said.

Pearson glanced at him as if he thought it an odd thing to say. Then, with his tongue in the corner of his mouth, still keeping his opinions to himself, he looked over at the dog. "I guess we better get back," he said. The dog threw a look at the woods, then up at his master. "Any time you need somethin," Pearson said, "you just phone me, hay? Number's in the book. John Pearson. I got a pickup truck, might help you clear all this owt." He flapped his right arm in the direction of the junk outside Mickelsson's back door—cardboard boxes and trash from the basement.

"I may take you up on that," Mickelsson said.

Pearson turned away, the dog turning with him and trotting alongside him through the gray, knee-high weeds, moving like a dark leaf carried along on a stream. Only after they'd vanished into the woods did it occur to Mickelsson that he'd forgotten to ask who it was that was supposed to have seen the ghosts, and when, how often, how long ago. Not that it mattered. It was interesting, faintly—living in a house that was supposed to be haunted. Perhaps in fact some childish, irrational corner of his brain had hopes of seeing them. He imagined himself casually telling his colleagues at the university that he lived in a house where there were supposed to be ghosts, dropping it at Jessica Stark's dinnertable, for instance. But though he was interested in the whole idea of ghosts, in a distant, rather academic way—casually interested in psychic investigation and what prescience might possibly imply about the freedom-determinism issue—interested, that is, as a professional philosopher and occasional reader of paperback books (*My Passport Says Clairvoyant, An Experience of Phantoms, Physics and Psychic Research*)—the idea that he himself might ever meet a ghost was, alas, unthinkable.

The image rose up in his mind of Pearson's blurry, gray-blue eyes, his masklike, lurid face with its tuft of goat-beard. That he chose not to have much to do with people seemed evident. It was perhaps for that reason that one couldn't tell whether or not he was joking, could no more know for sure what he was thinking than one could guess the opinions of a tree. He was a warning, Mickelsson thought, staring blankly, unconsciously poking at the ashy tobacco in his pipe. Karl Jaspers again; the idea that solitude in Nature may mean a temporary replenishment of selfhood, but to remain solitary is to risk impoverishment—to risk vanishing like a cloud dispersed, or sink like old man Pearson into the woods. His gloom deepened. Having fled to this house, he could not imagine finding his way back.

Abruptly he cleared his throat, put his pipe in his pocket, dusted off his hands—he could not remember now what he'd been thinking—and started back toward the house.

Back in the room he'd chosen as his study he returned to the dusty but interesting business of unpacking his books and old papers. He came across the notecards for a piece he'd started some years ago, and then for some reason dropped, on Dada and modern political recklessness. The cards were yellow, the ink, from a ballpoint pen, blurred and fading. He'd written the notes when he was teaching in California. He remembered the sharp thrill of the discovery: that the Dadaists, as early as 1915 —the final "apes of Zarathustra," one of his notes proclaimed—were expressing exactly the same disgust and despair one found in the graffiti on university walls in 1965: "Stop everything!" Nineteen fifteen, when his father was eight years old, his grandfather still brooding by medieval reasoning on problems already a century defunct; 1915, when his father was perhaps already inclining, subtly, non-rationally, toward the unmeditated, neither theistic nor anti-theistic love of life—love of cows, pigs, chickens, horses, ducks, goats—that would shape his character and perhaps, for a time at least, Peter Mickelsson's own: a time when farming was sweet, no sound but the gentle creak of harness-leather, the occasional hiss of steam, and the horizons of consciousness were walnut groves, hedgerows and hills.

The movement known as Dada came into being in Zurich in 1915 and eventually exported its people, "art," and outbursts to wherever an audience could be attacked. The name Dada is French babytalk for anything to do with horses, including horses' fecal matter, and like the movement, the name had no direct positive significance. Dada was in its outward form a nihilistic protest against everything. According to a Dada manifesto, its "position" was:

> *No more painters, no more writers, no more musicians,
> no more sculptors, no more religions, no more re-
> publicans, no more royalists, no more imperialists, no
> more anarchists, no more socialists, no more Bolsheviks,
> no more politicians, no more proletarians, no more dem-
> ocrats, no more armies, no more police, no more nations,
> no more of these idiocies, no more, no more, NOTHING,
> NOTHING, NOTHING.*

Another note:

> *Dadaist Arthur Craven, invited to lecture at the Exhibition of Independent
> Painters in New York in 1917, appeared drunk and proceeded to belch and
> swear at his audience. The address was concluded by police when Craven began
> to strip. (Cf. lecture from inside diving bell.)*

He had intended to argue that Dada had won, more terribly than the
Dadaists—lovers of suicide though they were—had dreamed they might.
Another note:

> *No social emotion is more vital in America today than a sense of personal
> helplessness, uselessness, and impotence. Everyone more or less has the sense
> of existing in the shadow of vast uncontrollable structures, impervious to
> human desire or need. (To elaborate: computers, I.R.S., Pentagon, etc.)*

Under the notecards he found, ironically, a sheaf of his grandfather's
sermons: "The Responsibility of the Lilies of the Field," "A Father's
Harsh Love," et cetera. He got a vivid image of the old man pacing in
his study in the manse, his right hand making furtive little gestures that,
strange to say, would expand only slightly, if at all, when he rose behind
the pulpit on Sunday morning to attack his congregation. (He was a
small man, doll-like. It was odd that he should have conceived large sons.)

Under the sermons, and under his own ream of notes on Martin
Luther, then notes on Nietzsche, near the bottom of the cardboard box
he was unpacking, he found a photograph he couldn't remember having
seen before. It was a color snapshot of his wife, Ellen, lying on a sofa, in
a black dress, their one-year-old son sitting beside her, smiling at the
camera, dressed in red trousers and a striped blue and white shirt. Ellen's
hair was straw-yellow, and she was thin, surprisingly pretty. He had not
remembered for a long time how pretty she'd been in those days. He felt
his throat constrict, as if the bright irretrievable past were a poison in
the air. It was not grief he felt. That would come, perhaps, but it was
not there yet. The pretty young woman and the equally pretty child
might almost have been strangers—touching, interesting: the lines of the
woman's face soft and intelligent, the child's smile serene. In a sense, of

course, Mickelsson remembered a great deal that instant, remembered that the setting was an apartment they'd had at the time in California, and that when he—or someone—had taken the picture (it was in some respects more a deduction than a memory), an uncle, his father's brother, who had died just a few months later, had been visiting, seemingly hale and hearty. But what he felt, it seemed to him—felt like a physical sensation, a jolt—was that favorite old puzzler of philosophers, the perishability of time. Days, months, years, whatever their vitality, could be swallowed into nothingness. The endless, green Wisconsin summers of his childhood, the joyful, anxious years of graduate school (he remembered the print, the texture of the paper in the Kant he'd pored over in his library carrel), then twenty years of teaching—and more important, more shameful, the vast plain of time he'd had with Ellen—all that charged, sunlit span could shrink up and vanish leaving nothing but a few sharp-edged boulders, frozen images drained of emotion, or of all but the bloodless, child-faced spectre of emotion. . . . He pressed his thumb and first finger to his forehead, pushing hard, as if seeing if his flesh still had feeling—squatting among shambles, books and papers and the long-forgotten snapshot—straining to get his mind around the fact that such vitality could vanish from the earth. "So this is death," he thought. Not that it was a useful, philosophical thought. He felt grief edging nearer, still unreal, mere potential, like some hazard ahead of him on a path through woods after dark.

That night—after he'd finished his weight-lifting, push-ups, and exercises, the athlete's regimen he'd followed for years, cowardly plea against mortality—lying heavily on his back under the covers, alone in the darkness of the big, quiet house, staring up at where the ceiling would be if he could see it (still wearing his glasses, as if imagining he might turn on the light again and return to the book on the bedside table), Mickelsson at last felt the sorrow, or rather self-pity, that he'd known would come. Tears welled up, and he reached up under his glasses to wipe them away with two fingers. He remembered his father and mother dressed up for church, young and handsome, with lively eyes. Now his father was dead, his mother an old woman, pale, wrinkled, bent like a foetus, hardly a visible trace of what she'd been in her prime. (Not that she wasn't happy, he reminded himself. Too bad the gift was one she'd been unable to pass on.) He remembered fishing on a lake somewhere with Ellen and the children—California or Nevada; they'd travelled a good deal, in those days—mountains above them like huge chunks of coal, throwing a long shadow. Then he remembered Ellen at some party, holding forth, glittering, everyone watching. Her neckline plunged; no one could fail to notice. Yet her face was what they watched.

The empty old house became more solid and stiff around him, more still. Though he couldn't see the ceiling, he knew exactly where it was, heavy to his imagination as a slab of stone. His eyes were now overflowing, though the tears seemed to him, or to the part of his mind standing back, observing, not warranted. He heard a train passing, far below him, a sound that recalled to him his earliest childhood. (A railroad had cut through his father's woods, a mile from the house. He would lie awake listening, in the middle of the night, when his mother and father were away visiting, or attending a meeting of the Grange. His grandmother would be down in the kitchen, reading her Bible. The house was of stone. Branches of fir trees scraped softly against the walls.) After the train passed—it took a long time—the silence seemed deeper than before. He could be afraid, he thought, if he let himself; could give way to fear as he'd done as a boy, walking down the pitchdark country road under a roof of creaking oak-beams, walking faster and faster, then running. But though the thought teased at his mind it did not reach him, quite. He watched it like a stranger, an alien spirit, curious and grieved but not tempted. One grew up, alas; came to see things plainly, with detachment. One gained things, one lost things; eventually one died. That was Nature's process. He thought of the formerly grand hotels in the Adirondacks, where he sometimes went to write, summers—he was probably the last of his kind to do that, haul his truckload of books to a decaying mountain "camp," an immense old log lodge held up, in its age, by its great stone fireplaces; where he would settle in, pondering now the printed page, now the vastness of trees, lakes, mountains, sometimes going on long Nature-walks like some nineteenth-century Christian optimist—finding, among other things, once-grand hotels that had sunk back into brute, unconscious life, giving way to sumac, pines, and beeches until hardly a sign remained of where those hotels had stood. One learned to accept. That was the real death, Mickelsson thought, closing his eyes, irritably reaching up again to brush away tears. (It was not the mountain camps or the vanishing of time that brought tears to his eyes now. It was the thought of his daughter standing on the third-floor sun-dappled balcony of his Adirondack hide-out, her long skirt moving a little in the breeze, her torso bent forward as she whistled down to the young German shepherd, who yipped and pranced, unable to find his way up to her.) Well, never mind. For the moment, anyway, he was on his own. He must manage.

An image of old Pearson from higher on the mountain floated into his mind. For a moment, just before he dropped off to sleep, he imagined he heard someone walking, slowly, as if puzzled, from room to room downstairs in the dark. An unpleasant sensation came over him, as if he were suddenly someone else, full of physical discomforts and anger. When he concentrated, the sounds and the strange sensation stopped together; or rather, the whole thing evaporated, like meaning from a word in a dream.

5

Though he was eager to get down to fixing the house, he was prevented from it, temporarily, by the fall semester's starting up—not to mention lack of funds. His situation was now so hopeless that he'd for the moment given up entering his checks. Bouncing was more or less inevitable. God damn the theater, he thought again and again, meaning his wife's absurd "investments"—most of them gifts, it had turned out, to down-and-out actors too childish to make sensible use of them. But the fault had not been hers alone. It was Mickelsson himself who'd bought the big house in Providence, the thousands of books, the Peugeot. He would accept the necessity of writing whining letters, making wild promises, praying that something would turn up, though nothing would.

"How can it be that bad?" Tom Garret asked once in the mailroom, his smile pleasantly baffled. Garret had ten kids, and nowhere near Mickelsson's salary. To his credit, he made no pretense of feeling pity. "You must make at least twelve hundred a month after taxes. And all those textbooks. Don't they bring something in?"

"We lived high," Mickelsson said, giving Garret one of his gloomy, significant looks. The look suggested yachts, gambling casinos.

Stubbornly Garret smiled on, like ole massa making light of his slaves' complaints. He swept his hands out to the sides, palms up. He smiled harder, in fact, his round cheeks bunching up, and said with maddening Southern gentility, "Everybody's got debts. But with the money you make . . . When's the last time you sat down and really tried to figure it all out?"

"Tom," Mickelsson said, half turning away, controlling anger, "believe me, you've got no idea."

"If I were you," Garret said, "I'd get a graduate assistant, and I'd have him or her lay everything out in black and red. . . ."

Whatever more he said, Mickelsson did not hear; he'd left the mailroom.

It was true, of course, that Mickelsson was not very clear on where he stood. Adding up his bills—those he could find (he had them stuffed everywhere, in part of his bookcase, all over his desk, in brown manila envelopes under his desk)—then looking at the month's statement from the bank, he would get chest-pains, and his head would cloud with confusion. He should certainly work out some plan, some schedule; but one could see at a glance that it was hopeless. For years his accounts had been neat and exact. Then Ellen had taken over. The thought of now unsnarling it filled him with anger and despair: he simply couldn't do it. Sometimes when it seemed to him that he hadn't written a check in weeks, so that there must be a fair amount in the bank, he would write a great swatch of them and mail them away with a prayer. Mostly he'd just send a thousand to Ellen and, for the rest, would let Nature take its course; that is, he would wait for the sheriff. He'd known in advance all Garret had to tell him, and something more, that Garret had not dared imply: that in a way he was purposely burying himself in debt and financial confusion. It was part of his general anger at the world, or in Heidegger's special sense *die Welt*—the Establishment, conventional values and expectations. Whether or not he approved of the feeling, he felt like Gulliver among the Lilliputians. He had deigned to behave like an ordinary man, buying what the TV told him to buy, giving what his wife in her position as lady-in-the-world demanded, and now here he was, a giant entangled in strings. Rather than snip all those strings one by one, with the patience of an ant, he would die and rot on the hill where he was tied, let his sweet death-stench drive the Lilliputians from their island.

Rhetoric. It was his joy and salvation, not that it paid the bills. It was his cynosure in the rift between *Welt* and *Erde*, the inviolable domain of the mad superman, the L-13 balance between words and things. It was indeed a kind of madness, of course. If one posed the problem in George Steiner's way (recalling Thomas Mann's), as one between a classicism harmonically "housed" in language and a modernism in which the particular no longer chimes within an overarching universe, Mickelsson's rhetoric was his noisy pox on both the many-mansioned house and the sticks-and-stones exile shanty. As Luther had hated the long dark shadow of the Pope, and as Nietzsche had hated Luther, Mickelsson hated everything, everybody, every remotest possibility. He hated works, he hated grace, he hated the retreat to love in all its permutations, from Eleanor of Aquitaine's Court of Love to the darkling plain of Matthew Arnold. He therefore despised his bills, was made angry and frightened by the very idea of debt. He would not think about it.

Not only was there, in addition to all his former burdens, the $224 a month that must go to house payments, and another $20 for fire insurance—required by the bank (fire was the only insurance he carried)—he'd also had to lay out $700, plus insurance, registration, and licensing, for a misshapen, cranky old Jeep. He'd met Tim Booker on the street, down by the Acme Market, on a bright September morning when the air had a smell of winter in it, and Tim had said, grinning, delighted to see him, "Hay, you geared up for snow, Prafessor?"

Mickelsson had laughed sociably. "I guess winter's right around the corner." The smell in the air had been the only evidence of it. Not a leaf had turned, and nights were often so warm he had to sleep with the windows open.

"Up there where you are," Tim said, "they'll be drifts ten foot deep, and that's if the winter's a light one!" He made it sound like praise, as if Mickelsson had done something masterful in choosing such a troublesome place to get to. "I hope you've gaht something to plow your driveway owt!"

Mickelsson had looked at him thoughtfully, half smiling because Tim was infectiously smiling; but he was feeling anxious. Heaven knew he couldn't afford a truck and snowplow! What were they these days—five, six thousand dollars used? For a moment the very thought of having to lie to the bank for more money made it hard for him to breathe. (He thought of Finney, Rifkin, his wife and children. He, a man with his name in *Who's Who*, walked around even now in shoes with holes in them; all his collars and cuffs were frayed. Sometimes students, usually young women, would point it out to him and laugh.) He said, though in fact the idea had only now occurred to him, "I've been thinking of trading the Chevy for a Jeep, if I can find one that's not too expensive." He glanced at Tim.

"Might be a good idea," Tim said. "In fact I might know of one, if you're interested." He shook his head and laughed. "It's naht much, but I'm pretty sure the feller'd sell 'er cheap. Fahrmer I know down in South Gibson, cousin of my wife's. It's only gaht forty thousand miles on it— but tell the truth they're mostly in granny-gear, pulling loaded stone-boats over new-plowed ground." He laughed again.

"You think it would run? I'd hate to lay out—"

"Oh, I'm pretty sure it would *run* OK. He's taken pretty good care of it, if you don't mind a wired-up tailgate and a couple of windows that won't roll down. You know these fahrmers." Again he laughed, clapping his hands as if he'd told an extremely funny joke. Though the laugh seemed as open and innocent as a boy's, Mickelsson, still half smiling, eyed him narrowly.

After an instant Mickelsson asked, "You're sure it's not haunted or anything?"

Abruptly, each for his own reasons, both of them laughed, and Tim reached out to put his hand on Mickelsson's upper arm, the gesture of an athlete, winner to loser. "Isn't that something?" he said. "You hear the story about the feller who stayed there all night and it turned his *hair* white?"

"Not me," Mickelsson said. "Nobody tells me anything." But he felt good now, relieved and cleansed, the whole thing behind them.

And so he'd driven down, following Tim's directions, to the farm outside South Gibson, where Tim's wife's cousin Charles Lepatofsky had

the Jeep. Lepatofsky was a smiling, chatty man, fat and short, with over-sized nose and hands, thick curly hair peeking out at his collar and matted on his arms, almost hiding his tattoos. He had his four- or five-year-old daughter with him, a silent, shyly smiling red-head, something wrong about her eyes—maybe just a dreamer. Lepatofsky automatically put her up on his shoulders, not asking if she wanted him to, hardly even glancing at the child in fact. Automatically she put her hands around his fore-head, carefully not covering his eyes, and they started across the neatly mowed back yard toward the weeds beyond. Mickelsson walked with them through brittle, high grass and ragweed down a lane thick with rasp-berry and elderberry bushes, past a shaggy pony and two brown horses, part of an old tractor and an upside-down truck, up a hill to a sagging, paintless barn with its door wedged shut by a locust post. Without taking his daughter from his shoulders, the man tugged hard at the post, veins standing out on his forehead and wrists.

"Are you your daddy's pal?" Mickelsson asked, holding one finger to the girl's face, close to the chin. She did not look at him.

"Lily don't talk much," Lepatofsky said.

Now he had the brace-post unwedged. After Lepatofsky got the door open, Mickelsson cautiously stepped in and then stood—shocked, to say the least—simply looking.

"There she be," Lepatofsky said.

"Yes, that's right," Mickelsson said, slowly nodding.

From the looks of it, the Jeep hadn't been driven in years. It was moored by cobwebs heavy as ropes and weighed down by mounds of pigeon droppings, so mud-stained and weed-specked it looked as if it had been sunk in some marsh and, long afterward, salvaged. One back tire was flat, and one side panel had been banged in in three places, as if a crazed ram had come after it.

"Ain't much, is it," the man said, and smiled, then winked. "But you gotta admit the price is right." He wore his sleeves rolled up, a crushed pack of cigarettes under one of them, on both arms large tattoos.

"You think it still runs?" Mickelsson asked. He couldn't tell whether he was delighted by the thing or horrified. It would be a shocker, down on the university parking lot, if he could get it that far. (He imagined Jessica Stark or some handsome young-lady graduate student climbing into it, heading, in Mickelsson's company, to some party.) On the other hand—perhaps because of its oversized tires, or because it stood all alone in the rotting, empty barn, wide bars of dusty light draped over it—it looked like the largest, most hard-worked, somehow most *serious* Jeep he'd ever seen. It was a 1973 Wagoneer, Lepatofsky told him. A snowplow came with it (he had it in the "grodge") and it also came equipped—Lepatofsky said it as if he thought it very special—with a brand-new chrome-covered trailer hitch. "Tell you what we'll do," Lepatofsky said.

"Lily and me will pump up the tire and we'll drive you owt for a ride."
He winked at his daughter. For the first time, the little girl looked
thoughtfully at the professor.

While Mickelsson waited, his hand on his pipe, moving slowly around
the Jeep, studying the rust and the blistered whitish-yellow paint, the
plastic, red-haired troll-doll hanging from the rear-view mirror (the Jeep
also had side mirrors, one of them broken), Lepatofsky, with the child
still on his shoulders, went back to the house for an old tire-pump. It
took him half an hour, sweating like a horse, the girl pressing her palms
against her knees beside him, to get the tire up high enough to run on.
At last, leaning the pump in the doorway and taking his daughter's hand,
he said, "OK, hop in!" When he'd gotten into the driver's seat and settled
Lily in his lap, he looked over at Mickelsson, waiting. Mickelsson looked
at the dirt on his own seat, a quarter-inch thick, thought of wiping it off
with his handkerchief, then sighed, grimaced, and, taking the pipe from
his mouth for a moment, climbed in. Perhaps for Mickelsson's benefit,
Lily reached up and tapped the troll-doll, making it swing. She smiled to
herself.

The motor roared to life at the second turn of the ignition key—it
had been driven more recently than Mickelsson had thought, apparently
—and Lepatofsky, twisting around to look out the back window, backed
the Jeep, coughing and bucking, out of the barn. "It needs to warm up,"
he said, and winked. The engine did settle down, after a minute, though
not to the point of hitting on all of its cylinders. He drove straight down
to a shallow, reedy swamp, shifted to low-low and four-wheel drive, and
started through it. Water oozed up onto Mickelsson's shoes, making him
lift his feet and glance at Lepatofsky. The daughter smiled. Mickelsson
sat rigid and unbalanced, hanging on with both hands, feeling slightly
injured by the child's amusement and thinking how it would feel to have
to walk, with the child smiling at him from Lepatofsky's shoulders,
through all that muck to dry land. Just outside his window a ratlike
thing—a muskrat or small beaver—paddled away in alarm, its eyes rolled
back.

To Mickelsson's amazement, the Jeep inched on through the water
and reeds and at last climbed to solid ground. Lepatofsky shifted out of
low-low and grinned.

"Jesus," Mickelsson said, and slowly lowered his feet.

"You telling me," Lepatofsky said, and laughed with relief, winking
at his daughter. The whole side of his face moved, as if the wink were
a tic.

For all his talk about the price being right, he hadn't yet mentioned
one. Now, when Mickelsson asked him about it, he said, "Seven hundred,
firm."

"I see," Mickelsson said. Then, after a moment, "That's fair, I guess."

He studied his pipe. "I'd been thinking of trying a used-car lot, maybe, where I could trade in the Chevy. . . ."

"That's up to you, a course," Lepatofsky said. "I can tell you right now you won't get a Jeep like this at a used-car lot, with a snowplow and everything. Not for seven hundred. If I was you I'd just keep that Chevy for a spare. The plow alone's worth seven hundred."

He gave that same argument again and again, mostly in the very same words, as they drove around. They rode up a logging trail, up and down steep banks, once up and over a partly fallen stone wall. "It's built high," Lepatofsky said. "You won't get hung up, that's *one* thing." To Mickelsson's slight annoyance later, they didn't think to try it on the road. Lily reached up, from time to time, to reposition the troll-doll.

"OK," Mickelsson said at last, his heart anxious but his expression grim, "I'll take it."

Slowly, dreamily, not making a sound, the child clapped her hands.

The first time Mickelsson drove the Jeep, after it was his own, two tires blew out and he discovered that, though it was terrific at negotiating swamps and stone walls, it had a maximum road-speed of sixty miles an hour downhill. According to his careful, neat figures, it got nine miles to the gallon. (Fear leaped up in him. He would be ruined!) Nevertheless, he retired the Chevy to his own empty barn—not as empty as Lepatofsky's; there were dried-out, twenty-year-old bales of hay, coils of rope, lengths of pipe and scattered, rusted farm-machinery parts—and, partly for style's sake, partly to get the old vehicle in condition for the difficult haul when snowtime came, Mickelsson cleaned up the Jeep and made it his regular means of transportation back and forth from school. "Hey, wow!" students would say when he pulled into his parking slot, and sometimes they'd come over to look at it. Witlessly, shyly, the red-haired troll-doll, still swinging on its short, rusty chain, would grin. He must remember to take that doll back to Lepatofsky's daughter, he reminded himself now and again. But he kept forgetting.

The university was thirty-five miles—more than an hour's drive—from the house on the mountain. He liked that, the distance between his two worlds. He could clear out his head, driving to school in the beat-up Jeep. (He'd left the Peugeot in Providence with his wife.) It was late September, no sign yet that the leaves would soon be turning, but when he set out, mornings, the house and mountain would be surrounded by fog, so that he had to poke slowly, carefully down into the valley, across the iron bridge, and up to the highway heading north out of the mountains into New York State. Sitting high above ordinary drivers, fists closed tight on the steeringwheel, shoulders thrown back and chin thrown forward, like a king fallen on hard times, he could think at leisure about his classes and appointments, remind himself of letters he had to write (he was badly behind, the desk at his office deeply buried), and make mental lists of books he must pick up at the library. He'd thought from time to time of installing an FM radio in the Jeep, but so far he hadn't done so, and it seemed to him increasingly unlikely that he would. Wind in his hair, morning sunlight gleaming in the swirls of fog and on patches of glass-smooth river in the valley below and to the left of him—here and there, rising through the fog toward visibility, a barn with high silos, a village of white houses, a neon motel sign precariously craning to the level of the Interstate—he felt himself changing as if magically from whatever he was on the mountain to Mickelsson the teacher, the colleague, the committeeman.

Not that he was much of a colleague, he would admit. After a year at this place, he knew hardly any of the people he taught with—five or six in philosophy, one or two in English, Jessica in sociology, perhaps a half-dozen others, more faces than names; but he was closer to these people, sad to say, than to any of the people he'd taught with in California or, before that, Ohio, not to mention those he'd met during his Fulbright year in Germany, none of whose names he remembered. (He saw his former friends from California occasionally at philosophy conferences, where they struck him as odd dressers and prematurely aged, full of crackpot West Coast opinions—thought as an effective physical impulse or "charge," and so on. His friends from Ohio, Hiram College, he never saw anywhere.) As for other people he and his ex-wife had known, Mickelsson had put them, through no fault of theirs, almost wholly out of mind. The thought of Providence, with its beautiful old trees and dark-brick buildings, its classy, troubled students, its long, drunken parties and gloomy flirtations, above all its oceanscape, at one time so dear to Mickelsson and his children—the thought of Providence filled him with such a feeling of waste and hopelessness that he preferred to consider the whole place swallowed by the Atlantic.

But if strictly speaking he was a colleague to nobody, he knew better, instinctively, than to admit that fact too openly to himself. Sometimes after telephone conversations with his wife, whether the tone she took was haughty or cajoling, he sensed how precarious his hold was on the world. He must find something to live for—his work, his students—otherwise sure as day he would wake up some morning strapped down hand and foot, full of guilt and dim, dreamlike memories of himself in garish dress, solemnly bent to impassioned, tearful conversation with a mouse in a trap or the shattered remains of a dog beside the road. PHILOSOPHER CLAIMS DIRECT ENCOUNTER WITH BEING! It was a harmless lunacy. He was inclined to believe he was at his best when "not himself." Nevertheless, any hint that he was slipping could make his fingers tremble. And so— as he'd drunkenly told Jessica the night he'd stayed late—by stubborn acts of will Mickelsson shaved in the morning, read his journals, soberly prepared classes. Let those things slide, as already he'd let his writing slide (a book on the ethics of genetic manipulation, several articles, a paper for the March convention of the A.P.A.—all very current and important, but nothing his heart was in), and he'd be doomed, subtly and irrevocably called into the shadowy world he felt always not far off, as close and dark and ingeniously patterned as the woods on the mountain above him. Closer. As close as the walls of whatever stark, inhospitable room he happened to be standing or sitting in in the old, allegedly spirit-ridden house.

And so, soberly, knowing what he was doing, Mickelsson acted the role of teacher, committeeman, jovial colleague. (His right hand left the steeringwheel, gesturing, trying to make things plain to the windshield.) It was in fact a character he had always enjoyed and could enjoy even now, with certain reservations, so long as he knew he could take it off, like his suitcoat and the annoyingly narrow tag, "Ethicist," when he left for home. Mickelsson had always been a friendly man, or so he believed, but he was not in a mood, at this stage of his life, for socializing. He was indeed in a period of redefinition, reassessment, or perhaps, to be accurate, mourning.

Mickelsson frowned and slowed down a little. A hitch-hiker, illegal on the Interstate, held out a thumb to him; a tramp-faced man in a long brown coat. Mickelsson slowed more, then changed his mind and sped up again. As the Jeep passed him, the hitch-hiker slowly, as if ominously, shook his head.

Period of mourning, Mickelsson thought, and nodded, lightly tapping the steeringwheel with the heel of his fist.

Jessica had been seated on the couch across the coffeetable from him, leaning toward him, lightly frowning, her eyes darker than usual in the dimness of the room. She'd turned out all the lights but the entryway light, the light in the kitchen (throwing its bluish fluorescent shaft over the far wall and the tall, evil-looking African drum), and the light on the fern-stand just behind his chair. The couch she sat on floated, sectioning off one quarter of the room. Beyond her he could make out wide French doors, a vase of silk flowers, a painting. It had not seemed to him that night that she'd turned off lights to make their talk more romantic, though now sometimes he wondered if he'd misjudged—missed a chance. Feeble as it was, the light behind him made her gold chain and eyes—slanted a little, like an ancient Persian's—gleam like whitecaps at twilight or coins found in childhood. He wondered if a woman as large as she was—perfectly proportioned, but goddess-size, nearly Mickelsson's size—had trouble buying clothes. He drank slowly and carefully, pacing himself, taking no risks.

"Why do you say you're a failure?" she'd asked. "What are you—fifty—forty-five?"

"I know it sounds like self-pity," he said, "or too much gin."

She dismissed it with a wave.

"Of course I've got very high standards," he said. He opened his hands, then once more clasped them lightly between his knees, his feet square on the floor like a farmer's. Her long, slim legs, the grace of her left hand draped over the couch-arm, made him feel heavy, wide as a truck; yet he did not feel ugly tonight. In fact, no doubt because she watched him with interest, he felt handsome. The sportcoat he wore had just come from the cleaner's; the pale blue shirt was the first he'd bought since he'd left Ellen. He reached for his pipe, found it still half full of tobacco, and felt for his matches.

"Usually when people of our age say they're failures," she said, "they're telling the truth. In your case, I don't believe it."

" 'Our age,' " he mocked.

She laughed. "I'll say this: you've got your act down pat."

"I don't mean it as an act," he said, then grinned. "Probably you're right."

"What were you like?" she asked. "I mean, when you were younger."

"You wouldn't have cared for me," he said. Now he had his pipe lit.

She waited.

He shook his head as if in admiration of the young man he'd been. "I was a name to conjure with, in my grad-school days," he said. "I'd played a little football as an undergrad, which people still remembered—I may have mentioned that." When he glanced at her, she nodded, and he saw that he'd mentioned it too often. "Well, now that I threw myself into it, I found I was pretty good at book-work too," he said. "Did a dissertation—published later by Temple University—on Luther, Nietzsche, and the modern predicament. Got some pretty fair reviews." He scowled, mock-petulant. "Nowhere important, to tell the truth. *Philosophy Today*. 'A bold and original contribution to the Nietzsche reassessment'—that sort of thing. It really was, in fact." He made his face modest but tucked his thumbs under his armpits. "I don't mean to brag."

Jessica rolled her eyes.

He said, smiling again, still mock-modest, "I showed in great detail how Nietzsche—and Nietzsche's deep-down hatred of Martin Luther—lies behind every contemporary philosophical leaf and flower. Nietzsche *is* contemporary thought, in a way. He's the trunk whose branches are Freud, Sartre, Bergson, Wittgenstein, Heidegger—whatever still thrives on that maddening sap." He cocked one eye as if surprised and displeased by the pun, then waved it away with the backs of three fingers.

"So the book was good, in fact."

"Not bad," he admitted.

But the book had not been linguistic, he explained with a sigh, which had been sufficient reason, in those days, for dismissing an argument unread. His present chairman believed even now that analytic philosophy was philosophy enough, much to Mickelsson's disgust. He pursed his lips, rubbed his palms together, and decided to tell her of his first run-in with Tillson, at some party soon after Mickelsson had arrived here. Tillson had said—eyes bugging, mad smile twitching, his index finger six inches from Mickelsson's chin—"Do you realize that, of the jobs announced in this year's *Proceedings*, only twenty per cent are *not* in analytic? And do you realize how many of that twenty per cent are not in *ethics*? I do not say, *believe* me, that ethics is an insignificant concern! Heavens no!" He leaned closer. "But statistically speaking it is not exactly the central fascination of our time!" He'd jerked forward, laughing, spitting out cracker crumbs and tiny bits of cheese, his head returning to its rightful place, level with the hump on his back. "He must've been drunk," Mickelsson had later said to friends. "No, no," they'd said, "that's just his way. You'll get used to old Tillson!" "I hope not," Mickelsson had answered sternly —his deportment (he would have to admit, looking back) self-righteous, bordering on ridiculous. Well, so be it.

"Tillson's probably a better man than you think," Jessica said, and looked down at her sherry glass. "I can't judge how good or bad he is as a philosopher. But his students like him."

"He's got me there," Mickelsson said, and gave her his crazed grin.

"Why are you smiling?" she asked. "Does it please you that some of your students dislike you?" He could say this for her: she did not come at you crooked, like a wolf, but straight, like a striking Alsatian.

He leaned back in his chair and locked his fingers together over his paunch. "Students are a necessary evil," he said.

"Really? Is that what you think?" Though her expression was noncommittal, her eyes nailed him where he sat.

"No," he said. He brazened it out with a smile, but if there was someone invisibly keeping score, he thought glumly, Mickelsson had lost another point.

It had been something that the work of a young philosopher should be noticed at all, and his book had in fact received praise from philosophers of the kind whose respect he most valued. (His wife had put it succinctly, not meaning to hurt: "Old men.") And it would not be quite right to say that from there his work had gone downhill. He'd written two textbooks which had remained in print for several years and a short, quite brilliant book (in Mickelsson's opinion) which looked at medical ethics from a more or less Darwinian point of view. He'd known, of course, that in taking that long-abandoned tack, scorned by Nietzsche and dead in ethical theory at least since 1903—G. E. Moore's demolition of naturalism (Jessica suppressed a yawn)—he had been asking for it. That had always been part of the game, for Mickelsson. He had not guessed how "controversial"—that is, how deeply hated in some quarters—his book would be. (He found himself glaring at Jessica as he said this; she smiled blandly back. Was it possible that she wasn't listening? He leaned closer, glaring harder.) Nor had he guessed the depths to which his critics would be willing to sink. He could show her reviews. ("Please don't!" she said, raising her hands as if to fend him off. So she was listening. To some extent. He hurried on.) He should have expected it, their shrill, mindless wrath. He himself had dislocated Nietzsche's great, dark secret, how in his rage at those who had "stolen Christianity"—those holiness perverters who had reached their obscene peak in Martin Luther—Nietzsche had purposely couched his in fact liberal Christian philosophy in language designed to make burgher Christians squeal. What Nietzsche had done to Christians, Mickelsson had done to the surds of Academia, and he'd reaped the same harvest: scorn and indignation. He could tell himself that his friendlier reviewers were right about him: if he was occasionally careless, at times drawn too far by his love of rhetoric and inclination to shock, he was nonetheless a better philosopher—bolder and more original —than a vast majority of the nit-picking dullards one encountered in the so-called discipline these days. Though his enemies were intent upon injury and insult, he could defend himself with his old football-field combativeness. Yet there was no denying that the attacks had surprised and wounded him.

He found himself staring at her downright angrily, as if it were she who'd scorned his book, and at once he changed his expression to what he recognized—too late—as an angry grin. He reached for his drink, discovered it to be empty, and stood up. Together they went to the kitchen, Mickelsson talking again, gesturing with more fury than he let into his voice, Jessica trailing, leaning on the door as he opened the gin, then the vermouth. When he'd put ice in his glass and reclosed the refrigerator door, he leaned on the kitchen counter, meaning to continue here, but Jessica—eating a cold hors d'oeuvre, chewing with her mouth open— moved back into the livingroom, and, hardly aware that the choice had been hers, he followed.

Well, after the initial jolt (Mickelsson continued, his voice and manner more reasonable now, his shrug mature), after the first bloody spray of polemics, he'd let it go, dismissing the gnats' complaints against him, commending their tiny souls to God. Extravagantly praised in other quarters, sought after by well-paying popular magazines where few real philosophers had a chance to get a hearing, he had underestimated the extent to which, personally and professionally, he'd been undermined.

Jessica yawned, smiled and shook her head apologetically, then reached down with one hand to slip off her shoes. She brought her feet up onto the couch beside her and leaned back.

His book, he told her—not meeting her eyes now, aware that he was abusing a privilege, turning her interest into an excuse for letting out bottled-up anger that probably had nothing to do, in fact, with the reception, all those years ago, of his ethics book—his book, he said, had come out ten years before that annoying piece of foolishness, Edward O. Wilson's *Sociobiology: The New Synthesis*, with which his work was now carelessly linked. A tic pulled at his mouth, beginning a sneer. He raised his hand to cover it.

"I'm really not yawning because I'm bored," Jessica apologized, fighting yet another yawn. "I haven't been up this late since God knows when. Kenya, I think." She glanced at him. He imagined her towering above a crowd of admiring Kenyans.

"I should let you get to bed," he said, and swallowed a yawn himself. Just when he thought he had the yawn beaten, his mouth, of its own volition, opened wide, like a fish-mouth. "Whoo-ee!" he said, then clenched his teeth. They both laughed.

"I like being up this late," Jessica said, "though I'm badly out of practice. It's like being in college again."

"Women do that too?" he asked. "Sit up all night talking philosophy?"

Her expression went sly, the eyes more noticeably slanted. "Not philosophy, usually."

"No, I wouldn't think so. Too smart for that." He smiled one-sidedly and winked.

"That's it," she said. "So go on with what you were saying."

"I can't believe you consider it all that interesting," he said. He leaned toward her, meaning to bully her a little.

"Not in the way you'd like." She smiled back. "I'm interested in why you get so angry when you talk about ideas."

He studied her, then shook his head. "Pure ego," he said. "I hate it when I don't get due praise."

"Everybody does." She shrugged.

He said, "It's more than that, really. The sociobiologists make my skin crawl."

"Brings out the old football-field combativeness," she said. She mimicked his look and tone so well that he was thrown into confusion. He raised a knuckle to his mouth and looked at her. He'd known actresses, friends of Ellen's, who could do that, nail every nuance of tone and gesture.

"Well," he said, blushing, hastily recouping, "it's not as bad as being linked with that crank Ayn Rand."

"Surely no one links you with Ayn Rand!" Jessica said, and laughed.

An odd fact struck him, so that again he felt confused. Jessica's legs were densely freckled—and so, he noticed now, were her arms and the upper part of her chest. The lower part, revealed by her V-neck, was tan, or bronzy, dotted only here and there. Her face, too, had only a few freckles—on the cheeks and nose. Yet her hair was almost black. . . . No, dark chestnut, silver-streaked. He'd spent hours with her—tonight and earlier, at other parties—yet he'd missed what any child would spot at once, that Jessica had the strangest skin in the world, unearthly but beautiful, as if she were a figure built up of precious metals and then transformed, imperfectly, into an ordinary mortal. Her freckles were buried level after level, like stars in the Milky Way: she was a thousand colors, like some dense impressionist painting. Strange! He tried to remember what they'd been talking about. She watched him as if trying to read his mind. At last it came to him.

"We're closer than you might think, Ms. Rand and I," he said. "It's not all that strange. Nobody can be wrong all the time." He leaned over his knees again. "In the ethics book I wrote, I described my approach as 'survivalist.' A grave tactical error, I know now." He shook his head, glanced up at Jessica, then back at the pipe in his two hands. "I don't know how much you know or care about Rand's ideas. God knows there's no reason you should. Anyway, both of us reject the kind of relativism that reduces 'the good' to 'the habitual.' And what's more important, both of us maintain—though by a different chain of argument—that the life of an organism constitutes its standard of value. What promotes and enhances the organism's life is 'good' and what threatens its life is 'evil.' That much we have in common, but in the end there's all the difference in the world between Rand's ideas and mine." He broke off and shrugged, suspecting he was growing tiresome.

"Such as?" she asked. She sat poised, half smiling, delicately balanced —as it seemed to him—between interest in what he had to say and fear that he would lecture all night.

Mickelsson sucked his cheeks in, hunting for a way to put it briefly. "Well," he said, "such as this. I claim that by our very nature human beings value the *idea* of human life more than we value our individual lives. That's what I sometimes call the Nietzchean 'foundational moral experience,' the immediate human sense of life's sacred quality, if you know what I mean—the explanation of the way our hearts lift when we hear of examples of the so-called 'supreme sacrifice.' Soldiers who die to save their buddies, things like that. Ayn Rand thinks survival is an absolute value, which it is, rightly understood. What she fails to see is that *individual* survival is a *relative* value, at least for highly evolved life-forms —us, whales, dolphins maybe, probably gorillas. . . . Nietzsche says somewhere, 'The world is full of things people will die for.' It's obviously true. What I've done is help explain why. It's an important idea, especially just now, in this stupid, pragmatic, improvisational age—"

One moment her thoughts seemed miles away; the next, Jessica was saying (diving at him like an eagle, he thought): "Your hands are shaking."

"It's true," he said, looking, abruptly laughing. "I get fired up."

"I think you're angry at yourself," she said, studying him with that cool, level gaze of hers. "But I'm not sure why, yet."

"You're very psychological, you people of the tribe of Freud. If I see evil and stupidity in the world, you check out my potty-training." All at once, as if he'd decided it was time to leave (he'd decided nothing), he stood up. Then, as if on second thought, he drifted around the coffee-table and the couch she sat on and moved with his pipe to the French doors. She sat behind him now. He did not turn to see if she were watching him. The doors opened onto her back yard and garden: immense dark trees against a starry sky, below them shapes he couldn't identify, flowers or bushes, something that might be a grape arbor. When he lit his pipe, the face that briefly glowered back at him from the glass was unexpectedly puffy, disheveled. "I've wasted a lot of time," he said. He shook out the match, then gestured impatiently. Dissertation and committee work, university politics, reviewing, the editing of unimportant articles and books by other people, the teaching of courses in which, especially of late, he felt no interest . . . And as for his true work, his philosophical writing . . . Deep down, he believed the worst his unfriendly reviewers had to say of him. He was fond of quoting Collingwood's line: "All widespread errors contain some truth." Clearly there was, at some level, something very wrong with the philosophy of Peter Mickelsson. Such a mood did not make continued effort—Hegel's *aufheben*, Nietzsche's *sublimieren* —an easy leap.

He turned toward the couch, where she sat perfectly still, not as relaxed as she pretended, watching him. "Middle age," he said, and gestured vaguely. (He had a definite pot belly and touches of dead yellow and iron gray in his hair; he had a forehead as wide and flat as a bull's, three or four broken vessels in his cheeks from too much drinking. . . .)

"What's the matter?" she asked.

"What?"

"Why did you sigh like that, just now?"

"Did I?" He grinned, lest her concern steal too much advantage.

She met his eyes. Her eyes, normally gray, were black now, stalking the darkness where he hid. "Were you thinking about your wife?"

"I don't know. It's possible." He had not been. "I suppose I was." After a moment, he nodded. He remembered that Jessica's husband had died.

She asked, "What do you think went wrong? Were you to blame?"

Mickelsson pulled his lower lip up in between his teeth and tensed his forehead, tempted by her friendly curiosity, knowing they weren't playing the same game. He glanced at her. She was smiling—queenly, he thought: Scheherazadelike—and in some not quite sexual way seductive. She reached past her skirt and feet to pat the couch. "Come sit," she said.

He moved toward her, turning over possibilities behind the mask of his smile.

"Why the guilt?" she asked. "Did you leave her for someone else?"

"No," he said, "certainly not." He ran his hand over his face. "It's true that I cheated on her, as they say. I hurt her plenty, and plenty of times."

"And did she cheat?" Jessica asked.

He breathed deeply, then put down his pipe, put his elbows on his knees, and lowered his head into his hands. If he told her all this he would certainly lie; how could he not? He'd do everything in his power to make himself look good, seduce this beautiful soft creature beside him with his pretended virtue, and then hate himself more, and eventually get found out and be hated for his lies or, worse, pitied. . . . He was painfully conscious of Jessica's foot just inches from his leg. His penis stirred, waking up.

"She started it," he said at last, almost a whimper.

After a moment he felt her foot touch the side of his leg.

"So why the guilt?" she asked. "Why all the misery?"

Tears came to his eyes—guilt, self-hatred, an ache of desire he was afraid to act on, even half drunk as he was.

"Wouldn't it help to talk about it?" she asked. She let him sit silent awhile, then asked, "You still love her, is that it? Part of you wants not to be here?"

"Oh, I want to be here, all right," he said.

"Part of you. I know. Don't think I haven't been through the same, though with a death it's—" She broke off.

Furtively, Mickelsson wiped his eyes, then gently lowered his left hand onto Jessica's foot. He was startled to find it bare; he'd thought she had stockings on. The foot was cold, very smooth, the bones delicate. A tremble of desire—almost a shudder—came over him, and the ache at the root of his groin was now fierce. "I'm not sure what makes me feel guilty," he said. "It's the way I always felt with her." He moved his fingertips to Jessica's ankle and then a little beyond. With her other foot, firmly, she stopped him.

Ellen had not been a student of philosophy but "a theater person," as she'd liked to say with a wry twist to her mouth. A literature student—comparative literature—who had moved, by the time she was in graduate school, entirely into drama. It was in graduate school that Mickelsson had met and married her. Since her special interests were Ionesco and Beckett, whom she took to be "dramatic philosophers"—he'd been unable to help making fun of that—her concerns and his had, in her opinion, overlapped. He told Jessica of his remembrance of how Ellen would read his papers in graduate school, her school-marm glasses low on her small, white nose, her sensuous, sharply defined lips compressed. They had lived, in those days, in one of those dreary university quonset huts, which Ellen had made brighter, more livable (though strange) by painting the plasterboard walls gray and gold and hanging framed sheets of crudely sketched costume designs by a girlfriend of hers (of whom Mickelsson had felt jealous) and a framed theater poster, also by a friend (of whom he'd also felt jealous), for Euripides' *Medea*.

She had found somewhere, probably in Chicago where she'd studied as an undergraduate, a grotesque old voodoo-doll, a two-foot-tall monstrosity of vaguely Mexican design, which had come (she told friends) full of jelly-beans. "Jelly-beans?" the friends would say, glancing at Mickelsson, who would grin and look down. "Contraband. Jelly-beans are illegal in Haiti," Ellen would say. Her eyes would widen dramatically and she would smile as though there were stagelights on her. He had loved, at first, her slightly crazed sense of humor, her native theatricality. Later, when he'd come to see how it imposed itself, how it refused all restriction, thrived on havoc—anything for effect, as if all the world really were a stage and one's sole obligation this side of the grave were to keep the very chairs and drapes amused—and when he'd come to see, too, what black, bottomless depressions followed when the chairs and drapes remained stiffly unsmiling—he'd begun to find her theatricality less appealing. Not that he'd discouraged her. It was the only real talent she had, in his opinion. (He glanced at Jessica and caught her frowning, slightly evasive.) Ellen had refused to keep lists of any kind (even her class notes were a jumble), refused even to make a shopping list or save her grocery receipts so that he could look them over. Her dresser drawers had no system whatever, so far as he could tell, and no matter what he did—whine, shout, or tease—she had never voluntarily closed a closet door. Yet they'd adjusted, more or less. She would say, back in those happier days, removing her school-marm glasses and staring at the wall of the quonset, "That's interesting, Mick! You remember that place in *Enrico Quattro* . . ." If he pointed out, gently, that her reading was wrong, indefensible, she would smile with a kind of eagerness, almost wildness, that should have warned him clearly of all that was to come. She never had what Mickelsson would call intellectual insights. Ideas, true or false (she hardly cared), were, if anything, suggestions for gestures, stagelighting, props. There she did have, he thought, a kind of genius. Heidegger would have loved her. *The rift! The rift!*

Ellen had taught part-time in the local public school, snatching graduate courses as she could and doing well in them, to Mickelsson's surprise. (She never studied until the last minute and immediately after the exam forgot—maybe consciously demolished—everything she'd learned.) Mickelsson had been on fellowships, not so readily available to women in those days, and it had thus been Ellen who'd earned the money to pay their bills, though it was Mickelsson, of course, who'd had to sit down and add them up and write checks or apologies. He had disliked the arrangement, to say the least, and had sometimes started quarrels, never on the subject at the heart of his anger, his dependency. She didn't want a husband, he sometimes told her, she wanted an accountant. "That's the kind of thing men are *good* at," she'd said, instantly close to tears. It was not just the damage to his male ego. He liked buying books, especially those fine, gray Oxford editions—books he looked forward almost hungrily to reading, at the time he bought them, but then, more often than not, was too busy to read. To Ellen, who held the purse-strings, Mickelsson's habit of buying books, some of them in languages he hadn't yet learned, seemed lunacy. (He smiled, self-mocking, as he told Jessica this; her returning smile let him know she understood those eager-young-philosopher feelings.) Ellen had preferred to use books from the library and save her money toward a trip "abroad"—it was Poland she had in mind (*fantastic theater,* she said)—or, later, when it was clear that, by the nature of his profession, they would never be world travellers, never have a "get-away apartment" in New York, preferred to spend her money on the kinds of things *she* liked, if in fact they must be holed up in this hell-hole wilderness—plants, a used Jaguar, furniture, a piano (though neither of them could play), and theater trips.

("It sounds as if you were a real shit," Jessica said matter-of-factly. "I guess I was," he said.)

He could happily have lived out his life in some attic room or country shack so long as the walls were lined with books and in all that really counted he could live like a king. But he was beginning to see that by his overhasty marriage to a shallow, childish woman who cared only about objects and empty sham (her extreme interest in theater now seemed to him pitifully significant and of course a little sick—all theater people were, he'd decided, sick), he had forever put that noble ideal out of reach. He hadn't had the nerve to strike out directly, and Ellen, by some instinct too deep for cunning (it was only now, saying it to Jessica, that he understood this), Ellen had clung to her power while she could.

Once, still in graduate school, he'd broached with Ellen the subject of his getting a part-time job himself. As an undergraduate, he'd pointed out, he'd worked as a bank teller, a farm hand, a salesman of World Book Encyclopedias. Ellen's reaction had been one of surprisingly heated indignation. She shook her fork at him—they were at supper at the time. "You have the potential to be one of the world's great philosophers!" she'd said, leaning toward him. "Do you think I intend to allow you to throw all that away for a few measly dollars?"

He'd looked at her in surprise, his own fork poised halfway between his plate and his mouth. "Ellen, that's ridiculous!" he'd said, and tentatively smiled. Her look was so intense, eyes widened, mouth open, head thrown far forward, he couldn't tell whether to laugh or back off in fear.

"You do, Mick," she said. "I know!"

For another instant he'd met her eyes, that stare so absolute it looked more like acting than like life. "But suppose I don't," he said. His voice went thin with nervousness, and abruptly he began to wave his fork, forgetting it still had spaghetti on it. "Suppose I turn out to be this perfectly nice, perfectly ordinary philosophy teacher at some college in Nebraska?"

"You *won't,*" she said, almost a shout.

Now it was he who leaned forward, almost shouting. "I damn well could," he said. "Such things happen. You've worked out our whole life like it's a play, that's what you've done! What if I'm miscast?" The instant the words came out, he'd wished them unsaid, because he'd seen that he was right: to Ellen the whole shebang was theater, with all the once-for-all-time deadly seriousness of theater; and he'd seen too—though he couldn't have said in what way her expression changed—that she was suddenly realizing that it might be true, all she'd been taking for granted about him might be fantasy.

She lowered her fork to her spaghetti and turned it around and around, looking at her plate, winding the spaghetti but not raising it to her mouth.

"We have to face reality," he said, speaking softly now.

She glanced up at him for a moment. "Fuck reality," she said.

The rest of the night she'd hardly spoken to him. She sat in the wicker chair in what served as their livingroom, bent over a book, a pencil in her mouth like the bit of a bridle, her brow knitted, pretending to be deeply engrossed in her reading but seldom turning a page. The cat, Horace, lay curled up, sleeping against her feet. Mickelsson had been tempted to ask if she was writing a new life-drama for them, but he'd decided he'd better not. When he'd finished the dishes he'd hung around for a while, cleaning and recleaning the counter top, rinsing out the cat dish, straightening up the canned goods in their cupboard. At last, drifting nearer to where she sat, he'd said, "Well, I guess I better hit the books."

"OK," she said. "Go do it."

He stood looking down at her, thinking—injured—that all he'd asked was the right to do a little part-time work, earn a little money he could spend as he pleased. Surely her little drama could accommodate that! But all right, he would withdraw the suggestion for the duration. "Look, Ellie," he said, "I'm sorry—"

She looked up at him, blank, pretending she'd forgotten the whole thing, then pretended to remember and waved him away. "Forget it," she said. "Go hit the books." She smiled.

Perhaps that really had been the end of it. She'd never again mentioned her expectations for him. In the years that followed they'd moved more and more toward separate lives, he becoming stuffier (as he saw it now), increasingly self-controlled and bookish, Ellen increasingly taking on the free-spirit habits and dress, not to mention the neuroses and easy liberalism, of her theater friends. They met for meals and sometimes read the Sunday *New York Times* together (it was strange to think, now, what pleasure they'd gotten out of the Sunday *New York Times*—or mushroom soup, or limejuice—it was like trying to remember one's original feelings about *Dumbo*, or *Snow White*). Occasionally they'd gone to parties together, where, as in other things, they went separate ways. She still read his papers, some of them anyway; and he, for his part, checked in from time to time on her theater activities. With all his heart he encouraged them. Intellectually, as he could not help telling her when she pressed for his opinion, she was hopeless. She seemed to understand that it was true.

("Jesus," Jessica said. Mickelsson thought about it, then abruptly rose and went out to the kitchen for more gin. This time Jessica waited on the couch. She was reclining, her head back on a cushion, when he came back and once more sat beside her. Outside, a chorus of birds now warbled and cheeped.)

No one could have been more pleased than Ellen when his work met with success, or more fiercely defensive when his work was, she thought, undervalued. But each of them had less and less sense of what the other was up to. The pattern they'd developed in graduate school had continued throughout their life together: Mickelsson working long hours in his study or hurrying off to meetings at eight at night or seven in the morning, Ellen—full of energy, smiling like a model (though she was now somewhat heavier and wore her blond hair long and straight)—teaching junior college, keeping tabs on her theater groups, and dealing, in her reckless, unsystematic way, with the world, the house, the children. Thinking back, he could more or less understand what had happened between them. Her recklessness and indifference had forced him to compensate, taking on the manner of a stickler, a harper on detail, a gloomy bully. "Oh, Mick," she would say when he suggested that perhaps they might plan their week's meals (they were forever having to throw out rotten food), "you *know* I'm no good at things like that. Besides, I *hate* it, knowing that Wednesday I've got to eat hamburger, come hell or high water. Maybe we could get a pig!" (They were living in a faculty apartment at the time.) If he mentioned, rather coolly, her habit of allowing the children to go to bed in their clothes, or, worse, sleep wherever they happened to fall, like leaves— they often slept that way until Mickelsson found them and carried them to bed—she would answer with a sigh, waving away the smoke from her cigarette, hardly looking up from her magazine, "I know, they're growing up just like *animals*."

In California—San Francisco—she began to do, besides her teaching and occasional reviewing, a little directing, "very experimental"—actors who dressed like clowns or mimes or wore nothing at all (skinny or lumpy, misshapen bodies he found it painful to look at, so that at times he desperately longed for the cigarette that—ironically, considering what was happening on stage—he was not allowed); plays without scripts, frequently with no props but toilets. (Nietzsche on Zola: "the delight in stinking.") It was all unspeakably boring, not to mention annoying, to

Mickelsson, though he praised her for her work; all the more annoying for the fact that it took place in what had once been a church. He would have dismissed the whole business as insane, but apparently serious people took it seriously, among others a young man who never wore shoes but edited some famous university-based drama magazine, for which he invited Ellen to write articles, which she did. Mickelsson had for the most part kept out of the way, now and then raising an ironic eyebrow but in general reserving judgment. It was the early sixties; the world was coming apart at the seams. Whether the "new theater" was part of the world-wide collapse or part of the moral reconstruction he couldn't make out. Possibly both, he'd thought. He'd read her articles, hoping to be enlightened—sometimes he helped her with the proofreading, as she helped him with his—but her writing had left him more puzzled than before. Either the articles were gibberish (as he suspected) or they required a background of knowledge he lacked. They were loaded with concern, a frantic social consciousness he was inclined to admire, though with misgivings. Every paragraph was filled with what someone like himself, if he didn't know her, would call gutter arrogance and pseudo-Maoist cant. But he *did* know her, knew the honest ferocity of her devotion to the deprived, knew what strange creatures she proudly brought home with her to their ramshackle, bare-roomed Mission-district house. They would sit up, after Mickelsson went to bed, smoking pot and softly laughing, talking about "The Man." (He'd thought at first they meant himself.)

Ellen, in the company of her theater friends, would be radiant, as if supercharged with electricity (like the Frankenstein monster, he'd secretly thought). She organized fund drives to help defend them from "the Establishment," helped them organize non-Equity "companies," all of which went bust within three months or disappeared at once, taking the money with them. Some of her friends were rumored to be rapists, even murderers. (If he showed horror or indignation, she was ashamed of him.) He remembered trying to talk one night with a man called "the Hammer," from Los Angeles, or, as they all insisted on calling it, Movieville. He no longer remembered what they'd talked about, probably the revolution. He remembered only that the man wore an expensive three-piece suit and a wide, gray and green polkadot tie, and that whatever one asked him, he would sit for a long time, maybe twenty full seconds, meeting one's eyes, and then would answer in one sentence alarmingly strange. Mickelsson had wondered guiltily—not too carefully hiding his irritation —whether the man was hostile, high on drugs, or just crazy. Was it possible that he was right, even brilliant—speaking not words but the very *Grund des Wortes*, or rather, underground? All the others, including Ellen, seemed to look up to him, though apparently what he did for a living was not open to discussion with outsiders.

That, an outsider, Mickelsson had certainly been. (Someone had once said to him casually, apparently meaning no offense: "Athletes are notoriously conservative, aren't they? 'Anything for the team,' and so on?") He had kept his distance, faintly suggesting his disapproval, no doubt, and sometimes, alone with Ellen, risking a scornful little joke. It was not a crowd in which Mickelsson could easily dominate, as he liked to do. He might be taller by a head than the rest of them, but neither his books nor his football days impressed them. In their presence he felt like, at best, a member of the Cattleman's Association, or a small-time Republican politician. He served drinks (to the few of her friends who drank), found ashtrays for them—all with exaggerated courtesy—and retired as quickly as possible to his study. If they were planning to blow up a bank, he would rather not know.

It would have been easy to dismiss the whole thing as a conceivably useful craziness, a repugnant but necessary step in society's evolution; but every now and then he'd met someone who made all his doubts seem shameful. One typical winter San Francisco night, half fog, half rain— foghorn moans coming in off the Bay, deep electronic animal sighs—a knock had come at the door, timid but persistent, around three in the morning, and Mickelsson, in pajamas and bathrobe, had at last irritably gone down to see who it was, the old cat Horace at his heels. Ellen was out, not yet back from one of her parties. He'd opened the door a few inches, with the chain attached, and, looking out, he'd seen a middle-aged bum with two old bulging suitcases. He was bald, spectacled, with heavy-lidded Oriental eyes, dressed in a ragged shapeless brown three-piece suit twenty years out of fashion. Where the watchfob chain should be he had a ratty piece of twine. The man was nearly bald, around his ears tufts of steelwool hair. He wore thick glasses; the whites of his eyes were yellow.

"Hello," the man said. "Is this the Mickelsson residence? I'm sorry to disturb you so late at night—"

"It is," Mickelsson had said. The street beyond the man was absolutely still, no lights anywhere but the streetlamps.

"My name is Geoffrey Stewart," the man said, and smiled apologetically. "Your wife, that is, Mrs. Mickelsson, suggested . . . I'm sorry to trouble you—"

Reluctantly, Mickelsson unlatched the chain. "Come in," he said. For all his irritation, he'd opened the door wide, as if sensing—correctly, he would later understand—that the man would not enter if the invitation seemed half-hearted.

"I'm sorry to trouble you so late at night," the man said again.

"No trouble. Come on in."

The man obeyed and, not yet setting his suitcases down, looked up the long stairway, then into the livingroom. "Beautiful house."

Then the name clicked. Mickelsson said, "Are you Geoffrey Stewart the poet—from Chicago?"

The man grinned, his head bent forward, as if the question might be harder than it sounded. "That's me."

"Come in!" Mickelsson spoke somewhat more warmly now, gesturing in the direction of the livingroom. "Can I get you something to eat? Something to drink?"

"Noooo thanks," Stewart said. He looked down at the cat. "You must be Horace," he said. His eyebrows slid upward. "Helloooo, Horace."

Geoffrey Stewart, street poet, was said to be the author of things like "Hell no, we won't go," and "Hey, hey, L.B.J., how many kids did you kill today?" It was also said that, to avoid income tax, and thus involvement with "the criminal government," Stewart earned and owned almost nothing. (His two suitcases, Mickelsson would discover, contained not clothes but pamphlets.) Mickelsson said, "I'm pleased to meet you!"

"Same here," Stewart said, and smiled. "I read your book." Carefully, fussily, he aligned his suitcases with the entryway wall, where they wouldn't interfere with people's passage, then clasped his hands together in front of him and followed Mickelsson into the livingroom.

Two hours later, when Ellen came home, they were sitting almost knee to knee; they'd been talking about politics, religion, ethics, race, aesthetics. Stewart was serene, gestureless, his manner that of a pastor in his study.

"Geoffrey!" Ellen cried, running somewhat drunkenly to lean down and hug him as, awkwardly, he tried to rise from the couch and greet her. Their heads bumped and both of them laughed. "This is Geoffrey Stewart," she said, turning with a dramatic sweep of her arm toward Mickelsson.

"I know," he said.

"Geoffrey!" she cried, and hugged him again, then immediately burst into tears. Mickelsson had gone out to the kitchen to fix her a Scotch. It was morning now, ocean-clear sunlight falling over the overgrown garden behind the house.

They hadn't slept at all that night or the next day; or rather, only Ellen had slept, and that just for an hour or so. While Mickelsson was fixing pancakes for the children—then five and two—Stewart had played old hymns on Ellen's piano.

"They taste all crumbly," the boy said—Mark—looking up mournfully, as if it were really no worse than he'd expected. His hair had at that time been yellow, like Ellen's.

"They're supposed to taste crumbly. They're made of all-natural, stone-ground wheat-flour," Mickelsson said. "You're lucky they taste at all."

Both children pouted, touching the pancakes with their fingers.

"Come on," he pleaded, bending down to be level with them, pretending to look hungrily at the syrupy mush, "give it a try! Two-three *hup!*"

Thoughtfully, experimentally, his daughter poked his nose with her syrupy finger, then laughed.

In the livingroom, where the piano was, Ellen was saying, slurring her words, "Geoffrey, doesn't it bother you that when people like you are living in poverty, people like us have Baldwin pianos?"

Stewart smiled. "The world's got to have pianos," he said.

He'd stayed four days, the first stranger in years to make friends with grumpy old Horace, and an instant uncle to Leslie and Mark. Mornings and afternoons he talked at schools and at San Francisco State (Ellen's arrangements), burning money and flags, speaking of pacifism and "the message of Jesus." He spoke—sternly, without gestures—of the Jews killed during World War II, the first real test of modern society's right to survive. Not that it was all brand new. The Germans had been mass-murdering Africans for years, killing every eldest son to keep the tribes in control, so that when Hitler arrived the machinery was pretty much in place. As for L.B.J. . . . And so on.

Mickelsson had gone to listen to him every time he could, the first professed revolutionary he'd met who wasn't visibly crazy. Then, as suddenly as he'd arrived (they'd thought he was in the livingroom reading the paper), Stewart had vanished. F.B.I. men had come to the house to ask questions. "How long have you known Mr. Stewart, Professor?" "Do you know his present whereabouts?" "Have you ever been in Seattle?" They would not explain what the problem was. For the first time, Mickelsson had fully understood Ellen's helplessness and anger, her impatience with "so-called Reason."

Though he still disliked the plays her friends did—plays her writings (and many other people's) gave what Mickelsson considered a kind of fraudulent legitimacy—plays which looked for inspiration to the French (whom, one and all, Mickelsson with whole-hearted bigotry believed and frequently declared to have been back-stabbers, fakes, and perverts at least back to Caesar's time)—Mickelsson was a great deal more sympathetic than formerly to her aims. Though aims and means were, in Mickelsson's opinion, inseparable, for the sake of domestic tranquillity he kept quiet, insofar as he was able, about Ellen's preferred means. That Ellen's friends were awakening audiences to the crimes of the age seemed to him unlikely. If anything, he thought, her Thespian warriors were playing the part of Stalin's "useful idiots," not raising consciousness (as the slogan makers of a later decade would love to say, innocent of any suspicion that they were quoting Carl Jung) but stiffening the resistance of a decadent society, hurrying up the inevitable clash, plowing and fitting the ground for dragons' teeth. He might have thought it was his duty to protest, had not the Establishment seemed, by its violence and wonderful stupidity, so eager to deserve every pint of the bloodshed that was coming. The scent of war was everywhere, not just in the San Francisco area. And so he had sat at the desk in his upstairs study overlooking the street, writing papers, preparing classes, listening with the back of his mind for trouble in the children's bedrooms, and letting Nature take its course.

Ellen thrived on it. Sometimes, he would swear—though all talk of the occult was to him claptrap—she would get a kind of halo or glowing aura when she and her friends brought off (and escaped alive) a particularly offensive "production." Sometimes none of them, Ellen and her friends, would sleep for days, plotting against audiences or reviewing their successes. Then, inevitably, the reverse swing of the pendulum would come, the crash, as they called it. She would lie in bed crying, clinging to him as, in his childhood, he or, later, his younger sister and cousins, non-swimmers, would cling to an inflated rubber tube at the swimming-hole. "Oh God," she would wail. "Oh God, Mick, take care of me!" He would explain to her, holding her, what he thought was going on psychologically, how the psyche was never fooled by ethical simplifications: the more fiercely one lied, however noble the purpose, the more fiercely the genetically programmed sense of human decency struck back. He would stare up at the ceiling, stroking her hair, cradling her as he would a child, explaining, explaining. By the time he got it clear, so that she could not help but understand, she would be sleeping. Even if she'd fully understood what he told her—he believed even now that what he'd said was true—she forgot it all as soon as she was back with her friends, "those dumb sons of bitches," as he too often described them. Her depressions, at first infrequent, then more and more common, became darker. Sometimes when he came home from a lecture or convention he would find that Ellen had been in bed for two days and nights, leaving the children to fend for themselves. "The kitchen," he would tell her, quietly, sternly, "looks like a God damned municipal dump." "But what am I supposed to *do*?" she would wail. "I'm so fucking *depressed*." She saw an analyst twice a week, which made Mickelsson seethe. (Mostly the cost, he would now admit.) Everyone knew she saw an analyst twice a week. "Come the revolution," Mickelsson said, "the first middle-class parasites to go will be the analysts."

Then the decade had turned; they were now in Providence—after one year in Heidelberg, Germany—good for him and, sadly, good for her. San Francisco was dead. The Actors' Workshop had moved to New York and promptly failed; the mime troupe was mostly in jail, or so he'd been told. She had begun to put up posters—in her study, in the kitchen—about women's rights. He'd been largely in agreement with what the posters said, with one or two reservations, and they'd sometimes, like superior people, joked about it. He hadn't understood that the complaint was personal. He did the dishes, some of the cooking, some of the housecleaning. She'd never wanted to be in on the handling of the money, or so he'd thought; he'd given her an allowance. "Like a *child*," she said once. "But, *Jesus*," he said, injured and astounded, "Jesus Christ!" Full of doubts, because Ellen was inexperienced and impetuous, he'd given her control of their finances. It was a burden he was glad to be rid of, of course, though he worried. And even now he had not fully understood that she considered him an absolute, unreconstructible male chauvinist pig. Then came—though they'd somehow missed it in San Francisco, or so he believed (now he sometimes wondered)—liberated sex. She'd gone to conventions on contemporary drama and had "slept with people"— both women and men—as she was careful to report. (It had been happening for some time when she finally brought it out, both of them drunk, sitting happily in front of the fireplace.) His world reeled; then he began to do the same at philosophy conferences. On principle, he thought. *Versuchen wir's!* ("It's a fact," he would sometimes tell male friends, when he was as blurry of eye as an ocean creature, "the most sexually ravenous beasts in the world are woman philosophers." He would leer crazily—so he saw himself—like his strangely innocent football friends, long ago, when they talked about "beaver.") Unlike Ellen, he was unable to bring himself to report his sins, even drunk. When they had fights about Ellen's playing around—a phrase that, inexplicably, filled him with rage —it always seemed later that it was not her infidelity that brought on the fights, nor his guilt at his own unconfessed infidelity, but the gin they'd drunk. It had seemed not in the real world, as real human beings, that they attacked each other, but as brightly painted puppet-like creatures in an eerie projection, a dream-world where blows (they had often come to blows—Mickelsson holding back, doing damage enough, Ellen laying in on him with everything she had, pitifully girlish, though sometimes he came out with a puffy face) had no force, whatever their violence, and words, whatever their viciousness, would prove hard to remember later. In the morning they would be careful of each other, as of people who've been wounded and will never again be whole. He understood only now, he believed, what had really been going on. They'd both been idealists. They'd been brought up, both of them, in families where fidelity was assumed, the marriage bond inviolable; and when they'd left that pattern, following the fashion of their friends and time (Ellen smiling, Mickelsson looking dangerously intense), enjoying the usual excitement of the chase and the cheap thrill of liberation, they'd become like lost children. Decency striking back. They'd become anxious. Soiled. (She too had known it. He remembered how one morning, after he'd fallen asleep dead drunk on the livingroom carpet, he'd awakened to find that she'd laid out tulips in a circle all around him.) Mickelsson's greatest pleasure, toward the end of their marriage, had been lying in bed with her, holding her quietly in his arms as she slept. If dawn had never come, or the next night's party, the next philosophy or drama convention, they would doubtless have lasted forever, like their parents.

"Is she happier without you?" Jessica asked.

"On the whole," he said, then quickly raised his hand, palm out. "No pun intended! Purest accident!"

She shook her head, excusing it. "As my aunt Rose used to say, 'God spare us.' " She tried to hide a yawn.

He put his hand back down onto Jessica's foot. "Anyway, yes, she's happier. I hope. Fine young buck to keep her company—another 'theater person.' I pay them handsomely to stay out of my hair."

She studied his eyes, suspicious. "How handsomely?"

"Thousand a month," he said. "Most months."

"That's crazy!"

He shrugged. "It's all I can afford."

A tuck came to the corner of her mouth, making the dimple show, and after she'd thought for a moment, she said, "You're establishing a precedent, you know. When you get into court you'll be stuck with it."

He made his face worried. "You think I should've hit her with a hammer?"

She shook her head slowly and looked up at where the wall met the ceiling. "I think you should try to be more serious about all this."

He squeezed her foot, then playfully ran his fingertips halfway to her knee. "First thing tomorrow," he said. It came to him, all at once, that the room had grown light. The birds were singing like crazy. "Gee-whillikins," he said, looking at his wristwatch, "it's time for you to get up and jog!"

She laughed. "No chance! You want to sleep in the guest room?"

He checked her eyes. "There's only one bed in the world I want to sleep in right now," he said; when her face showed panic, he added quickly, though it was not what he'd meant to say—and perhaps, he would think later, not even what Jessica had wanted him to say—"and that's at my apartment."

"You won't fall asleep driving there?" She frowned, eyelids partly lowered.

"How far is it? Half a mile?" He shrugged and leaned forward as if to get up, but he didn't yet.

"You've been drinking, though. Are you sure you're awake enough?"

"I'm terrific," he said. "Listen, don't see me to the door. Stay right here. Close your eyes. You need a blanket?"

She shook her head.

Now at last, reluctantly, he did rise. He moved toward the head of the couch, where he could look down at her face. Her pallor startled him. What if his keeping her up all night made her ill? Jews were a sickly people. Brilliant and good-hearted, but prone to allergies and infirmities. He pointed at the bridge of her nose as if his hand were a gun. "Close your eyes," he said. "I'll let myself out. The door locks automatically, doesn't it?"

"Mmm," she said. "To tell the truth, I really am fading."

"Good. Sleep, then. You're sure I can't get you a blanket?"

She moved her head, just a little, from side to side on the couch cushion.

"You haven't closed your eyes," he said.

She smiled. Her eyelids fluttered, then lowered. She seemed asleep already.

He bent down, thinking of kissing her on the lips, then kissed her on the forehead. As he straightened up, he saw a shine on her cheek—the path of a tear. He stood as if frozen in a slight bow, startled, his hands clasped in front of him. After a moment he took his pipe from the coffee-table and hung it between his teeth, then crossed silently to the door and let himself out.

Mickelsson sighed, coming out of his dreams and memories, finding himself in Binghamton already, without any sense of how he'd gotten there. The shadow of the Jeep on the road beside him darted along too quickly, like something overtaking him. Traffic churned around him—pickup trucks, buses, hurrying cars—demanding his full attention as no doubt it had done for miles now, though his mind had been elsewhere. He hunted for his pipe, stuck it in his mouth mechanically, eyes on the road, and lit it. Monday. Plato and Aristotle at ten. Ruefully, he shook his head.

Now the campus opened out in front of him, an immense factory-complex of aluminum and brick. Possibly the ugliest campus in America. So he had thought when he'd first arrived, shuddering at his fall. He could not say that, with increasing familiarity, the campus had become more pleasing to the eye. But his heart calmed at sight of the place, exactly as—after his hours of classes and conferences—his heart would calm, late tonight, when he burrowed into the darkness of the Endless Mountains.

Plato and Aristotle at ten. A course for beginners.

Taught by Peter J. Mickelsson.

Incredible.

6

"But what was 'Plato saying,' really?" he inquired of his class, or rather, looking over them, one eyebrow lifted, inquired ironically of the empty blackboard at the back of the room. He leaned forward, waiting, though they all seemed persuaded that the question was rhetorical—bent over their notebooks, pencils poised, ready to write down and underline and adorn with multiple exclamation points whatever it should turn out that, according to Professor Mickelsson, Plato was saying. The semester was only three weeks old. Most of his students were freshmen or sophomores, shining-faced innocents waiting eagerly for wisdom, or what they took for wisdom—things they could write down and make use of in life, like algebraic method or the rhyming saws one picked up, as they'd no doubt learned by now, in the Anguish Department (" 'Forlorn!' The very word is like a bell . . .")—each of them dressed in the uniform of the age, formerly the uniforms of streetworkers or cowboys, bleached-out jeans and workshirts their mothers had bought them (so Mickelsson imagined) at Saks, watching him with interest, hair-triggered to laugh if he should happen to make a joke, or groan if he should ask them to take out paper for a quiz, and groan again when he said "Time's up!" Only one of the students in this class, the would-be suicide he'd met during the summer, Michael Nugent, was a junior—not that one would have guessed. He showed no sign of the typical junior's amused, glossy confidence. He seemed, if anything, even more earnestly out after wisdom than his classmates, watching Mickelsson like a crazed hawk, now grinning, now showing fear, sometimes looking around in troubled rage, as if, for some reason, he'd come to hate it that he'd been born a carnivore yet could not help seeing his classmates as chickens and mice.

Mickelsson was seated, as usual, on the front of his desk, his pipe in his hand, his heavy right leg swinging. On the tree outside his window, a half-dozen leaves had turned bright yellow. Two young sparrows darted back and forth near the glass as if trying to get a look at the clock. Alan Blassenheim, probably the brightest of this semester's crop—though hopelessly, frantically in love with his own wild, undisciplined opinions and mildly corrupted, Mickelsson suspected, by a business-world background (his father was "in plastics") that would tend to make him unduly quick to compromise, too easily satisfied by the stylish and commercial—poor

Blassenheim looked powerfully tempted, almost driven, to raise his hand, whether or not he was sure he knew the answer. He had the ways of an athlete: Get in there and fight, don't think! Mickelsson averted his eyes from Blassenheim's, lest he lead the boy into temptation.

"Put it this way. It may or may not be, as Miss Mariani points out . . ." He nodded polite acknowledgment toward the girl who'd raised the issue—a young woman thin of arm and leg, large of face, heavy of eyelid. She sat hungrily smoking a cigarette, awkwardly knocking the ashes off onto a makeshift ashtray of folded notebook paper. "That is," he said, "it may or may not be that, as I. F. Stone argues, Socrates was a fascist and Plato, as his defender, must have been more or less the same. It's a question we can hardly judge directly, of course, since none of us was there." He smiled and they dutifully smiled with him. "All we have is Plato's writings, so the only question we're competent to deal with is, 'Just how fascistic is Plato's *Republic*?' "

He paused for an instant, making sure of their attention. Most of them were writing furiously in their notebooks. Miss Mariani made a show of looking interested, as if her question about Plato's fascism had been, for some time now, a matter of concern to her. Not that he blamed the poor girl. It was a bitch, trying to learn what to ask, what to think, what to do to get attention. It was cruelly unfair and always had been, the whole teaching-and-learning business. He wished the whole lot of them back in Eden, where all you had to know was the difference between apples. "You'll notice that Stone is very quick to use phrases like 'Plato was saying.' Should that bother us at all? Any reasonable objections?"

He waited, hoping for any hand but Blassenheim's or Nugent's, the terrible two. Nothing, of course, not even from them, and of course nothing from poor Miss Mariani. He sighed. "All right. Plato—'the dramatist,' as we called him earlier, as some of you may recall—" He smiled; they smiled. "Plato, or Socrates, or some Socrates invented by Plato and not necessarily to be confused with either Socrates or Plato—*some*body, anyway—argues in *The Republic* that the masses can't be trusted. Is that fascism, in itself?" They waited and, when the pause lengthened, looked up expectantly. "At least we can grant that it's an excusable mistake," he said. He raised his pipe to his lips and pulled. It was out. "Think of Hitler's Third Reich." Usually when you dropped an allusion to Hitler their interest increased, as if the subject guaranteed that now, at last, you must say things worthy of their notebooks. "A mass of citizens full of ignorant opinions, mainly, of course, 'the Wagnerian morass,' as Nietzsche calls it, anti-Semitism" (Nugent nodded quick, angry agreement). ". . . a madman willing to make use of anything for his own aggrandizement . . ." He found the matches, lit one, and held it above the pipebowl, hurriedly moving the flame from side to side. "To what extent can we pin such things on Plato? Certainly *The Republic* has no room for a Hitler; Socrates explicitly condemns that kind of thing, and he speaks persuasively on how it comes about, how the mob wants simple answers and the strong man, the bully, comes along and offers them."

"Just like Reagan," Nugent said, pretending to be talking to himself. Mickelsson decided to ignore it. There was much one might say of Mr. Reagan as bull to the Nietzschean "herd"—Nietzschean buffoonery vs. Hollywood buffoonery, that is, "harmonious classicism" housed in cowboy good intentions and fangless wit. But it was hardly to the point.

"Try this, then," he said. (Nugent was still muttering.) "Does the fascism we're annoyed by lie in the stupidity of the masses, that is, their preference for cheap solutions backed by force—mental fascism? Obviously, Socrates frowns on that too." Some of the class nodded. "But think, now. Perhaps we can nail Plato yet! Possibly the problem was deeper, the very concept, however blurry in the German mind, of transcendent ideals against which multitudes of people can be measured—Gypsies, Poles, Jehovah's Witnesses, not just Jews, though mainly Jews, certainly. Was the problem—the tendency toward fascism—the belief in 'transcendent ideals' against which whole groups of people, as I was saying, can be measured and found to be 'defective'? Transcendent ideals—immutable forms, the Realities behind Actuality: as some would put it—are much frowned upon these days. Even Heidegger, whose philosophy gave a certain comfort to the Nazis, had no patience for transcendent ideas; and the feeling's standard—the existentialists, the so-called hermeneutics . . ." He watched the class write down *existentialists, hermeneutics.* He swung his leg.

"Plato's the philosopher who taught us about transcendent ideas, so if it's true that they're the problem, then Plato has to go—maybe go live in the woods with the expelled poets." He smiled. "Well, what do you think?" After a moment he glanced at the blackboard, thinking of writing the question down. *What do you think?* There was nothing there but the NO SMOKING sign someone had written and, in Mickelsson's hand, Wednesday's assignment.

"Notice what we've said here; let me put it to you again," he said. "Maybe there's something *always* wrong with transcendent ideas, something 'deeper' than the particular situation. Anything bothersome in that statement?"

Nugent had his eyes screwed up. He seemed almost on to it, but he wasn't yet sure. As for the rest, they watched Mickelsson like children struggling—some of them irritably—to figure out the rules of an unfamiliar game.

"Well, all right, let it stand for now," he said. "To continue the argument—" (Dirty trick, of course; Socratic.) He glanced at the window. The birds were gone. "In principle, nothing's more beautiful, we may feel, than the strict idealist view of things. But the question is—" Blassenheim's hand went up. Mickelsson pressed on: "The question is whether the Ideal exists in actuality or only in our clumsy, moment-by-moment emotions—continually shifting potential; in other words 'out there' or 'in here' or both: God's voice, so to speak, or the opinion, on a particular Tuesday, of some human—or both at once. Am I leaving things out?" He waited. No response. "Put it this way. Darwin might say—and Aristotle, as we'll discover, might partly agree (if the terms were made clear)" —he smiled, ironic—"that the Ideal is everlastingly evolving, so that in effect there's no such thing as an absolute, static Ideal, only the shifting implications of *Being*. But if that's *always* true, a fact independent of our personal existence . . ."

It was impossible to go on ignoring young Blassenheim's hand. One knew pretty well what tack he would take, but no matter; nothing was happening anyway, and one could always work one's way back to the point at hand. Mickelsson nodded, giving Blassenheim the floor, the same instant glancing at Nugent, who smiled with sudden enlightenment and jerked his head, raising his hand, then drew it back down. His queer pallor and large, seemingly lashless eyes had the odd effect of making him appear to be watching the proceedings from far away—ancient Ireland, perhaps—though he sat among the others, presumably in the same dimensions of time-space.

Blassenheim looked at his desktop, deferential, and raised his eyebrows as if to make his face look still more meek, though his accent— Long Island Jewish—suggested to Mickelsson a kind of tough-kid irreverence, perhaps originally a defense against an overprotective mama and Long Island schoolteachers just like her. He glanced left and right, like a basketball player about to make his move, and he spoke slightly out of the side of his mouth, his *s*'s thickly liquid, almost *z* or *sh*. "But isn't it two different questions, really—whether there's even such a thing as an Ideal and, if there is, whether an ordinary person can perceive it?"

"Yes, of course," Mickelsson began. It was a good point, if the boy could figure out what to do with it, nail the old epistemological issues, who can know the Ideal and how, and separate out the content issues, are the ideals situational or transsituational? He should give the boy some help; but his thought hung, snagged, on Blassenheim's comfortable use of the word *perceive*. He'd grow up to be a lawyer, big firm in Manhattan. He already had the look. Clean cut. Shiny brown, abundant, blow-dried hair.

Blassenheim hurried on, deferential and aggressive. "If Darwin's view is right, there's nothing inherently good about a creature that survives except the fact of its survival." He rolled out his hands, as if bargaining. (The Darwin argument faintly rang a bell; then Mickelsson remembered: his own book.) The boy said, "But how can you be sure that Reality doesn't have, like, built-in standards? Like maybe the closer a creature gets to one of those standards, the better its chances of survival."

"That's conceivable, of course," Mickelsson said, startled by the queer direction the boy had taken. (Heading for Bergson?) He really ought to stop and get back on track, or at least make some effort to sort out the many possible claims the boy seemed to be making. Perhaps in response to Mickelsson's expression—a one-sided smile he only now became aware of—the class was showing signs of boredom and amused contempt, the usual effect when Blassenheim trotted out one of his theories, though they all liked him. (In all fairness, they were equally bored by Mickelsson's theories, or even Plato's, if the presentation lacked punch.) The blond girl-athlete, Brenda Winburn—swimming team, if Mickelsson's memory served—was staring out the window. She was, he'd long since discovered, the class nihilist, not that the word was within the range of her vocabulary. "I guess if people want to believe that, they might just as well," she would say, hollow-voiced. Such bleakness of heart in one so young was disturbing, and Mickelsson rarely called on her if he could help it. Sometimes, turning to her side of the room, he would find her large, sullen eyes settled on him—beautiful eyes, shiny as dark glass—and he would wonder in brief distress whether there were perhaps something he ought to be saying to her, some phrase he had at hand, insufficiently valued, that might transform her way of seeing. She reminded him a little of a bird in winter, round head drawn in toward the shoulders. He knew better than to brood on it. He'd seen enough to know that philosophy follows chemistry. If she stared at him with the cool detachment of a wood-nymph, or someone terminally ill (he got a memory-flash of his father in the hospital), it was not because she'd been musing too long on, say, Spengler.

Miss Mariani was still watching him with large-faced interest. She had not noticed, apparently, that the discussion of I. F. Stone's charge was, for the moment at least, dead. Harry Kaplan in the back row passed a note to the red-headed girl beside him. Weber? Webster? She opened it, glancing up nearsightedly at Mickelsson and, seeing that she'd been caught, blushed. He returned his attention—thinking he might quickly get rid of them—to the opinions of Alan Blassenheim.

"I take it you're suggesting," he said, "that there is indeed a 'divine plan,' a sort of 'museum of eternal forms,' as a certain reading of Plato has it"—he shot a look at Blassenheim, telegraphing the punch and half smiling to soften its effect when it came—"and Nature, by random evolutionary groping, struggles to find her way to those forms one by one." He glanced at Nugent, then back, as he added, "More or less like the roomful of apes at typewriters, trying to stumble onto *War and Peace*."

Here and there students snickered, Nugent among them, not necessarily because they'd understood. (*Out of control,* he thought; he couldn't even handle the discussion of freshmen.) Blassenheim blinked, not yet fully aware that his suggestion had been made to appear too silly to pursue. Mickelsson felt at the back of his mind a troublesome struggle of contradictions: annoyance at the too easy laughter of the young man's classmates, and a twinge of pity for Blassenheim, whose suggestions, after all, were more interesting than any those who laughed at him were likely to come up with; a touch of impatience at the fact that, year after year, one covered the same old ground; but also a surge of impatience with himself, not just for losing the thread, falling into chaos (there was a time when he'd have laid all this out clearly, with contagious excitement), but also for striking out at poor Blassenheim. He thought of his own son Mark, unhappy in college, an eager, nervous boy whose teachers had no appreciation of his gifts—his sweetness of soul, his devotion to ideas, his monkish diligence and care. It was not, he was certain, the opinion of a doting parent. Mickelsson knew the university world, its shoddiness and self-absorption; and he'd seen the boy's carelessly graded papers.

The thought of his son brought with it a clammy sensation it took him a moment to identify: the visit of the I.R.S. agents, their alarming knowledge of everything in his life, including the fact, trivial in itself, that Mark was involved in anti-nuclear demonstrations. Their visit had been more than a month ago now. He'd heard nothing since. Alas, nothing from his son either.

"I don't mean to dismiss your suggestion too hastily," Mickelsson said, struggling against inertia—struggling and, at the deepest level, failing, dealing with Blassenheim's murky, difficult notions by a magic trick: deliberately changing the issue. "It may well be that the universe is filled with ghostly forms waiting to be realized. But if they aren't yet realized—or, worse, if they should happen never to be realized—it would seem necessary for us to figure out in what sense we can claim they exist."

Quickly, Blassenheim said, wildly improvising, darting up his hand to give his speaking legitimacy, apparently unaware that his point had been palmed and pocketed, "I understand your objection, but maybe that's where, like, consciousness differs from the rest. Maybe it's wrong to talk about *physical* objects and eternal forms—the perfect zebra, say." He smiled and shrugged, opening his hands again. "But maybe with thoughts it's a whole different business. Like mathematics, for instance, or chemical formulas. Like the number *two*. It was up there for millions of years before anybody thought of it, right? It's built into, you know, like, the structure of things." He folded his arms, closing the hands on the well-developed shoulders.

"Well, not really, not exactly," Mickelsson said and pretended to smile. Should one drift off to Wittgenstein—words as names, words as functions? He sighed and glanced at the clock.

Now Michael Nugent had his hand up, his pale eyes a little like those of an I.R.A. killer, or so Mickelsson imagined. "Are you saying the 'eternal verities' that Faulkner talks about, there aren't any?"

Mickelsson started to answer, then paused, arrested by a hunch that the boy was speaking ironically, scoffing at Faulkner's hopes. He met Nugent's eyes and believed the hunch correct. "All I *meant* to be suggesting," he said, looking down at his pipe for a moment, "is that 'Plato's Ideas,' insofar as we can call them that—" He paused again, glancing at Miss Mariani, who sat smoking hard, writing in her notebook. She breathed the smoke deep, then let it seep out. He'd lost his thread. Then it came back to him. " 'Plato's Ideas' "—he spoke directly to Nugent— "have a fascistic tendency only if we argue that the universe is hopelessly unreasonable, so that the rule of reason in human society is unsupportable, absurd." Abruptly he got up from the desk, went to the blackboard behind it, and picked up a short piece of chalk from the tray. "If death, for example, is a regular and predictable feature of our experience," he said, raising the chalk but not yet writing, half turning back to them to finish his thought, "so that the wish to avoid death and make life worthwhile is also one of our experiential facts—" He shifted his eyes, wishing he hadn't mentioned death.

Quickly Mickelsson made three boxes, put a checkmark in each one, then drew a shadowy box-with-checkmark above them, with dotted lines radiating down from it, one to each box, like heaven's love.

"If *anything* is constant," he said as he made his picture, "then that Something transcends particular experience, though it's also immanent *in* experience"—he jabbed his chalk at the checks in the lower three boxes—"and we have a chance, at least, of figuring it out." He drew spectacles studying the boxes:

"As for Mr. Faulkner's rather general notion of 'eternal verities,' well, the impulse is fine, but the language lacks the kind of focus we look for in Philosophy 108." He smiled. Part of the class smiled with him, mirroring his grimness. He felt, for an instant, the sensation of a younger, more impartial teacher: benign and powerful, as if ideas were what counted. Nugent glanced, pink-faced and alarmed, at the students to his left, perhaps checking to see whether they resented his asking questions, making trouble. Brenda Winburn went on staring out the window. She was not the only one, it came to him. Several, mostly those in back, were glancing from time to time at the clock. The notebooks he could see were filled with doodles. (Woe was Mickelsson. They were on to him all right. Their evaluation-of-the-instructor forms would be blistering.

> Knowledge of subject matter: *Fair.*
> Presentation of subject matter: *Poor.*
> Interest in students: *Stinko.*

He would do the sensible thing: forget to hand out the forms.)

His pipe had gone out. "Put it this way," he said, letting his shoulders droop, avoiding Nugent's eyes. "One reading of Plato—not a very good one, necessarily, but a common one, and one to which Mr. Blassenheim would seem to be inclining us—says eternal forms exist 'out there,' like lures in a fashion magazine. Darwin would say, if you pushed him to it, that the way to *be,* for zebras and human beings, exists not 'out there' but inside, respectively—or should we say exists *largely* inside?—zebras and human beings. Our nature, in other words, would be, for Darwin, not some goal we're aiming at—the way a farmer aims his tractor at his red handkerchief when he turns that first furrow"—the class looked blank —"but our whole animal history and the whole grid of our genetic potential, including possible but as yet unrealized mutations. If we're more loving than zebras, he'd claim, it's not because God is Love and we're closer to God than zebras are; it's genetic programming: our children are more helpless; they need families and tender care for their survival. If there's a form for human beings, he'd have to say, it changes with every evolutionary leap. Reason can figure it out, if it stays alert, or so we hope." He pointed at the picture of spectacles on the blackboard. "But here's the tricky part. In actual fact—that is, in practice—by 'reason' we always mean, consciously or not, 'elite reason,' the reason of people who've cut themselves off from farming or shoemaking or selling insurance to study 'reason.' We mean people who've devoted themselves to logic, mathematics, the traditions of human thought, and can therefore make some claim to knowing what they're talking about. You can see the problem. I don't know anyone who'd strenuously deny that some human beings are smarter than others; but it's hard to know for sure who the smart ones are—it has too much to do with class, unexamined teaching methods and learning theory, and so on. And if the form for human beings exists mainly 'in here' "—he pointed at his chest with his pipestem —"in all of us, each with his own somewhat special program—or to put it another way, if it exists 'out there' only in the sense that the chessboard on which a particular game is played exists transcendently 'out there' " —he saw that they were lost in his verbiage but decided to trudge on— "then it seems risky to leave the definition of what we are, or ought to be —that is, what game life ought to play—in the hands of just a few, the reason-specialists, the philosopher kings of *The Republic.*" An image of his neighbor John Pearson came into his mind. The mysterious, possibly misanthropic smile, the eyebrows that went out like gray-black wings. He continued quickly, brushing past the image: "This is an argument often raised against Plato in recent years, ever since the philosopher Bertrand Russell cracked the door to it. Gordon Past's book, for instance, *Enemies of the Open Society*. It's an argument almost always overstated, as it is by Past; but there may be a sense in which it's valid. The Germans allowed themselves a very small brain-pool during the Second World War. They'd even have killed Einstein, if they could have gotten him to come home. Meanwhile, in America, it was a fifteen-year-old boy who figured out a practical way to build the superfortress. In other words, we may be wise to distinguish between Plato's idea that there are transcendent truths and his metaphoric political notion of how society might get at them." An odd whininess, he noticed, had invaded his voice. He pushed on. "Looking for the truth isn't fascistic. It means giving in to open-minded-ness, subjecting one's opinions and prejudices to analysis and rigorous argument. On that score, you might look at the *Parmenides*. Plato's suggested means—the reasoning class in *The Republic*—may be something else, in practice anyway. On that point . . ." He let it trail off.

Miss Mariani was smiling. It was exactly as she'd always thought.

Inevitably, both Blassenheim and Nugent had their hands up. Mickelsson again glanced at the clock—two minutes left—then nodded, decisively, at Blassenheim.

"But isn't it true," Blassenheim asked, "that all that really proves is that Plato had a sort of aristocratic bias, like the modern, like, capitalist? He couldn't believe that a Jew like Einstein or a fifteen-year-old kid might be the real philosopher kings? I mean, some things are right and some things aren't right, that's all there is to it. If an evil government survived for a million years, it would still be evil."

Again Mickelsson nodded. "Of course it would," he said. "By definition. The problem is—"

Again Nugent had his hand up, furiously waving it.

He realized with a start that Brenda Winburn was staring at him, her large, dark eyes still as gun-barrels. Perhaps it was only that the others were gathering their papers and books, ready for the bell. Her stare was murky with shadows, like that of a child on drugs, though he doubted that it was that. He had an irrational sense that in a moment she would break out of her terrible lethargy of soul and shout at him, or snarl like an animal, expose him as a quibbler, an obscurer, a time-server, a fraud. Along with his fear of her came a sexual stirring. Michael Nugent's face was white, his hand stretched up, desperately reaching. That instant—fortunately—the bell rang. With the back of the hand that held his pipe he touched his forehead; then he smiled, as if grudgingly, and nodded his dismissal of the class. Most of them, as usual, went out shaking their heads. As usual, he'd fooled only the smart ones.

. . .

He was halfway to his mailbox when Alan Blassenheim caught up with him. "Terrific class," the boy said, grinning crookedly, not meeting his eyes.

"Thank you," Mickelsson said. Faint panic stirred in him, a minute sickness near his heart.

"I really like that way you do that, make us think for ourselves." He shook his head, falling into step with Mickelsson, then brushed his rich, dark hair back with his fingers.

"I guess that's what it's all about," Mickelsson said.

"I was wondering," the boy said. He glanced over his shoulder. "Maybe you could give me a list of books or something."

Mickelsson smiled, unconsciously checking the hallway for familiar faces. "Fine. Drop by the office sometime."

"Yeah, sure. OK." The boy hesitated an instant, knowing he'd been dismissed, then continued beside him. After a moment he said, "I was thinking about that thing you quoted from Collingham that time, how all widespread errors contain some truth. I got to thinking, you know, since there are all these people that believe in God—"

They'd come to the mailroom. Rogers, in history, looked up from his mailbox, saw Mickelsson, and mournfully grinned. "Peter," he said, "are you invited to Blicksteins'?" He glanced at Blassenheim, politely and sadly registered his existence, then looked back at Mickelsson.

"I'd forgotten all about it."

Rogers laughed as if wearily, colored light sparking off his silver hair and glasses. "I thought you might have. Or rather, to tell the truth, Jessica thought you might have."

Without meaning to, Mickelsson frowned.

"See here," Rogers said, looking up at him more carefully and raising a hand, palm out.

"No, no, that's fine. I'm glad you reminded me," Mickelsson said. "It slipped my mind, that's all." He smiled, reassuring, then turned his attention to fitting the key into the mailbox.

"Well, see you, then," Rogers said.

Mickelsson nodded and, with his left hand, waved. It occurred to him that Tillson, his chairman, might be invited; an unpleasant thought. He dismissed it the next instant. It was a dinner party, small; and Blickstein knew a fool when he saw one.

As he glanced over his mail, Mickelsson was aware of Blassenheim awkwardly hovering at his elbow. Consciously, a little guiltily, he blotted the boy out. Bills, ditto sheets, various letters, one from the American Society of Aesthetics. He thought of leaving the student newspaper, then on second thought lifted it from the floor of his box. On the front page he found a picture of his student Brenda Winburn in her swimsuit, poised for a dive.

"It's funny to think of professors having private lives," Blassenheim said. Mickelsson half registered something odd in the tone, but his attention was focussed on the girl. She was raised up on her toes, her legs chunkily muscular, her breasts much smaller than he'd have imagined. Her expression was intent, unreadable, as if she were deep in meditation. At her back there was a large, inexplicable shadow, as if she had broad, dark wings. When he glanced at Blassenheim, he saw, in the instant before the boy looked away, that Blassenheim had been studying him hungrily. To cover his surprise, Mickelsson tapped at the picture with his pipe-stem. "Pretty girl," he said. "Smarter than you'd think."

Dutifully, Blassenheim looked at the picture.

Mickelsson closed the mailbox and turned to leave. "Stop by any time," he said, his voice accidentally stern, "we'll work out that list."

"Yes sir," the boy said. Though he did not seem satisfied, he smiled.

Mickelsson felt, suddenly, a physical heaviness, a leadenness of limbs and heart, that it took him a moment to understand. This afternoon at three, he must cope with his graduate seminar in medical ethics. He remembered how he'd been himself, in his days as a graduate student: the hungry ambition, the awful heart's wail for wisdom and justice, the moral outrage in the presence of soulless pedantry. Not that his freshmen and sophomores were so different, or his children, even when they'd been small, no more than five or six. Maybe one was born with it. One of those infant and childhood diseases, often fatal. He got a sudden painful memory of the Minnesota football team, sitting on glossy, battleship-gray wooden benches in the locker-room at half-time, listening to old Deer-lock's harangue. Team-spirit, honor, courage, shame. Faint in the distance, the marching band peeped out its snazzy syncopations. After a moment, a faraway crowd roar reached the locker-room, not like something now happening (back then) but like something from a dream, an old, old memory. *Gim-me a M! Gim-me a I!* . . . The black smudges on his team-mates' cheekbones were like Indian war-paint playfully smeared on the faces of children at a party.

As he turned the corner, starting down the hallway toward his office door, he glanced up for some reason from his impatient perusal of return addresses and saw that Nugent had gotten there ahead of him. His heart sank, and, without entirely meaning to, he put on an expression of harassed irritability. There was another young man with Nugent, a tall, handsome black boy in a tank-top, his hair in corn-rows. Mickelsson had a feeling they'd been in earnest conversation and had stopped at sight of him. They stood not far apart, their heads inclined toward one another, watching him approach. He nodded, a quick little jerk of the head, and looked back down at his mail, letting them know he was busy. At his door, with his right hand closed around the keys in his pocket, Mickelsson reconsidered and turned toward Nugent. If he and Nugent could have their conversation, whatever it was, here in the hallway, he might get finished with it quickly.

"Hi, there," Mickelsson said and, in spite of himself, grinned.

Nugent bowed with exaggerated formality and blanched a little, as he always did when directly addressed. "Hi," he said. He looked confused for an instant, then said, overcoming fear, "Professor Mickelsson, I'd like you to meet my friend Randy Wilson." He reached out and touched his black friend's elbow, exactly as one might touch the elbow of a younger sister or, perhaps, a girlfriend.

"How do you do," he said.

"Hey, man," Randy said, and shyly reached out his hand.

Mickelsson shifted his Plato's *Republic* and the letters he held from his right hand to his left and extended his right hand for an ordinary handshake, then quickly readjusted to a power-to-the-people shake. Though he couldn't have said why, his heart sank more.

"Randy's in dance," Nugent said.

"That's wonderful," Mickelsson said—rather stupidly, blinking. He felt caught in one of those contemporary tragedies of the kind his ex-wife especially favored, the kind in which you laugh and laugh until the grossly predictable horror swings in. Who else would the sorrowing, suicidal white boy choose as best friend—no, lover—but a black boy in, of all things, dance? Murderous cliché! How easy it was to find roads to catastrophe!

But it was the real world, not theater; scuffed, fake-marble floors, taped-up *New Yorker* cartoons on the office doors. All might yet be well. Randy had fine, supple muscles, enormously wide lips, such apparent sweetness and childlike timidity one could not help hoping for the best. He was already fading back, delicately allowing Nugent privacy for his conversation with the professor.

Nugent said, "I just wanted to say, that was terrific, the way you handled that."

"Oh?" Mickelsson said, and waited.

Randy Wilson stood ten feet away from them now, sidling away still further, reading the notices on Libby Tucker's long bulletin board, his hands on his buttocks, perfectly pressed to them like limp leaves, the elbows perfectly parallel, oddly widening his shoulders.

Nugent glanced at Mickelsson's office door, then away, as if aware that Mickelsson had decided not to let him in. "All that crap about Ideal Forms," Nugent said, "and Nature struggling toward God's Ideas."

"Mmm," Mickelsson said, and waited.

Nugent stood oddly still, his chin thrust forward, the bone-line disturbingly visible, troublesome as the sound of one's own heartbeat in bed. The tracery of his veins showed under the skin. "Everybody wants to

go back to the simplicity of childhood," he said, and smiled as if in p
"They're scared of the modern world, you know? Want to get bac
innocent, sweet Nature, William Wordsworth. They don't underst\
what we came out of—superstition and craziness."

Mickelsson's smile became fixed. He began, almost against his will, to
pay attention. He couldn't spend much time on this; he had yet to finish
his preparation for the medical ethics class. But Nugent was a strange
young man, no question about it.

"Look at the world—the Church is a would-be mass murderer. I mean
the Pope's medieval craziness on abortions—no place for them, even to
save a woman's life! Higher education in full retreat, or if it tries to
stand firm—like Greg—he was my chemistry teacher . . . someone murdered him. Got into his apartment and—you know the one I mean?" He
began to blink rapidly.

Mickelsson nodded. He'd heard something about it; not much, though
it had been in the papers.

"I mean," Nugent said, his voice breaking, and suddenly jerked his
forearms out to the sides, the rest of his body motionless, "what we need
is devices for present-day survival, you know what I mean?" He stretched
his lips in a failed grin, one angry, superior intelligence to another. "I
used to be in engineering—"

Mickelsson nodded again.

"We need *inventions*, that's what I think. But not space-shuttles,
smaller computer chips, artificial blood. All that's been tried." With a
wave he dismissed Technological Man to outer darkness. "Did you happen
to read a book by Dr. James J. Lynch, called *The Broken Heart: The
Medical Consequences of Loneliness*?"

"I've heard of it," Mickelsson said, lying, hoping to avoid a long
discussion.

Nugent's head tucked in abruptly, as if he were suddenly going into
a fit, and his arms cringed back from extended position, then closed on
the straps of his small, dark green backpack. He pulled it off with clumsy
haste, unsnapped the top, dove in with one hand, and after a moment
came out with an orange-red paperback book. "I thought you might like
to look at it," he said. "I'm sorry about all the underlinings—" He
pressed the book toward Mickelsson's chest. Automatically, unwillingly,
Mickelsson took hold of it. The boy said, his eyes on Mickelsson's forehead, "What Dr. Lynch argues—well, it's here on the cover." He pivoted
around to stand beside Mickelsson, almost pushing against his shoulder,
pointing with two white fingers at the blurb: "Dr. Lynch brings together
striking evidence that companionship is an important life-force."

"Interesting," Mickelsson said, and, as the boy released it, accepted
the book.

"People like what's-his-name, the kid in our class—the pretty one—"

"Alan Blassenheim," Mickelsson said, reserved.

"Well, anyway," Nugent said, "anyway, it's easy to say we'd have been happy if we'd lived fifty years ago, or in ancient Judah, whatever—try to resuscitate a bunch of dead ideas—"

He felt a queer, sentimental urge to touch the boy's arm, say something like "Listen, take it easy!" Instead, he looked thoughtfully at the cover of the book.

"It's all about heart attacks, and the reason why they happen," Nugent explained. "Most people don't realize how important it is, for our very survival—"

"I'll be interested to read it," Mickelsson said.

The boy went white, as if slaughtered by some thought, and his red, seemingly lashless eyes blinked rapidly again. "It was good, the way you handled that, that shit-ass crap—"

Mickelsson went on looking at the cover of the book. "Come on now," he said (he heard in his own voice Rifkin's whine), "I was equally hard on *you*."

"That's true, but I don't think you understood what I was saying. I mean, I didn't make it clear."

He stood in calculated silence. Then he cocked his eye at the boy. "You can't blame me if I'm a little confused, Mr. Nugent." He allowed a little gentleness into his voice. "You give me this book about loneliness and, I take it, heart disease, and at the very same time you ask me to squash a fellow student like an insect. What will it lead to, such scorn of one's fellow human beings?"

The white face went red, and the girlish mouth came open. "I didn't mean—" he began. It was the start of a lie, but he quickly caught it. Anger replaced fear, but then he caught that too. Of their own will, his shoulders heaved in a monstrous, meek shrug. He had large, shining tears in his eyes. "I just thought you'd like to read—" he said, and indicated the book in Mickelsson's hands.

"Mmm," Mickelsson said, "yes I would." He nodded. In fact, it was true.

The black boy, Mickelsson noticed now, was watching them, eavesdropping. Into Mickelsson's mind, against his will, came an image of the two of them going at each other, naked in some foggy green meadow— spectacular cinema in the style of *Barry Lyndon*, done on cheap Kodak celluloid that would fade in a couple of years, as *Barry Lyndon* had done (so he'd read in some newspaper) to pink or violet. He felt a great, depressing rush of guilt. Nugent was no dolt. If by some miracle they could get on the same wave-length, he thought—then cringed in disgust at the word *wave-length*, then frowned at his snobbishness.

"All I meant," Nugent said, watching his face, "is, everybody hates it that the modern world's so civilized and boring and generally safe, so crushing to the human soul and imagination. Everybody wants to get back to simplicity. Windmills, tide-power, little communes in Vermont. Nobody has the faintest understanding of, well, you know, the *awful* part, the perdurable evils." The catch came to his voice. Mickelsson squinted at him, thinking about the word *perdurable*. Nugent waved, almost gasping with frustration. "When I hear that business about how everything's evolving toward Wonderful, and things—"

"I know how you feel," Mickelsson said. He looked down at his mail.

Nugent stepped back from him, almost military. "Right," he said, as if in answer to some remark of Mickelsson's. "I realize you do. I know what you've been through. I know everything about you." He looked away, embarrassed. "OK! You've got a lot to do, I know. . . ." He half turned to leave, his eyes hanging back. "By the way," he said, "you never answered that note I left you, at your apartment."

"Note?" Mickelsson said. Though he flushed with guilt, the truth was that he did not remember, that instant, Nugent's note under his door.

"Well," Nugent said, and bowed, formal again, preparing to go. He suddenly waved, nearly a salute, and—flashing his unnaturally small, white teeth—smiled. Mickelsson watched him retreat, followed by the black boy, down the hall.

As he was unlocking the door to his office, the feeling came over him that someone—some further nuisance—was waiting inside. The feeling was so strong, however irrational, that he hesitated before turning the knob. The phrase *perdurable evils* drifted into his mind, and he shook his head. Then he remembered, and for the first time really noticed, that even stranger phrase: *I know everything about you.*

The office, when at last he opened the door, was empty. Sudden depression flooded through him. He looked again at the letters in his hand. In the left-hand corner of one of the envelopes he found the name "Bauer" and a Florida address. No doubt because his mind was fixed on his university context, not the house in the Endless Mountains, he could think of no one he knew named Bauer and dropped the envelope, along with the others, into the chaos of papers and unopened envelopes on his desk.

7

It was the dean himself who opened the door for him, grinning, his muscular, round face tipped sideways, chin neatly cleft, his right hand reaching up to seize Mickelsson's upper arm. "Come in! Come in!"

Blickstein's suit was tight at the shoulders, his neck thick as a boar's. He'd been a wrestling coach and professor of phys ed, some years ago, before he'd gone into full-time administration. Not that Sheldon Blickstein was your common jock. He had a sharp, crafty mind and seemed to read everything, though he was shy about his knowledge and had cranky spots. (He believed and for some reason often insisted that Homer, the epic poet, was a woman.) His Ph.D. in education was from Columbia. As a student, people said, he'd been an activist, helping to seize buildings, shouting about peace and justice. Nonetheless he'd been a champion wrestler and had a tendency even now to put his hand on the back of your neck or on your shoulder in a way that suggested feeling for a hold. Mickelsson felt his body coming alert, cautiously balancing. The dean swung around on his small, neat feet, extending his short and powerful left arm in the direction of the carpeted stairs leading up to the living-room. "Come up! Come right up! We were afraid you'd gotten lost!"

"I'm sorry," Mickelsson said, "I didn't realize I was late."

"Not at all! Good Lord, no," Blickstein said, but now his right hand was on the small of Mickelsson's back, groping for advantage, gently pressing him toward the stairs. The entryway was tiled, vaguely Spanish; the livingroom, partly visible above, was what Mickelsson's ex-wife would call American academic—dark panelling, indirect lighting, a vast superfluity of books. The house smelled richly of food—beef, onions, potatoes, garlic, herbs. On the wall at the top of the stairs hung a black and white photograph of an old shed and trees. For an instant Mickelsson's heart caught: he thought it was one of his son's. It was not, of course; probably by someone famous and expensive, perhaps a photographer who had influenced his son.

"Beautiful house," Mickelsson said.

"*We* like it," Blickstein said, warmly grateful.

Talk filtered down from the livingroom and, from somewhere to their left as they started up the stairs, kitchen sounds, blurry as sounds under water. As Mickelsson's eyes came up level with the room he saw, indistinctly, gathered in small groups here and there, some seated, some standing, the usual crowd—the Rogerses; the Bryants, in English; Tom and Mabel Garret, in philosophy; one tall, young couple he'd never seen before, both blond and scrubbed and ill-at-ease; and over on the couch, just looking up at him from intense conversation, old Meyerson and his wife and—Mickelsson's heart paused, thoughtful—Jessica Stark. They both smiled. Tillson, Chairman of Philosophy, was not present.

"You know everyone here, I take it," Blickstein said; then, tipping his head in the direction of the young couple and raising his hand like a classy waiter offering a table, "Have you met the Swissons?" Mickelsson drew his eyes away from Jessica.

The new couple bowed formally, exactly together, shyly smiling. The woman had a long white neck and huge eyes. When she blinked it was something from Walt Disney. Mickelsson approached them, extending his hand. "Peter Mickelsson," he said heartily. He spoke, he realized an instant too late, as if he meant to overawe them. Blickstein's influence frequently did that, made him clumsy. As the young man reached out, slightly effeminate, for Mickelsson's hand—giving him that covertly eager look, boringly predictable, Swede meeting Swede—Blickstein delicately poked his head in between them, saying, "Britt Swisson's a composer— you may have heard of him—and Katie here's a soprano. They're the catch of the year, believe me!" He winked. Now the young woman took Mickelsson's hand, squeezing his fingers much more firmly than her husband had done, her oversized eyes not meeting Mickelsson's, gazing instead at his tie, as if perhaps there was a spill on it. Her skin had a waxen look.

"Glad to meet you," Mickelsson said, somewhat lowering his voice. "I look forward to hearing your work."

The young man smiled, glancing at his wife. He had dark vein-shadows in his forehead and on the backs of his hands. The flesh under his eyes looked bruised.

Blickstein asked, rapidly brushing his palms together, looking up at Mickelsson, "What are you drinking? We have pretty much everything, I think."

He asked for a martini and, as Blickstein hurried away, delighted by the choice, moving as if weightlessly for all his bulk—ritually touching people's elbows as he passed—Mickelsson returned his attention to the couple. He was aware that, behind him, people were beginning to talk again. Fred Rogers' wife appeared with a tray of hors d'oeuvres. Mickelsson accepted one, a pastry shaped like a butterfly, with some kind of spicy meat on it.

The young woman's name had already escaped him. "So you're new with us," he said. The Swissons bowed and smiled, two china figurines.

"We just arrived last week," the woman ventured, as if speaking took great courage. Her voice was soft, like a young child's. "We've been touring, you know." Her eyes blinked shut, then opened wider.

"You haven't found a house, then?" Mickelsson asked.

"Noooo," she said, and smiled hopelessly, her head tipped sideways, like the head of one of those divinely meek saints in a fourteenth-century painting. Her husband, when he smiled, revealed bad teeth—yellow fissures and pits. It was a startling effect, as if a beautiful-woman mask were removed to show a skull. As they talked about housing in Binghamton, Edith Bryant edged in on them, a woman of over sixty, maybe close to seventy, red-headed and merrily wrinkled, bold-featured as a puppet. She was licking sauce or cheese from her fingers.

"You should just *taste* this, Peter! Hmm-huh! Dee-luscious!" Her voice was husky, intimate; her whole face twinkled. She cut her eyes up at Mickelsson coyly. "Ah we to understand that you *really* plan on *livin* out in those *Endless Mountains?*" She turned in a spasm of camaraderie to the Swissons, insisting on including as many as possible. "Don't ya'll just *love* that name—the Endless Mountains?" She insisted on the slightly self-mocking *ya'll* as urgently as she insisted that they all have a wonderful time—a little-girlish grand old lady craning her powdery face toward the Swissons, eyes sparkling still more brightly, throat-cords straining. Fixing again on Mickelsson, she crooned, "I bet you just *love* it, Peter. The Endless Mountains! Isn't that something from Poe or Hawthorne? Romantic *gloom* and all? I am most certain Zarathustra would approve!" (Edie Bryant was, she would tell you if you asked her, just a plain old gal from Atlanta. Here people were well-to-do. Her husband, who seemed much more classy, vaguely Bostonian, hailed from Pittsburgh. He had not worn, tonight, his Tyrolean jacket.)

"I suppose he would," Mickelsson said carefully, not wishing to be drawn too far.

Blickstein arrived with his martini, with two immense olives, and Mickelsson took it from him, bowing.

Edie touched the Swisson woman's arm with her fingertips and threw a bright, seductive look at Blickstein to make him stay. Blickstein waited, obediently smiling, furtively tucking in the front of his shirt. "Peter's found himself a farm that overlooks the *very Susquehanna!*" She cast her eyes toward an imaginary mountainscape, her head drawn back grandly, her right hand—fingers aflutter—drawing in the mountains' details. "Well, I for one *approve!* Ya'll know that's where *Coleridge* wanted to have his *col*ony? And where Captain John Smith found those Indian folk that were the model for Rousseau's 'Noble Savage'? And to think!"—her attention was on Mickelsson again—"you live right *there,* on that river so romantically, so *very* poetically yearned after! Why just the *idea* makes me cry!"

"Wonderful place to live!" Blickstein said, shaking his head as if with envy. "Wonderful! Oh, excuse me." The shirt and belt were where he wanted them now. He backed away, remembering some errand.

Edie flashed her smile, permitting him to leave, then, rearing back, fastened her jewel-bright eyes on Mrs. Swisson. "Listen, honey, why don't ya'll drive down sometime and see it all," she challenged. "Might truly inspire you. So much beauty! And when the leaves get themselves into autumnal dress—my! It's rather like Vermont, only broader." Her head swung toward Mickelsson. "Peter agrees with me, don't you?"

"I guess that's a pretty good description," he said. Though he forced a smile—he did in fact like her: the brazen energy of the woman, the tyrannical insistence that they be merry—he felt like someone listening from beyond the grave, come back for a visit, weighed down, faintly pained by the trivia of all he's lost. Not that he blamed Edie. (It occurred to him now that he'd missed some party she'd invited him to. He could not have said by what subtle gesture she reminded him of it. She bore no grudge, she was letting him know; but she hadn't forgotten.) Why was it important, he wondered, that they all have a wonderful time?

Again Edie touched the Swisson woman's arm, though the woman had shown no sign yet of fleeing. Edie's eyes enlarged with interest. Her tightly curled, orange-red hair glittered, metallic, each hair exactly the same color as every other. Her head trembled a little with palsy. "I b'lieve one might call it *spiritual* country—though to my mind it's downright peculiar, what with the Mormons starting up there and all. Why, Peter, you're dwelling on *holy land*! That's where Joseph Smith had those *divine* visitations, where those *fabulous* tablets were given into his *very hands*." She scrunched her face up to a self-scorning smile. "I know Peter knows all that stuff."

"They've got a monument I drive past," Mickelsson said. "Small, pretty shoddy. You'd hardly notice if it weren't for the historical marker."

"Mercy no!" Edie agreed, and now it was Britt Swisson's arm she fondly reached for, widening and brightening her eyes again. "And there's *more*. *That's* not the whole of it by a long shot! Did ya'll know there are oodles of Pennsylvania Dutch out there? Entire villages of witches of the most vicious order?"

"Is that true?" Britt Swisson asked, glancing up at Mickelsson and raising his glass.

"When you get to know Edith—" Mickelsson began.

"I swear to God," she blurted, pretending indignation, reaching out as if to bat at him. "It's *forever* in the paper!" She caught Fred Rogers eavesdropping on the conversation and quickly brought him in on it, frantically waving at him. "Wait just a minute. You help me out, Fred. *Fred* will tell you the *God's truth*," she explained to the Swissons. "Fred's a *historian*, he knows *everything*." She smiled, mocking both herself and Fred, but, all the same, bursting with pride, smug about being his friend.

"What's the debate?" Rogers asked, smiling, leaning his silver head into the group, one shoulder forward. He had a face shaped for pathos, even when he smiled; a long sad-clown mask gently bearing up under the sorrow of things.

The Swissons glanced at each other, each timidly hoping the other might answer.

"It's true, isn't it," Edie said, "there *are* Pennsylvania-Dutch witches in Susquehanna?"

"Witches, Klansmen, rattlesnakes . . ." Rogers waved his drink, indifferent and mournfully amused. To the Swisson woman he said, "I heard your recital the other night. What a sweet, sweet voice!"

Her face lit up, and her husband smiled, once again revealing the pitted, patched teeth, and slowly raised his glass, looking down. Edie Bryant leaned forward, fascinated. "Oh *shoot!*" she said, her false teeth clacking, "I *missed* it!"

Mickelsson backed off, looking critically at his nearly empty drink, then drifted as if aimlessly toward Phil Bryant and Tom Garret, who were discussing, as usual, university politics, or anyway so it appeared from their expressions. Maybe this time it was whales, or the horror of having to choose between Carter and Reagan. That was the main subject everywhere, these days. Even if the survival of the world depended on it, as some people claimed (Mickelsson had his doubts), it was a dreary business. Before he'd moved far enough to have fully committed himself to their conversation, he paused, drained his martini, ate the olives, and glanced around. Jessica Stark, still talking with the Meyersons, caught his fugitive glance in her direction, gave him a little wave, and smiled— one quick, brilliant flash—then returned her attention to the old people. She looked, as she always did at parties, expensively handsome—a burgundy dress cut low but made modest by a lacy white blouse, her deep brown, slightly graying hair swept up and pinned with an ivory comb. Though her complexion was dark—heavy tan over her freckles (Jessica had a mother in Florida, he remembered)—her cheeks were flushed, as if she'd been running. Her eyes, in the shade of her dark lashes, were pale tonight, a lucid, unearthly gray. She sat as if riding the couch sidesaddle, bent forward with interest, bringing her height down to the level of the old people. Her back was supply curved in a way that made him think of pictures of beauties from the twenties, though the curve was less extreme, her knees together, prim—somehow falsely prim, he thought, like a tomboy dressed up in silk stockings and diamonds—and she made no flapper's pretense that she was less than, as they said on TV, full-figured. Above all what made her no twenties beauty was that rich darkness set off by her strange, gray eyes—a darkness of gold and browns and amber, lustrous as the sherry in the glass dangling forgotten in her dark right hand. When she laughed she tipped her head back, baring her throat, and a dimple appeared on one cheek, flickering like light. The famous David Meyerson sat far back in the couch, bleary-eyed, cackling, saying something in Yiddish—"*bobbe-myseh*"—flapping a hand at Jessica. A gleaming, gray plastic hearing aid protruded from one large, liver-spotted ear. His wife, beside him, smiled vaguely, timid as a mouse.

"Refill?" Blickstein asked, appearing beside Mickelsson and taking the glass from him before he could answer.

"Thank you," Mickelsson said, then on second thought followed the dean toward the kitchen. Behind him he heard Tom Garret saying "Why *not* believe in dragons? If they really were a possible evolutionary move, hydrogen sacks, helm of terror, and all the rest—" He would be grinning with wide, innocent eyes and squirrel cheeks, his chin lifted as if willing to take a punch. "Oh, faddle, Tom!" Bryant said in his English-professor voice, sweet and deep as a bass viol, "give a little credit to human imagination!" If Mickelsson had known they were talking of dragons (Garret often did that, something of an embarrassment in a representative of the Philosophy Department), he'd have gone over and put in an opinion.

Blickstein's wife, Gretchen, was at the stove, pink-faced and anxious, peeking under a pot-lid, holding in her right hand a glass of wine over ice. Perspiration glistened on her forehead. At the sink a tall, slim, auburn-haired girl in a black dress and white apron stood scrubbing pots and pans. She had the water on, plunging down through steam. She looked too old, somehow too classy to be a student, but he couldn't think why else she'd be working for the Blicksteins.

"Oh, Peter," Gretchen Blickstein said, smiling as if he'd caught her at something. "How wonderful to see you again!" She lowered the pot-lid, wiped her hands on her apron, and reached out to take his. "Let me *look* at you!" she said, and tipped her head, smiling fixedly. Her hand, like the rest of her, was plump and soft.

Blickstein, at the refrigerator, poured from a sparkling glass pitcher into Mickelsson's martini glass. A thick-furred gray cat stood at his feet, looking up into the light from the open refrigerator door. "You know Agnes Warren?" Blickstein asked, inclining his head in the direction of the girl at the sink. "She's helping us out tonight. Agnes, this is Peter Mickelsson. Philosophy."

The girl turned her head, brown eyes flashing a look of what seemed hatred.

"How do you do?" Mickelsson said, taken aback.

"Fine, thank you," she said softly, almost inaudibly, and returned her fierce attention to her work.

With the side of his foot, in a movement as soft as the cat's fur, Blickstein pushed the cat away, then closed the refrigerator door.

"Now you boys go back out and mix," Blickstein's wife said. "Dinner will be ready any minute." She smiled and waved her hand, shooing them.

He took the drink from Blickstein and, after one glance back at the auburn-haired girl, moved with him into the livingroom. "The young woman, the one that's helping you," Mickelsson said, then hesitated, hardly knowing what he meant to ask, "is she . . . a student?"

"It's an interesting story," Blickstein said. "Well, *interesting* is not quite the word. You don't recognize the name? *Warren?*" He whispered it.

Mickelsson raised his eyebrows.

The dean smiled, or rather winced, giving his head a little shake. "Remind me to fill you in." He broke away, hurrying over to Tom Garret and Phil Bryant to check their drinks, then pick up the empty hors d'oeuvres tray from the glass-topped coffeetable. Mickelsson paused to sip his martini and survey the room, then for some perverse reason went over to Mabel Garret, the hardest woman in all Binghamton to talk to. She stood at the bookshelves, head bowed, reading titles, her shoulders pulled inward inside her shawl—dull black as a Bible—as if she were cold. Darkness seemed to come out of her, though he knew it was only her habit of hiding where the light was most dim.

"Hello, Mabel," he said.

"Hello."

"How are the children?" She had ten of them, all adopted—blacks, "native Americans," Vietnamese, children with handicaps. Her children were all he had ever gotten her to talk about, and then never more than a sentence or two. He wondered if she ever talked to the children themselves. He supposed she must—not that she would need to, necessarily. She emitted a kind of enfolding warmth, for all her remoteness and secrecy. A weird lady—as if some mist-covered bog had taken human shape.

"Fine," he thought he heard her say. She glanced up, briefly smiling, giving him a definitely significant look, though God only knew what it signified. She often gave him significant looks, as though there were some secret bond between them, perhaps something from an earlier life. She believed in such things.

"And *you're* fine?" he asked.

She studied him for an instant, then returned her attention to the books, not answering. Much of what Mabel Garret did was, by ordinary standards, rude. Suppressing a flicker of irritation, Mickelsson glanced across the room at her husband, still talking in his soft, upper-class South Carolina accent with Phil Bryant. Dean Blickstein stood listening, smiling down at Tom Garret eagerly, tensely, as if ready to grapple with him— all in fun, of course. He was tucking in his shirt again. Mickelsson sipped his drink, then turned his attention to reading the backs of books.

"You should go talk to Jessie," Mabel Garret said.

When he looked at her, she was reading book titles as before. He wondered if conceivably he had only imagined that she'd spoken. He raised the martini, thoughtfully sipping it, studying the side of Mabel's face.

The table was dazzlingly bright, like a field of ice and snow: crystal glasses, cut-glass candlesticks, gleaming china and silverware, pure white linen napkins and tablecloth. He thought of the communion table of his childhood. Steam poured up from the serving dishes or formed droplets on their shiny lids.

Mickelsson discovered, not exactly to his surprise, that Jessica had been placed beside him. He would be conscious all through dinner of not brushing against her arm. Jessica handled the seating arrangement well, he'd have to grant. She smiled like an old friend from Boy Scout camp, delighted to be placed where she was, and made small talk, once or twice touching his forearm as she parried some bullying Mickelssonian joke. As quickly as possible—as if to take the pressure off him, sensing the confusion he felt in her presence—she turned her attention to Phil Bryant, seated to her left, asking him with just the right shade of interest about his year abroad. One could feel the charge she carried, some intense native energy; but at the moment she had it closed in, securely capped. He was conscious of how large they were, Jessica and he, in comparison to the others, except for Bryant. It made him ask, when she turned to him again, if she'd ever done anything in athletics. "Only Rugby," she said, giving him a smile and a slow wink, as if she'd read his mind. Then she turned back to Bryant. (*Fucking little tease,* he thought.) Once the side of Mickelsson's knee touched hers, and they both drew back quickly, Jessica giving him a glance, then smiling.

The Swisson woman—he managed to catch her name now, Katie—was to Mickelsson's right. She held her fork daintily, as if fearfully, like an astonished bird invited to dine with tomcats. She looked up with exaggerated interest, head tipped meekly sideways, whenever anyone spoke her name, asking for her plate, passing asparagus, pouring wine into her glass. To make her feel less a spectator, Mickelsson inquired, "You have children, Ms. Swisson?"

She shook her head, chewing, trying to swallow quickly.

He told her about his son at U.V.M., excellent photographer—perhaps she'd heard of him? (it was impossible, in fact)—and his daughter Leslie, taking classes at Brown, though a highschool senior, planning to enter McGill next year to study French. He glanced at Jessica. If he was behaving like a fool she hadn't noticed. She was deep in conversation with Phil Bryant and Gretchen Blickstein. Yet the back of her head struck him as alert and too still, as if she were eavesdropping on his talk.

"French! How interesting!" Kate Swisson said, looking up at him, wide-eyed.

Mickelsson shook his head. "You know what it means," he said, mock-morose. "She'll go off to Paris and fall in love with some miserable Frog and that's the last I'll see of her."

She laughed, large eyes grown larger. It struck him that, though he'd meant it as a joke, he'd spoken with some vehemence, as if in fact he were furious with his daughter, not to mention the French. He wondered if it were so—that he was angry at his daughter, that is. It was true that she never phoned, kept losing his number. Like her mother, she was congenitally disorganized. He could phone her, but the chance that Ellen might answer put him off. He realized that the table had fallen silent and said, to cover himself, "It's surprising how close you can feel to a daughter, and how little you really know her."

"Peter! You, a man, expectin to understand *women*?" Edie Bryant cried out, across from him, brandishing her fork. Her eyes sparkled like the cut-glass candlesticks. "Perhaps shortly after the Second Coming!"

"Why, Edie," her husband said, to Jessica's left, his voice even more than usually melodious (he was fond of quoting Shakespeare, and his fifty-year-old Yale songs could make a turnip cry), "you sur*prise* me!" He paused just an instant, then added, "Again!"

They all laughed, even Mickelsson, as if it were a wonderful piece of wit. He wondered, inwardly tumbling toward darkness, if it were possible that they all laughed, as he did, from politeness hiding disgust. It didn't seem so, he thought, furtively glancing around the table—though certainly it had to be politeness with old Meyerson, who never heard anything anymore, not even the town's many churchbells, against which he'd once lodged complaints. He sat next to Gretchen Blickstein at the foot of the table, wheezily laughing with his eyes shut. His wife, beside him, watching him like a hawk, suddenly dabbed at the corner of his mouth with her napkin. He pulled angrily away and said something in German.

"Don't worry," Jessica said, *sotto voce*, speaking past food, "she'll hate it at McGill. Believe me! She's like you." She touched the corner of her mouth with her napkin.

"Like me?" Jessica and his daughter had never met.

"Intuition," she said; "maybe a little simple deduction." She smiled, then suddenly returned her attention to the conversation to her left.

Dinner wore on, painfully like every other dinner he'd ever been to, here, in Providence, in California, in Ohio: predictable compliments, jokes, earnest fragments of discussion, the usual little flashes of sexuality or annoyance between husbands and wives, husbands and other husbands' wives; the usual spilled wine and quickly poured salt; the usual sudden, deep pauses. For a time Mickelsson was free to let his mind drift. Blickstein, to her right, had taken over conversation with Kate Swisson, bending over his folded hands toward her big, frightened eyes, grinning like a jack-o'-lantern, the chandelier and candlesticks reflected in the lenses of his glasses. Mickelsson found himself musing idly on the curious distance between this world and the world he'd be driving back to later tonight: here fine clothes bought in New York or London or at very least Fowler's Department Store in the local mall; there in the mountains . . . The image of John Pearson rose again in his mind: faded blue workshirt, bib-overalls, heavy boots. . . . What would the old man think, walking in on this—the glittering silverwave, the china, dirty now, the once-sparkling wine and water glasses smudged by lips and fingers? (It would be different with the real-estate salesman Tim Booker. Tim would be delighted.) Beyond the lace-curtained windows of the Blicksteins' dining-room, Mickelsson could see only darkness. The conversation droned as if the dinner were taking place in a room at the bottom of the sea. The girl he'd met in the kitchen was clearing plates now, speaking to no one, meeting no one's eyes. When she reached past him to take his plate, Mickelsson drew back to make it easier for her and said, "Thank you." She showed no sign of hearing. Perhaps it was something about the way she moved, slowly raising the plate and drawing it toward her; the thought of rattlesnakes leaped into his mind.

He must shake this mood, he told himself. These people were his friends.

Blickstein said, leaning forward to look past Kate Swisson, his cheeks and jaw as muscular as his arms, "Pete, how's my boy Nugent doing?"

"No problem, so far as I can tell," Mickelsson said. Blickstein was looking at Jessica, making sure he hadn't interrupted. It was curious that Blickstein remembered the young man and knew he was in Mickelsson's class.

Tom Garret said, leaning toward them across the table, pivoting on his elbows, his short, thick hands folded for prayer in front of him, "Nugent? Is that somebody I should know?"

Everyone was listening.

The dean was embarrassed. "Well," he said. His right hand made a kind of brushing motion, but he couldn't seem to think what to say.

Gretchen Blickstein, at the foot of the table, called out, "*Now* I remember what I wanted to ask! Fred, whom are you voting for?"

Rogers smiled sorrowfully and considered his plate. He looked up with sagging eyes at Mickelsson, then solemnly raised his spoon to clink it three times against his water glass. "My friends," he said like a funeral director, "friends and dear colleagues, in these trying times—"

"Hear, hear!" Phil Bryant said, and clinked his glass with his spoon, his handsome, wrinkled face grinning all over.

"No speeches!" old Mrs. Meyerson said, batting her hands about, crazy as a loon. But the majority was against her.

In the livingroom after dinner, while Blickstein poured liqueurs, Tom Garret sat down in the chair beside Mickelsson's, cocked his knees out, and leaned toward the coffeetable, smiling his amiable Southern smile. His skin glowed. "Pete," he said, "how's Al Blassenheim doing? You've got him in P and A, right?"

"He's doing fine," Mickelsson said, turning.

Garret grinned, waiting for something more, then looked down. "Terrific kid," he said. "I had him in Philos and Lit. He did me a wonderful paper on Wallace Stevens. 'Beauty is momentary in the mind,' so forth and so on—you know the passage. 'But in the flesh it is immortal.' "

"Yes, he's still working on it," Mickelsson said a little testily (he disapproved of the Philosophy and Literature course) and glanced over at Jessica, who was watching them. When Garret raised his eyebrows, Mickelsson explained, waggling his hand, not wanting to make too much of it, "He's not resigned, if you know what I mean. He'd like to have it both ways."

Garret nodded, grinning. Jessica asked, "What do you mean, Pete?"

"Oh, you know. He'd like to take the view that evolution stumbles blindly, but also he'd like to believe that after Nature's done her stumbling, God gives out grades. What survives is not just what's fit but what fits God's plan."

"That's sort of nice!" Jessica said.

"It is," Mickelsson said.

She looked at him thoughtfully, still smiling, her shadowy Oriental-Icelandic eyes narrowed, then over at Blickstein, who was coming toward her and Edie Bryant, carefully carrying their liqueurs. The small glasses glinted—dark, colored flames.

"But wouldn't it be interesting if it were true!" Garret said, mainly to Jessica. "The whole universe just atingle with forms, waiting for matter to come up to them!"

"Like eggs waiting at the end of the cosmic fallopian," Phil Bryant said, drawing up his chair. He chuckled heartily, like one who's said something risqué, and glanced at Jessica.

Garret said, grinning, punching the air high above his shoulder, like a spectator at a racetrack, "Come awn, dinosaur! Come awn, Pax Romana!"

They all laughed, even Jessica, bravely agreeable. With her right hand, perhaps unaware that she was doing it, she fingered the softness of the couch beside her.

"Pax Romana?" Blickstein asked, eagerly grinning, handing Garret his glass.

"Just havin a little joke with the boys, sir," Garret said. He once again sat still and formal, stocky, toeing out, his wide mouth impishly clamped shut; one could hardly believe that an instant ago he'd been clowning.

Blickstein gave Mickelsson his glass, eyebrows still lifted, waiting for enlightenment. A spark of red danced on the rim of the glass, then vanished.

"Philosophical discussion," Mickelsson explained. "Whether or not Plato's museum can be restored."

"Ah!" Blickstein said, and straightened up, delighted that such things should be discussed in his livingroom, then looked around to see whom he'd missed.

"Well, you know," Garret said, abruptly serious, still speaking mainly to Jessica, one had a feeling, though it was Mickelsson he looked at, "it's easy to dismiss these ideas kids have, put them away in little boxes marked 'Kant,' 'Hegel,' 'Whitehead,' and so forth and so on. Kids don't know how much arugment's already piled up against 'em. But I like the way they keep comin and comin, like termites. One morning you wake up and look around and—no castle!"

"Termites don't eat stones," Phil Bryant said, and chuckled.

Garret glanced over at him, friendly. "Sir?"

"Castles are made of stones," Bryant said. His grin showed large and perfect teeth. He'd been an officer under Patton in World War II, had directed the mission stealing gas from ambulances for Patton's famous drive. "Termites don't eat stones." He gave another little laugh.

Garret seemed to give it serious thought, his eyes fixed on the rose in the cut-glass bowl on the glass-topped coffeetable. "What you mean is," he said, jabbing a finger toward Bryant but not looking up from the rose, "*so* far there is no definite physical evidence that termites eat stones."

"I read in the paper that there are termites that can eat cement," Gretchen Blickstein said.

Jessica smiled and tipped her head with interest. No one else seemed to have heard her.

"That reminds me," Mickelsson said, "that house I bought, down by Susquehanna, Pennsylvania—it's supposed to be haunted."

They all looked at him, expecting a story—or all but the Swissons.

"Britt and I don't believe in ghosts," Kate Swisson said.

"I do," old Mrs. Meyerson cried out sharply, and considered saying more, then hushed. Her husband slowly turned his head and looked at her, as if startled to discover her still there.

Jessica said, tilting toward Mickelsson, "Tell us about it, Pete! Are you serious?"

He told them what he knew. He was surprised himself at how little he'd bothered to find out.

Though he knew it was foolish, Mickelsson refilled his martini glass. As he poured from the pitcher, now more water than gin, the young woman who'd helped out was putting her coat on to leave. "You do this kind of thing often?" he asked. When she said nothing, he glanced over his shoulder. She had her lips clamped together in stern concentration, buttoning the coat—black cashmere, fairly new or else very well cared for. She bent her head forward, drawing her flowing auburn hair from under the collar and shaking it out behind her. He put away the pitcher, closed the refrigerator door, and asked again, "Do you do this kind of thing often?"

Suddenly she looked straight at him. "I'm sorry, I'm not good at talking to people yet," she said. Her eyes were filled with tears. Then, turning away, she snatched her white scarf from the back of the chair and was gone.

"Hey, wait!" he began, then closed his mouth.

It was not that she'd attacked him; she'd somehow made it clear that it was nothing personal, not his fault. But for all that, the hand that held the martini was shaking so badly he had to put the glass down on the counter. How terrible, he thought, that the universe should be so charged with pain and rage! *Universe, universe, universe,* he heard his wife's voice hiss, the voice so clear, so "real," so to speak, that he turned and looked past his shoulder. The room was empty—more than empty, he thought: drawn back from him like a cowering beast; it seemed if he moved nearer it would strike. Some thought trembled at the edge of his consciousness, some familiar idea turned at a strange new angle; but try as he might, straining his attention like a man trying to read a clue in charades, he couldn't quite spring it. He got his pipe from his coatpocket, packed it and lit it, and at last, feeling calmer, took his martini from the counter and started back to the livingroom. He remembered the young woman's eyes as she spoke to him. Had she been raped? Newly released from prison? Had she lost a child? He got an image of her standing in the shadow of the woods above his house, motionless. Then it came to him that, imperceptibly, her image had confused itself with that of another angry young woman, his student Brenda Winburn, watching him patiently, with an expression he could not read. "Not *me*," he whispered inwardly, meeting the sullen, witchy eyes. When Mickelsson realized he was talking to himself, he immediately forgot, if he'd ever known, what he'd been thinking.

Jessica said, "I understand your friend Dr. Bauer is being sued for malpractice."

Mickelsson looked up, slow-witted from drink, and saw what he should have known, that there was nothing snide in it. "Bauer?" he asked, then remembered. "That doesn't seem likely," he said, forming the words with care.

They were among the last remaining. The Rogerses, Swissons, and Meyersons had left over an hour ago, the Garrets maybe half an hour later. Now the Bryants were at the top of the stairs leading down to the entryway, where for the past ten minutes they'd been talking with great animation to the Blicksteins. Gretchen Blickstein looked asleep on her feet, but the dean, smiling and punching out diagrams in the air, made up for her. His shirttail bulged out in front, but he seemed not to notice, enjoying himself immensely. "That Blickstein's got energy," people said. "I wonder if he ever sleeps."

"I'm sure she's not guilty, if that's what you mean," Jessica said, and shrugged. "But she *is* being sued; some young woman died in childbirth. It was two or three years ago. The doctor's lawyer is a friend of ours— that is, mine." She saw his look of disbelief and came straight at him. "These things *happen*, you know."

Mickelsson shook his head. "Maybe so," he said. "I would've thought, the way they seem to feel about Dr. Bauer—" He was suddenly conscious of two things at once, his attraction to Jessica and the distance he had to go to reach home. He didn't feel too drunk to drive, exactly, but his eyelids were leaden; perhaps he'd have to sleep beside the road. He thought of trying to proposition her; but he said, voice lowered and a trifle stern, "Everybody you talk to in Susquehanna speaks highly of 'the doc.'"

"I'm sure that's so," she said, half smiling, watching him. She sat finely balanced, legs crossed at the knees, her smooth-muscled body alert and calm, like a slightly displeased schoolteacher, or some superior life- form in a sci-fi movie, observing but carefully not meddling. "Yet there *are* some pretty strange people down there, I'm told."

"Me, for one!" Mickelsson said, hitting his chest with the inside of his fist and laughing, playing maniac.

She looked cross for an instant, then reconsidered, frowning down at her hands folded on her knees. She moved her right hand to touch the gold chain on her left wrist, making light blink. "You're right, it's none of my business," she said. "I'm sure they're fine people. It's just that it's so far from—" She hesitated, trying to find the word.

"The city's bright lights," he offered, gesturing with both hands, suggesting a kind of umbrella of light in the air between them. Gin made what he'd meant for irony seem anger, but she seemed not to notice.

"Maybe that's it. I worry about people getting too far out of touch."

"Turns 'em into witches," Mickelsson said, and grinned evilly. Also gives them heart attacks, he remembered, but didn't say it. He pulled uncomfortably at his pipe. Dead again.

"It does, you know? Not literally, I suppose." She blushed slightly. "OK, you've made your point. I'm not to worry about you." Her smile made the dimple show. Her eyes, pale as the arctic, met his steadily.

"I'm grateful to you for worrying about me," he said, and gave her an embarrassed nod. It was the last thing in the world he'd intended to say. He set down the glass, pocketed his matches, and stood up. He felt a moment's unsteadiness. "Well—" he said.

"You're right," she said, leaning forward and rising too. "I have a nine o'clock class in the morning!" She took a step in his direction, then looked startled, maybe dizzy. Without knowing he would do it he held out his hand to her, as if to help her over slippery ground.

"Why, thank you!" she said, and smiled as he'd never seen her smile before, as if, for the first time in years, she'd been taken by surprise.

He could barely stay awake. He caught himself broadly weaving on the Interstate; if the police had been out, he would certainly have been arrested. But it was worse after he turned off, nosing toward the mountains. The road was tunnel-like, the sky overcast, as if a hand had been lowered over the world, blocking out the stars. Again and again he had to slow suddenly for curves he hadn't remembered, the guardrail to his right stark under the headlights and surprisingly close, beyond that the drop-off to the invisible Susquehanna. He had the sensation, not unusual when he'd been drinking, that nothing was quite real, a feeling borrowed from one he had at movies or at plays Ellen had dragged him along to— a sense that, looking away from the road and the darkness of the mountains, he might see people around him, a rapt audience looking where a moment ago he too had been looking, at the road, the darkness of mountains. It was a feeling he always found freighted with meaning, not that he didn't understand it well enough, and know what it was worth—the old Christian Platonists' idea of the *theatrum mundi,* reality as a shadowing forth, a clothing or fleshing out of something behind it, except that, of course, how could there be anything behind it? All the same, he had the sense that if he drove with all his might into a concrete abutment, he might, like an electron breaking free of an atom, crash through the stones into lightless deep space, clarity, absolute freedom. It was a thought he wouldn't have bothered with sober, and even now he half scorned it. And yet it was always the case, he found, that when intellect dimmed down and something older took over, the notion seemed faintly worth regard: by trees, stones, sky, he felt distanced, as if by words. He felt removed from the essential in the way a black and white photograph is removed from the barn it represents, perhaps a barn no longer standing, or as a star still visible may be removed from its present actuality: spectacular red flash, white dwarf. In this queer situation, he must survive by close attention to details he had no confidence in, the phantom steeringwheel, the phantom road. And must do it, alas, with his whole body tricking him toward sleep.

Dreams tugged more and more persistently, and, awakening with a start, his eyes snapping open from a protracted blink, he would swerve hard, overcompensating, then swerve again. He drove more and more slowly, bent forward over the wheel. "Have to be careful," he said aloud, but thanks to the gin he felt no alarm. A peculiar calm came over him, in fact, as he moved into the hug of the mountains rising immediately to his left and, more distantly, across the narrow valley, to his right, comforting shapes as much felt as seen, closing in more and more snugly, like huge friendly milkcows on his father's farm many years ago, drawing him gently along the fenced, grassy lane toward home. He thought of Jessica, or rather saw her in his mind, tossing her head back, laughing.

Then suddenly, right in front of him, he saw two men in long black coats. They swung around, swift as startled bears—at first, in fact, he registered them as bears. The image of their open-mouthed, button-eyed faces stayed frozen in his mind as he slammed on his brakes, skidded crazily toward them, tires spitting gravel, then shot left toward the ditch beyond the left-side shoulder, trees leaping out at him, white in the headlights, then skidded again and shot right toward the guardrail, then back, with a violent jerk, toward the road. When the motor died, the big Jeep sat beached at an angle to the macadam, half in the ditch, shooting light up into the trees. He sat clenching the steeringwheel, shaking. He looked back at last toward where he'd seen the two men. For all the darkness, he saw everything clearly—the gray of the road, duller gray of the guardrail, heavy blackness of weeds and treetrunks. The two men had vanished. He thought a moment, then rolled down the window and called out, "Hello?" The sound of his voice clanged in the stillness. No one answered. He called, "You all right, back there?" Again no answer. The shaking in his arms and legs had become just a stirring now, his flesh entirely weightless. The two men would be hiding in the ditch, he imagined, or in the woods across the road. No sound. Nothing.

Strange that they wouldn't answer. He was aware that he was beginning to feel afraid before he knew why. Perhaps they were up to something. He forced himself to wait three or four minutes longer, then started up the Jeep, shifted into low-low and four-wheel drive, and half let the clutch out, preparing to drive up out of the ditch. There was a strange noise, something wrong with the engine, he imagined, and he shoved the clutch in again. The noise continued, growing louder. He switched off the key, then extinguished the lights. Even now it took his drunken brain another moment to understand that the noise came from outside somewhere, a whining engine roar, a little like the sound of an earthquake—he'd experienced small ones in California. Then he saw what it was. He blinked, half convinced he was hallucinating.

One close behind the other they came over the hill and down the narrow macadam road past Mickelsson; two of them, huge trucks black as midnight, driving with their lights off. He hadn't the faintest idea what they might be—one wild thought after another went through his mind. Huge army trucks on midnight manuevers, he thought, remembering the great caravans of his World War II childhood; but those trucks hadn't driven with their lights off, and not on high-crowned narrow back roads.

If these were army trucks they weren't on maneuvers anyway, but up to something more serious: one could tell by the whine that they were heavily loaded. Trucks moving nuclear waste? Not likely. They'd stay on 81, wary of hijackers. What then? He thought of switching on his head-lights. Only when his hand refused to move did he realize how afraid he was. The second truck wailed past, a huge black rectangle solid as con-crete, slowed for the curve at the bottom of the hill, brakelights darkly glowing like rubies, then vanished. Mickelsson continued to hear the wail for what seemed a long time. At last, all his muscles weak, his head full of confusion, he started up the motor and carefully pulled up out of the ditch. The troll-doll hanging from the rear-view mirror swung lazily. It was an ugly thing, but for some reason it made him think, with a pang of grief, of his daughter.

He parked behind the house. His body still trembled, and there was pain in his chest. He massaged it with one hand, rubbing slowly but hard. With a part of his mind he was aware that a herd of deer stood on the cant of the mountain above him, just this side of the trees, watching. At last he opened the door of the Jeep and got out. As he approached the back door, sorting through his keys in the dark, he heard his phone ring. He thought immediately, once again—or perhaps was thinking just *before* it rang—of his daughter. Who else could be calling him at two, maybe three in the morning? His son, perhaps; or Ellen, if something terrible had happened.

None of the keys seemed to fit the back door. The phone went on ringing. Four rings. Five. He tried the keys again, one after another, slowly and systematically, growing angry. The phone stopped ringing.

Furious, knowing it was his drunkenness that made the keys not fit, he gave up on the door and leaned back, looking around, wondering how he might break in. The house rose high in the night above him, like a docked ship, black as the mysterious trucks against the starlight. There were faint noises inside the house, creakings and settling sounds, not unlike sounds from the movements of a large animal stirring in its sleep. To his left, just this side of the high, darkly frowning triangular wood-pile delivered two days ago, stood the door to the debris-filled workroom. Once he'd noticed it it seemed to call attention to itself, almost beckoning, like a door in a horror film. Carefully he moved toward it, then tried the knob. It opened. There was a rush of fleeing mice and—so he thought for an instant—a scent of bread baking. Almost at once the scent decayed to something else, an excessive sweetness a little like the smell of rat poison, or like the anal scent of devils' breath Martin Luther used to catch a whiff of, now and then, in his rooms. He decided to leave the door open, air the place out, and when his hand, feeling along the wall in the darkness, came to a window, he decided to open that too, to get a cross-draught. The smell of clear air bursting over his nostrils made him try one last time, before the other scent was gone, to identify what it was. He felt it right at the edge of his memory, but the scent, as it weakened—full of devils' slyness—changed again. Molasses cookies, he thought; mingled with the cloying scent of flowers at a funeral parlor.

He got a vivid, bleak memory of his younger sister's funeral, the casket set up in the family livingroom, in front of the high, clumsy windows with their old yellowed curtains of dusty, brittle lace. He stood looking down at the shiny white satin cushioning on which her body lay propped, miraculously straightened out—in life she'd been twisted by polio (he wondered, now for the first time, whether those who'd prepared her had had to break bones to get this doll-like serenity)—and his father's boyhood friend, still his best friend, a man named Hobart, who had a farm just down the road, had stood with his hand laid on Mickelsson's shoulder. There had been others in the room, he could not remember anymore who they were, and in the kitchen there were women, various neighbors, who had brought food—casseroles and baked goods.

He shook off the memory and, feeling his way, continued through the workroom's blackness. It was not properly a part of the house but the lower story of a wing oddly jutting out behind the rest, its small back window looking up at the mountain. He paused for an instant, hearing something, then realized it was only the rumble of a train in the valley. The door from the workroom to the livingroom was open; the lock hadn't worked in years. His feet found the buckled place on the livingroom floor.

When he switched on the light in the livingroom another memory jumped into him, another time and place where yellow light had leaped up on walls in exactly this way, like the first frame of a movie, starkly revealing black, curtainless windows. It was the office of his Providence psychiatrist, Dr. Rifkin; small, horse-faced, hair parted down the middle.

"These patterns you feel emerging, do they alarm you?" His voice resounded as if the room where they sat were stone.

"It bothers me that they're elusive," Mickelsson said. He rivetted his gaze to the doctor's scuffed shoes. "I just get them plain and then suddenly it's as if someone's turned the kaleidoscope."

"Tell me this: Would *I* be able to see them?"

"I could prove to you that all maple trees have the same number of leaves," Mickelsson said, evasive, "just as all human beings have the same number of arms and legs, except where something's been torn off."

Rifkin thought about it, no doubt concentrating on the words *torn off*. Mickelsson glanced at him, reproachful.

"All right," Rifkin said, waggling his hand, his tone impatient, "maybe you're right about maple trees." He risked a little grin. "What does it mean? Is Somebody sending us a message?"

This time Mickelsson's look was rather more than reproachful. They'd spoken before of Wittgenstein.

"Try it this way," Rifkin said irritably, and leaned forward. "Is it bad that you're unable to read the message? How does it make you feel? Guilty?"

"Uneasy. I don't say there's a message."

Rifkin smiled. "Uneasy. That's natural, isn't it? You're a professional philosopher."

"Most philosophers don't think dead animals are trying to tell them things."

"That's true. That's a point." He nodded, paused, then nodded again, as if seeing the problem in a new light. "Tell me about that—how it feels when dead animals talk to you."

"I can't remember."

"Come on now. You remember *that* it happens. So *how* does it happen?"

Mickelsson cleared his throat. "It's like trying to remember a dream. I'm walking along, thinking nothing, daydreaming . . ." He sank into silence.

Rifkin waited. Then after a moment: "Make an effort, Professor!" His face was childishly stern.

Mickelsson was unable to remember what they'd been talking about.

He seemed to remember the whole conversation clearly now, standing alone in the livingroom of the new house. Perhaps because now the pressure was off. He seemed to remember the doctor's every gesture, though perhaps this too was phantom and illusion. But even now he could not remember or imagine what it was like to hear a dead animal speak. The mouth did not move, certainly. Perhaps it had something to do with the eyes.

He remembered his wife's saying—calling late at night—"Talked to any interesting cadavers lately?" Anger had risen in him, he could almost have killed her; but he'd understood how painful and frightening it had been for her. " 'Madman Mickelsson,' they say. Can you imagine how that makes me *feel*?" She'd been standing in the kitchen, hugging herself, though the room was of course not cold. "What about the children? What about Mark? You're making him crazier than *you* are."

"I'm sorry," he said. He felt no emotion at all.

In the kitchen, Mickelsson made himself one last drink. He was wide awake now. Since he had no gin, he fixed Irish and water. He sniffed the water suspiciously, but all was well; no rabbit had fallen into the reservoir as yet, or if it had, it was not yet smellable. He must remember to do something about his water supply. He thought of placing a note to himself on his refrigerator, where he had paper and magnets, but feeling through his pockets he found no pencil, only his pipe, which he took out and held in his hand. It crossed his mind that he might call his daughter; but according to the clock on the oven it was quarter to four.

With the drink in one hand, his pipe in the other, Mickelsson wandered from room to room, still in his suitcoat, scowling thoughtfully, his step just noticeably unsteady. In the livingroom he paused a moment, thinking of putting a record on the stereo—an excellent set, the first thing he'd bought after he'd left his wife—but he decided against it. Though he was thinking nothing, merely sizing things up, trying to shake the vision of those two black-coated men, inseparable in his mind from the nightmare trucks, he did not want Beethoven or Mozart intruding. He moved on, touching things, in his mind the image of the two men whirling around to face his headlights. He saw the image as a photograph his son might take, black and white, grainy. Soon he found he could see it only as a photograph, not as it had been. He raised his glass, looking at the hand that held it—steady as a rock, he discovered to his surprise.

He concentrated, smoking now—puffing fiercely—on how he meant to change the house. He'd paint the bedrooms white, or maybe get wallpaper, fill the rooms with antiques, make farmerish chests of pine and cedar; he'd wallpaper the livingroom and put down hardwood floors all downstairs, or maybe spruce. The workroom, he'd decided long since, he'd make a diningroom: white plaster, dark, exposed beams. Assuming the I.R.S. didn't seize it, maybe attach his earnings as well. Assuming he could somehow pay his old bills and his wife's expenses, take care of his children . . .

Images of the party drifted into his mind and out again—Blickstein bowing, European-style, to old Meyerson, Jessica sliding her eyes away, sly. He found himself recalling a different party, months ago; an image of his hunchbacked, gray-bearded chairman, above his head the fake rough-cut beams of his kitchen. As always, he was flashing his crazy, twitching grin, his two knuckly hands reaching out toward Mickelsson as if to persuade him that he, Tillson, was the soul of reasonableness. It was the first and last party at Tillson's that Mickelsson had attended. "But Greek!" Tillson wailed, and let out his skinny, nervous laugh. "We're not Harvard, you know!" He switched his eyes to the others, all facing him, tentative antagonists, then looked back at Mickelsson, and his tic-ridden face came forward farther, even with the hump. He blinked rapidly and strained his smile wider, as if Mickelsson's dullness of comprehension might perhaps be overcome by sheer energy and good will. "What *use* is it? *That's* the question! Let us say just for the sake of argument that our students actually learn the stuff, which I'll tell you in all honesty *I* never did, not that I didn't pass the tests, you understand, just as I passed the courses where presumably you couldn't get by without Greek—and this was at Princeton, which was supposed to be 'boss,' as the kids say, ha!—but believe me I wouldn't know an aorist tense if it ran up and bit me; in fact to tell you the truth I'm not sure I ever really got the *letters* straight, though believe me I was good enough at other things

—logic, for instance, all the intricacies of math, linguistics—" He swung his eyes from Mickelsson to the others, laughing but not joking, then hurried on, almost stammering in his eagerness to retain the floor: "But say for the sake of argument they actually *master* the stuff. What good is it? If we've learned anything at all in the last fifty years of philosophy, it's that even in English practically nothing we say makes sense. So why Greek? Why not talk gibberish in the language we were born to? You trying to make them root-and-berry Heideggerians—'dis-close,' 'com-pre-hend'?" He laughed wildly, perhaps delighted by his rhetoric, and looked around again. "It'll kill us!" He pointed at Mickelsson's chest. "It'll kill our F.T.E., drive students away. And it won't do much for the society either. What's a philosopher for if it's not to help people, in his clumsy way—help society clean up its act? Your book, now, *Survival and Medical Ethics*—ha ha! Thought I didn't read it, didn't you! *Your* book—that's philosophy for our *time!* Pop-philosophy, you may say—ha ha! nonetheless—"

"But I do read Greek," Mickelsson said, reserved. *Pop-philosophy, you little fucker?* Then he remembered that he himself had called it that.

"All right, so you're one up on me, I readily concede it. Actually, I manage to stumble through the stuff myself. But we're talking practicalities—shrinking enrollments, pressure from the state. We're talking headcount, dollars and s-e-n-s-e. And the tyranny of the Christian theological tradition." Suddenly an edge of pious anger was in his voice. "That's what it all comes down to, I'm sure you realize."

Tom Garret said, standing in the wings of the conversation, "What about discipline? I always liked the argument 'The study of Greek is good discipline for the mind'?"

"You're kidding!" Tillson said.

Garret shrugged, grinning, his glasses blanking out his eyes. "I never know until I see if people laugh."

Old man Meyerson shook his head, too deaf to hear more than every fifteenth word. "Greek tought iss the foundation," he said. He raised his long, crooked finger.

"Long before the Greeks there was algae," Tillson said, "but nobody makes us start with algae."

Mickelsson raised his martini and gazed down into it, looking for water separation. "Are you seriously proposing," he asked, "that we stop encouraging our majors to take Greek—for fear we might lose a couple?"

"God save me from people with standards," Tillson said. "Better dead than ill-read, right?" His eyes widened. "Listen, don't get me wrong! I have a personal fondness for Greek. Heck—"

"So long as I'm advising, I'll keep pushing Greek," Mickelsson said. "Harder than before, since my view's in the minority." He raised his glass to drink.

"I hope when it comes right down to it you'll ease up," Tillson said, tipping his head, weakly smiling. "Some students, sure. But a lot of these kids—" He put his hand on Mickelsson's arm. "I realize you're bull-headed. I like that about you, up to a point."

Rage moved up through Mickelsson, starting under the tips of Geoffrey Tillson's fingers. "I'll push. Count on it," he said. Quickly he turned and left the kitchen.

Stupid, Mickelsson whispered now, meaning himself, not Tillson. Dr. Rifkin would no doubt be interested in that rage. "What," he would say, "does Greek have to do with the Great Cryptogram? Is it possible that God still speaks Greek?"

It was true that that night, more than a year ago now, he had begun to hate Tillson, or perhaps, more precisely, that night he'd found a hook for the hatred that had risen in him spontaneously, right from the beginning.

It was true that his anger made no sense. One could always tell one's students, "Learn Greek," and the best of them would do it. Why should he be threatened by a timid little hunchback who controlled nothing, commanded no one, hardly even published? What could it mean, this animal fury that rose up at sight of the man? He thought of the Marxists in Jessica's department, *real* nuisances, simultaneously dolts and maniacs, programmed, it seemed, to fly into rages at the mention of certain words. "Feminist!" one of them had suddenly shouted at a party last year at the Bryants', bursting like a whale out of a serene, pale sea. "If she's a feminist, I'm Napoleon!" Everyone had looked at the man, or at the envelope of space around him, their eyes dulled, expressions patient. Only Mickelsson, the newcomer, had been surprised.

Was it true that in the plays of Shakespeare, Seneca rumbled down underneath, and beneath that Aeschylus? And beneath that the creature who once slept, restless and brooding, in the Giant Bed of Og? Maybe one of Garret's real-life dragons?

Craziness. From Greek, Latin. From Latin, French Spanish English and the rest. From the top vertebrae of some ancient beast, the grossly enlarged, holed bone that made the human head.

It had to do with the house. It had been, once long ago, something else, perhaps just a saltbox—the room he meant to make into a dining-room and the dark, ravaged attic above it. Should he make it what it was —tear off the whole immense addition, spacious rooms, spreading porches? By some act of not quite unthinkable magic bring back the world as it had once been?

Dream thoughts. Foolishness. Cunning evasion of present grief. How pleasant it would be to call Ellen on the phone, talk to her awhile as if nothing had changed.

. . .

He seated himself in a chair beside the acrid-smelling woodstove in the livingroom and stared at the Dutch door leading to the kitchen. All at once in his drunkenness, as it would seem to him later, all he could see was that large, neatly painted hex sign: tulips and oakleaves and birds not found in nature, around them a black band harshly unornamental. Was it meant to keep out evil, he wondered, or to lure it in?

He listened, for some reason, as if he'd let some sound pass unregistered. But there was nothing, inside or out. Unsteadily, he rose and made his way to the hex to study it. One eye on each of the two birds looked out at him, vaguely hypnotic. When he squinted he discovered that the design made a blurry, disturbing face. He thought about that. Was it simply his drunkenness, or was it possible that the face was meant to be there, perhaps had some occult use? He squinted again. It did seem to have a hypnotic quality. Was that possible? He'd read something somewhere about the cobra's gaze, some disorienting effect on the balance of the brain's two lobes. He had no faith or particular interest in witchcraft, but by all accounts something went on in these mountains, presumably something one could identify with physical causes, once one figured out the tricks. Was the shadowy face intended to, in some way, give special powers to occupants of the house? Or on the other hand to harm them? He thought of the gray cast to Dr. Bauer's skin.

It made sense, he thought, feeling a stir of excitement. The dark reputation of the Sprague place was solid; everyone around seemed to have heard of it. And no theme in folklore was older than the notion of the deadly sign or magic writing, bearer of some curse. Perhaps the whole secret of the Sprague place was right here on this door!

He was no doubt thinking foolishly, melodramatically, but he groped his way to the kitchen, where in increasing excitement, as if rising to some formidable challenge, he sharpened a butcher knife. The image he'd seen through half-closed eyes was fixed in his head, reminding him of something, nothing he could put his finger on, but unpleasant. He tested the blade against the palp of his thumb, then returned to the livingroom and decisively, scrape by scrape, cut away the hex sign, leaving a halo of ragged wood. When he was finished, he carefully cleaned off the knife, using soap and water, as if even the wood and paint shavings might be dangerous, put the shavings in the garbage, then put the knife back in its drawer, neatly aligning it with the other knives, all good cutlery, sharp. These too, for some reason now obscure, he'd bought almost immediately after leaving his wife. He found that his glass of whiskey had disappeared, no doubt set down someplace. He was in no condition (turning slowly around, looking in all directions) to think out where he'd left it. He fixed himself another, definitely the last. The image of the face was still clear in his mind, still proffering its challenge. Now it reminded him of Tillson.

He stood wide awake, still looking around, grave, firmly planted. He was aware of the emptiness of the house, and its foreignness. He found himself moving again from room to room, bare dry walls, bare dry floors, most of the house devoid of furniture, stark. His shadow moved beside him, head lowered, large back round. Because the light fixtures had offended him—cheap, machine-etched fleurs-de-lis, a fake antique wooden-wheel chandelier, machine-painted globes hung from phoney brass—he'd removed the fixtures, leaving bare bulbs. Every stipple and crack in the ceilings called attention to itself. His footsteps, however carefully he walked, resounded. When he leaned close to one of the curtainless windows, cupping his hands against the light of the room, looking out, he saw nothing, just the dark, low curve of mountains. There was no evidence that anyone was alive but himself.

In the workroom, prospective diningroom, he absent-mindedly made an incision with his thumbnail, then pulled off a small swatch of wallpaper. Once he'd pulled it from the wall, the wallpaper divided magically into separate layers, dusty-backed, light, as if they'd never been glued. He held in his hand nine separate dry pieces, all queer to the touch as dead moth-wings. He drew them nearer, to look at them more closely. The first one was gray with a faded pink flower design, more like stitches than like paint, the whole thing so carefully made to look like cloth that it struck him now for the first time that in the old days, maybe the eighteenth century, it must indeed have been cloth, not paper, that people put on walls. He was vividly aware all at once of not just the age of the house but the *time* it contained: generations of people who had made lives in it, had periodically pored over samples of wallpaper, debating, arguing, finally choosing; and then new people coming in, as he had done now, people who had perhaps laughed scornfully at the wallpaper they found there, or had touched it wistfully, regretting its age and dinginess, knowing they would never find anything as nice. The next piece of wallpaper was light brown and dark brown, again made to look like cloth, and the next was what had probably once been wine-red, with an intricate stripe and flower pattern. All three of these oldest pieces had been, almost certainly, paper for a livingroom. It was perhaps at this point that the room had begun to change functions: the next two pieces might be either livingroom or bedroom (one green, one blue), and the next two seemed patterns one might pick for a diningroom. The most recent, no longer at all like cloth—a bright pattern of chickens, corncobs, and yellow dots, then another of teapots and salt-shakers—could only be paper for a kitchen.

He felt a pang of regret that he'd so casually violated those generations of decisions: happy renovation, then gradual, almost unnoticed declines; regret even that he'd scraped away the hex sign on the door between the livingroom and kitchen. "Well, no matter," he told himself aloud, then stopped to listen.

The house around him was as still as a dried-out seashell.

He looked at the pieces of wallpaper again, startled for some reason. A tingling came over him, some chemical change that increased rapidly, then came rushing up his spine like a spring bursting out into the light through the side of the mountain. The room changed its color and a rumble filled his ears: it was as if he were fainting. He reached out to steady himself and had the illusion, all at once, that he was seeing the whole history of the house: weddings, funerals, births, deaths, battles. . . . In the rush of images one detail stood plain: a boy with gloved hands throwing a poisoned, apparently dead rat into the stove, then widening his eyes, covering his ears against the animal's screams. Pain shogged through Mickelsson, as if he himself had become the burning rat—but it was something else, something that doubled him over and filled him— filled the whole room—with a high wind of emotion, something like insane rage. Almost at once, the feeling subsided, the vision passed.

He stood blunt-witted, motionless, staring at the vivid bits of wallpaper. All was well; silent. He could hardly believe the thing had happened to him—certainly nothing like it had ever happened to him before. He felt frozen, as when one awakens from a nightmare unable to move a finger—the body's memory of ancient millennia, someone had once claimed; the stillness that saved our small forebears from passing sabre-tooths.

It came to him that he must have fallen asleep on his feet. It was a dream.

Now he was able to move again, first his hands, then his shoulders and head. His spine felt icy.

He shook his head, staring hard at the pieces of wallpaper, sorting them like cards, unconsciously testing, he realized after a moment, like a child fearfully teasing a snake behind glass to see if it will strike. Nothing, not the faintest stirring now. He closed his eyes, reaching up to rub the back of his neck where it ached as if from a cramp, and remembered Tim Booker's joke about the man who'd stayed in the house all night "and his *hair* turned white." For some reason—as if, without his help, his mind were snatching at alternatives to the nightmare—he thought of the swan-and-water-lily wallpaper in his bedroom when he was a child. Blue, white, and silver. He remembered his grandmother combing her long hair, then remembered his bachelor uncle's cough, at six in the morning, when he got up and dressed and, grumbling to himself in Swedish, went out to start chores.

Still a little shaky, but oddly sober, Mickelsson wandered again to the livingroom, squinting, trying to call back more. It was as if he'd buried the nightmare already, deep in the gloomiest room of the brain's ancient dungeon. He sat down, sucking at his pipe, unaware that it was out. His stomach was filled with dead butterflies.

He thought of Jessica Stark, the remarkable way she'd smiled when he took her hand, reopening possibilities. He must tell her about all this—the two men on the road, the trucks, the hex that was a face. . . .

He remembered something more: his grandfather, one gray afternoon, standing in his black suit at the rural mailbox, a package of newly arrived books under one arm, probably more volumes of Martin Luther. His head was tilted, listening to faraway, muffled thunder as if he imagined the thunder to be speaking.

Suddenly the thought broke through again: What was behind that sudden, dreadful nightmare? Just some childish image of death? Small-boy idea of Hell?

What of the possibility he'd been stubbornly refusing to acknowledge all this while: that it had not been a nightmare? He raised his drink.

When he'd sipped, he check-reined his head back, trying to work out the crick in his neck, and the next thing he knew he was sitting on the couch with his two hands closed lightly around the whiskey glass, and outside the windows it was mid-day. He'd been dreaming something, some room full of beautiful colors. Someone had said, "I'm sure you're not guilty!" Moving his head by accident, not yet awake, he'd shattered the dream, scattered it back into electrons. He would never dream that exact same dream again.

8

Thomas's Hardware was the most prosperous business, possibly the only prosperous business, in Susquehanna. Owen Thomas, the proprietor, was shy and retiring, fine-featured, scholarly, a man of forty or so, with a daughter majoring in art at Penn State, whom he mentioned proudly, with careful restraint, whenever reasonable opportunity arose. The store was a pleasant place, bright and airy, for though it was crammed with goods—tools, rope, pipefittings, hasps and hinges, woodstoves, picture frames, drawer after drawer of bolts, screws, nails, racks and display cases of fishing equipment, Coleman stoves, hunting knives and guns—it had sixteen-foot ceilings of light gray stamped tin and large, uncluttered front windows. It looked out on the parking meters, broken asphalt, and worn red brick of Main Street, beyond that a waist-high stone wall and then nothing, a sunlight-filled drop-off where thirty years ago one would have seen the grand vaults and arches of a turn-of-the-century depot, at one end of it a restaurant of glass and wood, said to be one of the finest in America. In the failing antique store a block up the street, there were yellowing pictures of the restaurant: grand Victorian gables and cupolas, tables so elegant they seemed to float, and beyond the far windows a spectacular view of the river. Studying the pictures in the dust-specked dimness of the antique store, Mickelsson had understood, in a kind of daydream, exactly what the town had been like in those days, how the huge old houses on the side of the mountain—now gray and warping, every shutter askew—had been mansions then; how the brick streets had rung with the *tock* of horses' hooves and the whispered chatter of early cars. Susquehanna had been, he'd heard somewhere, a repair station for steam locomotives. Money had poured in, and pride of place. It must have seemed to the people of the town that it could never change, a settlement so glorious and well-to-do, so solidly established. Those who worked for the railroad, whether as linemen or as railroad engineers or as officials in sunlit offices filled with large, brass-studded leather chairs, had been heroes; it was the weak younger brothers who ran the post office, the barbershop, the hardware store. Now those heroes—except for the richest, who'd moved away—were employees of their once-humbler neighbors, the pharmacist, the man who sold household appliances, the people who ran the declining lumberyard, the real-estate office, the dry-goods store. "Vanity, vanity, all is vanity!" the preachers sang here as in other towns, or so Mickelsson imagined, recalling the great, spare church of his childhood. He imagined the people all nodding in solemn assent.

Mickelsson looked through wallpapers, borrowed four books to take home with him and think about, then bought white latex paint and two rollers, a dropcloth, and a plastic mixing pail. While the woman at the register rang them up, he caught sight of the tools on the wall along the left-hand side—saws, hammers, files, such a wealth of power-tools that for a moment, somewhat to Mickelsson's surprise, farmboy greed leaped up in him. His father and uncle had spent all their lives building and un-building, converting barns from one use to another, horsebarn becoming chickenhouse, sheepfold becoming pig-shed—or constructing inventions of one sort or another, first drawing pictures far into the night at the round oak diningroom table: a heavy wooden frame with a track-slide loader for the buzz saw, a double-gated contraption for loading sheep, clunky wood-and-iron gadgets to fit on tractors or trucks or to lift his grandmother's wheelchair onto the porch. It occurred to him only now that all that labor had been play, however solemn their faces, however they complained about time and the work still awaiting them. Lifting a sabre-saw, feeling the heft of it, Mickelsson recognized his hand as his father's hand. They were the same size and shape and had much the same freckled redness; the only real difference was that his father's hand had always been barked, scabbed, cracked, and calloused, always at least one fingernail discolored by some mishap. He remembered a chest his uncle and father had let him help them make when he was seven or so, a pine chest longer and deeper than a coffin, no nails or screws, just wooden pegs, locust. It had served as a windowseat through most of his childhood; later they'd used it to hold cow-feed. In the bright, pleasant-smelling hardware store, the discovery that his father and uncle, all those years, had been playing, enjoying themselves—making art, in a way—came over Mickelsson like an awakening. He felt an extravagant inclination to pity himself. What foolishness his life was, in comparison to theirs! But the likeness of his hand to his father's hand distracted him, made him feel, almost un-willingly, a surge of joy.

When he looked up from his daydream he saw Owen Thomas and a customer, a man in a hunting jacket and a Wheel-Horse cap, sorting through a tray of small, brightly colored plastic objects, something to do with electricity, just a little way down the aisle. When Thomas smiled at him, politely nodding, Mickelsson held up the sabre-saw and said, "Fine collection of tools you got here!"

"Cost you an arm and a leg these days," Thomas said, smiling privately, more shy than before. It was clear that he knew how Mickelsson felt. Maybe it was a similar feeling that had kept him in the hardware business, made him run it so well. For that matter, maybe it was that feeling for objects well-made, tools both beautiful in themselves and in their uses, that had inclined Owen Thomas's daughter toward art school. Again he saw the present lining up with the past, like one image superimposed on another.

Thomas straightened up, holding out a handful of the plastic things to his customer, who looked them over through the bottoms of his bifocals, apparently counting them, his mouth fallen open, showing yellow stump teeth, then took the objects into his two cupped hands, nodding, still looking a little baffled, and carried them to the register. Thomas came over to Mickelsson. "How's that place of yours coming?" he asked.

"Lot of work to be done," Mickelsson said. He smiled.

"I guess there would be," Thomas said. Though he pretended to speak ruefully, he obviously understood Mickelsson's pleasure in the prospect of getting at it. "I guess the doc never had much time for fixing things. Mostly hired kids around town. You know how that is."

Mickelsson chuckled, man to man, still pleasantly conscious of the smooth metal handle of the sabre-saw in his fist. He lifted one eyebrow and lowered his voice. "You wouldn't believe that place," he said. When Thomas glanced up at him, he continued still more softly, "Not a wood-screw in the house that wasn't slammed in like a nail!"

Thomas smiled and shook his head. He seemed prepared to draw away, as if afraid he was imposing, but for the moment, tentatively, he remained where he stood. Mickelsson couldn't help but think it was because the man felt friendly toward him. If so, it was mutual. Even at the university—perhaps especially at the university—there was no man Mickelsson felt more comfortable passing the time with. He said, glancing back at the rack of tools, "I oughtta buy everything you've got here. I haven't got a thing, up on the hill. Been living in apartments."

"That's one thing about houses," Thomas said, "there's always something needs fixing."

On impulse, furtively, as if Ellen might walk in on him, Mickelsson took a screw-driver from the rack, then a pair of pliers, then a wreckingbar. Frowning, making a difficult decision, he studied the handsaws. Thomas reached up and drew one from its hook, wiped a speck of dust from it with the tip of his finger, and held it toward him, handle first. "If you're not a real full-time carpenter . . ." he said, and let his words trail off.

For the next twenty minutes, increasingly pleased with himself, though increasingly anxious as well, Mickelsson—with Thomas giving advice when he needed it—chose tools. When they took them, together, to the register and added them up—skill-saw, sabre-saw, electric drill, hammer, wrenches, dust-mask and goggles, level . . . more tools of various sorts and sizes than Mickelsson had ever owned before—he found, not really to his surprise, that he'd spent two hundred dollars. He had half a mind to have Thomas throw in an electric belt-sander, but he decided he could wait.

It even crossed his mind, as he stood idly waiting, his hand resting on the wallpaper books, that maybe he ought to get a rifle. Why not? His father had taken him hunting as a boy; the memory rose in his mind with wonderful vividness—creeks, trees, sunlight, squirrels scampering along high, leafy branches, the sky bright blue, like the ceiling at his parents' church. He'd never been hunting since. Ellen had hated guns. Her irrational fear of them had gotten under his skin, her weird conviction— only now did he fully realize how weird it was—that Mickelsson was a man too dark-spirited and moody to be safe with a rifle in the house. He shook his head. Odd what a man could take for reasonable and natural, if the poison was slipped in subtly enough, over a long enough period of time. Nevertheless, he would not buy the rifle, handsome as it was with its blue-black barrel and gleaming, machine-carved stock. He had far too much to do to be thinking of hunting. He got out his checkbook and took a ballpoint pen from beside the cash-register. Strange to say, though he'd been trying to live dirt-cheap these last months, skimping even on groceries to justify having bought the Sprague place and sending all he could to Ellen, whose expenses seemed greater than ever these days, Mickelsson, parting with two hundred dollars (Thomas had rounded off the bill), felt jubilant.

As he made out the check he said, "Owen, I meant to ask you. What would I do about getting a well drilled?"

"You got water problems?" Thomas asked. His right hand paused a moment, then went on helping the left put Mickelsson's purchases in paper bags, then fit the bags into two large cardboard boxes.

"Not yet," Mickelsson said, "but I expect them."

"I guess first you need a dowser," Thomas said. He straightened up, looking around the store for something.

"That how they do it?" Mickelsson said.

"Around here they do. You know John Pearson? I thought he was in here, a minute ago." He leaned to his left, trying to see past counters to the rear of the store.

"He's a neighbor of mine," Mickelsson said.

"He's supposed to be the best. I don't know, myself."

Mickelsson reflected. At last, slightly smiling, he said, "He dropped by, not long ago. Wanted to sell me firewood. Mentioned something about the house being haunted."

Owen Thomas looked at him, then decided to smile, looking away. "They say a lot of things, up there in the mountains. No TV reception."

They both laughed, then stopped. John Pearson had stepped from behind a counter near the back and stood with his tufted chin raised, trying to see them with those bad eyes of his, trying to separate their shapes from the glare of the windows.

"There he is," Thomas said, and returned to his packing.

Mickelsson hesitated, then moved down the aisle toward his neighbor. "Hello, there," he said.

Pearson studied him, at last recognized him, and nodded. He stood even now with his chin slightly lifted, whether from near-sightedness or from some mood that was on him, Mickelsson couldn't tell. In his square right hand Pearson held, clamped between his thumb and first two fingers, a length of black stovepipe.

"I understand you're a dowser," Mickelsson said.

"Use to be." Pearson jerked back one side of his mouth for a grin.

"You don't do it anymore?"

"I might. Can't tell."

They studied each other. The back of Mickelsson's neck tingled. He forced a grin and said, "I'm not sure I follow."

He would wonder later if the old man hadn't waited longer than he needed to, as if enjoying Mickelsson's discomfort, before saying, "Sometimes it works, sometimes it don't. You never know, these mountains."

"Yes, I see," Mickelsson said. He felt himself breathing again and was once more conscious of the bright, pleasant store around him, clean coils of rope, red wheelbarrows, hickory-handled hoes and garden-forks. Pearson's boots were lumpy, permanently wrinkled; in his rolled-up cuffs there was sawdust. "I'll tell you why I ask," Mickelsson said. "I've been thinking of having a well drilled, if I can—if there's reason to think I'll hit water."

Again Pearson cocked back one side of his mouth. It was probably accidental that the grin looked scornful.

"I thought maybe if you could drop by with your dowsing rod, or whatever you use—"

"Can't do it for a while yet," Pearson said. "Maybe come October—"

"That'd be fine—"

"And I don't guarantee."

Mickelsson's smile had become stiff. "That's fine too. I understand, a thing like dowsing—"

"Cost you twenty-five dollars."

Mickelsson stopped smiling. "I don't know," he began.

"Always charge the same thing, whatever I dowse for—water, gold, dead people. I don't say it's worth it, not by a darn sight. But I guess you'd pay more for a plumber, come to that. Any darn fool can lay pipe." If he was joking, he didn't show it.

Mickelsson tipped his head. "But a plumber guarantees his work," he ventured.

"That's what they'll tell you," Pearson said. He raised his left arm, ready to move Mickelsson aside as he would a bob-calf. "Wal, glad I run into you, Prafessor."

As the old man started toward him, aiming for the register beyond, Mickelsson said, backing off a step, "All right, shall we say early October?"

"Sometime in October," Pearson said. "See how things go."

Mickelsson accepted it. Anyway, it didn't matter; he'd have no money this fall for well-drilling. He walked with the old man toward the front of the store, where Owen Thomas was now putting the two large boxes, along with the wallpaper books and paint, on the carpet of the right-hand display window. Pearson set the stovepipe on the counter.

"Get any squirrels?" Mickelsson asked.

Pearson looked at him blankly, as if the subject had never been mentioned between them. Mickelsson squinted, then realized that the man was, of course, just deaf.

He drove home the back way, past the large brick Catholic church—most of the people of Susquehanna were Catholics, those who lived in town; legacy of the railroad days, Italians and Poles, a few Irish and Welsh—then up past the old brick hospital where the doctor had worked, a schoolhouse-like building shabby and morose in a clearing just beyond the shade of huge trees, its back walls perched at the edge of a cliff that dropped away sharply toward ash-pits. He passed large, sagging houses, then smaller houses, once the homes of men who'd worked the railroad beds, houses now mostly empty, caving in, stripped of their doors and windowframes. Where houses were still occupied there were snowmobiles in the yards, and torn-down motorcycles. Photographer's heaven, he thought, and felt a pang of lonesomeness for his son. He remembered the photographs stacked, still wrapped in brown paper, in the livingroom of the house up on the mountain. They'd made his small apartment in town look like an art gallery, not any picture there more than two feet from another. Here he could spread them out, give them their due. They were splendid things, the whole set a gift from his son last Christmas: bicycles leaning against old shed walls, a plastic watering can among cinderblocks, dying trees, a spiderweb, portraits of friends, portrait after portrait of his sister. . . . As he turned onto the road leading to his house, Mickelsson found himself thinking suddenly, his stomach tightening, of his daughter. It was as if the photographs had made her more real to him than his memories could. The memories themselves became photographs. His mind fixed on one of Leslie at seven, struggling to read the *Babar* in French that Ellen and he, in their youthful folly, had bought for her. Ah, how determined they'd been to give their children culture, introduce them to languages early, while their minds were flexible! So now, though still a senior in highschool, his daughter was taking her second year of French literature at Brown, a lover of the snide, superior, hopelessly unlovable French.

"I don't really mean I hate the French," Mickelsson said aloud, tossing up his hand in a French-style gesture for the benefit of whatever ghostly visitors might be listening beside or behind him in the Jeep. Then, hearing himself speak aloud, he scowled and thought, *How strange, this liberal intellectual timidity, this craven Judeo-Christian cowardice. Of course I hate the French!* At once he thought of Jean-Pierre, the exchange student who'd lived with them in Providence, and felt repentant. (He thought, in the same movement of mind, of Luther's dangerous doctrines —and Heidegger's on "national character." If his heart agreed, it ought not to.) Though it was true that Jean-Pierre was full of ignorant opinions about America—for example saw the zucchini in the overgrown, untended garden (they'd been away on vacation) and said smugly, in his execrable English, "Ah, ze Americains, zay will nevair undairstand wiz vegatables, not?"—it was also true that a gentler, more tender-hearted creature never sallied forth on earth. "Very well," Mickelsson negotiated, opening his right hand as if to show those around him that he saw their point of view, "I like the French all right, some of them. But you'll admit, they're an exasperating people." He cringed from a memory of Leslie, then fifteen, sitting on the couch in the livingroom with Jean-Pierre, kissing him with a passion Mickelsson would have thought beyond her years, no light in the room but the flickering glow of the fireplace. They had managed without a word to make Mickelsson feel that he himself was the guilty one, walking in on them in his slippers. "Perhaps I was," he said aloud. The image stayed with him—his daughter's startled, indignant face— until he consciously replaced it with another: his daughter in her night-gown, stretched out alone on her stomach in her bed, looking up from her poems of Victor Hugo toward where Mickelsson stood filling the doorframe, again in his slippers and robe. It was long after her bedtime, two in the morning.

"Hi," she said.

"You're supposed to be asleep," he said, tiresomely parental.

She flopped over on her back. Her eyes, shiny in the light of the door-way, were like dark mist, or maybe the deep blue of mountains toward nightfall. "You know something about French?" she said. He made the mistake of waiting. Her silver-blond hair fanned out beside her—her body, under the flannel nightgown, alarmingly thin but developing toward womanhood. She said, "It makes you see things a whole different way. Like a *cheval* is a completely different thing from a horse, but it *is* a horse, and so the next time you look at a horse you see *more*."

"Leslie," he said, "it's long past your bedtime."

She smiled and closed her eyes. *"Je t'aime, Papa,"* she said.

He'd arrived at his house now. He pulled over to his mailbox, praying that there would be no mail.

He must start writing something, he thought, walking up to the house. Its shadow fell over him. Something worth real money, this time. Such things were possible, not even prostitution. The world stood more in need of philosophy than it believed. Just get the world's attention, that was the trick—a mighty, zinging style (he was capable of that), an initial focus on matters of common, maybe prurient interest. He would be mocked, of course; he was mocked already. But there was much that could be said, starting with such subjects as rape, the modern return to witchcraft, the grotesque tendency he saw in his students to be willing to believe in anything, from the Great Green Soup Cure to saintly levitation—or believe in anything but the fundamental goodness of life. (He was conscious of standing back from himself, watching and listening to himself. The self he watched and listened to was florid, heavy. It gestured in angry jerks. His grandfather, influenced by Luther, would call the thing a devil. Mickelsson was powerless.) It could be done, he thought. There was hope. There was always hope! He would get out of all this—nothing to fear but fear itself, et cetera. He would start at once, begin the first chapter this very evening.

He (they) began to pace. Unconsciously, he'd set down the mail on the kitchen counter, one or two envelopes spilling onto the floor. Bills.

The next morning he was at Thomas's again, getting wallpaper rolls, paste, and brushes. He would start immediately, he thought, but then for no reason changed his mind and carried the whole Kaboodle down to the cellar to store till the proper mood was on him. "First a little writing," he said aloud. *Little control here. Everything in order.*

He'd meant only to stop in for a six-pack, to help him with his writing —he was naturally rusty, after all this time—but the bar had trapped him. It was more like a London pub than anything he'd ever before seen in America—no etched glass, no fine woodwork, no ornamentation but the off-and-on Schlitz and Genesee signs—but the sounds and feeling were much the same, despite the blare of country music on the jukebox: the aqueous roar of talk, both adults and children, the occasional yap of a dog, the thick haze of smoke like heavy silt. The woman at the bar called him "sweetie," sliding him his Scotch and telling him the price, which was surprisingly low. After he'd paid, he moved carefully into the darkness of tables, each table covered with a red and white oilcloth and furnished with a dark, stamped-tin ashtray. The place was packed—farmers, stubbly working people, women with blackness in their eyes and mouths, fat female arms and thighs white as flour—and he'd almost adjusted to standing up, leaning on the dark back wall, when someone waved to him, shouting something—in all that ruckus he had no idea what it was the man shouted—and he made his way, pushing past the sea-sunken clutter of chairs, to where the man was making space for him. The man, young, wearing a blue workshirt, stood up and reached across toward him with a tanned, muscular arm. "Hay, Prafessor!" he shouted—the words just barely came through—"so you've fownd the waterhole!" Mickelsson realized at last that it was the real-estate salesman Tim.

"Say, Tim!" Mickelsson shouted back. "Small world!" He looked at the woman beside him. Blond, big-bosomed, slightly drunk. She seemed young to be drinking; only a little past his daughter's age. He tried to think of Tim's last name but couldn't. "Is this the wife?" he asked.

"Naw," Tim said, laughing with boyish pleasure and shifting his handshake to a power-to-the-people shake. "This is Donnie. She's my cousin."

"One of his many, many cousins," Donnie said, and held her soft, plump hand up to Mickelsson. Mickelsson let go of Tim's hand to take Donnie's. She said, "You're the one that bought the ghost house?"

"That's it. I'm the one," Mickelsson said. He drew back the chair across from them—the tables were so crowded he could draw it back only a few inches—then wedged himself into it. He raised his glass in wordless salute, then took a sip.

"Any trouble yet?" Donnie asked, leaning toward him and eagerly smiling. Her dress was a light flowerprint, almost transparent, wide open at the throat and plunging; no bra. Her white cleft instantly aroused him. He thought guiltily of Jessica Stark. The girl's face, in spite of the slight look of drunkenness, was as innocent and open as a child's. Compared to Jessica, she was as common as a kitchen sink.

"Not yet," he said, and shook his head as if in disappointment.

"I can see you've settled in," Tim said, as if proud to have been a part of it.

"You're really not at all like that other one," Donnie said, and with slow strokes patted his arm, approving.

It was because of the way she laughed, he'd realize later—and the way she looked at him—that he didn't quite notice what she'd said. He imagined her white, undersea-soft body in his bed and in some way understood that it might not be impossible to arrange.

Something bumped his feet and Mickelsson leaned over to look under the table and see what it was. A child was crawling past them, a fat, very dirty little girl. She smiled at him, then crawled on.

"Boy, talk about weirdos!" Tim said, and laughed. "I guess you didn't know him?"

"Know him?" Mickelsson asked. Because of the noise—the general talk and a sudden peal of laughter two tables away—he had to ask it again: "*Know him?*"

"He was something," Donnie said, "though I guess it's not something you should laugh abowt." She laughed, then made her face drunkenly stern.

"I think they said he came owt from Sunny," Tim said. "Course he didn't live here. Whole different situation, and he wasn't in philahsaphy either, I don't think. Psychology, was it?" He looked at Donnie. She didn't know.

Tim grinned and shrugged. "So you haven't seen the ghosts yet," he said then. "I guess I'm naht real surprised, to tell the truth." He raised his beer and swallowed a swig of it, then set it down and glanced around the room, wiping his mouth with his hand. "I guess the thing is, a town like this, crazy stories are abowt all there is to keep things lively. You wonder if there's any truth to any of it."

Mickelsson nodded, agreeable, then raised his eyebrows and asked, "Any of what?" Tim apparently didn't catch it.

Donnie's foot—she'd taken off her shoe—came to Mickelsson's. At first he thought it was an accident, but the foot remained, and then after a moment her toes came up to touch his ankle. He glanced at her. One would swear the foot and the girlish, wet-mouthed face were unconnected. It was a pretty face, he began to think. Small, dimpled chin; light brown, myopic-looking eyes. The blond of her hair was unconvincing, but the dark lashes weren't exactly convincing either.

"What a weird idea," she said, "living in a house with ghosts in it!" She laughed. Her foot came back to the toe of his shoe and pressed several times, rhythmical.

Mickelsson nodded, for some reason not sure even now what she was signalling. He knew, of course, but his mind kept going over it, rechecking. He found he couldn't remember at all what they'd been talking about. Someone bumped his shoulder, pushing past him toward the bar, and leaned over to shout in his ear, "Ex*cuse* me!" Mickelsson glanced up and nodded, then raised his glass and drank. The man moved on. His gray underpants showed above his trousers, outside his tucked-in shirt.

"Warren, that was his name," Tim said.

Now Mickelsson remembered what they'd been saying. "You happen to recall his last name?"

"I think maybe that was his last name. I only saw him once or twice, myself. I remember people said he was very interested in the stories about your house." He smiled.

"I guess that's not so strange, necessarily. Any particular stories?"

"Oh, well, you know," Tim said. He shrugged again, then after a moment's thought took the stainless-steel ballpoint pen from his shirt pocket to play with it. "Man with a lot of questions, everybody said. That's all I know. I guess he thought he was being pretty canny, and I guess maybe people had him on a little. They'll do that, place like this. At the time they were still smahrting from the things that feller Skinner said— B. F. Skinner. He grew up here. Put all the local dirt in his autobiography —whorehouses all up and down Main Street, things like that. Fahr as I can say, it was mostly true, but you know how it is. Things look different when somebody writes 'em owt on paper."

"So what happened to the man?" Mickelsson asked.

"Warren, you mean?" Tim asked. "Or Skinner?"

"I don't think we should talk about it," Donnie said. She was rhythmically pressing on Mickelsson's shoe again, smiling and meeting his eyes.

Mickelsson looked thoughtfully from one to the other of them, trying to make out whether or not he too was being teased. He could no more tell than with old Pearson.

"I meant Warren," Mickelsson said.

Tim shrugged, pursing his lips, then raised his beer and finished it.

"Really, I don't think we should *talk* about it," Donnie said. She smiled and glanced past her shoulder.

Tim made his hand into a gun and pretended to shoot himself in the head.

"He shot himself?" Mickelsson asked, leaning forward.

"Well, not exactly."

"Someone else, you mean—?" He smiled, covering himself, in case it were all just a joke on him.

"That's about it. Of course nobody's saying there was a connection. But you know how people talk." Tim gave his head a little jerk and smiled, apologetic. "I don't know how I got off on that. You're nothing like him, and the whole thing's just silly anyway. It happened up in Binghamton, the murder, I mean, and the man had never been down here more than three or four times."

"More than *that*," Donnie said.

"Well, six, maybe."

"Now you're getting closer, anyway," she said.

Mickelsson drained off his Scotch and held the glass up to look at it, still brooding on whether or not they were having him on. Maybe they thought if you told a man his house was haunted, then filled his head with vague, scary stories . . . He thought again, as he'd been thinking off and on for a week, of that brief, violent nightmare, if nightmare it was. Was it possible that they'd somehow planted that in his mind too? Strange sense of humor!

"Jeez," Donnie said, looking at her little gold wristwatch, "I've gotta go! Prafessor, you wanna walk me home?"

"If you like," Mickelsson said after a moment's hesitation, looking at Tim.

The boy was still playing with the pen, popping the point in and out.

"OK, Tim?" Donnie asked.

"Sure," he said, and grinned. "Catch you tomorrow?"

"Tomorrow," she said, and kissed the air in his direction.

As soon as they were outside the door, Mickelsson asked, "Maybe you'd like to come up to my place. Have a little nightcap?"

"Are you kidding?" she asked, and smiled, then took his hand.

He glanced at the Jeep, the troll-doll dark and still behind the windshield, as if hanged, and decided to walk.

She lived in an apartment on the fourth floor of an old brick building overlooking Main Street and the river. The first floor was Reddon's Drugs; the rest of the building consisted of apartments no doubt much like Donnie's, approached by the darkest stairway in the world, a long row of battered metal mailboxes on the first-floor entryway, then nothing but an occasional fly- and paint-specked bare bulb, a railing worn smooth by decades of use. On her door there was a white plastic rose. His growing erection pressed painfully against his trousers.

"Safe and sound," he said when she'd unlocked the door.

"You wanna come in?" She looked up at him, her eyes in shadow.

He hesitated. "If you're not too busy," he said.

She smiled. "This *is* my business. You mean you didn't know?" She looked at him with innocently widened, maybe mocking eyes, then pushed the door open and reached for his hand. He followed her in. She flicked the lightswitch by the door and the room leaped forward—a purple-carpeted livingroom furnished in K Mart and Goodwill, plastic imitation-lace curtains bright as barnacles on the windows, faded and water-stained tannish wallpaper with an obscure pattern of glossy places like stretch-marks on a woman's abdomen. The kitchen was to his left, separated from the livingroom by a rounded, dark oak arch. An old refrigerator clanked and hummed in tune with another sound, possibly an electric clock. There was no light in the kitchen except what fell from the livingroom, draping over part of an old sink and stove.

"Nice place," he said.

She laughed.

He walked over to the window looking out at the street and drew back the curtain a little with the side of his hand. Her window looked down on the lighted iron bridge, the long dark curve of the Susquehanna River, and what remained of the huge, locked-stone depot. Directly below him lay the street. No one was out, though it was not all that late.

"Drink?" she asked.

"No thanks." He was feeling distinctly uneasy now. It was obviously no place for a sober professor of philosophy, an ethicist at that. He could hardly believe it was happening. Looking out at the bridge, the asphalt-patched street, he thought about disease, stories of prostitutes and murder. His erection was increasingly painful, and a kind of trembling had come over him. The air was hot and muggy. He was beginning to sweat.

A light went on behind him; she'd opened the refrigerator door. She stood for a long time looking in, then closed the door and came to him, carrying a beer. "You mind opening this for me?"

He accepted the bottle from her—it had a twist-off cap—and opened it. "I have a feeling you cost a lot," he said.

She shook her head. "Depressed area." She winked, then raised the bottle to her lips.

"Mind if I smoke?" he asked.

"Anything you like." She glanced at him, coy. "But no hitting, and nothing really really yuk."

"I'm not into yuk," he said. "Actually, I'm pretty puritanical." He thought a moment, studying a bruise on her shoulder, then said, "Listen, I really have to ask this. How much?"

With one hand she unbuttoned the top of her dress and—almost shyly, he thought—exposed one blue-white breast. She studied it, thoughtful, and after a moment, without lifting her head, raised her eyes to him. "Not too expensive," she said. Her smile was calculated, but not quite hard, despite the fake eyelashes—not quite professional (though Mickelsson was admittedly no judge). Her youth was increasingly disconcerting. In fact he was suddenly filled with dread, wondering what his solicitous friend Tim had gotten him into. When he put his arms around her, drawing her close, his trembling became violent. On her forehead there were droplets of sweat.

In the middle of the night Mickelsson awakened alone in a strange, musty bed, roused by a sound of angry shouts not far away, somewhere below and outside. He sat up, trying to minimize the creak of bedsprings and figure out where he was. Even the shouting outside was not enough to block from his mind the return, all in a rush, of images of her body—breasts, buttocks, mouth—and his own, shuddering and heaving, driving into her. He was once again semi-erect. "Asshole!" someone yelled not far away. There was a sound of breaking glass, then several shouts at once.

The livingroom door was part way open, letting in enough light that he could be certain the girl had gotten up and left him, and that his clothes were still on the chair at the foot of the bed, apparently untouched. As quietly as possible he got up out of bed and went to his trousers. The wallet was still in the right rear pocket, and his money, he found when he looked, was still inside. Now he wasn't so sure his clothes hadn't been touched—something was wrong—and he checked his valuables again. All there. He drew on his undershorts and trousers, put his arms through the sleeves of his shirt, and, disguising his erection as well as he could, started for the livingroom.

"You OK?" she called, an instant before he emerged.

She was sitting in the overstuffed armchair by the window, reading. As if self-consciously, she took off her glasses.

"What's all the noise?" he asked. Flasher-lights jarred the darkness beyond the window. He moved closer to her to look out.

"Saturday night fights," she said. She smiled. "I guess it's hahrd to imagine that kind of thing where you come from."

He bent toward the window. "What do you mean? Boxing?" He knew it wasn't that.

Out on the lighted street there were thirty or forty young men, a few young women, and several policemen. They seemed to be doing nothing, just standing there shouting.

"They do that all the time," she said. "Haht nights, they come down owt of the mowntains in their pickup trucks and drink beer till they're all sweaty and mean, and then they stahrt hitting. It's no hahrm, really. You could go owt there and walk right through them, they'd never touch you."

"What a crazy place to live," Mickelsson mused aloud.

One of the policemen was trying to persuade one of the young men to get into a police car. The young man stood with his arms folded, shaking his head. He was far too big to push.

"You know, you shouldn't have come here," the girl said. "You should go back wherever you were, while you've still gaht your looks."

When he glanced down at her, she was smiling. Delicately, with two fingers, the pinkie raised as from a tea-cup, she unzipped his fly.

"I thought you said I could walk right through them and they'd never touch me."

"*They* wouldn't. At least I *think* they wouldn't." She lowered her gaze to her magazine, maybe taking note of what page she was on. One could have sworn she actually did not know she was reaching in, closing her hand on his stiffened penis. His heartbeat quickened.

"Who would?" he asked.

"How would *I* know? Do I look like a newspaper? All I know is it's not good, you being here."

"In this apartment?"

"No, that pahrt's all right." She smiled again. She had a chipped, blackened dogtooth, just noticeable when she forgot and smiled too widely. "What's not good is when you leave and go back to that—house."

"Is it the house I should be afraid of?"

It was the craziest conversation he'd ever been party to. His mind seemed wonderfully clear, but split in two.

Now she laid aside the magazine and stood up, opening her robe. "I don't know what you should be afraid of. If I were you I'd be afraid of"— she met his eyes for an instant—"everything." She pressed closer, one hand drawing his penis out of his pants.

It struck him that she wasn't at all afraid herself. Surely the whole thing was some damned country joke. Her light blue robe—something like polyester, very prim, the kind of thing a good suburban wife would wear when driven from her husband's bed by snoring—fell from her, and she rose on tiptoe, almost climbing up onto him. He bent his knees and lifted her in his arms. "Oof!" she cried, then laughed. He slipped in like magic. On the carpet at his feet, to the left of her chair, there were scattered records—Wings, Elton John, Stevie Wonder. She arched her back, leaning away from him, breasts rising.

"How much do I owe you?" he asked, breathing hard, still upright and wearing his trousers and shirt, plunged inside her, his two hands on her waist.

She moaned, shaking her head, closing her legs still more tightly around him. "I don't know. Five hundred? How much can you afford?"

"Jesus, not five hundred!" No doubt his voice showed his fright.

"Make it a hundred then. Times are hard."

"How about twenty-five?"

Her eyes rounded. "That's really insulting!"

"Fifty?" A drop of sweat got in his eye.

"Ninety. You aware of how much time I let you have?"

"I can't! Really! I've got terrible financial troubles—you've got no idea! Seventy-five?" He tried to blink the sweat away. No use. She too was sweating. He could hardly hold her.

"OK," she whispered, and suddenly clamped herself like a fist around him, alarmingly strong. "OK! Oh, Jesus! *Sold!*"

Afterward, when he was zipped up again, hardly able to reconstruct how the whole thing had happened, sick with anxiety—and with guilt, too, since it was now clear to him that the girl was no more than a teen-ager—Mickelsson asked, handing her the check she'd finally agreed to accept from him: "Tell me something. Do you do that often? Upright like that?"

She laughed and held the check to the light. "How often does a poor country girl get seventy-five dahllers?"

His visitors were long gone when Mickelsson got home that night, or rather that morning; the sky was already beginning to lighten, and birds were singing in every bush and tree, like poor Mickelsson's heart. It was not that he'd ceased to feel guilty. Intellectually he had no doubt that what he'd done was very wrong, inexcusable in fact, and no doubt that if there were in fact a God, He ought to be shot for creating a world where young women so sweet and essentially innocent could be turned into playthings of masculine pleasure. But when he climbed out of the Jeep, giving the troll-doll a playful little tap to make it swing, it was not solid ground but dewy air he stepped on. It had of course not escaped his attention that she'd outrageously tricked him: she'd as much as told him so herself. And it was not that he'd forgotten how much money seventy-five dollars was in his present straits, or how far it was beyond her usual fee—as she'd mischievously let him know. But the truth was, he liked the trick, liked its bold, teasing wantonness—liked it almost as much as he liked her sweaty, plump young body, or the way she'd somehow banished from his mind all fear of going limp, or her oral expertise, or her shyness when he'd come out of the bedroom and caught her with her glasses on. He liked the way she'd said "Depressed area," luring him into her trap— no country bumpkin, she, with language like that; a reader, as he'd seen, of *Cosmopolitan*. Above all, perhaps, he liked the way she'd let her feeling for him slip out, her suggestion that harm might come to him here, and the faint hint that she'd be sorry if that were to happen. So Mickelsson, smiling to himself as he walked toward his house, went over in his mind every moment of the time he'd spent with the girl. Once again, he found, he was in a state of semi-erection.

Getting his keys out—letting his hand, inside his trouser pocket, rest longer than necessary against his partial erection—Mickelsson went suddenly still all over. The door, which he was sure he'd locked behind him as always, stood open. Fear crackled through him, and without thinking he stepped back at once behind the chimney, out of view. He listened for a long time, heart racing. It seemed to him he'd never heard the old house so still before. At last, slowly, stepping carefully on the flagstones, he moved back to the open door, then in. For a full three minutes he stood, hardly breathing, in the kitchen, listening with every nerve. It took another five minutes for him to move, freezing each time a board creaked, to the closet in the study, where he groped in the darkness until his hand found the silver-headed cane. Then, with the cane gripped like a bat, he switched on the study lights.

It was like a scene from some junky movie: books torn from the shelves, papers and manila folders everywhere. He could hardly believe he hadn't sensed the condition of the room as he crept in; but of course that was not what he'd been watching for: every sense had been tuned for one thing, the dangerous intruder. He began to breathe normally— somehow he knew, the minute he saw the mess, that whoever had come was now gone.

And of course he was right. They'd looked for whatever they were looking for behind the couch cushions, in the bedrooms, everywhere. He touched nothing, intending to call the police—merely stood looking at the jumble, room after room. Then, with the telephone receiver in his hand, he began to think clearly. The police would know—like everyone else in Susquehanna, no doubt—where he'd been, and why his visitors had felt free to take their time. He saw again the crowded bar—men, women, and children, even dogs and, no doubt, cats, though he'd seen none. Nowhere in town could he have stood out more plainly, except possibly in one of the churches. The realization was comforting, in a way: it was not necessary to believe that Tim or Donnie had purposely set him up. Someone had seen what was happening at Tim's table, had seen the professor go out onto the street with Donnie. . . .

He hung up the receiver, frowning, the call unmade, and began a more systematic, more intelligent search of the house. Nothing was missing—not his typewriter, not the stereo—nothing, so far at least, but three cartons of Merit cigarettes and all his pipe tobacco.

"Kids!" he said aloud, and almost laughed. He knew, suddenly—or so he imagined—what they'd been looking for. He was a professor, one of those strange outsiders you read about. They'd been looking for dope! Now he did laugh, self-consciously, oddly like an actor—so he thought even as the laugh poured out. He thought of their mad dream as they tore books from his shelves, their hope that one of the books would prove hollow, full of Quāaludes, or coke, or marijuana. On impulse he went to check the refrigerator. Sure enough, all his beer was gone. He went to the livingroom and opened the closet, below the stereo, where he kept his whiskey. Wiped out.

"Paltry!" he said aloud, raising his right fist at the lighted windows onto the porch.

All his body was charged with imperatorial scorn (the light in the sky was reddish yellow now, and the roar of the waterfall across the road was like a rumble in his brain), but, for all the acting, a part of him drew back. He remembered faintly, not in words, something odd about the bathroom, where he'd gone earlier to relieve himself. Now, in front of the toilet, bending close to the bowl, not quite sure what he was after, he got a scent of alcohol. The kitchen sink smelled the same, but more noticeably of beer. He went out, on a wordless hunch, to check the garbage cans. Nothing; but the hunch was stronger in him now. He walked to the cluttered, overgrown ditch behind the barn across the road. He stood with his head bowed, hands behind his back, looking down at new bottles glinting in the red morning sun. He made no careful count, but he was sure. They were here, all those bottles that had been stolen from him. He moved down, as if someone had suggested it to him, toward the burdock patch between the barn and the pond and waterfall, and began to bend down the burdock stalks with his right foot. Within fifteen minutes he'd found the three cartons of Merits.

There were more things to think about than he could possibly deal with, tired as he was. Someone had torn his house apart and had tried to make it look like the work of kids. He began to feel uneasy again about Tim and Donnie.

The worst part was humdrum. He needed a drink, and they'd poured out all he had.

He walked back up to the house, the world around him like a blurry old movie. He remembered mornings in Heidelberg. Drunk and hungering for a drink at 6 a.m. The grass gave gently under his feet as he crossed the yard. Birds warbled fiercely all around him.

There was no reason to think they'd had anything to do with it, Tim and Donnie. The bar had been packed. Who could know what crazies had been watching him through the gloom? Yet it was true that if he were a native here he might know. They all might know. He thought again of calling the police.

He was still thinking of calling the police when he lay down on the couch in the livingroom for a moment to think, maybe grant himself a few minutes' sleep. When he awakened—from a series of dreams about Donnie—it was late afternoon.

9

"Hi, Pete! Finney here!" The line sputtered and crackled in protest. In his mind Mickelsson saw the bloated, lead-gray face, here and there suffused with a dark red blush, and the gray, swollen paw, also blush-splotched, with rings on the fingers and tiny curling hairs, the hand fatly clamped as if for dear life around the shiny black receiver.

"Hello, Finney."

"Listen, we've talked with the lawyers of the lady—ehhh, thank you, Shirley, no, I'll get back to him—we've talked with the lawyers of the lady, nothing fancy, just boilerplate, and I figured I better touch base with you, sort of see if you still got your socks on."

Mickelsson waited. He was in the middle of the third page of the blockbuster book he was determined to write. The study around him was only partly straightened up. He had no time for fooling with housecleaning: his mind was wheeling, careening with ideas—thanks to Donnie Matthews (he'd finally remembered the last name he'd written on her check). Even when he was deep in thought about what he was writing, the memory of the girl was all around him in the air, and for all his weight and furious concentration he felt as if he were floating. He must see her again—he'd decided that even before he'd left her. Once, picking up his week's supply of Di-Gels at Reddon's Drugs, a scent drifting over from the rack of perfumes, colognes, and nailpolishes had caught him unawares and he'd believed he might have heart failure. He'd hunted through the bottles, trying to discover which scent it was that so powerfully brought her back to him, but before he could isolate it his nose had become confused. He wished he'd stolen something from her—a hankie; even a button would have served. She filled his writing with power and life. It was a strange and wonderful effect. Sometimes he would stop and, dreaming of her, would masturbate.

"You hear me all right?" Finney asked.

"I can hear you."

"Good, good. I went over the settlement you proposed and they were very professional about it. They didn't laugh." Finney laughed, explosive. Mickelsson could see his chair yawing back precariously, his fat left arm flying up in the air as if inviting an audience to laugh with him. "They were brilliant, in fact, considering it takes three of 'em to figure out who should go pee. Ha ha! They listened to that dream-scheme from Candysville, offering the lady the Taj Mahal if it's not too much trouble for her, otherwise you could give her the Empire State Building and the Brooklyn Bridge, and after it's over they have the alligator balls to look solemn, as if maybe it's not enough."

After Finney's pause had lengthened for a moment, Mickelsson brought himself to ask, "What did they say?"

"Well, the lady lawyer—Lincoln, that's her name, no shit—she folds her hands like she's in Sundayschool and she looks very concerned. You offer your former spouse, free gratis, for just existing—a dubious virtue, all things considered—the house and the car and fifteen hundred a month, which is more than you make, if you'll come out of the clouds for just a second and think it over, more than you make after taxes, not to mention the taxes you forgot to pay last year—"

"I didn't forget."

"Just playin with ya, kid. You're offerin her more than you make, that's the point, plus house, plus car, books, paintings, records, swimming pool— and your wife's lawyer is very concerned that your wife might not be able to get by on that."

Mickelsson sighed and, to keep himself from reading over what he had in the typewriter, covered his eyes with one hand. "Why not?"

"Well, you know how it is these days," Finney said. "Kids in college, no scholarships—why should they need scholarships? Rich professor's kids, right? And all the lady's expenses, not to mention her friend's—she sent me a breakdown; I'll slap it in the mail. Heat bills, travel expenses, food and clothing, liquor, car repairs, doctor bills, life insurance—hundred thousand dollars on you, that's how much she values you; I bet it makes you proud!—but of course she can't pay it, where'd the little woman get money like that?—also lawyers' fees, three of 'em, gotta be well-protected. Put it all together it comes to about double what you offered her, champ; otherwise no dice."

"That's crazy."

"What the fuck does she care?" He laughed.

Mickelsson could see him, self-consciously chortling, blue eyes smouldering, angrier at his client than at his client's ex-wife—not without reason, from a lawyer's point of view.

"So what am I supposed to do?" Mickelsson said.

"Cancel the offer, the whole ball of wax, that's my advice. The money you've been sending her, don't send her another thin dime, drive her ass into court and let the judge decide."

Mickelsson sucked his lower lip in. "Maybe I should give her a call," he said, "try to reason it out."

"Do that. Good luck to you!"

There was a pause.

"Probably not such a hot idea," Mickelsson admitted. He leaned forward onto his elbows. After a moment he said, "I just don't see why she doesn't take it. She must realize it's fair—more than fair—and the best I can possibly do."

"That I doubt she believes," Finney said. "What did you make on the speakers' circuit—three, four hundred a night?"

"That was years ago, when I had a book out and people had heard of me."

"So write a book. You forget how to type? And what about those summers? June, July, August you just sit on your can, go live in some fancy hotel in the Adirondacks and watch the birds and bees, maybe paddle a boat around and try to find some late Redskin ass. You could be doing your duty as a father and ex-husband, maybe get yourself a job with the merchant marines, a little highway construction. Take some inches off."

"That's bullshit, Finney."

"Isn't everything, ole pal? Listen, don't yell at *me*. Lady's got a right to dream, understand? And you gotta admit you invited it. You offer her the moon and a ton and a half of fingerpaints, no wonder she wants you to throw in a rag to wipe her hands on." He laughed again. When he laughed, Mickelsson remembered, Finney's face would begin to shine. One of these days he'd have a stroke.

"I just want to do what's fair," he said. "It seems to me she shouldn't have to move to a smaller house or even cut down on expenses all that much. If she'd just be reasonable—"

"By what standard, Professor? You got a book somewhere tells you what's reasonable and what's not?" Mickelsson could see him bending forward in his chair, leaning on his desk, picking up a pencil, getting serious. Finney was breathing harder now, his belly crowding his lungs. "Maybe you found someplace in the Bible that tells you how much the Lord allows? Believe me, you're dreaming! Two years now, you been dreaming like a baby. Little cottage in Eden, with a cleaning woman comes in two times a week—that's what you think your wife deserves; she's a human being, right? Little lower than the angels? What if the money to pay for it just doesn't exist? Nowhere in the world? Never mind, what's right is right, you've got your dream. Am I on to you? But what about *her* dream, since we're ignoring reality and all its pigshit tedium. Why should she settle for a miserable fucking cottage, nobody interesting to talk to but a couple of big bossy angels, maybe a snake. You hearing me, Professor? You on my wave-length? In a perfect world you wouldn't need me, that's granted. But unfortunately we're dealing with a world made of crap, world of cut or be cut, so if I was you I'd start listening to a little advice."

Mickelsson said nothing. It struck him that it wouldn't be easy to get back into his writing.

"Don't send the lady another thin dime. Let her see you're serious.

She'll negotiate—no choice! When she's hungry enough she'll go to court for a settlement and the judge'll award her maybe ten thousand tops—probably less, all things considered. You can always send her a little more if you get conscience pangs. Hell, you can give her every penny you make, but as your lawyer I can't let you commit yourself to going to prison if you should hold a penny out."

"All right, I won't send her any money for a while," Mickelsson said.

"Now that I call reasonable."

"But when we get her to court, the offer I've already made stands."

"And that I call *not* so reasonable. But OK, OK. We'll play it as it lays. Say, I see your kid got his kisser in the paper."

Mickelsson sucked in his upper lip. "I didn't catch it, I guess."

"Yeah, one of those 'protesters arrested' things. I'll slap it in the mail."

"Do that. I'd like to see it."

"I bet you would." Finney laughed.

Mickelsson hung fire for an instant. "What does that mean?"

"Nothin, pal! It's been a long time since you've seen him, right? He looks terrific, believe me. Peak of health!"

"I'm glad to hear it." His mind remained snagged on Finney's laugh. At last he said, "What was he protesting?"

"Nukes, I think. Seabrook or Yankee, one of 'em."

"I see." Mickelsson nodded. His fingers played absently with the phone cord. "Do send the clipping. I'm sorry I missed it."

"Will do, pal," Finney said. "Keep fit, now. Anything else?"

"I guess that's it."

"OK, then. Keep in touch—I hate surprises. Bye-bye!"

"Good-bye," Mickelsson said.

When he looked over what he'd written he saw that he'd been right. It had terrific drive, a quality one could only call magical, easily the flashiest piece of argument he'd ever pulled off. But the mood had left him. The very room around him looked dead, as if whoever lived there had moved. Again he reread his pages, struggling to get the feeling back. Rhetoric like a delicate tracery of ashes.

Late that afternoon it began to rain, a gray, smoky rain that moved back and forth against the mountains like curtains, and Mickelsson's depression increased. For all his work, he'd gotten out only another half page, and he did not need an objective friend's eye to know that it was worthless. He forced himself to quit. A day like this—lurid gray sky, gray rain, gray hills—would be a good one to waste on finishing the straightening up of the mess his visitors had left. He went to the cabinet under the stereo for the one bottle of Gordon's gin and the one small bottle of Martini & Rossi with which he'd replaced all the liquor he'd lost, paying with a check he was pretty sure would bounce, though he had, really, no idea. He fixed himself a large martini, then moved dully from room to room, putting things back into their drawers or onto their proper closet hooks, shoving the furniture back where it belonged, then sweeping and dusting, stopping every fifteen minutes or so for a sip of his drink, finally putting his books back on their shelves, this time imposing, as he hadn't done before, some measure of organization. The size of the stack of bills on his desk made him sick. He wouldn't think about them. When he came across the silver-headed cane in the hallway, where he'd left it that night, he stood looking at it for a moment, then leaned it up against the rickety coat-and-umbrella rack as though it had for him no more special meaning than any other familiar household object.

Housecleaning finished, he went down to the basement to look over the still-unopened boxes of tools he'd gotten from the hardware store in town, the great stack of wallpaper rolls, the paste and brushes. The basement—cellar was more properly the word—was damp, full of smells of decay. The beams overhead had patches of gray fuzz on them, like lichen or dampened ash. The stone walls literally dripped, probably not leakage from the rain outside, and the cardboard boxes, brand new a few days ago, were soft to the touch. Leave the wallpaper rolls here much longer and they'd be money down the drain. He carried them, armload after armload, up to the kitchen and nested them on the long, formica-covered counter. He must get busy soon at fixing the place up. He remembered as if from a different existence how eager he'd been to get at it all, just a week ago. Now his decision to write that blockbuster book made his plans for the house an annoyance, though of course he must carry them out; otherwise the waste of money would be criminal. He stood sipping the martini, finishing it off, his shoulders drooping, stomach falling heavily forward as in some Beardsley drawing (no doubt even now he was flattering himself: his trousers were limp, baggy, and soiled; his shoes were damp and shapeless and had a rancid smell), gazing wearily at the wallpaper rolls, their patterns hidden inside their white wrappers—patterns he'd brooded on, considering and reconsidering, though now he couldn't remember which ones he'd chosen—and he was filled with such weariness and misery he could hardly understand why he'd left the apartment.

He went to the refrigerator for more ice, then to the cabinet under the stereo, and made a second large martini, then wandered back to the study to look over his writing. All the interior of the house was gray, like the gloomy, fading afternoon, but his study, where the bills were, seemed the grayest room of all. Outside his window the birdbath was coming apart in flakes, like the treasures of Venice, and the large, orangish roses had been shaken and shattered. Rain was still falling, a lead-gray, luminous mist.

At last it came to him that, though his eyes had been going over and over the typewritten sentences he'd been working on, his mind remained stubbornly fixed elsewhere. His hand went to the telephone receiver: he would call Information and get Donnie Matthews' number. But then he changed his mind and drew his hand back. He leaned his elbows on the desk in front of the typewriter, rested his chin on his interlaced fingers, and closed his eyes, shutting out the stack of bills, trying to think. The instant his eyes closed he realized he was slightly drunk. No wonder, of course. He hadn't eaten all day. He would go down to the restaurant in town and get supper. He switched off his worklight, pushed back his chair, and got up. He carried his drink with him to the hall, where he meant to get his raincoat, then changed his mind and went into the bathroom to wash and shave, then to the bedroom for a clean shirt—surprisingly frayed at the cuffs, but the best he had—a relatively unwrinkled ascot tie, and his dark blue sportcoat. (Two buttons were missing, but no one would notice if he remembered not to button it, which he would, since the coat had grown too small.) When he was dressed and had looked himself over in the mirror, he went downstairs again, finished the drink, put on his hat and raincoat and took the cane from the umbrella stand. He had no umbrella, but no matter. The rain, as if to please him, had stopped.

He locked his doors carefully—thinking of his visitors—then walked carefully, stepping between puddles (he had no rubbers), to the Jeep. It was now nearly dark. The house, when he switched the Jeep lights on, was all rough elbows, frowning eyes.

After he'd parked the Jeep on Main Street, in front of the bank, directly across from those who watched the intersection from their old wooden bench (he did not feel inclined to salute them, this time), Mickelsson, succumbing to a sudden impulse, turned west toward Reddon's instead of east toward the restaurant, hesitated for a moment in the doorway, then, swinging his cane, moved quickly past the battered mailboxes and up the stairs. "I'll just ask her if she's had supper yet," he said to himself, "or if perhaps she'd like coffee." He began, whispering, to rehearse what he would say. "Evening, Miss Matthews. Remember me?" The stairway was full of cooking smells and the tinny noise of television sets. At one of the landings a woman's voice cried out, startling him out of his daydream, "How many times I got to tell you, Robert?" Mickelsson slowed his step, at first out of alarm, then from interest in learning what it was that Robert kept forgetting; but the whining voice that answered was far away, another room perhaps, and the woman, when she spoke again, had moved farther from the door. He continued up the stairs. Halfway up to the next landing he stopped, with his hand on the railing, to catch his breath. He could see her white plastic rose.

He had knocked several times before he was willing to believe she wasn't in. Even now it would not be accurate to say he believed it. He had thought, not quite consciously, that all reality had been magically on his side: the fact that he hadn't eaten, so that it was necessary (more or less) that he come into town; the fact that the rain had opportunely stopped. . . . He put his mouth close to the door and called, "Donnie?" With his ear against the wood he knocked again. He stepped back quickly and glanced past his shoulder as the door to the apartment behind him opened. One eye and half of a dark, splotched face looked out. He nodded and touched the brim of his hat. For three or four seconds the eye went on staring. Then the door creaked shut.

At the restaurant, just after he'd given his order to the waitress, a voice at his shoulder said, "Professor Mickelsson! How's everything going up there?"

When he turned, raising his head, he saw and, after an instant, recognized Tim's boss, Charley Snyder. The man was spiffied up, downright distinguished-looking, suit and tie under the raincoat, big white grin on the darkly tanned face. For some reason it hadn't until now dawned on Mickelsson that the man was more than commonly well-off, though of course he'd seen those Snyder Realty signs everywhere and had once heard Snyder joked about: someone, one morning at the Acme Market, had been telling some out-of-towner how Marie Antoinette, hoping to escape to America, had bought up thousands of acres of northern Pennsylvania. The woman at the cash-register had winked at Mickelsson and said, "Just like Charley Snyder." He had laughed, of course, but he understood now, seeing Snyder dressed to the nines, that the joke was more true than not. The man had a large onyx ring on one finger. His raincoat and the suit underneath looked like something in an ad from *The New Yorker*.

"Hello, Charley," Mickelsson said, and reached up his hand to shake Snyder's. "Care to join me?" He tilted his head, indicating the unoccupied chairs.

"I could do that, if it's not any trouble," Snyder said, giving him a brief serious look.

"By all means!" Mickelsson said. "Good to see you!"

"I'm meeting some friends here," Snyder explained, looking toward the door, then back at Mickelsson. He began to take off his raincoat. "We usually meet over at Dobb's Country Kitchen, but some of us thought, well, you know. Support local business."

They both laughed. Snyder folded the raincoat carefully and hung it over the back of a chair, then seated himself next to Mickelsson. "I'll just have coffee," he said to the waitress, who had appeared with her pad from nowhere.

"The coffee's really terrible," the waitress said.

"I don't mind," Snyder said, and smiled.

Mickelsson watched her swing away, moving past empty tables to the louvred doors into the kitchen. It was no doubt true that the coffee was terrible. Its slightly scorched smell filled all the restaurant.

Snyder leaned forward onto his elbows. His cufflinks—onyx, like the ring—blinked. Mickelsson, smiling back into Charley Snyder's smile, was aware of ambivalent feelings. He was a hard man to dislike—even, despite his business, a hard man to distrust—but Mickelsson, tonight at least, with the thought of Donnie Matthews not far back in his mind, felt irritation at Snyder's easy handsomeness. The man made Mickelsson feel as overweight as he was, and worse yet, as homely. Mickelsson smiled, realizing what a figure he cut. His face was puffy. Even in his prime, before it had begun to turn yellow and iron-gray, his hair had been too carroty to be anything but odd, and it had never been trainable. His neck was like a bull's, his shoulders so large as to be slightly grotesque, an effect increased by his habit (he saw this moment, with the heightened clarity that comes of too much gin) of choosing suits too small for him. He couldn't even feel a comfortable intellectual superiority. Snyder was at peace with the world, and evidently rich. He knew his business at least as well as Mickelsson knew his. Like water in some old-time torturer's chamber, gloom was rising in Mickelsson, threatening to drown him. He smiled more intensely to dispel it.

"Well, what do you think?" Snyder asked. "Is the old house haunted or not?"

"That's an interesting question," Mickelsson said.

The man glanced up at him, as if surprised that he should hedge.

"What's the story on this man Warren?" Mickelsson asked.

Snyder interlaced his fingers on the tabletop and looked thoughtful. "I doubt that there is any story," he said. "He came down and made some kind of study of Susquehanna—for all I know he was interested in the history of railroads. Maybe he was in folklore. He was as nice a man as you'd hope to meet. Nothing strange about him, just an ordinary professor. Good-looking, young . . . I'll tell you my theory. The whole thing's socio-economic."

Mickelsson waited, eyebrows arched.

"Most of the people in this town, or anyway the people I deal with, they're as middle-class as anybody. But we've got more than our share of poor people, and the thing about the poor is, they compensate, if you follow what I mean. Holy Rollers, lower-class Catholics . . . When life disappoints them, they improve on it. You know what I mean: Heaven, all grievances redressed. But also other things. They make up for their lack of real social power with imaginary power. Witchcraft, strange legends people whisper to one another—" His right hand made a faint, dismissive gesture. "I don't blame them. I'd probably do the same, in their circumstances." He sadly shook his head. "Well, anyway, when that man Warren died, it was a godsend for people like that, you know? Rumors began to circulate on the kinds of questions he'd asked—probably most of them he'd never actually asked or even thought of—and little by little his death became a proof of, well, the power of the Devil. Something like that. My own opinion is, he happened to be murdered, up there in Binghamton, and it had nothing to do with Susquehanna."

Mickelsson said, "I understand he asked a lot of questions about my place—the Sprague place."

"I imagine he must have. It's the best legend we've got."

Mickelsson nodded. "Just about the only legend." He smiled.

"Well, no, not really." Snyder stopped, looking up at the waitress, who'd appeared with his coffee.

She set it down carefully. "You're sure you don't want anything else?"

"Not yet," he said. "I'll be eating later, when the others come." He looked at Mickelsson. "Do you want coffee? It's the best in Susquehanna." Snyder and the waitress exchanged smiles.

"No thanks," Mickelsson said. "I may have some after I eat."

"It's almost ready," the waitress said.

"Fine," he said, and nodded.

She left.

"So go on," Mickelsson said. "There are other legends—besides the one about my house?" He blushed, embarrassed about calling the place "my house."

Ruefully, Snyder smiled. "You mustn't judge Susquehanna by what its crazies think."

Mickelsson waved as if to say, "Never dream of it."

"Well, we have a man that can fly." He raised his hand like a policeman signalling Stop. "No broomstick," he said, "pure will." Suddenly he grinned. "That's all I can tell you. It's interesting, of course—strange and amusing. But it would give you the wrong idea about this place, take my word. You want to know what we mainly do here in Susquehanna? We try to bring in industry. It's no pipedream. Really isn't. We're on a main railroad line—even Scranton, it's just a side-line—but trains do go through Scranton. If Reagan's elected . . . I don't mean to talk politics—"

Mickelsson waved away objections.

"Well, as to your house," Snyder said.

The waitress arrived with Mickelsson's open roast-beef sandwich. Meat, soggy white bread, potatoes; all covered with brown-gray gravy.

"I'm sorry," the waitress said, "did you order a salad? I didn't bring you a salad, did I?"

"It's fine," he said. "I did order a salad, yes. Maybe if you could bring it later—"

"I'm sorry. You wouldn't believe how confused things are tonight!"

The tables were still mostly empty. Snyder smiled.

"Later will be fine," Mickelsson said. He thought suddenly, with terrible lust, of Donnie. He glanced at his watch. With his fork poised to plunge into the mashed potatoes, he said, glancing over at Snyder, "You don't mind?"

"Eat, for heaven's sakes," Snyder said. "I'd join you, but since I've arranged with my friends—"

Mickelsson ate. After a minute he abruptly put down his fork and asked, "Do you have many thefts here in Susquehanna?"

"Never," Snyder said. "Literally. Drive up and down your road, you'll see signs on farmers' stands telling you how much pumpkins cost, or squash, whatever, and nobody there, just a basket full of money. Nobody steals a nickel. It's a funny thing, in fact. Tourists come through, from New Jersey and so on. *They* don't even steal. Why do you ask?"

Mickelsson cut into his roast beef. After a moment he said, "Somebody broke into my house."

"You're kidding!"

Mickelsson shook his head.

"Did you call the police?"

"Well, no—" He shrugged.

Somehow it seemed to him that Snyder knew the whole story, or at least understood why he'd chosen not to call the police.

But Snyder chose to feign innocent indignation, or at any rate so it seemed, at first, to Mickelsson. "You should have called them! How come you didn't? What did they get away with?" He was angry, his eyes hard-looking, more slanted.

"Nothing, really," Mickelsson said. "They pretended to steal my liquor and tobacco, but actually they didn't." He explained the details— the smell of liquor in the sink and toilet bowl, the bottles in the ditch behind the barn, the cartons of cigarettes in the weeds down by the pond. He'd never found the pipe tobacco.

Charley Snyder studied him as if he couldn't believe that Mickelsson was telling the truth. The waitress arrived with the salad. Neither of them looked up at her. At last Snyder said, "I'd certainly call the police if I were you. Doesn't sound healthy at all."

"Why would they do it, though?" Mickelsson asked. "And who would do it?"

Snyder got out a cigarette, paying such close attention to tamping it and lighting it that there could be no doubt that he was baffled.

"Are you a Mormon?" he suddenly asked.

"No." He remembered his food and began to eat again.

"Ever write about the Mormons?"

"Never."

Snyder sucked deeply at his cigarette. Nervously, Mickelsson got out a cigarette of his own. "I don't say they're behind it," Snyder said. "I don't say anything. For all I know, what you smelled might just be some kind of chemicals. We'll get that, now and then. But say it was your whiskey. If you or I were to work over a house—looking for something, or whatever we might be doing—and try to lay the blame on kids, by stealing all the liquor and tobacco . . ."

"We wouldn't throw them away," Mickelsson suggested. "Whereas the Mormons—"

"That's it," Snyder said. He frowned at some new thought. "On the other hand, if somebody wanted to lay *blame* on the Mormons—"

"It was pure luck that I found the cigarettes and bottles," Mickelsson said.

"Maybe," Snyder said. To Mickelsson, the man looked shifty all at once. He dragged on the cigarette, then quickly blew out smoke. He said, "There's an alternative theory. It really was kids, and after they'd drunk up a certain amount they got panicky and threw away the rest and hid the bottles."

"And the cigarettes?"

"Maybe they were afraid to take them home—thought they could hide them and come back and smoke them when it was safe."

"Maybe," Mickelsson said.

"Why not?"

"That's true. Why not?"

"It's easy to hate the Mormons," Snyder said. "They've got a strange idea of history. Nothing's more offensive to the ordinary mind."

"Maybe," Mickelsson said, half smiling at the odd idea.

"Well, anyway—" Snyder said, and hastily scraped ashes off his cigarette.

The front door opened and several people came in, well-dressed, like Charley Snyder, though none of them quite up to his style. A chinless, otherwise quite pretty woman was the apparent leader. She looked around the room, head lifted, dark coppery hair grandly falling. When she saw Charley Snyder she pointed at him, turning to speak to the others. The whole group floated, smiling, toward the table where Mickelsson and Snyder sat. They might have been schoolteachers on a visit to New York City, or Presbyterian elders coming in for tea after a meeting. Mickelsson went on poking in his food.

"Ah, here are my friends," Snyder said to Mickelsson, at the same time raising his hand as if imagining they hadn't yet seen him.

"Oh?" Mickelsson said.

"As I mentioned," Snyder said, "a lot of Susquehanna is solid middle-class. These people you've been getting stories from . . ." He grinned, then drew the ashtray toward him and meticulously crushed out his cigarette. Then he rose from his seat, moving back the chair with his left hand, and, taking a step toward her, kissed the chinless lady on the cheek. They talked and laughed, the whole crowd of them—six or seven—soon becoming part of it. Tall, distinguished bright-eyed birds with glossy feathers. Mickelsson concentrated on eating, giving them a chance to move on to a table of their own. He was still a little sullen from the two big martinis, and for other reasons too he was hoping he wouldn't get trapped here. But inevitably Charley Snyder made introductions. Mickelsson rose, with his mouth full, his left hand patting his mouth with his red paper napkin while his right reached out to shake hands with one, then another and another. He did not listen to the names.

A man with a long nose, a black moustache, and a sunken mouth said, "Peter Mickelsson. I heard you'd moved here. Aren't you the one that wrote—"

Mickelsson endured it all nobly. He adjusted once again his idea of Susquehanna. They were as clever and lively as middle-class people any-where—teachers, owners of small businesses, dentists. . . . They were moderate of voice, earnest; one could imagine them at meetings of concerned citizens. They were meeting tonight, it seemed, to discuss once more the long-stymied possible renovation of the decayed stone depot to make it a shopping mall and theater center. There were various possi-bilities—a grant from the Appalachian Regional Conference, help from HUD, certain private philanthropists in Philadelphia. The small, bony, very businesslike woman who'd at once filled him in cocked her head at him, no doubt sizing him up for usefulness.

"Would you care to join us?" the chinless woman asked.

He wondered if she knew that he was seeing—or at any rate had once seen—the town prostitute. Improbable, he thought. They would not readily believe that such a thing existed in their fair city.

(Cruel and uncalled-for, he thought. They were good people. Not pious or self-righteous. They were honored that Peter Mickelsson, philosopher, should be their neighbor, fellow citizen. If they were to learn that he'd gone mad over a prostitute, they would not crackle with indignation; they would be sweetly distressed, dismayed.)

"I'm afraid not tonight," he said. "Another time, perhaps?"

They all spoke at once, insisting that he be with them next time.

The man with the long nose said, "I didn't actually read your book, but I hear it's very good. God knows it's needed! I'm a doctor myself." He smiled meekly, his eyes fixed on Mickelsson's forehead as if there were a ruby there. Perhaps there was. More veins popped every day.

"Well, if you'll excuse me," Mickelsson said. He laid down his tip beside his plate, one corner of the dollar bill peeking out. He would pick up his check at the counter.

"I'm so glad to meet you," the woman who seemed to be their leader said, and took his hand again. "If you ever need anything—"

"Thank you," he said. He bowed to the others, almost clicking his heels like one of Nietzsche's Prussian officers. "Thank you!"

It crossed his mind—a wave of distress—that the woman meant it. If he should ever need anything, she would be there. They would all be there. It made him stoop a little, backing away from them, falsely smiling. One might say, if one were mad, "I'd love to stay longer, but there's a teen-aged girl I must go fuck." A shadow fell over him, almost a physical coldness. The chinless woman herself, down under those stylish, medium-expensive clothes, was no doubt beautiful. Ironically, Mickelsson's infatuation made every woman in the world seem sexually attractive. *Fool, fool!* he thought. When the waitress hurried past him as he waited to pay his check at the counter, he managed to brush her thigh, so lightly she didn't seem to notice, with the back of one hand.

Out on the street again, his right hand closed snugly around the silver lioness-head, Mickelsson found the sidewalk and pavement almost dry, here and there a large, dark, glassy puddle that sharply reflected the bluish-white neon of the Acme sign, the colors of the traffic light, the headlights and taillights of an occasional passing car or truck. The sky overhead was black and starless. He walked to his Jeep, intending to drive home, but then, standing in the street with his hand on the handle of the door, he frowned, second thoughts tugging at his coattail. The beep of an old car approaching on his side of the street startled him from his reverie, and he pressed closer to the Jeep, though in fact the car had plenty of room to pass. Right beside him the car slowed still more and beeped again, and, scowling into the dimness of the car's interior, he made out, in silhouette, a big man leaning close to the steeringwheel, waving at him, and on the passenger side, nearer to Mickelsson, the ghostly image of a white-faced, smiling child. The taillights were halfway up the hill, bound for Lanesboro, before it came to him that the driver of the car was the man he'd bought the Jeep from, Lepatofsky. Belatedly, Mickelsson waved.

He decided to see if Donnie had come home while he was eating. He could see from here a faint light in her front window, suggesting that she might be there. Giving a decisive little tug to his hatbrim and glancing once, furtively, at the watchers on the bench, he turned from the Jeep and walked quickly to the entrance of her building, stepped inside, then paused for a moment, touching the tip of the cane to the floor but not leaning on it, the fingers of his right hand restlessly playing, closing and unclosing, on the cane-handle, his heart as weighty as some dead thing at the bottom of an elevator shaft. The lightbulb in the entrance-way had burned out; one looked up, as if from the bottom of a pit, at the dim glow of some bulb not visible at the top of the first steep rise of stairs. Except for the faint sound of television sets, the building was asleep. Though his mind had come to no decision, he began to climb the stairs. Like a thief, he kept close to the walls, where the treads of the stairs were less likely to cry out. At the third-floor landing, the floor below hers, he stopped again. Then, firmly setting his smile and removing his hat, carrying it in his left hand, he climbed the rest of the way to her landing and door.

Though he knocked and repeatedly called out to her, not too loudly, no answer came from the apartment. Once he thought he heard someone moving about inside, but he couldn't be sure. Here, as at his own house, beams and boards creaked, futilely searching for a comfortable position. No light came out onto the threadbare carpet below her door. The longer he stood there, memorizing the grain in the door panels, the more sounds he became conscious of—refrigerator motors, fans, air-conditioners, TV voices and music, a regular clinking sound he couldn't identify, the faraway mewing of a kitten.

At last he put his hat on, nodded to himself, and, closing his right hand on the worn-smooth railing, started back down to the street. When he stepped from the entrance-way, the bench people were still there. He climbed into the Jeep, laid his cane on the seat beside him, and started up the engine. "Well, no luck," he said aloud. He U-turned and started up the steep hill leading to the outskirts of town and eventually his house, but then on second thought pulled over, two wheels up on the sidewalk, yanked on the emergency brake, and turned the lights off. He sat thinking, talking to himself, then abruptly got out, closed the door, and, swinging his cane almost jauntily, like an English banker, climbed the steep sidewalk until he came to the alley behind the building containing her apartment, where without a glance to left or right he turned in. He moved past garbage cans and huge, square bins, past rusty, louvred ventilators and metal-faced doors, and stopped directly below the black silhouette of a raised fire escape. Nowhere in the darkness around him was there any sign of life. A television voice cried out, "Stop right where you are, Ferguson!"

He tested in his two hands the security of the canehead's fit to the cane, then reached up as far as he could, trying to hook the bottom of the fire escape and pull it down. He was short by a good three feet. He tucked the cane under his arm and went back to the nearest garbage can. It was full, and when he moved it water sloshed in the bottom, but he lifted it, trying not to get garbage on his clothes, and carried it, as quietly as possible, back to the fire-escape extension. Standing on the can-lid, he found he could reach the fire escape with ease. It would not budge, perhaps frozen in position by old rust. "Bastard," he whispered. He pulled himself up on the cane, holding it with both hands, so that his feet rose off the garbage lid. Still nothing—at first. Then, as he was about to call it quits, something gave: with a faint sandy groan the extension tilted a little, then sank gently toward him. He swung free of the garbage can and, when his shoes touched solid ground, climbed hand over hand up the cane until he caught hold of the fire escape itself. With one hand he jerked the garbage can out of the way. Seconds later he was up on the

tar-and-pebble roof, where he could look in through the windows of the third-floor apartments. How he would get to her bedroom window, still a floor above him, he did not know, but he was convinced now that he would make it.

Carefully, so that no one below might hear him, he crossed the roof, keeping low and avoiding the third-floor apartment windows. There were four of them, three of which were dark. As he passed the one lighted one —lighted only by the flickering bluish fire of a television set—he raised up enough to peek in. He saw a clutter of bulky, dark shapes—an immense old wooden wardrobe with its doors hanging open, shapeless, colorless clothes draped on the doors; overstuffed chairs that looked rotten with age, some of them piled high with unopened boxes and plastic-bagged electronic parts; several TV sets in various stages of disassembly; a sturdy antique piano-table piled high with odds and ends (jumper cables, new-looking plastic clocks, a stack of dirty clothes); a round-front dresser with glass handles, also cluttered; an old-fashioned glass-doored bookcase packed tight with old magazines. Exactly in the middle of the room, with his back to the window, sat the man who had collected all this—an immensely fat man wearing steel-rimmed glasses and what appeared to be a policeman's hat. He had on a filthy gray workshirt with the sleeves rolled as high and tight as they would go; the rest of him was hidden from Mickelsson by the overstuffed chair the fat man sat in and the steamer trunk beside it, piled deep, like everything else in the room, with junk.

Preparing to duck his head and move on, Mickelsson nearly missed the most interesting thing of all. Later it would seem to him that it was the first thing his eyes landed on, and that, by some quirk that only a Dr. Rifkin could explain, his eyes had moved away from it, the brain refusing to register what it saw, flashing Will Not Compute. Stacked among other things on the steamer trunk, right by the man's bloated, hairless left arm, lay a glass refrigerator tray filled with money: packages of bills wrapped in colored paper bands, packages of the kind Mickelsson had dealt with in his undergraduate days, when he'd worked as a teller at Wisconsin Farmers Trust.

Now, though Mickelsson had made no sound, the fat man's head began to turn. The profile came into view, small-nosed, small-chinned, alert. Mickelsson waited no longer but ducked below the window ledge and flattened himself as well as possible against the sooty brick wall. He held his breath, listening, but if the man in the room was moving—rising, coming to look out—the noise of the television masked the sound. Minute after minute he waited, still as a rock. Just as he was deciding it would be safe to move away, he heard the soft rattle, directly above him, of a window-shade being pulled down. His muscles locked and for nearly a minute he held his breath. At last he did breathe again, but still he did not move. Even when he heard the television channels switching he remained as he was; the fat man might well have a remote-control switch. It was equally probable that he had a gun.

He looked straight up and realized, after he'd stared at it a minute, that what jutted out above him was the iron-mesh floor of a fire escape. It went directly past her window. He should have known, of course, that there had to be a fire escape, though he could not have hoped it would give him immediate access to her room. He had not noticed it before only because its darkness blended in with the black-brick darkness of the building. For an instant, desire leaped in him; but then he thought again of the probable gun, the probable genius of the fat hoarder's paranoia. It was unlikely that she was there; maybe she'd gone on vacation with his seventy-five dollars. In any case, the chance that she might be there hiding all evening in her apartment with only one dim light on, was not quite worth his life.

He stayed motionless for what seemed to him another twenty minutes, then carefully made his way back to the edge of the roof and the fire escape leading down to the alley. The escape extension creaked loudly as it lowered him the final twelve feet. Was it possible that it had made this much noise before? "Ah, the mind, the mind!" he whispered. Dogs barked sharply, two or three of them, down by the garbage he must pass. He held the cane like a bat and moved confidently toward them. At the first fierce swipe—it fell harmlessly on the lead dog's shoulder—the dogs fled, yipping in indignation.

Only when Mickelsson was seated in the Jeep, reaching for the emergency brake, preparing to drive home, did it occur to him that the man was, of course—or perhaps had once been, some years ago—a thief. Mickelsson was so frightened he could only sit trembling, so loose of muscle it was as if he'd turned to milk. But even as he sat helpless, sick with the knowledge that he could have been killed, a strange, evil dream came over him. He would watch for the man, and someday when he saw that he was out of his apartment—sitting on the watchers' bench by the traffic light, perhaps (he had a feeling he'd seen him there)—Mickelsson would hurry up to his apartment window and break in, and his financial troubles would be over. Acid welled into Mickelsson's throat and he fumbled through his pockets for a Di-Gel. He imagined himself going to the post office—as in fact he would do three days later, not quite intending to—and looking through the Wanted posters, hunting for the fat man's face.

As he reached the edge of Susquehanna, the night became alarmingly dark. A suicidal deer leaped out in front of him, but Mickelsson, as if he had known it was coming, hit his brakes just in time and missed it. "Bastard," he whispered, as if the deer were part of the conspiracy.

His mailbox showed up, stark in the flame of his headlights, and he remembered that he hadn't looked into it in days. He pulled over, opened the metal door, and reached in. There was, as usual, a great pile in it, gray as conch. Bills. Envelopes from collection agencies. He dropped it angrily on the seat beside him and, a minute later, carried it into the kitchen with him, where he threw it on the stove top—the formica counter was crammed with earlier mail and wallpaper rolls—intending not to look at it. But something made him stop and finger through it. There was a small pink envelope with flowers on the back, on the return-address corner one word: *Matthews.* He tore it open.

> *Dear "Professor":*
>   *Your fucking check bounced. (Excuse the pun.)*
>   *I guess you think that's pretty funny!!*
>   *My* Frends *will be in touch with you.*
>   *D.*

He went to the telephone book and found her name. He let the phone ring fourteen times before he quit.
   He wrote:

> *Dear "D":*
>   *I will give you not only seventy-five dollars but my very life. I am deeply and profoundly in love with you.*
>   *I told you I have terrible financial troubles, but I have means of dealing with them. Believe me, my love, my precious darling, I will make you happy!*
>   *Adoringly,*
>   *M.*

He tore it up. Never before, except when drunk, had he behaved so stupidly. He wrote a long letter to his ex-wife, then tore it up.
   He painted all the next day (a teaching day; he called in sick) and most of the night in the upstairs bedrooms, white on the walls, battleship-gray on the wide-boarded, uneven floors. His muscles ached fiercely, especially his back, forearms, and wrists, but the pain pleased him. He'd never known anyone who could put in longer, harder hours than he could, once he put his mind to it. It was perhaps not much to be proud of, but it was something. His heart tugged. (Whatever does not destroy me makes me stronger.) From time to time, struggling not to think about Donnie, or the thief, or the I.R.S., or his children, he brooded on Finney's complaint, the one solid thought his mind could get hold of. The portable radio chattered and sang like one of Luther's small devils in the corner; he listened only when talk of the so-called Presidential race came on.
   It was true, of course, that he was a foolish dreamer, as Finney maintained; that something, somewhere, had gone wrong with his fix on

reality. He was offering, in his proposed settlement, more than he could honestly expect to earn, never mind the debts or his own new expenses, which he recklessly increased from day to day.

Whether it was a common complaint or unusual he was unable to make out, but something in Finney's anger made him see that the so-called episodes—to say nothing of the present absurdity of his life—were the least of it. It was clearly true that the world was, at least in very large part, pigshit, Porphyry's rancid honey. He'd plodded through it, mired to the knees, year on year; yet he'd stubbornly refused to believe it.

He felt something beckoning at the back of his mind. He was rolling shining white paint onto the frames of the old louvred doors in the master bedroom, the whole room around him as white as snow, all except the stark, black windowpanes looking out on what might have been deep space or the center of the earth. It was perhaps the thought of Finney—all those jokes about Eden—or perhaps the whiteness that brought on the memory: he saw the church where he'd gone every Sunday with his parents as a child—shiny white walls, skyblue ceiling, on the wall behind the pulpit a large, naive painting of Adam and Eve in the garden, their private parts not visible, and looped around the tree a rather friendly-looking snake.

What his reverend grandfather had had to say about Eden he couldn't remember, probably nothing good, but it seemed to him now that his grandmother had told him a hundred times the story of those two naked people and the serpent. She told it with spirit, as she told all her stories, but no moral conviction; it had not been—in contrast to the story of God's calling Samuel in his sleep, or Noah's flood—a story full of meaning for her. She told it exactly as she told stories of her childhood in unimaginable Stockholm, or told the stories she made up to explain the pictures in his Charlie McCarthy coloring book. She told him, with ice-bright, merry eyes, how the snake had talked and Eve had bitten the apple and the pair had been thrown out of the garden, so that afterward human beings had to be farmers and storekeepers. So far as he could tell, the moral of the story was that because the snake had spoken to Eve, all snakes in the world ever since had to crawl on their bellies, perhaps so they'd be far from people's ears.

Every Sunday, once he knew the story, Mickelsson—then five or six—would sit, hardly hearing his grandfather's drone, gazing up, rapt, at the picture. It had never occurred to him that this was not the real snake, the picture not as true as a photograph, nor had it ever occurred to him, so far as he knew, that the story might not be a literal report of facts. He studied the expressions of the man, the woman, and the snake in wonderment—especially the snake: sad-eyed, misunderstood, suffering perhaps a premonition of the trouble to come but as yet knowing nothing, as innocent as the apple on the tree. He tried to imagine what the snake might be saying—that part was never quite clear in his grandmother's account—but nothing would come to him, not even a guess. He could not help but think it had all been a peculiar misunderstanding, though nothing of much consequence, since it was obviously pleasant to be a farmer or storekeeper, though it was sad that people must now wear clothes. (One could not discuss with his grandmother the oddity of wearing clothes.) When he was eight, the church—which had originally not been Lutheran but something else, vaguely pagan—had held a fund drive and, to Mickelsson's sorrow (also his father's and uncle's), the sanctuary had been changed, the wood stripped down and stained almost black, as it was supposed to be, according to someone, and an organ installed—a huge whale-mouth full of teeth—where the picture had been. He'd realized now that it was a bad thing to be thrown out of Eden, though it was nobody's fault, so far as he could tell. After the reconstruction—or sanctification, as his grandfather had called it—his uncle had stopped going. It was interesting to him now that the son of a Lutheran minister should be able to rebel so whole-heartedly. But perhaps in the final analysis his father had been the greater rebel. He'd continued going, but, from all evidence, only for the hymns—he gloried in singing and grieved at his son's inability—and for Sunday entertainment, and to visit his friends.

All the world had been thrown out of Eden at about that time, he knew now, by hindsight. World War II was on. Many of the older farmboys he knew, and even some grown men, his uncle among them for a brief period, had gone away to be part of it, and some were reported to be missing in action or dead. Sweden was said to be conspiring with the enemy. Collaborating. There had been movies to that effect. He would sit cringing, hot with guilt and shame, and at night, each time with astonishment, he would wet his bed. For years, even after he knew they were unjust, he'd been unable to get those movies out of his mind. At times—sometimes publicly, when he was drunk—he had blamed them for his choice of profession.

He and his family, cousins, and friends would sit hunched around the radio, dark and glassy-eyed, listening to Lowell Thomas or Gabriel Heatter report the news: bombings, planes missing, London on fire. No one had known that it was necessary to explain to him that Sweden was not at the heart of it. He'd explained, ragingly, on the asphalt school playground (he had often, in those days, argued with his fists), that his uncle had joined up with the United States Navy; but when Donald Warner—a face and name he would never forget—had said, "Sure! As a spy!" Mickelsson—that is, Mickelsson the child—had felt his heart sink.

Every time an airplane went over at night, he was sure that in a moment he'd hear the piercing, downward-slanting whistle of a bomb, and when the plane droned on, its dark sound innocently diminishing to silence, he was astounded by God's mercy. It was otherwise with trains, moaning through the woods at the far end of the farm, carrying weary-faced young soldiers. Sometimes in town, standing on the platform of the gray brick depot—torn down thirty years ago now—he had looked in at them with something like that wonder with which he'd looked up at the picture of Eden in the church. They sat crowded like animals in a stockcar on its way to Chicago, but they smoked and grinned, sometimes waved through the gray, greasy window at him, peculiarly indifferent to the fact that when they got where they were going they would have to shoot people, or possibly die. Every Saturday afternoon he saw people die in movies— sometimes actual people, in *Time Marches On.* The chatter of guns seemed not real, more like dream-noise; only the drums were real— absolute Being—rank on rank of goose-stepping soldiers, with swastika flags hanging down from the buildings, so many thousand soldiers that there seemed no hope for mankind. He held his older cousin's hand, white-blond Erik, who was to die in Korea. Later he saw pictures in *Life* magazine of mound on mound of dead people—Jews, he was told, though the magazine did not make it clear. Still later, in college, he had lain beside a half-Jewish, half-Italian girl, one of the cheerleaders, on a blanket over-looking a quarry. Suddenly, looking into her brown eyes, feeling the softness of her skin, he'd felt horror stir in him, as if a black shadow— Sweden's evil ghost, or the ghost of Dr. Luther in his final madness—had fallen over them. Whenever he went to movies about World War II— dog-fights, people shouting happily, like Boy Scouts, grenades exploding, bridges falling in—he felt sick at his stomach, as if he were looking at his childhood through thick, wavy glass. People laughed in the ocean-bed darkness of the theater around him, or leaned forward, flickering light on their faces. At times a kind of vertigo would come over him, a weakness of arms and legs, and he would leave. Once, in college, lying on his bunk in the dark with his hands behind his head, he'd asked his roommate, "Does it ever seem to you that everything you look at, it's in a mirror?" "No," his roommate had said, after thought. He hadn't expressed himself clearly, he'd decided. It was impossible that others should not have noticed. (He'd never heard of Plotinus, Porphyry, and the rest—thank God— though he ought to have suspected the whole thing from his grandfather's talk of Luther.) But then there were times, sometimes weeks on end, when even he himself forgot and swam comfortably, easily, through a world that seemed to him not insubstantial. After he'd married Ellen, that queer sense of things had more or less left him, and after his son had been born, the world had become for him positively secure. (By now he knew Nietzsche on consciousness: "a more or less fantastic commentary on an unknown, perhaps unknowable text.") The feel of grass when he hunkered down, rolling a ball to Mark, had such quiddity, such authority, one might have imagined time had stopped, and the sacramental moment toward which everything tended had arrived. When Mark's clumsy hands came together around the ball and he laughed in proud amazement— Ellen standing over by the day-lilies, a book closed on her finger, her bespectacled face turning its smile to them—it was as if the whole world cried out, delighted, changed to music, lively as an animal—the dazzling white walls of the neighbors' houses, the green lace of leaves overhead, blue sky.

At four in the morning, feeling a change in the darkness beyond the windows, Mickelsson decided he'd better quit. There would be another day for painting—and another and another. Days also for writing his blockbuster book. He'd do well to sleep. He put the lid on the paint can, sealed it tight with his heel, then washed out the roller and brush in the upstairs bathroom sink. The bones of the hand that had gripped the paintbrush ached like rotten teeth.

It gave him a queer feeling, moving around alone at this hour in the big, empty house, the house he was painting, preparing for nothing, "just the one of you," as the doc had said. He remembered distinctly, as if she were in the room with him, her girlish laugh. "Strange," he said aloud, then said nothing more, made uneasy by the sound of his voice. He turned out the lights, then—unconsciously massaging his right hand as he walked —went back to the bathroom to wash up, prepare for bed. He got a sudden image of the fat man's tray of money, then of Donnie in the musty-smelling bed, on her knees, her face buried in the pillow, her two hands spreading her buttocks for his entrance from behind. Like a suddenly shrinking aura, his emotion shrank inward and went dark. He stared into the mirror, brushing his teeth. Foam around his mouth, bags under his eyes, the hair on his chest yellow-silver. He was old, debauched, repulsive. No one would ever again see Mickelsson the athlete, big-chested, small-bellied, powerful but not yet fat of shoulder, not yet grossly fat of neck. He looked away. He spat, rinsed his mouth, wiped his face on the towel, then draped it once more over the toilet tank; he'd taken down the towel rack in preparation for painting the walls. He took from the medicine cabinet the sickly violet plastic-and-rubber gum-stimulator, dreariest curse of middle age, leaned toward the mirror again, and dutifully bared his fangs.

He awakened at seven-thirty with a strong sense that something was wrong. At first it seemed to him that the house was on fire, but when he put on his trousers, stiff muscles complaining, and hurried from room to room, he couldn't get even a whiff of smoke, though something else reached his nostrils, the baffling scent he'd encountered once or twice before, of bread baking, or cookies. It was weird: the smell was strong and all around him, like the smell of baking in his grandmother's house, in his childhood; much too strong to be explained by the trickery of mountain wind bringing smells in from the kitchens of his neighbors.

He'd look into it, see if one of the chemists at school could account for it. At the moment he had other things to think about. His sense of something wrong was more intense than before, and now it seemed to him that the wellspring of trouble was under his feet, in the cellar. Only after he'd turned the wooden latch and cautiously opened the cellar door did he realize what it was that he'd expected, the dim memory of a nightmare perhaps: he'd thought the cellar would be hip-deep in rattlesnakes. As he moved tread by tread down the cellar stairs, the center of evil seemed to shift to another part of the house. He stood for several minutes, with the fingertips of his right hand spread on the damp stone wall as if waiting for an earth tremor, then moved to the doorway opening to the cellar chute. The padlock was broken. It was here, then, that his visitors had come in; that was why the kitchen door, which had been open when he'd come in that night, had not been broken. All this time, ever since the break-in, the house had, unbeknownst to him, stood open. He would nail the thing shut, but not till he was rid of this sixth-sense certainty that something was amiss. He went back upstairs.

In the middle of the livingroom he stopped walking and looked around in alarm. If it was not fire or snakes in the cellar, it was a violent outpouring of electricity, some fallen power line, something wrong in the TV. . . . He closed his eyes.

No . . .

He had thought all this time that it was a force outside himself, invisible, crackling, so powerful it bent him almost double and made all his joints cry out with pain. If he'd believed in spirits he'd have said it was the angry native spirit of this place—the earth god, still smarting over the digging of the cellar or the reservoir higher on the mountain; or the waterfall god, across the road, annoyed by the frequent intrusion of tourists (through the livingroom window Mickelsson could see that there was a car out there now, its smooth dark top gleaming in the sunlight, the driver and his family no doubt out there littering, breaking branches from saplings, lining each other up for pictures against the falls)—but he did not, of course, believe in spirits. The malevolent shockwaves he felt all around him in the house must come from within.

No wonder. He, Mickelsson, had fled from the world's complexity to what he'd hoped might be Eden, and he'd found the place polluted, decaying—filled to the tongue-roots with low, slimy secrets: gossips, pompous asses, crudely cunning whores, con-men, idiots, mysterious intruders. He'd taken risks, like the merchant in the parable, who sold all his goods, or like the man who found the treasure on another man's land, and what he'd gotten for his trouble was neither paradise here nor freedom from his troubles in . . .

"Shit!" he whispered, and bolted to the window. The car he'd thought belonged to tourists was gone. Dark green, utterly without ornament. No doubt the Pennsylvania contingent of the I.R.S. "Shit!" he whispered more bitterly than before, and hit the wall with the side of his fist, so hard that his hand went numb.

As if it might help, he showered, shaved, trimmed the hair in his nostrils, cleaned his nails, then dressed as if for an English picnic, white sportcoat, blue slacks, blue ascot, white shoes, took the silver-headed cane and went out to the Jeep, ground the starter till it caught, then drove down, square in the middle of the road, to the Susquehanna bank. He hadn't hit them yet with one of his Binghamton checks. With luck . . . At the drive-in window he wrote a check for seventy-five dollars, drawn to "cash," and handed it to the woman. She gave him the money without a moment's hesitation, and wished him good-day. He drove back onto Main Street and parked in front of Reddon's Drugs, for all to see.

He knocked and knocked. Finally she called out, "Who is it?"

"Pete Mickelsson," he said. "I brought your money."

There was a pause, then she called, "What time is it?"

"Eight-thirty, maybe nine. Donnie, could I come in?"

"Eight-thirty in the *morning*?"

"I brought your money," Mickelsson said, leaning closer to the door. "I brought cash—the full amount. Donnie, I've really got to talk to you."

Silence.

He tapped at the door with one knuckle. "Donnie? Can I come in?" When she said nothing, he called, "Are you alone in there?"

Now she did answer, and to his surprise she was only a few feet from the door. Desire leaped in him, stirring in his chest and groin. "I can't let you in," she said. "Can you slide the money under the door?"

"Let me talk to you for just one minute. That's all I want—just to talk to you. No funny business."

"There's somebody here," she said, barely audible.

He thought about it, not quite believing her but trapped. "Can I talk to you later, then? When will you be free?"

"First slide the money under the door."

He smiled, then got out the bank envelope, removed twenty dollars from it, and slid the rest under the door.

Almost at once she said, "It's not all here."

"When can I see you?"

"Jesus," she whispered. From the way she said it he thought perhaps there was someone in there with her after all.

"Tell me and I'll slide in the rest," he said.

"All right, all right," she said. "How about midnight?"

"You're kidding." It struck him immediately that if she was serious he could stay with her till morning.

"No, I mean it."

He pulled at the twenty-dollar bill, then after an instant bent down and slid it under the door. "OK," he said, his voice thinned by emotion, "midnight."

As he turned from the door, still smiling, she called, "Hay, Prafessor, I just remembered something. I have to go visit my sister tonight. She's in the hospital."

His mouth opened of its own volition and he turned. At last he said, "Bullshit."

"It's the truth," she said. "Listen, tomorrow night, OK? Midnight tomorrow night. I'll make it worth your time."

There was no real doubt that she was laughing at him, both she and whoever it was she had with her, maybe fucking him upright even as they talked; yet, crazily, he wasn't quite sure. He thought of kicking the door in: it wasn't pleasant to think that some son of a bitch—he might never know which one—had listened to his miserable whimperings and plead-ings and would go out and tell all Susquehanna. Better to kick the door in than be a farmboys' joke and never even know whom to thank. She might admire him for it. He was not quite the crawling slave he seemed!

But it wasn't quite positive that someone was with her, and not positive that Donnie, if he kicked her door in, would ever let him visit her again. He turned, blushing, his right hand clenched tight on the handle of his cane, and, when he was sure he had his voice in control, said, "OK, then, tomorrow night. Good."

"Bring cash," she said, but the teasing voice was sweet.

"Don't worry," Mickelsson said.

At the third-floor landing he stopped without knowing why. Though it was bright daylight outside, one could hardly tell here whether it was day or night. He glanced down the hall into increasing dimness, then realized with a start what it was that had made him pause. The fat man, still in his police hat, was bending over at his door, trying to reach something on the carpet, apparently a pamphlet. There was no one in sight, and the fat man, caught up in the labor of bending, appeared unaware of Mickelsson's existence. In the dingy corridor the man seemed even more immense than he'd seemed in his room, but also more vulnerable. His face shone with sweat, and as he bent his knees a little, snatching at the pamphlet, breath-ing in gasps, he seemed about as dangerous as a beached whale. Upright, he'd be six feet tall, maybe more.

"Let me help you with that," Mickelsson said, taking a step in the fat man's direction.

The fat man jerked his head up, cheeks gray as ashes, flapped both arms wildly, and almost fell. Mickelsson froze, the fat man's steel-rimmed glasses aiming at him. By the time his heart had ka-thumped three times, Mickelsson understood that the man could not see him at all.

. . .

For two or three hours he tried to work on his book, but nothing came. He kept looking at his watch, as if tonight were the night he would be seeing Donnie; then he would remember that it was not, and would remember that somewhere—in some bar, in some store, in some sooty, run-down factory—some countrified oaf knew fat, middle-aged Professor Mickelsson's doting shamelessness. Some goaty-smelling cow-herd or plumber or electrician, young or old, fat or thin, bare-chinned or whiskery —some preacher, garbage-man, schoolteacher, lawyer—maybe the very man who'd murdered Professor What's-his-name, or the man who had torn apart Mickelsson's house—somebody, somewhere, had the word on him. For a minute the thought enraged him; then suddenly, as if some blockage in his brain had broken open, he was serene. Her naked image rose before his eyes, and he no more cared about the impression he made on the people of Susquehanna—or Binghamton itself—than Boethius cared for his prison bars, or some silver-eyed saint of the thirteenth century for his grotto's stench of piss.

Again—thesis-antithesis—in came the thought of his grandfather, his own tight-sphinctered, abandoned self (thus Rifkin, once), dryly correct and reasonable as clockparts. Abruptly, Mickelsson got up from his desk, got out his dropcloths, roller, and paint, and, every aching muscle crying protest, set to work. When he was able to write he would write.

His lunacy would wane, this preposterous, self-destructive business with Donnie Matthews. When he imagined himself married to her he almost might have laughed—would have, except for the sudden, sharp chest-pain he felt at the thought of losing her. Biological programming, he knew; nothing more. The older male turning to the potential child-bearer. God did not demand that one approve of being born a primate; He demanded only—and exacted—obedience. Ah, for a little common dignity, Mickelsson thought. He shook his head, ironic, lest some well-intentioned angel mistake his meaning.

Jessica Stark's late husband, in the photograph she'd one night shown him at her house, was young, almost comically clean-jawed, like Dudley Do-Right. He had smiling, slightly impish eyes, crooked teeth. Though he was a treeman—"forestry," she'd said with a tone of respect that struck Mickelsson as odd—he had a classy look suited to her own. He looked English, though he wasn't. An American from Michigan. But one could imagine him speaking with an Oxford accent, talking about cricket or Rugby with the Queen. Not that that was fair. He had one of those boyish, forestry-people names: "Buzzy." He did not look like a young man who'd played football, though perhaps, somewhere like Yale, he'd been on the rowing team. Shadowy and unreal as he seemed, now that he was dead, he had left, scattered here and there throughout the house, bold signs of his existence: African drums, long spears, painted masks. Much of his work, Jessica had told him, he'd done in Africa. "He wasn't exactly political," she said, "but of course because of the nature of his work he knew everyone."

One of her colleagues in sociology had been listening—it was a large party; otherwise, Mickelsson knew now, the man wouldn't have been there. "How could a man work in Africa and not be political?" he asked. He had a blunt, gar-nosed, tough New York face, a curiously arrogant way of lifting his pock-marked chin.

"*I* don't know," Jessica said. "Somehow he managed."

The man leered, smug, and in what appeared to be a rare burst of politeness decided to drop it. He let his hooded eyes drift over paintings, furniture, the drapes on the windows; then he floated away to find more lively conversation.

"Who the hell was that?" Mickelsson had asked. He felt again now the protectiveness—the witless leap of anguish like a dog's—that had stirred in him then.

Jessica said, watching her departing colleague, "Him? I'm not quite sure what his name is. Danytz, I think. One of the Marx brothers." She smiled, momentarily wicked, her dimple flashing, then put back her studiously fair look. Except for Jessica, the whole Sociology Department was Marxist. It was not a subject she cared to dwell on. "They're decent enough people," she said, and shrugged.

"I'm sure," Mickelsson said. The man who'd just left them stood grinning, jabbing his long, thick finger into a black man's chest. Apparently he and the black man were friends.

Jessica said, "Come, meet the Bryants. You'll like them."

Mickelsson had liked them a good deal, perhaps simply because Jessica liked them, or perhaps because that night Phil Bryant, in his melodious, down-cellar voice, had chosen to argue with Geoffrey Tillson about whales; and for all his scorn of Tillson, Mickelsson had liked Jessica Stark even more than before for the way she'd tried to help poor Tillson save face.

"But heck," Tillson said, his smile wildly twitching, "how can anyone come out against women's per*fume*? Never mind protein for the Japanese people—" He twisted his silver-bearded head toward Mickelsson and winked, then quickly, when Mickelsson gave him no response, poked his face back into Bryant's. When Tillson shook his finger, the cloth of his suitcoat pulled against the hump on his back as if the hump were stone. "Sentimentality will be the ruin of our civilization," he said, grinning crazily, as if afraid to let anyone know he really meant it, though his voice insisted. "You weep over the whales—big, intelligent mammals. Who weeps for the thousands and thousands of cows out there dying in Wyoming and Oklahoma to make Burger King Whoppers? Granted, steers may be comparatively stupid—but down with intellectual snobbery! They're feeling creatures! Did you ever watch a cow with her calf?"

"It's true, Peter," Jessica said, seeing Mickelsson's look.

Ruth, Tillson's wife, cried out sharply, "We're vegetarians, you know." Only when she spoke did Mickelsson notice that she was present—round-backed, big-bosomed, arrow-faced. Her shiny eyes seemed all anguish.

"Then you shouldn't approve of eating whales," Phil Bryant said reasonably. He stood comfortably erect, like the former army captain he was, and he smiled as if he took them all for fellow officers.

"We don't! Do we, Geoffrey?"

"But per*fume*! *That's* the issue!" Tillson raved.

"Oh, come on, Geoffrey," Jessica said, and laughed. Light seemed to gather around her.

Mickelsson backed off, briefly catching Phil Bryant's eye, then winking at Jessica as he turned to find other conversation.

"He's not a bit crazy," she'd said later. "He's self-conscious, so he puts on a show. I imagine we all sound fiercer than we are, at times." She gave him a sidelong glance.

Poor woman, Mickelsson thought now, almost prayerful. Fall coolness had come to the mountain, and he was down on one knee, putting a log in the livingroom stove. He would sleep on the livingroom couch again tonight, the bedrooms upstairs newly painted or in disorder, stripped down and waiting for his brush.

God grant her someone worthy of her beauty, he thought. Someone full of energy in bed, someone like his own . . .

Everybody's own, he corrected himself, and reached into his right-side pocket for a Di-Gel.

He put away the poker, closed the door of the stove, crossed to switch off the livingroom light, the last still burning, then stood a moment thinking, unconsciously rubbing his sore shoulders and arms. Now the sky was beginning to gray. If it weren't for the mountains, he might already be looking at sunrise. How peaceful it was, he thought, then realized he was mistaken. The house was full of noises and unnamable trouble. A wind had come up, a wash of sound just wintry enough to make things whisper and creak, much like voices. Something alive and almost certainly large ran startled through the cellar, knocking something from its place, a dull clunk, then fleeing. Then, somewhere across the valley or maybe up on the mountain behind the house, he heard gunshots, two in quick succession, then a third. He had a feeling there had been other gunshots earlier. He listened hard, almost not breathing, but except for the sounds of the house stirring, he heard nothing more.

He got a crystal-clear mental image of the fire escape leading to the girl's window.

He went over to the couch, lay down and pulled the afghan over him. When he was almost asleep, free-falling through space, hearing faraway angry shouts, he was jerked back to wakefulness by a roar of motorcycles on the road out front, or maybe in the rough field beyond—four or five of them, from the sound of it, crackling and whining like chain-saws digging in. *Kids,* he thought, annoyed as an old man. Of their own accord, his fists clenched and his back bent painfully. Rattlesnakes, housebreakers, animals in the cellar, big-chested big-cocked devils on dirt bikes . . .

He closed his eyes, praying that he be spared bad dreams.

PART TWO

1

"But isn't it true," Blassenheim said, his hand still in the air, lest anyone get the idea of interrupting him, "that Aristotle's just as much a fascist as Plato was, it's just their manners are different?" Michael Nugent slid his eyes toward the ceiling in despair. Blassenheim continued, registering Nugent's comment but not persuaded that he'd made any mistake, "Like in *Nicomachean Ethics*, where he tells us that 'courage' is the mean between 'foolhardiness' and 'cowardice,' what's his authority but his own aristocratic style—I mean, button-down collars, like 'Let's not make a *scene*, my dear fellow'—shit like that. I mean, what he's always saying is 'Be reasonable.' Just like my mother." The class laughed, all but Nugent, who dramatically clenched his fists and squeezed his eyes shut. Blassenheim looked around, pleased (on the whole), moving just his eyes, and remembered to lower his hand, then hurried on. "How do we know it's correct to be reasonable except that Aristotle says so? Look at the berserkers—you know, those Viking guys. They took this drug or something and when they went into battle they were crazy people, and maybe they'd get killed—lot of times they didn't, people were too scared—but either way the Vikings trashed all Europe. Or look at those guys in Vietnam that would throw themselves on a grenade to save their buddies—*that* wasn't reasonable, or even if it was, it wasn't why they did it. And the same thing for cowardice, only vice versa. How does Aristotle know it's not more reasonable than killing people? He doesn't even question it. All he's really saying is '*Our* kind of chaps don't *do* that kind of thing.' " Again the class laughed.

John Kalen raised his eyes from his doodle with a look of surprise. "That's stupid," he said. "Running away never solved anything!"

"Maybe not if an atomic bomb's coming straight at you," Blassenheim said.

The class laughed more loudly. Even Nugent half smiled, glancing at Mickelsson. Biamonte, in the right rear corner of the room, leaned over his desk, stomping his feet in applause. If he let this progress, Mickelsson saw, things would soon be out of hand. Yet he did nothing, merely turned to look out the window. The tree in the courtyard was a blaze of yellow now. Soon they'd be looking out at snow. The room was already like a classroom in midwinter, stuffy and overheated.

The memory of waking with Donnie came to him, her blue-white body a deadweight on his own, her hair silvery in the early-morning light. After he'd left her he'd covered six pages with single-spaced outlining and notes, then scribbled additions, before driving in to school.

When he turned back to the class, Brenda Winburn, in the chair-desk beside Blassenheim's, was slipping a note into Blassenheim's fingers, her face dead-pan, as if Mickelsson were some bullying but not very dangerous cop. Mickelsson thought about it, or rather, paused to register it—in the room's heavy warmth, no real thought broke through—then cleared his throat and asked amiably, "Are you saying, then, that 'it's all relative'?" A crazy thing to say, he knew even as he said it; an expression so cloudy in student minds one hardly knew where to start on it. It was a mark of his weary recklessness that he'd deliberately introduced the befuddling phrase—language that would blow up the arena, to paraphrase Whitehead.

But Blassenheim rushed on, like one of those movie-cartoon characters running on, oblivious, beyond the edge of the cliff. "I'm just saying it's not right, that's all. I mean, logic's got its place, like when you're a kid playing with an Erector set, but a lot of times it can trick you." More laughter. Mickelsson quashed it with a look. "What seems reasonable to a tsar," the boy pressed on urgently, leaning forward, almost whining, "may not necessarily seem reasonable to his peasants, but what can they do? He tells them, 'Be reasonable,' with all his cossacks around him with their swords and big black horses, so the peasants have to stand there and look reasonable."

Mickelsson shook his head. Class discussion was not his favorite mode, especially when the class contained a Blassenheim; yet he couldn't quite find it in his heart to squelch all this, get down, finally, to business. Perhaps, to take the optimistic view, he was mellowing. Or perhaps what Garret had said at Blickstein's party had gotten to him. ". . . they keep comin and comin, like termites. One morning you wake up and look around and—no castle!" Garret was a good deal more confident than Mickelsson that sheer unmethodical will could flatten castle walls. But Blassenheim's reckless eagerness—even granting its measure of exhibition-ism—was its own excuse. He could not bring himself, this early in the game, to call Time, start sorting through Blassenheim's morass of claims. In the back of his mind floated the thought of his own son, at least as urgent and concerned about Truth as young Blassenheim, though quieter, more restrained in his style; not that it mattered: his professors cut him down, or listened to what he said with their brains turned off, as Mickels-son was tempted to listen to Blassenheim, thinking all the while of how much there was yet to get through before midterm, then finals.

He said reasonably, hearing in his voice the tyrannical patience he'd used all those years on his wife, "So tell me, Alan. Where *is* it, if not from reason, that we get these value assertions you keep telling me we're in some sense right to make?"

He sensed the irritable impatience of the class. They were a difficult herd, one moment laughing, as if Time were Eternity, the next insisting that he for Christ's sakes get on with it.

Again Blassenheim gave that left-right glance like a basketball player's just before a shot—or no, something less competitive: the look of a waiter carefully threading his way through a crowd with a loaded tray, or a New York Marathon runner making sure he doesn't trip those around him. "I don't know," the boy said, "maybe the wisdom of the whole community, like, tested over time. You know what I mean?" His expression became silly, as if he thought he might have said that before, and he glanced at Brenda Winburn, who'd turned to stare dully out the window again; then he pushed on, seemingly despite his better judgment: "Like when Kierke-gaard talks about Abraham and Isaac, I think he got it wrong. I mean like *he* thinks what's good about Abraham's walking to Mount Moriah is that sometimes a person has to listen to God, metaphorically or whatever, and shut his ears to what the ordinary person might think. But what *I* think—"

"Now hang on," Mickelsson said, "we're getting a little far afield here. Let's go back to—" It was odd—startling—that Blassenheim had read *Fear and Trembling*. It was that thought that made Mickelsson pause and gave Blassenheim an entrance.

"Just let me finish," Blassenheim said, "just this one, like, sentence." He threw a panicky look left and right, checking the class. Nugent covered his eyes with one hand and stretched his mouth back as if he thought his classmate was, incredibly, faking stupidity.

Mickelsson helplessly shrugged, deferring to Blassenheim, or giving in to weariness, surprise at this unexpected turn of things, or to the stuffiness of the room. The boy could see for himself that the class had lost patience. (It was really with Mickelsson himself, he knew, that the class had lost patience. It was he that allowed the class to flounder, yet on quizzes gave low grades. In his mailbox this morning he'd found two more drop cards.)

Blassenheim said, "What *I* think is, all that's important about the story is it's a parable against human sacrifice, and what makes it right isn't that Abraham listened to the whisper in his ear, which was really pretty crazy, but that all these generations of scribes and revisers kept agreeing with the parable, looking at, like, their personal experience, and listening to the whisper of God in their own ears—and they left it in, so the parable got, like, *truer*."

Mickelsson felt gooseflesh rising. (He was admittedly an easy lay for notions of that kind. It was the point at which he and Nietzsche parted company. Say the words *common sense* or *community* and his eyes would grow moist, not that, in real life, he knew any community he did not hate.) "That's not bad," he said. He glanced around the room. Apparently nobody else had gotten gooseflesh. Blassenheim was looking at him in-tently, as if hoping for an A—not the common kind of A; an A straight from God. Michael Nugent, behind him, sat leaning on his fist, morosely waiting for graduation, success, old age. Susan Kunstler, behind Nugent, was asleep.

"Alan's got the start of an interesting idea here," Mickelsson told the class, feeling only a flicker of irritation at their sluggishness. (An idea that left much to be desired, of course; not exactly up on the metaethical, methodological, and epistemological issues central in philosophical ethics since 1903—but never mind.) He rose from the desk and moved toward the blackboard, looking around for chalk as he went. The light outside the window seemed to have brightened. "Let me try to rephrase it and develop it a little, in case any of you didn't quite catch it." He found a tiny pebble of chalk in the tray and wrote on the blackboard, *Intersubjectivity*, underlined it, then drew a line and, at the end of it, wrote and underlined *Verification*. "Now watch closely," he said. "Nothing in my hat, nothing up my sleeve . . ." Dutifully, without pleasure, they laughed.

As he spoke it came to him that Brenda Winburn, who'd seemed to be staring at him with fierce hostility—eyelids half lowered, long dark lashes veiling the eyes—was not seeing him, in fact, but gazing inward. Relief leaped up in him, and he began to speak more quickly and heartily.

Considering the heat, Mickelsson spoke with remarkable animation and focus, making circles in the air with the end of his pipe, putting Blassenheim's cloudy notion into language one could build on, make use of. Yet a part of his mind drifted free of all he said, half dreaming. Suppose it were true that God was really up there, a "lure for our feeling," as Whitehead, not to mention Aristotle, had fondly maintained—bespectacled old Jahweh, scratching his chin through his mountains of beard, watching Blassenheim climb carefully, shakily toward him, feeling his way around boulders, scooting downward now and then on loose scree. Mickelsson's voice resounded as in a cavern. He listened as if to a stranger, aware that he was in a sense talking in his sleep. At the edge of his consciousness, as on old, blurry film, he saw Brenda Winburn pulling herself deeper and deeper, with powerful strokes, like a pearl diver, down past the kingdoms of mammals and fish, down past the strangest of antique, blind serpents, toward God only knew what primordial, half-animate beast. He saw her reach out and seize something, and the next moment it seemed that what she held in her fist, swimming up, was the bright yellow courtyard, the tree.

He acknowledged Nugent's hand. He felt, though he did not hear, the collective groan.

"It's interesting, all that about shared community values tested over time," Nugent said. He sat rigid, slightly tilted to one side, stiff with concentration, his arms—poking out of the short-sleeved blue shirt—very white, his face and elbows pink. "But what I wanted to say is . . . it doesn't seem to me you can call either Plato or Aristotle a fascist." He was indignant that anyone should think otherwise. His pale, lashless eyes grew round. "The point is . . . the point is, Plato and Aristotle have a test you can try out on your own, like a repeatable experiment in chemistry. They start with the same assumption everybody makes, even dogs and cats, that some things may be true and some things may not be; only Plato and Aristotle are better than dogs and cats at thinking logically."

The pressure of his nervousness made Nugent's face redder and redder, and he began, just perceptibly, to sway, eyes rapidly blinking. Mickelsson lowered his gaze, lest his looking at the boy increase his discomfort. "It's bad to dismiss them out of hand," Nugent said, "dismiss the whole idea of discernible truth just because one doesn't want to go through the trouble of thinking." Blassenheim turned, injured, to look at Nugent. Hadn't Blassenheim stood up for Truth just last week, and Nugent, in his arrogance, made fun of the 'eternal verities'? Nugent hurried on, "It's the assumption that some things are true—discernibly true —that keeps us going, makes life even possible." He flashed a panicky grin, catching Mickelsson's brief glance. "I mean, that's where we get our sense of dignity, from the feeling that we're *good*, the feeling that our team's better than the other team. Angels of Life versus Angels of Death, things like that. But the thing is—this is what I wanted to say—even though Plato and Aristotle mean to be logical and reasonable, so you can repeat their processes, when you really look at it nothing ever works. It's as if between their time and ours all the names of the chemicals got shifted around, so that what we call oxygen is really lithium hydride, and . . . For instance, take the word *moral*. What's the connection between the way Plato uses it in the *Symposium* or Aristotle uses it in the *Ethics* or *Poetics* and how we use it now, when we say 'She hasn't got any morals'? Or take 'virtue.' "

Mickelsson raised his head, about to break in, but Nugent pressed forward, raising his voice a little. "They may work differently—Plato's like a poet, or the person who writes a national anthem, and Aristotle's more like a novelist, or a symphony composer—or anyhow that's how it seems to me. . . ." He looked proud of himself. No harm. For him it was an original insight. "But all the same when they say 'virtue,' they seem to mean more or less the same thing. If Kierkegaard uses it at all it's like somebody handed him the wrong test tube." *Kierkegaard, Kierkegaard,* Mickelsson thought. *Is that shit still "in"?* "Or what does a person mean by 'virtue' when he's talking about the greatest good for the greatest number? I guess Aristotle wouldn't say, any more than Jean-Paul Sartre, that people are necessarily born with virtues—if they were, Aristotle wouldn't have had to write that instruction book for his son—but in Sartre, from what I can tell, it's like virtue is something that just vanished out of the universe." *Sartre! Christ save us! Sartre!* "That's the reason Kierkegaard's so strange: he tells you right out that he doesn't know what virtue is, maybe it's God's whisper in Abraham's ear, maybe it's just insanity. I think he"—Nugent nodded toward Blassenheim—"might be right: maybe Aristotle really didn't *know* what he was talking about, he was just saying how we do things in Athens or wherever. He even uses that word—'we,' like 'the reason we believe'—as if he were speaking for all grown-ups. But if he *did* really know what he was talking about, it seems like it must be lost knowledge, like how to fuse brick. It's like what Kafka says, there's this machine that really used to work, but it doesn't anymore—something fell off and nobody noticed, or the parts are worn out and nobody knows how to make new ones. It's like words, language, ideas that used to make perfectly good sense—" He raised both hands, as if to guard himself from something invisible. "I realize it's confusing, the way I'm saying it, but—" He abruptly looked down, then with a jerk, his face whitening, sat back in his chair. "That's all."

There was an embarrassed silence. For a moment Mickelsson couldn't think how to break it. His stomach was in a knot. Some of the students were looking at him, waiting; some looked at the floor. He pushed from his mind the observation that too many chairs were empty. At last he nodded and said seriously, "Very good, Mr. Nugent." He couldn't seem to remember the boy's first name. After another moment he nodded again and said, "Very interesting!" He glanced around the room. "Anyone like to comment?"

Miss Mariani raised her hand, looking troubled.

"Yes?"

"Are we supposed to have read the *Poetics*? According to the assignment sheet you passed out—"

"Mr. Nugent's been reading ahead," Mickelsson answered. "Reading and thinking. A practice I commend to you."

Miss Winburn was again passing a note to Alan Blassenheim. Mickelsson gave her a look. To his surprise, she smiled brightly, her teeth large and perfect, startling against her tan.

Like someone who has just confessed some terrible crime, or avenged a murder, Nugent sat gravely still, with his eyes closed.

Mickelsson looked at the clock. "Well—" he said.

Sudden, loud rustling of papers and books, a raucous scraping of chairs. The students got to their feet—all but Nugent—and shuffled, beginning to talk now, toward the door. Then a strange thing happened. As the students filed out, Alan Blassenheim, passing behind Nugent, paused, looking down at him, then draped his hand for a moment over Nugent's upper arm. Nugent opened his pale eyes, throwing a look of alarm up to Mickelsson, who merely gazed back at him, hardly knowing how to respond. Blassenheim, unaware of the effect he'd set off, moved on, loose-limbed, graceful as a dancer, toward the door, turning once, smiling at something another student said, saying something in return. His shoulders, in the dark athletic jacket, were immense.

Now Brenda Winburn, moving in a kind of side-step between the rows of desk-chairs, glided behind and past Nugent, her tanned, amazingly smooth face turned toward Mickelsson. For the second time today, as if she and Mickelsson had some secret, she smiled. She turned from him, swinging her smooth hair, and, just behind Blassenheim, disappeared into the noisy current of the hallway. At last, abruptly, as if someone had told him to, Nugent stood up, wiped his forehead, then his eyes, looking at the floor like someone stunned, mechanically gathered his papers and books, and left. Only now did Mickelsson come to himself and rise to leave.

"What was that curious phrase?" he asked himself, then remembered. Angels of Life; Angels of Death.

He'd meant to spend no more than a few minutes in his office, just drop off his mail as he always did, ritually transport it from his box to his desk, glancing at return addresses as he walked, on the slim chance that there might be something he'd take pleasure in opening—a letter from his daughter or son, perhaps—then get out of there quickly, before some student could catch him and pin him to his chair with questions, requests for favors, reasonable demands he couldn't decently refuse. But almost as soon as he was inside the door, looking down miserably at his ex-wife's handwriting (a demand that he send money, he knew without opening it), there stood Tillson, poking his silver-bearded head in, smiling his murderous, fake smile like the Keebler Cookie Elf gone insane.

"May I speak to you, Pete?" he asked, and grinned harder, his eyebrows jumping up and down as if he were clowning, which he was not. He wore an expensive but rumpled black suit, white shirt, a tie with narrow stripes; a kind of hunchbacked dandy. No doubt part of what was wrong with him, Mickelsson had decided some time ago, was that it took so much energy to keep up the opinion that it was the world out there that was misshapen. Not a generous thought, Mickelsson would admit. But Blassenheim was right, why be reasonable?

"Come in," Mickelsson said, and, when Tillson had slipped through the door, not opening it farther, "sit down."

"Thank you!" Tillson said. "I'll only take a minute of your valuable time." He bent his knees to sit, but then, with his rear end hovering over the chair, two fingers of each hand raising the material of his coal-black suitpants to protect what little remained of the crease, he caught sight of the huge pile of mail on Mickelsson's desk and, eyes widening, cried, "Wow!" He was pointing now, looking at Mickelsson in disbelief.

"Saving it for a rainy day," Mickelsson said.

"Gosh, Pete," Tillson said, "don't you feel that's a little . . . unethical?" He flashed the grin again, slanty eyes glittering, like a fierce debater pretending he never shot to kill.

"No doubt," Mickelsson said casually. "Was that what you wanted to talk about?"

After an instant Tillson seated himself, once again flashed his exaggerated smile, and said, "Not directly." His tongue flicked out, wetting his lower lip. "I thought maybe we should have a chat about . . . Senior Personnel?" He tipped his head, letting his smile come in at an angle.

Mickelsson waited.

"You've been getting our notices?" He tapped the tips of his fingers together, eyebrows jerking, smile painfully stretched.

Mickelsson glanced at the pile on his desk. "I'm sure they're here someplace."

Tillson laughed thinly, as if gleefully, and nodded. "Yes, I know meetings are a nuisance. Personally, I *hate* them! But if we don't all of us pull together on this—" He leaned far to one side, smiling hard, never blinking, his whole body wearing an expression so oddly devious that Mickelsson was abruptly reminded of what Edie Bryant had told him, that Tillson had a wife and a mistress who knew each other, were in fact good friends. It was all very open and twentieth-century except that, she said, Tillson and the mistress were forever sneaking in extra assignations, not telling the wife. "That's ridiculous," Mickelsson had said at once, sorry to have lent his ear to such talk. "Isn't it?" Edie had laughed, innocently delighted.

The memory and Mickelsson's sense of guilt made him suddenly blunt. "You keep scheduling the meetings on Fridays," he said. "I don't come in on Fridays."

Tillson's laugh might lead one to wonder if he were actually making an effort to appear insane, but he splashed his hands open and stretched them, palms up, toward Mickelsson, begging him to show a little sense. "It's the only time the whole committee has free!" he said. "Gosh, I know it's not ideal—"

"*I'm* not free on Fridays," Mickelsson broke in. "Thursdays and Fridays are my days for research."

"Research is important, I grant you," Tillson said, "and believe me, we'd be nowhere if it weren't for the reputation we get from people like yourself! On the other hand, these matters of hiring and firing, tenure and promotion—we need your in-put, Pete. Golly, leave such matters in the hands of the department's weaker sisters, people like myself, ha ha—"

"I see your point, but I don't come in on Fridays," Mickelsson said. He put his arms on the chair-arms, as if to rise.

"Pete, you're being rigid," Tillson said sharply. He raised an index finger and shook it, fakely grinning. "You're new to the department, and of course you're a 'famous man' and all that, so we all like to give you the benefit of the doubt. But we have to work together—that's civilization. I know you're a man of principle, an idealist—" Accidentally but quite horribly, as if his face had gone completely out of control, he sneered.

Mickelsson looked hard at the man, confounded by the sudden conviction that Tillson hated him. It was no cause for alarm; Mickelsson had tenure and probably more clout, if it should come to that, than the chairman himself. Probably the discovery shouldn't even have come as a surprise to him: professionally, Tillson was of the enemy camp, a "linguistic atomist"—so he pretentiously styled himself. No wonder if he minded Mickelsson's success, such as it was, a success which must in any case seem to Tillson fraudulent, "a shrill pitch to the philosophical right," as some metaphor-scrambling fool had once written of Mickelsson's ethics book. And of course it was true too that Mickelsson had never pretended to feel friendly toward Tillson—had perhaps been, at times, barely civil. Nevertheless he was sickened for an instant by the realization that Tillson hated him. Not sickened for good reason; simply a cry of his genetic programming. Thanatos, vulnerability . . . a dreary business.

Now it came to Mickelsson that he was looking at the chairman— the black suit and too fashionable beard, the monstrous fake smile and piously tapping fingertips—with an expression of undisguised contempt. He had a choice to make: he could negotiate, take back that look of disgust, pour oil on troubled waters; or he could confirm the charge or, at any rate, innuendo—could admit to Tillson and himself at once that he did not care in the least what Geoffrey Tillson and all his kind, spawn of G. E. Moore and Bertrand Russell, might think.

Though Mickelsson had by now made his face expressionless—might even have seemed to a casual observer to be studying Tillson with a friendly half-smile—the truth was that a peculiar coldness, clammy as cave-walls, had come over him, an indifference that finally had nothing much to do with the nervously leering little scholar. Along with the indifference came a feeling of power, invulnerability like a dead man's. "Surely your feeling of righteousness is a little misplaced," he said. He watched Tillson's pink tongue dart across his lips again, silver eyebrows shooting up, then continued, "You know it takes me an hour to get in from Susquehanna, and an hour to get home again, and at least an hour for those meetings where nothing ever happens." Though Tillson was showing alarm, he pressed on coolly, "You know I've set aside Thursdays and Fridays for my own research and writing. You set up those meetings knowing I can't come to them—not even wanting me to come to them, I suspect, since my opinions would surely be opposed to your own—" He checked Tillson's eyes and took pleasure in the look of amazement there. "And then you come in and use my 'valuable time,' as you call it, complaining about my failure to attend."

Tillson's smile became crazier than ever. "What?" he said, straightening a little. His eyebrows stopped jittering, frozen in circumflex.

"I'm not interested in offending you," Mickelsson said. He felt his indifference increasing by leaps and bounds. "All I'm saying is"—he pointed at the calendar on the office wall—"you've scheduled the meetings for a time when I can't come. That's your mistake, not mine. And now, if that's all the business we have between us . . ."

Tillson raised his finger again, then changed his mind, leaned his head to one side, and slowly lowered his hand. "Mickelsson," he said, as if threatening, "you're a strange man. Stranger than you think!" He suddenly stopped smiling. "All right," he said, and abruptly stood up, fists clenched. His eyes glittered brighter than ever. "I appreciate your frankness."

Mickelsson rose.

At the door, Tillson said, "We shouldn't be"—he paused, hunting for the word, looking wildly dishonest as he did so—"enemies. I'll admit, now that we've talked about it, I may have been a little in the wrong."

Mickelsson nodded curtly, feeling redness in his face.

"We all have to try to get along, you know," Tillson said. "None of us is perfect."

"No doubt that's true."

Tillson thought about it, decided against comment—one hand went up furtively to the corner of one eye—and after a moment's further hesitation, he nodded sharply and left. Mickelsson's arms and legs began to shake. He bent over the vast mess of mail.

Only the back of his mind was aware that someone stood just outside his door looking in. "What was all that about?" Jessica Stark's voice asked.

"Oh, hello," he said. Guilt crawled over him. How fitting that she of all people should catch him at such a moment—Mickelsson the Viking, the Prussian Junker, reducing poor humpbacked Geoffrey Tillson to tears. Well, better Jessica than Edie Bryant.

Jessica was looking down the corridor after Tillson. Now she turned to look in at Mickelsson again. "Mind if I come in?"

"Do," he said, a little querulous. He picked up the first piece of paper that came to hand and, scowling hard, pretended to read. *Proudly, the Department of Music Presents* . . . He put it down again.

She closed the door behind her and stood half leaning against it, her left hand on the doorknob. "Is something wrong?" she asked. She wore, today, a beige turtleneck, dark brown skirt, skin-tight soft leather boots.

"No," he said, "nothing wrong," and reached for his pipe. It occurred to him that if he were dying of lung or throat cancer none of this would matter. His father had died of cancer. Pancreas. People had come in great crowds to the hospital; the windows and tables, even the floor at one end of the room, were jammed with flowerpots.

Mickelsson said, "I had a fight with Tillson, as I imagine you saw." He smiled sourly, then put a match to the tobacco in his pipe. "Poor bastard, he doesn't deserve me."

"Don't be silly," she said. He registered an interesting complexity in her tone. By an act of will she supported him as if instinctively, but clearly she had private reservations. He wondered if perhaps it was a trick she'd learned with her late husband.

"Well, anyway . . ." he began, then shifted: "So how have you been?"

She said, "You're trembling."

"You think I'm trembling, you should see Tillson!" He laughed, faking pleasure, and lowered the pipe.

Her eyes narrowed and one side of her mouth went up, not quite in a smile. "You like fighting with him, don't you." She came a step nearer.

"It's always good to keep in shape," he said.

"I think it's a little like a fifth-grader picking on a third-grader."

He stood stupidly gazing at her forehead. Her dark hair glowed; her scent brought a wave of unhappiness. He could think of no witty response.

She turned from him, irritably glancing at the papers on his desk. Something caught her attention. "Look," she said, "the Swissons are giving a concert." Then, after a pause: "You want to go?"

He looked down at the paper. *Proudly, the Department of Music Presents* . . . "I could," he said, suddenly thinking of Donnie Matthews. "Do you?"

"Sure," she said with a shrug, "why not?" She seemed to be working something out in her mind.

"I'll pick you up, then," he said, lifting his chin and sweeping one arm out like a Congressman performing.

At once he got an image of Jessica seated in her mink coat in his old, beat-up Jeep, but before he could take back his offer, she said, looking in horror at his desk-clock, checking it against her wristwatch, "Jesus! Gotta run!"

After she was gone, Mickelsson stared for a time at the mail on his desk, his mind a blank. When he came to again, he thought: *She's right; I should apologize to Tillson.* He took out his checkbook and hastily wrote a check to his ex-wife, addressed and stamped the envelope, and sealed the check inside. *Dear God, let it clear,* he thought. The letter from Ellen he dropped in the wastebasket unopened.

Then he saw the letter from Finney. He reached for it at once.

The photograph was startling. Young people of college age, some perhaps only highschool students, lay everywhere in attitudes of passive resistance; a few sat foetus-like, hands over their heads. In the foreground two angry-looking members of a SWAT squad were lifting a young woman by the hands and feet. They were helmeted, white billy clubs hanging from their belts. At the center of it all, the only protester standing upright, was Mickelsson's son. Though the picture was black and white, Mickelsson saw the boy's hair as flame red, flying out wildly in all directions under the top-hat. In one hand stretched out toward the photographer's camera, the boy held the remains of his Rolleiflex. His expression was solemn, the eyes just dark shadows, the mouth a straight line of resignation, as if the violence done to his camera had nothing to do with the police or, indeed, with anything terrestrial. The standing figure seemed ritually still and formal, clothed in the apparel of a by-gone age. It was as if he were not really there, a trick of light.

When he phoned the university, Mickelsson could learn nothing. Mark hadn't visited the dorm in a week; no one could say whether or not he'd been going to his classes. Somehow Mickelsson had known Mark would have vanished. He phoned Ellen. She wept. "You must be very proud," she said. "Ellen," he said, "try to be reasonable!" "For God's sake," she said, "why don't you die or something?" After that she cried for a long time and couldn't answer when he spoke. Then The Comedian came on.

"Is that you, Professor?"

"Hello, Willard."

He remembered the first time he'd seen the boy, out in the hallway of some grubby theater during the first intermission, lighting the cigarette in Ellen's cigarette holder, Ellen puffing furiously, sucking her cheeks in, bending her head to him—he was a good nine inches shorter than she was and as skinny as she was fat. Both of them were dressed in black and white and both of them wore dyed black hair. Neither of them had noticed Mickelsson standing by the ticket-table, drinking coffee from a paper cup, getting ready to say hello. He hadn't been expected, had intended to surprise and please her. It was an evening of plays—*Three Radical Plays for Women*—that Ellen had produced, and apparently Ellen and her friend agreed with Mickelsson that the evening was going badly. When Ellen, looking up past her smoke, had seen Mickelsson, she'd frozen, eyes caught in an evil wince. Slowly—ratlike, as it seemed to Mickelsson—the boy had turned to see what was wrong. That instant told everything. There was some fish he'd read about in his childhood: the male impregnated the female then docilely let her eat him. The boy touched Ellen's waist as he looked at Mickelsson. She apparently hadn't yet told him that she hated to be touched. All women, according to Ellen, hated to be touched, and all men were touchers. Women, she said, were lunar.

Willard said now, his voice crackling with emotion-held-in-check, "I should think you'd know by now that El doesn't appreciate these phone-calls."

"Good dog," Mickelsson said. He was thinking of German shepherd watchdogs, but the joke was admittedly obscure.

There was a pause; then the boy said, "If you have things to say to El, I'd be grateful if you'd relay them through me."

"I'll bet you would," Mickelsson said.

"In future, if you don't mind—"

"I do mind, actually."

"I'm not too interested, *act*ually, in what you do and do not mind."

One could imagine him thrusting his beard forward, eyes hooded. He would be standing bent-backed with the intensity of his emotion, maybe rising in slow, precarious rhythm onto the balls of his feet, then down again onto his heels. He wore pointy black shoes, black suspenders.

"Occasionally it's necessary for a man and his ex-wife to discuss the welfare of their children," Mickelsson said. "You wouldn't understand that, given your proclivity to fucking barren mares. Don't be needlessly offended! I'm impressed by your Jesuitical devotion to your, so to speak, sex object—"

The phone went dead.

Mickelsson hung up, then looked at the newspaper photo of his son again, then folded it carefully and put it away in his billfold.

His graduate class in medical ethics had eight students. It met in a windowless room on the library's fourth floor, around a dark, polished table. If he was lucky he did not have to sit next to or across from Gail Edelman, a bright young woman with whom, unfortunately, he had once spent the night. Generally, though the class was supposed to be a seminar, Mickelsson lectured, or rather, read from old notes. He would arrange the ashtray, pipe tobacco, pipe knife, matches, and notecards in front of him, hardly looking up as late-comers entered, and would skim through his notes, organizing his thoughts—he was never completely unprepared, in fact, but no one could doubt that for the most part he was winging it, not so easy with graduate students as with freshmen but possible as long as he alone held the floor—and when everyone was settled and the talk had died down, he would look up and say, formally—the formal tone indispensable to his ruse—"Good afternoon." "Good afternoon," they would respond, not quite words, more like a collective *Mmmm'n*. In just two weeks now their reports would begin, and he'd be off the hook, temporarily at least. If he had fifteen students, the maximum for the course, he'd be off the hook for good; but God sends only what He sends. In the brief moment when he looked up at them he got their placement, Gail Edelman in the far corner, where she often sat, these days, C. J. Wolters, his forty-year-old ex-highschool teacher across from him, fat Pinky Stearns profusely sweating to his immediate left, Janet Something to his right (it was hard to learn names when one never took attendance, never called on a student, never gave spot quizzes). . . . Of his eight students, only two, Stearns and Wolters, were male. In the old days, when Mickelsson had first begun teaching, nearly all graduate students in philosophy were men.

He lit his pipe, cool and reserved as an officer of the Gestapo, carefully squared his deck of notecards, and began.

"We observed last week that before we can talk seriously about ethics as they relate to any given field—law, education, medicine, whatever—we need some fundamental principles we feel we can trust. We've reviewed the common available options—Kant's imperative, Utilitarianism, R. M. Hare's philosophy of (as we called it) 'style,' and so on—and we noted the limitations of each position. The fact, for instance, that Kant, if you were his dearest friend and you went to him asking him to hide you from the police—Kant, if he acted by his principles, would turn you in. What I'd like to do today is set out—or anyway begin to set out—a system that may prove less vulnerable to reasonable attack, anything short of, as we mentioned, an *absolute* attack, such as Nietzsche's, though my approach, as you might expect, is Nietzchean"—he laughed formally —"a looking out from one window, then another." He laughed again. "The position involves four basic areas of inquiry: One: What? Two: Why? How? Who? When? Where? Three: Foreseeable effects? and Four: Viable alternatives?" He glanced at Pinky Stearns, to his left—yellow-bearded, puffy-faced, leaning on his hand, lost in thought or private sorrow. Wolters, across from Mickelsson, was writing furiously in his notebook, his left hand half raised, palm out, begging Mickelsson not to go too fast. Janet Something sat sideways, leaning on her elbow, facing Mickelsson. She had no notebook. She smiled and waited. The bitch had read his book.

"Let's begin with the 'what,' " Mickelsson said. He glanced at the card. "The *is* is father to the *ought*; or, to put it another way, the moral judgment is about what befits or does not befit the personal situation as it really is. Let me give a rather quick and—admittedly—cheap example. A good deal of discussion of capitalism and socialism is lamed from the start by a failure to identify 'what' it is that is meant by capitalism and socialism. Professor Robert L. Heilbroner points out that in much that is said about capitalism, the explicit assumption is that the United States is the most typical capitalist nation. Thus, Paul Sweezy, the American Marxian critic, says that the United States is a capitalist society, the purest capitalist society that ever existed. . . ." He took off his glasses, more impediment than help, and held the card up closer. "But as Heilbroner says, it might well be argued that the United States is not a pure realization of capitalism but rather 'a deformed variant, the product of special influences of continental isolation, vast wealth, an eighteenth-century structure of government, and the terrible presence of its inheritance of slavery—the last certainly not a "capitalist institution." ' For 'pure' capitalism, we should perhaps look to Denmark, Norway, or New Zealand. Obviously, making *those* countries our model will affect all subsequent analysis of the political, economic, or moral dimensions of capitalism. We start with a different 'what.' "

He set aside the notecard and glanced up at his students—all dutiful, most of them scribbling away like doomed prisoners writing for pardons they were sure they wouldn't get. Janet Something hadn't moved a muscle in all this time, staring at him with a slight, inscrutable smile. She was short and, more than that, built low. She was said to be a brownbelt in karate. Under her Oxford-cloth shirt she had, he imagined, voluminous steel tits. It crossed his mind (weirdly, for a quarter of a second) that he would like to be hit by her, even killed. They would be screwing. She would kill him the instant he came. The tall young woman with the Polish name and the hair drawn tight to her head, then frizzing out— she sat beside Janet—moved her left hand slowly back and forth, fanning away smoke from Mickelsson's pipe and her classmates' cigarettes. She seemed unhappy, dark circles under her eyes.

Guiltily, he turned to the next card.

"And obviously Russia is an equally dubious model of socialism," he said. "I assume you've all read Marx—if you haven't, please do! Anyway, you get the point. As the scholiasts liked to say, *Ex falso sequitur quidlibet*—that is, for those of you whose Latin is rusty"—mechanically, he smiled—" 'From false premises anything can follow.' As E. H. Hare points out—not to be confused with R. M.—a hundred years ago it was the established belief of the medical profession that masturbation was a frequent cause of mental disorder." He glanced up, smiled again, then again looked down. "Explaining 'what' masturbation was, medical experts in those days claimed it was an activity that caused an increased flow of blood to the brain and thus was enervating in its effects. It was supposed to produce"—he drew the card closer—" 'seminal weakness, impotence, dysuria, *tabes dorsalis*, pulmonary consumption, not to mention senility, stupidity, melancholy, homosexuality, hysteria. . . .' " He let his voice trail off, deciding against reading the whole long list. He said, "This is obviously a dim view of 'what' masturbation is, not that any of us here would practice it." No one laughed. "With such chaotic notions of the 'what' of masturbation—and thus as to what effects it could have—rational moral discourse on the subject was impossible."

He turned to the next card. Wolters again held up his hand, his cigarette between two fingers, to slow him down. Obligingly, Mickelsson paused for a moment. The fat woman, Rachel Something, at the end of the table, next to Gail Edelman, jerked her ballpoint pen from the paper she'd been writing on, looked at it, then angrily shook it. She whispered something to Gail, who, with a glance at Mickelsson, bent down for her purse. *Ah, poor miserable humanity,* he thought, *all this punishment —smokey rooms, broken pens, boring professors. . . . What crime could possibly warrant all this?* He thought again, just for an instant, of the night when, on one of his walks, he'd stopped at Gail's. He'd been somewhat drunk; she, surprised and nervous. Frightened, possibly? Had she thought he might, despite appearances, prove a rapist and murderer? In the apartment she lived in the ceilings were weirdly high, the wallpaper dark. The memory was too painful, too shameful, to allow further play. *What sufferings and humiliations people live through!* he thought. *Poor girl! Poor good, kind kid!*

He said, glancing down at the card, "On the subject of death there are similar definitional problems. Medically, death is not a moment but a process. Some organs may die while others live. At what point in this process do we declare that death has come? When, if ever, are we justified in preserving the living dead for the recycling of their functioning organs? Or take the area of sexual intercourse . . ." He caught himself just in time to prevent, or at least divert, an instinctual glance at Gail. He almost evaded the glance at Gail by a glance at Janet, but caught that too. Out of the corner of his eye he saw that, studiously, mournfully, Gail was writing something, clearly not class notes—he suspected it was a letter —in her notebook. He read: "It will obviously be telling if one immediately defines sexual intercourse as 'the marital act.' The widely respected moralist Richard McCormick"—he gave the words an ironic twist—"has written: 'Since sexual intercourse and its proximate antecedents represent *total personal exchange,* they can be separated from total personal relationship (marriage) only by undermining their truly human, their expressive character.' " He looked up. "Obviously, McCormick is answering, by his lights, the 'what' question regarding sexual intercourse. Either it is marital or it is objectively wrong." Now for just an instant he did look balefully at Gail. She was buried in her writing. "Do you think this is a good idea?" she had asked, distressed. He thought of Donnie Matthews.

His pipe had gone out. He held a match to it, his hand slightly trembling, then said: "Well, so much for the 'what' component in every moral decision." He looked up from his cards. The soft, pale white Jewish woman whose name he did not know was also accessible. His penis was as hard as a petrified tree. "It comes down to simply this: if we don't get reality right, if we *misunderstand* the case we're examining, all we say will be poppycock." He looked at his watch. Thirty minutes to go, then a fifteen-minute break. Could the watch be broken?

"Let's turn to the 'why' and 'how,' that is, ends and means." He was skipping cards now. He had several more on the 'what' component. He chattered as he hunted. "Take government, for instance. Every government is basically intended . . . Every government is basically intended to promote the common good, but the preservation of the government— as you all know, as loyal Americans"—he looked up for a second and smiled—"giving your money to support the I.R.S., the F.B.I., the C.I.A. —as you all know, the preservation of the government can easily come to seem more important than the common good it was designed to insure. If you look at history, you'll find this is a *pattern,* not an exception." Now he'd found his card. "Or take jobs. A job is a means to survival and, hopefully, personal fulfillment. But we all know how a job can become a man's life. Think of the popular term 'workaholic.' " He turned the card. "Or take wealth. Wealth is obviously nothing but a *means* to happiness and well-being. But when wealth becomes an end, as it often does, people under its sway will sacrifice both happiness and well-being—even life itself—for money." Impatiently, looking at his watch again, he turned to another card.

"Or take armaments. The avowed purpose of armaments is always to bring security and power." He almost flipped this card too, then changed his mind. "Tsar Nicholas the Second of Russia in his proposal for the first Hague Conference in 1899 spotted the fatal flaw in equating arms and safety: 'In proportion as the armaments of each power increase, so do they less and less fulfill the objects which the Governments have set before themselves. . . . It appears evident that if this state of things were prolonged, it would inevitably lead to the very cataclysm which it is designed to avert, and the horrors of which make every thinking man shudder in advance.' Think about that," Mickelsson said, looking up, "in relation to our present situation—sixteen tons of T.N.T.—atomic equivalent—for every man, woman, and child in the world!" For reasons not instantly clear to him, tears sprang to his eyes. "Think about it," he said, catching himself, forcing himself to smile. "If we were true philosophers we might well be terrorists, trying to bring down the nukes."

His son, in the photograph, stood eerily alone, framed by the two SWAT men bending to lift the girl. His hair, flying wildly in all directions under the top-hat, and his eyes, aloof and shadowy—his chin slightly raised, like that of a nineteenth-century prince posing for a painting—gave him a mad look, or rather, to be precise, the look of some good man profoundly wronged by people who could not know better, forgiving his persecutors and waiting, with a still and terrible rage, for his meeting with God.

"The question 'who,' " Mickelsson said, "enters into the calculus of ethics to make us address the following realities: What is right for one person may be wrong for another. What is right for a person now may be wrong for the same person at another time. Some persons are, in ethical calculations, worth more than others. . . ."

He remembered his ex-wife's sobbing on the telephone, his own senseless cruelty to The Comedian.

Then suddenly he felt nothing. As if from a distance, he heard his voice droning, changing now and then to a different drone, for emphasis, or irony, or to present a seemingly spontaneous example. He listened to himself like a man judging the performance of a colleague, then let his mind wander. He saw again the wary look on Mark's face, the look one might give to an injured boa-constrictor. The other Mickelsson talked on, paused for questions, told a joke. He forgot to give the mid-period break. No one objected, though Pinky Stearns glanced at him from time to time with tentatively unfriendly puzzlement. When the bell rang, Mickelsson glanced at his watch, startled. "Thank you for your patience," he said. "Thank you all for your patience."

He'd been seated in his office for more than an hour, with the door closed and the light off—seated doing nothing and thinking nothing, staring at the wall—when a timid knock came. He considered not answering, then thought perhaps it might be Jessica, whose conversation might be a comfort just now, and so he called, rather softly, as if he hadn't quite made up his mind, "Come in."

As soon as he saw the worried, uncertain way the doorknob moved, he knew it would be Nugent. "Christ," he whispered, then leaned forward onto his left elbow and swivelled around in his chair so that he partly faced the door. The boy opened it wide, not seeing him at first in the room's late-afternoon dimness. His black friend—Mickelsson had forgotten the name—was with him again. He looked in over Nugent's shoulder, and when he was sure that it was really Mickelsson there at the desk, he smiled and bobbed his head, then backed away, giving them privacy.

"Did you want the light out?" Nugent asked, hovering between the hallway and the office.

"It's fine. My eyes are tired," Mickelsson said. "Come in if you like. What can I do for you?"

"Thank you." He advanced a step or two, looking around the room as if to make sure no one waited in ambush. Then, apparently deciding he was safe, he closed the door behind him and came the rest of the way at a more normal pace. "May I sit down?" he asked.

"Be my guest," Mickelsson said wearily.

"I won't take long," the boy said, and seated himself, rigid as usual, folding his hands and locking them between his legs. He looked not at Mickelsson but exactly at the point on the wall Mickelsson had been staring at earlier.

Mickelsson got out his pipe and tobacco.

"I'm sorry about this morning," Nugent said. "I realize I wasted valuable class time and talked nothing but stupid nonsense." His lips trembled and it came to Mickelsson that, damn it all, the boy was going to cry again.

In spite of his annoyance—the feeling of claustrophobia that came over him every time the boy came near him—Mickelsson said, almost gently, "That's not true." He concentrated on his pipe, lest the boy throw him a look.

"I hadn't thought it out," Nugent said. "I lost my temper, sort of—all those things they were saying. . . . I'm sort of new at all this. I'm not a very well-educated person, as I imagine you've noticed. I've read a lot of novels and poetry and things—nothing systematic—and I've been pretty good at physics—I can tell you why the lifetime of a resonance particle is not necessarily the smallest possible unit of time—" He gave a choked laugh. "There I go again." Mickelsson could feel the boy looking at him now but kept his eyes on the bowl of his pipe, packing it, preparing to light a match. When he did, the flame was surprisingly bright, glaring on the glossy stipple of the wall. "Anyway of course it's not true that Plato's method is different fundamentally from Aristotle's—I finally read the *Parmenides,* as you suggested we should do, and I, I saw—" Suddenly he raised his hands to his face, not lowering the face, simply covering it, holding his breath, his red elbows shooting out sharp as knives to either side.

"Take it easy," Mickelsson said, gently but with distaste.

"I'm sorry," the boy whispered. His neck and arms were surprisingly small, and white, as if never touched by sunlight.

"Take your time," Mickelsson said, and sighed. "It's all right, believe me." Seeing that the boy was still unable to speak, he said, "Life's full of troubles, we all find that out eventually, but in due time we live past them." He got out his pipecleaners, took the pipe from his lips, pulled the stem off and busied himself with cleaning it.

"I know you have plenty of troubles of your own," the boy said, still pushing apology.

Mickelsson remembered the boy's saying, earlier, that he knew how Mickelsson lived, knew everything about him. He thought of asking now what Nugent had meant; it was never good to leave fingernail parings in the hands of witches, but instead he laughed and said, "Boy, you said it!" He looked sideways at Nugent, who had taken his hands from his face now and was staring into his lap. Mickelsson dropped the pipecleaner into his wastebasket, shook his head ruefully, and said, "I've been trying to deal with the I.R.S. They're incredible—simply incredible! They spy on me." He laughed. "No doubt that sounds like the height of paranoia, but it happens to be true. Every now and then they show up in one of those dark, unmarked cars and sit watching me. I suppose it's some kind of scare tactic."

"You're sure it's them?" Nugent asked, slightly turning, not quite raising his eyes to Mickelsson's.

"Well, pretty sure," Mickelsson said with a little laugh and relit his pipe. "I had a visit from them, not too long ago—came to see me at my apartment. The car they were driving then was pretty much like the one that comes by now."

"What are you going to do?" It did not seem just polite conversation.

Mickelsson saw now that perhaps he'd made a mistake, telling Nugent about that car. It might be construed as an invitation to friendship, an undermining of the teacher-student relationship. In the hope of blocking that development, he told him more. "Well," he said, falsely chuckling, "I thought it would be best to deal with the thing directly, so I shot off a note to the I.R.S. office most likely to be responsible, the one in Scranton, since now I'm living in Pennsylvania. I simply told them I know what they're up to and asked them to stop."

Nugent thought about it, no doubt privately analyzing, as Mickelsson had done over and over, whether it was a good idea or likely to make things worse. At last he said, just above a whisper, "Creeps."

"They *are* creeps," Mickelsson said, pleased to have been given the word for them.

Now a silence fell between Mickelsson and the boy. It was Nugent who finally broke it. "Well," he said, "I just wanted to say I'm sorry—and I'm sorry about making a scene here now, too. It's been a—" He stiffened slightly, making sure he had control. "It's been a bad year."

Mickelsson studied him. Nietzsche would say—or Freud, or any other man of sense—that the statement was an emotional con. He drew the pipe from his mouth and, against his better judgment, said, "I heard about your father. I'm sorry, Nugent."

The boy nodded. After a moment he said, "I also had a friend die, my chemistry teacher—he was murdered; you probably heard about it, maybe I told you. Professor Warren? He'd just gotten married a week before—"

A chill ran up Mickelsson's spine. Warren. That was it, of course: the strange, bedevilled woman he'd met at the Blicksteins' party. Evenly, he asked, "Wasn't he investigating something down near where I live, in Susquehanna?"

"I don't know about that," Nugent said. He closed one hand over his nose, breathing shallowly again, fighting emotion. "He was always looking into something or other. He had more energy than—" He fell silent and tightly closed his eyes. In a minute he would whisper again, "I'm sorry," and would cry.

To prevent it, Mickelsson said sternly, "It's been a bad year for you, Nugent. I'm very sorry."

"Well," Nugent said, and sniffled. Abruptly he stood up. "Thank you," he said, for an instant meeting Mickelsson's gaze.

"No problem," Mickelsson said, and waved his pipe. "Any time I can be of help . . ."

Nugent nodded stiffly, then turned, off balance, and hurried to the door. He fumbled for the doorknob as if unable to see it, then opened the door, half turned back, nodded stiffly again, then quickly stepped out into the hallway and closed the door behind him.

Mickelsson sat for a few minutes longer in the now quite dark office, thinking, or trying to think. A chemist. Then at last he heaved his bulk out of the chair, dropped the tobacco-pouch and pipe into his pocket, and settled his spirit on the long, lonely drive home.

2

Now that the leaves had turned, exploding in a variety of yellows and reds here and there broken by the dark green pines, the Susquehanna Valley and the mountains rising on each side of it were more beautiful than ever. In farmers' yards lay piles of bright orange pumpkins, and on every roadside stand, from Binghamton to Susquehanna, Mickelsson saw more of them—also apples, bright yellow pears, plastic jugs of cider. Here and there, seated on a porch or up on the gable of an old, gray barn, sometimes on a porch roof or sleeping against a tree, he saw pumpkin people—brightly dressed, straw-filled characters with jack-o'-lantern heads. Cars with New Jersey license plates cruised slowly up and down the mountain roads, pausing now and then to spill out tourists with cameras. Often they stopped outside Mickelsson's house, to take pictures of the pond and waterfall, the viaduct and river in the distance. Mickelsson kept clear of them, more reserved than any native. (He'd seen no sign, lately, of the dark green, unornamented car that had earlier come to spy on him.) Every night, deer came to look down at his house. Mornings, the grass would be white with frost.

Halloween came and went. He might easily have forgotten about Halloween—he'd lost all track of time, floating in it as in Nietzsche's sea of recurrence. If there were masks in store windows, Mickelsson didn't notice them. But two nights before the real one—if he wasn't mistaken about the date of Halloween (it had always been Ellen who tended to such things)—Mickelsson, driving through Susquehanna after dark, came suddenly on a troop of four- or five-foot-high witches and goblins, monster creatures, white-sheeted ghosts. They scattered away in all directions from the glow of the headlights. Hastily, Mickelsson laid in candy and apples, preparing for the blackmail of trick-or-treat, and just to be on the safe side padlocked the barn in which the old blue Chevy sat—in his country childhood, Halloween had been a favorite time for vandalism, especially the destruction of seemingly useless machinery. Then he waited, busying himself around the house and listening for a knock. His head was crowded with painful, happy memories—scenes, images, fragments.

Their first year at Brown, he and his family had been invited to a Halloween party given by some friends, the Vicos—the adults to drink, eat, and talk, the children to go out trick-or-treating together, maybe ten, fifteen kids. Marla Vico, famous for her sewing (she'd later turned professional, opening a store), had "created" something for his daughter Leslie; none of them except Leslie had seen it. Leslie, nine or ten, never wore anything at that time of her life but overalls, some old workshirt, and a baseball cap, her long blond hair stringy, always slightly tangled, usually (like her face and hands) not quite clean. Her greatest happiness was to visit her grandparents' farm in Wisconsin, often with a girlfriend, sometimes with her brother, who liked it less, and devote herself to fishing, pigs, and horses. He and Ellen had not strongly disapproved of her ways; even if they had, nothing much could have been done about her. She'd been as stubborn and independent as she was winsome.

So they'd arrived that night at the Vicos' steep-roofed, ultra-modern house with its lush plants, mysterious lighting, and invisible stereo, Leslie in her usual country-hippy garb, and after a few minutes Marla had gone off with the girls of the children's party to the master bedroom. Joe, Marla's husband, took the boys. When the girls emerged, with much fanfare, all the children transformed, Mickelsson's eye had fallen instantly on Leslie, knowing her at once and, in a way, not knowing her at all. The room had been filled to the brim with noise—ooh's and ah's, exclamations and cries of laughter—but he had felt as if he and Leslie were standing in a great silence. Marla had dressed her as a fairy princess: silver crown, light blue dress nearly floor-length, large transparent wings that seemed lighter than air. Her hair, around the eye-mask, was brushed and shimmering, lighter than the wings, and her face had been subtly colored, so that she looked a little like a doll, or a Sumerian goddess. He stood motionless, baffled as by a psychic vision, and he was not himself until his daughter came to him, obscurely smiling, and, raising her star-tipped silver wand, lightly—impishly—touched him with it on the nose. He stood grinning, dazed. Then the boys came tumbling out from the second bedroom, Joe Vico behind them, Mickelsson's colleague in philosophy; pirates, cowboys, a portly banker with a Godzilla mask, then Mark, his son, dressed as some formal, scientific-looking man, bald, with a long white beard and a kind of scarf draped flat over his shoulders. Though there couldn't have been more than six boys in all, they roared like school letting out. Mickelsson, abruptly coming to himself, had joined in with the laughter and extravagant but not inaccurate praise. Then, before his heart was ready, the children were off trick-or-treating.

Everything he'd seen, smelled, touched that night was alive, unforgettable, transmuted by his vision of Leslie. Marla had made some kind of fish in aspic; other women, including Ellen, had brought other things. There was a black chocolate cake with whipped cream and cherries; a large fruit salad that made a picture of a witch. He looked at everything with reawakened vision, the innocent eyes of a child. For all his love of talk—especially his own talk—Mickelsson, that evening, had been unable to follow the conversation and had taken no real part in it. In his mind he saw his daughter approaching strange doors: such beauty as the man in the doorway's glow had never seen before, beauty that might reasonably turn him at once from a furniture salesman or professor of economics into a kidnapper or rapist. Little comfort that the party was led by Olympia Vico, sixteen, and guarded on all sides by sixteen-, fifteen-, and fourteen-year-olds. Everyone in the room where Mickelsson sat was talking of Marla's genius with needle and thread. Mickelsson kept stroking the fern beside him as if he thought it were a dog, often nervously glancing at his watch, and at last he'd said casually, "I think I'll just drive around and see how the kids are doing." No one seemed to notice the oddity of the remark. No one seemed worried in the least about the children.

He drove up and down street after street and saw no trace of them. His heart began to pound. He seriously examined how a murderer might capture fifteen children all at once and leave no sign outside his door. Then at last he spotted them and at once pulled the car over to the curb and extinguished the lights. His son was bowing grandly, swinging down his top-hat to reveal the pink cloth bald dome, and the man and woman at the door were laughing. His son was obviously the star, the leader. His daughter was nearly at the back of the flock, just another child in dress-up. She was smiling and slapping the hand of the girl beside her as Mickelsson had seen black people do on TV.

When he returned to the party, one of the men from the Art Department was doing a sword-dance, and Marla Vico was flamboyantly playing the piano. Mickelsson thought her beautiful. Then he noticed that all the women in the room were beautiful. Let the demon of eternal recurrence come speak to him now!

He remembered other Halloweens, at Hiram, in California, the sad one in Heidelberg where they couldn't find masks, no matter where they looked (only the children had taken it in stride). He remembered the Halloweens in graduate school, when they were poor; how they'd watched the glass dish of M&M's beside the door, praying they wouldn't give out. . . .

Suddenly he remembered, only for a moment, a rather different occasion.

He wasn't certain how old he'd been. Nine, maybe. And he was no longer clear on exactly what had led up to it. He was in fourth grade. His teacher was Miss Minton. He hated her as he'd never hated anyone before or since. For some reason she'd sent him to the coatroom, or rather, led him there by the ear—a particularly grisly punishment because no one after second grade was ever sent to the coatroom. (He understood it now. Proper form would have been to send him to the principal, but Miss Minton was notoriously cruel, maybe crazy; the principal would not have supported her, or anyway not to her satisfaction.) He could remember vividly only one thing from his year with her: "Sssmart, aren't you! Oh yess, you're *sssmart!*" Her lips shook, a hairy, warty lump on the upper one. She was a stupid woman (so Mickelsson had believed), and no doubt, overgrown and stubborn as he was, and a smart-aleck besides, he had challenged her more than he knew. He remembered, though he couldn't recall details, that he'd mocked her, made fun of her, mimicked her; and he knew that the wilder she became the more stubborn and despairingly reckless he grew. No one quite believed him about her or, so far as he knew, took his side. It was no trifling business. Once when he had had his desktop open and was munging around inside for a book, she, passing down the aisle, had slammed the desktop down on his forearms with all her angry might. When the school nurse came—Miss Minton couldn't prevent it—the nurse found his left arm was broken. Mickelsson had believed absolutely at the time—and tended to believe now—that he'd given his teacher no provocation. In any case she'd lied, or tried to, saying he'd fallen while running—wicked child—in the classroom. Much as all the children feared her, someone had told on her, and at last, bitterly weeping, blaming Mickelsson, Miss Minton had admitted what she'd done. When he'd complained, theatrically crying, to his parents, faking more pain inside the cast than he felt, they'd insisted that he must have done something very wrong—"There's two sides to every story," his father said, not ungently but with finality—and the principal had pretended to hold the same opinion. (She'd been as kind as she was able to be. The principal had suggested, in subtle ways, that if he endured through this year he would next year have Mrs. Wheat, who would make up for it all —which in fact had proved true.)

Miss Minton would slap your hand with the ruler—so hard that the fingers would sting for minutes—if you said "Hell-o-copter" instead of "helio-co-peter." She would also hit you with the ruler if you said "stuff," as in "books 'n' stuff"—"except when you're talking about Thanksgiving," she said. ("That's not 'stuff,' that's *stuffing*," Mickelsson had said scornfully. She'd hit him with the ruler.) She also hit you for reading "David Cooperfield," as she called it. Why it was wrong to read *David Copperfield* she did not explain; perhaps because he read it through arithmetic class—but he loved arithmetic and had finished and handed in all the book's exercises weeks ago. Pretty clearly her madness had in it, among other things, something twistedly sexual. When she'd finally admitted slamming the desktop on his forearms, she explained to the principal that she'd done it because he was "playing with himself." No one questioned this, though the physical contortions the claim suggested were extreme—as extreme as his small-boy prudery and shyness.

Miss Minton was not pretty. She was thin as a rail from the collarbone up and from the knees down, and a blimp between. She had such warts as would not be tolerated in the work of a painter who claimed to be realistic, and from half the warts, as from the rest of her body, came soft moss. Her hair was black, her face chalky white except for artificial colors here and there. She was unpleasant in every way, and when later that same year she had died of a brain tumor, Mickelsson had not been as sorry or forgiving as he'd pretended.

And so, locked in the coatroom that afternoon, Mickelsson, still with his arm in a cast, had begun to look through the art supplies—mainly white paste and construction paper, brushes and dried-up tempera—then look (not for the purpose of stealing) through the other children's coats. Eventually, in the broomcloset, he'd found Miss Minton's coat, boots, green felt hat, umbrella, and purse. In the purse he found her make-up. When Miss Minton opened the coatroom door at four o'clock—he had never fully intended this to happen—she met a creature wearing her own coat, hat, and boots, a face painted to look as if it had horribly shattered, splashing blood. That was not the worst. In the creature's right arm, Miss Minton's umbrella was raised like an axe. It came down on her. She would remember nothing more for several hours.

Now all the children began to scream. He chased them with the umbrella, screaming back at them, terrified, trying to make them stop. It seemed the whole world was in reeling, finny commotion, flopping end over end. And then the black janitor, Mr. Pierce, was holding him in his arms, talking to him quietly and squeezing the air out of him. Miss Minton, laid out flatlings with her face turned toward him, over by the coatroom door, was talking. The words dribbling out between her parted lips made no sense.

No one had knocked yet at Mickelsson's door. He decided to sit down in the front room with a book, to make doubly sure he didn't miss them when they came. The clean lines and colors of the candy and apples weighed on his spirit. Still no knock, no laughter in the yard. He was too far out in the sticks, perhaps. No one even crept up to soap his windows. Was it possible that Halloween was last week? Next week? In the end he put the candy away in plastic bags in his refrigerator. For days after that, he ate apples from the bowl in his livingroom or from his pockets.

He'd been driving to the university, during this period, no more often than he had to, and avoiding people, as well as possible, when he was there. Occasionally he broke this pattern, always to his later grief. Once, travelling down a hallway he seldom used, and glancing in through an open office door, he saw someone he recognized, a young man he'd met at a party somewhere and had enjoyed talking to—they'd talked about football. He glanced at the name on the door—Levinson—then waved and called in, "Hi there! How's it going?"

The young man turned his head, looking startled, then pleased to see him. "Hi!" he said. "Terrible!" He laughed, but the left side of his lip jerked up, forming a sneer not meant for Mickelsson but for the world. He was wearing one of those Greek off-white sweaters—more off-white just now than it ought to be, slightly ragged at the cuffs and too short.

"What's wrong?" Mickelsson asked seriously, at once genuinely concerned and sorry that he'd stopped.

"Ahgh, nothing," Levinson said, regretting that he hadn't answered, *Fine, just fine!* He raised a hand to his curly, dark hair, not to touch it but to place the pencil he'd been writing with up behind his ear, like a grocery clerk. "I'm getting killed, these gas prices. I've been here eleven years as an associate professor, and all I'm making is twenty-one." Again his lip lifted in the involuntary sneer. "My son's in Boston, with his mother. It was a bitter divorce—very painful. I really love him." His eyes flicked angrily away from Mickelsson's. "I drive up and see him every two or three weeks."

"Jesus, I'm sorry," Mickelsson said.

Levinson shrugged, an exaggerated heave of the shoulders. "Fucking oil companies. Reagan as President, it'll be a whole lot worse."

"He hasn't really got much chance, has he?" Mickelsson asked.

"Don't kid yourself!" The sneer-tic grabbed fiercely this time. His eyes roved the room. "They should've been socialized twenty years ago. Oil companies. Well, what the hell, at least I'm working." Now Mickelsson remembered who Levinson was: one of Jessica's Marxist colleagues in sociology. He felt a brief impulse of coolness toward the man, then lost it. Levinson looked like a college freshman, but battered, permanently injured. His Jewish nose was so hooked it looked broken in the ring. "I had a dry spell for a while. Jesus, it drove me crazy."

"I know how that feels," Mickelsson said, raising his hand to the doorframe.

"Working on Nietzsche," the young man said. "It's something that might interest you. I'd be glad to let you see it, maybe get a few comments, when I get the thing in shape."

"Ah?" Mickelsson said, both interested and reserved.

"I've been working on pain"—he sneered and smiled at once—"how to put it to work for you. Nietzsche was on to it as early as *The Birth of Tragedy*. Not *really* on to it yet, but on to it."

"Yes, that's true."

"The sublime as the artistic conquest of the horrible."

Mickelsson nodded.

"You think you'd be willing to look at it?" The young man's eyes settled on him only for an instant, then roved again.

"Sure I would," Mickelsson said. "Of course!" It was a point at which he might easily take his leave, but he remained, for Levinson's sake, not for his own. "I've never known exactly what I think about that particular doctrine," he said. "Problem of 'Physician, heal thyself.' "

Levinson drew the pencil from behind his ear, as if unconsciously considering writing down some note on the lined white pad on the desk in front of him. "What do you mean?" he asked.

"Oh, you know. The whole question of 'sublimation.' Freud's kind, that's easy; but Nietzsche's, I'm not so sure." It struck him that if he went any further he'd be there all afternoon. "Well, anyway," he said, "good luck."

"Thanks," Levinson said. Then: "You mean you think it's possible?"

Mickelsson smiled. "God knows I *hope* it's possible."

The young man thought about it, then said, lifting one eyebrow, "Good luck."

Every spare minute he could find, all through October, he had worked on his would-be blockbuster book, the book he'd begun with such joy and confidence in the first radiance of his infatuation with Donnie Matthews, but which seemed to him now, like the costly, difficult affair itself, sometimes unbalanced, never really sensible, though at moments as glorious as the autumn weather, the sweet smell of change in Donnie's hair and breath. At his worst moments he found the project, like the love affair, embarrassing, enslaving, and insipid.

When he was unable to write, he worked—sometimes far into the night—on the house. He had reason enough for gloom. His son was still missing; and it had been weeks since he'd sent money to his ex-wife and daughter, though he'd caught Ellen up on her house and car payments. When he glanced through his mail, usually without opening it, at least half of it consisted of letters from collection agencies. The Acme would no longer take checks from him—he'd bounced there repeatedly—and even Owen Thomas looked ill-used whenever Mickelsson got out his checkbook, though Thomas did still take his checks, accepted them almost graciously, all things considered, perhaps from kindheartedness or timidity, perhaps because of the large amount of business Mickelsson did at Owen's store.

Winter would be trouble, when he had to pay for fuel oil, more wood, and the various extras that inevitably settled in with cold weather. The automatic transmission in the Jeep was behaving oddly, noisily clunking whenever he shifted into drive; some lawyer in Providence was threatening to sue him for fifteen hundred dollars, an old litigation fee Ellen had for some reason refused to pay three years ago; and Mickelsson was no closer than ever to paying off the I.R.S.—the fines and penalties mounted daily: fourteen thousand a year was about what they'd come to; so Finney claimed. He had, in short, reason enough to be discouraged. At times he angrily wished the whole thing done with, wished some supernal referee would blow a whistle and declare him out, bankrupt. But he was beginning to learn that financial ruin, like death, is not a moment but a process, a slow, merciless grinding down. Sometimes not even an expert could say, in a given case, that ruin has now come, or ruin, though close at hand, has not yet arrived. He sent away for, and obtained by means of lies, a Master Charge card, which meant that his checking account would be guaranteed up to three thousand dollars. He also received, in spite of his execrable credit, an American Express card. Ellen, as a separated woman, could get no credit at all. The news that this was so—news Mickelsson got through a joking phonecall from Finney—filled Mickelsson with righteous indignation, a sentiment Finney did not share. "Prods her ass one step closer to the courthouse, ole pal," Finney said. "Look at it this way, ole pal ole sock: you didn't make the world, so mafriend you're Not Guilty. Whatever falls in your yard, put your fucking flag on it!" Though he had always despised Jake Finney's worldview, and suspected that even Finney himself despised it—exactly the worldview of Martin Luther, but with no otherworldly alternative—he could not deny, in those moments when he allowed himself sober reflection, that he'd already adopted it in practice. His chief personal expense these days, greater even than the expense of his house, was a seventeen-year-old prostitute.

Sometimes late at night, especially when he was drunk, he thought about the money he'd seen in the apartment of the fat man. Hardly knowing he was doing it, he would go through in his mind how one might run three hard steps from across the hallway and smash the tall door in, sometime when the fat man was down on the street, then rush over to the chest beside the fat man's TV chair, gather up the money and be gone, all in less than a minute. He envisioned it so clearly it might have been a memory floating up out of the gumbo at the bottom of his mind. Then, realizing what he was thinking, half seriously toying with, he would shudder like a sick man and whisper, "Stupid!" or, sometimes, "Insane!" When he was in downtown Susquehanna he would catch himself gazing thoughtfully up and down the street, seeing if the fat man was out. He never was. Sometimes, going up the dark, narrow stairway to Donnie's room, his coat collar turned up, his hat flat on his head like an Indian's, he would pause, in spite of himself, at the landing on the fat man's floor.

She no longer charged him seventy-five dollars a visit. She'd grown somewhat fond of him—or so he hoped, since his heart was slaughtered by just the rustle of her dress, the little joking pout she put on when he lost his erection, or the way that, making a face, she would cross her eyes. But she was, she insisted, a professional, and would not "put out" for less than twenty dollars, or spend the whole night with him for under sixty. (She would not accept checks.) Before Donnie, he'd never visited a prostitute, neither did he any longer know anyone who did, so he had no way of telling whether or not she was cheating him. She probably was, he supposed, but he was afraid to press. Once when he cautiously touched on his suspicion that the price was exorbitant, she said, "Why don't you check with the police?" She knew him, all right! The thought that the police might burst in on them some evening or afternoon (which somehow seemed worse) made him sick with dread. When he was teaching classes, the approach of that thought would make everything he was saying fly at once from his mind. He would imagine dire headlines: UNIVERSITY PROFESSOR HELD FOR CONTRIBUTING TO DELINQUENCY OF MINOR. PHILOSOPHER CAUGHT WITH SEVENTEEN-YEAR-OLD GIRL. He would rack his brain, standing there empty-headed in front of his class, too sick at heart even to remember to take a Di-Gel. Sometimes he could do nothing to get his wits back but go over to the window and stand for a few minutes rubbing his forehead and staring out.

His fear of the police and his distress at how much his addiction was costing him were by no means the only griefs she gave him. He worried about disease. He thought of poor syphilitic Nietzsche, who in 1889 had run into a street to throw his arms around the neck of a horse as its master, like some brute from Dostoevski, was beating it to its knees, after which moment "the Antichrist" was never again sane—the best mind in Europe reduced in one instant of passionate sympathy ("I am not a man, I am dynamite") to rubble, one at last with Jesus of Nazareth as Nietzsche had understood him—Jesus the "idiot." No one went mad from syphilis anymore, of course, or so Mickelsson believed. Nonetheless, he knew that Donnie Matthews wasn't careful, and some of the people with whom she dealt looked—to say the least—unhealthy. He worried as much about her as about himself and couldn't help furtively checking up on her at times —rather frequently, in fact—finding reasons to loiter in front of Reddon's Drugstore, as if waiting for a prescription, or chatting with Owen Thomas on the sidewalk in front of his hardware store, conveniently nearby. He couldn't bring himself to go sit on her landing—she might get angry, and her anger was a terrible thing—but he knew by now all the people who lived in the other apartments and could pretty well tell who her customers were. (Sometimes he would say, unable to help himself, "You're a hard worker, I'll grant you that. *Five* this afternoon?" She would roll her eyes.) They were a ghastly company, Donnie Matthews' clientele, not just filthy, scarred, pimply, but downright deformed. Get them all together in one room, it would look like a Fellini cast party.

"Mostly the good-looking people don't need me," she said with a little shrug when he mentioned it. "Everybody puts out, these days. You ain't heard of the Pill? My people, they're naturally the desperate ones. Love for the unloved." She smirked. "I should get that printed on a card."

"The Mother Seaton of the demi-monde," he said.

Donnie looked uneasy, as she always did when he used unfamiliar expressions.

He said, "How can you *do* it, though? That one tonight. No bath for at least a year, I'll bet, and a week's growth of whiskers, and—"

She laughed. "I know. That fucking *thing* in his eye."

He rolled toward her. "Well, how *can* you?"

"A person has to get ahead," she said. "That's the American Way." She pursed her lips, looking at him. Gently, coyly, she poked his nose with one finger. The gesture filled him with an almost sickening, guilty desire. "You're jealous," she said.

"God knows!" Mickelsson said, and took her hand.

The house, in any case, was beginning to be beautiful, and he was thankful for its demands, since, to some extent at least, work on the house, besides toughening him up, kept him from making a fool of himself downtown. The newly painted and wallpapered rooms, though for the most part still empty of furniture, gave the place the brightness of a New England inn, even when the day outside was dark, as days in the Endless Mountains often were. He'd found junk light fixtures, which he'd patched and polished and fitted with clearglass bulbs. The brighter and trimmer the house became, needless to say, the more absurd the legends of its haunting seemed—legends still obscure, since while everyone in Susquehanna claimed to know the place haunted, no one so far had been able to tell him any more than old Pearson about who might be haunting it or why. Some thought it was the Sprague ghosts who troubled the place; some thought it was the ghosts of the people who'd lived there before the Spragues. The U.P.S. man, when he came by with the fruit trees Mickelsson had ordered, claimed he'd heard an entirely different story, one no longer very clear in his head but given to him on the best authority— something about buried treasure, or perhaps a mysterious grave . . . a curse, possibly. . . . "Well, no matter," Mickelsson had said, smiling, turning back to his work, which was, that day, the sanding of the downstairs floors. He must put the whole stupid haunting legend out of his mind.

He could not entirely drive from his consciousness the strangeness of what he was doing, fixing the place up when he had no one but himself to do it for; but he carefully kept himself from thinking too much about that. Even more studiously he kept himself from thinking about his son. Ellen had had a card from him, from Rochester, New York. She had the police out hunting him.

Mickelsson received a letter from his daughter—a long, chatty one that he read over and over until he knew it by heart, and between readings, kept on his pile of manuscripts on the table in his study. Though the letter was in English, only a few hints here and there of her increasing inclination to shift to French, it seemed to Mickelsson that she spoke to him already in a foreign tongue. The letter seemed all surfaces, as if the words were not windows into her thought but mirrors, maybe rapidly moving mirrors made of steel. Strain as he might, he couldn't hear the sound of her voice in the writing—whether it was the letter's fault or his own, he couldn't tell. He would stand by the curtainless window of his study, holding the letter in his two hands, reading through it slowly, word by word, as if he were brain-damaged, and though a thousand thoughts pressed through his mind—dream-thoughts crowding like shadowy deer through a meadow at night—none would stand plain. She assured him that Mark was all right; he knew what he was doing if anyone did in this crazy, *fichu* world. Then she spoke of a young man named David as if Mickelsson should know him; spoke of her new doctor, a chiropractor and nutritionist, and of the theory of chiropractic: electrical circuits, stimulation of weak organs. He, Mickelsson, should take vitamins, she said, especially vitamin E, for the heart. She included a list of the supplements he needed, with dosages. "Well, Papa, *bon soir*," she ended. "*Baisers . . .*"

At last, thoughtfully, he would fold the letter and put it back on its place on his study table, then move as if aimlessly, to the kitchen, to put on another pot of coffee. While the percolator snorted and rumbled, he would stand at the back door, his hands in his pockets, looking up at the colorful, thinning leaves, thinking calmly—coldly and indifferently, as if it had nothing to do with himself or his son—how queer it was that the soul in isolation, no matter what the stimulation of the world around, should shrivel up, like a plant perfectly healthy except for its signal leaf, and die. It was no queerer, of course, than the familiar fact that to a person in love the world, however drab, comes alive, full of music and soft voices.

It was by no means just poetry. As the book Nugent had pressed upon him made abundantly clear, with pages and pages of statistics and charts, one's very life depended on the sometimes sped-up heartbeat one experienced when close to loved-ones (also, to some extent, one's sped-up heartbeat in the presence of those who offend). If it was true that people occasionally died while making love, it was far more true that people died for lack of it. Reading through Nugent's book, case after dreary case of cardiac fatality in the single, the unhappily married, and the divorced, Mickelsson had begun to feel like a man encountering his own obituary. At first it had seemed that Donnie Matthews, costly or not, would prove his salvation, but no such luck: the quite violent heartbeat rise during young people's sexual coupling, and the moderate heartbeat rise during older people's coupling, were both found to be beneficial. The sexual coupling of an older man and a younger woman, especially one not his marriage partner, was apparently only a little less deadly than cyanide. In the end, of course, the heart's real, physical demand for love was not just a matter of sex: the heart—whatever the mind's objections—demanded company, security, trust. By the time Mickelsson was two-thirds of the way through *The Broken Heart,* he found the chest-pains caused by his anxiety so great that he dared not read further. All he could do was glance hastily at the last few pages to make sure that at the last minute the author didn't take it all back. Alas, he did not. Mickelsson resolved to eat less, drink less, smoke less. Even so, if Dr. James Lynch was right, Mickelsson was a walking dead man.

He was over that original anxiety now, for himself at least. He was resigned to the likelihood that he would die soon—even morbidly interested. It would solve a good deal. But with every passing day he grew increasingly uneasy about his missing son. It was not, of course, that he thought the boy might be lying hurt somewhere, or dead. His mind refused to entertain such thoughts (though one of Dr. Lynch's statistics unnerved him: four out of five of those who die between the ages of fifteen and twenty-five die by accidents, suicide, or homicide). Yet he couldn't help but worry—indeed, Peter Mickelsson was worried sick—about the long-range effects of the boy's decision to go underground. Not the danger that he might be caught for something, and imprisoned, or shot; these things, though he thought of them, had not yet impressed themselves on Mickelsson as real possibilities. He worried that Mark's heart, like his own—but far nobler than his own—might be broken.

He shook his head, raising his hand to his chin, touching the stubble of whiskers. Perhaps things were not as dark as he imagined. What if it was the influence of some young woman that had made Mark disappear? Some beautiful, flashing-eyed, nutty radical. *Let it be that,* he thought. He almost came to believe it; it made the rest—the extremity of disappearing—make sense. Yet his gloom remained, deep and sodden. A flock of birds floated high over the trees on the mountain above him, drifting like specks of ash.

There was, sometime during this period, a queer piece of news in the Binghamton paper. Early in the morning someone had discovered, less than thirty miles from where Mickelsson lived, three perfect circles, each a hundred yards wide exactly, cut into the forest just off Route 17. Within the circles, trees, wildlife—whatever had been there, apparently—had been ground to bits. Federal investigators called in to study the strange phenomenon, the article said, had ruled out wind damage, flood, and human vandalism. Asked if they thought the circles had been made by UFOs, the investigators said, according to the paper, that that seemed at present the only available explanation. Mickelsson reread the sentence. That was, sure enough, what it said. The article mentioned that similar circles had been found in the same area two years earlier. Mickelsson pulled at his mouth with two fingers and read the whole thing again, expecting that this time he would surely find it was a joke of some kind;

but it was apparently not a joke, at least in the mind of the newspaper people. Strange business!

The following day when he went in to teach, Mickelsson waited for someone to mention the peculiar article—more and more peculiar, as he thought about it: though they'd treated the story as front-page news, the news people hadn't even bothered to print a picture. Surely in a case as bizarre as this, a couple of aerial photographs . . . To his surprise, no one said a word about the article until Mickelsson himself brought it up; and even then, as it seemed to him, they showed only the feeblest interest. Fred Rogers, the historian, when Mickelsson met him just outside the mailroom, smiled as if bravely withstanding life's woe, sadly amused by Mickelsson's concern. "We get a lot of that," he said. "Binghamton's one of the hot spots, apparently. I guess you're familiar with the Port Crane Center for the Study of UFOs?" He flipped tragically through his envelopes, sorting as he spoke.

"You're kidding," Mickelsson said.

Rogers glanced at him for an instant, then back at his mail. "No," he said, as if seeing no reason anyone should think he might ever be anything but serious. "You haven't seen the trucks? I imagine you'll see one, sooner or later, tooling down the highway. Port Crane's not far from here, up on Route 88. They're beautiful things, those trucks—enough to make you want to study UFOs yourself. Big vans, very official-looking. Sign on the door, siren, red flashers, radar dish on top, computers inside . . ." Suddenly, woefully, Rogers laughed. "Peter, you should see your face," he said.

"I'm sorry," Mickelsson said, and made an effort to look sober and sensible. "I guess it never—"

"Yes," Rogers said, glancing down the hallway, preparing to move on, "it's curious, all this. Well, there are lots of strange things in this old world. 'Falls,' for instance. That's the one I like—frogs falling out of the sky, or blood, or fish . . . stones. . . . Most people say it's hogwash, but nobody says that after they've seen one."

Mickelsson lifted an eyebrow, not quite willing to ask the question.

"Oh, sure," Rogers said, shaking his head and patting his pile of mail as if the proof were right there. "I saw the fall of little stones out in Chico, California—maybe you read about it; it made a lot of the papers. I was there the second day. 'Right out of a clear blue sky,' as the saying goes. It was most peculiar, believe me. Made you blink your eyes a bit. There were scientists there, state police, newspaper reporters. We just stood there with our hands folded and looked. Even in Chico nobody believed it except the people who were right there and saw it. Poured down out of the sky as if there were somebody up there with a dump-truck, except not that fast and not that steady, sometimes nothing for a while, then one or two stones, then bucketfuls. The way they hit the ground they seemed electrically charged or something—blurry, as if with heatwaves. Very odd, but then when they'd settled they just lay there, commonest stones in the world. People make up theories, but they never explain anything. Waterspouts, for instance. But nobody tells you how the stones pulled out of the ocean by waterspouts get carried along in the sky to a place as far inland as Chico, or how come the stones are invariably the local kind, different from even the stones you'd find forty miles away." Rogers smiled and shook his head, raising one hand to discourage protest. "I know. I know. You'd be surprised, though, how many thoroughly studied cases there are of these mysterious falls—though I must say, in these matters 'study' seems a little irrelevant. I'll tell you my favorite one: a fall in St. Louis—1967, I think. Five and a half tons of cookies in unmarked plastic bags." He laughed, and Mickelsson risked laughing with him. "Thorough investigation," Rogers said, "local police, U.S. government, chemists and physicists from Washington University. None of the airlines would admit they'd lost a cargo of unmarked, plastic-bagged cookies—I suppose I wouldn't either, if I were the guilty airline. But it was pretty clear that it wasn't a case for ordinary explanation. All the cookies fell on one man's property, not so much as a cookie-crumb outside the line. Flattened his garage."

"I must say—" Mickelsson began, then floundered.

"Obviously it doesn't much matter whether you believe these things or not," Rogers said. "They don't seem to have any earthly effect on anything, except possibly on a few people's mood when the thought dawns on 'em that the universe occasionally kids around."

"You actually believe, then—"

"As I say," Rogers said gravely, patting Mickelsson's arm, excusing himself, "belief's a luxury. I'm just a historian. I like to know things really happened, if I can, or really didn't happen, and I analyze what happened or didn't if I can. If I can't, I don't." He grinned. "Anyway, except to those who think they've seen these things, it doesn't matter much—unless, of course, taking firm stands on doubtful matters gives a particular person pleasure."

"I suppose that's true," Mickelsson said as Fred Rogers moved away.

When he asked Jessica about the UFOs, she shook her head and said in a tone of regret that she'd thrown out yesterday's paper without reading it. Except for Mickelsson, no one had mentioned it to her. "Wasn't there something like that a couple of years ago?" she asked. Absently, with a quick, soft gesture, she brushed her hair back. When he told her what the paper had said, she nodded. "Funny."

"Well, puzzling," he said.

"Oh, Peter, why worry about it?" she asked, and smiled. She touched his arm.

"I'll stop," he said, hunching his shoulders and touching his fists together just under his chin, "as soon as I know it's safe."

At the university bookstore, later that day, his eye chanced to fall on a book displayed on the sale table. *Phenomena: A Book of Wonders.* His very discovery of such a book at just this time—he was sure it hadn't been there a week ago—seemed to him that moment as strange as the UFO circles or Freddy Rogers' "falls." It was a large book, full of etchings and surprising photographs. He bought it, carried it back to his office, closed the door, and guiltily paged through it. Falls, missiles from the upper regions, strange disappearances, mysterious mutilations, spontaneous human combustions, anomalous fossils, shared visions, human beings that glowed, phantom music and voices . . .

He frowned, surprised at his eagerness to believe. *Error is cowardice.* —Nietzsche. And: *The religious have a thirst for foolishness.*

As if it were a *Playboy* or *Hustler*, he put it in the back of his desk drawer, where he could look at it more carefully later, taking his time.

The report by the fat woman, Rachel Morris, in his medical ethics class that afternoon, was on abortion. It was reasonable and meticulous. She was a better researcher and a clearer thinker than, just from looking at her, he would have guessed. She efficiently covered the legal and philosophical history of the subject, then began, with a certain amount of fervor and no obvious stupidity, her own ethical analysis. There was nothing anywhere in what she'd said so far that one could nail as wrong. There were a few cheap shots, for instance a mocking quotation of Billy Graham and a blistering aside on the recent papal directive banning abortion for any reason; but on the whole she followed out her central argument, based on the premise that in ethical calculations not all persons are of equal worth, with reasonably good sense.

Yet as Mickelsson listened, making an occasional note to himself, he felt restless, crotchety. It was not just her style of delivery, though he would admit that that gave him problems. When she'd come into the windowless room, ahead of nearly all the others, she'd taken, for the first time this semester, the chair at the center of the table, opposite him, and had laid out her things—ashtray, cigarettes, notecards, tissues—as if in conscious parody of him; and she was dressed more formally than he'd ever seen her before, high-heeled shoes, stockings, a dark blue satiny dress, several strands of beads. It was probably because she was nervous, he thought; yet once the paranoid notion crossed his mind that she was mocking his own formality, he could not entirely shake it. It was likely, he knew, that she meant no insult—indeed, that she was imitating his style because she admired it, thought it worked. But because he did not very much like her, really, it was difficult to believe that she felt anything but dislike for him.

When the whole class was seated, Pinky Stearns at the far end of the table, Wolters next to him, the women clustered, as if accidentally, at the opposite end of the table from the men, Ms. Morris began her report with what seemed to Mickelsson a sort of lidded belligerence, smoking hard as she read, lighting and jabbing out cigarettes almost without looking at them, her fleshy mouth overneatly pronouncing every word—her nervousness again, probably—her eyes oddly narrowed behind the glasses. Though she couldn't be thirty yet, she had the look of those middle-aged, blond, overdressed and over-made-up Jewish women mocked—always to Mickelsson's confused distress—in a thousand movies. Her upper arms were fleshy, pale, and soft, her hands small, dimpled, neat. The way she sucked the cigarette smoke far into her lungs and held it there, only gradually letting it out with her words, made him want to break in on her report and talk to her about cancer. Despite his fear that it might worry her, he avoided looking at her, leaning on his elbow, shading his eyes, staring hard at the paper on the table in front of him, with its few neatly pencilled notes. It was a once-a-week three-hour class with a fifteen-minute break in the middle. His misery was so great—his right hand furtively rubbing his chest—he wondered if the class might be the last he ever met.

Part of what made him restless was his sense that she was working toward an argument for abortion on demand, an argument that, for all its popularity, even present legal dominance, filled him with fury. She began with the claim, legitimate enough, that a mother with four children dependent upon her is of more worth to society, including her husband, than is an unborn foetus; and she moved, not unreasonably, to a claim that any mature human being, given society's various kinds of investment, should take priority over a foetus. (He wondered if she would find it equally easy to argue if she used the words *unborn child*.) In general, she seemed fair, even-handed. She was properly annoyed by extreme "feminist" arguments that describe the foetus as a "cannibal"; she rightly noted the possible implications of a widespread practice of aborting when the foetus is not of the parentally desired sex, among other things the possible consequences of population imbalance (but she treated the matter too flippantly, he thought: "If present correlations remained constant, a United States with many more males would have a lower life expectancy, fewer church-goers, higher crime rates, and more Democratic voters"); and she neatly side-stepped the trap involved in turning all anti-abortionist feeling into cheap religiosity or male-chauvinist-piggism—though she couldn't resist those little raps at silly Billy and the Pope.

Nevertheless, Mickelsson had to concentrate on not wringing his hands, and, furtively glancing around the room, he saw that he was not alone. At first the battle-lines seemed male vs. female, a condition that would not have surprised him. But on closer inspection he saw that at least two women were similarly uncomfortable with Ms. Morris's position —which finally did indeed turn out to be a defense of abortion on demand, "for the avoidance of the needless humiliation of women, too frequently socially disadvantaged young women; and for the sake of social justice, since only the female must suffer the pain of childbirth and, in our society, the shame of unwed-motherhood." One of the women who seemed displeased was the short girl, Janet, daughter, Mickelsson suddenly remembered from his first conference with her, of Orthodox Jews; the other was the tall Polish woman, who stared at the table in what seemed acute distress. He wrote himself a note to bring up, when time for discussion came, Dr. Bernard N. Nathanson.

After the break, which was unusually quiet—not surprisingly; abortion was always a touchy subject, even for those who thought they knew what they thought—Pinky Stearns asked, frontally, the first question. "I notice you don't say anything of murder."

Mickelsson sighed.

Ms. Morris was ready for it, of course. She sucked deep on her cigarette, lowering her eyelids (evilly, one might have said, but it was obviously nothing but the gesture of one threatened, attacked), and said, "To many people capital punishment is murder, or war is murder, just as, to other people, abortion is murder. But we traditionally make a distinction between killing by the society and killing by the individual." *A stupid distinction*, Mickelsson thought. He thought of Heidegger, cloistered in his university, encircled by disciples, sending out his praise, however qualified, of the Third Reich. Why *not* prefer murder by a Raskolnikov? Not that anarchy was an answer either. *Stop everything!* No more painters, no more writers, no more musicians . . . Ms. Morris was saying: "In the case of abortion, of course, it can be argued that the thing killed is not even fully human." She threw a look at Mickelsson that, in spite of himself, he found touching—the uncertain young girl looking out through the eyes of Portnoy's mother. Hesitantly, like an umpire under duress, he nodded, the curl of his lip no doubt showing his distaste. Stearns fumed but was too stupid, or maybe too angry, to spot the weaknesses in her response. He shook his puffy, filthy-bearded head, an impressive display of disgust and perhaps right feeling, but not an argument. In this much, anyway, Heidegger was right: judging philosophy by the standards of science is like judging the capacity for survival of a fish out of water.

Gail Edelman said softly, looking gently at Ms. Morris, perhaps to avoid looking at Mickelsson, "I suppose one might argue that the problem's partly one of sped-up modern time." Her hands made a tent on the table in front of her. Her voice was an almost inaudible tinkle. "As Professor Mickelsson has often pointed out, morality is based on reality, including our knowledge that our conduct has future implications." She smiled a weak, frightened little smile, perhaps intending to tell Ms. Morris in advance that eventually she meant to support her position. Gail's dark hair was cut short, her Irish-Jewish features perfect, china-doll-like, beautiful in the way a museum piece is beautiful. Her eyes—

black irises, and whites that were faintly blue—were astonishing. It had occurred to him, the night of his drunken visit to her, that Helen of Troy might have had such eyes; they were as striking, in a different way, as Jessica's. The girl said, "The problem is, when social roles and social premises are changing with lightning swiftness, as we all know they are, these days—when one cannot tell what the acceptable and defensible norms are—one's wisest choice may be to argue one's own life-necessities, since . . ." She looked down, as if troubled by a mental conflict. "Of course the difficulty is that, in acting in a way that seems best for the self, leaving the welfare of the other to the other's self-defense, that is to say, the future, we may in fact be poisoning our *own* future self. . . ." She broke off, the outside ends of her eyebrows sinking, as if she were convinced that no one would understand her. No one ever did, no one ever had. She allowed the tent shaped by her two frail hands to collapse.

Mickelsson said, though not entirely sure what she was trying to say, "That's a good description of the problem, I think." He swept the table with a glance, then focussed on the hands of the Polish girl, knotted in front of her, on her notebook. Her tightly pinned hair seemed more frizzy than usual, the lawless ends catching the light, making a kind of halo. He said, "Sometimes, in practice, we're so hopelessly confused about the total situation we have no choice but to act on self-interest. Which is fine of course, as long as we fully understand what's in our interest." He glanced at Janet Something, who, unobtrusively but not timidly, had her hand up. "Janet?"

"I'd like to know what *you* think," she said. "I was watching your face—I guess we all were—" She glanced around, then back at him, the barest suggestion of a smile touching her lips. "I guess I think everything Rachel said was true"—she brushed the hair back from her eyes, quickly, stiffly, almost a karate chop—"but I felt something important might be missing."

He waited, hoping to lure her on.

She seemed to consider waiting him out, then gave way. "I was thinking of that doctor in one of your articles," she said, "the pro-abortion doctor who became the head of an abortion clinic which performed, if I remember, sixty thousand abortions without a single maternal death."

"Bernard Nathanson," he said, and nodded. For the first time he realized that, all this time, watching him, inscrutably smiling, she'd been an ally. "Go on," he said.

"Well, as you say in your article—I guess probably everybody's read it—Nathanson helped get the liberal 1970 New York State Abortion Statute passed, and then suddenly he quit the abortion clinic." She shrugged. "That's all I meant to say." She shrugged again.

"I don't see," Ms. Morris began, then looked at Mickelsson, betrayed.

Mickelsson looked down at her notecards to avoid her face. "Nathanson's problem," he said, "as he explained in an article for the *New England Journal of Medicine*, was that the foetuses he and his associates vacuum-cleaned out were alive: living human beings, capable of feeling pain, struggling against death—every bit as alive as newborn babies. Sixty thousand of them. He never stopped believing in abortion, at least in certain situations. He just stopped performing them."

"But you agree," Ms. Morris said, her head very still, her dark eyes burning into him, "that an adult female human being is a more meaningful and socially valuable person than a foetus." No hardshell Baptist was ever surer of his ground. Her troubled eyes insisted on the irony of it all: that it was Mickelsson's own position on the inequality of persons that underlay her argument. "I mean," she said, inclining her head toward him, "*isn't* a grown woman of more value than an unborn *thing*?"

He hung fire. "Sometimes," he said at last.

She paled. The ex-highschool teacher, C. J. Wolters, looked at Mickelsson, not sure what to write in his notebook.

"I'll tell you a funny story," Mickelsson said suddenly. He let his eyes rest on the tall, thin Polish girl's hands. "Last spring as I was trimming the hedges around my house"—it was a lie; in fact it was something he'd read in a newspaper—"I disturbed a bird's nest—a robin's nest. An egg fell out on the ground, and when I picked it up it felt heavy. For some reason—I'm not sure why—I cracked it, then opened it up, and behold, what I found inside was a tiny, living bird. I was a little upset. I'm a farmboy, I have experience in these things, and I knew there was no way in the world I could keep that little robin alive—eyedroppers and all that, if they did anything at all they'd just prolong the misery. I didn't want to leave the baby bird to be eaten by snakes or to be found by my neighbor's cat or dog; and though I myself felt pity for the thing—the way it opened its bill to me, blindly hoping behind those sealed-shut eyes—I knew the mother bird would never accept it, now that it had my smell on it. So I put it down gently on the ground and put the heel of my shoe on it and crushed it."

Ms. Morris stared.

"As I say," he said, "a funny story." He opened his hands and raised his eyebrows, apologetic. "It was only a bird." He smiled, then glanced at the Polish girl, then quickly down. She looked gray. So that was it, he thought. He'd walked into it but good, this time.

"So you're against abortion," Pinky Stearns said sharply, triumphantly aiming his cigar at Mickelsson.

"I didn't say that, in the first place," Mickelsson said, equally sharp, perhaps hoping to throw the guilt onto poor Stearns. "I happen to be *pro*-abortion, within limits. And in the second place, what *I* think has nothing to *do* with it. We're talking about ethics, not personal opinions."

"No one's mentioned the question of ensoulment," the mousey brown-

haired girl next to Gail said abruptly, but no one, not even Mickelsson—
though he heard her—noticed.

C. J. Wolters said, holding his hand up, palm out, to keep Mickelsson
from answering too fast, "What I'd like to know is, what should we think
about abortion, and why?"

No one seemed aware of the misery of the Polish girl.

Ms. Morris said, "That's what my whole report deals with."

A mousey blond girl, whose name he did not know, seated next to the
mousey brown-haired girl—the blond girl had never before spoken in
class—said, bored-looking, speaking in a comically flat Midwestern accent,
"All Professor Mickelsson's saying is that if abortion's too casual it's
dehumanizing. A society where people can kill people 'on demand,' so
they don't have to go through the embarrassment of explaining why, is
a crappy society." Was her glance at him hostile?

"I suppose that's it," Mickelsson said.

The tall Polish girl took a slow, deep breath, and still none of them
seemed to notice.

"Anyway," he said, "that's it once we've added in the individual
agony, fear, guilt, anger, and helplessness, the things that make abortion
a philosophical issue in the first place."

He suspected that only one of them understood for sure what he was
saying. Perhaps "one" not including himself. *All truths are for me soaked
in blood.*

In the parking lot he found he had congratulated himself too early on
escaping the campus without having to deal with Michael Nugent. As he
was getting out his keys, preparing to heave himself up into the Jeep, a
voice called out, "He was investigating some kind of fraud."

Mickelsson turned to see who it was that had spoken, not imagining it
was himself who'd been addressed. Thirty feet away, in the middle of the
asphalt between rows of cars, looking at him or maybe past him, he saw a
gangly, rather tall, very white-skinned young man wearing white slacks,
blue jacket, a broad-brimmed hat canted over one eye. Perched on the top
of a dark van nearby, maybe twenty feet beyond the young man in the
hat, he saw a graceful, broadly smiling Negro boy. It was only because he
recognized the Negro that he recognized Nugent, then an instant later
recognized that the words were meant for himself.

"What?" he called.

"I don't know if it had to do with chemistry or not," the young man
called, "but I know he was investigating some kind of fraud."

Mickelsson looked down, gathering his wits, wondering why it was
here, on the high parking lot overlooking the campus, dark blue waves
of mountains in the distance, that Nugent and his friend had chosen to
waylay him. It seemed strange, to say the least, that Nugent should wait

for him here, in this isolated place, and then shout his information from thirty feet away. After he'd mused a moment, Mickelsson put the keys back in his pocket and walked over to Nugent—since apparently Nugent did not wish to come to him. The black boy went on smiling, his elbows on his knees, then tipped his head up to look at the sky. Towering black clouds were moving in, drawing together, tumbling. Occasionally one of them would brighten with buried lightning, then go dark again. There was as yet no sound of thunder. The trees above the parking lot were perfectly still. In a moment the smallest branches would begin to move, and after another moment it would begin to rain. Mickelsson's shadow fell over Nugent.

"You mean Professor Warren?" Mickelsson asked.

Nugent blinked rapidly, then nodded.

"How do you know?" Mickelsson asked.

"I talked to some people," Nugent said. It was clear that no amount of prodding would make him more specific.

After a while Mickelsson asked, "Something to do with the university, you think? What was his interest in this fraud?"

Nugent shrugged as if it hardly mattered to him, but his eyes showed interest. They stared straight into Mickelsson's. Disconcerting.

"That's all you know? He was investigating some fraud?"

"I guess that's right."

Now he did hear thunder, a low, long-drawn-out roll that made him think of his grandfather, in those final years, listening as if God's voice were in the sound.

"You think it was just intellectual curiosity?" he asked.

Nugent seemed to ponder the question, then finally said, "He was a clown, in a way. The sort of person who liked to go on—you know—intellectual benders. I remember he told me he was a member of an ashram in Boston for a while, after he'd abandoned conventional religion —he was at Harvard then. Later, when he was teaching at Riverside, in California, he got into Rolfing and the Alexander method—I forgot what all. I don't mean he was stupid, or just a joker, or anything like that. When I say he was a 'clown' all I mean is—" He stopped smiling and rolled his eyes heavenward, grotesquely, as if saying what he wanted to say, getting it just right, took total concentration and God's help. "You know how it is in the circus. The acrobat does something, and the clown tries to imitate it, but the clown's not human, like the acrobat, he's just this creature with straw in his head. That's why clowns are at the same time funny and sad: they imitate exactly what human beings do, and if the *Nicomachean Ethics* were right, they really would become human. But no matter what they do they remain just clowns."

Mickelsson smiled crossly and, still with his head down, looked at the boy up-from-under, reserved. The black boy on the van was still looking up into the darkness of the clouds, watching them with fascination, as if their movement were writing. "I guess I don't really follow," Mickelsson said.

Nugent gave a quick, eager nod, as if that were completely understandable, exactly as it should be. "I just mean that you have to *believe* things, to be human—you know? You have to feel that things are *true*. A clown is someone who'd give his soul to believe, if he had one, but he never can, he just goes through the motions, harder and harder, to no avail. We laugh at him because we recognize that, in a limited way, that's how we are too. That's what I was trying to say in class, about Kafka and the lost language and everything."

Mickelsson thought about it—thought, tentatively, hastily, about many things. "And Warren was a clown," he said at last—vapidly, waiting for something more.

Nugent nodded; two quick jerks. "I didn't understand it at the time—and I don't mean I was wrong to admire him. Gosh no! When he got married . . . I guess you've probably heard he was homosexual?"

"I hadn't, but—" He dismissed it with a wave.

"But that was typical, you see! The Truth of Science, Liberal Causes, Marriage and the Family . . ."

"Mr. Nugent," he said—again the young man's first name had escaped him—"you seem to be telling me that *you* have no beliefs, *you* feel like a clown. It seems to me that with a mind like yours—an extraordinary mind, if you'll forgive my saying so—"

"Mind! Oh yes, certainly!" He was smiling, ready to burst out any moment into raucous laughter. "Mind! No question!—e to the $i\pi$ equals minus one; this is the absolute proof of God's existence! Shall I demonstrate?"

Mickelsson reached out and touched his arm. "You stole that," he said.

Now the leaves were moving, filling the air with a whirring sound. One second ago the trees had been as still as marble. Western light slashed in under the darkness, yellowing the drab brick buildings below, burning the aluminum verticals and windows of the towers.

Nugent jerked his arm back. "Nobody *wants* to be a clown," he said, "except Emmett Kelly, who was human."

Now the rain began, huge warm drops falling softly and neatly, as if aimed.

3

That Friday morning (all but the oakleaves had fallen now, and the smell of November was distinct in the air, all but the scent of woodsmoke, which would only come with the month itself in Pennsylvania), Mickelsson slept late. A little before noon a knock came at the door. He lay waiting for whoever it was to go away, but the knock came again, and, changing his mind, he got up, put on his slippers and robe, and hurried down to answer. He was hung over from drinking while he worked on the house, the night before, and his arms, his back, and the backs of his legs ached from pushing too long and hard at his weight-lifting, just before he'd fallen into bed. As soon as he opened the door he saw that he'd been mistaken to come down. On his front porch stood two young men, wearing ties and long black coats. Their plain black, carefully polished shoes looked like government-issue, and both young men had their hair cut short, like marines. He clung to his first thought, that they were I.R.S. men, or maybe F.B.I. men come to speak with him of Mark, bring him some news or warning; but he knew all the while that that was wrong. There was something drab, even pitiful about them. They wore no gloves, and their faces, especially the noses and ears, were red from the cold. Their breath made steam.

The blond one said, "Mr. Mickelsson, we're representing the Church of Jesus Christ Latter-Day Saints. We understand you recently paid a visit to Salt Lake City—"

Whatever the young man said next Mickelsson didn't hear. He stared, a confusion of emotions leaping up—horror, anger, morbid interest. It was true that he'd visited Salt Lake City, but it was three or four years ago, an aesthetics conference. How had they found out? Some student? Faculty member? Their network didn't miss a trick, he'd give them that. Or was it possible that they used the line on everyone, since more often than not whoever they talked to would at one time or another have visited that exalted tourist trap? If the person they talked to happened not to have been there, no harm: the sober black foot was in the door. Did they have psychologists working for them, he wondered—people who figured out the angles of entrance, understood the insidious advantage of taking the prospect off guard, addressing him by name, seeming to know all about him, past and present? Did they have sales-pitch classes, conferences on seduction, persuasion, intimidation? It was a shocking idea, but they probably did, he decided. It was the 1980s; the world was on its last legs, Armageddon close at hand. No time for the messengers of God to be scrupulous or shy.

He realized that almost unconsciously he'd said "Yes," nodding, admitting that he had once visited Salt Lake City, yes. Perhaps, the blond one said, he would like to know more about the Mormons. Again Mickelsson failed to react. He could have told them he knew a good deal about the Mormons. He'd had a student, some time ago, who'd broken away from the Mormon Church and had been hounded for months by their soft-spoken, black-suited squads. He'd had a colleague in California who'd been hounded in the same way for fifteen years. Mickelsson thought of the underwear he'd been told their women wore, marked with holy gibberish and never taken off, not even in the shower—a sin against life, if it was true, he would have told them—and once, in a motel somewhere, he'd read a ways into their incredibly dull bible, the adventures of the archangel Moron. He knew the good that could be claimed for their company—their music, mainly (according to Ellen, it was vastly overrated); also the fact that they were family people, unusually successful in business and agriculture, non-drinkers, non-smokers, statistically more healthy and longer-lived than any other group in America. He would even grant that sometimes, as individuals, they were apparently good people, no real fault but dullness. The daughter of a family of Mormons had been a babysitter for his children when they'd lived in California. Perhaps these two young men at his door, if Mickelsson got to know them, would seem to him as admirable as his California neighbors. In all fairness, he couldn't condemn them for coming to him as missionaries. They all had to do it for a year of their lives, or so he'd been given to understand—always in twos, each for all practical purposes a spy on the other. Indeed, it was possible that they earnestly believed whatever foolishness it was they came with. Zeal and credulity were common among the young. Ecology, politics, animal rights . . . He thought of Alan Blassenheim and then of his own son, as pale as this pink-lipped young man now explaining to him the desperate condition of humanity—speaking not by rote, quite, but not altogether from the heart, either; prepared to be harshly interrupted and sent on his way. The dark-haired, red-nosed young man beside the blond one stood leaning slightly forward, looking at Mickelsson, listening to his partner with keen interest.

"Listen," Mickelsson said, raising both hands, "I'm not interested in this." He might have mentioned the cold they were letting into the house, but he said nothing, embarrassed at not inviting them in. Maybe that was why they wore no gloves or hats, part of the strategy worked out in Utah. Eastern States. Zone B.

"I realize you're busy," the blond one said, and gave him a smile as general and mechanical as the smile of an orphan, "but I'm sure if you could give us just three or four minutes—"

"I'm sorry, I really can't," Mickelsson said, and started to close the door.

Suddenly the one with black hair spoke up—the back-up man, the hard-sell. "Everyone's busy," he said and, smiling genially, cut the air with the side of his hand. "If we told you we could teach you a foolproof system for living to be a hundred, that might be different, right? Or if we told you we could make you a millionaire, no ifs or buts, no tricky fine print, you'd jump at it—anyway most people would!" He laughed, almost handsome. Mickelsson closed the door a few more inches, but the boy was no fool; he knew if Mickelsson had really meant to close it he'd have closed it. "You think I'm going to tell you that spiritual things are more important than earthly things like health and wealth. That's what other faiths will tell you. But the way we look at it, the whole thing's interrelated. You'll understand what I mean, Professor. Aren't you the author of *Survival and Medical Morals?*"

The hair on the back of Mickelsson's neck stirred.

The boy went on quickly, smiling hard, no doubt sensing that he'd set off a wrong reaction, "Survival's what we're here to talk about, Professor." Again he gave the air a slow, sideways chop. With the gesture, his craned-forward head moved like a snake's. "Isn't it possible that if people live as God intended them to live, they're likely to live longer, much healthier lives? Let me quote you some statistics about the Church of Jesus Christ Latter-Day—"

"Wait a minute," Mickelsson said, feeling his face flush, his right hand closing the lapel of his robe against the cold. "I know the statistics. I know the whole pitch. I already told you I'm not interested. Now good-day."

The boy blinked, then nodded. After an instant he said, "Thank you. Good-day, sir." He smiled in a way he apparently intended to seem friendly, but he didn't quite make it. Sour grapes, scornful superiority crept in.

The blond one showed relief. "Thank you for your time, sir."

Mickelsson closed the door.

The unpleasant aftertaste stayed with him for hours, like the indistinct memory of a nightmare. It was still at hand, coming over him in occasional flashes, when John Pearson drove up around four that afternoon, with the long-haired black dog in the seat beside him in his pickup. He got out stiffly, held the door for the dog, then closed the door and stood looking at the house. Some kind of object, a forked stick—a dowsing rod—dangled from his angular right hand. Mickelsson went out to meet him. "Hello," he called as the old man approached.

"Hod-do," Pearson said. He gestured to the dog without speaking, and at once it sat down beside the old man's left boot and stared as if thoughtfully at Mickelsson.

"Fine weather we been having," Mickelsson said.

Pearson seemed to consider the remark, glancing at the sky—gray, wintry clouds, yellow western light shooting under them, capping the mountains. "Had a little time on my hands," he said. "Thought I'd try to rustle you up that water."

"Good," Mickelsson said. "Anything I can get you?"

"Gaht it all right here," he said, and gave an impatient jerk to the dowsing rod. He looked up at the field behind Mickelsson's house, then, after a moment, back at Mickelsson. "Everything going all right here?"

"Everything's been fine," Mickelsson said. He gestured toward the trash bags, scraps of lumber, and crumbled shards of sheetrock piled more or less neatly near the firewood. "Been trying to fix the place up a little," he said. He was aware that his smile was less than modest. Anyone who glanced through the windows would be sure he'd had professionals in.

Pearson puckered his gray lips, not quite bothering to nod. Then, pointing to the woodpile: "I guess you know that wood ain't seasoned."

"Isn't it?" Mickelsson said.

"Burn that stuff in your stove, you'll wreck your chimley." He walked over to the wood—the dog moved with him—and, reaching down with two fingers, twisted off a small branch from one of the logs. "Pure green," he said. "Two months ago this stuff had birds in it."

"I guess I didn't realize," Mickelsson said.

Pearson shook his head as if in wonder, one side of his mouth pulled back. "Better let me bring you down some seasoned," he said. "Leave this just set here for a year or so." He glanced at Mickelsson. "I guess you ain't used to country livin." He grinned.

"Not for a long, long time, anyway," Mickelsson said.

"Wal," Pearson said. He looked up at the field behind the house again, then down at the dowsing rod, getting ready to start. The dog sat watching him, waiting for some command.

Mickelsson asked, "You mind if I come along and watch?"

"Suit yourself," the old man said.

They started up across the yard, past the overgrown garden, toward the field.

The old man walked with a look of concentration, his lips pressed together, the dowsing rod straight out in front of him, level with his pelvis, his thumbs aiming straight forward on top of the rod's two arms. Occasionally the end of the rod dipped, but apparently not to the old man's satisfaction. He walked with stiff, long steps, as if he were pacing something off. For all his concentration, he seemed to see nothing in the low weeds on the ground ahead of him but stepped awkwardly on small rocks, sticks, and ant-hills, adjusting his step without noticing. He walked straight across the field, parallel to the road, then, at the stone wall along Mickelsson's north line, turned and set off at an angle, up toward the woods. At the top of the hill, almost in the woods, he stopped pacing and, after a moment, sat down on a stump to rest. The dog sniffed his boots, then trotted away, darting here and there, keeping them in sight, searching for birds or rabbits.

"Seems like the land's gaht a spell on it," Pearson said.

Mickelsson studied him, trying to make out whether or not he was joking, but the old man's face showed nothing, staring out across the brightly painted valley in the direction of the viaduct. It seemed unlikely that he could see that far, with those blurry eyes. The river, under the gray sky, was silver and mirror smooth. Pearson turned his head to look at Mickelsson. "Funny you ain't seen them ghosts yet."

"I guess I'm not the type," Mickelsson said.

The old man grinned, then turned away. "Everbody's the type," he said. "Most likely you see 'em and don't notice."

Again Mickelsson said nothing. It was queer, he thought—though not all *that* queer, at Mickelsson's time of life—that in the classroom he stubbornly resisted ideas that made no sense, ideas half formed, unjustifiable, while here, standing in damp yellow leaves, he accepted John Pearson's crazy opinions as if nothing could be more obvious or natural. Or was he kidding himself, talking of a classroom Mickelsson who no longer existed? When was the last time he'd insisted, in class, on his students getting anything right?

Pearson's thought had drifted elsewhere. "Down there right acrost the road from your house," he said, pointing, glancing for a moment at Mickelsson to see that he had his attention, "they use to have the Susquehanna ice-house. Pond was a whole lot bigger then. Use to skate there, when I was a boy—me and all my friends. Used the ice-house to warm up in. They had apples there too, crates and crates of 'em; keep 'em cold through the winter. Sometimes kept bodies there, for burying in the spring. That was supposed to be a secret. Summertime we'd bring a bunch of boards and nails and make a diving-board. All that land there growin up in woods use to be pasture then—smooth pasture except for some thistles and boulders, right down to the edge of the pond. Old brother and sister that use to live in your house had a cowbarn and a silo right by that pear tree. Maybe you can see the foundation, if your eyesight's good. Burned down the same night the ice-house did. Drunken kids, likely; some of them rascals from up above the woods past my place. That was a long time after the murder and all. People use to come here from miles arownd just to swim in that pond." Again he glanced at Mickelsson. "Sometimes the brother and sister would set on the porch and watch, though they'd never talk to you, never said a word, and nobody never said a word to them neither. Strange people, not right in their heads. I guess a little slow."

"Sprague, you said their name was?" Mickelsson said.

"That's right. Can't quite recall their given names. I think the woman's was somethin like—" He looked at the sky for a moment, then said, as if reading it, "Theodosia."

Mickelsson raised his eyebrows.

"Yep. Some kind of religious name. All them old-timers had religious names. More strange religions in these pahrts than a man could shake a stick at."

"I believe I'd heard that," Mickelsson said. He remembered his visitors and asked, "Are there many Mormons left? I had a couple drop in on me this morning."

Pearson's look was rueful. "Not many, but people say they're comin back. You see a lot more of 'em on the road, these days, and I hear they been dickerin for a big old house in Montrose"—he turned his head, one eyebrow raised, to examine Mickelsson—"Quackenbush place, up against the church, white house with pillars and a big round porch in front. Back in 1900 it was a bank, they say. Oldest house in Montrose. They won't get it. Nobody likes to sell to 'em."

Mickelsson nodded. "I've seen the place."

Pearson looked down at the dowsing rod. After a minute he said, "Cryin shame."

When it was clear that he wouldn't continue unprodded, Mickelsson asked, "About the Mormons, you mean?"

"They're clubby," Pearson said, and squinted. "There's somethin unnatural abowt people all hangin together like that. The Baptists, now, they may be mean sons of bitches, but there's no way they're ever gonna take over the world. Too ornery. Can't get along well enough to get organized. Even the Catholics, they don't really make you nervous. Half the things they do in the world the Pope says they shouldn't, but they go right ahead and do it anyways. You don't have to worry about people like that, at least no more'n you'd worry about a common Presbyterian. But the Mormons, now—" He stared at the dowsing rod, lips compressed, trying to come up with exactly what he thought, and at last brought out, "Clubby."

"Well, they're healthy, you've got to admit that," Mickelsson said, and grinned. "They live practically forever."

"Yup." Pearson nodded. He looked out over the valley for a minute, then turned to squint up at Mickelsson again. "You seen those churches the Mormons gaht?" he asked. "I saw a picture of the one down in Washington, D.C. Big white thing, looks like they built it for one of them science-fiction pictures. Bunch of white spires that go pokin up like forktines, golden angels on top blowin trumpets. I tell you, I don't think I'd care to do business with a God wants a church like that. Wants to scare you and let you know your place—right under his boot. Those churches over in Europe, now—those cathedrals—they're a whole different thing. They make you think of a God that's *mighty* powerful, *mighty* impressive, but they let you know he's gaht some human in him; there's a chance if you talked to him he might know English. Same with the Methodist and Presbyterian churches, they let you know God's gaht his human side; and the Baptist churches, hell, anybody that can do card-tricks could take over for *that* God. But the God that thought up the churches of the Mormons"—Pearson shook his head as if sorry he had to say it—"he must've come down here from Pluto."

"Well, I imagine the Mormons do a great deal of good in the world," Mickelsson said, glancing toward the woods.

"Sure they do. Same as ants and bees." He leaned forward and, after a moment, stood up. "I suppose they're all right," he said. "Somebody thinks he knows how to get through this world alive, I take off my hat to'm." He held out the dowsing rod, adjusting his grip, preparing to march down the mountain.

"I take it you're neither a Mormon nor a Baptist," Mickelsson said, smiling. "Or a Catholic or Presbyterian," he added.

Pearson turned to stare at him. "I'm a witch," he said. "They didn't tell you that?"

Mickelsson stared, for the hundredth time uncertain whether or not he was having his leg pulled. "I guess I heard there were one or two of those around," he said, carefully not giving Pearson the satisfaction of a questioning look.

Pearson nodded soberly, staring down at the forked stick in his hands. If he'd been teasing, the mood had now left him. "This country's seen it all," he sighed, and slightly shook his head. "I imagine it's something to do with the darkness, the way the clouds are always there, or if they happen to break for a half a day it's like a miracle." He raised his head to look across the valley. "People joke about it having a spell on it, this country, specially fahrm people tryin to make somethin grow out of them rocks. But it does have, I always thought. Maybe gaht a whole lot of spells on it, layer on layer of 'em, clear back to the time of the Ice Age. Prehistoric animals, when they were driven owt, put a spell on it; Indians, when the white people came along, they put a spell on it. Then the Pennsylvania Dutch, then the railroad people, now the Polish and Italian dairy fahrmers . . . Course none of the spells do a thing, that's the truth of it." He narrowed his eyes to slits. "Mountains don't care," he said. "They're like a old lean cow, they give you what they can, and if it ain't enough they let you die and they forget you. Maybe dream you, once in a while, that's my theory—bring you back for a minute, like the Spragues down there."

"There's more life in the place than you'd think, though," Mickelsson said, falling in with the old man's mood. "Every night around dusk the deer come out, great big herds of 'em. They stand up there grazing almost to the first morning light."

"Yup," Pearson said, "lotta deer, all right. Bear too, though you'll never see 'em. Plenty of skunks, too—them you will see, owt crawling around your woodpile, lookin for bees and beetles. Coons, possums, thousand different species of birds . . ."

"Rattlesnakes," Mickelsson said.

"Hob-goblins," Pearson said.

They looked at each other as if reassessing. At last Pearson grinned and looked away.

It was dusk when Pearson finally found strong water, or claimed he had, right beside the garden fence. They marked the place with a stake and went into the kitchen to settle up. The dog stood just outside the door looking abused, and in brief consternation Mickelsson wondered if by country manners he should invite the dog in. Immediately he dismissed the thought. It was odd how in everything he did with the old man he felt foolish. A problem of the different languages they spoke, no doubt, every word and gesture half foreign. While he was writing the check, Pearson fingered the scraped place on the door.

"I see you scratched off the hex sign," he said.

"Yes," Mickelsson said. "You think it was a bad idea?"

Pearson shrugged. "It's yore howse now." He hung his rough hands on the bib of his overalls and looked into the livingroom. "You got a buckled floor," he said. "I don't recall seeing that before."

"I've got to fix that, if I can figure out how," Mickelsson said. "According to the doc, there's a spring under the house."

Pearson's mouth dropped slowly open and he pointed at the floor as if imagining it was he who was having his leg pulled. "You gaht a spring," he said slowly, "right under the howse?"

"That's what I was told," Mickelsson said.

"Well, I'll be damned," Pearson said. He pointed toward the kitchen door and the darkness beyond. "You got a spring right there under the floor, and I spent half the afternoon owt there wandering around in the weeds with a stick. . . ."

"Jesus," Mickelsson said, dawn breaking.

Pearson's eyes widened, and then suddenly both of them were laughing. The old man's normally gray face darkened and he laughed as if he could barely get his breath. Mickelsson leaned on the refrigerator, shaking.

"Jehoshaphat!" the old man said, clacking his false teeth.

Mickelsson bent over. He brought out, "Talk about city slickers!"

"Lord, I should charge you triple!" Pearson roared.

"I told you I've been away from the farm a long time!" Mickelsson said.

"Long time is right!" He drew back now, both of them getting their laughter into partial control. "Well," Pearson said, "if it was anybody else I'd say you owed me a drink!"

"Good idea," Mickelsson said, and, with one more whinny, wiping his eyes, went over to the cupboard for glasses.

They drank in the kitchen, Mickelsson unable to figure out whether or not it would be right to invite the old man into the livingroom. "Craziest thing I ever heard of," the old man said, and they laughed again.

Sometime into their second drink, Mickelsson asked, "By the way, how's your wife?"

"Etta Ruth died," Pearson said. "Happened three weeks ago Wensdee."

Mickelsson set down his glass. "I'm sorry." To his horror he realized that his lips were still smiling.

Pearson waved it off, not meeting his eyes, his expression stern. "No need to be. She was sick with that cancer a long time." Still looking stern, he stretched his lips in a grim, fake smile. "Spring right under the howse," he said, "and old John Pearson out there stompin through the weeds! Lord Jehoshaphat, that's a good one!"

That night, though he hadn't arranged ahead, as she liked for him to do, he went down to see Donnie. When he knocked on her door she called brightly, from a distance, probably the bedroom, "Who is it?"

"It's me," he said.

When she spoke again the brightness that had been in her voice was gone. "I can't come to the door, I'm taking a bath," she called.

He was almost certain he heard male laughter. He stood motionless for a moment, his head angled toward the door, his right ear almost against the panel. It was odd, these games they'd begun to play. It was the money, no doubt. To Donnie, he was a goldmine: even if she wasn't overcharging him, he was one hell of a regular; and so, even though it visibly annoyed her that old Mickelsson was always there, like God— annoyed her that he should spy on her, feel jealous of her, run on and on about his worries concerning her, her seeming lack of all normal connections (parents, young friends), her seeming indifference to the well-known dangers of her shady profession—she played along, ministered to his soul's prissiness as she would minister, if the profit seemed sufficient, to any other of her customers' kinks (he'd found bite marks on her shoulder one night—broken skin, ugly swelling, such a mess that he'd begged her to go see a doctor, which of course she'd refused to do), so that now, because it was Mickelsson calling to her, she claimed, like some maiden of the suburbs, to be taking a bath. No wonder the pustuled, crooked-toothed, hairy beast beside or on top of her laughed! Shamelessly, absurdly, Mickelsson went along with his own side of the stupid pretense. "How long will you be?"

Murmured consultation. Perhaps they purposely made themselves heard, to mock him, to let him know no one was fooled, neither there in Donnie Matthews' big, dingy apartment nor anywhere else in Susquehanna.

"Make it an hour," she called.

"OK, good," he said, nodding formally, actually reaching, in the dim, filthy hallway, for the brim of his hat. "Ten o'clock." He turned, scowling angrily, gripped the cane by the shank, just below the head, and started down the stairs.

The streets of Susquehanna were quiet, unusually empty. After the last few days' heavy storms—rain that had torn away most of the leaves, transforming the mountains from riotous color to the ominous slate gray of high, rolling waves in some sombre Winslow Homer—the weather had turned cold, so cold that tonight bits of ice shone like quartz in the darkness of asphalt and brick underfoot, on the walls of buildings, on the electric and telephone lines draped across the street, stretching away like a staff without notes toward the dully glowing iron bridge, the perfect blackness of the river below. He turned in that direction, deciding against the tavern up the hill, source of the only sound he could hear in all the town, or the only sound except the dull clunk that reached his ear each time the traffic-signal turned from red to green. People were laughing, back there in the tavern, and the jukebox was playing, so far away, all of it, it might have been sounds from his childhood.

At the bridge he turned left, moving toward the unlit, broad, flat span that had once been Susquehanna's famous depot, engine-repair station, and restaurant. The sign, up above his head, dimly lit by stars—COMING SOON! SUSQUEHANNA PLAZA!—was cracked and chipped, getting hard to read, like the rusty old sign one saw on the way in from Highway 81, VACATION IN THE ENDLESS MOUNTAINS. As he looked up at the sign, his eyes, without willing it, made a sudden shift to the stars beyond, the dusty white light of the Milky Way. Something bright, diamond-like, moved slowly across the sky from west to east, maybe an airplane without the usual lights, more likely some Russian or American satellite, Telstar, or whatever: odd that he no longer had any idea what was up there. He remembered—he hadn't thought of it in years—what excitement everyone had felt in the beginning, in the days of Sputnik I and Sputnik II, the martyred dogs, the great American end-over-end flopper: days of miracle! —the arrival of Christ in Glory could not have been more astonishing than the passage of those sparks across the heavens, one of them mournfully blinking on and off. They would stand in their yards, in suburbs and small towns or in the stillness of farm pastures all over America, looking up like sheep, empty hands hanging down beside their pockets;

here and there some father with a child in his arms would point up, whispering in awe, "See, Timmy?" or "See, Mark? See?" and the child would gaze solemnly at the finger.

"The heavens declare the glory of God," Mickelsson's grandfather would intone dryly, and Mickelsson's father would sit beaming in his pew, far more convinced than the old man in the pulpit that it was so, though Mickelsson's father would not definitely acknowledge God's existence. "Could be," he would say, when pressed, "could be." He believed in cats around the milkcan cover on the cowbarn floor, where he sploshed warm, new milk; believed in pines—he'd planted thousands of them—Canadian geese, slow-swaying Holsteins moving up a lane, heavy old Belgians pulling the log-sled. . . . Sometimes on Sunday afternoons, if Mickelsson had no highschool football game, the whole family would drive to the state hospital to visit his uncle, who'd gone crazy in the war. "Shell-shock," the family said, and everyone would nod sympathetically; but somehow Mickelsson had known the first time his grandmother said it that for some reason she was not telling the truth. It was not until many years later that he'd learned what had really happened. "Poor dear," his mother said, "it's a shame he couldn't have died right there! What a burden to carry all the rest of your life!"

From the moment they passed through the high iron gates of the hospital grounds, nothing was real: time slowed down, shapes took on an extraordinary sharpness and a seeming weightlessness, or every shape but his uncle, who stood in his bathrobe and pajamas, unkempt, hollow-eyed, as firmly centered and infinitely heavy, though small of stature, as some innocent, terrifying image in a nightmare. Though he was thin, his whiskered flesh sagged on his face (that was the effect of some drug he had to take, Mickelsson's father said), and his hair was bristly, littered with something scaly, dandruff-like, though apparently it was not dandruff. But none of that had been as troublesome to look at as his eyes.

"Well," Mickelsson's father would say as they drove home again, "I thought Edgar looked better, this time." "Did you?" his mother would say, giving him a glance. "Well," his father would say, as if it didn't much matter, really; eventually all would be well, that was the nature of things. Optimistic fatalist.

Mickelsson found himself standing in perfect darkness, in the pitch-dark shade of an abutment that rose steeply to give its heavy rock support to what was now empty air, below it the vast flat landfill floor that was once to have been the plaza. A perfect landing place for UFOs, he thought, and for a moment his memory entertained images from the final scenes of *Close Encounters*. In the blackness a few feet below him, invisible water lapped at the gravel, stone, and trash he stood on. For all the cold, the river had a smell, a fetidness like human bad breath. Across the flat, still river the black mountainside was beautiful with yellow houselights and cold white streetlights. The lights of a truck came slowly down the street, parallel to the river, then vanished behind trees and buildings. He half remembered, then brushed from his mind, the trucks he'd seen driving with their lights off. Maybe he'd dreamed the whole thing. A drunken nightmare.

He breathed deeply, clearing his head. How many times in fifty years, he asked himself, self-consciously, trying to pull back his earlier, sweeter mood, how many times did a man stand pondering in the night beside some river, remembering former nights, former rivers, counting up his losses? A man was never more alone, he thought, than when standing by himself looking at the lights of a community across a river, or across a lake, or from the deck of a ship. Had he thought exactly that same thought before, in exactly those same words, perhaps years ago? No, it came to him, he'd read them, or something like them: James Boswell looking at the stars before going up to his latest mistress. What a life! He turned to look up, ruefully, at the lights of Susquehanna.

And what if, for once, he, Mickelsson, were *not* to go up to his mistress? What if he were to take one small step toward bringing his life into control—reassert his dignity? It was community that kept one well and sane; that was the message of the book Michael Nugent had forced on him. Community was what he'd lost, leaving Providence, and what he'd fled, leaving Binghamton, and what called to him now in the form of yellow lights rising straight up the black wedge of mountain, lifting toward the lesser, gentler darkness of sky and embedded, icy stars.

He moved, frowning with thought, out of the shadow of the abutment onto the wide, gouged-out plaza site. His foolish infatuation was the heart and symbol of all that was wrong with him, his increasingly desperate embrace of chaos. It was she that made a clown of him, in Michael Nugent's sense, the imitation lover who gallantly allowed the whole town to laugh at him—anything for love!—middle-aged Mickelsson dressed up in ascot and threadbare formal coat for his teen-ager lady of the dark chipped tooth. Had he indeed gone mad, he asked himself. "Love for the unlovable." Surely it was not true that he was one of those! Though he'd almost not dared to think about it, Jessica Stark had shown by certain signs that she was not entirely indifferent to him, there was at least a faint chance. Gail Edelman, dropping her gaze when he glanced at her, smiling at him with a hint of special interest when he politely passed the time of day with her—neither he nor she showing by any word or sign that they remembered the night of his drunken visit. . . . It was of course not real love that he felt for Donnie Matthews but some irrational need, some sickness. Rifkin would know. (He had not yet mentioned the matter to Rifkin.) It was his firm persuasion, as an ethicist—or almost firm—that one could choose right conduct, will the higher man's self-mastery, if one would, in spite of the witless heart's wail.

He stopped walking, standing in the middle, now, of the gouged-out desolation. It was true, he saw with sudden clarity: he must not go to her! His children and ex-wife had need of his money, the money he was squandering, these days, on Donnie Matthews. He stood with his hands pushed deep in his overcoat pockets, his shadow, thrown by the street-lamps above, stretching across the bulldozed span of gravel and bits of ice-speckled brick. It was decided, he would not go. He would walk back to the Jeep and drive home. Relief flooded through him. There was hope for him yet, then! Slowly, somewhat against his will, he drew his left hand from his pocket and raised it toward his face for a look at his watch.

Ten o'clock! Panic rushed up into his chest and all his wisdom melted. "Shit," he whispered, and began to walk with quick strides back in the direction of the bridge. It was surprisingly far away. After a moment he began to run. He began to breathe hard, then cough as he ran—too much smoking—but he continued to run.

When he was inside her apartment, the door closed and locked behind him, he shook his overcoat loose and let it fall to the floor, Donnie Matthews staring at him with eyes full of alarm. He stood cocked forward like a maniac, breathing in gasps and rubbing his chest with his clenched right fist.

"Peter, you shouldn't have run," she said, "you knew I'd wait for you!"

She wore a white, Greek-looking dress and the amber beads he'd bought for her, no shoes on her small, perfect feet. Her skin shone, lightly perspiring from her recent bath; her hair was still slightly wet. She put her arms around him and pressed the side of her face to his chest, pushing his fist away, taking its place, moving her cheek against him hard, massaging him. "Peter, poor, crazy, crazy Peter," she murmured. He wrapped his arms around her, clinging for dear life. Her left hand moved to his erection, then unzipped his fly, freeing his straining penis. His heart whammed still harder. Unquestionably, she'd be the death of him. She slid down on his body, sinking to her knees, and took him in her mouth. He straightened up, arching his back, still gasping for breath. When he began to thrust, she rose, lifted the skirt of her dress— she had nothing underneath—and climbed up onto him, helping him in with one hand. Tears ran down his face. How many men's sperm did that warm cave contain? That was Peter Mickelsson's community: a thousand dark, writhing lives, unfulfilled, unfulfillable. He came, her legs froze around him, and—this time, anyway—he did not die.

As she put up with other things, she put up with his talk. Lying on his back beside her, early in the morning, after sleeping for hours without moving even a finger, like a dead man—one arm under her head now, the other thrown across his eyes—he told of old Pearson's visit, then of the visit of the Mormons.

"Strange people," she said, and opened her eyes for a moment as if thinking something unpleasant.

"Why so?" he asked, then lowered his wrist to his eyes again.

"I don't know. How can they *believe* that stuff? I mean, it's *all* a lot of bullshit, but with those other religions you can see how people might be taken in, because the weird stuff all happened so long ago. But Joseph Smith! People around here actually knew him—knew what an asshole he was. My own great-great-grandfather had dealings with him, or so my grandfather used to say. Said he was tricky as a snake."

"You had a grandfather?"

"Most people do. He lived in Lanesboro when there were still Indians around, except the Indians lived in Red Rock. There used to be this Indian that would come into town once a year, or maybe twice, I forget— he didn't live with the others, in Red Rock, he lived in the woods. He'd go to Mireiders' Store—it wasn't Mireiders' then—and he'd make a big pile of all the things he needed, and he'd find owt how much it came to and then he'd walk back into the woods and he'd come back owt the next day and pay his bill in gold coins. My grandfather had a dream one time, that the Indian dug the coins owt of a bank up by the viaduct. He always meant to go look there and see if the dream was true, but he never got around to it, and when he died he'd never showed anybody where it was."

"Do you have parents?" Mickelsson asked.

She was silent for a while. At last she said, "The Mormons always play like they're stupid and sweet, but really they're mean sons of bitches, or anyway most of 'em are. I guess even the sweet ones have to know what the other ones are doing, and I guess if they put up with it they're naht so sweet either."

He smiled, still with his eyes closed, hidden under his arm. "What do they do, these mean ones?"

"Torture people. Harris them."

"Harass."

"Well, however you say it."

"How do you know they harass people?"

"I know, don't worry." She spoke petulantly, as if she didn't know, in fact.

Mickelsson drifted toward sleep for a moment, then drifted back up into consciousness, thinking of the shabby, pitiful Mormons at his door. "They're a strange people," he said. "We all work from premises we can't fully defend, but the Mormons are true, deep-down absurdists."

"Mmm," she said; then, after a moment: "What do you mean?"

He turned his face to hers, then rolled over toward her, conscious of how huge he was, in comparison to her—how wasted, gross. No doubt that had to do with his heart's choice of her: since he paid her, it need not concern him that he was old and fat. He stroked the side of her forehead and cheek with the fingertips of his right hand. She stopped him, holding the hand in hers. "What do you mean, 'absurdists'?"

"They're people that know that nothing makes sense, the whole universe is crazy, or so they claim, but they go right on acting as if things make sense." He drew his hand free of hers and touched her face again. Could it be true, as Ellen claimed, that all women hate to be touched? He said, "The Mormons start with this insane, made-up history—Jesus Christ coming to someplace like Peru, where he meets not only Indians but also white people who look exactly like Charlton Heston playing Moses—and out of this craziness they make a huge, rich church, complete with army and police, or anyway so people will tell you out in Utah; they make a whole new style of architecture, new theory of the universe, new system of family relationships. . . . It's an amazing accomplishment, when you think about it. They've stepped out of normal time and space, and so far as you can tell, most of 'em aren't even aware of the fact."

"All religions are like that," she said. Again she stopped his hand.

"I don't know. The Mormons seem pretty special. Anyhow, they take care of each other. There's something to be said for that."

"I'd just as soon take care of myself," she said, and closed her eyes.

He drew his hand back and lay still, looking at her eyelashes, the faint suggestion of veins in her forehead, feeling gloom rise in him, recalling to him its cause, that soon he must leave her.

It was true, Mickelsson thought: she really would just as soon take care of herself. A true, natural feminist—unless perhaps she'd gotten her ideas from TV. All at once he thought he understood something. She would talk with him for hours as if with interest, sometimes closely watching his face as he answered some question she'd put to him, exactly as she would do if she cared about his opinion, that is, loved him; yet she insisted, over and over, that she did not love him—*liked* him, certainly; liked everyone, why not?—but love: no; never. She's wrong, he thought, and felt his heart lift. She's lying to herself, from her fear of entrapment. How she could love him—how anyone could love him—was a question he did not feel up to this morning; but suddenly he was absolutely sure that she did indeed love him. In the crisp morning light, the cracked paint on the window sash was like writing, like some form of Arabic. His eyes moved on to the wallpaper, dark gray and green on a base so yellowed it looked scorched. The tight wallpaper design looked as though it, too, might be writing. He looked at the pattern of veins in her chest and thought—not quite seriously but seriously playing with the possibility—that at any instant, if in some way his mind-set could be minutely shifted, she too would be language, all mysteries revealed.

"I have to go," he said.

She nodded, still with her eyes closed. "I'm glad you came."

He eased up onto the side of the bed, reached down for his socks, and put them on, then got into his undershorts and shirt.

She asked, half sitting up, "Peter, could you hand me that plastic pill thing on the dresser?"

He did. It was a pink plastic, numbered birth-control-pill dispenser. She thanked him, got out a pill, then whispered, "Shit."

"What's the matter?" he asked.

She shrugged. "I forgot my damn pill yesterday," she said. "Don't worry, I'll just take two today. It's all right. Don't look so panicky!" She laughed, delighted by the no doubt old-maidish look of horror on his face. "It's all right, believe me. It's happened before. Don't worry about ole Donnie, kiddo! She's strictly professional!"

"Christ, I hope so," he said. He put on his shoes.

She lay back, moving over into the middle of the bed, now that he was out of it, and spread her legs wide. She smiled, not enough to let the broken tooth show. "Think of me," she said, then pursed her lips as if to kiss the air.

"Don't worry," he said gloomily, cinching his belt. He turned his back to her, his heart growing heavier, darker by the moment, as much with guilt and self-revulsion as with sorrow; he counted out the money and slipped one corner of the stack of bills under the base of the elf lamp on her dresser; then he picked up his hat, cane, and overcoat in the living-room, fixed the nightlatch so the door would lock behind him, and let himself out.

He hardly noticed when someone on the stairway said, "Morning, Professor." But then it came through to him, and he stopped, looking down the third-floor hallway in the direction of the two black-coated young men. At the fat man's door they stopped walking and, looking back, saw him watching them. The dark-haired one smiled and nodded a second greeting while the blond one reached toward the fat man's door and knocked. Needless to feel alarm at being caught coming out of her apartment, he saw now. *They* wouldn't tell. In all probability those poor shabby innocents didn't even know what kind of business she ran. (Do them good, he thought; one night with Donnie Matthews. Both of them together, so they could spy on each other, keep up the ole support system.)

He heard the fat man's voice, then the door opening on its chain. Odd that he would open it at all, Mickelsson thought. No doubt after a time one grew lax. He put his left hand on the bannister, his right holding the cane by its silver head, and started down.

Around eleven that morning he was roused from desperately needed sleep by the jangling of the phone. He got up, shaking his head, rubbing his eyes, clearing his throat to get his voice operational, crossed to the phone on the bedroom wall and answered. When he heard the voice at the other end, he at first thought someone must be playing a prank on him. The voice was absurdly nasalized and flattened, almost exactly the voice of Bugs Bunny, but the accent was desperately low-class Italian, too extreme by many degrees to be real, and the words the voice spoke were so comically mad—or such was Mickelsson's first impression—so un-prompted, simultaneously hysterical and bellicose, reminiscent of the long-ago radio-days wackos who lived on Allen's Alley, that he smiled as he listened, trying to think who would do this to him, until little by little the smile decayed and he understood that the maniac on the line was serious.

"Professor Mickelsson?"

"Yes."

"My name is Ernest diSapio, that's right diSapio as in 'sap,' but don't count on it; I'm with the Internal Revenue Service, Scranton office, and I have here on my desk a letter allegedly written by you to this office on October twelfth. You claim in this letter that the I.R.S. has been harassing and bird-dogging you, according to your presumption because you dint pay your taxes in seventy-nine or even file them properly as the law pre-scribes. I wunt go around making charges of that nature if I was in your position, Professor, but that's neither here nor there. I'm now calling you to tell you two things, which the first is, we don't bird-dog, we don't need to, because the power is with us as you will see if you keep vilating federal law and trying to play cat and mouse with the Service, in fact we dint even know you was in the area and no longer in Binghamton, New York, until your letter let it slip. And which the second is, I have now been personally assigned to your case and I strongly advise you to cooperate in the fullest."

"Who is this?" Mickelsson asked.

"My name as I said earlier is Ernest diSapio, and I'm an agent with the Internal Revenue Service, Scranton office, P.O. Box 496, Scranton, Penn-sylvania."

"Wait a minute," Mickelsson said. Tentatively, he smiled.

"I would like you to be here in my office between nine and eleven on Monday morning, November seventeenth, with a fully documented account of—"

"Hey, hold on," Mickelsson said, his anger rising now. "I don't know if this call is a joke or not, but I teach on Mondays, and I have no intention—"

"I can show you pretty quickly that this is no joke. I have the power to swear out a warrant for your arrest. If I was you, Professor—"

"Listen, Mr. Sapio or whoever you are, I don't know why you're taking this tone with me, but I assure you I don't like it. It may be that all you ever deal with is criminals, in which case I'm sorry for you, but

I am *not* a criminal, and I must ask you to keep a civil tongue in your head." He was trembling a little. In a minute he'd be shouting.

"You're not a criminal, I'm glad to hear it. In that case I'm sure you will have no objection to meeting me in this office between nine and eleven on November seventeenth. The address—"

"Slow down, God damn it!" Mickelsson shouted. "As I've told you already, I teach on Mondays. Besides that, I have no information to give you, everything I have is with my lawyer, you'll have to talk with him."

"Mr. Mickelsson, I don't want to play games with you. In my book you're a skip: you moved from Binghamton, New York, without sending us notification; in 1977 you filed but neglected to pay your taxes, and in both seventy-eight and seventy-nine you filed late and again have not paid. Now you may have explanations for all the above, but since you dint see fit to give them in your letter of complaint to this office, and since your attitude is clearly hostile to the work of this office—"

"However that may be," Mickelsson said, controlling himself, suddenly aware that the maniac really might have the power he claimed, "I cannot give you the information you want; you'll have to talk to my lawyer. I'll give you his name and phone number."

There was a pause. At last diSapio said, "Very well. Let me have 'em."

He gave the man Jake Finney's name and number.

"All right, Professor Mickelsson," diSapio said, "I'll be back in touch. If I was you I'd get a lawyer in Pennsylvania. You're gonna need it."

"I'll do that. Thank you." Just before diSapio hung up, Mickelsson remembered and said: "One more thing. You say the I.R.S. has *not* been spying on me? I'm sorry to bother you, and I'm certainly sorry to have accused you falsely, if I have—I don't blame you for being cross, I suppose—but there's been someone, so to speak, keeping tabs on me, one of those dark green unmarked cars. . . ."

"Not us, Professor. According to my records you're separated from your wife. Maybe she's put a private dick on you."

"That's not her style," Mickelsson said, mostly to himself.

"Sorry I can't help you," diSapio said. Suddenly his voice was friendly, amused. With the change in tone he seemed to Mickelsson more than ever the voice of the Reich: savage, primordial, merciless.

"Well, thanks."

"I'll be in touch."

That afternoon when he tried to work on his blockbuster book, he found his mind was cement. Not only could he not write, he could see no value in anything he'd written. He remembered how pleased he'd been by some of the pages stacked beside the typewriter, but reading them over now, trying to give them every benefit of the doubt, he thought he must simply have been insane. It was, when one thought about it soberly, the stupidest project imaginable—a blockbuster philosophy book! He turned off the electric typewriter—all the time he'd spent looking at his finished pages, he'd allowed it to hum to him—then stood up and raised the sheaf of papers in his hand, about to throw them in the wastebasket. At the last moment he changed his mind: perhaps another day they wouldn't seem so bad, would at least seem revisable. He put them back beside the typewriter, face down. He would work a little more on the house.

That night he began on the hardest of the jobs he'd set himself, the transformation of the crooked, unheated workroom into what would be, eventually, his diningroom. It had seemed an almost impossible job all those afternoons and nights when he'd stood looking in at it, sipping a drink, thinking about what had to be done. There was a double sink to be taken out; a workbench; crude, cheaply stained pine cupboards and shelves; wallpaper and one stretch of panelling to be torn away, then linoleum flooring and the waterstained false ceiling. But once he'd put his gloves on and begun to tear into it with the wreckingbar—his pipe and a glass of gin for company, on the portable radio some newscaster talking about Reagan's vast support in Texas and his "undisclosed plan" for freeing the hostages—the work of demolition went more quickly than he would have thought possible. The shelves and cupboards had been carelessly put up and came out easily. The sink was not much harder, and the panelling came off in three fierce yanks. The fiberboard ceiling panels broke away like cake, and, climbing once more onto his rickety chair, he began on the wallpapered plaster and lath. By four in the morning, when he was on his third glass of gin and the ceiling was half down, his neck and shoulders numb from his exertion, he began to make discoveries. (He'd turned off the staticky radio long since.) At the far end of the room every second beam was missing, and those that remained were support-braced and blackened by fire. Even more interesting was the fact that here, as nowhere else in the house, the nails were square. It was the oldest section, then, as he'd suspected. Probably this room and the attic above it were all there had been of the house for a good many years. No wonder it had gone through so many wallpapers, so many changes of function.

He worked in a kind of dream, almost a trance, the room so full of dust that he could barely see. He wore a mask over his nose and mouth, goggles over his eyes. His pipe and the glass of gin on the floor in the corner of the room he'd covered with his handkerchief. From time to time he stopped to replace the filter in the mask and clean the goggles, but increasingly it became an idle gesture: even with the door open, propped against the woodpile, the turbulent dust and floating wallpaper chips made the room so dark and murky it was like working at the bottom of the sea.

He would not remember later what thoughts came as he worked.

After painting, sanding, making various fairly extensive repairs to the other rooms, he was used to the way the mind drifted freely when the body was engaged; but never before tonight had it been quite like this. It was not just the gin, the heavy darkness of dust through which he moved, wandering half lost in a room only fourteen by twenty—though both the gin and the dustcloud no doubt had their part in it. Lath and plaster, breaking away from the beams, opened squares of darkness like revelations. He stared deep into them but could see nothing, neither attic roof nor sky. With each tear-away of plaster and lath, dirt fell down into the room as from a shovel (he thought of Freddy Rogers' stone falls), struck the floor with a thud, and billowed upward again, pushing up like smoke all around him. In his mind he saw the dog floating through weeds like a black swan on a lake, and saw Pearson marching along the mountain with his dowsing rod, his whole soul and body intent on the discovery theoretically impossible for him to make. Witchcraft drifted into Mickelson's mind and seemed to him normal, not surprising: he imagined Pearson bent over a table where there were gloves, perhaps fingernails, speaking the name of the person they belonged to, drawing her toward him through the night. He tried to think where he'd gotten that image—something he'd seen, or possibly something someone had told him. But nothing came. Pearson had been joking, no doubt; so Mickelson had by now convinced himself. A "waterwitch," maybe; not really a witch. Yet in the dark, dust-filled room it seemed clear that no joke was ever wholly or solely a joke, not even what Rogers had called the "kidding around" of the universe. Whatever it occurred to one to say—anyone—was at some level true. At any rate, this much seemed sure: that Pearson was at one with the world in a way Peter Mickelsson was not. He knew without looking where the dog had gone off to, knew even what was happening under the ground. He thought of Pearson's words, "Most likely you see 'em and just don't notice." It was a theory that Mickelsson had encountered before, that psychic insights are for the most part trivial: a vague intrusion of someone else's personality, foreknowledge of a speed-trap, or that a letter of no real importance will be waiting in one's mailbox. His grandfather, after the arrival of his gift, had for the most part had visions as clear and detailed as applecrates on a hayrack, but there were times all he got was hunches, like the hunches of a blind man.

He found himself imagining—staring into the dust—the outlines of a shabby woodstove at the far end of the room, a gaunt, middle-aged woman in a gray dress bending down beside it, reaching toward a woodbox. In her right hand she had a wadded-up hankie. Had she been crying, perhaps? That was how the fire would have started, yes. A woman full of troubles, no longer alert, an unsafe old stove . . . He could know a good deal about the house, if he let himself. Long before the doomed brother and sister had lived there, there had to have been other generations, people who'd grown old in the house when it was only a one- or two-room saltbox. He thought about what kind of man would have built the place—cleared the trees, dug the foundation, notched the cornerbeams and nailed up the walls. Perhaps a young settler not even in his twenties, proud of himself, joyful in his freedom from dull New England parents, or parents back in Germany—a young man with a blond young wife as charged with animal vitality as he was, a big-smiled, big-bosomed, strong-legged young woman he fucked every night till the roof shook. He imagined it so vividly his genitals tingled; meanwhile the unhappy woman in gray—some long-forgotten cousin or aunt, perhaps, or some Wisconsin neighbor—stood at a dark, thick table, kneading bread. Her hands moved with an odd ferocity, as if driven by inner violence. He could smell the bread-dough, sweet and yeasty. The woman's head was bowed, her black hair rolled up and pinned. Between the two narrow cords at the back of her neck lay a dark, deep valley.

Then for a while he seemed to think nothing at all, simply watched the wreckingbar stab deep beneath the plaster and lath and pry them free. Once he barked his knuckles and swore; yet in a way he was pleased, remembering his father's hands, and his uncle's. Once, reaching down for what he thought to be a large scrap of wallpaper, he discovered with a start—as if the wallpaper had magically changed in his hand—the picture of Jesus looking sadly toward Heaven, a beautiful young man with no hope for humanity or himself. He thought of his son's look of sorrowful detachment as he rode in the Marin Riding Show, winning prize after prize, a born athlete—his sister clapping wildly and shouting herself voiceless, Mickelsson beaming, his weight-lifter arms folded on his wide chest. "Son, I can't tell you how proud we are!" Mickelsson had said as they drove home. His son had said, "Thanks," and without another word had turned to stare out the window. "Did I say something wrong?" Mickelsson had asked his wife. She'd smiled, her large teeth brilliant, as always, and had said nothing. His only consolation was that Leslie too seemed baffled, her expression as thoughtful as a cat's. And now, as if there were some connection, Mickelsson's thought drifted to the un-beautiful, earnest young Mormons pressing through the world with red noses and ears—like ants, like bees, as Pearson had said—urging their gospel of safety in numbers, organized conspiracy against death and the Devil, Utah's vast army of locked-together minds. They would prevail, no question about it. They, with their plain, shabby clothes, their dull eyes, were the Future, the terrible survivors. They were good with computers, wonderful at business administration; no unruly habits.

While he was thinking this—concerned, really, about his own situation, and even that not quite consciously, his attention unfocused, only dimly aware of why the Mormons so bothered him in his present mood—

a man adrift between yellow-lighted worlds like a dustcloud mindlessly wandering in space, toying with the possibility of collapsing into a planet —Mickelsson thought he heard a woman's voice say, angrily but desperately hiding her anger, "I'm not well, I guess," and then another voice answering with a grunt. Surprised, Mickelsson turned his head, straining to pierce the room's dimness, but there was nothing; a dream-voice, some old memory. He shook his head as if to wake himself, then sucked in breath and stabbed hard into the plaster and lath, prying away a great hunk above the door into the livingroom. "Dad?" someone said, making Mickelsson jump. But no; another dream. As the wall-section fell he heard a clink such as coins might make, or old brass jewelry. He got down off the chair, stepping clumsily because his legs were overtired, and bent down to sort with his gloved hand through the trash on the floor. After a moment, he found something and raised it toward his goggles to study it more closely: an old-fashioned wooden cheesebox with a sliding top. He forced the top open; then, removing the glove from his right hand, still holding the box up close to his goggles, poked inside with two fingers. The box was full of keys.

Mickelsson carried the box into the livingroom, carefully closing the door of the dust-filled workroom behind him. Slipping off his goggles and mask, he bent by the lamp in the corner to inspect his find more closely. It was evident at a glance that whatever doors, gates, trunks, or boxes the keys had once opened, whatever treasures or keepsakes they had guarded—whatever hands had turned those keys or reached in for the keepsakes—had long since vanished from the earth.

That instant a crash came from the cellar, right under his feet. He strode to the cellar door, determined this time to catch the damn thing, whatever it might be. He opened the door, switched the light on, and thudded on wobbly legs down the steep, narrow steps, almost falling in his haste. He stopped at the bottom and looked carefully all around. Mouldy, crooked beams, the filthy oil furnace, shelves crammed with rusted, mouldering paint cans—all he had left from the mountains of junk that had lain here when he came . . . He could see no sign of an intruder. The shadows seemed to peer back at him, like children in hiding, but nothing moved. Was it possible, he wondered, that rattlesnakes could come into a cellar and, in its warmth, stay awake through the winter? Not likely. He would get a book from the library, try to find out. Probably it was rats. Carefully, step by step, he went back up to the kitchen, watching and listening all the way. In his gloved left hand he held an old rusted key, the teeth blurred away to nothing. He imagined he smelled freshly baked cake. Then the scent was gone.

4

Before the concert, Mickelsson and Jessica had drinks at her house. He could hardly tell what he felt as he pushed the lighted-up button that rang her doorbell—guilty, shoddy, angry at having been put in this position of fake respectability, at the same time miserably unworthy: she was a beautiful woman, he a laboriously cleaned-up derelict; for all he knew, he had the clap. Not that he'd noticed any sign yet. Matter of time.

But as soon as she opened the door and gave him her smile, at the same time taking a step back, saying "Hi! Come in!"—Mickelsson tipping his hat to her like a big friendly sheriff—his churning emotions settled; he felt safe. Her hair flowed around her shoulders, and her tanned and freckled skin was radiant. She wore a white blouse and string-tie and tweedy light brown trousers, part of a suit—the coat lay on the arm of the couch. She held her fingers apart as if she had wet nailpolish on them, though he could see none. The clear kind, perhaps. "I'm running late, as usual," she said. "Do you want to fix us drinks? I'll just have sherry." Before he could do more than mumble "Fine, OK—" she was off down the hallway, calling over her shoulder, "Still raining?"

"A little," he said, opening the doors of the Swedish-modern cabinet where she kept her small store of liquor: Beefeater gin and the cheapest vermouth available, X-brand bourbon, one good Scotch, an assortment of circusy, undrinkable liqueurs, a bottle of Harvey's Bristol Cream that had probably been there for two, three years. He decided on straight gin for himself and took out the Harvey's for Jessica. He noticed that his cuff was ragged, almost fringe. "Could turn to snow," he called, then rose, setting the bottles on top of the cabinet, and headed toward the kitchen for ice.

"You really think so?" she called back. "My shoes will be moosh. I suppose if I can find my what's-its . . ."

Mickelsson laughed, still morose but coming around, unable to help himself. "Boots?" he offered. "Galoshes?" He dropped three ice cubes into his glass, then returned to the livingroom. Just as he finished filling her sherry glass, Jessica reappeared and sat down in a wide brown overstuffed chair, slipping off her shoe so she could tuck her right foot under her left leg. When she reached up for the glass he held out to her, trying not to let her see his ragged cuff, it struck him that the lift of her arm was exactly like a ballet dancer's, yet natural, unconsidered. "What a day!" she said.

"Fights with the Marxists?" he asked, bending closer, looking down at her like a surgeon. He stole a peek at her bosom, then backed off, drink in hand, and lowered himself onto the couch. It had come to be a frequent topic with them, the Marxists in sociology—in Mickelsson's opinion the stupidest so-called professors he'd ever met (not counting Levinson, perhaps), though in fact he had no evidence except for what he'd seen of one or two of them at parties—that and his invariable experience of Marxists elsewhere, both alive and in print. In Jessica's view, or so she claimed, they were at worst no more than a nuisance, "sincere and earnest, whatever else," she kept insisting, though once she slipped and referred to them as "like a squadron of mosquitoes in the bedroom." When pressed she would admit that possibly someday they might prove a threat; she broke their solidarity. Not too serious a threat, presumably: except for the elderly chairman, she outpublished the pack of them, and in debate, if she chose to (she probably would not) she could whip their asses—Mickelsson's expression, or President Jimmy Carter's; anyway, not Jessica's.

"I'll tell you," she said, "you should be grateful for a chairman as smart and good-hearted as Tillson!"

"And good-looking," he said.

There was distance in her smile. "That's not exactly his fault, you know."

He bowed, Oriental. "Dumb thing to say; most sorry." He raised his glass. "Cheers!"

She touched his glass with hers. "And may the concert not be awful!"

They sipped ritually. He asked, "You think it might be?"

"Well, you saw the Swissons at the Blicksteins', how they hide behind each other. 'After you, dear!' 'After you, dear!' That kind of thing could get pretty embarrassing on stage, maybe a contest to see who can make less noise."

He smiled, studying her. "Whose idea was this concert, anyway?"

"I guess I asked you," she said. She raised her shoulders and arms dramatically. "Well, somebody had to do it." She laughed.

"That's true," he said, and nodded soberly. "You did the right thing."

"Anyway, I'm sure it will be wonderful," she said. "Aren't they supposed to be famous or something?"

"We're all supposed to be." He shrugged sadly.

She laughed again, then raised her drink and sipped it.

He found himself bothered by the tone she was taking toward the Swissons. It was true that they weren't instantly charming, but if they were excellent musicians, as they were said to be . . . Something about her view of them struck him as unpleasantly—secular. Not just irreverent; something deeper, that he had no word for. Clinical. A tendency to look at human specimens—perceiving nothing wrong in it—under an unfairly revealing light. Yet that wasn't it either; she could be more just than he was—as she was, for instance, about Tillson. Were all women like that? Was it the case that men were all, like young Blassenheim, idealists— lovers of the Good, even when, like Mickelsson, they denied its existence, and therefore eager to give the benefit of the doubt, and made miserable by each inevitable lapse of flesh and brain—while women, for all their otherworldly attractiveness, were cold-blooded realists, indifferent to the rainbowed, celestial crypt, even at the noblest peaks of poetry or the loveliest moments in music planning out which hat to wear shopping? It was the opinion, he thought gloomily, of a male chauvinist pig.

It had been The Comedian, Ellen's friend, more than Ellen himself, who had made him aware of how strong that impulse was in him. "You really believe that, don't you," the young man had said, smiling, far away. Mickelsson no longer recalled what his offense had been, but he remembered meeting the young man's brown eyes and understanding with a shock that he, Mickelsson, was indeed, as the young man implied, a kind of living fossil, wrong through and through. Mickelsson had drawn back into himself and the rest of the night had refused to come out. "Stop sulking," Ellen had said when the others had gone home. She flashed her smile, as wide and impersonal as the smile of a model in a Sears catalogue, and later, at something like two in the morning, she and the young man had gone off somewhere. It seemed to Mickelsson now that he'd been sulking ever since.

". . . like my husband," Jessica was saying, slightly smiling, looking down. "What a bum."

He awakened to the realization that, for all her smile, she was speaking carefully, controlling strong emotion, imagining Mickelsson to be listening with the interest and sympathy his expression seemed to show. *Less bum than I am*, he thought, fraudulently smiling on. He had a sudden sharp sense of the dead man he'd never known, a gentle personality adrift everywhere in the room, in the black leather chair, the tall African drums (he realized with a shock how absurd it was that all this time he'd felt superior to a man who knew trees, black African languages, the politics of ecology). . . . Jessica above all, touching her collarbone with the tips of two fingers, as if she were feeling a light pain there, was an expression of the dead man's taste.

"But of course he was always the soul of tact," she said, turning her shadowed eyes on Mickelsson. "Saying exactly what you meant was uncivil. You can see where that put me. South Borneo."

"You're tactful in the long run," Mickelsson said. "Just trickier."

She thought about it. "I hope that's true."

Woefully, he thought of the big, battered Jeep truck waiting outside in the rain, the front license plate dangling from one screw, the right front mirror angling out—as it had been when he'd bought it—like a broken dodo's wing.

"What do you think?" she asked. "Shall we go or have another?"

He pursed his lips and lowered his eyebrows in a comic frown. It seemed to him conceivably an invitation to spend the evening, miss the concert. His eye fell on the stereo—futuristic, expensive, another tactful observation from beyond the grave. If she was as blunt as she claimed to be, he was a real dunderhead; the more he tried to figure out her signals, the more confused he became. He remembered how when he was moving his hand on her leg she'd stopped him, in no uncertain terms, with her foot. He looked at his watch. "I guess we'd better get going, if we're going," he said.

He couldn't tell whether her smile was one of relief or just bafflement. He leaned forward, preparing to stand up.

"OK," she said, still smiling indecipherably, "I'll get my coat."

They rose together; he couldn't tell which of them had caused it, and even now he was toying in panic with the idea of staying. The idea of their future fell away like the corridor in one of those Texas super-motels he'd stayed in from time to time when attending conferences; but whether that was bad or good he couldn't tell. While she searched through the closet beside the front door, Mickelsson put on his own coat. At the far end of the hallway, the bedroom door was open, dim light falling over the bedspread of fringed yellow-gold. Her dead husband, watching solemnly from the edges of the room, would approve. "Be good to my wife," he would say, as Mickelsson had said in his heart to the young man who was able to be not just lover but friend to *his* wife. *Ah, that this all too sullied flesh would melt, thaw, resolve itself. . . .* He cleared his throat.

Jessica slipped her gloved hand between Mickelsson's waist and elbow and gently laid the fingers on his arm. When they stepped outside, they saw that the rain had turned, as he'd thought it might, into softly falling snow. The Jeep, to Mickelsson, looked sullen and defensively self-righteous, as if thinking of the height to which the lady must lift her leg if she intended to get in. A dog stood on the sidewalk twenty feet away, looking up at them from something it had been sniffing. It lowered its head, apologetic, and moved off.

"What a beautiful night!" Jessica said, raising her face so the snow could fall on it.

Outside the Jean Casadesus Auditorium they saw everyone they knew, all dressed to the nines—the Bryants, Edith in a mink stole, Phil in the shabbily expensive attire of a British lord; the Garrets, Mabel in drab, funereal black, Tom in a black turtleneck sweater and a brown sport-coat, a prominent spot of blue paint on his otherwise impeccable French bell-bottoms; the Meyersons; the Blicksteins; several of his students. . . .

Conversation roared like a sea around them. Suddenly, Tillson was at Mickelsson's elbow, bowing and grinning, speaking in the cracked voice of an adolescent: "Good to see ya, Pete! Gosh, Jessie! Good to see ya!" He grabbed her right hand in both of his. "Isn't this exciting?"

She nodded, smiling, resting her left hand on Mickelsson's back. "Isn't it?" she said. Mickelsson nodded and smiled.

"Well, I better get back to my place on line," Tillson said, giving his head an extreme sideways jerk. "God bless you! Happy evening!" He fled.

"Poor Geoffrey!" Jessica said, and smiled.

It was true, as Freddy Rogers had observed at the Blicksteins', that Katie Swisson had a "sweet, sweet voice"—sweet, pure, elegant, and young. But Mickelsson found it unpleasant to watch her. She seemed unhealthily pale, as did her husband at the piano, but that was the least of it. She had a queer way of striking her notes with the tip of her nose and her eyebrows, and she sang bent forward at the waist, hands eagerly clasped, eyes overlarge and bright, as if to say, "Isn't this delightful? Isn't this *fun?*" She wore a narrow-strapped, low-necked teal dress that looked to Mickelsson remarkably like a slip, and on the bun at the back of her blond head she had pinned a dark red rose. Her husband's piano playing was if anything even more self-conscious than her singing. He leaned far back and occasionally shook his head as if to say, "Oh no! Oh no!" or nodded as if to say, "Oh yes! Oh *yes!*" then brought his blond head sweeping forward dramatically, as if to butt the piano, then at the last moment stopped, jerked his head up with an open-mouthed look of astonishment at what he'd nearly done, tossed a smile to his wife, who seemed to take wonderful pleasure in his antics, and leaned far back again as if to make the audience believe it was not *he* who made that curious tinkling in the treble.

"There's the answer to the energy shortage," Mickelsson whispered. "We could strap some kind of machine to them, run the lights or something."

Jessica raised one finger to her lips.

He closed his eyes, thinking if perhaps he only heard and did not see, all would be well. But alas, in his mind they bobbed and weaved as grotesquely as ever. When he opened his eyes again and glanced around, it seemed that in all the audience he alone was unenraptured. He leaned slightly toward Jessica and whispered, "Ah, I get it! It's Art!"

She pointedly did not hear him, sitting with her head lifted, smiling with appreciation. Christ but she was beautiful! Fake as hell, just now; but beautiful. He thought of speaking further but decided against it. She seemed actually to be enjoying it, though it was she herself who had warned him that it might be awful. Once or twice she nodded and almost laughed with delight. It was a fact, perhaps, that the whole thing was ridiculous, but he'd better not trust his judgment. Though he'd had only one glass of gin, it had been a good-sized glass, and on an empty stomach. He would give the audience the benefit of the doubt. Anyway, music had never been his language. Spiritual insensitivity, no doubt, like Faust's. Deaf to even the noblest arguments. *See, see, where Christ's bloom streams in the firmament!*

He tried to listen to the words of the song, since some of them at least seemed to be English, and after a moment he discovered that it was something old-timey, not Shakespeare, but something vintage:

> *"Stay me with flagons,*
> *Comfort me with apples,*
> *for I am sick with love!"*

Mickelsson threw a look at Jessica, saw that she was still all attention, then slouched down in his seat.

"*With lu-uh-uh-uh-uh-uv!*" Kate Swisson sang. Her eyes had that glistening, lidless look embarrassingly common among Swedes.

All around him students, professors, and townspeople listened reverently, as they would listen to the solemn intonings of a Carter, Anderson, or Reagan on TV. Some of the people around him were smiling, little teary glints in their eyes. He sighed. "Don't make a scene," he cautioned himself. "Culture is not for everyone." He let his eyes drift again over the audience and suddenly came alert. The brown-eyed young woman he'd met in the kitchen at Blicksteins', widow of the murdered chemistry professor, was here at the concert with the dean and his wife, sitting between them like a daughter, the dean's arm on the top of the seatback behind her, just barely not touching her, nestled against her hair. The young woman sat with her forehead resting on her hand, the elbow on the seat-arm, so that her eyes were hidden, perhaps allowing her to sleep or, conceivably—he smiled at the thought—cry. Then it crept over him that she *was* crying. "Fool," he told himself, clenching his fist. He thought of how he'd blindly trod on the Polish girl's feelings in his graduate medical ethics class.

Kate Swisson sang, smiling frantically,

> *"The voice of my beloved!*
> *Behold he cometh, leaping upon the mountains,*
> *skipping upon the hills. . . ."*

Idiotically, the piano made jumping noises in the bass, and all around Mickelsson, people laughed. He craned his neck, making sure it was not that something had happened on the stage, but no, it was the music; all was normal, if any of this hoity-toity foolishness was normal—the Swisson twins grinning happily, both of them swaying like Muppets on TV. He thought, abruptly smiling, of what Donnie Matthews would think of all this, or Tim. "Faggots!" she would say, and that would be that. But at once he backed off. They were not his people either. As soon as the dining-room was finished, he thought, he must have a party. That would be a good time, as long as the party weren't too close to Christmas. He wasn't quite up yet to full-fledged Christmas feeling.

Perhaps his son would show up, stay for a while with Mickelsson, talking about the nukes, straightening out old problems. It was surely not unthinkable. What rage he must have felt when they'd smashed his camera, what absolute bafflement, given the trust in life Mickelsson had done his best to instill in him. They would talk, perhaps shout, as when Mickelsson had tried to make him not afraid of horses. He saw the horse rearing, his son flying off, terrified and helplessly enraged. Mark had been seven or eight then. It was at one of those riding stables, snowy mountains in the distance. "For Christ's sake, it's only an *animal*," Mickelsson had yelled, trying to drive his son to courage by pure fury. "I hate animals," Mark had yelled back, crying, looking wild-eyed, crawling away on all fours from his father as if he, Mickelsson, were an animal, the most dangerous and stupid of them all. Mickelsson cringed, remembering it. But Mark had indeed overcome his fear—had become a fine rider, secretly proud of himself.

Perhaps it was possible. It would make sense, all things considered. Mark would appear from nowhere, like a deer from the woods or the first midwinter robin. He would be bearded, duffle-bagged, loaded down with books and pamphlets. And what if the boy were to meet Donnie? He felt a blush stinging his face.

He must definitely have a party, show off the house. He began to work out in his mind what date the Friday two weeks before Christmas would fall on. Election Day was next week, the fourth. . . .

Without warning, the Swissons' song stopped, and everyone began to clap. Jessica, beside him, clapped with what surely must be genuine pleasure. Britt Swisson rose from the piano to bow—he seemed almost to be laughing—and the clapping grew louder. From here and there throughout the auditorium came whistles and shouts of "Bravo!" It was, by God, an *event*, Mickelsson thought. The Blicksteins' young woman was leaning far forward, clapping violently. Perfectly together, like two grinning dolls, the Swissons bowed and bowed. Then at last the clapping diminished and died, and Britt Swisson went back to the piano. He and his wife watched each other, nodding to an inaudible beat, nodding like two children about to leap into the flip of a jumprope; then suddenly, exactly together, they started singing and playing. Mickelsson lowered himself in his seat a little and sullenly closed his eyes. "*I am come into my garden, my sister, my spouse,*" Kate Swisson sang, her blue eyes round as saucers.

. . .

"Who would've believed from meeting them," Phil Bryant said when intermission came, "that the Swissons would turn out to be comics!"

Mickelsson, for civility's sake, said nothing. He thought again of old Pearson's idea of the Mormon God, alien and terrible, watching the activities of humanity with the detachment of a spider.

"They must've had the *most* fun working up their act!" Edie cried, bending toward Mickelsson and Jessica to make herself heard.

Jessica called back, laughing, "You make them sound like a vaudeville team!"

"But what else?" Edie cried, tossing her curls and merrily batting the air; then, turning to draw in Mabel Garret, "They're a team, Mabel, aren't they? Nobody doubts they're *artistes*, of course!"

Mabel said nothing, smiling rather oddly at Mickelsson, her brown eyes hooded, as if she'd heard some terrible rumor about him and had not yet definitely made up her mind.

"Well I *approve*," Edie said, dictatorial. "Whatever says that serious art can't be playful? Why, isn't all art play?" She turned suddenly to Mickelsson. "What do *you* think, Peter? *You* know all about aesthetics!"

"Yes," he said, slightly bowing, like a count, intentionally off register.

She smiled as if it were exactly what she'd hoped he would say, and as she turned back to the Garrets, then quickly to her husband, realizing just an instant too late how difficult it would be to play off doom-faced Mabel, Mickelsson backed off a step, getting out his pipe, and edged into the chattering, smiling crowd, toward the double doors. When Jessica glanced at him, as if surprised at his abandoning her to the Bryants, Mickelsson smiled and held up his pipe as explanation. She made a face, then turned back to Edith.

In the commons outside, it was still snowing, large flakes falling softly, thickly, so that the tower of the Ad Building was a barely visible wedge against the night. Large and noisy as the crowd was, both inside the building and here, spilling out past the doors behind him, there was no one about on the commons. Under the long lines of goose-necked lamps the falling snow bloomed brighter, the whole scene forming some pattern he recognized. It came to him at last: ballet; London; his daughter Leslie in the seat beside him, holding his hand, leaning forward with an expression of intense concentration, taking in the dance just as, once, in Paris or Rome—some old, high-ceilinged, inexpensive hotel—she'd sat up suddenly in the darkness, bending forward intently, as Mickelsson and Ellen abruptly broke off their love-making.

He gripped his pipe between his teeth and raised a match to it. As he did so, it came to him that something was standing just behind him in the darkness, almost at his elbow, though most of the others stayed close to the building, out of the cold. When he turned, he saw Tom Garret smiling at him sociably.

"Oh, hello, Tom," Mickelsson said. "I didn't know you smoked."

"I don't," Garret said, and grinned, holding up both hands to show that they were empty. "Can't afford it; too many mouths to feed. Just came out for the air. Enjoying the concert?" From his cherub, squirrel-cheeked grin it was clear that he, like Jessica and the others, was having a dandy time.

Mickelsson blew out smoke and half turned away. "I guess I must not be in the mood," he said.

"That'll happen," Garret said lightly, as if Mickelsson's remark were not evasion but familiar truth. "Sometimes the waters just aren't flowing."

For some reason the observation stirred Mickelsson's feelings. He was reminded of old John Pearson, marching up and down the mountain with his dowsing rod; and he remembered Pearson's saying, "Seems like the land's gaht a spell on it." Mickelsson cleared his throat and said, "I see the Blicksteins have their friend with them."

Garret nodded. "Yeah. I guess they take her everywhere."

Mickelsson moved closer to him. "Why is that, do you know?"

"You didn't hear?" Garret asked. He brushed snowflakes from his nose.

"I know her husband was murdered. That's about all I know."

Garret looked out into the empty commons. He stood with his arms folded on his banty chest, stomach thrown forward, and he rocked back and forth on the balls of his feet. "That's about all anybody knows," he said. "Awful thing." His tone was oddly light, conversational, though it was clear enough that he took the matter seriously. "They'd only been married a month or so, very happy, and so forth and so on."

"I'm sorry. What was the connection with the Blicksteins?"

"The husband worked part-time in Blickstein's office, some kind of administrative assistant or something—rest of the time in the Chem Department. I guess the Blicksteins got friendly with 'em."

"And nobody has any idea who killed him?"

"Apparently not, or if they do they're still keeping it under their hat." He leaned his head way over, looking at Mickelsson. Garret's hair and shoulders were white with snowflakes. "Worst part of it is, it was apparently someone the Warrens knew. I forget the details. The girl was away at the time, visiting her parents or something. Mabel can tell you the parts I've forgotten. Husband was alone in the apartment, let in the murderer, apparently had a chat with him, and so forth and so on. You'd think the police could solve a thing like that." He shook his head.

"Awful," Mickelsson said. "Let *him* in, did you say?"

"Him, her, them . . ."

He thought of asking if it were true that the man was homosexual, then decided against it. Anyway, Nugent wouldn't have been mistaken about that.

In the lobby behind them the lights flicked on and off. Mickelsson put the palm of his right hand over the pipebowl, the palp of his left thumb over the hole in the stem. "I meant to ask you," he said as they went in together, following the crowd, "I'm having a little party December twelfth, Friday. Do you think you and Mabel could make it?"

"I'll ask her," Garret said, smiling. "Off-hand, it sounds great."

"Nothing fancy," Mickelsson said, waving his pipe. "Just a few friends."

As they rejoined the group at the auditorium door, Edie Bryant was saying, smiling, her wattles shaking like fringe, "Well, Jessie, there they are, two people sharing a talent. I'll grant them that. Now, Phil and I, we're as diffrunt as night and day. Outside the sanctuary of the bedroom, all is war." She winked at Jessica, wicked. Bryant smiled, raising his jaw a little to put on more dignity. Tom Garret, arms folded over his chest again, looked down at the carpet, grinning to himself.

"Phil," Mickelsson said, "and Jessica, I wanted to ask you this too." He took her elbow. "I'm having a little party on December twelfth; that's a Friday. If you're free that night and you'd like to come—"

Jessica smiled as if wonderfully surprised and pleased but drew her arm away.

For reasons Mickelsson didn't fully think out, the second half of the concert annoyed him much less than the first. He could have found reasons enough, of course. There was the distraction of Jessica's emphatic coolness beside him, as if he'd somehow insulted her—whether by leaving her for a smoke outside, or by showing too little respect for Art, or by some other mistake, heaven knew. In any event, the discomfort she caused him made the music seem comparatively unworrisome. He glanced at her occasionally, showing his puzzlement, wordlessly asking for explanation; and though she didn't see fit to explain to him, she did at least partly relent, patting his hand, then returning her own hand to her lap and resting it with the other.

And part of his increased appreciation, no doubt, had to do with the effect of the music on the Blicksteins' young friend. She listened with such a rapt expression—head lifted, one diamond ear-ring shooting off needle-sharp arcs of colored light—that it occurred to him to wonder if perhaps the young woman was herself a musician, hearing things inaudible to the common ear. He made a greater effort to feel what the others were feeling. He began to nod, furtively tap his toes inside his shoes, raise his eyebrows in appreciative surprise, smile when those around him smiled.

Once he turned his attention to it, the whole idea of using "serious" modern musical devices ("tone rows," "clusters," whatever musicologists would call all this) for comic purposes seemed to Mickelsson rather interesting. Mickelsson knew nothing about the details of music. For all his Lutheran heritage and his father's special love of singing, he himself had never been musical, as a child; in fact he couldn't carry a tune. Not that he hadn't made efforts to inform himself; part of his game was writing articles in aesthetics. He'd read an occasional book—a life of Mahler, another of Berlioz, the memoirs of Shostakovich. But he would hardly have ventured an opinion on Mahler, Berlioz, or Shostakovich in the company of musicians.

Yet for all that, as he listened to the Swissons' music he began to develop a theory.

The devices Britt Swisson used in his compositions were mainly of the kind an ordinary, uneducated listener (like Mickelsson) would describe as "noise"; discord, scrambled rhythms, an occasional little passage of what might have been jazz, another that might have been the slightly "off" thumpings and poopings of a German town band—passages leading nowhere, ripped from their context, not so much "music" properly speaking as fragments of sound, glittering objects from civilization's music dump. Surely these devices had entered the vocabulary of contemporary music in the first place (he reasoned) because they gave expression to feelings left unsatisfied in the rhythmic, melodic, and harmonic tradition descended from, say, Bach and the eighteenth century. (It was true that in philosophical circles the emotion/expression theory of art had been taking quite a beating lately; but Mickelsson's money, despite the current fashion, was on Collingwood and his gang.) And surely those unsatisfied feelings—the loss, alarm, paranoia, and vulgar passion in modern music— were none other than the emotions the Enlightenment repressed: the universal or at least very common human sense of vulnerability, encircling chaos, cosmic indifference. Discord and noise, in other words—bits of musical chaos partially ordered by the composer but allowed to stand as chaos, uncancelled or reformed—Being in the rift—were the musician's expression of the godless, all-but-universal modern world-sense: the rage and alarm of an accidental consciousness stripped of its comforting illusions. It was fitting, it struck him now, that Kate Swisson should have said to him, all righteous sobriety, "Britt and I don't believe in ghosts"; but also it was the usual modern bullshit, for what was the meaning, intentional or otherwise, of Swisson's comic use of devices invented out of fear and anger if it was not mockery of the devices by misapplication, to demonstrate, by mimicking them, how childish they were in their existential wail—to reveal them, without mercy (but also with no hard feelings), as theatrical rant and hand-wringing? Once all pretensions to tragic grandeur were dashed, once the very scream of "the ungodded sky" was shown for what it was, a self-regarding *Waa*, what could be expected but—what else was possible than—a return to good humor, classical sociability in place of the Romantic yawp? In other words, "Ideals," as one used to say— value assertions with rounded edges—rushing up into the world as from a wellspring? (To say "We don't believe in ghosts" was an act of truly

MICKELSSON'S GHOSTS / 258

shocking vulgarity. Who was ever quicker to talk about ghosts than the civilized, the effete genteel, the English? Only the opposite assertion, "We *do* believe in ghosts"—except if it were said by a madwoman—could be more vulgar.)

Little by little Mickelsson came to be so taken by his theory that he began actually to enjoy the music, even its overwrought performance. Tentatively, he smiled, nodding his approval. He knew well enough how Ellen's theories, many of them published in *Modern Drama* and *The Educational Theatre Journal*, could make crap intellectually majestic; and he remembered how, when they'd gone to Cornell to decide whether or not Mark should go there, and had visited the conspicuously expensive art museum, Mark had said, looking around at the sculptures, paintings, drawings, and photographs, "Any freshman that comes here would know right away that it's all stupid, but I bet you after four years of art education, he's not sure anymore." Mickelsson knew, in other words, how aesthetic theory can steal the wall from the aesthetic object. Nevertheless it seemed to him that his theory of the Swissons' music was right, not just concept juggling, not just an exercise, on his part, of the age-old human inclination to make peace with even the most outlandish opinions of the tribe. True, it was possible that the stuffiness of the place had mellowed him: audience heat and the scarcity of oxygen made it harder and harder to keep from yawning. And no doubt he'd been influenced by pity for the Warren woman. It was always tempting to reason away the defects of an essentially benevolent community. Nevertheless he smiled and nodded now—even raised and lowered the toes of his shoes—with firm commitment. Jessica glanced at him, still reserved, even sulky, but tentatively pleased by the improvement in his attitude. He considered reaching for her hand. The same moment, he saw, close to the stage, right in front of Katie Swisson's teal-colored shoes, his student Alan Blassenheim. The sight of Blassenheim warmed Mickelsson's heart almost as a glimpse of his own son would have done. The young man's dark, soft-looking hair, set off against the stagelights, had purple highlights and a rainbowed halo at the edges. Mickelsson was reminded of the half-despairing Jesus in the dust-obscured picture from the workroom floor. It was true, he reflected; Blassenheim was a classic case: the desperate good boy, eager to please, lifted up beyond the physical now, devoted to the Best, whatever in the world the Best should prove to be. His devotion alone witnessed to its existence. Perhaps it was the same with his son. Ah, the pity! With all one's heart one longed to give young people the key to it all, but . . . He saw in his mind the blackened wooden cheesebox and its cargo of rust-pitted, hundred-year-old keys, keys once so precious that someone had actually buried them in a wall! He shivered, smiled, then stifled another yawn. Blassenheim had his head turned, apparently conscious that Mickelsson was behind him. Mickelsson bowed across the intervening rows with exaggerated sociability.

Automatically, when the song ended and the applause began—he couldn't remember a single note of it—Mickelsson joined in.

"Cheer up," Jessica said in his ear, possibly meaning to injure—her scent rushed to his heart—"it's almost over."

"I like it," Mickelsson said. "They're very good."

She gave him a sidelong, utterly inscrutable look.

He smiled, clapping on, thinking about her anger and the scent of her perfume, distinct, yet too subtle to identify with any earthly flowers, landscape, weather. . . .

Kate Swisson bowed and bowed, left, right, center, smiling at the students in the front row. Alan Blassenheim, broad-shouldered, handsome as a latter-day Hercules or Apollo, clapped with his hands above his head, like a Greek dancer. At last the audience stopped applauding and settled back for more. Mickelsson glanced at his watch and thought, mistakenly, that it had stopped.

The clinking of the piano suggested one of those dread-filled moments in a horror film, or an awesome shot in a space-buster, star sparks plummeting toward the camera. With a wild look of either madness or terror, Kate Swisson wailed in *Sprechstimme,*

> *"In the timelessness,*
> > *the spacelessness of heaven,*
> *after 33,000 performances of Handel's* Messiah,
> > *I cried out.*
> *In utter desperation I forced my way*
> *through masses of bodiless spirits*
> *that surrounded the throne.*
> > *There was a clamor of voices,*
> > > *all wanting to get out.*
> > > *I was not alone!"*

Mickelsson laughed. Very clever! Interesting! Not at all with the intention of sleeping, he closed his eyes and slept.

He dreamed he had a long, friendly conversation with his wife. The dream was in vivid color, and his wife wore a dress decorated exactly like a wedding cake, sugar-white, as blinding as snow on a sunny, cold day. Her hair was once more its original golden yellow. They were the best of friends, as close as two children together, and everything in the dream was filled with light, rich and surprising, like morning to a very young child. The village where they found themselves had brown streets, bright yellow and red flowers in windowboxes, and red brick houses like those in a young child's picturebook. He heard her say clearly, with such sweetness his heart went light with joy, "This way, Mick." She lifted off the ground, flying like a candied angel on a string. He too began to fly, but then, high above the lovely picturebook world, he suddenly realized that he'd lost the trick of it.

He jerked awake, reaching out to catch himself, and looked around, startled, crushed inward by the auditorium's darkness, though the dream-voice was still in his ear. To his outer, merely fleshly ear, Kate Swisson sang, in her overly meticulous, phoney way:

> " 'But there's nothing here in my book,' God said,
> 'nothing but miserable lives,
> of toil and tears and human suffering.
> Look here,
> there is an opening for a black
> unemployed, unskilled, uneducated laborer,
> who will go from job to job,
> from booze to drugs,
> from woman to woman. . . .' "

There was a pause, a rising melodic phrase on the piano, and then:

> " 'Halleluyah! I'll take it!'
> God smiled
> and I was born again."

With a tavern-piano glissando and three funky chords, the concert ended.

The people around Mickelsson clapped and clapped, some of them shouting "Bravo! Brav-*i!*" or whistling. He saw Gail Edelman, in an aisle seat to his left, lean forward with shining eyes, clapping and nodding. She was dressed in light blue, like a highschool girl, and had on rouge and lipstick. Alan Blassenheim and his friends, then some older people, stood up and clapped with their hands in front of their faces. He saw that the Rogerses, Garrets, and Tillsons were standing, then the Blicksteins and the girl. Jessica got to her feet, brushing the seat of her skirt as she rose. Mickelsson rose too. "Brav-o!" Jessica's eyes were shiny, glinting. "Brav-o!" Mickelsson shouted, cupping his mouth, then clapped harder, cupping his hands to get maximum noise.

In the lobby, afterward, pressed against the wall, out of the crowd's way, Tom Garret said, "I hear you're the Cupid behind the Great Romance."

"Me?" Mickelsson said gruffly, "What romance?"

Garret pointed, the ceiling lights blanking out his glasses as he did so, and when Mickelsson turned to look he saw his student Alan Blassenheim with his arm around the waist of the class nihilist—as he'd thought her once—Brenda Winburn. Blassenheim was laughing, holding forth to those around him, gesturing with his free right hand and arm. He looked grown-up tonight; successful young lawyer or politician. Brenda's eyes were hooded, her expression unreadable, yet there could be no denying that her own right arm was clinging to Blassenheim's waist as if for dear life, and when suddenly she smiled at him, looking at his forehead, one saw that there was definitely something going on. If the smile made her beautiful—changed her completely—no one was quicker to notice than Blassenheim, pulling his chin back, grinning and widening his dark brown eyes as if Brenda Winburn were his personal creation and now, watching her, he were amazed at how he'd outdone himself.

Mickelsson said, "They're in my class together, if that's what you mean."

"The way *I* hear it," Garret said, his smile going up into both plump cheeks, "you practically commanded the thing. Isn't that the truth, now?" Again his glasses became silver blanks.

Mickelsson glanced at Jessica, who smiled, reserved. *Damn stiff-necked bitch*, he thought. In her shadow, Mabel Garret, ancient and elfin in her drab black dress, was looking at Mickelsson with an expression so clouded and unfriendly that a shiver ran up his back. He glanced at Garret. "I guess I don't know what you mean."

"You old *yenta*," Garret said, smiling on and clamping a hand on his arm. Then he too saw his wife's expression, and his smile went as blank as his glasses. Michael Nugent's face emerged from among the others, staring hard at Mickelsson, as if harboring some grudge. His face was so white it looked as if he'd powdered it. Belatedly, Mickelsson raised his hand to wave, but Nugent had disappeared, fading like a fugitive back into the press.

"Well," Jessica began, unaware of whatever it was that was going on with the Garrets—but that moment Tillson broke in on them. He had his short, big-bosomed wife in tow, her face triangular, sad-eyed, long-suffering, at the moment bravely smiling. Tillson firmly gripped Mickelsson's hand, his silver-bearded head thrown forward, his grin and eyebrows twitching. "Wonderful concert!" he piped, shaking Mickelsson's hand as if Mickelsson were responsible. Then, as if to cover his exaggerated friendliness toward Mickelsson, he reached in past him to shake Phil Bryant's hand. "Wonderful concert!" he cried, and gave his head a sharp sideways snap. Bryant smiled vaguely. "Interesting poem, that last," he said, but Tillson didn't hear, swinging his face around toward Jessica and crying, "Shall we try to catch the Swissons for a drink?"

"I don't know," Jessica said. She gave Mickelsson a look, then turned quickly back to Tillson: "Yes, let's!"

Mabel Garret said, with her usual madwoman abruptness, "We have to go home. Tom can meet you if he wants to." She gave a quick, shy smile. "All those kids, you know."

"Oh!" Mrs. Tillson said—the first thing she'd said to any of them— "I'm so sorry!" She pressed her hand to her heart. "I'd hoped—" Tillson leaned in, nodding urgent agreement.

Mabel ignored them, staring hard at Mickelsson. "Peter," she said, "don't go home tonight. Stay with someone in town."

"What?" Jessica said.

Mickelsson waited. Something had happened inside his ears; perhaps he was hearing the roar of his own blood.

"I have this feeling," Mabel said.

"What do you mean?" He grinned but raised his fist to his chest, pressing in, having a little difficulty with his breathing.

"I don't know." She suddenly laughed and raised her hand to her eyes.

Tom Garret leaned into the group to look up at Mickelsson. "Her hunches are sometimes uncanny, Pete."

When Mickelsson looked back at Mabel, she was already turning, fixing the shoulder-strap of her large, lunky purse and moving off quickly, fleeing her friends' attention.

"Are you all right, Peter?" Jessica asked.

"I just think I'll get a drink of water," he said.

Two hours later, after food, martinis, and several cups of coffee at the Firehouse Five—the Swissons saying no more than two words to anybody there, even Edie Bryant—and after dropping off Jessica with a kiss on the cheek ("Thanks, Peter!" "No, no, thank *you*," both of them feeling, it seemed to him, like traitors, though he couldn't make out even now where it was that the evening had gone awry)—Mickelsson, driving up the winding mountain road, just escaped being slammed into a ditch by a dark, expensive-looking car. For all the speed with which the car came at him— barrelling straight down the middle of the road, headlights undimmed, blindingly lighting up the snowfilled night—for one violent, ephemeral instant as the two cars slid crazily around each other, nearly overturning, Mickelsson saw in the beams of his headlights the face of the driver who'd nearly killed him. Fists clenched at the top of the steeringwheel, her ashen face thrown forward toward the windshield, almost striking it, wide-eyed and white in her black overcoat, sat the large, pleasant woman who'd sold him his house, "the doc."

He stopped the Jeep as soon as he was able; but whatever was at her heels gave the doctor no quarter: her taillights shot away down the mountain road, around sharp, falling corners, under overhanging limbs, then plunged between stone banks and trees and was suddenly out of sight.

5

He was too upset to sleep. Every time he closed his eyes he saw again those sudden, blinding lights in the curtain of white flakes, slicing out of nowhere, less like a car than like a speeding UFO, and he felt again that sickening yaw of weightlessness as the Jeep snowplowed sideways, climbing—leaping like a wolf—up the wall of the high, soft snowbank and stones underneath, teetering, tilting far over as if to topple, then righting itself. The other car too had gone sideways up onto the snowbank, rolling part way over onto the door of the driver's side, sending out an arc of white glitter like spray from a motorboat, roaring like a train as the metal caved in, the headlights aiming down, his own aiming straight, from slightly above, at her windshield. It felt to Mickelsson like the whole spin-out of his life reduced to one timeless instant—his financial ruin, his sick infatuations, his self-destructive smoking and drinking, his professional collapse. . . .

He stripped to his underwear to lift weights for a while. That often helped, at times like these. Partly it helped his ego; in more concentrated fashion than his work on the house, weight-lifting kept the middle-aged thickness of trunk mostly muscle, burning away the gin fat; kept his arms and thighs toned up, free of undue flab or, worse, plain old-folks'-home weakness. And then too, there was the drug effect, better than any gin or marijuana in the world: sucking in air, swallowing great gulps right to the bottom of the abdomen, bending and, with a loud cry of *hup*, lifting, holding, and after a quick shift of balance, throwing the press. . . . The pain came quickly, and then almost as soon, the human morphine that shut it off. Human morphine, hyperventilation, the bestial sense of steadily increasing goon power—what could beat it? He felt he could kick down trees, drag elephants by the tail.

He lay off for a while, puffing, swinging his arms, rolling his shoulders to quiet the muscle spasms. He wiped sweat off his hands, face, and neck with the rag, vigorously rubbed his scalp and the back of his neck, then squatted for perhaps two minutes, closing his eyes. It was a good thing, keeping the old corpse in shape. Tended to encourage non-violence. He'd said once to Ellen's friend The Comedian, "I've got half a mind to break you in half." "I do be*lieve* you have half a mind," The Comedian had said, blinking slowly, grinning one-sidedly in his panic, "and I see you also have the muscles." Almost by accident, as if the pipsqueak's wit were directed at someone else, Mickelsson had laughed.

He stood up again, loosened up the machinery—his whole body was soaking wet—and went back to it. After half an hour more he quit again, this time for good, rolled the weights back into their corner with his foot, then went into the bathroom, rinsed out the sweat rag, and showered. When he finished he found that even now he wasn't ready to face bed, so he put on his glasses and bathrobe and began wandering through the house barefoot, unconsciously opening and closing his paintbrush- and hammer-calloused hands, looking at objects as if he found them unfamiliar: the brushed steel face and knobs of the tuner and amplifier he never used—he switched them on, then immediately off again—the junk furniture he'd gotten to tide him over; magazines on the coffeetable, not a magazine in the stack that he would actually read without a gun at his head, except maybe *The New Yorker* for its cartoons, which he'd probably read already, he couldn't remember. He picked up the top *New Yorker* on the pile to check but then stopped, seeing again the whitened face behind the windshield sliding past him, crazily listing; and again he wondered, his skin crawling, what could have so frightened her? Where had she been?

With regard to the second question, where she'd been before he'd met her on the road half a mile below his house, the possibilities were not exactly rich. She could have been coming from here, his place, formerly hers, or she could have been coming from somewhere farther up the slope, or (less likely) somewhere beyond, the other side, deeper in the backwater wilderness of ridges, high lakes, and fog-bound valleys.

He'd driven up to the top several times, exploring, back in early September and October, and he'd tried a number of the back roads through valleys suddenly opening out behind, dirt roads descending quickly and recklessly, like spring-fed creeks. He'd seen very little to occupy anyone here on his own mountain, and it was doubtful that she'd come from much farther. A trailer or two, with immense woodpiles and jitneys in the yard, dark mongrel dogs that came out to yip and howl in indignation as you passed; here and there small tarpapered houses in the woods, no electric lights in most of them—places taken over long ago by squatters: shy, wolf-eyed people, watchful and still as bears as your car cruised by; and here and there he'd made out big, empty houses like dried-out gray skulls, houses the local children no doubt told stories about, once-grand, now-crumbling nightmare places, some furniture still left in them, perhaps in summertime the favorite old chair of a rattlesnake. Once, long ago, these high ridges had been farmed.

It was hard to believe that it could have been from higher on the mountain that the doctor had come, but the alternative was even more difficult to deal with, the idea that right here at Mickelsson's house the doctor had met someone or something that had sent her flying. Again and again as it invaded his thought he dismissed the idea, then found himself pausing to listen. At last, angrily, hoping to be rid of that feeling once and for all, he took the flashlight from the shelf at the head of the cellar stairs and searched the house inside and out. There was nothing to be found.

He poured himself a drink, but after one sip discovered that his stomach was too sour to put up with it, and poured the remainder down the sink. His mind was still weird from the weight-lifting, catching movements that weren't there, at the periphery of his vision. At last, one by one, taking his time, he turned the lights off—he'd turned on every last light in the place, even the watchlights on the barns—and with no light remaining but the lamp on his bedtable, he shrugged off his bathrobe, then picked off his glasses, pausing once to listen as he did so, his brow deeply furrowed—listening not only with his tufted ears but with the nerves of his back and the tips of his fingers. Then he crawled meekly under the covers, turned off the lamp, and lay belly up with the back of his head on his hands, elbows out, keeping his ears free. He stared at the pitchdark ceiling as if he had no intention whatever of going to sleep.

In the valley the 3 a.m. train went by. He listened as it sang along glens and cliffs, sliding eastward toward New York City, a huge, humming, dark-iron snake. Once there had been glowing-steel passenger trains on this line, rushing yellow windows. No more. He thought of New York's lights, not many of them now, cavelike alleys, tombstone-dark buildings. The train must be a hundred cars long. Lonesome sound, as the folksongs liked to say. How empty it made the night!—alas, an emptiness not just physical. Peter Mickelsson was no longer a child on the Wisconsin farm, cows scattered like old gray boulders across the moonlit pasture, hushed with rumination. Time had actually done to him what old people in his childhood had jokingly spoken of its doing—eyes glittering, as if merry— had poured the magic out of the world like well-water from a dipper. For him as for all those country songwriters and weary black blues-singers, not to mention high-class tragic poets of former times and places—Greece, Japan, China—or brooding philosophers, Diogenes in his barrel, Marcus Aurelius knee-deep in chickens, Boethius in jail—the day had come when suddenly the obvious goodness of life, the splendor in the grass, innocence of eye and ear were vanquished, gone as if they'd never existed, like Occident light from a Stoic's leaded window or spirit from a father's blue eye. How did human beings go on after such things—family deaths, ruin, the collapse of marriage with a woman once loved. . . .

It was unthinkable that nothing could be done about it. That was why Ellen and her friends had despised him, in San Francisco. They would sit "rapping," drugged, far into the night, sprawled on the floor and on the lower reaches of the furniture, or flung like sated jackals on the lawn in back, dreaming up grand schemes to make the world a softer place. He would bait them with Nietzsche: "The wish to eliminate suffering is the wish to eliminate life," and, "Pain is a good part of what holds societies together." He would mockingly suggest—but he meant it more seriously than they knew—that they'd misunderstood human nature. "You've forgotten about *Schadenfreude*," he said—he loved pulling fancy language on them, dropping it casually, as if any half-educated fool ought to know the term.

One of her friends, a tall, black-bearded young man named Vince, was particularly offended by all he said and stood for. "Far out!" he would say, looking up-from-under with foggy blue eyes, maybe trying to focus his minotaur-bulky shape. "Like, man, how can you go to, like, a great play—*King Lear* or something—and not come home horrified by the cowshit all around you?" From the darkness of the lawn beyond where Vince sat came a faint, weary chorus of yeah's. Ellen said nothing.

"Art makes heavy the thinking man's heart," Mickelsson said. "Nietzsche." He might easily have used Nietzsche in their defense, of course—for instance his idea on the imposition of form and order as a cause of suffering—but the temptation to defend was not strong.

The night in which they plotted and grieved over the oppressed was ironically sweet and still. The house looming against the stars was grandly Victorian, pre-fire; it was on the other side of Twentieth Street that the smaller, newer, though equally shabby buildings began. To the left of the house from where they lay in the yard (or, in Mickelsson's case, stood) an immense old evergreen pointed darkly at the moon.

"Don't you have something to do, Peter?" Ellen asked.

There was no arguing with them. Because reason had been misused by corrupt forces in the Establishment, Ellen's friends now scorned the use of reason, scorned self-analysis, even rational self-defense. They would not talk, would only sneer or attack, bully both their enemies and each other.

In their filthy little playhouse, ex-Protestant church—walls of black, a few spotlights, tape-recorder, old cracked folding-chairs for the audience —Vince and a black called Errol appear on a coolly lighted set which consists of a lamppost, a wheelbarrow, and a mirror, the two of them in shabby clothes, Vince (tall, bearded, with knobby knees and elbows) leaning on the lamppost, center stage, Errol pushing the wheelbarrow around and around him, for no apparent reason. Occasionally, Vince looks in the mirror; he will not let Errol look. Sometimes they do the play with words (mostly obscenities), sometimes as mime. Vince (this is the play) hates the audience. When he uses words he calls them "dumb mashed-potato fuckers," "wet, middle-class steamy shit on an onion roll," et cetera. (Vince has a flair for the vividly vile. This does not necessarily make him likeable.) Errol begins in agreement with Vince, gradually shifts to preferring the audience to Vince, decides to abandon the stage. Vince will not allow it. Errol has *always* been on the stage, and the audience is a bunch of et cetera, et cetera. Errol slips off his boots and makes a dash to join the audience; Vince shoots and kills him. (The death is frighteningly convincing.) The End. When the performance goes well, the audience feels insulted, financially and artistically cheated, hurt, diddled with, confused (What does it mean? What is the symbolism of the mirror? Who is Vince?), sickened and enraged.

Does the play raise the social consciousness of the audience? Who knows? Sometimes the troupe barely escapes alive, and this, Mickelsson sees plainly, begins to be their kick. One day, not long after Geoffrey Stewart, the street poet, has denounced them, talking of "the imitation of Jesus Christ," Ellen's crazies see, by whatever epistemological means it may be that convince them, that they must work not on middle-class audiences but directly on the oppressed. The ordinary black on the street must learn to let it all hang out, quit repressing, stand up and shoot. San Francisco street theater is born.

They put on whiteface, wear odd costumes: a fat, rich Wall Street banker's attire, the *kosmoi* of a wealthy, aristocratic lady (cigarette holder —Ellen's, ironically—and lorgnette); they go up to gentle, ordinary blacks who are minding their own business, maybe walking the kids in Golden Gate Park, and the actors engage the innocent victims in improvisational dialogue. There are flowers everywhere, the smell of new-cut grass on the rolling lawns between eucalyptus trees, the smell and soft wind of the Pacific.

"Hey, nigger!"

The man tries to edge away, shooing his kids ahead of him. It's not necessarily that he thinks he's in danger or even that he doesn't understand what they're up to; he may even understand that they're doing it all for his people's good. He's no fool, he reads the paper—during his lunch-break in the basement at I. Magnin's, or at the Legal Aid office, where he's a lawyer, head of the housing attack force—it's just that, for himself and his kids, he wants no part of this.

"Hey, you! You-boy!" They move in on him.

He knows this foolishness better than they do, these high-assed kids with their mission and their expensive acting lessons. His grandfather was a make-'em-sweat preacher in Georgia: "You! Sinner! You wid dat bottle!"

The black man in the suit and tie, holding his two children's hands, knows the game. Who doesn't? Since they've cut off his escape, he tries asking them to leave him alone, please. He tries to reason with them. His kids are afraid now. Bystanders pause to watch, a few drawing near. The actors and actresses are ecstatic. The street play has begun! If they're lucky, punches will ensue, people will throw stones at them. Mickelsson, sick with disgust and pity, fades back into the crowd.

"Why do you stay married to her?" a friend had asked—Carol, a female grad student in poly sci at Berkeley, whom he'd often talked with over coffee or sitting on the grass by the library; nothing heavy, though both of them had thought about it.

"I keep hoping it's just a passing phase," he said.

She looked at him, waiting in the soulful, non-directive Rogerian way that had been popular at the time.

"And then there's the fact that we've got kids," he said.

She nodded.

"I keep pretending it's not happening," he said, and ruefully smiled. "I rarely see their 'performances,' and when I do, I pretend each time that this one's probably exceptional."

"Sounds like they all are."

He nodded, looking down. He loved her large, solid knees.

He had been right at least that with Ellie it had been just a passing phase. Today she lived in a mansion of sorts and gave tea-parties. If she directed or produced a play, it was *The Seagull* or *Krapp's Last Tape*. She was no longer one of those who struggle against the way of the universe, the unalterable outward drift of wreckage, the greenhouse effect here on this one piece of junk—the irreversible rise of CO_2 in the atmosphere, the accelerating transformation of everything on earth to rot. "Betrayed!" her actors cried now, without hope, shaking their well-trained, long-fingered hands up at the spotlight. Perhaps in a deeper sense she was still up to her old tricks, drugging the world with beautiful might-have-beens. (Nietzsche on Art: "Humanity owes much of its evil to these fanatical intoxicates.")

He rolled his head on his pillow. The irony was, he missed those awful days in San Francisco—missed Ellen's stupid, passionate friends. Believers.

"He that reflects not in his heart," the ancients said, "is like the beast that perishes." Not true. Everything is like the beast that perishes.

There were sounds downstairs, something rhythmical; like walking. When he concentrated, it stopped. He rubbed his eyes. It was nothing. No doubt the brain still kidding around after its surcharge of laboring blood, too much weight-lifting.

Poor Jessica.

She'd been young, happy, travelling far and wide with her handsome tree-scientist—today Nigeria, tomorrow some committee of the United States Senate—and now all at once, reluctantly, she was surveying with her nervous, flashy eyes the paunchy host of bachelors and cast-offs for some arm not unduly unpleasant to lean on as she drifted toward declining beauty, old age.

Mickelsson closed his eyes tightly, saw strange things, and reopened them, despairing of sleep. He must put his student Michael Nugent on to Nietzsche, it occurred to him—Nietzsche for recognition of the central "perdurable evil," as the boy would say, the essential human character, "so delicate, sensitive"—what was the phrase?—"so delicate, sensitive and something-or-other that we have need of the highest means of healing and consolation." Nietzsche for nihilism transmuted, "the new way to *Yes*."

He turned his head to look down the hallway through the partly open door, trying to penetrate the darkness. In a kind of waking dream he seemed to hear voices, two of them. Not really voices; sounds of some kind. He could not make out words. It was queer, those voices, or voice-like sounds—possibly some taut wire picking up a radio signal. It was—Tom Garret's word—uncanny. Except that no, it was not uncanny, that was an exaggeration. One could make it uncanny by thought, make it like one of those experiences recorded by the hundreds in the book he had hidden in his desk—but he refrained.

Again, suddenly, so vividly that he might have been dreaming it, he saw lights coming at him, lighting up the trunks and lower branches of trees on each side of the road's banked shoulders. He sat up straight in the bed, head rammed forward. It filled his windshield, seemed to fill his very skull with whiteness, rushing him like a blinding burst of water down a flume in the California mountains, and he felt again in his stomach and chest the sickening sideways sweep of the car in its miraculous, high-speed, roaring do-si-do around the doctor's. He wiped his forehead and lowered himself onto his back again.

"Better get some sleep," he told himself gruffly.

He took a deep breath and closed his eyes. When he opened them again, it was quarter after three. Was it possible that only fifteen minutes had passed since the last time he'd looked at the luminous dial on his wristwatch?—his son's wristwatch, rather, a gift or loan just before Mickelsson had left. It was certainly too late to get up and phone Jessica. That was what he wanted to do, all right—tell her what had happened as he was driving home, not just the near-accident but also who it was that had been hurrying so, in the middle of the night, coming down the mountain from God knew where. It would be a comfort to puzzle with Jessica over Mabel Garret's seeming foreknowledge of the event—a strange woman; he'd always thought so.

He rolled his head on the pillow. At the first thought of Jessica, his penis had begun to stiffen. "You're not a well man," Rifkin had said. Mickelsson thought: *You should see me now, Doctor.* He put his hand on the erection, encouraging it. *Jessie, Jessie, Jessie.* All right, it was not just comforting talk he wanted of her. He wanted her naked here beside him, or under him. He began to move his hand. He imagined that incredibly beautiful body with the clothes stripped away, imagined her kneeling over him, glistening, the full breasts finally revealed, dangling above him, the collarbone like wings, the perfect wet mouth, gray eyes like Homeric seas. As if she were really there he felt her lowering herself onto him, then felt himself coming. He clutched the sheet to the mess and, overwhelmed by disgust and gloomy wretchedness, shifted to the edge of the bed, where it was dry.

As always when he'd made imaginary love to her, what he felt now was not relief but shame and revulsion. If any man had ever been truly in love, he thought, he, Peter Mickelsson, was in love with Jessica Stark. (Rhetoric; bullshit. Could nothing stop the Thespian antics of the mind?) But he was thinking: he understood now the agonies of the silly courtly-love poets, moaning and groaning over the holy unattainable. Or Nietzsche hopelessly mooning over Cosima Wagner. It hadn't been like this when Mickelsson was young, with Ellen. He'd been handsome then, or anyway, well-built; he'd thought highly of himself. Now he was gross, a proven failure, with no place to go but further down. (Bullshit, bullshit.) Thoughts crowded his head, as if to show more plainly his depravity. Always concepts, opinions, past history and books between himself and things. He thought of the whole absurd courtly-love scheme, and its Platonism: how the lover was the poor hopeless worm, writhing, writing verses in secret, hungering for the divine, and how the lady, if he was lucky, came to him like God, with grace. It was true—the misery of the lover, at least. All the rest was changed. The lady might pity him. He'd seen signs tonight that if he played his cards right she might sleep with him, though her reserve, even wariness, was hard to miss. She was no starry-eyed kid. Paradise, everlasting joy . . . Women were people too; that was the crushing wisdom of modern love. He had nothing to offer: big, maybe dangerous animal. In the end—and it wouldn't take long—he'd be discarded. If he loved her less, that might be tolerable. (Something phoney in that thought too. He would refuse to notice.) If one were young and stupid, blindly optimistic . . .

Idly, bending his anger around to where perhaps it would do most good, he thought of suicide. It made a certain kind of sense, theoretically. He longed every day for his old life with Ellen, especially when he remembered her as she'd once been; but that was over, wrecked, and in a way he wasn't sorry: with Ellen, or with those casual pick-ups at conferences, he'd never have experienced the pure pig sexual joy he'd found in Donnie Matthews—nor would he have met Jessica Stark. No magazine fold-out showed the likes of that lady sociologist—such was his opinion—and if he could not have her, at least not in the absolute way his soul demanded—if he could not own her absolutely, grow old with her, be loved by her without a trace of reservation, as if he were spiritually of equal worth . . .

He jerked his head, fighting the everlasting sick rush of thought. He would not kill himself, not because he was cowardly but because, like an old bull standing in a field among flies, he didn't give a shit.

He breathed deeply, listening to the wheeze from too much smoking, then again thought of Mabel Garret's precognition, or hunch. He frowned, turning over onto his side and staring deep into the darkness down the hall, eyes unblinking, trying to decide whether or not he believed in hunches. He believed in his grandfather's hunches, certainly. Odd that one could believe the particular case but doubt the principle. Perhaps as he and Jessica discussed these things, he could edge her toward what it was that had gone wrong between them, an evening that had started out so well, as it had seemed to him. In his mind he again saw her slipping her shoe off, sitting on her foot. He thought again, with a sinking feeling, of Donnie Matthews. Shabby business. He was troubled now by the realization that had come to him the last time he'd been with her, that she felt for him more than she admitted to herself. Only a few days ago the realization would have filled him with joy. He saw again in his mind her sweet, childish pout—something slightly common about it, something studied—studied before a mirror, no doubt; modelled on the pout of some Grade B actress. He moved his right hand to cup his penis and testicles. As if she were there in the bed beside him, he smelled her scent, partly from a bottle, partly sweat. How strange it was when one compared it with the tastefully expensive scent of Jessica Stark!—yet even the dim memory of Donnie's scent had the power to stir in him the beginnings of a new erection. Ah, Love, joiner of the unjoinable! He thought of Kurten's theory of Neandertal extinction and closed his eyes. He closed his hand around his cock and moved the hand slowly.

Poor Blassenheim! Poor Brenda!

Without wishing to, invaded, though he glared and shook his head against it, he thought of the Swissons, the Garrets, the Bryants, finally the Tillsons—saw them all in his mind's eye so sharply it was as if they were there in the room with him, gathered like visitors at a sickbed. As if hunting for something, or alerted to danger, he looked carefully from couple to couple, still moving his hand. The Swissons, shyly smiling exactly together—except that the woman's smile was less shy than the man's, as her handshake was stronger, and the man, hard as they played at their game, cared more in the end about music than the woman did; one could see it in the trouble-lines fencing in his eyes. He thought of driving his cock into Kate Swisson. The thinking part of his mind tick-ticked on. *Parts mixed unequally* . . . They were doomed; he knew it as surely as he knew his name.

The Garrets. He could form no definite opinion about the Garrets. Good people, certainly—ten adopted children; and Tom was always, in his mild, Southern way, a man of liberal concern. (Mabel he would take from behind, up the anus. He drove the vision out, disgusted.) Strange pair: Tom, genteel aristocrat turned into a liberal verging on radical and living up here in the land of deep snow, with ten young children of a variety of races, married to a secretive, maybe psychic Russian Jew. One could make a life, of course, of strange ingredients. Nevertheless, it was indeed very strange. He had a feeling Jessica, if she should choose to speak frankly, would make short work of them, or at any rate of their chances—though why he thought this he couldn't say. Of this much he was sure: when he was young he had believed, like Alan Blassenheim, in Truth, the great rock foundation of everything. It had seemed to him obvious that if one "behaved in accord with what one knew to be true"—an expression that had not then seemed puzzling to him—one would be safe, for all practical purposes invulnerable. But now he'd grown confused, like a once-carefree bob-calf come of age. The clearer his thought—the more rigorous his categorical distinctions—the more angry and confused he'd grown. It was as if he had stepped out of a room which for the time he'd been inside it he'd known to exist, and could now not find his way back to it—couldn't find it on any map, couldn't even find its theoretical justification, its chemical and mathematical possibility in so-called reality. He believed now in systems, an anarchy of truth-systems spinning like the components of independent molecules—believed in them intuitively, as he believed in root propositions—but he was no longer altogether comfortable with tables and chairs. Tom and Mabel Garret, old-name Southerner and immigrant's child . . . ten children of several races, whom they sat up with, perhaps sang Southern ballads to, or *Mottel der Operator*, perhaps read *The Wind in the Willows* and *Charlotte's Web* . . . They were good people, and he liked them, but at the center of their life lay something that troubled him. He'd run across a phrase somewhere, Darwin or one of his followers: "The blind daring of Nature's experiments . . ." (Beetle-browed Neandertal marrying handsome Cro-Magnon, producing mules, dying out . . .)

He lost his train of thought. His eyelids were heavy. Perhaps he would sleep after all, except that his cock was huge now, still blindly hunting.

He mused with some twilit part of his brain on the arrangements of the Bryants and Tillsons. The Bryants had been married for thirty-one years, brutally mismatched as they seemed to be. (Edie had mentioned tonight at the Firehouse Five that their anniversary was coming up. "Three decades of holy deadlock and one year to spare," she'd said. "Most marriages that last very long are three-legged stools." The Swissons, holding hands, had looked interested for a moment.) Perhaps the truth was that the Bryants weren't as badly mismatched as they seemed—and seemed to believe themselves. Was Phil really so classy, she really (with her noble old blood-lines) so vulgar? He was a fine shabby dresser and good at quoting poets, especially Shakespeare; but then, who wouldn't be after twenty, thirty years of teaching Anguish? What he really cared about—what made his cheeks redden and his voice take on a quaver, what made him jab at the tabletop with a manicured index finger—was university scheduling, parking regulations, the careless policing of the faculty cafeteria. When his cheeks reddened, Edie would gently put her hand on his arm, not pausing to look at him, dropping not a word from the gently self-mocking monologue she was delivering to Jessica and the Swissons. Sometimes Bryant called her, as if ironically, with scorn, "my little chickadee." It occurred to Mickelsson now for the first time that perhaps they loved each other. Phil the stunningly handsome young officer, Edie the dazzling Southern belle. Instantly the thought turned in on him and depressed him. He noticed that with the fingertips of his right hand he was feeling the pulse in his left wrist. He moved his right hand back to his crotch.

What the Tillsons felt for each other Mickelsson couldn't guess. She loved *him*, all right. (Now it was Ruth that he imagined coupling with. He imagined her crying out.) Ruth Tillson was the classic betrayed, still-doting wife. Every time Mickelsson had glanced at them, the poor big-bosomed, sad-eyed woman was clinging for dear life to her hunchbacked husband's arm. She never spoke, it seemed, if she weren't sure in advance that he'd agree. She'd spoken passionately only once all evening, leaning in toward the red-bowled candle at the center of the table as if almost forgetting that Tillson might be watching. The flame lit up her face and the cleavage between her fat peek-a-boo tits—brightening, dimming, intensifying the darkness of the tables, heavy beams, broad old staircase behind her. "Coffee and Coca-Cola," she said, "will be the ruin of this country. It's everywhere, you know." She pointed at Mickelsson's pipe. "Are you aware that tobacco is cured in *sugar*?" Then she drew back, touching her hand to her cleavage, calming herself. Mickelsson registered as a fact for possible future use that Geoffrey Tillson strongly disapproved of coffee, Coca-Cola, and tobacco. He wondered if Tillson's mistress had been at the concert tonight, somewhere in the shadows, smiling at her hunchbacked, silver-bearded lover and his pitiful wife, her dear friend. He wondered if she smoked, used sugar.

In a moment Mickelsson would be asleep, the erection hunting through the world on its own. The voices he'd been hearing were now distinctly dream-voices, though the words were still unintelligible, a mumble like wind on an abandoned beach; and the people he'd gone with to the Firehouse Five (he could feel himself falling back from them, easing himself out of the light from the red glass bowl on their table) were no longer entirely fitting in with the waking world's ways. Something he imagined Edie Bryant to be saying, when he brought himself awake enough to think about it, turned out to have to do with leaks in numbers, which in turn had something to do with his father's death. All at once, in this faintly unpleasant half-dream, he heard Jessica laughing. Evidently something had just cancelled every trace of unhappiness in her life. Perhaps her husband was alive after all, had never been dead; it had all been a casual bureaucratic mistake. He began to thrust, against his will, his heart quickening, and exploded inside his dream of her. That instant a door opened, and the sounds coming through made him think of sweet

Mexican sunlight on clean white tile-and-stucco walls. Mickelsson concentrated, listening with every nerve and hair, but nothing would come clear. ("Wait here, please," someone said.) He wiped the sheet on the cold wetness and tried to make out what he was thinking.

Then, in the hallway outside his bedroom, he heard breathing, then footsteps, the creak of floorboards. He jerked himself awake—fought his way up out of sleep as from drowning and opened his eyes, half sitting up. Even wide awake he felt disoriented, as if he'd come to himself in a different house. Somewhere downstairs a child was crying. The sound was real, unmistakable, though of course it was impossible that the house should have a crying child in it. He looked around, trying to think how he might prove to himself that he was or was not awake. The crying stopped.

The footsteps kept coming, slowly, not at all furtively, the ordinary footsteps of stiff and uncomfortable old age. It was surely not a dream. Just outside his door a hoarse, somewhat feeble voice asked crossly, "You in there?" A moment later, a bearded old man with red-webbed, milky, near-sighted eyes and no teeth except a few in the front poked his head in at the door. He did not look at Mickelsson or seem to recognize his existence, but peered into an almost empty corner of the room, the corner where Mickelsson had placed an antique hatrack he never used. After a moment, touching his beard and muttering something, as if he'd made a mistake, had caught himself in a moment of senility, the old man drew his head in and backed out of sight. Mickelsson listened for the sound of the old man's movement down the hall, but though he strained every nerve, he heard nothing more. At last he realized that, dream or vision, whatever it was, it was over. The old man, if he'd ever existed, had finished or abandoned his errand long ago.

6

By the time Peter Mickelsson reached his office the following morning, the snow had almost all melted. Except for frail icicles hanging from eaves and trees, they might have been back in September. Birds ran up and down on the wet, gray-brown lawn outside Mickelsson's window; more birds watched from the bare branches, now and then flying down by paths as determinedly straight as guy-wires to join the activity of the birds on the ground or drive a few timid ones treeward. Students walked around in sweaters or light coats unbuttoned down the front. The day warmed more and more.

He'd arrived earlier than he'd needed to, feeling lively for some reason—perhaps his near-accident on the road last night had somehow gotten the old juices flowing—and he decided to see if, in the forty-some minutes he had available before class, he could make a small dent in the great pile of unopened mail on his deck. Casually he began to sort through the envelopes, intending to deal first with whatever seemed most urgent. Thus he came upon the letter with the name *Bauer* in the upper left-hand corner, and a Florida address. This time he recognized the name at once as belonging not to some professor he'd forgotten but "the doc." According to the postmark, the letter had come nearly two months ago. He opened it.

She was planning to be in Susquehanna in late October or early November, she wrote. She had business, a legal matter that he might perhaps have heard about—she believed there had been some mention of it in the papers—and it had occurred to her that she might perhaps drop in on him in case he'd run across any problems in connection with the house—questions she'd failed to anticipate, difficulties she, after fourteen years in Susquehanna, might be able to help him resolve. If he wanted her to visit, he should write to her sometime soon at her Florida address.

Mickelsson read the letter through again. It was hard to imagine what sorts of "problems in connection with the house" she had in mind. But on one score at least, the letter relieved him. He had not just imagined seeing her last night—almost scattering atoms of the doc and her car (himself and his own car as well) from Susquehanna to Montrose. Today, according to his desk calendar, was October 27th. It was apparent, then, that she really had been up at his house, or somewhere nearby, and had

been frightened by something. Useless to try to puzzle out what could
have frightened her, knowing as little as he did.

No sooner had he told himself that it was useless than he knew he
was mistaken and reached for the phone. He finally got hold of Jessica
not at her office but at her house.

"Jessica," he said, "this is Peter Mickelsson." He put his voice on
intense polite. "I hope I'm not calling you too early?"

There was a pause, then she laughed. "Peter, what's the matter?"

"Nothing. I was just afraid I might have—" He thought about her
question, imagining her look, then suddenly, throwing caution to the
winds, asked, "Do I sound as bad as that?"

Again she laughed, this time thoughtfully. "First you tell me 'This is
Peter Mickelsson,'" she said, "and then you ask me, at half past nine in
the morning, if you're calling me too early. You know I get up with the
sun."

"I guess I forgot." He glanced at his watch.

"So what *is* the matter?" she asked.

"It's really nothing," he said, and got out his pipe, set it on top of the
pile of mail, and began to hunt through his drawers and pockets for
matches. "I just need to ask you a question you may possibly know the
answer to. Also"—he paused, then again took a chance—"I need to tell
you I had a wonderful time last night."

"Thanks. I did too, mostly. What was the question?"

He stood up to open the file-cabinet drawers and look for matches
there. "You remember mentioning that Dr. Bauer—the woman I bought
my house from—was being sued for malpractice? Do you remember the
name of the people suing her?"

Waiting for her answer, he momentarily forgot his hunt for matches.

She said, "I don't think I ever really noticed the name. I could find
out, if it's important."

"Could you try?" he asked, and, abruptly remembering, returned to
his hunt.

Jessica asked, "Where are you—in your office? How long do you plan
to be there?"

"Another thirty minutes, then I have class. When it's over—it runs
for an hour—"

"I'll get back to you before that," she said. "Bye."

"Thanks, Jess," he said. "I can't tell you how—"

She'd hung up.

Magically, matches appeared in his shirt pocket. He lit one and hurriedly raised it to his pipe. *Sugar,* he thought, and abruptly smiled. Crazy
bastard! He thought of the big old-fashioned couch in Tillson's office,
how sometimes when you went there Tillson would be lying on it with
his shoes off, his hand on his forehead in the gesture of some nineteenth-

century heroine. With his suitcoat off, his suspenders loose on his white shirt, gray bags under his eyes, so dark one might have imagined he had lupus, he looked like a doll that had been meant to be comic, one of those apple- or potato-people, but had somehow come off unfunny, obscurely depressing, Rumpelstiltskin not destroyed by his own anger but merely beaten, dwindling toward old age.

Five minutes later Jessica called back. "Hi. Listen, the name of the girl who died was Deborah Vliet, but the people who are suing are her parents. Her maiden name was Sprague." When Mickelsson said nothing, she said, "Hello?"

"I'm here," he said. "I guess you caught me off guard. Sprague's the name of my ghosts." He half laughed.

"Ghosts?" she echoed; then, remembering: "Oh, that. Mickelsson, could you possibly divulge what this is about?"

"Tell you when I see you," he said. "Have to make another phonecall now—at least I think I do. You wouldn't know where these Sprague people live?"

"I imagine with a little detective work—"

"Never mind, I can do it."

"All right," she said, less than satisfied. If she was still full of questions, she contained them. "I'll see you right after your class, OK? You'll be there?"

"Sure," he said. "Good." By the time he got to good-bye, she'd hung up.

His second call he made to his neighbor John Pearson. The phone rang and rang. Just as Mickelsson was about to give up, the old man answered. He'd been out in the yard; something about a ram who'd hanged himself trying to break through an American-wire fence. When Mickelsson was able to get around to his question, the old man said, "Shore I know where they live. Right up the road about a mile and a half from me. They're my next-door neighbors except for one place between, Dudaks'. Course I don't see much of 'em. Odd bunch. Wouldn't be suing the doc if they wasn't. Tell the truth, I'm surprised they ever heard about lawyers. But you know how it is. People on Aid know more about lawyers and gettin things for nothin than people like you and me do."

"Sprague doesn't work, then?"

"Oh, he works accordin to his lights, I s'pose," Pearson said. "He's old."

When it was clear he didn't intend to elaborate, Mickelsson asked, "Do you know if they're any relation to the Spragues that lived at my place?"

The line hummed and clicked while Pearson considered the question from various angles, or so Mickelsson imagined. At last the old man said, "I s'pose they musta ben."

. . .

For the first time all semester, Brenda Winburn was talkative that morning, an effect of her romance with Alan Blassenheim, no doubt. Perhaps his admiration gave her the necessary confidence, or perhaps his apparent liking for Mickelsson had seduced her, made her willing to play Mickelsson's game a little. "Did you see the article in Sunday's paper," she asked, "about the brothers who'd never known each other and were brought to America to be part of a study of identical twins?"

With a nod Mickelsson encouraged her to continue.

Though her look was still distrustful, as if prepared for lack of interest, scorn, or ambush from Mickelsson, Brenda continued with considerable ease and poise, her hands flat on the desk-chair top, one over the other. Her blond hair was drawn back tightly and tied in a bun, giving her small, almost lobeless ears a stranded look. On another day it might have seemed bizarre, but today the aliveness of her face—the blush of love, one might as well call it—made it difficult to think of her as anything but pretty. "One was named Stohr and the other was named something like Yufe," she said. "One was raised a Nazi, the other one Jewish. They never saw each other since soon after they were born, but when they met at the airport they were both wearing steel-rimmed spectacles and double-pocket blue shirts with epaulettes, they both had little moustaches, they both flipped through magazines from back to front and had a habit of keeping rubber bands around their wrists. . . . I forget what else, but the similarities were amazing."

"It's an interesting phenomenon," Mickelsson said. He added with a smile, lest he drive her back into her reserve, "I'm not sure I get your point."

The class, taking its cue from him as always, waited politely. Even Nugent seemed to hold down his anger a little, keeping his face passive, his chin resting on his slightly loosened fist.

"Well, I was just thinking," she said, "maybe when Aristotle was doing all that taxonomy he was aware, to some extent, that things were more set by Nature than his—you know—moral philosophy admitted. Maybe he just didn't make the connection, I guess that's possible. But maybe, setting down those different kinds of fishes and crustaceans or whatever—maybe he had an inkling that human beings have certain basic natures too, and that"—she glanced at Alan Blassenheim—"ideas . . . all that sort of thing . . . different kinds of actions . . . don't really count much. Maybe our ideas and philosophies and all . . ." She looked down at her hands, calculating whether or not she ought to say it, then looked up and said, "Maybe all that is just cosmetics, if you know what I mean. Sort of just . . . polite behavior, like when whales or wolves touch noses or chimpanzees groom each other."

The class looked from her to Mickelsson. He resisted the temptation to take the idea from her and bend it to the purpose of the course. "I'm not sure I follow the argument," he said.

"It's not an argument," she said, suddenly smiling, and shrugged. "It's just that, for example, this man Stohr, the one that was raised a Nazi, he was one of those Hitler *Jugend*, if that's how you pronounce it, and when he was young he saw movies that said Jews were cockroaches and had to be gotten rid of, and then after the war when the Russians captured him and made him look at those pictures of the death camps and things, he felt confused and guilty, and he changed his mind to the same extent everybody else did in that situation—he didn't really have any choice at all—but in all the important things, like what kind of glasses and shirts to wear—"

"Important things?" Mickelsson asked, raising his eyebrows.

She smiled, alarmed, and waved her left hand. "You know what I mean," she said.

Nugent slid his eyes toward her, scornful, murderously impatient.

Blassenheim raised his hand.

"I'm not sure I do," Mickelsson said, and decided to grant Blassenheim the floor.

"Nobody's saying that killing people isn't important," Blassenheim said, and threw a look at Brenda to see if his defense was acceptable to her. "The question is why people do it, or don't do it, whichever. We talk about people as doing what they do because they think of it as right, or at least, like, expedient. Like Plato's principle that nobody chooses to do what he thinks will bring him pain. But she's saying—Brenda's saying —maybe that's wrong. Maybe people choose ideas by style, they just sort of helplessly go with whatever's in the stores that season—sort of a general 'go with the group' adaptation—but when they're dealing with *little*, more *specific* styles, like when they choose their clothes, like their shoes and shirts and glasses, that's more like straight genetic programming." He sat back and waved his hand, just an interpreter, not committed. Predictably, the class was amused.

"You really think blue double-pocketed shirts with epaulettes are programmed in our genes?" Mickelsson asked.

"You know," Blassenheim said, "maybe not that directly." He waved again.

"Interesting," Mickelsson said, smiling at Blassenheim as if playing chess with him. They'd moved a long way from Aristotle, but no matter. "And what does that do," Mickelsson asked, "to our theory of the Good? Are moral judgments and aesthetic judgments of the same kind? Are the Nazi ideal of human nature and the liberal ideal just alternatives of taste?"

Though he addressed the question to Blassenheim, it was Brenda Winburn who answered. "It wouldn't necessarily mean absolute values are wrong," she said. "God might have rules a snake can never figure out." She leaned forward like a daughter pleading—as if Mickelsson and Reason were stern authorities who could be gotten around by bright eyes and a timid smile. As was no doubt the case. "If some genius figures out and tells us about a divine idea but it's against human nature—how people really are, I mean, with all their programmed individual differences—it can't last, he won't be accepted."

"Ah!" Mickelsson said, and raised a finger as if shooting the ceiling, "then in effect the 'moral absolutes' "—playfully, he put on a German accent—"can exist, if at all, only in the actual behavior of human beinks!"

"Not necessarily," she said at once, narrowing her eyes. "Only the moral absolutes we're capable of achieving. Maybe that's why people are so restless and weird."

Mickelsson smiled, his eyebrows lifted, as if unable to believe he'd been beaten fair and square. "Well done!" he said, grinning; and taking careful aim with his index finger, he shot Brenda Winburn in the nose.

Nugent had his hand over his mouth. Mickelsson gathered his books, realizing that he'd been caught, and, seeing that they were out of time, gave a nod, dismissing the class.

As the students were filing out he said to Blassenheim, who stood dawdling, waiting for Brenda to get her pen capped and tucked into the proper compartment of her purse, "It's not fair, you know, you two ganging up on me like that."

"We didn't really plan it," the boy said. He stood with his head drawn back a little, smiling uncertainly, as if with part of his mind he would like it to be thought that they *had* planned it.

"Like termites, these students," Mickelsson said, speaking past the pipe and waving both hands, wiggling the fingers. "They keep coming and coming, and then one day you look around and—no castle!"

Alan and Brenda laughed pleasantly, as if from a great distance, then drifted toward the door, where Michael Nugent stepped aside for them. Mickelsson saw with a sinking heart that Nugent was waiting to ask some question.

"It's interesting the way you handle class," Nugent said, walking beside Mickelsson as he hurried back to his office. Nugent's long legs moved oddly, yet with a curious grace, like the legs of a giraffe at the zoo. One hand was pressed hard to his chest as if to stanch blood. "I guess I don't understand it, exactly, but it's interesting." He threw his head forward for a look up at Mickelsson's face. "I mean, you don't really say what's true, really, though you say it in your books."

Mickelsson remembered his intent to put Nugent on to Nietzsche. "Maybe I don't actually *know* what I do in class," he said, and smiled.

Nugent waited, floating along beside him with his arms lifted a little —he carried no books today—his face, at the end of his long, white neck, like the face of an alarmed sunflower. It crossed Mickelsson's mind that Nugent's worsted jacket was exactly like his own.

"There's a philosopher I've been meaning to recommend to you," Mickelsson said, squinting at the boy. "Friedrich Nietzsche. Your remark about the way I teach our class made me think of it. Like many intellectuals, he had a profound distrust of the uses of intellect, or, as he'd prefer to say, 'consciousness.' "

Directly ahead of them as they walked down the sidewalk toward the library building, one of Mickelsson's colleagues, Lawler, the Aquinas man, came tentatively barging, walking straight down the middle of the sidewalk, his nose in a book. Edward Lawler was the soul of oddity: though he was apparently not religious, he was a specialist in medieval philosophy. He was short, five-two at most, and unhealthily fat, balding. The little hair he still had was gray. Like Tillson, their chairman, Lawler never wore anything but black—black suits even shabbier than Tillson's. (Sometimes, driving past his house, one would see him on his porch steps wearing his bathrobe, reading a book.) His shirts, on the best of days, had only two buttons left, though it was said that for special occasions he could dress like a prince. Weddings of his most beloved students, funerals . . .

"Hello, Edward," Mickelsson said.

Lawler walked on, not looking up. "*V'yanna,*" he said. God only knew what language it was. Lawler was a master of languages. There was hardly a known one he couldn't work out, given time. When they'd walked a few steps further, Mickelsson looked back. Lawler had stopped, belatedly understanding that someone had addressed him, and stood bowing formally, oddly military, still buried in his book. "*Guten Tag!* Hi, there!" Then—still without really seeing them, it seemed—he waddled on. Mickelsson smiled.

"Lawler," he explained to Nugent. "Brilliant man—philosophy. You must work with him sometime."

"I'm taking his course," Nugent said. "You signed me up for it."

"Ah!" Mickelsson said.

They walked on.

Thinking about Lawler, Mickelsson had completely forgotten now what they'd been talking about. For all he knew, they might by accident be walking toward the market together—except that he noticed that they were heading toward the library building, which fact brought back reality, dimly.

"I'm afraid I forgot what we were saying," Mickelsson said.

Nugent smiled palely and nodded. "We were talking about Nietzsche —and our class."

"Ah yes." He pursed his lips, walking more slowly for a moment. Nugent adjusted his pace. "There was something that bothered you," Mickelsson said, not remembering, playing the odds.

"Well, they were talking about 'moral absolutes,' that's all," Nugent said, "the idea that they're built into Nature, and so on. Which is a long way from talking about values as human assertions. I guess I thought that girl—what's-her-name, the swimmer—was sort of *on* to it, how human beings can see only what they're constructed to see, and maybe it's entirely wrong, maybe green is really yellow, in God's eyes, but since there's no way human beings can know it, it doesn't matter. If our actions aren't *informed*, they're not really actions. I was surprised how you handled it, that's all."

"Yes, right," Mickelsson said. "Yes, I remember now. I was saying I may not *know* what I do when I teach. It's obvious that teaching should be thoroughly rational—" He glanced at Nugent to see that he was listening, not brooding on miseries of his own. "But Nietzsche's not convinced —in certain moods, at least—that we're at our best at our most rational." He raised his hand, blocking objection. "Let me explain. Think about bodily functions. Imagine what it would be like if we had to be aware of the breakdown of fats"—he glanced again at Nugent, asserting his professorial authority—"that is, imagine how it would be if digestion was something *we* had to do. Consciousness, Nietzsche would say, has nothing much to do with what's most efficient in the working of the body. The question, he'd say, is why consciousness is needed at all. Nietzsche acknowledges the phenomenon of consciousness and supposes it developed —'fortunately'—only late in the evolution of the human species. In other words, he thinks we're often better off without it—playing it by ear, as they say. That's not the *whole* story. It doesn't account for his idea of the 'true hero'—the poet, philosopher, or saint."

They'd come to the library-building doors. Mickelsson held back, letting Nugent enter first. Nugent held back, too, unsure of the rules, then hastily stepped forward. When they were inside, Mickelsson looked around at the door, making sure it was automatically closing, then moved on.

He said, "He was a German, of course, and the son of a Lutheran minister, which put him in a good position to see how troublesome strict rationality can be. Still, there's something to be said for his uneasiness. He has an interesting remark on human language. 'In general,' he says"— Mickelsson slowed his walk again, smiling his fixed smile, and put the back of his right fist to his forehead, striving to get it right, though he'd quoted it a thousand times—"'in general, whenever primitive man laid down a word, there he believed himself to have made a discovery. How different it really was! He had hit upon a problem, and thinking he'd solved it'—it goes something like this; I'm afraid I'm paraphrasing slightly —'thinking he'd solved it, he in fact only raised an obstacle to its solution. And now,' Nietzsche says—something like this—'now, with every piece of knowledge, one must stumble over stone-hard, everlasting words —and one would rather break a bone than a word.'"

They'd come to the first floor men's room. Mickelsson stopped. "I need to go in here," he said, and pushed the door open. Nugent nodded and followed. Mickelsson braced up against the urinal, Nugent at his back, and said, "Nietzsche's whole philosophy—like modern positivism, and ultimately like nominalism—is based on a deep concern with language. The idea that if *you* can understand me, I must not be saying much." With his stream he wrote "*P J M*" on the cracked white wall of the urinal.

"Well," he said, "it's true, I'm a little lax in class. I'm glad to hear my students thinking about anything at all." He shook his penis, then put it back inside his pants and zipped his fly.

"I suppose I'd have to admit," he said, "I'm not very comfortable with undergraduates. 'Certitude is weakness,' this same Nietzsche says. In undergraduate classes one of the main things we do is offer an illusion of certitude." He smiled, almost nasty. "It helps the F.T.E."

"I *thought* that was what you were doing," Nugent said.

Back in his office, Mickelsson partly closed the door, leaving it only an inch or two ajar since Jessica would be coming, she'd said; then he went directly to his desk, where he rummaged through the drawers until he located his Susquehanna-Montrose phone book, found the number, and dialed the Susquehanna Hospital. Over the hills outside his window a gray wash of cloud had moved in, making the trees along the ridges and the weedy fields below more drab and dingy than they'd been earlier this morning—sickly, in fact, as if infected, mile after mile, with mange. The phone rang six times, seven times, eight. . . . He rechecked the number, thinking it impossible that a phone could go so long ignored in a hospital; but there was no mistake. He waited on, and at last a friendly, middle-aged female voice said, "Seskehenna Hospital, Hennessy speaking."

"Hello," Mickelsson said. Just then his office door swung open and Jessica came in. When she saw that he was phoning, she signalled him to go on, she'd wait outside, and started to leave, then paused as he waved her toward one of the chairs he had for conferences with students, gave him an inquiring look, then settled gracefully though perhaps not entirely at home there in Mickelsson's learner's seat, crossed her legs at the knees, and cupped the upper knee in both hands. Mickelsson was saying into the phone, meanwhile, "Hello. This is Professor Mickelsson out on Riverview Road. I wonder if I could talk to Dr. Bauer."

"Dr. Bauer?" the voice said. "We haven't gaht a Dr. Bauer anymore. We used to, but—"

"I know she's not with you anymore," Mickelsson said, "but I understand she was planning to drop by today. I'm the man who bought her house from her." He laughed, vaguely like an old friend. "If I could just get in touch with her—if there were someone there who would be likely to know—"

"Just a minute, Prafessor." Blips and buzzes hit his ear, then a husky male voice said with practiced haste and distraction, "Benton."

Now the other voice, the woman's, sounded miles away. "Dr. Benton, the prafessor that bought Dr. Bauer's howse is on the line. He's trying to locate Dr. Bauer?"

"All right, I'll talk to him," Benton said. Then, loudly, as if he distrusted phone-wire, "Hello?"

"Hello, Doctor," Mickelsson began.

Before he could say more, Dr. Benton called out, "Far as I know Dr. Bauer's down in Florida. If she wasn't, I feel pretty sure she'd've rung me. We used to be partners here. Is it something somebody else could help with?"

"No," Mickelsson said, and glanced at Jessica. "Is there anybody else she'd get in touch with if she came up?" He gave a little chuckle. "Actually, the reason I'm so persistent—I thought maybe I saw her."

There was a pause, three heartbeats. "If she was here, I'd be the first one to know."

"I see. Well, I'm sorry to have troubled you."

"No trouble, no trouble a-tall," Dr. Benton said.

Jessica sat frowning thoughtfully, eyes evasive, the side of her index finger pressing into her cheek, like a professor listening to a not very carefully prepared seminar report, as Mickelsson told her how he'd nearly been killed, driving home last night, then explained to her the theory that was beginning to take shape in his mind. When he finished, she went on staring for a time at nothing in particular—the pipe on the great stack of mail on his desk—then gave her head a little shake. She had a wonderfully sharp jaw-line, the handsome, sharp nose and Near-Eastern slanted eyes of the warriors of Darius—if one could believe the ancient polychrome brick frieze. He wondered if the ancient Persians had been a tall people.

"Strange," she said. Mechanically, making a comb of her fingers, she pushed a falling sweep of hair back from her temple. After a moment she asked, "But why would she have gone there without telling anyone? Her friends, I mean."

"I won't know that for sure until I've talked to her," Mickelsson said. "Or talked to the Spragues." He leaned back in his chair, looking at the door above Jessica's head, aware that she was watching him more sharply now, surprised and displeased by his suggestion. "According to my theory," he said, "she couldn't very well tell her lawyer what she was doing, your friend what's-his-name—"

"Bob Ceslik."

"That's it. If she told him she wanted to make a visit to the Spragues, try to persuade them to settle the thing privately, he'd have insisted on going with her, or more likely he'd have advised her not to go. You know lawyers. As for Benton or any other friends she may have—" He paused, casting about. "Maybe she was in too much of a hurry to see them, so she decided not to tell them she was coming. That's possible, she may have flown up and rented a car at the airport. The one she was driving was new and clean, the kind you'd be likely to get at a Hertz or Avis." He shrugged. "Or maybe, doing what she was trying to do, she felt uneasy— secretive. I don't know; I haven't thought that part out yet."

Jessica mused. "What I don't understand is why she was going so fast. No matter where she'd been—at the Spragues' place or at yours—it makes no sense."

Mickelsson smiled. "It would make sense if she'd been up at my place and seen the ghosts."

She shook her head. "I don't think so." She leaned forward in the chair, her head almost level with Mickelsson's. "I know you're not even considering the possibility. But just for the sake of argument, suppose that's what happened." With a quick, impatient movement of one hand, she waved away objections. "Suppose she went to your place, maybe be- cause for some reason she wanted to talk to you; she found the place dark, or maybe one light on somewhere, up in the upstairs bathroom, say— doesn't matter—something that made her think you might be home. So she got out of the car and went to the door and looked in, right? And saw something. We don't have to say it was a ghost. But we know she must have heard the same stories you've heard. Say she believed them— for whatever reason." She shrugged and again waved away objections. "The point is, no matter what she saw—make it the worst thing your mind can conceive . . . I don't know, some old woman in the kitchen, sawing the body of some old man into pieces—" Jessica laughed, startled by the image that had come to her, then hurried on: "She runs back to the car and gets the hell out of there. Flying, right? But after half a mile, would she *still* be flying?"

Mickelsson studied her, distracted from thought about what she was saying by the image of her earnest face thrown forward toward him, her hands palms up under her chin, level with her collarbone. He imagined her as a schoolgirl, straightening out her drama teacher.

"*I* wouldn't," she said, and poked the desktop with her index finger. "I'd drive like crazy until I knew I was safe, and then I'd slow down. And if she'd driven all the way from Spragues' when she met you—what*ever* it may have been that happened at Spragues'—"

Mickelsson nodded. "Interesting," he said. "But if something was chasing her—"

Jessica glanced at him, unpersuaded but willing to think about it. Then something else occurred to her. She asked, "Why is it you want to talk to her—or to the Spragues? What good will it do? You want damages for an accident that didn't happen?"

"I'd like to know what's going on, that's all," Mickelsson said.

"You feel threatened?" She leaned toward him again. "Look, why don't you just forget it? Write it off."

He smiled, ironic, unwilling to be bullied. "Maybe that's it. I feel threatened."

"You feel *some*thing weird, Peter. I realize you're Superman and nothing scares you. . . ." Again her look sharpened. "Is it the coincidence of the names—the Spragues who lived at your house, the Spragues up on the mountain?" A smile began to form at one side of her mouth. "Some kind of problem in ontology—if that's the word?"

"Maybe," he said, dismissive, and reached for his pipe.

She watched him pick it up, feel into the bowl with his grimy index finger, then put it to his lips. Still with her legs crossed at the knees, she began to swing one leg slowly, as if purposely to bother him. "You feel threatened right now, that's for sure." She smiled.

"You're a scary lady," he said, covertly sly, like a poker player.

"Maybe all women are." She shrugged.

Foul blow! Ambushed! He held a match to the pipebowl to evade her eyes. He decided on frankness, the old nothing-to-hide play. "All right," he said, "I feel threatened. God knows why. I like order."

"Hmmm," she said. He could feel her drawing back, preparing a new tack, less like a gambler than like an oral examiner briefly letting up on a student in trouble. "It *is* interesting that the names are the same," she said. "I doubt that it means anything, but it's interesting. I guess I know how I'd feel, if I were you. Here's this mystery of ghosts—even if you don't believe in ghosts, it must make you feel odd—and then you run into this second mystery, the mystery of coincidence. I think it would make me feel"—she shrugged—"as if something were creeping up on me. Make me feel vulnerable. And if I were feeling a little vulnerable already . . ."

"That could be it," he said.

She laughed. "Bullshit." Then abruptly she lowered her gaze. "So you still mean to talk with the Spragues."

He nodded, drawing in smoke, then letting it out with his words. "You want to come?"

Like sunlight breaking through dark clouds, Jessica smiled. "Not on your life!" After a moment she asked, "When do you mean to do it?"

"Right away." He leaned forward in his chair. "I'm sure you're right about why I have to do it—the feeling that something's . . . out of control. I suppose if I were sensible, understanding that fact would be enough." He looked at her soberly. "You're sure you don't want to come?"

"I couldn't, Pete," she said. She caught a corner of her lip between her teeth, weighing the question in her mind. "I have appointments and meetings all day long, and anyway, if I went with you, how would I get back? It's an hour out to your place, so if you drove me back it would be an hour in to town and an hour home again, for you, I mean." She shook her head. "It would make no sense."

"I don't know." He shrugged. "You could spend the night at my place. I have a guest room—of sorts. I have to come in again tomorrow."

She met his eyes, then seemed embarrassed at having done so. "I don't think so," she said.

"All right." He stood up. "I'll let you know how it turns out."

"Do!" she said, rising, then turned to the door. As she opened it she looked back at him. "Be careful?"

"Certainly." Like a Prussian officer, Mickelsson clicked his heels and bowed.

"Oy," she said, and rolled her eyes.

After she was gone he put on his light overcoat, walked out to the parking lot, and drove to the parking-lot gate. As he was about to pull onto Campus Drive he saw her coming across the lawn, running with surprisingly long strides, waving. She was tall and broad-shouldered, like a man, but ran with a woman's special grace—ran, he thought, like a warrior-goddess out of Homer. He rolled down his window. When she reached him she laughed, out of breath, and called, "Hey, I changed my mind. Is that all right?"

"Hop in!" he called back, and laughed with her. Jessica hurried around the front of the Jeep, still smiling as if delighted and also dismayed by what she was doing. He reached across to the passenger-side door and unlocked it. She swung herself in.

"Could we stop off at my office for just a minute?" she asked. She was breathing hard. "I didn't have time to put a sign up to cancel my appointments."

"No problem," he said. He felt two things at once, emotions distinct and simultaneous as two colors on a flag: a flash of annoyance at the age-old inconvenience of womanhood, and a flash of joy at her having left in such a hurry to catch up with him.

Later, driving down Highway 81, he asked, "By the way, why were you mad at me last night?"

"Was I?" she asked.

He gave her a look.

She half smiled, then frowned, gazing through the windshield again, and after a moment lowered her eyes to the large, graceful hands in her lap. "You should have invited me to your party before the others," she said. "That would've been common courtesy." She looked at him, her shoulders hunched inward, her face a living history of the Diaspora—morose, legalistic, gentle. The thought of Donnie Matthews came into his mind, then the memory of all those nights he'd sat up, pretending to work, checking the clock now and then against his will, wondering where the hell his wife was and glad he didn't know.

The sky darkened increasingly as they wound up into the mountains. Here and there they passed parked cars or pickup trucks, probably deer-hunters, he realized when he saw two men standing in a field with guns. On the backs of their Day-Glo orange jackets they had hunting tags. As he passed his house Mickelsson pointed, telling Jessica, "That's it! That's where I live!" She looked out, then rolled down her window to look back at it after they'd passed. "It's big!" she said. "I had no idea it was so big! It seems odd, though—a man all by himself . . . a house like that . . ."

"I have grandiose taste," he said. "Who knows, maybe I'll meet some little angel, have sixteen kids."

"You should. You'd be a wonderful father," she said. She shook her head. "I don't know. A house like that, I'd go bonkers."

An awkwardness settled between them, or at least on Mickelsson. It was as if Donnie Matthews were right behind them, in the back seat. He drove her from his mind. Jessica was distant again, as if sorry she'd mentioned children, or her fear of big houses. Mickelsson sighed and shook his head. He doubted that his daughter and son would agree about his gifts as a father, ignored and abandoned as they must feel. And angry, perhaps. Certainly it was anger in his son's case; otherwise he'd have called.

He glanced into the woods at the side of the road as if expecting something. There was nothing, of course. Treetrunks, a tangle of bare branches, a few gray leaves. The light had a dead look. They passed a tarpaper shack with the windows broken out, the driveway grown up in weeds. The climb was steep now. He shifted down.

"It's funny," she said, "how much land there is in this country . . . that nobody lives on."

"It's desolate, all right," he said. He glanced at her. "It bothers you?" She thought it over. "Of course." She stole a glance at him.

He slowed, passing John Pearson's place. Though he'd still had his dairy just a year ago, one would have thought the barns had stood abandoned much longer, the old gray silo tipping precariously away from the cowbarn, the doors hanging partly off the track like half-knocked-out teeth. The house was asbestos-shingled and dark, patched layer on layer, surrounded by rusting bits of machinery, an old wringer washing-machine, small outbuildings. The front yard was fenced, and in one corner four sheep with black faces stood watching the Jeep pass. Where they went for shelter he could not guess, unless the open, rusted cellar door gave the answer. It was a queer idea, obscurely depressing, the thought of sheep muffling around in an old man's cellar. Behind the house, neatly stacked across the space of half an acre, stood cord on cord of wood.

On the next mailbox he read, in black paint, *Dudak*. He said, "Spragues' should be the next place up."

She nodded. She sat turned partly sideways, her right arm reaching

as if casually toward the dashboard, the hand resting there with fingers spread wide. Whether she was afraid he would drive into a ditch or afraid of something else was not clear, but he wouldn't be surprised if it were the country itself that troubled her. Now the mountain was wooded on both sides of them, and there was snow on the ground, glittering ice on the branches overhead. The road switchbacked sharply to the left, over a stone bridge spanning a deeply gouged creek, a fall that made the heart gasp, then climbed more steeply for a minute or two, then levelled off. He saw a mailbox in the distance, cocked back from the road like a pistol hammer, and as they drew nearer he made out an opening between trees, a two-rut lane that, except for the mailbox, he probably wouldn't have noticed. There were car tracks. He stopped the Jeep at the entrance to the lane and sat for a moment looking in.

"Peter," Jessica said, then didn't finish.

He could see no house, at first; then, as if by magic, out of the fallow gray of trees and brush the drab gray rectangle of the house emerged, the windows unlighted, no smoke coming out of the chimney. Not far from the house, leaning heavily to one side, sat a fat, gray car, perhaps a Pontiac or Oldsmobile, a relic of, at the latest, the 1960s. It was certainly not that car that had left the tracks. On the left side it had no tires. Now he began to make out smaller buildings, all as gray as the house—something that might be a garage or chickencoop, something that might contain pigs or a shaggy old pony. In high weeds at the side of the house there were butane tanks. Mickelsson leaned forward, looking up through the windshield, searching all around, and confirmed the suspicion that had come over him: no phone line, no electricity.

"Are you sure there's someone living here?" Jessica asked.

"I guess we'll find out," he said. He shifted into low and four-wheel drive, and the Jeep nosed slowly in.

They saw when they came up beside it that the house was, like his own much grander house, a T-frame: behind the two-story front part, curtainless, paintless, plain as a box, a porched back part ran out, reaching deeper into the woods. The whole house was up on blocks—trash lay underneath, and more trash in great, rotting mounds toward the rear—and the rear extension was crooked, bulged outward, the back wall fallen among corncobs like a square nose sniffing.

"All out," Mickelsson said, and opened his door. Jessica nodded, compressed her lips, and opened the door on her side. Dogs began to bark, noisy and frightening as a volley of shots, but when Mickelsson looked around for the source of the racket he saw at once that the dogs, leaping up at the chicken-wire wall of a lean-to shack, could not get at them. Something lay at their feet. He looked away.

"It's all right," he said, meeting Jessica at the front of the Jeep and taking her elbow.

She nodded, watching the ground, stepping carefully, the dogs barking more and more wildly, snapping at the air, as the two of them moved toward the porch. Mickelsson kept his eye on the paintless door as they approached it, but in his mind he continued to see those leaping, rolling-eyed, half-starved hounds, and on the dirt floor by the dogs' feet . . . whatever it was . . . a head of some kind, a horse or cow, perhaps; he didn't much care to know which.

"This is a crappy idea," Jessica said softly as he brought up his fist to knock.

He did not allow himself to think about it, but brought his knuckles down hard, three times, against the wood.

The man who opened the door was shrivelled and bent forward like a monkey, maybe five feet tall, not a quarter-inch anywhere on his large, lead-gray face unwrinkled. He might be fifty, or he might be a hundred. He had a wrinkled, spit-stained cigarette in his hand, pinched between two arthritically swollen fingers, and smoke came out of his nose and mouth as if his meagre, dried-out insides contained smouldering rags. He wore a thick, filthy sweater full of holes and snags, and over it a tattered denim frock, white-seamed with age. His gray hair was stiff and went out in all directions, and though he'd recently shaved, every crack on his chin and lower cheeks was full of bristles, feathery and silver as frost. He looked out through the screen with an expression of sharp curiosity, perhaps alarm, and even when Mickelsson said "Hello!"—smiling, his voice as hearty as a farmer's—the man said nothing. "My name's Mickelsson. I live down the road a ways, down by Susquehanna," Mickelsson said.

Perhaps the man nodded; it was hard to be sure. Then he turned to look up at Jessica with the same animal curiosity he'd shown as he sized up Mickelsson. At last he smiled, showing naked gums and one last yellow tooth. "I know who ya are," he said—a high, thin whine, merry grin like a boy's. "Come on in!" He pushed at the door and, when it stuck, kicked it hard with his boot. As the screen swung out he stepped back, making room for them to pass. Jessica stepped in as if completely at home, then stopped, two steps into the room, to wait for Mickelsson. The old man slammed the screen door, then the wooden door, and came in behind them. "I see you down there at the doc's," he said. "Yore place is right down under my place." His head came forward, tongue lolling, as if he meant to make an obscene suggestion. "Sometimes I hear you, workin away in the middle of the night."

"I do that sometimes," Mickelsson said. He spoke loudly, on the presumption that the old man was deaf.

Jessica stood looking around, smiling vaguely, at the dark, filthy kitchen—dishes in the sink, the dirt on them caked as if it had lain there

for months; grocery bags full of garbage along the walls; patches of linoleum torn away or worn through; on the sagging ceiling and upper walls,
immense dark stains. In the center of the kitchen stood a long pine table
filled to the last inch with boxes of cereal, mason jars, an open milk-
carton, dishes, silverware, balls of string, jumbled piles of sewing, bits of
mail. Everything in the kitchen was the same color, the bone gray of long-
fallen timber.

"Gwan along into the parlor," the old man piped, waving in the direction of the doorway beyond them. "It ain't as bad in there. If you need—"
He broke off to cough, doubling over, covering his mouth with the hand
that held the cigarette.

Carefully, they picked their way toward the parlor. The room, when
they reached it, proved as messy as the kitchen and cold as a barn, but at
least it was lighter here, sunlight pouring in through the curtainless windows. The old man, still coughing, took a stack of magazines and old
clothes from the sofa between the two windows, making just room enough
for the two of them, then, when they were seated, took a waffle-iron from
the plywood-patched seat of a wooden chair opposite and sat down himself, facing them, four feet away. Again he showed his gums and his single
up-stabbing tooth in a smile. "Make you a cup of Offaltine?" he asked.

"No thank you," Mickelsson said.

"I had coffee just before we left," Jessica said. Her eyes moved from
corner to corner of the room, half fear, half sharp disapproval.

"Good," the old man said, and laughed, poking his tongue out. "I
doubt we could find it ennaway!" Then he leaned back in his chair and
just looked at them, smiling sociably, tongue lolling again, waiting. At
the far end of the room a door opened—the old man did not turn to look,
merely watched his guests in amusement—and an old woman with a haggard face and snow-white hair poked her head in, then drew it back again
quickly and closed the door. "That's Mother," the old man said, and
gave a laugh. "She don't like comp'ny. It ain't that she don't like 'em,
really. She had a stroke, while back. She thinks she don't look good."

"Poor thing!" Jessica said. The fear and disapproval sank away as if
by magic, replaced by a troubled look.

"Wal, we all got our crosses," the old man said. Then: "So you went
and bought the doc's place." He drew the cigarette to his mouth and
pulled at it, sucking the smoke in deep.

"Yes, me and the bank," Mickelsson said, mechanically smiling. He
sat unnaturally erect, partly to give Jessica room, partly for fear that the
sofa might give way if he put his full weight on it. "I understand you
used to have relatives living there."

"That's right," the old man said. He was quiet a moment, smiling and
nodding, letting smoke drift out. He studied Jessica, considering whether
or not to say more, and at last said, "Great-uncle and -aunt of mine.

Uncle Caleb and Aunt Theodosia. Some people say they're still down there." He coughed.

"As ghosts, you mean?" Jessica asked, turning away from him, looking toward the door where the old woman hid.

"That's it, ma'am." He laughed, then looked mock-stern. "They was never close with the rest of us. That's why it got 'em. There's Spragues all through these here mountains from one end to th'other, but they didn't want no part of that. They had no use for kin."

"It?" Jessica asked, turning back to him, frowning a little, leaning forward.

The old man looked blank.

"You said, 'That's why *it* got 'em.' "

Sprague stretched his lips out, lifted his hand a few inches, then dropped it to his knee again. "Didn't mean nothing by it," he said. "Sometimes people just get taken over, ya might say. By their moods or suthin. Some kinda feelin that's in the woods." He looked to Mickelsson as if for help. "You know, there's us and there's all that other. If people stick together, take care of their own—"

Mickelsson nodded. "It's not always easy, though. You, for instance, way out here in the wilderness . . ." He just missed saying "sticks."

The old man nodded, smiling again, then came to. "Oh, we see people," he said, abruptly defensive. "I got a brother Bill over there in Gibson, and a sister in Hallstead. They come by here now'n again, with the kids and all. We see people, all right. Not like we used to, now that Mother ain't so well and the car don't keep runnin. But Bill's a mechanic, my brother. Soon's he gets over here, he's gonna take that old automobile apart and get it runnin just like new."

Mickelsson nodded. He was sure the car had lain dead in the weeds for years.

Jessica asked, looking at the old man's hands, "How do you do your shopping?"

"Oh, I walk in, usually. Lot of time people will pick you up, you know. Everybody knows us. We been livin here sixty-seven years. Course soon's the car's fixed I'll start drivin again."

"How far *is* it?" Jessica asked.

"Bowt five mile," the old man said. He smiled, little fires in his eyes, as if something about her tickled him.

Now the door at the end of the room opened again, and the old woman's voice came out, fretful. Her words were slurred, not easy to understand; her false teeth were noisy. "He walks all the way in and he walks all the way back with a big box of groc'ries. Don't *nobody* pick him up."

Jessica straightened up, trying to get a glimpse of the old woman.

The old man smiled. "*She* don't know," he said. He leaned forward and winked. "I fly, that's the truth of it. I been granted the gift of flight."

"His heart's bad, too," the voice called. "All them cigarettes."

"Now, Mother," the old man called, grinning at his lap.

Jessica stole a look at Mickelsson.

"One of these days he'll be dead on the road there like a woodchuck, nobody find him for two, three weeks, and here I'll be all by myself up here, can't even do for myself."

"Lord God protect us from crabby old women," the old man said. He tipped his head up to smile at the ceiling.

"But you do have company sometimes, don't you?" Jessica asked, leaning forward again. "I thought I saw car tracks out by the road in front, as if somebody had been here not too long ago—yesterday, maybe, or last night."

The old man thought about it, grinding out his cigarette in an aluminum frozen-pie plate on the floor beside his boot, then shook his head. "Nope."

"You sure?" Mickelsson asked. His voice was accidentally stern. "I noticed them myself."

The old man lifted his chin, his eyes narrowed, on guard. "Ain't seen nobody in a week," he said. "Mebby that car that sets and watches us."

"More like a month," the old woman shouted from her place behind the door.

Mickelsson frowned. "Maybe just somebody turning around in your driveway," he said. "What kind of car is it?"

"Kids, mebby," the old man said, and nodded. "I don't go out and mess with 'em."

Now Jessica stood up, her movements too smooth and restrained, as if she thought herself in danger. "Well," she said, "it certainly was nice of you to invite us in. If there's ever anything we can do for you—that is, anything Peter . . ."

"We get a lot of kids up here," the old man said. He spoke quickly and peevishly, lest they not let him say it. He too got up, bending far forward, pushing down hard on the sides of the chairseat with his arms. "Give 'em half a chance, they'll burn you out."

"Really?" Mickelsson asked. Now he too was standing.

"Yup. They got a gang. Burn people's houses and barns down for money. Whole thing was in the Seskehenna paper."

"And you think—" Jessica began.

He was leading them back through the kitchen now, making his way between garbage bags. "That's right," he said. "But tell the truth, they don't scare me. We're pretty well protected." He turned, head bowed, to smile back at them. "See this?" he said. He reached up to seize a rope near the kitchen door—a dark, frayed rope that went up into a hole in the ceiling above. "Give this rope a good jerk," he said—he suggested a pull without carrying it out, then pointed through the grimy kitchen window—"and out there in the dog-house the door on the side there pulls open, and out they tumble."

Jessica leaned down by the window, pressing her hands against her knees, to look. "Are they dangerous?" she asked. Even bent over she was taller than old Sprague.

"Wal," the old man said, smiling, "there's worse dogs and better dogs, but I'll tell you this: they're hungry."

Mickelsson said, "You really think there's somebody that wants your house burned down?"

"Sure I do!" Though he continued to smile, his cheek twitched. He reached into his shirt pocket for his cigarettes, and his knobby fingers came out with just one, as if he had them in there loose. "There's Dudak and Pearson—they'd like to get my land if they could grab it off cheap. And there's the doc." He raised his eyes to meet Mickelsson's, then smiled, pretending the look was not a challenge. "She's a killer—that's right. Believe me, I know! And *she* knows I can prove it in a court of law. We been goin at it a long time now, her 'n' me." He hesitated, studying Mickelsson, still smiling. "She stole that house, ya know. Stole it right from under my shoes."

"My place?" Mickelsson asked.

"That's it."

Jessica asked, "What happened?"

The old man held a match to his cigarette and sucked in, then coughed. When he was able to talk again, he said, "It's a long story, but the long and short of it is, there was some taxes on the place and she paid 'em and took it, just like that."

"You couldn't afford—" Jessica began.

"She was quicker, that's all," the old man snapped. "Got there to the courthouse before I ever knowed what was doin." Again a coughing fit came over him, ragged smoke-clouds spewing from his lungs with each cough.

"Hmm," Jessica said. She had her hand extended toward him, getting ready to say good-bye, but now she changed her mind.

"Don't matter. Comin to the end of it," the old man said. "She's got a hex on 'er."

"She's got—" Mickelsson began, drawing back a little.

"Never mind who put it," the old man said, then laughed, eyes crazily merry. "People just never do learn, do they?" He seized the doorknob, turned it, and opened the door for them. "Glad you folks come up," he said, bobbing his head at Jessica, then at Mickelsson. "Now don't be strangers!"

Across from the porch, the bony hounds were leaping at the fence again, snapping and barking as if in rage and despair. Powdery dust clouded at their feet, obscuring the head on the floor.

"Shet *ap!*" the old man yelled, and flapped his arms at them, to no avail. To Jessica he said, "Say hello to the ghosts for me, missus."

"I will," she said, forcing a smile. She stood looking out at the dogs.

"Don't you folks fool with 'em," the old woman's voice called from somewhere nearby. "You leave *them* alone, the spirits'll leave *you* alone!"

"We'll be careful," Mickelsson called. "So long!" He waved, in case the old woman was somewhere where she could see him.

"Take care, now," the old man said, and reached as if toward a cap. "I'll be seein ya." He winked. "Someday ye'll look up in the sky and there I'll be." He flapped his arms like a bird.

Jessica smiled. "All right," she said.

They crossed to the Jeep, neither of them glancing at the head thrown to the dogs. When the motor caught, Mickelsson waved one last time, then backed out. At the road he stopped, shifted into low, ready to start back down the mountain, but Jessica said, "Look, Pete! Look at the snow in the woods! It's full of paw-prints!"

He saw that it was true. "He must've freed them for a while," he said. "Presumably sometime after last night's snowfall."

"Or sicked them on someone," Jessica said.

"Like for instance the doc," Mickelsson said, slowly nodding.

In his mind's eye he saw the black dogs bounding along like deer beside the doctor's car. He saw Pearson's ram jerk his head up suddenly as the dogs came flying through the fenced-in yard, bellowing, and saw the ram take off, heading in blind terror for wherever the dogs were not.

"Yes," Mickelsson said, and nodded. "That must be what happened."

They sat side by side on the couch in his livingroom, staring into the crackling, sputtering fire in the open-doored stove, Jessica with her shoes off, one foot tucked up under her, the back of her head resting lightly on Mickelsson's arm. Her face was solemn, like that of a child listening to the stories of a grandfather. When he moved his hand on her shoulder or arm, she did not stop him. His groin ached dully, and every now and then a light shiver passed over him. Her left arm lay along his right upper leg. He concentrated on willing her to move her hand to his crotch. No luck.

Except for the fireplace and the nightlight in the kitchen, the whole house was dark. Outside, it was snowing a little. Jessica's sherry glass sat untouched on the glass coffeetable, Mickelsson' abandoned martini beside it. How she'd gotten him on the subject of the ghosts Mickelsson couldn't remember.

"So what was it like?" she asked. "He just came into the bedroom and looked at you?" Though her tone was impatient, she was serious, interested.

"As I said, I'm not really sure he was there at all. Anyway, he didn't look at me." Mickelsson touched his forehead with two fingers. The scent of her hair and the nearness of her mouth impaired his capacity for thought. He said carefully, "He said something to someone—not to me, I think; someone he expected would be there—and then he looked embarrassed, as if he realized he'd made a mistake, and he went out."

"You don't even remember what he said?"

"Something like 'Are you there?' or, 'You in there?' "

"So then what? He turned around and saw you?"

He smiled at her bullying. "I don't think he ever saw me," he said. "I'm not at all sure I saw him either, you know. The mind's a queer business. People see things that aren't there all the time—crazy people, people on drugs, people who are asleep and don't know it, people who've been hypnotized. . . . When you think about it, it's a wonder anyone's certain of anything."

"Maybe so, but really," Jessica protested, "you can tell at *some* level when what you're looking at isn't really there."

"I couldn't—not this time—though common sense makes me assume it wasn't. I don't know." He stared hard into the fire, reliving the memory for her benefit—the bearded old man shuffling in on him, staring with near-sighted, red-webbed eyes at the hatrack across the room. "I remember wondering at the time if maybe I was dreaming," he said. He glanced at her. "Or crazy."

"What did you decide?"

"I couldn't tell. I think what I pretty much decided was—" He closed his eyes for a moment, trying to make out whether or not he believed what he was about to say, not that it mattered, then finished: "It wasn't craziness. Something real, possibly not a ghost. It could be, I think, that I was tuning in on something from the past."

"Spooky," Jessica said, and sat forward in order to look into his face.

"Spookier than a ghost?"

She shook her head. "It's all pretty spooky, if you ask me." She considered, then settled back against his arm, snuggling in. With the thumb and first finger of her right hand she caught the wing of her collar, pulling it up almost to the tip of her chin, then letting it fall back. She glanced at him. "Don't pick," she said, and lightly slapped at his hand. Unconsciously he'd been playing with her sleeve. Her eyebrows lowered and her expression became comically studious, eyes glittering and darkening as the firelight and shadows moved. "You could be right," she said at last. "I read a book, the autobiography of one of those psychics who work with the police. He talked about what he feels and sees as he works, and it's a little like what you describe. It's as if he's in two different rooms at once, two different times—you know what I mean?" She checked his eyes, though why he should fail to understand her plain English was unclear to him. "He sees the people standing around him—the police, for instance—and he sees something else just as clearly, the way when you're driving down the road and imagining something, you see the road, but you also see the thing you're imagining." Again Jessica leaned forward to see him better. "Did you feel anything funny? In your body, I mean? Did you feel *old*, for instance?"

Mickelsson shook his head. "Not that I remember."

"Maybe it's different with different people," she said. "Are you sure you don't remember?"

He thought of Dr. Rifkin. "I've tried. I can't."

As if disappointed in him but grudgingly forgiving, she lay her head back on his arm again. "I wish you'd pay closer attention to things," she said. Then she turned, rolled her eyes toward his, and smiled, as if afraid if she pushed too hard he might get balky and be of no use to her. "But it is interesting." She rounded her eyes still more. Then abruptly sober: "If only I could make out what it means!"

"It has to mean something?"

"God knows it doesn't *have* to," she said, "but maybe it does. Why is it *these* ghosts that people get glimpses of? Is it possible they're trying to warn us about something? I know that sounds dumb—I don't mean it, exactly. I think. But why is it this particular house that's so alive? Or maybe it's *you*—something about you, or people like you. . . ."

"Tell you a different theory," Mickelsson said. "It all started as a haunted-house story by a bunch of kids, and when I heard the story, being more or less 'suggestible,' having a history of delusions of this kind—"

She declined the gambit, clenching her fist on her knee. "But I don't think it *is* 'nothing.' There's something about the house that feels . . . I mean, it's a nice house, it's beautiful. But there's this strange"—she frowned, then slid her eyes at him—"there's this smell, Peter."

"Probably the spring in the basement," he said. "It rots the wood."

"Are you crazy? It smells like *cake*."

He shrugged, apologetic. The uncivil forthrightness no doubt had its advantages, but it was wearing.

Jessica looked at him, then patted his arm as if conscious that she'd slightly hurt his feelings. "You *have* noticed it, haven't you?" she asked.

He'd had, he knew now—one after another—strange sensations he'd dismissed at the time: fantasies of indistinct voices, smells, an occasional sense of people near him, observing, nodding. . . . Suppose it were not just flickering dream-work but something more active. Suppose they had, whatever it might mean, some kind of stake in him.

He felt her hair brushing lightly against his wrist, tickling it, and when he breathed in deeply he again smelled her perfume. Lilacs? He was stirred, as one always is, he thought; but at the same time he was hurled deeper into the pit of himself. He imagined himself making love to her, huffing and blowing away in the bed upstairs, both of them mmming and groaning with delight, Jessica generously faking by the ancient Rules of Order for sexual politicians. He remembered for no reason what old man Sprague had said: *Sometimes people get taken over. . . . Some kinda feelin that's in the woods.* That was what was happening to him, the reason he was beginning to see ghosts.

He shuddered severely enough that Jessica noticed. She turned to him and, like someone reaching out to touch a nervous stallion, put her hand on his chest. "Are you cold or what?" she asked.

Down in the valley the train was rumbling through the darkness with its freight of lost childhood.

Abruptly, to free himself from the sweetness of her touch, he leaned forward, reaching for his pipe on the coffeetable. He got a match lit and held it over the bowl.

"Don't pull away, Pete," she said, as if she were now the injured one. She leaned forward too, moving her left arm around behind him and pressing her right hand flat on his chest, over his heart, where the pain was. She drew back a little, away from the pipe-smoke, and blew at it.

Against his will, he savored the calm spreading out from her hand. So it had once been with Ellen. Age-old story. He said, "I was thinking about what old Sprague said, the feeling that's in the woods. I know what he means." He scowled, bold sign of sincerity, though he had no intention of saying what was in his mind. No more cowpastures apparelled in celestial light. That was why he hated it when her judgments of people were clinical, unwilling to consider anything not physically there: because she was right. "Why are you massaging my chest?" he thought of saying. "What's it to you? Except that maybe someday your chest may ache. Good long-range investment." His chest ached more, and the magical healing power of her hand—so it seemed—became all the more annoying. Christ, what wouldn't he give for Jessica to be in love with him! But he'd learned what Jessica, of the tribe of Freud, had no doubt always secretly known. No love, just fuck. He decided to put the pipe down; he could survive for at least a few minutes without it. What difference? He said, "It's not like entropy—not like simple loss of energy, simple giving up. It feels more like something alive, like those dogs, or rattlesnakes." He looked at her forehead. The side of her breast was touching the side of his. They were inching up on the time of decision. Someone must make the first move. Was the game already started?

"I'm dull company, I'm afraid," he said. "I'm sorry." Cheap move, but piss on it.

She put her finger to his lips, leaning close. Her eyes were distant and thoughtful. She placed her mouth where he had no real choice but to kiss it.

. . .

Mickelsson lay beside her, trying to think, trying to come alive. Not that his body was asleep, non-functional. His body was a massive contradiction, his erection immense and violent, the rest of him—his fingertips and lips, even his large, cold feet—so timid, so constrainedly gentle, as if robbed of life-force by the ache in his heart, they were almost nonmaterial. The smoothness of her skin, the fullness of her breasts—pale underneath, glorious with tan and color toward the shoulders—her perfect nipples, the dark, soft bush between her legs, all took his breath away: beauty beyond his wildest dreams. Yet his heart was drowning in wretchedness. "Pete, it's all right," she crooned, as if knowing his mind. She was lying on her side, her breasts touching his arm and chest. His sense of doom hovered over him like a foreign presence, worn out, icy with indifference. Yet here was this body of his in a state of jubilee! He hardly dared to touch her breasts, though he touched them, first with his fingers, then with his lips and tongue, hungrily. *Women hate to be touched. Women are lunar.* She kissed the top of his head, then his eyes, nose, cheeks—sweetly, tentatively, as though she knew the slightest error would make him draw away again, feeling foolish and fat. Oh, she was good— A-plus, five stars—no question! Or could it be that she was still unsure, afraid of him, holding back out of timidity? He moved his hand from the softness of her belly to her crotch and to his astonishment found it wet, more than ready for him. Rarely in his life—either in his married life or in his occasional affairs, even with Donnie Matthews—had he encountered such seeming evidence that he was desired. His mind, with all its doubts and considerations, switched off for a moment, his penis stealing his brain's blood—*ah, Nature! ah, Devil!*—and his heart, like an animal beaten and shouted to activity, began to labor, sending reverberations through his body. He eased himself up over her and touched the lips of her vagina with the tip of his painfully throbbing cock. His heart hammered crazily now; he realized again that he could die. She raised her head from the pillow and, as if doing some magic charm, kissed him four times, quickly. Then he eased himself into her. They both gasped and almost laughed, and her arms came around him, clinging, as he clung to her. Her legs locked around him like jaws. Soon a motion he could not control came over him—over her as well—a terrible mechanical power he'd never in all his years been taken by, a mighty and yet effortless rocking that made him feel shaman-like, as if the curtain of illusion had parted and they'd fallen to the beginning of things. Her face shone, her smile wide. When at last the explosion came, he felt light, as if turned from heavy flesh into thin, shining air. Now he did at last laugh, and pressed his cheek against hers.

"Wow!" she said into his ear. "Wow!"

. . .

He slept, heavy as a bear in winter, more serene than he'd felt in a long time. Then—perhaps hours had passed, perhaps only minutes—he found himself desperately laboring up from slumber, gasping, full of fear, trying to make out what he must do. Then he was in the room, and understood that the shouting came from Jessica in her sleep. She was crying out with stinging, crackling anger, such blood-curdling rage that he was afraid to touch her and awaken her. Though the room was silent now, he realized that he'd heard the words clearly: *"Get away! Just fucking stay back! Let me be!"* It was like the voice of someone else. From all he knew of her, he could not have guessed her capable of such tones. She was still tense, he saw, and grinding her teeth like one of Luther's devils. He rose up on his left elbow to touch her upper arm, then gently, cautiously kissed the side of her face. She was sweating as if with fever.

"Jessie," he said softly.

She murmured something, still angry, but she relaxed a little.

Half an hour later it happened again. "Jessie, Jessie, Jessie," he whispered, moving his hand on her head as though she were a sleeping child. He listened to the name in the darkness, the sound nosing out into the room as if in bafflement, trying to make sense of itself. Jessie? Jessie? One thought of, if not Shakespeare, fat wives of rabbis, or bitchy little English schoolgirls in perfect banana curls. What had it to do with this soft-faced midnight changeling? "Poor Jessie," he whispered. Whether or not she'd been faking her pleasure, or yelling out at *him* that pure, ancient hatred, she was another poor miserable damned mortal. *Jesus*, he thought, *what a stupid fucking existence.* He blinked away tears. A moment later, he realized that his hand was no longer moving on her head; he'd drifted off. *All are faithless, saith the angel.* He stroked Jessie's head from front to back twice more, then gave in to gravity.

7

He had been working at his desk for some time when he heard the upstairs toilet flush and knew Jessica was up. According to his watch it was nine-thirty. That was late, for her. He wondered if it meant that she'd slept peacefully at last. The thought stirred anxiety, and he looked back at the papers spread before him.

A few minutes later a knock came at his door, and he called, "Come in." The door opened, and Jessica stood there in his white terrycloth bathrobe, tentatively smiling, one hand on the doorframe. She had on no make-up but had brushed her hair. A confusion of emotions rushed over him. Except for Donnie, he hadn't seen a woman in her morning's natural beauty for a long time: clear-eyed, human, nothing about her doll-like or prepared. It was so much like being married that he couldn't make out whether the sight filled him with happiness or misery. (His cock had no such problem. It stirred like an old dog waking up, looking around.)

"Hi," she said.

He nodded. "You must have slept well."

"I did." She came to him, put her hand on his shoulder, then moved her palm, massaging the muscle. After a moment she bent down cautiously and kissed him. When she'd straightened up again she gazed into his eyes —only for an instant, but purposefully, as if to tell him something— perhaps: everything can be changed, *Nichts ist wahr, alles ist erlaubt.* Now she was looking at the papers in front of him, covertly reading, ready to look away and play innocent if she must. Her eyes raced. "What are you working on?"

He put his left arm around her, then moved his hand to her left thigh. "I've been more or less *un*working," he said. His right hand waved off grandiloquence. "For a while now I've been fiddling at what I like to think of as a sort of blockbuster philosophy book, something to make the best-seller list and earn me a fortune." She was amused, cautiously interested, sliding her eyes at him then hurriedly back to the paper, still reading. "I'd start out," he said, "with superdramatic stuff: the graphic presentation of an imaginary case of child-molesting and murder committed by a quadraplegic nine-year-old, then a rape with ice-tongs, intended to cover up a devilish cloak-and-dagger conspiracy by government agents and the nuke people; and after I'd established my *raison d'être . . .*" He put his right hand over the page she was reading, his fingers spread wide. She smiled and mugged Not Guilty! "But this morning it came to me that the only really good parts so far are the roaringly dull ones. 'Consequently,' 'To the contrary' . . . So I've been sitting here crossing things out."

"Who needs wealth, right?" With the back of her hand she snowplowed mountains of rubies to oblivion. "As long as you've got your happiness, and paid-up health insurance . . ."

He laughed. His erection was becoming a problem.

She slipped from his one-armed embrace and went over to the window. Her arms were folded, drawn in against her chest. "It's beautiful out," she said.

A soft snow was falling, mounding up over the birdbath, settling on the dark branches of the pines. The morning sunlight was bright again, deceptively warm-looking; the cloud cover had rolled away.

"Want me to make breakfast?" she asked.

"I can do that." He made as if to push back his chair.

"No, really, I'd like to. You work a little longer—that's what you'd be doing if I weren't here, right?"

"I'd probably still be up in bed, hung over and groaning."

She laughed. "Eggs? Scrambled?"

"Sure. Terrific. There's bacon, I think. Peppers and onions in the bottom drawer of the fridge."

"I'm sure I can find things. You drink coffee in the morning?"

"I finished off half a pot already." He pointed at the cup.

"I'll make some more." She reached across him, took the cup, and went out, closing the door behind her. That pleased him, her closing the door. Ellen would never have done that. He'd have had to get up, after she was gone, to close the door himself, and would have felt, as he did so, petty, unsociable, spinsterish.

For a minute or more he sat staring at his page, his eyes going over and over the words, in his mind the image of Jessica at the window, her buttocks and legs strong under the tightly cinched, overlarge bathrobe, her jaw—when she turned her face to him—clean-lined, cheekbones high. With one hand he moved his erection over into the looseness of one pantleg, his fingers lingering a moment as he thought about going out and propositioning Jessica. Then, though the image of her was still in his mind, he began to get the sense of the words on the page and began to be interested. The old dog yawned and settled down to rest. Mickelsson picked up his pencil and slashed out a paragraph, then began writing in his small, meticulous script, more and more rapidly, in the margin. *Over,* he wrote, running out of space, and flipped the paper to continue on the back. He was so deep in thought he did not hear the sizzling of bacon or smell the rich effluence coming from the stove until she tapped on his door again and opened it. "Ready?" Hunger leaped in him, and he pushed back his chair.

They ate in the as yet unremodelled kitchen, large, gray, astir with chilly draughts. The chill seemed to him more pleasant than unpleasant; but then, he was fully dressed, wearing a sweater, whereas Jessica wore nothing but his terrycloth bathrobe. While she ate with her right hand, forking in her food like a teen-ager in a hurry, she held the collar closed around her neck with the left.

"Jessie, let me get you a sweater," he said, and rose from the table.

"I'm all right," she said, looking up as if he'd broken her train of thought. "Don't let your eggs get cold. Anyway, I can't put a sweater over *this*."

"My sweaters are big," he said, moving on toward the entry-hall where, if he wasn't mistaken, he'd left his old black sweater with holes in the elbows. He found it where he'd thought he would, and returned to the kitchen. "Hands up," he said, as he'd said long ago to his children. "Hang on to the cuffs."

She turned to look up at him, unpersuaded and inconvenienced, then obeyed. "Jesus, the *fuss* you make about things," she said, then laughed, her last sounds muffled by the lowering sweater.

He allowed his fingertips to graze her breasts as they passed, and when her face popped out, he kissed her, then stood back to look. "It's definitely you!" he said, wagging both hands, limp-wristed.

"Who else?" she grouched, then looked down at herself. It might indeed have been someone else, a hobo who'd recently lost weight. She did not smile. "So anyway," she said, "eat your eggs." She pointed with her fork.

He hurried to his chair and sat down. He liked her in the ratty, baggy sweater. He smiled, watching as she laboriously rolled up the cuffs. "You'll admit, it's nice to be warm," he said.

She said, wrinkling her nose, "It smells of turpentine." He knew that instant that nothing of Buzzy's had ever smelled of anything if he could help it.

When he'd cleared away the dishes, piling them in the sink, and they were seated, each working on a third cup of coffee—the sun risen higher now, pouring into the kitchen from the entry-hall, making one bright place on the wall and floor, throwing the rest of the room into greater darkness—Jessie asked, breaking what had grown to an extended silence, "What did you make of Mr. Sprague's talk about flying?"

"Do you mean do I think he believed it?"

She shrugged, then waited.

"They have funny ways of joking, around here. It used to throw me, but I guess I'm catching on." He added after a moment, "It's not like anyplace else I know of. I suppose if I were a sociologist—" When she glanced up at him, he moved his head as if nudging away objections. "All I mean is, everyplace has its own oddities, things that make people feel part of the group."

"Nearly all human beings joke," she said. "It's one of the defining characteristics."

"I know." He raised his cup, cautiously sipping. When he'd lowered the cup again, he said, "But it's something you especially notice in Susquehanna. Maybe it's a way of denying that the whole place is moribund. Anyway, it seems unusual how much joking goes on. At the check-out counter down at the market, at the post office, on the street . . . There's a farm, over by Gibson, where they have these strange-looking long-haired cows, they look like musk-oxen or something. One day when I was passing, the farmer was out with them, breaking open bales of hay, and I pulled over and asked him what kind they were. He looked at them, very thoughtful, pulling at his chin, you know; then he looked at me, as if puzzled that I didn't know, and he said—very serious—'Them's mice.' I laughed, but not him. You'd be surprised how long it took him to admit they were Highland Something."

"He must've liked your company," she said.

"He *looked* like a smart, discriminating sort of man."

She sat very still, gazing at her coffee, smiling. Only one tapping finger showed her restlessness. "It's funny, though. He sounded as if he meant it, about flying."

"No doubt he's used it for years," Mickelsson said. "In fact somebody else here mentioned to me once they've got a man in these parts who flies. Maybe Sprague's used that joke so long they've all come to believe it."

"Pray he doesn't try taking off from the roof sometime." The finger tapped on.

He put his hand over her hand to stop the barely audible drumming. "I wonder if I should have offered him the use of my car," he said, and watched her face. "The blue one, I mean. It just sits there in the barn, doing no one any good—"

"Are you crazy? If he went over one of those . . . moraines or whatever they call them, those big bluffs up there—"

"That *would* be flying," Mickelsson said with a grin, then at once put on charity. She was a sucker for Christian charity, he was beginning to see. She'd been hanging around with the bleeding-heart Marxists too long. He wondered what would happen if he pushed it a little. "It did cross my mind that he might hurt himself," he said gravely. "Not that I'd care about the car . . ."

"I understand." An instant after she spoke, she looked at him, suspicious. He smiled benevolently and signed the air with three limp fingers, like the Pope. "Jesus," she whispered crossly, not even pretending to smile, and looked away. "You really are crazy," she said.

He'd finished his coffee. She still had half a cup, too cold to drink. "Shall I put on another pot?" he asked, his voice bright, trying to pull her out of her mood.

She shook her head. "I hate coffee."

He sighed.

Uncomfortable as he was feeling—all this formal informality, these complex games they both somehow kept losing—he minded nonetheless that it would soon be time for her to leave; minded it more with each small failure. He hunted for something to say that might keep her longer, but it was hard to concentrate. He found himself haunted by images of Donnie Matthews. It was of course true that he could drop his little nightlight just like that, put all that behind him, a sordid but ultimately trifling affair of the sort human beings, shitty beasts that they were, were prone to get mired in. But even as he thus consoled himself, he knew it was not as true as he might wish. He couldn't imagine himself telling Jessie about Donnie, nor could he imagine continuing this . . . whatever . . . with Jessie without confessing. Neither could he imagine—despite the brackish taste that came with the thought of Donnie, all those Di-Gels rising in armed revolt—that he could simply stop visiting Donnie's apartment, put behind him forever the thought of holding her slippery, pale waist in his two hands, screwing her upright like some animal he'd grabbed from the pen, his trousers around his feet, his sick heart slamming.

Remorse rose into his gorge. Jessica too he'd grabbed from the pen, if he admitted the truth. Or they'd grabbed each other. If she was sorry for him, and attracted, she was also repelled, at very least distrustful. He again slid his hand over the tabletop toward her, inviting her to take it. After a moment, she did. Her hand was surprisingly warm and soft. The old dog stirred.

"Do you teach today?" he asked.

Rising out of some dark thought of her own, she asked, "What's today? Tuesday?"

"If I haven't lost track."

Looking sadly at their clasped hands, she said, "I don't go in on Tuesdays. But I have some editing I should do, work for the magazine. And there's a meeting I promised to drop in on tonight. . . ."

"It's nice to have you here," Mickelsson said.

She thought about it, carefully not looking at him, then nodded. The next moment, changing her mind, she raised her shining, sea-gray eyes—was it tears that made them shine?—then abruptly looked down again. "I guess I should get dressed."

"You could," he said. "Or we could go back upstairs and, you know . . ." He pressed her hand.

She stood up with him, then moved into his arms. "OK," she said, a smile bursting over her face. "I give in."

They lay spent and at peace again in one another's arms, talking, much as he would talk with Donnie, early in the morning—except, of course, that it was not the same at all, so different that from time to time his jaw muscles would tense, and part of his mind would formally resolve to tell Jessica everything, get it out in the open, let her think whatever she might think. Once she caught him at it.

"What?" she asked. Her dark head was on the pillow, facing his.

"Mmm?" he said, fake innocent.

"What was going through your mind just then?"

"Childhood sorrows. Misery of old age."

"Bullshit."

He closed his eyes to avoid those two dark lie-detectors. "Nothing, really."

She traced the side of his face with two fingers. He remembered that he needed a shave. She said, "What was that funny look? Tell the truth."

"Secret," he said at last. "I'll tell you sometime. I promise."

"OK." She seemed to let it go at that, but then, tracing the lines of his face again, she asked, "Somebody else?"

"Nothing like that." He grinned, then leaned toward her to kiss her nose.

"You shouldn't let it bother you, Pete," she said, and turned her face away from him to look up at the ceiling. "I'm not demanding." Her expression was sombre. "Even if I were your wife, I wouldn't be demanding." She smiled and briefly glanced at him, sad. "It's wrong for people to hurt each other—cause jealousy, things like that. But also, someday we'll be eighty—you know?—and we'll have nothing but the past." She pouted a moment, narrowing her eyes. "I have to be kind to that eighty-year-old woman."

Mickelsson pondered it, or tried to. "Does that mean 'Never let a sexual opportunity slip'?" he asked. "I'm not sure what you're telling me."

"People must do what they must," she said, "and if what one must do would hurt someone, one must be sly."

"It's a good enough theory," he said. "Works well for parents, anyway. Personally—"

She put her finger over his lips. "It's not good to talk about it." She studied his face as if figuring out the phrasing for her question. "Tell me more about Ellen," she said.

He said nothing for a while, brooding on Jessie's theory; then he sighed and closed his eyes. "I don't know what to tell you. She was good-hearted, always giving people presents." He frowned, staring up at the ceiling now, listening to the silence of the house, the snowy world beyond. "She would've made a good minister's wife in some small town in Indiana. Making up baskets of goodies for the poor, teaching knots to the Girl Scouts. I'll tell you a story.

"Once a friend of ours—man in the Philosophy Department with me

—got hit by a bus when he was out one night, drunk. It just sort of nudged him, but it broke some bones and so on. He was famous for his drunks, and at the time of the accident everybody got suddenly righteous about it. Perhaps it was a Warning, a Blessing in Disguise, et cetera. No doubt they were right, but it was offensive. There he was lying in the hospital, one leg in traction, bunch of his ribs broken so he didn't dare laugh—a crazy, bright-eyed Irishman who no more intended to mend his ways than . . . He kept propositioning the nurses, wanted them to put up the screens and climb up on top of him. Some of them were tempted! You'd have to know him, of course: boyish, quick-witted . . . So there he was, horny and so dried out he was seeing the Devil. . . . One night at visiting time Ellen went to see him, with her front all swollen as if she were pregnant, and when she got into his room she stepped into the john and emerged with a big red lighted candle and a tray with a glass and a bottle of Jameson's on it, and potato chips and dip—" Mickelsson's eyes filled with tears. They had more to do with the saying of it than with the remembering.

"You miss her a lot," Jessie said, her sincere look of sympathy as artful as his story.

"She was a nice girl," he said, a whimper escaping with the words. "She married badly."

"I imagine it was somewhat more complicated," she said. Her glance told him that she could have said worse.

He turned his head away, sick unto death of bullshit, especially his own. "Well, anyway—"

For several minutes, neither of them spoke. Furtively, Mickelsson blotted his tears with two fingertips.

"Marriages are hard things," Jessie said at last (somewhat ponderously, he thought) and breathed a sigh. "My husband, Buzzy, was a great believer in presents. When he went someplace without me, which happened at least every month or so, he'd always bring back something crazy—native beads, bone headdress, expensive gowns. He often bought clothes for me—in fact he'd hardly let me buy them for myself. Which was nice, in a way; flattering. But also it made me feel like one of those motorcycles they put more and more lights on. He loved me, I'm sure, but he could never find the balance. At parties he'd always be there near me, hovering around, earnestly listening to everything I said, as if he'd never heard it before. I suppose in a way I was grateful. But sometimes when he'd smile that fond, practiced smile at me, as if to say to all the people, 'Oh, isn't she lovely! Isn't she brilliant,' I'd be tempted to push those crooked teeth in." She grinned, then quickly made her face apologetic. She met Mickelsson's eyes.

"He was a good man," she said solemnly. She put her hand on Mickelsson's chest, fingering the graying, curly hair. "He always wanted to be lord of his own house, though. A little like you, with Ellen. There was really nothing you could do about it. I'd fight him, argue with him, but it was impossible to get him to understand. He had a good trick. If I'd say one cross word—not to mention throw a dish at him—Buzzy would sulk for a week." She smiled, meaning to lighten it, but her eyes showed the old irritation. "He used to do these *things* to me. He'd say, 'Jessie, dear, call Dr. Brown for me, will you? Tell him I can't make my appointment this afternoon at two.' As if I were his secretary! Or, 'Jessie, would you mind fixing dinner for three? I'm bringing old Dornsucker home.' I'd be up to my ears in work, you know—writing some article, or whatever. . . . I don't know how he ever got it in his head that in marrying a Ph.D. in sociology he'd bought himself a lifetime cook. I never gave in—at least not completely—but it was strictly one of those no-win situations. He was so sure he was right! Sometimes I'd show him articles in magazines—the fiercest feminist tracts I could find, things any normal wife would laugh at. He'd settle down in his black leather chair and put his horn-rimmed glasses on—he was never what you'd call a scholarly man, though he'd picked up somewhere an incredible amount of information about trees. . . . So anyway . . . he'd read the article very slowly and carefully, and when he'd finished he'd lay down the magazine and look at me, and after a while he'd say, 'Ver-ry queer.' 'But what do you *think*?' I'd say: 'I mean, don't you think there might be something *to* it? The old where-there's-smoke-there's-fire principle?' Buzzy would shake his head, maybe pull at his collar, and after a minute he'd settle himself and nod and smile and say, 'Ver-ry queer.' " She sighed and slid her hand to Mickelsson's belly. "What the hell. We made a life of it. I loved him terribly, especially when other women fell in love with him— which they did like flies around a honey-pot. Opening up the fronts of their blouses and leaning close, to talk. He never seemed to notice. What a dummy he was! That was part of why I loved him."

She turned her face away.

"How did he die?" Mickelsson asked.

"Smoked too much, like you," she said. "Lung cancer." She sniffed. He hadn't realized she was on the verge of crying.

"I'm sorry," he said.

"Death is death," she said, suddenly bitter. "It doesn't matter all that much what the cause is. I'll tell you this, though. If I were ever to marry again—"

(Alas, poor Mickelsson, pricking up his ears!)

". . . it would be to someone wise and gentle and ugly, someone not famous or likely to become so; someone like—" She broke off abruptly, no doubt suddenly conscious of how far that description came from fitting Mickelsson.

"I'm ugly," he said. "I can work on the rest."

She laughed as if flooded with relief at his not having been hurt by her carelessness. Her hand moved gently on his resolutely sleeping cock. She said, "You're crazy. You're the handsomest man I know."

He played the words over and over in his mind, baffled. What would make her say such a thing? He felt a little chill of panic.

Silence fell between them. It was Jessie who finally broke it.

"Everyone was wonderful when he died—the Bryants, Blicksteins, people I'd never really known, friends of Buzzy's. Your colleague Edward Lawler. You know him, don't you?" She raised her left hand to wipe her eyes.

"One of the best," Mickelsson said. "I didn't know Lawler and your husband were friends."

"Buzzy had a thing for intellectuals. And of course there was no one else here who could speak those African languages he knew. They'd have lunch together and talk Swahili or something. I guess Professor Lawler enjoyed it too. He strikes me as a lonely man."

"I suppose that's so," Mickelsson mused. It surprised him that the thought had never occurred to him, though as she said it now he knew it was true. Never in all the time he'd been here had he seen Edward Lawler at a party; he'd never even heard him mentioned except in connection with his learning. Was he married? A widower? Mickelsson imagined the handsome young man he'd seen in the photograph at Jessica's, smiling with his lips closed to hide the crooked teeth—the charming, universally admired Buzzy Stark—seated in the faculty cafeteria with immense, short, black-suited Lawler, a man so shy, or so filled with distrust, one could hardly tell which, that he never ventured out without a book between himself and the world, some heavy old tome from which he never for an instant glanced up, even when, in one language or another, he said hello. There was something childlike, even weird, about Lawler's parading of languages, a sort of boyish showing off. But that was part of the beauty of the man, that unworldliness, innocence like an angel's. Had he looked up from his book while he and Buzzy talked their Swahili or Waringa? Probably not. Stark would be leaning forward, animated; Lawler would be sitting erect, slightly sideways to the table, mechanically sliding his fork into his potatoes, raising it to his mouth, lowering it again, his eyes on the book in his left hand, occasionally moving the food into the side of his mouth to bring out a few timid words, not as if conversing with Stark but as if reading aloud. It was his loneliness, perhaps, that made him seem so distant, so medieval, in fact so generally grieved and dismayed by everything around him, insofar as he saw it at all.

"So Lawler came to see you," Mickelsson said.

"More than that," she said. "He took care of everything—the burial plot, casket, funeral, the works." She thought a moment, or remembered. "I didn't want anything to do with it, it's always seemed to me so pagan, and anyway I was a wreck." She rolled her head on the pillow. "Boy! But somebody has to do those things, and Edward understood how I felt without my mentioning it. He was really good at it. The funeral was beautiful, simple and . . . elegant. Buzzy would have liked it. He always liked elegance—fancy cars and clothes. . . . I guess Edward knew that. Maybe it was one of the things they had in common."

"Strange, isn't it," Mickelsson said, "the friendships that spring up. Lawler, this positively frightening intellect, and your husband—not that I mean to say—"

"I know," she said. "I've thought about that too. It makes me feel rotten that I was never able to satisfy him that way. But I suspect he didn't really *like* too much brain in a woman. At any rate, I know he was always surprised when he ran into it. Maybe I wasn't as smart as I thought. I may have bored him, tagging along like a kid sister, my eyes glazing over when he talked about trees—the way his glazed over when I talked about shopping in Entebbe or witchcraft in modern Nigeria. . . ."

Something came awake in him. "You knew the languages too, then?"

"Of course," she said. She smiled and gave a suggestion of a lying-down shrug. "I'm a Jew!" That last was too hard for him. On second thought, it was all too hard for him.

"Are you *crazy?*" he said. She didn't seem to notice that he was mimicking her. He rose up on his elbow, feeling sorrow partly at what Buzzy Stark had failed to see, partly at his own ignorance of African languages. He bent over her slowly and kissed her.

Mickelsson made lunch, feeling superior to Jessie's late husband. He made what he made for himself almost every day, as for years he'd made it for his children: baked, open-faced sandwiches of cheese, peppers, mushrooms, tomatoes, and onions, a little oregano; hearts-of-lettuce salad with the spiced buttermilk dressing Ellen had discovered long ago in San Francisco; and coffee. When he served it to her—at the low, glass-topped table in the livingroom—the diningroom was still unfinished—she looked up from the *New Yorker* she'd been glancing through, took off her glasses, and raised her eyebrows in surprise. "Hey," she said, "it looks *good!*"

When they'd begun on the sandwiches, he asked, "How are you doing with your Marxists?" He thought of Levinson, grieving, driving to Boston every two or three weeks to see his son. Guilt passed over him like a cloud.

"We get by," Jessie said, and shrugged. She stopped to pat the side of her mouth with her paper napkin. "I'm a thorn in their side, but so far so good." She took another bite, bending down close to the plate inelegantly. She was not careful to eat with her mouth closed.

"They've got no reason to cause trouble," he said.

"That's easy to say if you're not one of them." She smiled, still chewing. "I'm not good around fanatics. I don't keep my mouth shut. I bait them. I tell students quite frankly what I think. Bad department citizen, as my chairman says." She stopped chewing, squinting at some annoyance. "He's right, but they make me furious." She bit into her sandwich again and waved her left hand, keeping the floor. "How can they say things they know to be grossly oversimplified, and say them with such conviction —even feel such apparently authentic indignation when you dare tell them they're crazy, as if *you* were the one telling lies?" She gave her head a little shake to drive the hair back. "There's one of them, David Reese— very young, very nice boy really"—she stopped, eyes widening, and picked a crumb from her blouse—"except that he's bonkers. He works like a dog, really dedicated teacher, students in there in his office all the time. . . . He makes 'em work like devils, not always the way you might wish he'd make them work—half of them can't write an English sentence—but they all get A's. . . ." She took another bite, chewed, then drank her wine as if it were grapejuice—all with hardly a pause. "I've tried to talk to him, because he seems nice—mild, kind eyes, good smile, real gentleness. . . . Believe me, it's like talking to a Martian." She shook her head, then rubbed her fingers on her napkin.

"I know," Mickelsson said.

She looked up.

"I don't know about Reese, but I know about fanatics. They really are Martians. There's a philosopher named R. M. Hare, very popular these days. He's got some interesting things to say about fanatics. Points out that, essentially, their code isn't moral, in the usual sense; it's aesthetic." He looked down, aware that he was telling her more than she was interested in hearing. He picked the last piece of onion from his plate with his fingers and ate it. It occurred to him to wonder if Jessica minded the smell of onions on one's breath.

"Go on," she said.

"Listen, let's go for a walk," he said. "It's beautiful out—getting warmer. I could show you the waterfall."

"Why not?" She rose at the same moment he did, and they carried their plates to the kitchen.

It was true that the day had warmed considerably; by evening much of the snow would have melted. He took her gloved hand in his, leading her past the large, still barn, past where his night visitors had thrown his bottles and cigarettes, down the drifted meadow and along the winding path through pines and low brush to what had once, according to his neighbor John Pearson, been the pond of the Susquehanna ice-house. The sound of falling water was much louder now, almost a roar—not a true, natural waterfall, but water pouring over the break in the high spillway, plunging into a dark basin edged with ice, from there rattling away down the steep, shale-and-icicle-lined glen.

"It's pretty," she said. "Isn't this close enough?"

Ahead of them lay a makeshift bridge of boards mounded in snow, patches of gray wood showing through. In the snow on the bridge and around it there were deer-tracks and the triangle tracks of rabbits.

"It's nicer from the middle," he said. He let go of her hand and took her elbow. She tried to pull away. He held on. "Don't be afraid," he said. "See? Deer have walked across it." He pointed to the tracks.

"Nothing doing," she said. "I'm not a deer. Do I *look* like a deer?"

"A little." He grinned.

She stared at him, then tried harder to pull away. "What are you, nuts?"

"Take my word for it," he said, "it's perfectly safe. I've walked across it a hundred times." He gave a little tug at her arm, moving her two steps toward the bridge. "Come on," he said with a laugh, "you're acting like a city slicker."

"I *am* a city slicker, God damn it." With a sudden sharp jerk she pulled free of him. She moved three long steps back from the water, then stopped.

He stood still, looking at the snow between them like a hunter. "It's a wonderful feeling, looking down from the bridge," he said. He held out his arms. "I hate for you to miss it. Come on. Don't be a coward!"

"*You* go look down."

He thought, then shrugged. "It's pretty from here too," he said. He put his hands behind his back and, after a moment, moved toward her. Though he was sure she would run at any moment, she held her ground. "I'm sorry," he said. "Maybe we can come in the summertime, when it's more peaceful and you can see the boards." He smiled, then cautiously put his arm around her.

"Maybe," she said. She stood rigid.

"Of course in the summer there are rattlesnakes." He turned back to the water.

They stared together into the churning, dark basin, watching gray water from above plunge in. Beyond the basin bare willowtrees shone, dripping wet. There seemed a faint red aura around them.

"It's spooky here," she said.

He nodded. At last, some of the rigidity leaving her, they turned, together, moving farther away from the water, up the snowy bank. He said, "What I meant to tell you before, about this argument by R. M. Hare . . ." She kept walking. He took her gloved hand once more in his. "The thing about aesthetic arguments is that there's no resolving them. One can debate whether a trumpet's been played badly or well, but if one person loves the trumpet and another person claims it sets his teeth on edge, there's no use trying to reason it out. *De gustibus.*" He glanced at her to see if she was bored. He couldn't tell. "What R. M. Hare points out is that in some ways the affirmations of, for instance, a Nazi are like aesthetic preferences. A Nazi's a man who has a certain ideal for human nature—or anyway so he claims—just as one might have an ideal for the sports car: precise steering, vivid acceleration, reliable brakes—"

He broke off. She said nothing, walking with deliberate steps up the snowy hill toward the outbuildings and house. "Nazis have an ideal," he said, speaking more hurriedly. He could not have explained why it seemed to him important that he convince her. "Insofar as the Nazi's not lying to himself—and they almost always are—the Nazi would say that even he himself, if it were proven that he has 'the inferior qualities of the Jews,' as he thinks—he himself in that case should be exterminated. The Nazi, insofar as he's not lying to himself, is a man who will let no ideal—least of all liberal concern for others—stand in the way of his vision of good." Because she'd paused, he glanced at her and saw that she was looking up at where the road wandered into trees. He said, "Your Marxists are more like Nazis than they like to think. That's all I'm saying."

"Mmm," she said. She asked, "Pete, are there wild animals around here?"

"Nothing that would eat you. There are supposed to be bears, but all people ever see is the tracks." He dropped her hand and got out his cigarettes. He held the pack toward her. She shook her head, then looked up at the trees again. He lit one for himself and hauled in smoke.

They began to walk again, three feet apart, not holding hands, rising through stubble and snow toward the barns and road.

"Your Marxists believe in manipulating people—for people's own good, of course. It's that that makes them like Nazis." He waved the cigarette, then on reflection took one last drag and threw it away.

She shook her head. "That's stupid," she said. "They care very much about people and . . . social justice."

He bent down to scoop up the makings for a snowball. "Maybe. But they're just as much social idealists as the Nazis were." He packed the snowball tigher and tighter, not looking at it, gazing up at the house. "To use Kantian jargon," he said, "the liberal's ideal is a kingdom of ends in which all citizens are legislating members. The liberal won't violate his fellow citizens' freedom because freedom is the social value he believes in. Your Marxists don't believe in that ideal for one minute."

"I don't know what you're talking about," she said. She stared at the snow and stalks of weed ahead of her. It was clear enough that he was making her angry; it wasn't clear what he'd done wrong. "They *care* about people," she said again.

"Sure. Like the Grand Inquisitor."

"Peter, let's drop it, OK? Let's talk about something else."

"Why?" He reached for her hand. She pointedly ignored him.

"Because I hate being bullied," she said.

"But I'm on your *side*, Jessica!—against the Marxists." He slammed the snowball from glove to glove.

"It's not a war," she said. "They're my colleagues. I wish I'd never mentioned them."

"All I'm saying is, they manipulate people—exactly like the capitalist managers they—"

She broke in, turning, squaring off at him. "Peter, for heaven's sakes *drop* it!"

When he looked down at the snowball he'd been packing all this time he saw that it was as solid as a rock.

"Jesus, you really are far-right," she said. "I'd been told that about you, but I must say, I'm shocked!"

"I *hate* the far right," he said, thrusting his head forward in surprise. He forced a laugh, squeezing the snowball with his right glove. "I also hate the middle." He looked up at the sky, raised his two arms, and shouted at a circling hawk with all his might, " '*I hate your feasts and celebrations! Show me righteousness flowing like a river!*' "

She backed away from him, eyes wide with alarm. Furtively, she glanced at the snowball, packed into a deadly weapon.

He could think of no defense but a crazy laugh. "Prophet Amos," he said, and let the snowball fall from his hand. Then, after a moment—she continued to stare at him—he said, voice quavering, "It's funny. I was told that *you* were far-right—'to the right of Adolf Hitler,' I think was the phrase."

She went on looking at him. Abruptly she looked down. "Let's go back to the house," she said.

He grinned stupidly and extended one hand toward her. "I'm not bad at all, if you'll study the matter fairly. I never say 'if and only if.' "

They endured another silence.

"It's true," she said at last. "You mean to be helping. You don't mean to be making things harder."

He waited on. The air smelled of spring, though it was nearly November. At last—for some reason it made him feel a wave of sorrow—she took his hand.

When five o'clock came, she decided—or perhaps, in some subtle way, they decided together—that she wouldn't have him drive her in tonight after all. The meeting wasn't really all that important. He would drive down to Susquehanna to pick up something for supper. She would stay, make a few phonecalls while he was gone.

He parked the Jeep beside a meter across from the Acme and got out, then stood a moment at the side of the street, lost in thought, something deep in his mind calling to him for attention. He came to himself with a jolt and stepped back toward his Jeep. Though there was still snow in the gutters and up along the buildings, the street to his right, in the direction of Lanesboro, was filled—or so it seemed to him at first—with motorcycles, their headlights bludgeoning the night, their opened-up tailpipes roaring. On closer inspection, it appeared that there were only six, in fact, and they were by no means the threatening monsters he'd first thought them. The lead cyclist waved as he passed, or raised his black-gauntleted fist in a way that seemed perhaps friendly; and though Mickelsson couldn't see the face inside the helmet, it came to him that the rider was his friend Tim. Tim, he remembered, had said that his bike was blond, and so this one was. Too late for Tim to see, unless in his mirror, Mickelsson, smiling, raised his fist. Only now, as the rest of the cyclists rumbled past, did he realize that the car parked behind his Jeep was the town's one police car, and that one of the town's two policemen was sitting in it, the cowboy-style hat almost to his nose. Mickelsson had heard the man's name from time to time, something odd, hard to remember—Tacky Tinklepaugh, it came to him. Stupidest name imaginable, for a policeman. No wonder the boys came down off the mountains and did pretty much what they pleased. Mickelsson, realizing he'd been staring—and that Tacky was staring back—bent slightly toward the windshield and gave a salute. The policeman, fiftyish, baggy-eyed and red-faced, maybe drunk, gave him a thumbs-up sign.

Mickelsson crossed the street.

He chose porkchops, canned applesauce, brussels sprouts and green peas, and a Sara Lee cheesecake, then pushed his cart up to the check-out counter. As the woman was ringing up his groceries, a soft voice said behind him, "Hi, Pete. You havin a party?" He hesitated an instant before turning.

"Donnie!" he said. "I never see you here!"

"Gotta eat," she said, and shrugged. She smiled, looking in the direction of the check-out girl, as if uncomfortable talking with Mickelsson in front of strangers, or maybe friends, he would hardly know. In the store's fluorescent lights, Donnie's hair, skin, and clothes looked washed-out, and a pimple on her forehead called attention to itself. He looked at her hands, small and pretty but very white, hanging limply on the push-rail of her grocery cart. She leaned toward him a little—was it possible, he wondered, that she *meant* to be overheard, though she pretended otherwise? "When you comin up and see me?"

He couldn't help glancing at the check-out girl. Sure enough, she was spying, expressionless.

"How much is it?" he asked, though the total showed on the register.

"Eight twenty-seven." She smiled politely.

He thought, blushing, that that was surely too much, but he quickly got out his billfold and reached in for the ten, all he had, and gave it to her.

"You should come by," Donnie said softly.

He could feel the blush deepening. He took his change from the check-out girl, lifted the grocery bag in his arm, and then—horribly, he knew, as if something had happened to his face—turned to Donnie and winked. She simply looked at him. He moved quickly to the door and pushed through it, not looking back.

Up at the house, as he was getting the groceries out of the sack, still blushing, unable to stop, Jessie said, "Pete, do you mind if I ask you something?"

Once again his heart lurched. Perhaps everything that had happened down at the Acme was right there in his face. "What?" he asked, and bent over the heavy paper bag to look in, as if some small treasure might have hidden itself at the bottom.

"What's all that mail in your study? Some of it's months old, and not even opened."

He picked up the porkchops to carry them over to the counter beside the range. "It's just junk," he said.

"It sure doesn't look like junk," she said. She leaned far to one side, trying to get him to look at her directly. "There's a stack of things from the I.R.S., and a ton of letters from collection agencies—"

He leaned on the counter and looked at the floor between them.

She said, holding out one hand, shaking it in his face, "Do you realize the I.R.S. can put people in prison? They love it when it's somebody famous like you. Puts the fear of God into the common folk."

"Alfred North Whitehead, one of the greatest philosophers of our time, refused for years to answer his mail from the I.R.S."

"Good for him," she said. "You can bet he got his name in the paper! Listen to me, Pete. You may think I'm just another Jewish neurotic, but believe me, you've gotta get your shit together."

He shrugged wearily.

"You're in real trouble, aren't you." She pouted, thoughtful, looking at him. "The divorce, I suppose . . . back taxes, obviously . . ." When he said nothing, looking down at the glossy, pink porkchops, she said, "That's why you wanted to write a best-seller philosophy book." She laughed, then stopped herself and came nearer, hesitated a moment as if wary of him, then came up and put one hand on his arm. "Look, why don't we just tear into it? I'll help you. *Let* me help—not just with answering the mail, necessarily. I have quite a lot of money. I don't mean I'm rich. . . ."

He drew back. "You know I can't take your money."

"Why not? Too proud?"

"Of course. But it's more than that. I'd be a bad investment."

She made a face, irritably dismissive, then watched him again. "I didn't exactly make the offer in my role as brilliant businesswoman."

"Forget it," he said. "You can help me with the mail if you want to, yes. Help me write whining, stalling letters. But not till after supper."

"It's amazing that you can eat."

"Are you telling me you're too upset to?" he asked.

"It's not *my* life."

His smile was no doubt sour, a little miffed. She put her arms around him.

"We'll fix you up," she said. "Trust me."

The words seemed to move through his head and chest, pursued by the shadow of Donnie Matthews.

He asked, "How do you like your porkchops?"

After supper they worked for hours, or rather Jessica worked, like the secretary she'd said she disliked being cast as, during her years with her husband. Mickelsson sorted through envelopes, staring blindly, managing to get rid of one from Donnie—he'd failed to notice it before and had no idea what it contained, certainly not a request for payment, since ever after that first mistake he'd paid cash. Jessie, sternly bent over the desk, wearing glasses now, made lists, depressing columns of figures, then drew the electric typewriter toward her and asked for typing paper. He opened a new pack, pilfered from the department, and set it on the desktop beside her.

"Dear Freddy's Refuse," she read aloud as she typed, "I'm terribly sorry my check to you, dated September third, failed to clear. There seems to have been some mix-up at the bank, which has not yet been straightened out. I thank you for your patience and can assure you that if you will be patient a little longer . . ."

"You know, it really is hopeless," she said at one point, taking off her glasses. "All those debts from your *old* life. Can't you just . . ." As she turned toward the chair by the window where he sat, he fixed his gaze on the sill, his ashtray filled with cigarette butts and dottle from his pipe. When he said nothing, she said, "Cancel that. Nothing's hopeless, not even you. We'll work it out."

"You can see why I let it lie there," he said.

"It didn't lie there, it accrued," she said.

He heard her crank another sheet of paper into the typewriter, then start typing. She made the thing sound like a machine-gun. Without a pause in her typing, she asked, "Is the stuff at the office as bad as this?"

"Better and worse," he said. "Hardly any of it is bills, but most of it takes longer, more complicated answers. Requests for letters of recommendation from former students—some of 'em I'm not even sure ever were my students, but who knows? Requests to give lectures, usually for no money, usually to a hostile audience. Appeals from the Teachers' Union, letters warning me that my subscriptions to tiresome magazines are running out—"

"If there's no money in it," Jessie said, cranking out the sheet, cranking in another, "throw away the letter and forget it."

"It's that bad." He sighed.

She was silent a moment, not typing. Then she asked, taking off her glasses again, "Pete, are you aware that the I.R.S. has taken a lien on your house?"

He said nothing, staring out the window into blackness.

"Mickelsson, you need a lawyer."

He smiled, thinking of Finney. "I know."

The rat-a-tat-tat of the typewriter began again.

They sat on the couch, the room dark around them except for the flickering light from the woodstove, the stove doors open, the screen in place. He said, thinking now of Phil Bryant, who was forever quoting Shakespeare,

> *"That time of year thou dost in me behold*
> *When yellow leaves, or none, or few, do hang . . ."*

She smiled. "What a whiner you are!"

He intoned nasally,

> *"Miniver Cheevy, child of scorn,*
> *Mournfully assailed the seasons,*
> *Cursed the day that he was born . . ."*

She raised a finger to his mouth. "It'll all come out in the wash, you'll see." When he kissed the hand, she drew it away, then lowered it to his stomach. "I didn't know you were a memorizer of poetry."

"Only things I read as an undergraduate," he said, "and only gloomy things, of course. I guess I knew all along I'd eventually spin out. No doubt that's the reason for my interest in Dada, some years ago—though I misinterpreted my motives. I thought it was civilization that was falling apart. '*Wheeling and wheeling in the widening gyre—*' "

"I hate poetry," Jessie said. "Did I ever mention that?"

He looked at her, forgetting himself and smiling. "*Nobody* hates poetry! That's like hating air, or chamberpots."

"*I* do," she said. "The only poem I ever memorized in my life is '*Thirty days hath September, April, June, and November*'—that's as much as I ever did learn of the thing. Even that I hated, especially the word *hath*."

He leaned away from her for a better look at her face. Though as a matter of fact he liked poetry, not that he'd ever been terrific at understanding it, at least by Anguish Department standards, her revelation delighted and baffled him. It was as if a door had suddenly appeared in a familiar room, opening onto rooms he would never have guessed the existence of. "You're kidding," he said. "All those paintings in your house, the fancy record player, all the culture and class—" He twisted the words toward irony. "Admit it, you really like *some* poetry."

"Absolutely not." She spoke with surprising vehemence.

"You're kidding," he said again; but he felt his smile fading and couldn't bring it back.

She withdrew her hand from his stomach. "I shouldn't brag about it," she said. "I guess I was badly educated, or there's something wrong with me." She made her eyes large and batted the lashes. "I'm a whiz at math, and I *adore* the novels of Jane Austen."

He laughed and kissed her cheek, but he was astonished.

"You're disappointed," she said. She interlaced her fingers and turned her hands palms down, looking at them sadly.

"No, I'm interested," he protested. "I've known people who *say* they hate poetry, but then they lean close to the jukebox and listen to words like '*My gal took my heart and she stomped that sucker flat*'—and then we're on to 'em. But to *really* hate poetry, knowing what you're talking about . . . No doubt you had some traumatizing childhood experience— some maniac in the woods who hung down from a tree and told you 'Little Miss Muffet.' "

"Funny, aren't you. You should be in pitchers."

"Sorry."

"It's probably true that it was poisoned for me," she said. "All those earnest, terribly cultural rabbis' daughters with the boyish haircuts and the pretty black eyes, beating time up in front of the room with a pointer and sing-songing Blake's 'The Tyger.' And then the recitation on stage, on Parents' Day—little girls folding their dimpled little hands. I never would do it. Shit. They could've killed me, I absolutely wouldn't. OK, buster, why are you smiling?"

"Smiling at the Jessie you used to be," he said. "I like her."

"You wouldn't have. She was a blood-drinker."

"I wish I'd known her. I feel cheated."

She relented a little and put her hand over his. After a while she said, "What were you like?"

"A monster."

"You were big for your age?"

"Mammoth—but not fat. I was scared to death of girls—as I would've been of you. That's why I played football. I thought it all out, very philosophical even then. If I played football, even if I wasn't very good, they would come to me." He paused, then corrected himself, "That wasn't all of it. I had a best friend, Punk Atcheson, who played on the team. And I had a certain amount of hostility in me. I liked slamming into people."

"Why, Peter?"

He moved his left hand back and forth over hers, closed on his right. If he waited a long while before he answered, it wasn't that he minded telling her; it was simply that he hadn't looked back at those feelings for years, and it was surprising to discover that, now that she'd reminded him, they were all still there, ready to spring back into his heart, both the joy in violence and the guilt. The glow on the walls was steadier now, the flames in the stove giving way to red embers. "Our family was considered somewhat queer," he said, then lowered his eyebrows. Again he corrected himself: "Maybe the truth is I *thought* my family was considered queer, because that's the way *I* considered it." He thought of telling her how ever since that business with Miss Minton there had been people, both children and adults, who were afraid of him. Instead he told her, "My father was a dairy farmer—wonderful man, no problem there—though as a matter of fact the psychiatrist I used to go to back in Providence wouldn't buy even that: thought the old man only showed me his best side, with the result that I was stuck with an impossibly noble model. But he was wrong, the psychiatrist. It happens that my father really was noble. He was the most universally beloved man I've ever known." He paused.

"Go on."

He took a deep breath. "Well, he was a very good man, and I'm grateful to him for it. I've had friends, Jesuits, and one black Protestant friend, really a friend of Ellen's—Geoffrey Stewart, the one I told you about. . . . It's good, having a model of perfection. If you don't measure up, then you don't; but at least it's there, it exists. All the words in the world—all the rules and prescriptions—they're not worth sour apples compared to . . . When my father was dying, the whole countryside was there in his hospital room. He was supposed to have only three visitors at a time, but the hospital gave up. His room was so filled with flowers and plants you could hardly move, and every night my mother would take some of the flowers to other people's rooms. The hospital was like a greenhouse, from one end to the other. We caused an ant plague. No joke. I suppose if I minded anything about it it was that I, a mere kid . . . I couldn't compete. He was a singer; voice like an angel. He was shy about his voice, but when he let it out, it was golden. I think I've never heard a better one, though I admit that may be blind love. Anyway, all his singing friends were there, and all his farm friends, and people from the stores in town—there was even this banker he used to go to for loans every spring. I used to be scared of him. . . .

"Anyway," Mickelsson said, "it wasn't my father—or my mother either—that made me feel odd. I had an uncle Edgar who went berserk during the war. He'd been peculiar all his life, in various ways—very secretive, also fussy, punctilious. Wouldn't speak English: beneath his dignity. But when the war came, and people began to talk about the Swedes as collaborators—not too openly, but somehow you knew they were talking . . . Certain movies, maybe. Uncle Edgar joined up, to everyone's surprise, and set off, mad as a hornet, to vindicate the race, or at any rate that was the family interpretation. He was a Seabee, one of the 'old men,' as they were called. They'd go in before everybody and build the landing strips. On some island in the Pacific something went wrong: he started machine-gunning his own people. My theory is it came to him that everyone was evil, the Americans as much as the Japanese— but I don't know, of course. Projection, my psychiatrist claims. Maybe so. They sent him home, and he spent fifteen years in a V.A. mental ward. When they finally released him he was crazier than ever, but he was no longer violent—probably hadn't been in years. After he was back, he almost never said a word to anyone, and if he did speak, it was almost never English. He visited us in California, a time or two. He'd sit up with Ellen half the night—I'd go to bed: every time he came he'd get me drunk—not on purpose; I couldn't keep up. I'd hear them out in the kitchen, Uncle Edgar gibbering away in Swedish, Ellen saying, 'Ya, ya, ya!'—she didn't speak a word of Swedish, but maybe with Uncle Edgar she thought she did. He gestured a lot. I'd stare at the furniture, trying to keep it from swimming around, and I'd hear them going on and on, the crazy old Seabee taking nectar from her hand. . . . Of course that was long afterward. I meant to explain why I felt the way I did in highschool."

"So explain," she said and smiled. She squeezed his hand.

It was almost dark now. He thought of putting on another chunk of wood but did nothing.

"I guess the horror of it was, he got off, more or less. He knew what he'd done, killing those people. It has something to do with Nietzsche's idea of pity—I'm sorry I keep prattling about Nietzsche."

"You don't," she said. "Or if you do, I haven't really noticed."

He said, "Nietzsche thought the pitier becomes infected by his pity— becomes weak, like the person he's sorry for. What he forgot to mention is that the pitied person becomes weaker than before, from his shame at degrading the one who pities him. It's true."

"Which is why you won't take a loan," she said, looking smug.

"Once the offer's made it's already too late."

She shook her head and rolled her eyes toward God. "You see," she said to God, "he's hopeless."

"And then there's my grandfather," he said.

She stifled a yawn, turning her eyes to him.

"For years and years he was a stern, boring Christian minister. I suppose I might not think him so boring if I knew him now. He was a good Luther man; had the whole hundred volumes in German. Anyway, in his seventieth year he got the gift. Did I tell you all this?"

"What gift?"

"According to the story, he was standing beside the marsh on my father's place, watching my father and uncle fish, when suddenly, there in the water, exactly like a reflection, or so he claimed—or is said to have claimed—he saw my great-aunt Alma clutch her throat and suck for air and die. He said to my father, 'Alma's dead. Heart attack, looks like.' My father and Uncle Edgar hardly knew what to say, they argued back and forth, but the old man made his claim with such conviction that eventually they pulled their lines and went home. Aunt Alma was dead, exactly as he'd said she'd be.

"After that he had these visions all the time. He knew trivial things—that a tire would go flat, or a dog would get mange—but also important things: he saw the hurricane Agnes weeks before it came. Various things like that. Believe me, we could've made money off him."

Jessica extracted her hands from his and got up to put a log on. Sparks flew, making her jerk back. When the fire settled, she put the screen in again. She came back and sat once more beside him, not so close now, cautiously erect. "Did you ever *see* any of this?"

"Everybody did. It was common as ducks. It was so common the family didn't even talk about it except if some stranger came, and then they'd get interested again."

Now the wall was bright once more, flames leaping in the stove.

"Strange," she said. They sat for several minutes without speaking, Mickelsson painfully conscious that all the talk was about himself. Then she leaned back onto his arm. "He just saw things, clear as day, and they were always true?"

"It was more complicated than that." He hesitated, then gave in. "Sometimes he saw things clear as day; sometimes he saw things but not the things you wanted him to see. Once a cousin of ours called. Her father was very sick, down in Florida. She wanted my grandfather to tell her what to do, that is, whether or not her father was really dying. My grandfather said, 'I don't know. I can't see it. If I were you I'd just go back to the kitchen and finish supper.' There was no way he could know she'd just left the kitchen, where she was making supper, to use the bedroom phone." Mickelsson smiled to himself, flooded now with memories, more than he could tell her. He said, "Sometimes he'd get things in dreams, all muddled and distorted. And sometimes all he'd get was hunches. He'd ask himself a question—'Is so-and-so going to happen?'—and he'd give himself an answer—'Yes it will'—and if it really was going to happen he'd have a powerful hunch that Yes was right. He almost never made mistakes, like those psychic guessers in the *National Enquirer*. There was one broad area of exception—the usual one, I guess. If he wanted very badly for something to happen, he would sometimes have a false hunch; so he was unreliable on important matters involving himself or his family. And sometimes he couldn't tell ordinary dreams from psychic dreams. It was a tricky gift—just like ordinary sight—in the sense that it could shade off from certain to doubtful. Some things he saw the way you see things on a bright, clear day; other things he saw as if in fog, or at night during a thunderstorm. He moved back and forth through time like a prophet, as if one really could slip out of time into eternity. He did see things, there was no doubt of that. If he saw a thing happening—plainly saw it—then if it was something in the past you could be sure it had happened exactly as he said, and if it was something in the future, then all the armies in the world couldn't prevent it. Pretty often the vision was trivial, as I said. He'd know what his birthday presents were before he opened them. He'd mention things he'd read in the paper before the paper came."

This time when Mickelsson stopped speaking, Jessica said nothing, and she was silent for so long he turned his head to look at her, to see if he'd put her to sleep. She opened her eyes as he did so, looking straight into Mickelsson's, and said, "You want to know something? I think *you're* psychic, Pete. I've had a feeling all along that you might be, but what you tell me about your grandfather makes me sure of it. I think that whoever it was that came to your bedroom was actually somebody."

"I don't know," he said.

"Listen, let's try something." She was suddenly wide awake. "Tell me something you can't possibly know. Tell me something about my mother!"

He laughed. "*I* can't do that. She walks with a limp, she has trouble sleeping, her hair's very white—"

"That's *right*, Peter! That's *good!*"

Again he laughed. "All I did was guess her age."

"Oh, Pete," she said, petulant, still determined. "Well, let's think of something else." She was silent for a moment. Then: "Tell me what will happen to the Spragues."

Reluctantly, he closed his eyes. All he could see was an image of flickering light from the woodstove, which his mind somehow imposed upon the doors and windows of the old, gray Sprague house up the mountain. As the image began to feel nightmarish he opened his eyes and said, "I forgot to tell you one thing about my grandfather's second sight. Anything he saw, if it wasn't absolutely trivial, was horrible. He never saw somebody winning his race, or a woman being handed her healthy new baby. He saw railroad bridges buckling and the train spilling over. He'd get an image of a wrecked car sitting beside a highway, and a young girl's head in the grass. He'd get an image of somebody's child screaming, running out of the house with her nightdress on fire. That's how it is with psychics, or so I've read. It's somehow pain and death that cry out to be noticed; the rest floats by and gets forgotten—maybe sufficient to itself."

"How awful!" Jessica said. Then immediately, so that once again he was almost alarmed by the quickness of her mind, "What made you think of that? Did you see something frightening when I asked you to tell me about the Spragues?"

"Definitely not!" he said. "Look, no more of this game, OK? It's creepy."

Jessica pushed her head against his shoulder. "You're right. I hereby renounce all creepy games." She sidled her eyes toward him. "You want to go to bed?"

"Let's!"

But the game was not quite over. In the upstairs bathroom, brushing his teeth, the cold water plunging noisily into the sink, Mickelsson had a thought that was almost a voice. It was a line from Nietzsche. "*This* life is your eternal life." It was a line he'd never understood, nor did he understand it now. Nietzsche's whole doctrine of eternal recurrence was a bafflement to him and, so far as he could see, to everybody else, even Kaufmann and Danto. But tonight, the line had the odd effect of sending a chill up his spine and drawing him to the window that looked out onto the field at the back of the house, between the house and the rise of the mountain. It was a soft, warm night stirred by gentle breezes and lighted by a full moon. Fifty feet from the house, directly in line with the window where Mickelsson stood looking out—bending closer to the glass now, startled—someone, a farmer, from the looks of it, was digging a hole. Mickelsson's thoughts flew into confusion and it took him a moment to realize that the man had no right to be digging there, on Mickelsson's own property—and another moment to realize that the hole was a grave. In the swaying weeds five feet from the head of the hole lay a small coffin, presumably a child's—too small, anyway, to be even a small woman's, too large to be the coffin of an infant. Without letting himself think further, Mickelsson spat out the toothpaste into the sink, grabbed his shirt and, without a word to Jessica—he'd forgotten she was there, in fact—ran through the bedroom, out into the hall and down the stairs, his feet hitting like thunder. He was halfway out the back door of the kitchen when he realized that the world had magically snapped into winter. There was no full moon, no gentle summer breeze. Overhead he could see only blurry stars, and in the field where the gravedigger ought to be there was nothing at all—short gray weeds, scraps of snow. Now at last he came awake to Jessica's cries of alarm from the house: "Pete! What's the matter?"

She was in the middle of the kitchen, the quilt from the bed clutched awkwardly around her. When he'd closed and locked the door, then turned back to her, she said, "What happened? You look awful!"

He put his hands on her arms. The kitchen they were standing in was not the kitchen he'd run through on his way outside.

"It's nothing," he said. "I thought I heard a bear, or a skunk or something. Let's go up."

When he at last lay down beside her, his skin against hers, the warmth and sweetness of it, and his residual fear, made him dizzy.

8

He'd been going through his fifteen-year-old Martin Luther notes and reading through his grandfather's yellow tablets on the subject, an activity which took him days and profoundly depressed him. How soon the best opinions of a normally intelligent, well-read man turned commonplace! Archaic, studiously eloquent—hiked up with *'tis*'s and *lo*'s and *yea*'s—the old man's broodings recalled the most vacuous poetry of his age: earnest, noble-hearted flounderings in the common bog. This morning he'd gone back to work on his own book, no longer a blockbuster—duller, he suspected, than the telephone book of an unfamiliar city, certainly duller than anything anywhere by Dr. Martinus. It was cruel that a rotten human being like Martin Luther should rivet one's attention, even now, after all these centuries, and the thoughts of a good man like Mickelsson's grandfather, hardly in his grave yet, as angels count time, should stupefy the soul.

Around noon Tom Garret had called him to remind him to vote, which Mickelsson promised to do, though in fact he'd forgotten to register. It gave him no grief. Carter had his faults, but it was unthinkable that the American people would be so stupid and self-destructive as to vote in Reagan. After lunch Mickelsson had worked on the house, still brooding more on Luther than on his own book, increasingly shocked by how powerfully the man's spirit worked on him, both the gentle side—copier of folk tales, translator of the Bible into beautiful, moving German, advocate of infinite gentleness in the teaching of children, doting parent himself—and the dark, terrible side, manic-depressive plunging toward psychosis, fighter, hard drinker, well of hatreds—the Italians, French, English, above all the Jews. Thinking about Luther—and himself, of course—he ate Di-Gels one after another. He was drinking while he worked, as his habit was. He'd drunk only beer, then at suppertime switched to gin and tonic. He turned on the portable radio to listen to the returns. By nine that night he was drinking martinis, as Luther would have done with great lust, if God had allowed their invention in time. He sat at the kitchen table listening in mounting astonishment to the evidence that the American people had gone mad. "Idiots!" he shouted, and slammed the table with both fists at once. He drank on, sometimes pacing, clutching at his hair with his right hand, swearing at the walls and windows. Carter conceded. Mickelsson hardly noticed that he was drunk—he could still see, still stand upright, still howl his anger, though his eyes were full of tears—but drunk he was: his heart bellowed for something, he didn't know what at first, and then he realized: the base, uncomplicated love of Donnie Matthews. His mind, inhibitionless, could see no objection. And so he found himself tapping importunately with his cane's silver lioness-head at her door.

Oh, he knew, he was cognizant, that it was debauchery. (He tapped louder, sweating gin.) He had become once more the suicidal Dadaist, representative hero and symbol of his nation—perhaps the secret center of all men and nations—fallen out of orbit, drifting like his civilization toward absolute catastrophe (all the professional predictors agreed, the U.N., the Carter Report on the Future, alas: by the year 2000 wide-spread starvation, plague, universal war, for all practical purposes the end of the world), all of which, however, he accepted tonight with mournfully comfortable fatalism. Let it come! Let the final explosions be colorful! ("And Lord, may my death be not painful!"—Luther.) It was the nature of life and always had been, insofar as life in the world was worldly: the beginning of things in the blood-washed breaking of membranes, the precarious middle span with its tortuous, ultimately futile imposition of order, the protracted close of life—entropy, chaos, the final loosening of the sphincter. *Alles ist erlaubt.*

He was banging hard now at Donnie Matthews' door.

"Who is it?" she called from somewhere not far away. Perhaps she was sitting in her chair in the livingroom, reading.

"It's me," he called back. "Are you free?"

"Just a minute."

He was leaning far forward, his left hand on his hatbrim, his right ear close to the door. He was unaware that he was leaning farther than balance would permit until he found himself falling, drunkenly tumbling, lashing out with the tip of his cane to protect himself, shifting his left foot at the same time, but somehow getting it wrong, so that the next thing he knew he was on the carpet, the thud of his fall still echoing like thunder, the door suddenly opening and Donnie Matthews looking down at him, surprised.

"Jesus!" she said, bending down toward him. "What happened?"

"Floor tipped," he said. "Or maybe it was solar wind."

"You're drunk!" she said.

"That's also a possible explanation." He was up on his knees now. She studied him with narrowed eyes, then suddenly decided to reach down for his right arm and help him.

"Come on in," she said, "before the neighbors see you."

He laughed and turned to look in the direction of the door at the opposite side of the landing. It was safely closed. Then, letting her help him a little, he entered her livingroom and stood waiting while she closed and locked the door.

"You really are something," she said, and smiled now. "Let me help you with your coat." He stood locked into balance, like an old horse asleep, while she drew the overcoat down from his shoulders, shook the sleeves from his arms, then folded the coat and laid it on the straight-backed chair beside the door. Then she came to him and put her arms around him. Her cheap, young-woman smell was foreign, as intensely "other" as the room. "Where *were* you all this time?" she asked. "I kept expecting you to phone or something." She was wearing striped pajamas and a gray bathrobe, attire that gave her a childish, innocent look that, when he thought of what she looked like naked, stirred him suddenly toward lust. Her hair smelled of shampoo.

"Sweet, sweet," he said, grinning, breathing heavily, moving his hands on her back and round shoulders, then down her sides to the smell of her back, then her ass, drawing her against him.

She moved one hand to his crotch, gently rubbing his growing erection through his trousers. "Come to bed," she whispered. "Fuck me."

In the bedroom she stood still as he clumsily undressed her, licking and kissing each part of her body as it came into view. When she was naked he kneeled in front of her, licking her treasure box, at the same time unbuttoning and taking off his shirt. "God, oh God," she whispered, gripping his head in her hands. Her knees went rhythmically out to the sides and in again. Whether her passion was real or only accomplished acting he did not care. He got out of his trousers and underwear and, still with his shoes and socks on, rolled with her onto the bed. Almost as soon as he entered her, lying on his back, Donnie on top, sitting upright, flapping her arms like a bird, he came, and before another minute had passed, he was asleep.

When he woke up, hours later, the first thing he knew was that his head was splitting, his eyes so sensitive that even the dim yellow light from the bedside table shot into his head ferociously, so that his eyes, as if of their own volition, snapped shut again; and the second thing he knew was that Donnie had his stiff penis in her mouth, slowly lifting and lowering her head, wetting it with her spittle, at the nadir of her move-ment taking his full length. If he came, he knew, his head would, that instant, explode into vastly greater pain; yet he could not make himself stop. His heart began to beat more rapidly, then more rapidly yet. He pressed the heel of his hand to his chest and breathed through his mouth. Her hair fell softly over him. Her right leg, young, magnificently shaped, lay next to his left arm. He reached over with his right hand and touched it, moving two fingers up to her wet vagina, then in. She wriggled, de-manding more, and moved her head up and down more quickly. Insane, he thought. Foul! Bestial! Yet it did not seem that. Even when he moved one finger into her anus, it seemed not ugly, not inhuman. "I love you," he said. He felt the pulsing in his left testicle that meant that in a moment he would come, and he felt the sudden increase of pain in his head that meant he *was* coming, then blinding, shrieking pain, Donnie clinging to him, sucking and gagging—and suddenly he was violently ashamed, disgusted beyond words, and was at the same time filled with fear, his chest and head screaming, on fire. He clutched Donnie's leg in a false show of passionate gratitude, to hide from her his wish that she were dead. She brought her face up to his now, smiling, and gave him a kiss that almost made him retch.

He lay still beside her, holding her, and for decency's sake, or kindness' sake, kept himself for as long as possible from asking if she had aspirin. At last, when he could hold out no longer, he said as if jokingly, "Wow, have I got a headache! You got any aspirin, honey?"

"I think so." She kissed his cheek, then rolled away from him, sat up, and went into the bathroom. A minute later she returned. "Here," she said. When he opened his eyes he saw that she held out three aspirin in one hand, a glass of water in the other. He raised his head from the pillow, and she put the aspirin in his mouth, then held the glass to his lower lip.

"Thanks," he said, lying back again, closing his eyes.

She straightened the covers, then crawled into the bed beside him, fit her body snug against his, and pulled the covers up over them both.

They lay still for a long time. His chest still ached, but his heart had grown calm again. Little by little the pain in his head sank to tolerable. He began to draw toward sleep—first the falling sensation and the sudden jerks as he grabbed for balance in indistinct dreams, then fitful, slightly deeper dreams—obscure, mumbling voices, uncertain phantom shapes.

"Pete," she said in his ear, "are you awake?"

"Mmm," he said. He resisted the climb back to consciousness. He felt stifled, desperately in need of rest. The headache, though reduced, was still with him. He imagined it as black, swollen, like corn-rot inside his skull.

"Can I talk to you?" she asked.

"Mmm," he said again. But he was back in the world now, miserable.

"You didn't answer my letter." When he said nothing, she said, "Pete?"

"I heard you," he mumbled. "I must not have gotten it."

"Oh," she said. That stopped her for a while, long enough for Mickelsson to drift back toward sleep. "Shit. I wish you'd gotten it," she said. Her tone was cranky, as if perhaps she suspected that he had indeed gotten it and had simply failed to open it. "Do you want to know what I wrote you?" she asked.

"Sure," he said. "What?"

"I'm pregnant."

He had his headache back. He let a minute pass, maybe more. She did not repeat what she'd said. She knew pretty well that he'd heard. At last he said, softly, neutrally, "I'm sorry to hear that."

They both lay unnaturally still.

"Mmm-hmm. I'm really late. Almost three weeks."

He had a distinct impression that he had reason to know that what she claimed was impossible. How long ago was it that he'd handed her that plastic box of contraceptive pills? But he'd lost all sense of time. The gin, probably. It would make his head hurt more to strain to re-member. "Sometimes these things fool you," he said. His voice let out a hint of the anger he hadn't earned a right to. "Sometimes just worry can do it."

"I'm never late. I'm like clockwork."

He could think of nothing to say, though he moved his hand on her arm, partly in the vague hope of comforting her.

She asked again, "What are we going to do?"

"I realize it's a stupid question," he said, almost keeping the annoy-ance out of his voice, "but why do you say 'we'?"

"You're the father," she said. She spoke, it seemed to him, with crazy conviction, like one of Jessica's Marxists.

He asked, "Doesn't that seem to you a slightly strange thing to be sure of, all things considered?"

"But you are," she said.

"Why me? Why not one of your Fellini freaks? Why not"—he snatched for a name. "Why not Tim?"

"Nobody'd believe that," she said. "Tim's a fag."

"That's ridiculous," Mickelsson said, offended now. "He's got a wife and child!"

"OK, maybe he did it once. But Tim likes boys, everybody knows that. Boys and whips and Jesus knows what—anyway, he's never done it with me."

"That may be or it may not be—" He lost his train of thought, trying to readjust his image of Tim. She was probably lying, but he was suddenly not sure. It flitted through his mind that the murdered man, Professor Warren, had been, according to Nugent, homosexual, and that Tim had known him. Some faint possibility that he didn't yet have words for made his skin crawl, and he wished his headache would let up for a minute, allow him to think. "I don't know about Tim," he said, "but God knows there have been plenty of others."

"That's not true," she said. "I let you think that, because you seemed to enjoy it, but the truth is I never slept with anyone but you. I was a virgin. I swear to God."

He squeezed his eyes shut, actually believing her for an instant; then he rolled his head from side to side on the pillow, wondering if all this could be a nightmare, in a minute he'd wake up. "That's easy to say," he said, knowing the futility of saying it, but plunging on, "you don't believe in God."

"Well, then I swear on my honor." Abruptly, as if the whole thing had been a joke from the beginning, she laughed.

He got up on one elbow, pain soughing through his head. "What the hell are you saying?" he asked angrily. "What *is* all this?"

"I'm telling you I'm pregnant and you're the father and I want you to help me," she said. No one would have guessed that a moment before she'd been laughing.

"And I'm telling you that's bullshit."

"Maybe so, but I bet you'd really hate having to prove it in court."

"Jesus," he whispered, and let his head fall back on the pillow like a stone.

Her body was rigid, and she'd drawn away from him a little. "All you ever think about is yourself," she said with surprising bitterness. "What am I *supposed* to do? A person has to take care of herself in this world. You say you 'love' me. Ha! You think I believe that for a minute? You use me. I'm just meat!" In a moment she'd be crying, sobbing with self-pity. And maybe it was to some extent justified, in fact. How he wished his headache would quit.

"You're not just meat," he said. "Don't say things like that."

"Then give me the money for an abortion."

After that, he was silent for so long that she again raised up on her elbow to look at him. He met her eyes, two bright glints in them, reflections of the pale snowy light beyond the window.

He said, "Do you want me to marry you?"

"Jesus," she said, and turned her head away.

"Do you?" he asked. "I'll do it, if you want—if my damn divorce comes through. I can push harder, get it into court."

Donnie shook her head, and he made out that there were tears on her cheeks. "I like you. OK? But you're old. I mean, I've got my whole *life* to live. I can't marry you. It would be stupid. You *know* it would. Your fucking *checks* bounce."

"We could deal with that. I'll work it out."

"No!" she said, and snapped her face at him, eyes widened. "Just give me the money for an abortion. Period."

"I don't really like abortions," he said. "Why can't I give you the money to have the kid and put it up for adoption—or raise it, if you want. I'd pay for that too."

"No, no, no. It *hurts*, having a baby. Sometimes people actually die. I guess you're not aware of that."

"They don't," he said, angry but controlling himself, speaking almost gently to persuade her. "At least not often, these days."

"Why should I chance it? You're crazy! *All* men are. If it was you,

you'd run and get an abortion just like that. But since it's not you, it's just some dumb countrified whore—" Now the tears were streaming down her cheeks, though they seemed to have nothing to do with what she was saying.

"Listen, think about it," he said.

"There's not that much time."

"Just for a little while longer. I could send you away someplace, somewhere where they'd take good care of you, maybe one of those church places—"

"No! Why are you *doing* this to me?" Her voice broke, and now she began to sob, her hands covering her face. He understood, all at once, just how frightened she was, and that instant he almost relented, but when he opened his mouth to speak his voice refused, locked stubbornly in his throat.

"I'm sorry," he said, trying to touch her, but she shrank away. His heart was all darkness, as if something had gotten into him. "Look, I know how you feel. But I can't do it. I just can't. I can't kill a baby."

"A foetus," she screamed, "it's just a foetus!" The scream sang through the apartment, shocking him to silence. She abandoned herself to sobbing. He lay perfectly still.

After his two nights with Jessie, his bout with Luther, and then that terrible night with Donnie, Mickelsson felt more anxious than ever, and therefore more than ever kept bullishly to his routines, including his refusal to deal with his mail. He did not resist when Jessie came to his office and asked if he were ready to let her help with the great, unstable mountain on his desk; he even threw himself into the work of helping her, summoning up for the moment the extraordinary powers of concentration he was known for, but only to avoid the questions in her eyes, only to avoid, insofar as it was possible, her touching him or drawing him out. That pile proved, as he'd expected it would, less alarming than the one at home had been: they found almost no bills, and the few that came to hand were of a kind easily dealt with—bills for magazine subscriptions, professional memberships, university traffic fines; nothing that had to be paid. He wrote, with her help, recommendations for former students he did or did not remember (some of the recommendation forms were far past the deadline and he could throw them away), wrote polite refusals to requests for articles and reviews, explained why he would not be able to give a speech to the parents of incoming freshmen on Exploration Day, and wrote brief, cool letters pointing out why he could not read and evaluate the books and articles sent to him, unsolicited, by aggressive philosophical strangers. When his desk was bare, they went for drinks at Firehouse Five, she pretending to feel triumph, as if his life were now all fixed—though from the moment she'd entered his office, he knew, she'd recognized that there was something wrong. He waited for her terrible Jewish nosiness and directness, but luck was with him: she closed her hand over his, patting it now and then, and she gave him searching glances sometimes between smiles, but for some reason she stayed off his case. His cheeks ached from smiling, and his mind wandered, dazed and full of dread, like a small child lost in the woods. Once, when he allowed himself a minor tirade against Ronald Reagan, calling the nation's new President "Herr" and allowing himself language he usually avoided, she said, slightly widening her eyes, pressing down more firmly on the back of his hand, "Peter, for heaven's sake take it easy!" She glanced around the restaurant. "I can't say I'm terribly fond of him myself, given his stand on abortion and so forth, but he's not worth breaking a blood-vessel over. I'm sure the republic will survive him."

"He's a shit," Mickelsson said emphatically, twisting his distress at the word *abortion* into anger. He was not shouting, but not lowering his voice either, which was no doubt why she glanced at the tables around theirs, good Middle Americans up to their usual tricks. He leaned toward her a little, speaking just loudly enough that the people around him could hear if they chose to, which he hoped they did. "All this budget-cutting crap! Can people really be so stupid they—"

"Pete," she said, smiling harder, leaning in toward the candle. The waiter, passing with a tray of drinks on his shoulder, glanced at her. Perhaps his name was Pete. "Are you feeling all right?" she asked.

"Don't you think sometimes righteous indignation is a perfectly rational response?"

"Maybe so," she said, and looked down. He blushed but stopped ranting. It was an interesting idea, the connection between rant and ill-ness, and for a moment the philosopher in him paused to consider it. He thought of Martin Luther in his final psychosis, writing tracts in sup-port of the slaughter of peasants who, inspired by Luther's own ideas, had risen in rebellion; then thought of the doctor's three unspeakable, potty-mouthed tracts against the Jews. He thought of Luther turning savagely against all his best friends, growing more and more obscene of speech, until his disciples, who did not blanch at "shitty" or "donkey fart" or even "Shit in your breeches and wipe your face with it," would not write down the exact words he said.

"What are you thinking?" she asked, bringing her face closer to get his attention. In the glow from the red-globed candle on the table, Jessie's mouth, nose, and cheekbones were strikingly Semitic. He was reminded of an image he'd gazed at once for a long time in the British Museum, a face on a coin. Strange, he thought, that centuries of human life should be present in a living face. *Et mortuus vivit!*

He said, "I was thinking of old Dr. Luther, if anything." He turned his hand palm up under hers to return the pressure of her fingers. "You're right, of course. There's nothing in Reagan to hate. Fly in a fly-bottle. It's depressing."

She laughed, though she understood that he was serious. "You should be *glad* we have no great demon to fight." She turned her head to look for the waiter.

He frowned, then calmed his heart and let it go. He thought of Luther sitting bolt upright in bed, his room full of devils, filling the place with their terrible stench. Emissaries of the Pope, who was in turn an emissary. No doubt the learned doctor had been crazy all his life. But it was the Renaissance; no one had noticed. He remembered Luther's remark on the Nuremberg citizen Herr Osiander, who claimed not to believe in poltergeists: "Osiander always has to be different."

"Idealism," Mickelsson said. "That's the great demon."

"We mustn't be sore losers," Jessie said, and glanced at the people at the table nearest them, a middle-aged man with curly sideburns and a choleric look, beside him a thin young woman with a slash of white in her carefully puffed hair.

"Well, anyway," he said, trying to put the evening back on track, if it ever had been, "we've got *my* affairs back in order." He thought of Donnie, raving, crying out for all to hear, *"It's just a foetus!"*

"That *is* good," she said, her eyes searching his face again, and again her hand came over his. With her free hand she signalled for the waiter.

Only when they parted, back in the gray-lit university parking lot, did Jessie come close to admitting that she knew something was wrong. She studied his eyes, then in quick decision rose on her tiptoes, her hands on the back of his neck, and kissed him. "Don't worry," she said, and smiled, searching his face. "It will all be all right. Give it time!" She kissed him again, lingeringly, then abruptly turned away, since there was nothing more she could do. Her coat flared out and she crossed with long strides into the circle of light from a goose-necked lamppost, then out into shadow again, to her car. How clean and fine her beauty was, he thought with a foundering heart. He registered, suddenly squinting into the darkness, that the night they'd made love he'd seen stretch-marks on Jessica's abdomen. He must pay more attention, he told himself. Break down these stinking prison walls.

For all that, he did not mend his ways. At home, he let his mail pile up as before; at his office, he stuffed it unsorted, unread, into his file cabinet, where Jessie would not see it. Rifkin would have been interested in that; not that Mickelsson needed a psychiatrist for help with the interpretation. The infant idealist in Mickelsson was holding out; it was nothing more than that. He wanted to be back with his wife and children, all of them ten years younger; wanted his father to come striding back from the grave, and his mother young and pretty again; wanted his promise as a philosopher to be all it had once been, or greater. He'd had, all his life, a dream about what life ought to be, and now, though all evidence was against the dream, he refused to renounce it. If not that life, he was saying in effect, then no life. He thought again of that ghastly phrase of Nietzsche's, "*This* is your eternal life."

To avoid thinking he worked on Luther—if what he was doing could be called work. One by one he brought Luther's books from the university library and piled them on the floor by his desk, along with his grand-father's old tablets. His simultaneous hatred and admiration grew day by day. He began to know the doctor's stylistic tics as he knew his own—indeed, he began to see, to his horror, more and more similarities between his own personality and Luther's. Sometimes, brooding as he worked on the house or as he walked the streets of Susquehanna, doing errands, he felt as if the old fiend were right at his shoulder, listening in; and once, in a drizzling winter rain, just as he was coming out of the hardware store, he actually thought he saw old Dr. Martinus in the flesh. It was one of those curious mental tricks one dismisses as soon as one sees one's mistake, but for the second or two of its duration it struck terror into his heart. There he was, huge and slovenly, as in the contemporary de-scriptions and the one famous painting. He was dressed in black, as he'd been in life, his back turned to Mickelsson, the coarse hands folded behind his prodigious ass, and instead of coat and hat he wore a hooded sweater, exactly what one might expect of a former monk. Mickelsson froze in his tracks, knowing already that it wasn't really Luther, yet staring on, stupe-fied, some dim, ancient part of his mind unconvinced. Then the enormous creature turned, as if aware of someone behind him, and Mickelsson saw that it was the fat man from Donnie's apartment building. Mickelsson gave a quick, jerky bow, touching his hatbrim, and hurried down the street toward his car.

He couldn't get the horror out of his bloodstream. A queer thought took possession of him: the unpleasant idea that once, before he'd stood religion on its head, that gross, foul-mouthed swine had from time to time heard confession—young girls who'd had venial thoughts, middle-aged lechers whose escapades had surely made young Martin lick his lips. There was a good deal to be said—as no doubt no one knew better than Luther—for his having gotten rid of that ugly institution; but then a queerer thought came: how comforting it would be, for a man in Mickels-son's position, to be able to pour out his soul to a red-faced lout of a priest whose lips were sealed!

He was building, today, the door- and window-frames for the new diningroom, beautiful cherry boards he'd gotten for a song from a farmer on the lower road, who had a home sawmill. As he worked, measuring, sawing, fitting—handling the tools with a skill and confidence he'd never known he possessed—he played with the idea of confession. "I'm in love with a beautiful Jewess," he whispered, rolling his eyes upward toward the confessional curtain. *Jewess* was to make Luther's lips curl and his genitals quiver. "Every day she seems more beautiful and more wrong for me—and I for her—just as the other woman I see, Donnie Matthews, seems more repellent."

Heavy breathing behind the curtain. "Who is Donnie Matthews?"

"A young whore, Father." He put woe in his voice.

"Ah!"

"Alas, I am not, in Kierkegaard's sense, 'pure in heart,' able to will one thing."

"Kierkegaard?"

"A somewhat older whore." ("Not funny," Jessie would say, and would shake her head.)

"I see. Continue."

The greater his desire for Jessie, he would explain, a desire heightened now by remembered images—the fullness of her breasts as she arched her back above him or swung from side to side, drawing him in deeper and deeper—the greater his sense of his worthlessness, her moral and spiritual superiority to him, even, alas, intellectual superiority. ("I've had carnal relations with them both, Father," he would say. And Luther: "Ah, ah!") He could not imagine making love with Jessie in the way he did, almost without shame or remorse, with Donnie. He could not say for certain that his sordid bestiality would be shocking to Jessie—it seemed unlikely, in fact—but he knew that he himself, at least, would be sickened by it, as sickened as he'd be by the most abhorrent acts of blasphemy. (Why he should hate blasphemy—copulation on church altars, or filthy jokes about Jesus—he wasn't sure. Not because he was in his heart still a theist, he thought. It had more to do with his childhood; the insult to his small-boy innocence and faith in goodness, insult to the ardent love all human beings feel, if only now and then, for righteousness.) In his mind Jessie had become for him (though part of him knew that it had nothing much to do with reality) a sort of Platonic beacon of immaculacy, secular equivalent to Luther's "Lord's Supper," the point at which the finite and infinite touch. And Donnie, poor kid, had become for him the soul and vital symbol of all things lubricious and lewd, meretricious, debauched, profligate and goatish—the dark side of Luther's symbolism of the privy in the monastery tower. The more he brooded, self-flagellating, turning his bullish will against itself—striking out in his mind first at Jessie, then at Donnie—the more angry, confused, and anxious he became.

He'd dropped his little confession game, it came to him; turning his poisons inward, as usual. No matter. A stupid game anyway. He finished tacking in the headstop and stepped back to admire the finished door. Even unstained, it was a handsome piece of work. He dropped his hammer in the makeshift toolbox and picked up the measuring tape.

Thoughts of his worthlessness in comparison to the image of himself

Jessie stirred in him—or recalled to him—made clearer old Luther's doctrine, and Mickelsson's grandfather's, of all flesh as filth. "The world not only is the devil's, it *is* the devil." And he understood more clearly now than ever before, it came to him—understood in his bowels—Luther's observation that never is God's wrath more terrible than in His silence. Nietzsche's starting point. That once mankind discovers that it has lost God, the only possible result is universal madness. If God is dead, Nietzsche had claimed, human dignity is gone, all values are gone. Cold and darkness begin to close in. If it were true that mankind is filth, and impotent, then indeed God, if He did not exist, would have to be invented. But for that, alas, it was now much too late. The knowledge that God is dead, and Heaven a fairytale, had settled and cooled like lava, becoming the ground. No alternative now but the old, mad Luther's imperious longing for death, the sad old fiend limping on gouty legs from room to room, shaking his fists, demanding release from this wicked virgin-shit world, and the sooner the better. (And might his death be painless.) It was too late now even to cry out, fervently indignant, for death. Peter Mickelsson was living in the cynical, long-suffering age Nietzsche had foretold. Rhetoric was exposed; and suicide—all human feeling, in fact—was rhetoric.

He thought, suddenly scowling to himself, of Jessie's distrust of poetry. He got a brief, silly image of Dante's Beatrice, sixteen years old, dressed for the 1980s, saying, eyes fakely widening, "Gee! Really?" No one any-more, not even a cheerleader, could be trusted to be a fool.

He lined up the sill horn and dado and tapped the sill into place.

"To tell the truth, Father," he said past the nails in his mouth, re-moving one, slanting it into the sill, then striking three times with the hammer, "there are times when it seems to me that if I ever do quit evading life—as eventually I must, since dying of woe is no longer a live option—if I ever do set my fat head firmly toward whatever future may be out there—I could hardly survive if my Jewess were not a part of that future. The thought brings me no peace, of course, only greater dis-quietude, almost—to be truthful—a feeling of existential horror." He took the saw from the box.

He thought of Luther's strange devotion to his ex-nun wife, "lord Kate," as he'd called her—with all the usual Lutheran complexity: the sarcasm of a man who knows himself pussy-whipped, but also the worship of courtly-love-in-marriage: "I would not swap my Kate for France with Venice thrown in." In the monastery (child of the Middle Ages and Renaissance) Luther had written lutesongs to God. Now he wrote them to both God and Kate. The most careful analysis, authorities said, could not figure out which was which. No man, Luther said, could be a true theologian who had not awakened with pigtails on his pillow. Well, Mickelsson had never aspired to theology. Or if he had, striving upward from marriage, he had stupendously failed at it.

"I have moments of respite, of course." He chuckled falsely, gesturing with his left hand as he finished a cut. "I find myself glancing into mirrors or store windows, sizing myself up, experiencing a brief little flare-up of self-satisfaction. At times, often after a conversation with Jessie at the university cafeteria or in the hallway that runs past both our offices, I am inclined to think myself a handsome devil, no more gone to pot than other men my age, my red hair still quite striking, in point of fact, though admittedly rather odd, yellowing out and unkempt, the freckles on my fat nose and this heavy, flattened forehead sort of merrily boyish." He tapped his forehead dramatically, then returned his hand to the frame-piece he was cutting. "In a shirt or sportcoat I still look passably athletic, it seems to me: broad shoulders, big chest—so long as I hold my stomach in. It's only in a trenchcoat or overcoat that I look definitely boxy, not to say rotund."

The curtain moved, Luther peeking out. Mickelsson struck a pose, then went back to his sawing.

"We're neither of us spring chickens, Father—Jessie and myself—though it's true that she's beautiful, perhaps right now at the peak of her beauty, and she'll no doubt look younger and healthier than I all her life." He frowned, losing his place, saving himself in the nick of time from sawing along the wrong pencil line. "All the same, I think I could fairly be called, given my height, broad shoulders, et cetera, an imposing sort of man." As the end-piece fell to the floor he tapped his chest with his left hand. "No woman need be ashamed to be seen with me." He sighed, studied the next cut, and began sawing. "Such is my extraordinary self-confidence, at times." He cleared his throat and continued, "Alas, more often, gazing at this same form, what I see is a blotched, shaggy monster, red of face, as if I were always angry, or a drunkard. I'm a rather heavy drinker. Did I mention that?" He rolled his eyes up toward the confessional. "And I've come to be increasingly aware of another disagreeable feature: my back has become rounded, Father. It's somewhat gone to fat. My eyes are what a former student of mine, a macrobiotic, called 'sanpaku,' white showing under the irises, you know, which gives me a kind of septic, jaded look. When this mood is on me, needless to say, it seems to me impossible that any woman, even Donnie Matthews, could conceivably be fond of me. And indeed she is not fond of me, of course." He waved the hand that held the saw, dismissing hope. "One more of her Fellini freaks."

"This is a very long confession, my son!"

"I know. I hope you've had supper."

A weary sigh, then a belch.

"At times, concerning Jessie," he said sadly, "my thoughts turn rather dark. It's clear, I think, that both of us are playing a morbid psychological game, consciously or unconsciously toying with one another—to put it in its best light, offering brief comfort—because neither of us is entirely prepared to meet the future. She loved, with whatever reservations, her dead husband; I, insofar as I love anyone, love my dear, lost wife. Down in the underground gloom where the light of the brain dims out, we both, I suspect, know that each is, to the other, safe. Not that that can be entirely true: if it were, I would have no problem, now, would I? Clearly my heart, whatever the state of hers, is to a baffling degree divided." He held up the frame to the opening. Not perfect, but planing would redeem it. He said, "In my worst moods, it's this that I hold against Jessica: I do not want her to pretend to love me if she doesn't, in fact, because only if I know she truly loves me will I be able to confront the possibility that I truly love her."

"There can be no doubt of it, my son. You are bedevilled."

"God knows! I'll tell you my worst fear. I wonder if, if I were to propose to her, she'd draw back in revulsion, revealing that all she has said and done has been just play or, worse, charity."

"Only Christ has charity, my son."

"Maybe. In any case, if she *has* been acting out of charity, I couldn't blame her. Her marrying me would be imbecile from every point of view. She's well-off. I, on the other hand, even if it were not for the alimony I've already offered my ex-wife, and even if I manage to straighten out my past, even if I should be able to rid myself of Donnie Matthews, as I hope and pray I'll do—not that it won't cost me plenty, in the short run—I, as I was saying, am a miserable pauper. Jessie is fancy, very refined—even counting her odd distaste for poetry. I, on the other hand, am a slightly cleaned-up country oaf. I have to wince, thinking of that concert we went to—I haven't told you about that, I think, but never mind. I made a fool of myself, muttering, destroying my neighbors' enjoyment. Even those mutterings that fortunately remained inside my head make me wince when I remember them—big redneck farmboy sitting there soberly reasoning with himself, the meaning of music is so-and-so, such-and-such—as if music, in any admissible sense, had meaning—while all those easily sophisticated people, even the kids, like my student Alan Blassenheim, less than half my age but trained in good Long Island schools, or maybe private schools, I wouldn't know . . . at any rate exposed to music of the classier sort . . . all those people sat back and simply heard what was there and knew as if by nature when to laugh or cry. Sometimes, after an experience like that, it occurs to me to wonder if it might be simply that I'm stupid."

"All of us are stupid. No help for it. Worthless, steamy filth—"

"I know, I know. In any event, it seems highly unlikely that Jessie would say yes to me, if I were to propose. I've seen how I frighten her at times. And even if Jessie's distrust of me should pass . . ."

Now he had the second frame tapped in. He sat down on the sawhorse, admiring his work, another part of his mind rambling on.

"It's part of my fanatic idealism that I wouldn't be satisfied, hearing her say yes, unless her answer were rational in the fullest sense, that is, fully informed. I can hardly imagine myself telling her about Donnie. Even if I did, and even if she were, grudgingly, to accept it, it would poison the ideal she too has a right to insist on. And as if that weren't enough, consider this: I don't want her to say yes unless she does in fact love me, heart and soul; and of course not even Jessie, clever as she is, can know whether or not she loves me as my fanatical heart demands until she knows my heart. You follow? Protestations of love are always about seventy per cent wild hope." He waved at the wall dramatically, showing his scorn of merely hopeful protestations. "Like a caster of spells, one proclaims as actuality what one wishes and, on the basis of present evidence, believes might eventually become actuality. I, however—unreasonably, querulously, foolish Platonist to the depth—I insist on a perfect exchange of love that cannot be until it is. I understand the trap; all the same, I'm trapped, like Epimenides the Cretan in his famous saying 'All Cretans are liars,' or like the madman who refuses to come down off his pillar until someone can offer him 'good reason.' Sometimes as I talk with her—once, especially, when we were standing in the parking lot, she holding my hand, her white scarf blowing in the wintry wind like the scarf of a kamikaze pilot"—with his right hand he showed the room how Jessie's scarf had floated—"I felt a sudden wave of irrational irritation come over me: actually it was resentment of the human condition, but at that instant my anger zeroed in on Jessie's inability to love me perfectly, without pity or reservation. My own capacity is of course no greater; but that thought was not in my head at the time. For no earthly reason, I have begun to suspect her of seeing other men. I laugh at myself; but once the suspicion has crept in, it has a way of lodging itself firmly, unevictable. Everything seems to confirm the suspicion. Sometimes when I phone her, even late at night, there's no answer."

Beyond the windows—he would tack up cardboard for tonight and glaze them tomorrow—it was twilight now. The day had been warm, springlike; he'd worked with only a sweater, not even needing gloves. But now a cold wind was rising: wind of a kind he had lately come to dislike. It would sing in the eaves and evergreens, inclining him to thoughts of hauntedness. Not that even now he was convinced that the house had ghosts. Nonetheless, the wind made him uneasy.

Martin Luther asked, "Do you repent these numerous and various sins?"

"I feel sorry for all the people I'm hurting," Mickelsson said. "That's my best offer."

And so in everything, even his feelings toward Jessica Stark, Mickelsson waited for some miracle, some burst of illuminating, all-transforming light out of Heaven—Luther's nearly castrating thunderbolt, perhaps—

and refused, until it came, to lift a finger. The only exception to this was his house. Every free minute he could get (he no longer even looked at the manuscript on his desk), he worked at transforming the place—putting down the diningroom floor, plastering, rewiring. He was spending money (theoretical money) as if it grew on trees, but since Owen Thomas said nothing, trusting him, Mickelsson was able to pretend not to notice. He had no idea how high his bill was by now. Hundreds, no doubt. He blinked the thought away as he blinked away the dusty sweat that ran in rivers down his forehead. If he stopped for a minute to pay attention to his affairs, Mickelsson believed, he would see his doom, solid as the house itself, all around him. With a recklessness Rifkin would have no difficulty explaining, he went on spending, hand over fist, never real money, credit at the hardware store, elsewhere plastic promises, burying himself—as all the country was doing, according to the papers—in a mountain of irredeemable pledges. He worked like a maniac. His wrists grew thick, his hands cut, barked, and swollen.

Rifkin would whine in his nasal way, "Isn't it just a new form of the old disease, Professor?"

"Maybe you're mistaken," Mickelsson said, pointing sternly, like a lecturer, at the empty air. "Maybe it's some kind of magic that I'm involved in. How do you get martins to come eat your mosquitoes? You build a martin house. I've listened too long to you sensible people with your life-withering sanity. What do you do with the impetuous, dangerous torrents of the soul? You try to dry them up!"

"Ah yes," Rifkin said, "freedom, holy self-abandonment!" Like a puppet he jiggled his head and waggled his two uplifted hands. Then, abruptly, he folded his arms over his chest.

"I'll tell you something," Mickelsson said, pointing the bight of his trowel at him, threatening. "All you say has been said before, millions of times. No doubt it was said by the tall, big-brained Neandertals before they vanished from the face of the earth—for all their love of order! I'll tell you what *we* say, the new breed of terrible invaders from the south: 'We philosophers and free spirits feel ourselves to be shone upon by a new dawn with the news of God's demise. Our heart flows over with thankfulness, amazement, presentiment, expectation. Finally! Our ships can embark again, and go forth to every danger! Every hazard is again permitted the inquirer! Perhaps there was never before so open a sea!'"

He broke off, banishing Rifkin from his livingroom. Just a few nights ago, going through a box of clothes his ex-wife had sent down to him in one of her fits of housecleaning frenzy or residual tenderness, Mickelsson had come across the full-length scarlet hunting coat he'd worn when his last so-called episode was upon him, a coat they'd bought long ago on Portobello Road, when they'd passed through London on the way home from that grim year in Heidelberg. He'd felt a brief jolt of fear, holding the coat up to look at it, and he remembered how he'd bawled, clinging to Rifkin in his dimly lit office, shamelessly clutching the cotton of Rifkin's shirt, bellowing like a bull in the slaughterhouse, while Rifkin, as if absent-mindedly, patted the red coat's shoulder, his eyes shifting from Mickelsson's face to the nurse who was preparing his shot. Poor humanity had need of its Rifkins, mock all it might. He'd considered throwing the coat away, but then its wrinkles and the dangling brass button at the collar had distracted him, made him forget his fear and remember instead how Mark and Leslie had run eagerly from shop to shop, streetcart to streetcart, or had pressed up close, timidly holding hands, to look up, mouths open, at street musicians. In the end, he'd taken the scarlet coat to the cleaners, along with other things in need of cleaning and trifling repairs. He must remember to get over to Montrose and pick them up. Anyway, he must get himself a Pennsylvania lawyer, the I.R.S. man had told him. Old Cook would be sufficient. How much big-city cunning did it require to acknowledge that one's client's case was hopeless?

It would not do, he understood, to think too hard about what it meant, this fixing of the house; yet he couldn't help toying with the idea he'd suggested to his phantom physician, that it was magic, not madness— if there was really any difference. Perhaps in a way he was doubling back into his childhood, as if playing with the idea of starting over. The first time he'd run a plane down a yellow pine board, watching the shaving curl up past his fists, he'd remembered with a clarity astonishing to him how his father had looked at thirty, his sleeves rolled up tight to his pink, freckled arms, his jaw thrown forward, lower teeth clenched around upper teeth. Sometimes his father would sing as he worked: *"In a cavern, in a canyon, excay-vay-ting for a mine . . ."* Mickelsson's uncle Edgar would move around, expressionless and straight-backed as a gorilla, as if sunk into his own grim meditation, but sometimes he would glance over in the direction of the barn or wellhouse where Mickelsson's father worked and sang, and one could see that Mickelsson's uncle was listening. Another time, when Mickelsson was working on his plumbing, fixing a leak under the bathtub, he got a sudden, wonderfully sharp image of his father down in the well with a trouble-light, his legs spraddled wide, shoes wedged into the wet stone walls on either side. He'd had the farts, Mickelsson remembered, and they'd all joked about it, especially his father: "If anybody'd dropped a match I'd've been blowed to Kingdom Come!" he said. It was true that, up at the top of the well, where Mickelsson, a small boy, lay on his belly fearfully looking down, the smell was horrendous. His father's red hair, just under the trouble-light, glittered and gleamed like new copper.

Still another time, prodded by an old rotten clothespin he'd just picked up from the cellar floor, Mickelsson saw his mother at the clothesline behind the house, reaching up, her mouth full of clothespins, to hang trousers, pair after pair, by the cuffs. Her hair, with the sun in it, was the color of Ellen's before Ellen had begun to dye hers black. Straw-yellow. His mother's stockings were rolled at the knees.

All that Thursday and Friday—his days for "research," as he'd told Tillson—he worked at plastering the new diningroom. It was indeed research, in a way (which was not to deny that he'd been less than forthright with Tillson). Dreams, memories, insights drifted into his head unbidden. He saw his sister in her coffin, dead of polio at nine. He remembered his uncle pouring gasoline over the pigpen, four dead sows inside—what it was they'd died of Mickelsson had now no idea. The corpses had been pushed together in a pile and old truck tires placed around them. Then his uncle had stood back and had thrown a match. There was a roaring explosion and a cloud of fire rushed outward and upward, almost to where Mickelsson stood holding his uncle's scabrous hand. Cousins squealed and ran back a few steps—Billy, Erik, Jeanette, Mary Ann—and from the center of the fire came a crackling, hissing sound, a rumble like a voice, and a thousand thousand sparks went flying up. His uncle's eyes, watching the fire, were a startling, glassy red.

When the plastering was finished, dark gray where he'd worked most recently, lighter, finally white, where he'd worked earlier, Mickelsson sat down on the rickety chair exactly in the middle of the room—it made him think of some play by Samuel Beckett that Ellen had taken him to— and with childish satisfaction looked over what he'd done. He went to the kitchen to get himself a beer, then came back and sat down to look again. Of all the repairs he'd made so far, it was the plastering that pleased him most. When the thought of his son came to him—still missing, no word—Mickelsson suddenly got up, turned off the lights, and left the room. He stood beside the telephone in the kitchen, his right elbow on the wall, his hand on his forehead, going over in his mind again and again the numbers that would ring his ex-wife's telephone. At last he admitted to himself that he was afraid to call her and went back through the livingroom to his study, where he sat down at his desk and put paper into the typewriter. He stared at the paper, not turning the typewriter on, then at last laid his aching arms on the typewriter and the whiskery side of his face on his arms. He'd been sitting there for some while, waiting out time like his poor angry student Michael Nugent, when it came to him—a shiver of dread moving slowly up his spine—that there was someone standing behind him. When he held his breath, he could hear whoever it was breathing.

He fixed himself supper, a cheese sandwich and a glass of milk, then went into the livingroom to eat and, afterward, sit pondering. Even now he felt watched.

Perhaps, he thought, he should get Jessica to help him with the Christmas party.

He went into the new diningroom to look at the plastering job one last time, stood there for twenty minutes, arms folded across his chest, then at last turned off the lights and went up to bed. He fell asleep listening for the phone.

It was at something like two in the morning that the phone did ring, and Mickelsson, waking suddenly from some unpleasant dream, stumbled naked from his bed to answer it. He realized at once, as soon as he reached the wall where the telephone was, that he should have brought a blanket to wrap around him.

"Hello?" he said.

"Hi, Dad." His son's voice was sweeter than ever to his ear, strangely cheerful—a cheerfulness possibly forced, he could never tell, but instinctively he accepted the pretense, if it was that. His heart lifted.

"Mark! Where are you?"

"I'm sorry if I worried you. Everything's fine, I'm OK. I just wanted to call, let you know things are all right."

"That's good! It's wonderful to hear your voice!" He was bent over, clinging to the receiver with both hands. "How are you?"

Mark laughed. "I'm fine. Really. Are you OK?"

"You know me. Like an old horse standing in the rain. How are you?"

"Dad," Mark said.

"I know. I already asked you that. It's so good to hear your voice!"

"I suppose Mom's been pretty worried. Did she call?"

"I called her, as it happens. She has been worried, of course. You should call her. How are—" He stopped himself. "It's so good to hear your voice!"

"I'm sorry I worried you," Mark said, "but things got sort of—heavy." He spoke the word apologetically, as if he'd gladly not use the street-talk if there were anything else. "I'm sorry about the Rollei. I guess Mom told you?"

"I saw the picture in the paper. Don't worry about it. You looked terrific! I didn't know you still had that hat. Do you need money? Is there some way the Rollei can be fixed?"

"I've got another camera now—an Instamatic. It doesn't make art— it's a real moron's camera, actually; I should be ashamed to be seen with it —but it's good enough for what I need it for right now, and it's easy to hide. I've got a line on something better, actually. If anything develops maybe I'll ask you for the money." He paused. "It's kind of a lot."

"Whatever you need, just let me know."

"Thanks, Dad. I will. Dad, you wouldn't believe this stuff."

"The police, you mean?"

"All of it." Mickelsson could see him smiling, slightly drawn back, maybe fiddling with the phone cord. "There were these people that came to U.V.M., representatives of Yankee. Kids would ask them questions, and they'd say, 'As representatives of a profit-making organization, it's obviously not in our interest to answer a question like that.' They were amazing. You expected them to lie, but they never lied about anything. They just refused to answer. It was a scary thing to see, all that arrogance —I mean the fact that they thought they'd get away with it. And the thing is, they *do* get away with it. A few kids may yell at them, but the nukes keep going up, and the alternatives—things like solar and wind and geothermal—they keep being blocked. Obviously they're not in a position to talk straight; all the facts are against them. But they figure if they don't talk at all they'll win, and I guess maybe they're right. Nobody really believes in Doomsday. People just go on, putting up with whatever they're told to put up with. It's suicidal."

"Well," Mickelsson said.

"I keep being amazed how hard it is to get people to listen. When we were at Yankee, sitting in, we'd talk with the oglers, tell them true horror stories—how the cancer incidence goes up fifty per cent in the area of a nuke plant for every one per cent elsewhere; how three of the nuke plants in New York State, and dozens elsewhere, are built on earthquake faults; how everything depends on the plant's emergency core-cooling system, and the thing's never really been tested—in this one small-scale test it failed six times out of six. You should have seen how the people we talked to reacted." He laughed sadly. "Mostly they just looked at the ground and shook their heads. Talk about walking peacefully into the ovens!"

"It's incredible all right," Mickelsson said.

Mark laughed. "Sorry to rant. Anyway, we're doing what we can."

"Look, don't do anything dangerous, OK?"

"You know me, Dad. Non-violent type."

"But it seems you have found it necessary to disappear."

"Don't worry. No violence directed at human beings."

"Buildings and machines?"

"Come on, Dad. They're no good anyway. Radioactive."

"That stuff's catching, isn't it? If a person gets too close?"

"Listen, Dad." Mark seemed suddenly distant. "Are you OK? Really?"

"Am *I* OK. Jesus!" But Mickelsson grinned in spite of himself, shivering. "I bought a house. Haunted. I kid you not."

"What do you mean?"

"Well, mainly I mean I bought this house. Let me give you directions to it, just in case. OK? You got a pencil?"

"What do you mean it's haunted?" His voice was worried.

"Have you got a pencil?"

"Sure," Mark said. "Just a minute." His voice went far away, the words unintelligible; he'd probably put his hand over the phone. Then: "OK, what's the address?"

Mickelsson told him, turn by turn. Then: "Mark, where are you?"

"I'm fine, Dad. Really."

"I know. I believe you. But how can I get in touch with you? Send you money, for instance."

"I'm OK. I really am."

"What if something happens to you? How do I find out?"

"Dad," Mark said.

"OK," Mickelsson said. "OK. Listen, honey"—he regretted the "honey," or half regretted it, but urgently pressed on—"it's all right to fight the bad guys, but remember, you've got a life—"

"That's not true, really," Mark broke in. "Nobody's got a life if things continue as they're going. I'm not sure you understand or, OK, agree; but it's all or nothing. I think it really is. I might be wrong. People like me have been wrong before. But if I'm right, I have no choice—you know, Dad? Look, I'm not a terrorist. I'd never hurt a fly. But they have to be stopped, people have to see what's really happening, and I'm not sure it's possible to stop them in the way I'd approve of. They're too big, whole federal government wrapped around them like eggwhite, feeding 'em. I think, well, it's a war for life. You know how proud you were of your uncle that lied about his age and went off to fight in World War Two? Well, this is a war for the planet. That's what I think."

"You say you're not a terrorist," Mickelsson said.

"OK, I'm a terrorist. I don't think of it that way."

"Honey," Mickelsson said. "*Honey*—!"

"It's OK, Dad. Really, it's OK. I haven't changed."

After a minute Mickelsson said, "I know. Listen. Be careful. OK?"

"OK."

"Listen—"

After a long pause, Mark said, "I'll call when I can. OK?"

"OK."

"Bye, Dad. I love you."

When he was able, Mickelsson said, "I love you too, Mark."

The line went dead.

"Good-bye," Mickelsson said.

In the morning he awakened pinned by his own immense weight to the bed, numb from head to toe, as if he'd gone to bed drunk and had never stirred all night long. It took him a good while to remember what was amiss; the phonecall. Then feeling flooded into him, the power to move. He thought at once of calling Ellen, then thought better of it. He thought of calling Jessie, then again stopped himself. "Christ," he

whispered, something like a prayer. He saw his son moving among dangerous, shadowy strangers far away—Utah, New Mexico, Colorado, North Dakota . . . wherever the nukes were; but they were everywhere. Some deep misery pulled at him, nothing he could put in words, though in a way he understood it: his son, stepped back from the world as he himself was, but more terribly, perhaps more hopelessly. Mickelsson would never again be as innocent as his son, or as loving of poor stupid humanity. He, Mickelsson, was old and crafty, or capable of craft. He, not his son, should be the terrorist. Passive resistance; very good, conceivably helpful. But he knew now, though he knew no details, that his son was beyond that—rightly, for all he knew. The gentlest child who ever lived.

Against his better judgment, overcoming his cowardice, he dialed Ellen's number. It was her friend that answered, The Comedian.

"Hello?"

"Hello. Willard?"

"Professor?" the voice asked.

"Is Ellen there?"

"She's out right now. Can I give her a message?"

In his mind, Mickelsson saw the young man bent toward the receiver like a Japanese, his black beard shiny, his shirt puckered in by suspenders. His voice contained a slight tremble. Fear, or concern for Ellen's welfare. Maybe hatred.

"Mark called last night," Mickelsson said. "Tell her he's OK."

"He called here too."

"Oh," Mickelsson said. Irrationally, he felt betrayed. "OK. All right then."

"Thank you for calling," the young man said. He spoke gently, as if concerned about Mickelsson's welfare too.

Not far away, Ellen's voice asked, "Who is it?"

"Good-day," the young man said.

Deliberately, almost without emotion, he struck the receiver hard against the wall to break the young man's eardrum, then hung up.

On the desk in his office he found a note from Lawler, asking him to drop by LN227—Lawler's office—at his convenience. After his Plato and Aristotle class (uneventful; they were working on their term papers now, and were content to let him lecture), Mickelsson went up to see if Lawler was in. He must try to make it brief. Jessie would be driving out this afternoon to help him set up for the party at his house. Would they make love? Desire and shame warred in his stomach. He took a Di-Gel.

By some computer mix-up, or perhaps by some odd preference of Lawler's, the office was isolated from the rest of the Philosophy Department offices, surrounded by the messy, oddly gray offices of mathematicians. Lawler's door was closed, as usual. No notes, sign-up sheets, or grade-lists were thumbtacked to the small, framed square of cork under the office number. No *New Yorker* cartoons, no posters or pictures, no decorative quips like the one on the door across the hallway from Lawler's: *What is the speed of thought?*

Mickelsson knocked and, after a moment, as if slightly alarmed, Lawler called, "Come in. It's open." The voice was high and thin.

Mickelsson turned the knob, opened the door a foot or so, and poked his head in. In the dimness of the astonishingly cluttered, book-filled room, Lawler sat turned sideways at his desk, thoughtfully chewing a pencil, looking down at the large volume he had open in front of him. Though he did not seem to have glanced up from the book, he said, "Ah, Pete! Sit down."

Mickelsson opened the door further and entered, gently closing the door behind him. Lawler was dressed, as usual, in his shabby black suit, his shiny steel glasses cutting into the sides of his pale, bloated visage. He was graying and balding—the gray hair unkempt, as if wind-blown—yet he was curiously baby-faced, as if nothing had ever happened to him, no griefs, no joys, no wind to dishevel him but the harmless wind of words. He sat in his old-fashioned mahogany deskchair with his lumpy black shoes resting on a low footstool—he was too short to reach the floor—and his posture was oddly prim, erect, a somehow quaint suggestion of the shy, brilliant fat boy he'd once been and, in some ways, was yet. An antique plush chair stood over by the bookshelf at Lawler's back, a chair that looked much too rickety to sit in, but the only one available. Mickelsson drew it up to Lawler's desk and warily sat down. The chair was not the only antique in the room, he saw now, as his eyes became accustomed to the dimness. Over by the window stood a tall grandfather's clock with a great brass shield for a pendulum and ornate brass disks above the face, gauges of the progress of the moon, perhaps; Mickelsson had no idea. Above Lawler's desk hung—or mournfully loomed—a large oil painting of a castle almost invisible in darkness and fog.

"How are things?" Mickelsson asked. He watched his colleague's face closely, with interest, to see if, this once, he would look up.

"Mmm, yes," Lawler said, and struck directly at his business, speaking in the fussy, at once timid and sober-minded fashion of a schoolboy certain of nothing in the world but his facts. Jessie had of course been exactly right about him: a lonely man cloaked and disguised in fat and abstraction. "I asked you to come by," he said apologetically, "because I'm rather concerned about our mutual friend or, that is, student, Michael Nugent."

"Oh?" Mickelsson said, and waited.

"Do you think he seems well?" Lawler asked. Startlingly, his eyes rose to stare straight into Mickelsson's with what seemed to him—perhaps he was mistaken—dreadful grief.

"He seems to me quite intelligent," Mickelsson said, hedging.

Lawler moved his hand in a minute gesture of impatience. "Yes, unquestionably. But I've been wondering, observing him—of course it's only conjecture. . . ."

"Yes, I see," Mickelsson said, and looked down. "Has Dean Blickstein talked to you, by any chance?"

"Nooo." There was a hint of alarm in his voice, as if he'd guessed what was coming.

"He's apparently going through a difficult time," Mickelsson said. He felt, all at once, awash in guilt. Here was Lawler, of all people, the great, aloof intellectual, distressed about the welfare of one of his students, while Mickelsson, superficially more social, by far more conscious of the world around him, even conscious, some of the time, of the parallel between his students' unhappiness and the unhappiness of his son, turned his back on his students as on everything else. He said, blushing, "According to Blickstein, Nugent's father died recently. The boy was extremely depressed by it; in fact it seems he attempted suicide. And then apparently he was hit rather hard by the death of one of his teachers, Professor Warren."

"Warren?" Lawler echoed vaguely. Again his voice was apologetic, as if the name were no doubt one he should know but, unfortunately, did not.

"It seems they were fairly close," Mickelsson said. "I'm not sure how close. Apparently, Warren was homosexual, like Nugent."

"Oh?" Lawler said. He seemed puzzled and a little dismayed by the revelation; he was perhaps not sufficiently of the world to have noticed Nugent's tendency. "That's a burden, I suppose, in our society." His mind was elsewhere. After a moment he said, looking down at his book again, "It sounds as if there's not much we can do. Is the boy getting counselling?"

"We could suggest it. I haven't, myself."

"Counselling might help, I suppose." He didn't sound hopeful. Perhaps he too had known his Rifkins. "Warren," he said, still trying to place the name. "Was he in our department?"

"Chemistry," Mickelsson said. "Nugent was in engineering before he came to us."

"Ah! I see! Yes, I knew that. Chemistry, then. I see. And you think they were lovers?" Lawler's face darkened in embarrassment.

"I wouldn't say that, though of course I wouldn't know. Just good friends, I think."

"Good friends. Yes, I see." He raised his right hand, unaware that he was doing it, to rub the space between his eyebrows, pushing up the bridge of his glasses, as if he had the start of a headache. "If there were only something one could do," he said. He seemed to be speaking more to himself than to Mickelsson.

"Yes," Mickelsson said.

Slowly, thoughtfully, Lawler began to nod. "Well, thank you for coming," he said. "I suppose all we can do is watch him, try to be whatever help we can."

"We can do that much, yes."

On the way back to his office, Mickelsson pressed his fist to his forehead, hardly knowing what he felt. Mainly he felt like a child returning from the principal's office, found guilty and not properly punished. "Very well, very well," he muttered angrily, but which of his failures he was confessing was not clear. One thing was certain. He ought to take Michael Nugent aside, have a heart-to-heart talk with him. *Ought*, he brooded. A stupid word, no force. A word for weaklings, Nietzsche would say. A word for survivors, something he apparently was not. No paradox, for Nietzsche. *The species does not grow in perfection: the weak are forever prevailing over the strong.*

Jessie arrived three hours later than she'd said, an annoyance not because he had anything planned but because it forced him to another painful recognition: she was one of those people who had a knack for making you worry. He'd pretended to read, glancing now and then at the clock beside the door, sometimes bending close to the window for a look at the weather—clear and frozen as a crystal—sometimes coming alert at the sound of a car, but then time after time the car went on past, another meaningless Not-Jessica, as Sartre would say. When she arrived, she came roaring up to the back door and beeped the horn twice (she drove something small and European-looking), and when he opened the back door and went out to her—no jacket over his T-shirt, hunching his shoulders against the bitter cold and rubbing his hands, whining but widely grinning, "Where were you, Goldfarb? I thought you were dead!" —she opened the car-door (the inside light went on) and called out, "Come on, Mickelsson, lend a muscle!"

The back of the car was piled high with boxes and paper bags which, after they'd carried them in and opened them, he found to be filled with Christmas decorations, napkins and tablecloth, a fruitcake from Texas, a large gilded menorah, which she set up in his window and filled with candles—what he thought of that he wasn't quite sure: he was no bigot, at least not in relation to Jews, and he didn't give a damn what his neighbors thought; but all the same, all the same . . . She'd brought a crèche, which she was now setting up on the coffeetable, handling the figures gently, like a child at her dollhouse, sometimes leaning back to study her arrangement critically, like a painter at her easel; and comparing his feelings about the menorah to hers about the crèche, a wave of self-revulsion rose in him. He leaned over beside her, resting one hand on his knee, and waved foolishly down at the glossy, brightly colored figures.

"Nighty-bye, Jesus," he said. She looked up at him, smiling, a sort of shadow moving over her features.

He nailed up the three Christmas wreaths she'd brought for the doors —the two large doors on the front porch, the smaller door in back—while she sorted out the Christmas tree lights and ornaments. "Where's the tree?" she asked, looking around the room as if she thought it might be there but behind something.

"I'll get the axe," he said.

Her eyes widened with childish excitement. "We're going to *cut* one?"

"Just like Joseph and Mary out behind the stable," he said.

Again the shadow passed over her face, but whatever was bothering her she quickly put out of mind (he knew pretty well what was bothering her), and, taking his hand, she stood up. They got their coats on—it was now almost midnight—he got the axe from the shed, and they plowed through the crunchy salt-white snow to the starlit woods higher on the mountain, where there were evergreens of every size and shape, none of them quite right when one looked closely. In the end they chose one almost at random. He could cut off boughs where they grew too thickly and wire them in place where the growth was too sparse. "You're *good* at that!" she cried as his axe bit in, slanting halfway through the trunk at one blow.

"As a child I was an axe murderer," he said, and grinned at her.

She shook her head, smiling. He had a sense that suddenly she was standing hundreds of yards away, observing him as if from another century.

He swung three times more and the ten-foot tree toppled, falling slowly, softly, as Jessie called, hands beside her mouth, "Tim-burrr!" They put their hands around one another's waists and stood for a long moment gazing at the fallen tree as if at some ancient mystery. Then, like two farm horses, they dragged it between them down the mountain.

As he built the stand for it, cutting, notching, nailing there in the livingroom beside the tree, Jessica fussing with candles, Mickelsson asked, "Jessie, how come there are stretch-marks on your stomach?"

He sensed her sudden stillness behind him. At last she said casually, "I had children. Two of them. Girls. I'll show you their pictures sometime."

"What happened?" he asked.

"They died," she said. "Ages three and seven. It was one of those boating accidents. A long time ago."

He waited for Jessica to say more, but no more came. He heard her move, behind him, to work on the candles at the further window.

"I'm sorry, Jessie," he said.

After a moment she said, "Me too."

He nailed the stand to the tree, clipped the excess boughs on one side and with picture-wire affixed them where they were needed. Then they moved chairs out of the way and, with a weight-lifter's heave—branches and pine-needles scratching against his face—he raised the tree and placed it. They put on the lights, Jessica fussily giving him directions as he leaned into the tree from the step-ladder, Mickelsson swearing a little under his breath; then they put on the ornaments and tinsel. When everything was finished they turned off the room lights and sat side by side on the couch, gazing like children at the Christmas tree lights and their reflections in the windows.

Mickelsson said, when they'd been silent for what seemed a long time, "How long ago was the accident?"

"Six years," she said. Gently, she squeezed the hand holding hers, telling him, he knew, to ask no more.

In his mind he formed the words, "I love you, Jessie," but then held back, suddenly repelled by the beauty around him, repelled by time and his inadequacy, the deep cruelty of life this Christian mystery was supposed to have transmuted.

"I think it's the prettiest tree I've ever seen," she said.

They did not make love that night, though they lay side by side on the rug under the tree, hardly talking, eventually sleeping, waking up stiff and half frozen a little after sun-up.

Twenty minutes after Jessica left, Mickelsson, coming into the livingroom from the kitchen, found a visitor sitting under the tree: a cat. It was as large as any he'd ever seen, almost lynx size, made more lynx-like by its bobbed tail, medallion of some old war. The cat was almost all white, sooty white from end to end except for a gray cap around the partly missing right ear and another gray splotch on the rump. One eye was half closed by tissue like Scotch tape. It had an odd lump on its belly, and the turned-inward, absent-minded look of something dying.

"Hello, stranger," Mickelsson said. His voice surprised him by its calm.

The cat sat on the rug between the tree and the woodstove, in the position of the Great Sphinx of Egypt except that the immense flat head was partly turned, watching him with yellow eyes. The cat's neck was almost as wide as his shoulders. He was motionless except for the stump tail moving slowly from side to side.

Mickelsson put his hands in his pockets. "So you're the mysterious noisemaker," he said. "I've heard you, my friend, knocking things down in the cellar. I must say, for a cat you're mighty clumsy."

The tail went on moving. The eyes, aglitter with pinpoints of colored light, never shifted from Mickelsson's face.

"Look," Mickelsson said, holding his right hand out. "I have nothing against cats *per se*. But you'll have to get over the idea that you own the livingroom."

Though they were fifteen feet apart, Mickelsson moved carefully, making his way to the chair by the stereo twelve feet from the cat. He could feel the quick ticking of some muscle or vein near his heart. His emotions were in a turmoil he had no time to understand. Slowly, carefully, he seated himself. For all his fear of the cat, he knew, with some part of his mind, that he was glad the cat had come.

"OK," he said, "so you've decided you live here."

The cat settled toward the floor a little, stating as clearly as he could have done in words that, sick and weary as he was, he was willing to deal. Abruptly but carefully, Mickelsson stood up again and moved toward the kitchen. The cat watched. Mickelsson went to the cupboard and took out a cereal bowl, then went to the refrigerator for the milk-carton, poured milk into the bowl, holding the carton with two hands to check the trembling, then put the milk-carton away and carried the bowl into the livingroom, watching that it didn't slosh, never looking at the cat. He moved toward where the cat waited and, four feet away, set down the bowl of milk. The cat had had dealings with human beings before, it seemed. It watched the lowering of the bowl, the withdrawal of the human hands, then closed its eyes. It would drink in its own good time. Perhaps it was from cats, Mickelsson thought, that human beings had learned the proper way of dealing with gods.

"OK," Mickelsson said, and sat down again in the chair by the stereo.

The cat went on watching him, eyes little slits, never glancing at the bowl of milk. His tail was still now. Then he turned his head away and, after a moment, began to lick his paws as if he'd lived here all his life.

Mickelsson waited, cold gray light hanging around them like a fog. The cat went on licking its paws.

He thought of his ex-wife. "You're my dearest, dearest, dearest," she had said to him again and again, year after miserable year. Surely it had been true. "What a good, good face you have," she had said, touching him. He'd felt the same about her. He couldn't remember why the whole thing had gone wrong.

He turned to look out the window. Across the road there were two hunters starting down through the weeds in the direction of the pond. He closed his eyes.

He remembered for no reason something his son had once told him about whales, how the mother would sometimes swim for miles with the calf cradled under her flipper, not for protection, not for any reason but fondness.

Mickelsson, if he were a decent human being, would be a terrorist in defense of whales, yes. Nasty, self-hired gun to the untainted and lordly. But in fact he would never be a terrorist in defense of anything, not even a writer of vituperative attacks, like his mental life's hero, the mad malicious cackler, dancing, screaming, blowing the cover of anti-Semites, whorish piety, and worshippers of the Reich—Fritz, crazed Fritz, whose dream of perfection was the wise, serene saint, but who himself achieved only the glee of the buffoon, maddening the devils of the moral majority with his cracked and fake-cracked murderous clowning, wisdom full of pranks: "Why I Am So Wise"; "Why I Am So Clever"; "Why I Write Such Good Books." . . .

On the rug between the couch and the woodstove, the cat feigned sleep. Across the road, not far off, the hunters' guns began blasting, *POOM POOM POOM*, like cannons.

9

Alan Blassenheim and Brenda were the first to arrive, triggering Mickelsson's familiar guilt about Nugent. He should certainly have asked Nugent,
if he was going to ask them. The boy had a desperate need of friends, as
even Lawler had seen, and he'd certainly done everything to deserve
Peter Mickelsson's friendship. It was all very well to say, as Jessie had
said when he'd mentioned his problem—but Jessie's opinion was not
fully informed; he hadn't made clear to her the apparent extent of the
young man's desolation—"Look, Pete, it's a party." She searched his face,
then said tentatively, "If you're really convinced that this Nugent would
be a wet blanket, then better to leave him out." The question was, to
put it in the mincing language of an ethicist, what would the probable
consequences be when Nugent learned that Blassenheim had been invited while he, Nugent, had been excluded? One could give oneself a
thousand excuses and palliations. Friendship was not duty, one should
consider the good of the group as a whole, et cetera, et cetera—but the
trouble was that Nugent, for all his brilliance, would understand none
of those excuses in his heart: his portion of unhappiness would be increased. Mickelsson couldn't even say with perfect honesty that in deciding against Nugent he had fashionably (however stupidly) set his own
good above another's. He would probably enjoy having Nugent here,
getting to know him in a slightly more relaxed atmosphere. No, he'd
given in to the side of his heart that was herd-controlled: Nugent would
require an excess of attention, limiting Mickelsson's freedom to dispense
hostly blessings equally on all. Now, seeing Alan and Brenda drive up,
he knew that he had made a mistake.

But Mickelsson's self-excoriation was brief. By the time he opened
the door for Alan and Brenda, he was already smiling, Nugent's unhappiness almost banished from his mind. They'd started out early, they
explained, blushing and laughing as they took off their coats. They'd
expected to have difficulty finding the place, but the map (Jessie's work)
was foolproof, and after stalling for half an hour, driving around sightseeing, wasting precious gas, they'd given up at last and driven—sheepishly, as Mickelsson had seen—into his yard. The minute they'd stepped
out of the car, Mickelsson's cat had vanished as if by magic. Mickelsson,
nowhere near ready for guests—Jessie, who'd promised to help him, had

been delayed—fixed Alan and Brenda drinks and allowed them to assist. They laid the white tablecloth in the newly finished diningroom, set up the candles, put out plates and silverware, started the mulled wine, set out the liquor and ice. By that time others were beginning to arrive—the ever-merry Bryants, wearing matching shepherd coats, holly in their lapels, the Garrets, the Rogerses, the Blicksteins and their friend (pale as a ghost, evasive of eye, but smiling), the Tillsons (Jessie had insisted that they be invited, really for Ruth's sake), Jessie herself—in a purple coat baffling to Mickelsson, queer and untamable as something in a New York store window, and obviously expensive—and with Jessie, Kate Swisson, who was unable to drive a car. Her husband was not with her, away on another tour, she said. She wore a full-length mink over a Paris designer dress, and bore a fruitcake redolent of rum. In her startling attire she suddenly seemed to him—whether authentically or not he couldn't tell—a creature from another world, the purlieu of movie-stars, TV personalities, maybe opera singers. (He wondered if it was Kate's odd attire that had made Jessica come as a gypsy.) Kate Swisson's shyness struck him differently now from when he'd first met her. If she was chilly and aloof, even when she smiled and bobbed her head forward on its long, white stem, her distance from the ordinary, common world seemed to him now (to his annoyance) perhaps not so much helpless as Olympian. The SUNY-Binghamton Music Department was supposed to be outstanding. It had two Tchaikovsky Prize winners, one of the finest opera departments in America—so they claimed—and a history of launching great chamber groups (and losing them)—the Guarneri, the Lenox. . . . Perhaps Ms. Swisson had a right to her mink. Whether or not that was so, he disliked her. She seemed to know it, smiling harder and harder at him, widening her gazelle eyes more and more, sinuating her long neck left, right, forward with increasing meekness. "Good to see you," he said, suddenly conscious that while his mind drifted he'd been glowering. He took the cake from her with his right hand, then stepped around her and, with his left, caught the collar of her mink as one would the loose shoulder-skin of a kitten.

"Thank you," she breathed, turning her head around at him, submissively smiling. ("Gratitude," says Nietzsche, "is a mild form of revenge.")

There was a knock at the door and he stepped over to answer it, still carrying the coat and cake. It was the graduate-student contingent, Wolters and Stearns, Ms. Cohen and Ms. Orinsky. "Come in! Come in!"

"This must be the place!" Christmassy laughter.

One moment, from Mickelsson's point of view, the house had been quiet, elegantly—maybe even exquisitely—prepared, the next it was abuzz with talk and movement, Edie Bryant raving about the Christmas decorations—"Nicer than the ones down in Rich's Department Store, that's in

Atlanta" (as she spoke, stealing the floor from Jessie's art, the candles and ornaments were instantly diminished to mere prettiness)—Mabel Garret drifting here and there in stony silence, picking up everything and looking at the underside, presumably to see who'd made it, Phil Bryant and Blickstein heatedly arguing over President-elect Ronald Reagan's proposed tax cut and decontrol of oil, Jessie and Kate Swisson talking earnestly about Binghamton child-care centers, though neither of them had children. (*Living*, he corrected himself, and fought a shock of gloom.) It struck Mickelsson, no doubt unjustly—he was liking Kate Swisson less and less—that she was coyly faking interest in having a baby. If he was right, Jessie was not fooled: sweetly cool, smiling, regal. He could not help feeling that some of the coolness was meant for him, though he'd given her no cause. He imagined his old friend Luther saying, with that scorn he'd always been a master of, "What a child you are!" "Old fart," Mickelsson whispered. Mabel Garret's dark eyes turned slyly to meet his.

Jessie wore a black floor-length dress with a low neckline and layers of gold chain. Mickelsson, when she'd come in, had squeezed both her hands, but though she'd smiled, she'd been reserved, like someone arriving at a party after hearing bad news. Had someone told her about Donnie? He could read nothing in her eyes. After the first instant, he decided on another, more likely explanation. That she took nothing for granted between himself and her was a kindness to him, a surprising bit of generosity; yet at some point—never mind what point, precisely—it began to verge on peculiar for a woman to hold a man still free, not responsible for the drift of her feelings, not to mention his own. His heart had leaped at first sight of her, Donnie Matthews and her troubles momentarily banished even farther from his mind than Michael Nugent. "What a lovely house," Jessie had said, more to Geoffrey Tillson than to him, as if she'd never before seen it. Was she ashamed of Mickelsson? She went over to study the Christmas tree ornaments she herself had picked out. Mickelsson had felt, in spite of himself, hurt. But then, as he was leading the whole crowd through the house, showing off his work of restoration, all but the diningroom, his eyes and Jessie's met, and Jessie winked like a conspirator, for the first time tonight showing affection. Bafflement on bafflement! A little later they'd accidentally come together in the doorway between the livingroom and the study, the doorway over which Alan Blassenheim and Brenda had hung mistletoe. They'd realized their predicament the same instant—they could feel the watching eyes— then abruptly had laughed, again the same instant, and had kissed briefly, like teen-agers. Her scent and the softness of her lips made his heart crash, his id, in its dark, grimy pen, bleating dolefully. "Merry Christmas," Jessie said, patting Mickelsson's shoulder, sisterly, then moving away.

"Should we light the menorah?" Mickelsson asked, catching her hand.

She gave him a look, a half-smile. Apparently there was some trick to it. Perhaps one couldn't do it without a rabbi. "Whatever," she said, and shrugged.

Tom Garret came out to the kitchen and set his mulled wine down to help Mickelsson chop onions. Tillson came too and stood by the outside kitchen door, drinking and smiling, his humped back to the woodpile in the snow. He said nothing, but eagerly laughed at all Garret and Mickelsson said, laughed as if he'd never had so interesting a time in his life. His laugh was like an old ram's.

The Blicksteins' young friend appeared at the kitchen door—gray of face, dark circles under her eyes—and said, "Mmm! Smells good in here! Can I help?"

"Ladies' night off," Mickelsson said, "but you can keep us company." Garret laid down the vegetable knife and fussily spooned the chopped onions into the waiting bowl, then stepped back—a quick little dance step—out of the way. Mickelsson pushed into the oven a heavy pan of pastitsio, made for him in Binghamton by the man who ran the Greek restaurant, checked the temperature setting and closed the oven door. The kitchen bloomed with food smells. He wiped sweat from his neck with a paper towel, then from the upper oven took a pan of hors d'oeuvres, which he quickly spatulaed out onto a plate.

"I could take it around for you," the young woman said.

He almost resisted; then, catching the look in her eyes, put the plate in her hands. "Thank you! Wonderful!" he said. "That does make it easier!" He gave her his crazed grin.

"How long does that take?" Tom Garret asked, uncrossing his arms for a moment to point in at the pastitsio and smiling.

It was interesting that Garret didn't know. He was one of those little Napoleons who give the impression of being thoroughly informed on every subject—the Iranian power-struggle, Queen Elizabeth's affairs of the heart, boat-building, tax law, Gödel's proof, Sumerian astronomy. . . . "Forty-five minutes or so," Mickelsson said, "assuming it doesn't catch fire, so we have to start over. Lot of oil on it."

"Forty-five minutes! That fast!" Garret said, pleased to have this new information. He recrossed his arms and tipped his head.

Garret's wife Mabel was standing at the kitchen door now—silent, as usual, remote from the rest of them as a woods creature, her head ducked, drawn in, her fingertips exploring the scraped place on the door where Mickelsson had scratched off the hex sign. What she was thinking no one could have guessed, probably not Garret himself. Somewhere beyond her in the livingroom Kate Swisson laughed falsely, tinkle tinkle tinkle, as she might laugh in a song, and Mabel Garret looked up, as openly curious as a child, black eyes widening, looking in the direction of the singer. Mickelsson was tempted to snatch a look, hardly aware of why it interested him; but there were more hors d'oeuvres to be gotten out, and anyway he'd be in there with the others soon enough. From the far end of the livingroom, or perhaps from the study, came the opening notes of a Christmas carol, maybe three or four singers, the grad students, no doubt. Someone was playing a violin. Then suddenly Dean Blickstein was planted at his elbow, as if he'd just materialized there, like Mephistopheles, smiling so hard his eyes were slits, holding a glass in each muscular little hand. "Ice in the refrigerator, Pete?" he asked. "I thought I'd just freshen up everybody's drink."

"Some in the refrigerator, some in the livingroom in the ice-bucket, and some in the plastic bag in the sink," Mickelsson said, and pointed toward the sink with his chin. Tom Garret backed off, grinning like a child who knows he's in the way, then retreated into the livingroom.

"Ah!" Blickstein said and, pivoting, went over to the sink. He nodded at Tillson, a little duck of the head like a wrestler's feint, and again the muscular face punched out a grin. "Holding up through the cries and alarums?" Blickstein asked.

Geoffrey Tillson chuckled, his head going quickly up and down like the front end of a jitney, and he stretched his glass toward Blickstein as if accepting a toast. Tillson had on a dark pinstripe, tailored and expensive; he looked like Rumpelstiltskin dressed for an audience with the Pope.

"What's it this time?" Mickelsson asked, about to step into the livingroom with his plate of hors d'oeuvres.

"Sociology, what else?" Blickstein said, half turning to face Mickelsson as his two hands, unwatched, deftly filled the glasses with ice. "Seems the Philosophy Department's not so good on Karl Marx. Sociology Department would like to teach the course themselves, get it right for once." He laughed. "Also the course in Contemporary."

"That's crazy!" Mickelsson said.

"You don't have to argue with *me*," Blickstein said, amused by Mickelsson's blush of anger, "and I doubt that Geoffrey here will give you much argument either." He winked at Tillson, then came away from the sink, Tillson silently laughing, head bouncing, behind him.

"What a bunch," Mickelsson said. "Poor Jessie!"

" 'Poor Jessie' is right," Blickstein said, and shook his head. For a moment the muscular smile froze, as if the dean knew more than he felt at liberty to say. Then the smile warmed again, and he shook his head once more and said, "They're feeling their oats—their 'minority appeal,' all the usual business."

"You're suggesting—?"

"Well, you know," Blickstein said, "they *would* like a solid Marxist front. They need it, really." He laughed and winked, then gave Mickelsson another sharp look. "If you asked me to predict, I'd say they'll move to get rid of her before the year's out."

Mickelsson stared, for an instant not sure of his bearings. Blickstein wouldn't be betting with such confidence if the process weren't already under way. "They can't do it, can they?"

Just inside the livingroom, at the edge of the circle where Blassenheim held forth, Tom Garret turned his best ear, apparently tuning in on Blickstein's words, though he continued to smile as if with interest at Blassenheim. Brenda Winburn, to Blassenheim's left, stood pressed up close to the young man's elbow, touching him.

"Theoretically they can't, and morally they can't," Blickstein said, and raised the glass in his right hand to give the air a little poke with it, as if ending the conversation with a period.

"But that's not an answer," Mickelsson said, refusing to let Blickstein past him into the livingroom. Tillson came up behind Blickstein, grinning, to listen.

"Pig-in-a-blanket!" Edie Bryant cried, almost a squeal of delight. "Did you make them yoahself or ah they the *frozen* kind?"

Mickelsson held the plate toward her and ignored the question.

"Well," Blickstein said, and hesitated, obliquely smiling. One could see that he was teased toward launching a lecture full of inside information—a sport he relished. "I guess you might say they've got us hostage, Pete. You have to remember the larger picture. The whole university system's under fire these days." He cocked his head, grinning, and looked up at the corner of the room. "Governor Carey comes in at the end of every year with his six-hundred-million-dollar revenue bonuses, and the people whoop with joy. He's no dummy, you know. He understands that if you close down a couple of mental hospitals, or two or three university campuses, overcrowd the prisons, even squeeze a few police and fire departments, you'll get a lot of people mad but you make a lot more people happy. He's figured out the leak in the Hobbesian theory of civilization. Self-interest does not necessarily lead to fine police departments, hospitals, and schools. It can as easily lead to some old man grinning like a monkey, stuffing his forty-dollar tax-rebate into his mattress. So he's got us on the run. From the whole university system he'll be cutting out *one-half the budget* this next year alone." Blickstein smiled as if that explained everything.

"Which means?" Mickelsson said, squinting. His wrists and knuckles ached. The murdered man's wife stood exactly in the middle of the livingroom, smiling fixedly, listening. In her two hands she held the empty hors d'oeuvres plate.

"Well," Blickstein said, as if surprised that Mickelsson couldn't see it, "here we are with these people we brought in—with the noblest of intentions—in the Holy Roller campus-under-fire days. Whatever their virtues or defects, they're *here*. In force. Well, so now we're reaping the whirlwind."

"Go on," Mickelsson said.

Blickstein shrugged, grinning sadly. "Their position's very strong. They can embarrass us, you see. Why?" He raised his eyebrows and, shifting his grip on the glass, held up one stubby finger. "*A*. They appeal to minority students—and they may be right that it's partly a function of their program's politico-philosophical orientation. Poor people always want clear, fast answers, preferably pious and rich with potential for bloodshed. No disrespect for the poor, you understand—far from it! But the stomach's an impatient organ, or, to put it another way, the injustice has always gone on too long already. So an attack on the Soc gang is a blow against the poor, you follow? And not only do we not dare touch them, we don't even dare make too much point of their existence, at least not if we're smart; because *B*."—he held up a second stubby finger—"they know how embarrassed we'd be if the taxpayers were to learn, in this conservative day and age—Reagan's 'moral majority' and all that—that our university's got a whole department, with the exception of one member, that's 'pinko.' Stirs visions of Iran, Afghanistan. This is no time for university scandals. We need every penny we can get from our friends the taxpayers, and you can be sure our new man in the White House will make it as hard as he can." Blickstein smiled at his audience, pleased to have made things clear but not taking undue credit, a servant of the general good. "So all in all," he said, "it seems safe to say that, when the time comes, we'll negotiate."

"I see," Mickelsson said, biting off his words. "In short, you'll let them fire her."

"I didn't say that," Blickstein said, half grinning, turtling his head in, lifting the ice-filled glasses up to shoulder level. "You know me better than that, Pete."

That was true, Mickelsson thought, pouting. He glanced across the livingroom at Jessica, who stood poised, smiling and talking with Mabel Garret and Ruth Tillson; then he glanced over his shoulder at Tillson, just behind him in the kitchen. It was a depressing thought that this man he scorned might soon be his ally, and Blickstein, whom he liked, his enemy.

"It's a mess, hey?" Tillson said, and nervously laughed. He sounded angry.

Mickelsson nodded, then remembered the plate in his hands and moved into the crowd.

The young woman whose husband had been murdered sat alone on the couch, the empty hors d'oeuvres plate on the coffeetable. When Mickelsson leaned down toward her with his filled plate, she shook her head. "Can I fix your drink?" Mickelsson asked. She'd hardly touched it, in fact. Again she shook her head and, for a second, smiled.

"Thank you for asking me tonight," she said.

"My pleasure."

"It's a wonderful house—and a wonderful party. It's always nice when there are students."

He glanced over his shoulder. Beyond the partly closed study door, the grad students were belting out "God Rest Ye Merry Gentlemen." It must be the historian Freddy Rogers that was playing the oddly mournful violin. He was missing; so was his wife. Mickelsson bent his knees, squatting down beside the woman. Her hair, he registered only now, was quite astonishingly beautiful, dark with red glints, like French-polished antique cherry.

"I'm afraid I was difficult the last time we met," she said.

"My fault, don't apologize. I wasn't aware, at the time, of—" They both looked down.

After a moment she said, "Susquehanna seems like such a peaceful place." She smiled, but tears had welled up in her eyes.

He could only study her, uncertain what she meant.

"I mean," she said, blinking, then touching first one eye then the other with the knuckle of her right index finger, "he was working on something here, you know. Looking into something."

Mickelsson nodded. "I'd heard that. Scientific project?"

"Oh no, I don't think so," she said, and glanced at Mickelsson timidly. "Something much more . . ." She searched for the word.

Gently, faintly ashamed of his prying, he asked, "You have no idea what?"

She shook her head, briefly smiled, touched her eyes again. "I'm sorry," she said softly.

"Don't be, for heaven's sakes. Please!"

As if she'd been carefully watching it all, Gretchen Blickstein drifted over to them, sat down beside the young woman, and took an hors d'oeuvre. "Lovely party, Peter," she said. She was built like a pigeon and had the same alert, unsentimental eyes.

"Thank you," he said, and began to straighten up.

The young woman said, "I know what he was afraid of down here. I overheard him talking on the telephone one night—he stopped right away when I came in. I don't know who he was talking to. He said something about a fat man."

"You mentioned this to the police?" Mickelsson asked, no longer meeting her eyes.

"I did, and they went to talk with the fat man, I think. It seems nothing came of it. But I know—*I know for certain*—"

"Agnes, dear," Gretchen Blickstein said, "don't! Please don't do this to yourself."

"I know. I'm sorry." She bowed her head, then put her hand over her eyes. Gretchen and Mickelsson exchanged looks; then Mickelsson straightened up.

Turning, Mickelsson said to Jessie, whom he found at his elbow, "Holding up all right, Jess?"

"Don't I always?" she asked with a small laugh. Her eyes looked tired, and the high cheekbones seemed sharper, more Indian, than usual. She took an hors d'oeuvre. The Tillsons and Mabel Garret hovered just beyond Jessie, timidly eavesdropping, like people not sure they were really invited. Tillson must have followed Mickelsson from the kitchen. Still trying to make friends.

"You do bear up, I must admit," he said. The grief in his voice startled him.

She gave him a look—angry?—then glanced at Agnes Warren. With the two smallest fingers of her right hand—in the others she held her hors d'oeuvre, and in her left hand her glass—she touched Mickelsson's arm, drawing him away. "Have you seen any more of the Spragues?" she asked.

He floundered, then remembered. The old people. Still he hesitated, trying to think what made her bring it up. Small talk, because she'd overheard Blickstein's dire predictions? Was she trying to make him look good in front of his department chairman? (Tillson was slinking off toward the Christmas tree to make some adjustment.)

"I haven't been back," Mickelsson said. "I suppose I should."

"I feel I ought to have done something," she said. "I hate it that he has to walk to town for groceries."

"Except when he flies," Mickelsson said.

"Oh, come off it, Pete." She looked smaller, like someone who's been scolded.

He touched her hand, trying to make out what was the matter. "You're right, I should figure out a way to help him."

"Perhaps he'll be too proud to take it," Ruth Tillson said eagerly, hoping it might be so.

Mickelsson looked at her, surprised to discover that she was stupid. "Perhaps," he said, and, with a glance of farewell to Jessie, still baffled by what she might be up to, what the devil she was feeling, he moved toward the circle where Blassenheim was holding forth. The boy was taller and broader of shoulder than everyone around him, his hair and features more burnished and alive, as if he were a visitor from some younger, healthier planet.

"Hors d'oeuvres?" Mickelsson asked, edging between Brenda Winburn and Phil Bryant. Both of them reached to the plate. Brenda's eyes were stormy, though she smiled as Mickelsson leaned near.

"I'll tell you the problem with that," Garret was saying, wagging his finger at Blassenheim and grinning, then taking a step toward him, unconsciously invading his space. "It's an admirable aim—*know thyself*, and so on—and in theory it's the only way to figure out values: look inside yourself and figure out what you are, what's possible and what isn't, then think out the necessary ideals for human beings." He was talking excitedly, a gesture for every phrase. Mostly he seemed to be arranging imaginary pots on imaginary shelves. Edie Bryant watched him with a fixed smile and widened eyes, pretending to think all he said was far, far beyond her.

Mickelsson shifted away a little. At times, especially when he held forth at parties, Garret allowed himself a surprisingly amateurish sloppiness, a Nietzchean "Let's try it!" that could look a little like a parody of Mickelsson's own method. It was silly that Mickelsson should permit himself annoyance, fond as he was of Garret. Yet he couldn't easily miss the fact that what he felt, watching Tom flail in, was undoubtedly similar to what a man like Geoffrey Tillson must feel, given his cool certainties, when listening to Mickelsson himself. If there was a difference, it wouldn't be evident at a glance to Tillson. That was what made Tillson so infuriating—that and the honor he somehow wrung out of the philosophy Establishment. Bookless as a jaybird, he'd nevertheless served on all the important A.P.A. committees. Somewhere on all the journal mastheads you'd find E. G. Tillson's name. He was on all the right sides, the sides that had won the day. For all one said, he knew the demolishing opposition in advance, opposition arguments one would never get time to isolate and, with careful, steady tweezers, unpack. One could always buttress one's ego with one's books, of course. But as Mickelsson often said when drunk—but by God he meant it—the first principle of Establishment philosophy was, "Never, never look carefully at another man's book!" Tillson, of course, had even less interest in Garret's ideas than in Mickelsson's. He moved off, smiling like a ninny, humming off tune, in the direction of the music.

None of the others, it seemed, had reservations about Garret's wit. The singer, Kate Swisson, listened with her head slanted far over, as if fascinated, gazelle eyes wide, her long narrow fingers draped casually over Blassenheim's arm, her soft lips puckered as if for a kiss. Hardly aware that his gloom was deepening, Mickelsson bulldozed the plate toward her, urging her to take an hors d'oeuvre. "Oh!" she said, smiling brightly, and, lifting her hand from Blassenheim's arm, wide eyes unblinking, carefully took the nearest on the plate.

"The trouble is," Garret said, twisting the cap onto an invisible pot, "trying to look deep inside ourselves is like trying to see the monster through the silt of Loch Ness."

Phil Bryant, with a floor-grabbing lift of the head, cleft chin thrust forward, tried to toss in a remark—"Wolves, thine old inhabitants!"—but Garret's rush buried it. "It looked very hopeful in the early days of psychoanalysis," Garret said, "nice, neat system of 'super-ego,' 'ego,' 'id,' 'conscious' and 'unconscious,' and so forth and so on. 'Extrovert,' 'introvert.' But I'll tell you what modern experiments seem to show." He pointed to his head, then to his chest, and grinned. "No connection." He held his hand toward Blassenheim, palm out, preventing anyone from breaking in. "I'll tell you a typical experiment. We take Brenda here and we wire her up—cardiograph, encephalograph, rapid-eye-movement tapes, and so forth and so on—and we put her in a room; then we take Katie here and put her in another room and give her random electric shocks"— he leaned forward quickly and touched her, as if to relieve her anxiety— "nothing that hurts, just enough that she feels 'em, right?—and we tell Brenda to write down guesses of when the shocks are being administered. You know what we find?" He grinned, his chin pulled back. "What we find is that all of her guesses are wrong, but according to the cardiograph and so forth her *body* knew exactly when Katie was getting zapped! So you see? No connection! What's happened is, we've evolved this massive super-ape brain—ape brain layered over snake brain layered over who-knows-what, each one foreign to the next, just foundation; no more real connection than there is between the bird's egg and the nest. I exaggerate, right? OK, OK. Point is, simpler brains may possibly know a lot of things we can't, things of certain kinds, the kinds of things Brenda here knows with her body. But once you've evolved the super-ape brain, well, except on rare occasions, what it does is it locks the body out. Good-bye, Eden!" With two fingers Garret showed the turning of a key in a lock. Lightly, merrily, he threw the key away. "Any way you look at it it comes out the same: you just can't get to the bottom of things. Matter, for instance." He leaned forward, grinning, to block interruption. "We're made of matter, right?" He grinned more widely, delighted by the strangeness of the universe. "Hey, listen, down to a certain point we are, but then we get to what's known as the sub-atomic particles, which in fact aren't particles or waves or numbers or anything else we can sensibly think of; they're just some kind of craziness, maybe Biblical demons." He laughed. "Neutrinos, for instance, neither matter nor energy. I can't even understand 'em when I find 'em in a book! Or quarks—we're told there are three quarks to a proton, and one quark is thirty times as massive as a proton. Help! How am I supposed to know *that* part of myself? Can't do it, that's all! Yet it could be there's something very powerful down there—Tillich's 'ground of being,' maybe. God Himself! We know there are some pretty wacky things in the world, 'More than your philosophy dreams of, Horatio,' "—he winked at the English professor, Bryant, and sprinted on— "the shroud of Turin, which could be, according to one theory, the kind of picture that's left by an atomic explosion, like the shadows burned into the concrete in Hiroshima and Nagasaki. Or there are, apparently, people who can move objects without touching them, even set walls on fire—or out-of-the-body experiences, 'Oobs,' as they call 'em, the kind of thing they've been documenting like crazy out at Stanford. And psychics, good old psychics, like the woman at Bank of America in San Francisco who writes down the addresses of people who've passed bad checks. It's all there inside us, in some sense it *is* us—that's the theory—and maybe the

Hindus are right that if we do the right yoga we can see it, grab right hold of it; but from a Western point of view it's as separate from us as the planet we stand on, we've just got to *ride* it, hopefully enjoy the ride." He turned, briefly glowing, a phenomenon himself, pleased with his oration, and looked at Mickelsson's scowling face, then Phil Bryant's absent-mindedly interested smile.

"I must say," Bryant said, "you don't seem to offer much hope for an eager young philosopher!" He laughed. So did Blassenheim, but with a gloomy look in Mickelsson's direction.

"In my view," Garret said, "philosophy's like any other human activity —just a craft." He raised his open hand as if setting a bird free. "For the kind of people who naturally take to it, it's a joy to work at, just like pottery, or leathercraft, target-practice—whatever. But the old idea that philosophers are doing something huge and wonderful, well, it just ain't so, or anyway not anymore. There's a great pleasure to be gotten out of getting a few ideas right—just as there's pleasure in getting your garden to grow, or in painting a picture of it. But it's no big deal. You want to be a big deal—" He turned to Blassenheim, grinning, threw his head back and reached up to put his hand on the young man's shoulder. "You want to change the world and be remembered, my friend? You want women to admire you and old school chums to say 'I knew him *when*'? Be Hitler! Be Joseph Stalin! You don't need philosophy to be good—common sense and a little common luck will get you by. But take ordinary nastiness and push it to the limit, turn common misunderstanding into a *great* misunderstanding, a profound stupidity—*that*, my friend, they will write *books* about!"

Blassenheim's smile had no pleasure in it, though if he knew the grounds on which Garret was teasing him, he didn't show it. "I guess I understand what you mean, sort of," he said—he was carefully not showing discomfiture at the hand on his shoulder, either, maybe even felt none, alas for him; a gentle soul to the sub-atomic core—"but isn't it true that if you wrote a good enough philosophy book you could answer in advance anything a Hitler might say?"

"It's already been written a million times," Garret said. "Nobody reads it. Out of print." He beamed. "Ninety-nine cents at Barnes and Noble."

"You mean, like"—Blassenheim searched, then suggested—"the Bible, Spinoza, Kant?"

Jessica joined the group. Mickelsson felt her there before he saw her.

"That kind of thing," Garret said. "Or *Peanuts, Beetle Bailey, As the World Turns*. People know pretty well what good is; they just don't care that much. Maybe when they're young they do—marching against the draft, throwing themselves down on logging roads to save the redwoods. . . . But it's hard to keep up your interest, and these days especially, some reason. Churches can no longer do it for you—at one extreme too complex and sophisticated, full of self-doubts, and at the other extreme too dumb. And novels—when was the last time you read a novel that made you feel young again? But a Hitler, or even a Khomeini—that wakes people up, makes 'em virtuous!"

"Inexpensive virtue," Mickelsson said.

"Listen, these days just a picture of a picture of a virtue, I'll buy it."

They all laughed. In Mickelsson's head, their sounds began to echo, as from a vault.

"Peter," Tillson said, materializing at Mickelsson's elbow, leaning into the group in apparent distress, "I think something might be burning."

"Good Christ, I forgot all about it," Mickelsson said, and hurried to the kitchen. Orange light leaped like a movie on the far kitchen wall, projected through the glass oven door. It was not the pastitsio, luckily; only the oil that had dripped over onto the oven. In another minute, the whole thing would have been an inferno.

With the help of Brenda, Jessie, and the Blicksteins' friend—he let no one else see—he cut the pastitsio and set it out on three large plates on the table, then set out the spinach salad, rolls and butter, white asparagus, red wine, and ice-water. Jessie approached the table—she seemed to float —with a lighted taper. When the candles were lighted and Mickelsson could think of nothing more to be done, he dimmed the center-light— he had a brief memory of midnight communion in his childhood—and began herding the crowd into the newly finished diningroom. It had until now been closed off, and it was a startling departure from the rest of the house: white plaster walls, black exposed beams, carefully wedged-in frames and casements, handmade doors and windows of cherry, on the walls above the two old walnut sideboards, dark red tapestries from Mexico, and framed photographs by his son. One would have thought it had cost him a fortune, this room. It had not—though it had cost him more than he could afford. Two hundred dollars to the farmer with the sawmill, for wood. All the rest he'd gotten, at a bargain, from the basement of Owen's store and the local antique store—neither of which, so far, he'd paid.

As he threw open the doors, revealing the feast, the sparkling white cloth, dazzling water and wine glasses, glinting china and silver, tall, fluttering candles over hills of holly—another of Jessie's contributions—a great, breathy *Ah!* went up, almost religious. No one moved for a moment, their faces bright in the candlelight, caught off guard. Jessie stood beside him, her hand on his arm, smiling as if the whole thing were in her honor. Across from them Brenda Winburn stood bent slightly forward at the waist, her hand in Alan Blassenheim's, her face aglow, eyes reflecting the candleflames, her entire being momentarily transformed—her tan darker, blond hair more brilliant—to an at once Mediterranean and unearthly beauty. Kate Swisson bent her long neck, chin lifted, her red lips eagerly smiling, to sniff the food. "Isn't it sensational?" she asked, turning to the couple. Janet Cohen the ever-ready, the one who'd read his book before taking his course, hurried down the table, her eye on the red plush velvet chair.

Now they all began to move toward chairs. "Sit anywhere," he said, kingly, "anywhere you like"—realizing as he spoke that it was a mistake; he should certainly have set out placecards. Jessie should have warned him. Yet they all made the best of it, laughing, choosing chairs, deflecting attention from his error by commenting on the crystal, the Christmas wreath centerpiece, the pastitsio. The graduate students, except for Janet, chose last.

Mabel Garret came in after everyone else, as if for some reason she'd been resisting—for it was not at the back of the crowd that she came but after the crowd, when it was no longer possible to stay in the livingroom—and after standing for a moment in her black dress, looking in at them, her frightened smile fluttering like a candle, her left hand groping unconsciously toward the doorframe, she quite suddenly widened her eyes, as if someone had touched her from behind, and opened her mouth for a cry that did not come. Mickelsson too was aware of something strange, an inexplicable cold wave, as if a door had been blown open in a nearby room. Tom Garret dropped the napkin he'd been in the act of picking up, jumped back, almost knocking his chair over, and tried to get to his wife, but he wasn't quick enough. There was a sound of rustling cloth, then a hollow thud, perhaps her head hitting, and she lay on the floor unconscious.

Mickelsson was the first to reach her after Garret. "Stay back," he commanded, pushing away whoever or whatever pressed over him, "give her room!"

"Is there a hospital around here?" Garret asked gravely. Already he was lifting her in his arms.

"What happened?" Edie Bryant called. "I didn't see it!"

"I bet it's low blood pressure," Ruth Tillson said. "*I* used to have that."

Hardly aware that he was doing it, Mickelsson moved Ruth out of the way with one arm, then helped Garret carry his wife into the livingroom, then into the kitchen, heading for the back door, the quickest route to where the cars were parked. Tillson had managed to get ahead of them to hold the door open. Jessie ran after them with an afghan. In the starlight her skin seemed stretched over her skull, elegant and alarming. "Wrap this around her, Pete. It's cold out." She draped the afghan over Mickelsson's shoulder. "I'll call ahead and make sure the doctor's there." He nodded.

"It's all right," Garret was saying loudly, over and over, to his unconscious wife, to himself, to the friends around them. "You people stay here. We'll call from the hospital, let you know what we find out." Then, to Mickelsson: "We'll take my car, it's behind the others. I'll give you the keys after we get her in."

"I'll bring your coat," Miss Orinsky told Garret, then ran back to the house.

"Alan, you come with us," Mickelsson said quietly, catching Blassenheim's eye. "Help Tom hold her while I drive."

Blassenheim nodded, one startled jerk of the head, then hurried around them to open the back door of Garret's Plymouth. When they had her inside, her head on Garret's lap, Garret fished the keys from the overcoat Miss Orinsky had just given him and handed them to Mickelsson.

"Be careful!" Jessie said at the car window, bending down to look in. Her skin was waxy gray in the dim light draped from above the back door. For an instant her high-cheekboned, wide-mouthed face subsumed the world. On the dark lawn beyond her, snow was falling. The Blicksteins and Bryants stood half in, half out of the kitchen, their visages dramatic —Edie above all, drawn to her full height, solemn, gray and white, like a death god. The others were at the window to their left, pressing against the glass like children. Mickelsson got the engine started and realized only now that he wished Jessie were going to be there to help. As he backed out, she was already on her way into the house to phone the hospital.

"What do you think happened?" Mickelsson asked as they reached the dark, icy trees at the edge of town.

No answer came from the back seat, and he glanced into the rear-view mirror. Garret was looking straight ahead. If he'd heard Mickelsson's question, he showed no sign.

For half an hour Mickelsson and Alan Blassenheim sat leafing through magazines in the chilly, dimly lit waiting room at the end of the Emergency Room hallway, an enlarged section of the hallway itself, listening to night sounds inside and outside—faraway footsteps, the clicking of fluorescent lights, distant trucks, voices of strangers. Except for a dark-bearded, early-middle-aged man in a brown coat and brown trousers who kept flipping through magazines in a distraught, bewildered way, licking his thumb each time he turned a page, they were alone in the waiting room—practically alone in the hospital, for that matter: there was the stocky, sixty-year-old nurse who'd met them at the door, chattering and solicitous—"Poor little thing! Wait here, please"—and the blond young doctor who'd come ten minutes later—"Tom Mowry," he said, holding out his hand. They saw no one else. "People complain that the hospital's not adequately staffed," the doctor said. He pulled his coat off and hung it on a coatrack. "They don't know what we go through just to keep up what we've got. Three of the doctors here have pacemakers. If they had any brains they'd be retired." Then, rubbing his hands together like a craps shooter, he went into the room where the nurse had put Mabel—conscious now, lying with her eyes closed, her husband seated beside her—nodded a quick, apologetic dismissal to Mickelsson and Alan, then closed the door behind him. They heard voices, and after a few minutes the nurse came out, went down the hall to a room at the far end, then returned to the room where the doctor and the Garrets were. Mickelsson called his house and talked with Gretchen Blickstein, then briefly with Jessie, telling them what little news there was, that Mabel was conscious and the doctor was examining her. Everything was fine at the house, Jessie said. The party was going ahead full-steam, the guests all still in the diningroom. Then Mickelsson sat in the waiting room again, fallen out of time, as he always felt in hospitals—half reading, occasionally glancing down the hall, the rest of the time half listening to voices in his mind, memories or dreams.

Once or twice when he looked up he saw that, in the darkest corner of the waiting room, the man in brown was looking at him, his mouth slightly open, in his eyes a puzzled, troubled look, as if he were thinking of asking Mickelsson some question. Then, changing his mind, the man would straighten his black, coarse hair with his fingers, and look at his knees.

Alan Blassenheim sat bent forward, a *Sports Illustrated* open in his lap, clearly a magazine of no interest to him, though apparently the others were even worse. Each time he turned a page he did it with an irritable slap, then grabbed the edge of the next page as if to turn that too, but on second thought went on reading. Whenever Mickelsson shifted in his chair, however slightly, Alan would look up to make sure all was well.

Mickelsson's eyes began to ache—the only lights were the lamp in the corner by Blassenheim and the dim light, a circular fluorescent, overhead —and he gave up for a while, dropping the tattered *Newsweek* back on the table and lowering his eyelids. He heard—or perhaps only saw, periph- erally—the man in brown stir in his chair. Mickelsson glanced over at him and saw him rising, as if with slight difficulty, like a man in light shock, soundlessly moving his lips. The man wandered down the hallway, his steps almost silent—probably looking for a men's room. Near the end of the hallway he opened a door and went in.

Mickelsson once more closed his eyes. He could hear faint, faraway machine sounds—pumps, furnace vents, refrigerators perhaps. Now and then Blassenheim turned a page. Otherwise, silence. He thought of Blick- stein smiling with interest as he predicted Jessie's advancing doom, and at the thought he felt a muscle in his face jerk. He heard someone groan, not far away, then realized that, in a kind of doze, he himself had made the sound. He glanced at Blassenheim, and their eyes met. They nodded like strangers on a train; then Blassenheim went back to his reading.

He decided to get up and walk. There seemed no one anywhere, though it stood to reason that on the floors above this one, the first floor, there would be sleeping patients in room after room. Looking in through a windowed door near the end of the hallway he saw the brown-coated man from the waiting room, seated at a glossy table, poring over a book. He had more books piled at his elbow. Mickelsson frowned, wondering what queer drama he was getting a glimpse of. He would no doubt never know. He found the men's room and went in. When he came out again, the man in brown was at the waiting-room end of the hallway, looking out at snow, or looking at his reflection in the glass of the door.

Finally the door of the room where Mabel lay came swooshing open and Dr. Mowry and Tom Garret came out. While Tom came over, the doctor smiled distantly and went to another room farther down the hallway, near where the man in brown had been. Blassenheim dropped his magazine on the table and stood up.

"Everything's OK," Garret said and smiled. "They're keeping her overnight, just to watch her."

"I take it you'll stay with her?" Mickelsson asked. "I'm sure we can find somebody to look after your kids."

"No need," Garret said, and raised his hand. "I'll run home and see to things, then come get her in the morning. She's asleep now—she'll sleep right through. He gave her a sedative."

"I'd be happy to babysit," Blassenheim said. He stretched his chin, self-conscious.

"Really no need," Garret said. He picked up his suitcoat from the chair-arm where he'd dropped it, then got his overcoat from the rack. Blassenheim went around behind to help him on with them.

"So did they figure out what it was?" Mickelsson asked.

"Yes and no," Garret said. He took a step toward the door, then paused. "Is this the way we came in?"

Mickelsson nodded, and the three of them moved together toward the door. The man in brown continued to gaze out, a book under his arm. He did not turn as they drew near. "And what was it?" Mickelsson asked.

"Well, it seems she 'saw' something," Garret said, and gave them an evasive grin. Mickelsson held the door. They went out into the cold.

"What d'ya mean?" Blassenheim asked.

Garret threw out his hands in an exaggerated shrug. "Believe me, if I knew what I meant I'd tell you. She doesn't know herself—I mean, she *does* know, but . . ."

Mickelsson stopped walking. "What?" he said.

Now Garret and Blassenheim stopped too. Garret's face was still smiling, frozen. "I really don't want to talk about it," he said. When they went on waiting, not accepting it, he reached out and touched Mickelsson's arm. "She saw a funeral, all right?" He shook his head. "She walked in that room where all of us were standing and instead of seeing us she saw these two people holding a funeral all by themselves." He laughed.

Mickelsson and Blassenheim waited.

Garret looked down, raising his fist to his lips. After a minute he said, "She took some Darvon earlier tonight—malrotated colon. The doctor thinks it may have been the combination of Darvon and alcohol. That could explain the fainting, too."

"I see," Mickelsson said. As he opened the car-door for Garret, he asked, "What kind of funeral, did she say? Who had died?"

"A child," Garret said.

Back at the house they said nothing to the others—it was Garret's wish—of what Mabel thought she'd seen; but in the kitchen Mickelsson told Jessie what Garret had said.

She looked at him, sharp-eyed as a bird. "How did you feel?"

"Well, I was interested, I suppose," he said. He leaned against the counter, swirling the liquid around and around in his martini glass.

"I should think so." She moved her hand as if to touch him, then thought better of it. "And you didn't feel anything—at the time she was seeing those things?"

"Or thought she was."

"Oh, stop it, Mickelsson." As if to take back the snap of irritation, she did touch him, lightly resting her hand on his arm.

He looked down. "I felt something, yes. A coldness, and fast-moving shadows."

She asked, "Do you want me to stay with you tonight?" Her eyes met his, then skidded.

"I don't know," he said before he'd stopped to think. "I mean, yes, but—"

She nodded. "It's all right. Stop worrying. Another time."

"It's just—"

Alan Blassenheim came into the kitchen for ice. He nodded, smiling one-sidedly, apparently thinking well of himself. Behind him, the Swisson woman poked her head in at the door.

"I wonder," Mickelsson said. Blassenheim glanced at him, seeing whether he was the one addressed. "I wonder what that man in the brown coat was there for. Eerie, somehow." When Blassenheim seemed not to follow, Mickelsson said, "The man in the waiting room, I mean."

"What man?" Blassenheim asked.

Mickelsson looked away as if guiltily.

Blassenheim rolled a look back at the Swisson woman; it was for her that he was getting the ice. "I guess I didn't notice," he said. "I wasn't really paying much attention."

Jessie met Mickelsson's eyes.

Then Edie Bryant was in the kitchen with them. "Git out! Git out! Everybody in the livinroom!" she called excitedly. "We're to have Freddy at the fiddle and Lady Kate will sing!"

"Thank you, Alan," Kate Swisson said, letting her head fall limply sideways, taking the glass of ice from him. "Now if I can just find some juice or something." To Mickelsson she explained, shyly smiling, flutteringly helpless, "It's my throat. It's like this all the *time*, these days. It just scares me to *death*." She touched her white throat with three long fingers.

"I'll find you something," Alan said. "I think there's some grapejuice."

"Alan," Brenda Winburn called from the livingroom, "are—you—coming?"

"I'm getting Miss Swisson some grapejuice," he called.

Mickelsson and Jessie moved into the livingroom as Brenda said, "*Mrs.* Swisson." Her eyes locked angrily on Mickelsson's for an instant. Then, guiltily, she smiled.

As soon as Brenda was out of earshot, Jessie said, "That young lady has a crush on you, Mickelsson."

"Jessie, that's silly. Look how jealous she is of Alan."

"That's at least partly for *your* benefit. She's a very proud young woman." She smiled, sliding a covert look back at Brenda. It was true, he saw, that she valued herself, and for good reason. But then what of Jessie, smiling down fondly at the poor innocent like some serene, possibly dangerous Chinese goddess?

In the corner of the room, with their backs to all the others, Tillson and Garret were in earnest conversation, Tillson's hand on Garret's arm, Tillson nodding, shaking his head, nodding again, speechless with interest.

10

When he awakened the next morning he was aware at once that the room was filled with bright, eerie light, and it came to him that, even as he slept, he'd been aware for hours that it was snowing heavily, a cold blizzard snow, wind whistling around the corners of the house, softly banging the shutters, knocking for admission. When he got up, shivering, and went to pull up the white windowshade, he saw, through the swirling clouds of whiteness, that snow lay deep on the porch roof and down on the lawn below, the road, the slope toward the pond beyond that, half hidden among pines—great unbroken drifts five or six feet deep, maybe higher. Even with the Jeep there was no possibility of his getting to school within the next day or two, assuming school would run, and if the icy snow kept falling and the wind kept blowing, no likelihood of his getting to school all week. All the shadows over his life—Donnie Matthews' pregnancy the darkest of all—must sit tight, bide their time. He remembered the blizzards in Wisconsin in his boyhood, how he and his cousins had dug tunnels through the drifts—labyrinths, large rooms, windows looking up at white light. Even his grandfather's mood would lighten on days like this. He remembered the cold white light in the old man's study in the manse, how the old man would stand, his shirt very white against the darkness of his suit, his white hands knotted behind his back, bent like a crow toward the window, almost smiling, his odd, bent nose aiming slyly to the left, teeth like a shark's, nostrils flared as if sniffing things his straightforward eyes refused to recognize. His white hair glowed. "God is merciful," he would say, apropos of nothing, as if the thought were unutterably baffling.

Even now Mickelsson could not quite help thinking of Donnie Matthews. It crossed his mind that this would be the time to go to her, bundle himself up like an Eskimo and laboriously struggle into town. No one else would be there. He could spend the whole day with her, work out calmly what they meant to do. More than the whole day. Several days, perhaps. They would make love, talk, make love, talk. . . . It was an at once appealing and sickening thought—the struggle into town perhaps the most appealing part of it. He remembered going out with his father and uncle for firewood in the winter, riding on the perfectly silent bobsled behind the shaggy brown Belgians, no sound but the whuff of wind and the creak of harness-leather, the collar bobbing slowly like an old man wagging his head from side to side, listening to music, the crupper now slack, now tight as a muscle cramp. He would explain to her his feelings, how it was not just a foetus but a child, his child and hers—not that he believed that it was knowably his; but no matter. A child. A living, suffering being.

Something silver, the top of a garbage can, perhaps, moved solemnly across the snow, hardly touching it, leaving no track that he could see. He thought of all he ought to do at the university, fight for his department's rights, protect Jessica, among other things—though the threat against her was not yet definite. Strange to say, he felt none of the anger at Blickstein he'd felt last night. Blickstein was, as surely as Mickelsson, an idealist at heart. But he had his job. It was as if years had passed since last night's conversation. He put on his glasses, slippers, and robe, and went downstairs.

The kitchen phone had no dialtone—predictably, he realized, and felt pleased. Here as upstairs, the snowlight was astonishing. Outside the kitchen door, where the woodpile should be, there was a mountain of sugary brightness. It was incredible that just a few hours ago there had been cars outside that door, and that they'd driven home on the road in front, now invisible, markless. Had Tom Garret gotten back to his wife at the hospital? Not likely. But no way to find out—no phone, no means of transport; he owned neither skis nor snowshoes. So he need not think about it. Even to get wood for the stove, he found, he couldn't get out through the back door but had to go out the front door, which opened onto the porch, and lug through deep snow around the side of the house to the woodpile and carry back fire-logs the same way he'd gone out. When he'd carried in four armloads, his boots, his gloves, all the openings in his clothing, were filled with snow.

From the few live embers among the ashes in the bottom of the stove he got a fire going. As soon as it began to warm the room, the cat appeared. The cat stood in the doorway between the study and the living-room, his large flat head low, tail back, as if stalking, carefully keeping his distance from the Christmas tree, then suddenly, without a sound, ran to the rug between the stove and the couch, looked around suspiciously, then settled himself. Instantly he looked as if he'd been sleeping there for hours.

"That's the way," Mickelsson said. "Make yourself at home."

The cat pretended to sleep on.

Mickelsson washed dishes and straightened up the house. The icy snowfall and wind had let up now, only an occasional gust driving a puff of white down the mountainside. He really could make it into town without much trouble. A mile's distance. An hour, an hour and a half at most. He thought of making lunch for Donnie. The Acme would be open, though few customers could be expected to come. He could make her something she'd never heard of, something wonderful but not unduly strange—bifteck au poivre, perhaps. He thought about how she would watch him, half admiring, half cross as he worked in her kitchen; but he continued straightening up the house, vacuuming, dusting, intending to set out but not yet doing it.

By noon the snowplow had still not opened up his road, which meant that there would be no mail today—no bills, nothing from the I.R.S., no angry letters from Ellen or her lawyers. He thought of the mail stuffed in the filing cabinet in his office at the school, another great burden of guilt he could dismiss, since there was nothing he could do: whatever lay there must lie on as it was until God and the county saw fit to clear the roads. Soon, it struck him, there would be a grim addition to the usual— the requests to send essays to stupid magazines, and so forth. Soon he would be getting appeals from the Ad Hoc Committee for the Defense of Jessica Stark, and just after each of them an even-handed letter of information from Blickstein, views from the mountaintop, gentle presentations of the larger picture, palatable ruin.

At three in the afternoon, the phone still had no dialtone. If he was wrong not to call his daughter and (not that he could reach him) his son, he could take no blame for his failure today, could not even smart at their failure to call him. Though the sun moved steadily from southeast to southwest, time was suspended; he need not even think of Donnie. God be with her, he thought, since nobody else was convenient. If God was off fishing in the northeast corner of the universe, or in bed with a cold, could Mickelsson be blamed?

"Maybe," Mickelsson said aloud.

Toward dusk the wind began to blow much harder and the drifted snow rose in clouds that blotted out the sun—swirling, slate-gray, blasting the sides of treetrunks with sharp needles. As night approached, anxiety stirred in him. It would not do to put off for too long his conversation with Donnie. He tried the radio, looking for a weather report. The whole band hissed and crackled with static, and all he could find was Christmas music, disco, and NPR's *All Things Considered*. He left the needle on the NPR station, then forgot to listen. Classical music came on without his noticing—an all-Wagner program, stirring, full of rattlings and weighty whumpings.

Now that darkness had fallen, the last of his pleasure in the snow-storm fell away. His agitation about Donnie Matthews' pregnancy—above all, his vexation at her daring to lay the whole freight of it on him and at his own fatuous acceptance of the burden—began to confuse itself with worry about his son, until now always so restrained and level-headed. Perhaps he was still that, but sorely provoked. What if there should be some slip-up? (He got up, heavy-legged, carrying a book—he couldn't remember having picked up the book or sitting down with it—and began to move through the house, pondering what he should move on next.) What could one do—actually *do*, within the limits of sane and humane liberalism—to block or expose the monsters, idiots and enforcers of the nuclear power industry? Could any politician, ever, anywhere, be shaken out of the dim-witted reasonableness and willingness to please that had gotten him his job in the first place—the turtlebrained patience or stupidity that enabled him to sit for months and years hearing sworn delaying and obfuscating testimony from the soft-spoken, nattily dressed nuclear devils—the new breed of extermination-camp scientists, the new breed of spectacle-rims-and-tooth-gold bankers, dutiful Eichmanns of the investment community—while every day new plants went up, and new patents for solar, wind, and wave fell before the threats, trickery, and cash of the hell people? He could feel his face reddening with anger as he thought about it. Partly Wagner's fault, probably, his heavy brasses still poleaxing the night. Mickelsson's hands clenched, squeezing the book, and his breathing grew labored. R. M. Hare had been wrong about the Nazis. The fol-de-rol of the Aryan aesthetic ideal—Wagner's—had been a ruse in support of a much more ancient and familiar human goal: unlimited pig-greed. Hitler was alive and well at Seabrook, and the rules had not changed. Survival of the fattest. What made one furious, of course, was not that these people were unfit to live. It was that only by becoming spiritually and morally one of them could one beat them. So it was that, by ever-quickening evolution, the species went from bad to worse. Good luck, my son! His anxiety scuttled back into musings more abstract and safe, not unrelated: thoughts of the tragically accidental human brain, so huge and self-absorbed that it was cut off from every vitality around it, even its loves, even the flesh and bone machine in which, complaining and scheming, it mushed from here to there and, dully, back.

Poor Mark! He looked up as if startled from the book he had been staring at, not reading. He was standing exactly in the center of one of the empty bedrooms, reading (or not reading) on his feet, like old Lawler. Outside the windows it was now deep night, the storm still woefully howling. On the radio a huge-voiced soprano was ranting. Thesis-antithesis: he remembered one of his son's gestures, how he would slide his hand lightly back and forth on the tabletop as he sat leaning forward, explaining in his soft, ever-reasonable voice the economics of death by radiation—for instance how eventually every stone of a nuclear power plant must become radioactive, too "hot" for human beings to handle, how the whole thing must be buried by machines that must then follow the plant into its grave, and how not one penny of the company's operating costs was set aside for that inevitable eventuality, though the expense would run to the millions. As he set forth, calmly, lucidly, his vision of the future— a world cheated and defiled, poisoned forever by present man's stupidity and greed—his fingertips moved smoothly back and forth, again and again, like easy-going skaters on a long, narrow pond in the country. Mickelsson's grandfather, similarly calm, had had, by comparison, only trivial images of Satan's majesty.

Mickelsson put down the book and went back downstairs. When he turned on the Christmas tree lights his funereal mood darkened more, but he let them burn on, as he let the big, warlike music of Wagner go on playing. It was an outrage that such a swine should write beautifully— not that Mickelsson claimed *Kunst Wissenschaft*. He'd tried to put out of mind Wagner's crimes against humanity, that year he and Ellen had spent in Heidelberg. The Germans had long since forgiven Wagner, he saw; but then, more than a few of them, it seemed to Mickelsson, had forgiven Hitler. In the laundromat he and Ellen had to use there were large, carefully painted swastikas. "The kids, the kids!" the woman who ran the place had told them in English, indulgently batting the air. In his impeccable German, Mickelsson had said, "The kids paint very professionally." In Austria, not far from the Eagle's Nest, he'd been invited to the home of a baron who had a painting of the Führer over his fireplace, two lighted candles on the mantel. Not that he hadn't met good people too, people who hated what Germany had done, even one woman who'd converted to Judaism so that when the soldiers came, herding Jews down the street, she would not be free to pretend it was not her business. Nonetheless, he distrusted every shopkeeper and bus-driver, the whole clean, dangerously law-abiding tribe. "*Das ist verboten!*" they would cry out as one man if some poor fool lit a cigarette where he shouldn't. They would rise again, fountain up, shining with terrible brightness, to the first Martin Luther or Wagner or Hitler who cried out to them, a tribe as wickedly high-minded as ever. Bäumler's Nietzsche—Hitler's Nietzsche— was still, to a surprising extent, the Nietzsche Germans knew: the altered, Jew-hating, war-monger Nietzsche whose *Also sprach Zarathustra* Nazi soldiers toted in their backpacks. Even more easily than they'd stolen and perverted Christ (in Nietzsche's view), they'd stolen and perverted the Antichrist. Mickelsson hadn't left a day too soon. His heart, when he came to the messy, disorderly streets of New York, had lifted like a yellow March kite.

In the kitchen he poured milk into a cereal bowl, then carried it into the livingroom to set down near the cat. As always, the cat ignored him, feigning indifference, though in the morning the bowl would be empty. "Hypocrite," Mickelsson said, but not with malice. It was a common fault. He thought of reaching out with two fingers to pet the cat's head, then thought better of it. For all the evidence of his warrior nature— the nicked ears, deformed belly and shortened tail—the animal seemed comfortable, serene; yet he could spring in a split second, Mickelsson knew—could explode in unholy outrage, hissing and slashing.

He stoked the fire one last time: red flames and embers, whiteness behind them, the air astir with heat waves as if reality were dissolving before
his eyes—he thought he saw Donnie Matthews' pouting white face in
the flames—and then, as he was uncomfortably turning away, he noticed
near the woodstove, on the brick and stone foundation, a pair of fur-lined
leather gloves. They were small, a woman's, and looked familiar. When
he raised them to his nose and caught the scent, his chest went light and
he realized that they belonged to Jessie. Odd that she should have left
them and not known it, cold as it had been when she went out to the car
last night. Freudian mistake, perhaps. He felt the softness of the fingers,
the leather warm in his hands, then smelled them again. Something eased
into his mind, something he'd been looking for before, he had a feeling.
He had seen, maybe thirty-five years ago, some horror picture about
voodoo; a white glove on a table, moving by itself as an old, old man
spoke incantations. In the night outside, a woman in a white dress, owner
of the glove, came sleepwalking down a long, straight road, under an
arch of trees. When the glove reached the edge of the table, the woman
was at the door. At the time, Mickelsson—twelve or thirteen—hadn't
doubted that such summonings were possible. If the world was all a show,
the flesh make-up and rags behind which vast energies played, why not?
He shuddered, then absently, dismissing the memory, folded the gloves
and laid them on the flowerstand by the door, where he'd see them and
remember to take them along with him to school when the roads were
plowed. He switched off the radio without noticing he was doing it; then
he wound the clocks, pausing for a long time after the last one, listening
to the wind howl—banging on the livingroom door like a dozen angry
fists—and looked down at the key in his hand, trying to remember what
it opened. It reminded him a little of the key to some old-fashioned
wind-up toy, something Leslie or Mark had played with, or something he
himself had played with as a child in his grandfather's study. He'd played
there for hours, though his grandfather had been cranky as a goat, family
stories suggested. "Grampa," he had asked once—meaning nothing large
by it (or so his mother believed), hoping to hear only of some particular
event, as when one day he had dusted the furniture in the livingroom
without being asked—"why does God love us?" "That," his grandfather
had said, looking furtive, cornered, "is a mystery."
Mickelsson glanced at the Christmas tree. The cat, when Mickelsson
looked over toward the stove, was gone.
"You all right?" someone asked.
"You know I'm not," another voice answered acidly, as if with familiar anger.
"Needn't snap," the first voice said, the old man's. He did not sound
apprised of how deeply that feminine anger burned, how long its festering
poison had been coaxed and tended.

When Mickelsson turned, slowly, as if to stir no breeze, they were standing there, perfectly still, the old woman's face bloodless gray, her eyes full of lightning. She wore a flowerprint housedress with a faded pink robe over it, her dark, graying hair brushed straight down, to the backs of her knees. Mickelsson reached out toward the wall to steady himself—exactly as Mabel Garret had reached out, he remembered. The old woman's carefully sealed-in fury was infecting him, it seemed. His stomach knotted tight, and a strangling feeling came into his throat and chest. The old man was in stockingfeet and workworn trousers, only a washed-out gray undershirt above, white bristly hair poking out like a hundred tentacles around the neck. Mickelsson knew him, then recognized him. It was the man in brown, from the hospital, but much older. His hair was parted in the middle and lifted at the sides, as if brushed. His beard was uneven. In his left hand he held a large silver pocket watch, which he'd apparently just wound and was now trying to read through his low-on-the-nose, thick-lensed glasses. His mouth was as lipless as an old razor cut. You could make out the white of his chin, like bread-dough, through the hair. At last he gave up on the watch and looked at Mickelsson. He seemed only a little surprised that he was there. For a moment it seemed that he would speak, but then the ghost worked his wrinkled, nearly toothless mouth—four or five long teeth in front, then nothing— as if trying to rid the inside of some taste. He turned his head, fumbled the watch into his pocket without looking at it, and moved toward the stairs. The old woman followed, clenching and unclenching her right fist, which had something in it, her eyes bright glints in the cavernous sockets, tiny glittering specks like wild-animal eyes lit up in the darkness of their lair. Mickelsson stood still as they moved past him, the two never glancing in his direction, watching the floor. In her spotted, trembling left hand the old woman clutched a fistful of the robe. With her right hand she dabbed at her mouth with what he saw now was a wadded-up hankie. When they were gone (he could hear them going slowly up the stairs) he remembered the clock-key in his hand, opened the glass door of the clock, and dropped the key inside.

"Well?" he imagined Dr. Rifkin saying.

"I don't know," Mickelsson said. "I'm not the only one, you know."

"Come on now," Rifkin said, and made a face as if he'd bitten into a lemon.

Mickelsson hovered, consciously refusing to come down firmly on either side. He thought of calling Jessie, then groaned, thinking of the face he'd seen in the flames. He must get money for Donnie. Had his mind's chaos progressed to such a point that he'd be willing to take a loan from Jessie? Acid and darkness rose in him and he thought nothing, slowly chewing a Di-Gel, then another.

Half an hour later, as he was drifting toward sleep, he heard the snowplow roar by. Along with the engine noise there was a soft swishing sound, almost the sound of a heavy old boat cutting water. It faded away down the road toward silence.

"Got to think," he whispered, knowing he intended to do nothing of the kind.

He had seen the ghosts. Was he afraid? He wasn't sure.

The sudden stillness of the house startled him, in fact for an instant terrified him, until he made out that it was only that the wind had fallen off, and the waterfall in the glen below was frozen.

That night he dreamed that he saw the old man up on the roof of the house, fixing the chimney. Something was wrong. The old woman came out onto the lawn below, walking stiffly, something behind her back. He woke up sweating.

As he was feeding the cat, two mornings later, the phone rang.

"Pete? Finney here. Thought I'd just touch base, see if you—me, still blood-brothers."

"Hello, Finney."

"Not bad, Pete. Nothin to complain about, anyway nothin terminal, except that it's God damn Monday. Listen, two items. First is, it looks like the squeeze play's working. She's makin the right noises, any day now she'll be singin like a camel. Keep the pressure on, OK? No talkee, no cashee!"

"Actually—" Mickelsson began. He felt a queasiness in his stomach and knew Finney had swung around in his chair.

"Her lawyers have agreed to a meeting in court," Finney said, and grimly laughed. "They don't like it, natch, but thanks to a little pressure from the court itself, which is thanks in turn to a little clever manipulation by yours truly (no applause, please! Thank you!)—I'll spare you the details (thanks, Shirley; Jesus; all right, tell the fucker I'll get back to him right away). . . . Let me tell you, Pete, the whole God damn world's comin apart at the seams, you aware of that? Begin's gone crazy and Sadat's still tryin to learn to imitate his fart; piss-ant politicians out there shaking the ash can—'You don't go long with me I'll blow up the world.' Not that I care. Be glad it's not *me* up there. I'd put my fingers in my ears and push the button with my cock. Actually, *don't* be glad it's not me. I been thinking of running for office, maybe. State legislature. No crap! Man needs to broaden his avenues of income, get more screws on more people, these troubled times. All that filthy corruption, it makes me sick that I'm not in on it. But OK, OK, we're still down here in the pigshit dealing with the piss quotient, right? You there, Pete?"

"I'm here."

"I was afraid you'd gone to sleep. Listen, try to groan a little when I talk to you, OK?" Finney laughed. "I keep getting the feeling there's nobody out there, I mean nobody in the whole fucking city of Providence, whole universe even. Isn't that weird? Finney at his lawyerdesk oinkin away, putting his feet up, puttin 'em down again, looking at the 'out' box, looking at the 'in' box, sweating and scheming, squinting his little eyes, and nobody out there—I mean nobody, nowhere, *nothin*. Little stirrings of dust."

"Finney, you should see my psychiatrist, Rifkin. He lives right near you. He's a good man."

"You tellin *me* I should see a psychiatrist! Believe me, no room in the schedule, I gotta keep runnin, cover my ass. OK. Thanks, Shirley. OK, where was I? Oh. Got it. OK, so all we're waiting for now is a court date, which is up to the court, you know; nothing I can do about it. So stay loose and stay in touch. That all clear, Pete?"

"How much warning—if we get this court date—"

"Couple days, maybe. Never mind, kid, we're getting down to payshit."

Mickelsson said, "How does Ellen seem?"

"She's alive. What can I tell you? Or if she'd dead she's still walkin. People will do that, you know. Walk around dead. Fucks up the census count. Listen, second item: I got a call from a sap named diSapio. Name ring your bell?"

"I know who he is," Mickelsson said, reserved.

"He's got a lien on everything you eat or evacuate—I guess you know that. I'm tryin to work something out with him, but it's likely he'll garnishee your salary any day now. He could keep you eating sawdust for years, if we're not careful. He's pretty crazy, from what I gather. One false move and suddenly you'll be a whole lot easier to find, if you take my meaning. Get yourself a lawyer in P-A, OK? And don't put it off, you got that? You want me to find you one, sing out."

"I'll manage it. Anything else?"

"That's it from this end."

"OK, I'll be in touch."

"So long, pal."

"So long."

"Man, you said it!" Finney laughed.

The other phonecall he received that morning he would discover to be important only later, though it fit well enough with the way his world was going; it was suitably depressing. It began oddly. Intending to telephone the Susquehanna Home Center to order hardwood, any odds and ends they might have, small stuff—he was not quite sure yet what he meant to make with it, chests, trinket boxes, plant-tables, maybe; something to make the house look less barren—he'd just picked up the receiver, the phone had not rung, when a voice said, "Professor Mickelsson?"

"Hello?" Mickelsson said.

"Professor, this is Michael Nugent."

"Oh, hello," Mickelsson said. He recognized the voice now, and felt a twinge of simultaneous guilt and annoyance. He imagined Nugent's coldly staring, rapidly blinking eyes.

"I guess you didn't look at the note on your door. I asked you for an appointment."

"I'm afraid I haven't been in," Mickelsson said. "We've been having a lot of snow out here, as I assume you've heard." He heard in his voice the cool, autocratic tone he too often took with students, and quickly made an effort to soften it. "What was it you wanted to talk about?"

"I'm sorry to call you at home," Nugent said. "It's about that term paper, for one thing."

"Yes," Mickelsson said, careful, knowing well enough where such openings generally led.

"I didn't hand it in, as I guess you must've noticed by now." It was the expected tone, half aggressive, half whiney, but unusual in its urgency, emotionally packed. Mickelsson wondered if the boy was drunk. "I really haven't got any very good excuse. I worked a lot on it, but I was getting later and later, and then . . ." In a strained voice he brought out, "I'd been having a lot of trouble with schoolwork. It's not that I wasn't interested. As I guess you know, I got an A average in your class up to now. And now *this*—" He couldn't finish. He seemed actually to gag on his wretchedness.

"Wait a minute now," Mickelsson said, growing alarmed. "Take it easy. What's the trouble?"

"It's not . . . I can't . . ." At last he was able to say, "I can't do the term paper, and I can't take the final."

Mickelsson pressed the receiver tighter to his ear. Nugent's voice seemed to be drifting off. "You can't take the final? Are you telling me you want an Incomplete?" he asked. "Look, if you've got a good reason, I'm not likely to object."

"What I was really wondering . . ." Now the voice was more controlled, less aggressive, still more urgent. "What I was wondering is, since I've been doing really well so far—I mean I've read all the work, and I got an A-plus on the midterm, and I contributed to class discussions, as well as I could, so you know I was serious—"

Mickelsson could see where the plea was heading. He was tempted to bear down, demand that the boy be just a little reasonable, but something checked him. The emotion in Nugent's voice was peculiar, different from anything he'd encountered before, even from poor mad Nugent. It was normal for students to plead for special favors; no doubt he'd done it himself in his college days, though he could remember no particular instance. But he somehow had a feeling that Nugent's distress was far beyond the usual, as if passing the course without writing the term paper or the final exam were a matter of life or death. And there was something else. The boy sounded changed, as if his mind had weakened, or he was drugged, fighting for coherence.

"A midterm exam is not exactly the same as a final," Mickelsson said, stalling. As soon as he'd said it he knew that by his tone he'd let Nugent know that the matter was still negotiable. He must quickly correct that impression, he thought, but then cringed guiltily from a mental image of timid, anxious Ed Lawler. *"Do you think he seems well?"* Mickelsson hadn't realized even then, with Lawler forcing his head to it, the full extent of Nugent's illness.

"Professor Mickelsson," Nugent said, rushing in, his voice tremulous, "I know it's not fair to ask—I mean, I know it's abnormal—" He gave an awful laugh.

Though he couldn't have said for sure how he knew it, he knew that Michael Nugent was crying. *Christ!* he thought, momentarily enraged, put upon one too God damn many times. But then instantly, for no good reason, he thought of Mark. "Listen, Michael," he said, almost as gently as he'd have spoken to his son, "what's wrong? What's all this about?"

Nugent said nothing. Mickelsson imagined him struggling for control, fighting the random contortions of his mouth, crying as Ellen had sometimes cried when she phoned, back in the days when she'd sometimes phoned. He felt a kind of sickness sweep over him, a strange and baffling feeling like absolute despair, the very soul's prostration. He knew what he should say, that he would give the boy an Incomplete, it was the best he could offer. Nothing else made sense, logically at any rate; but logic seemed not relevant. The boy's anguish, whatever its cause, was so strong that Mickelsson could feel it himself, a sensation of teetering on the rim of the abyss. The power of Nugent's distress was shocking, unheard-of. He said, "Suppose I give you a B-plus for the course, scrap the rules this once. Would that do?"

"That'd be fantastic," Nugent said. The way he snapped at it made Mickelsson more uneasy than before.

"Listen," Mickelsson said, "come talk to me next semester, all right? I must say, I was hoping you'd pull an A."

Nugent said nothing.

"Michael?" Mickelsson said.

There seemed to be no one on the line.

After he'd hung up, he thought, still feeling queasy, almost nauseous, how peculiar it was that he'd so easily caved in, not that even now he regretted it; his sense of Nugent's helplessness and misery was still very strong. No doubt he should have demanded that the boy at least give his excuse, he thought. But the thought was no more than a dutiful flicker; he felt, beyond reason or argument, that he'd done the only thing he could have done.

An hour later he still hadn't gotten the strangeness of it out of his mind. All his own troubles, confusing, unsolvable, oppressive as they were, seemed trivial beside Nugent's, though Nugent's hadn't even a name.

What the connection was he couldn't have said, though he sensed some definite connection: brooding on Nugent, he got a sharp image of his father and uncle and his father's friend Hobart kneeling beside a Guernsey cow. The cow was bloated, lying on her side against a fencepost. All around her, up and down the field, there were other cows in the same helpless condition, stomachs swollen, eyes rolling, lips breathing foam. They'd gotten into wet clover, he knew now, though at the time he'd known only what he saw. He'd been four or five. His uncle pushed his fingers into the cow's swollen side, just below the chine, no doubt counting down ribs, and then his father had raised a hunting knife—Mickelsson could see it so clearly it might have been a photograph—and stabbed with all his might. Foul air hissed out, spitting red-yellow liquid—a terrible, filthy mess—and the cow groaned, "Ooof!" In less than a minute the cow was on her feet, angrily tossing her head, mooing in high dudgeon, clumsily running away.

The memory released another. One winter night when Mickelsson was seven, he'd been awakened by a sound it had taken him a moment to identify: every cow in the barn was mooing, in eerie chorus. He'd gotten up and put his clothes on and had run into the kitchen—his bedroom was downstairs—just in time to see his father putting on his old tattered denim frock. They'd gone out to the barn together; a little later his uncle had come, red-nosed and dim-eyed, smelling of whiskey, his hands buried in the pockets of his sheepskin. The cows went on bawling, the strangest sound on earth, the sound reverberating in the big stone barn. His father had looked businesslike and solemn, moving along behind the gutters with his head bowed, trying to make out what the cows were telling him. When he came to the heavy piece of sheet-metal that made a bridge over the gutter, near the middle of the barn, the bellowing dropped off. Every cow's head turned to watch. His father looked around, then down at the sheet-metal under his boots. When he and Uncle Edgar bent to lift the metal away, they found, wedged in under it, a newborn calf. How or why it had crawled into that small, dark cave was hard to say, but by morning it would have been dead. The cows watched silently as Mickelsson's father lifted the calf and carried it over to the empty calfpen and laid it in the straw, then moved the mother cow from her stanchion to the pen.

It was hard to believe in the honor and nobility of the profession of philosophy when he compared it to his father's profession. Humble work, it might seem to some; but standing in his study, looking at the papers and unopened mail on his desk, he regretted his youthful inability, back when he still had choices, to grant proper value to such work. It might have made a difference. Perhaps as a farmer, a cabinetmaker . . . He thought of Heidegger's mythologizing of "the Folk."

He must call the Philosophy Department, he remembered.

By now Susquehanna had been "socked in," as the locals said, for nine days, the roads never open for more than a few hours at a time. It was still windy and bitterly cold—so cold that if one went outdoors without gloves on it was like having one's hands shot with a gun, first terrible pain, then numbness. The roads had at last been cleared all the way to the highway, but the semester was over; Christmas vacation was upon them. Two days after the call from Michael Nugent, Mickelsson phoned in his grades. It was irregular, but he hadn't been the only professor to give no finals, no last-minute conferences. When the secretary had taken down the grades and checked them twice she said, "Professor Mickelsson, I think Professor Tillson was hoping to talk to you. Can you hold while I see if he's in his office?"

"I'll hold," Mickelsson said.

A moment later, Tillson's old-ram voice was on the line. "Hello, Pete?"

"Hello, Geoffrey." He leaned his elbows on the limited bare space on his desk—he was phoning from his study—and gazed out the window in front of him at the gleaming white valley, blue-snow mountains in the distance. Though Tillson's voice was friendly, Mickelsson was conscious of waiting impatiently, almost crossly, for the phonecall to be over.

"How's the weather out there? I bet it's beautiful!"

"It is."

"God, how I envy you! I imagine the skiing must be wonderful!"

"I suppose so. I don't ski, myself."

Tillson laughed. "To tell you the truth, I don't either." He laughed again, then asked, "Listen, Ruth wants to know if you could come to a party. Just a few friends—the usual, pretty much. But you know how it is, Christmas season and all that. Also—" He hesitated, no doubt hoping to be interrupted. When Mickelsson said nothing, Tillson said awkwardly, probably grinning, cheeks twitching, "I thought maybe we could kill two birds with one stone, get some people together and have a talk about you-know-who."

"You-know-who?"

"Well, you know, the Marx brothers, as Jessie says." He laughed. "They really are becoming quite a nuisance, to tell the truth. They're not kidding, this business about wanting to teach our courses."

"Blickstein's putting up with it?" Mickelsson asked.

"Not actively," Tillson said. "But of course it's not his business to interfere."

"Ah, it's interdepartmental politics now!"

"*You* may not think so, and *I* may not think so," Tillson said. "I may as well mention another thing too, on the chance you haven't heard. They've begun their assault on Jessie."

Mickelsson took what Dr. Rifkin would call a neurotic's deep breath. "I'm not surprised."

"That's all you've got to say?" Tillson laughed again, this time caustically.

"It's all I've got to say at the moment," Mickelsson said.

Perhaps Tillson caught the sound of hopelessness in Mickelsson's voice. At any rate, he backed off a little. "Yes, I see what you mean. Well, as I say, it might be a good thing if we could talk, you and Garret and I, Phil Bryant, maybe Freddy Rogers, a few others, old Meyerson. . . . Mix business and pleasure . . ."

"When is the party?" Mickelsson asked.

"Friday night." Tillson's voice was lively again. "I know it's short notice . . . we'll have a little singing, egg-nog, that sort of thing—"

"Ah. Friday."

"That's a problem?"

"Well, *something* of a problem," Mickelsson said.

"You're out of town that night?"

Mickelsson seized on it. "I'm supposed to be. I'll see what I can manage."

"I do hope you will, Pete." He sounded hurt, trying to disguise the fact. "For Jessie's sake. We need your feistiness."

"I'll see what I can manage," Mickelsson said again.

"One other thing," Tillson said. "I know you don't always take time to read the papers." He paused, loath to go on, though he must. "Did you hear about that student of ours, young Nugent?"

Mickelsson closed his fingers on the telephone cord. Something stopped him from mentioning that he'd just talked to the boy. "What about him?"

"I'm afraid he's—killed himself. It's a shocking thing. Always terribly shocking when they're so young. Slit his throat in the dormitory bathtub—I think it was three days ago. It's a miracle nobody found him; apparently he might have been saved. Poor devil! You hadn't heard?"

"It can't have been three days ago," Mickelsson said. A soft hiss came into his brain, the sound of a TV after the station goes off.

"It was, I'm sure. I have a note here. Sunday evening; that's why he wasn't found."

"I see," Mickelsson said after a moment. ("Well?" he imagined Rifkin saying; and himself answering, "Just hang on a minute, will you?")

"I'm sorry to be the one to—"

"That's all right." His tone was sharp. To Tillson it would seem inexplicably so. Mickelsson would have said something to cancel the effect, but nothing came to him. It was as if his mind had stopped dead. Like Nugent's—if Nugent's had.

After a moment Tillson said, "Friday night then, around seven? You won't forget? I know it's short notice. You'll write it down?"

"I'll write it down," Mickelsson said, almost a whisper. He picked up a pencil from the desk and lowered the point toward a slip of gray paper containing some old, no longer intelligible notes, but he wrote nothing. He heard Michael Nugent's voice again, wretchedly pleading from the shadows for a grade. "*I know it's not fair to ask—I mean I know its abnormal. . . .*" He tried to think about it, but he could find no hand-hold. For an instant he had a vision of ghosts everywhere, all through the valley, filling all valleys, crowding every street—stewing, groaning, clutching their hands over business undone.

"Good, we'll be expecting you!" Tillson said. "Good-bye, then."

"Good-bye, then," he said.

The receiver wobbled in his hand as he hung up the phone. He went to the couch in the livingroom—the cat was nowhere to be seen—and lay down. Stretched out, shaky, he remembered how, after his sister's death, his father would come in, day after day for months and months, and lie down on the old swaybacked davenport at mid-day, when the work was heaviest, and sleep. So anguish was everywhere, he knew now, stretching across the earth and back into time, back to the large-brained, gentle Neandertals dragging their old and crippled from place to place, burying their dead in encircling flowers, bewailing life's sorrows with mouths incapable of more than two tight, flat vowels. Anguish among people, high apes and low apes, geniuses and fools; anguish among squirrels in trees when John Pearson blasted parents and children out of them; anguish of bulls on the slaughterchute; out at sea the huge, unimaginable anguish of whales. And now he knew, if he was willing to believe his eyes and ears, that it extended even to the kingdom of the dead. Not surprising, after all. One read about séances in the days of William James— wailing voices from various parts of the room, whimpering lost children wandering, crying out for long-missing toys; older voices trying to drive some message across, word of some letter, hiding place, unconfessed sin. Such was the fruit of all those eons of evolution, from hydrogen to consciousness: galaxies wailing their sorrow. Music of the spheres.

In this as in everything, Mickelsson thought—damning his self-pity but helpless against it—his father had been a better man than he was. He had grieved from love, over things he couldn't have prevented; not from guilt. It was guilt, self-hatred, that made Mickelsson's limbs too heavy to move. Theoretically their professions were similar, farmer and teacher. *Pastores.* The sheep look up . . .

He thought of his own favorite teacher in graduate school, McPherson.

He'd been fifty-five or sixty when Mickelsson had first known him; reputed to be homosexual, though one never heard any real evidence. A bachelor, Southern genteel, like Tom Garret, but of an earlier vintage—three-piece suits, Phi Beta Kappa key, both his house and his office crowded with books; one could hardly see the walls. He'd been notoriously stern. If someone dropped a pencil he would stop the class. But also he'd been famous for kindness, like old Lawler. Mickelsson remembered, with a flush of embarrassment, a cocktail party he'd gone to once, in his grad-student days, where he'd set himself down next to McPherson's chair and had made some rash, casual remark about A. J. Ayer. McPherson had bent toward him—he had a plate on his knees, a glass of whiskey on the floor beside his shoe—and suddenly it had come to Mickelsson that the man was listening, actually interested, as if he thought he might learn something. Panic flared up in him; he'd had nothing much to say about Ayer, really. He'd stammered, had felt almost faint for an instant; and then some kind demon had entered him and he'd found himself saying things he hadn't been aware that he knew—the slippage in natural law, why it implied not freedom but a bizarre randomness—McPherson nodding, jabbing his fork in the air in front of him—"Exactly!" or "Ah, but that's a moot point!" or, once, "Poppycock!" Afterward, back at the quonset hut, lying in his bed a little drunk, Mickelsson had realized that McPherson had granted him, as if nothing in the world were more natural and right, the first serious philosophical conversation he'd ever had with a real philosopher. He hadn't been able to explain to Ellen or anyone else the special, almost miraculous quality of that conversation. "Faggots are like that," Ellen had said, smiling her big, white smile. "Instant charm."

Toward the end, McPherson had gone nearly blind. The last time Mickelsson had seen him, his eyes, through the glasses, were like large, blurry eggs, and everywhere he went he had to be guided; but there were plenty to guide him—forty years' worth of students, all of them eager to exchange a few words with him.

It was a strange thing that, with models like McPherson, Mickelsson should have failed. Rifkin had given him a dozen theories, ways of letting himself off; but they were all, as McPherson would say, poppycock. Whatever might be true for other people, it was always the case with Mickelsson, he was persuaded, that in his darkest moods he saw most clearly. Only then did everything stand still for him, the patterns creep out from behind their obscuring foliage. Rifkin scoffed; but it was a first principle of philosophy that no hypothesis should be rejected if all the available evidence supported it, and search as he might, he could find no evidence that the primary fact of his nature was not selfishness, bestial self-love, blindness to the ordinary needs of those around him. "Come on now," Rifkin had said once, exasperated into showing his colors, "people are like that." He pointed with a rigid arm and finger at the waiting room. "You should *see* what comes through that door!" He spoke as if with scorn (the tone, Mickelsson understood, was accidental) of Dr. Freud's late theories, the universality of neurosis in human beings, the lifelong struggle of Eros and Thanatos, finally one thing, the incurable disease which began with the theft of the infant's feces, how every love afterward was an imperfect and therefore doomed sublimation of that first sweet shit-love. Mickelsson knew that Rifkin was wrong; philosophers had understood since Butler that psychological egoism was false. Against all Rifkin's philosophical backwardness, Mickelsson held up, like a cross against a vampire, the image of McPherson among his student-disciples, and also another, older image: his father standing against the sun, coppery-headed, a heavy black and white calf slung across his shoulders.

Mickelsson rolled over on his back on the couch, as if to turn away from the argument, and covered his tear-filled eyes with his forearm. That was where the image had come from, in paintings and books, of Satan cringing from God's light: from real human experience like his own, certain knowledge of inherent defect or self-betrayal. From somewhere came the thought of his mother, living with cousins now, for the most part staying in one room—lace curtains on the window, a bright red and yellow quilt on the bed, a highly polished mahogany chair and desk where she sat to write, in her slow, trembling hand, preparing her Sundayschool lessons. He had thought the room, the one time he'd visited her there, a wonderfully bright and pleasant place—but of course it was only because *she* was that, even now, shrunk to dwarf-size and bent almost double. "Well, of course sometimes I miss the house," she had said, and had smiled at herself indulgently, as one might at the foolishness of a child. Only now did the full force of what she'd meant come through to him—the big old farmhouse shell, not unlike this one, rotting away on its hill. All those years, more than a century, it had been full of life, but now, because there was no one left to want it—except her, his mother, a being as supererogatory as the house—it must sink back into Nature, as everything sank back, dead children, Michael Nugent, those huge white-elephant hotels in the Adirondacks. . . .

Abruptly, as if it were the couch that was sending him these painful thoughts, he threw his heavy right leg over the side, then his left, and with difficulty sat up. He rubbed his forehead with both hands, his teeth clenched together, then leaned forward and carefully stood.

He searched the room for some help or distraction, but there was nothing. It came to him that the whole room was subtly composed of threes—three pictures on the walls, three chairs, three cushions on the couch, three plants. . . .

He thought of going up to the bedroom and lifting weights for a while and started indecisively in that direction. Just ahead of him, in the kitchen, the phone rang. He decided to ignore it, but at once found him-self moving—rather quickly, considering the shakiness of his legs—to answer it. It would be Jessie; he knew it as surely as if he'd already heard her voice. Guilt washed over him.

"Hello, Pete?" she asked.

"Hi."

"Are you all right? Your voice sounds strange."

"I'm fine, Jessie," he said. "Little in the doldrums, maybe."

"Are you drunk?"

Her bluntness made him smile in spite of himself. "I haven't been drinking, but it's a good idea."

"It's just that your voice sounds funny," she said, still suspicious.

"I know. You mentioned that." He wedged the receiver between his cheek and shoulder and sorted absently through the papers on the coun-ter, mostly unopened mail.

"Poor Peter," Jessie said, suddenly all affection and concern, her voice as comforting as her touch would be if she were here. "It must be an awful time for you too. All those Santa Clauses with their laps full of kids . . . the Christmas music . . ."

"It will pass," he said. "Have you heard from the Garrets, Jess? Did Mabel get out of the hospital?"

"They brought her home day before yesterday. She's fine. Lots of tests. Nothing."

Belatedly he registered the phrase "an awful time for you too." He could summon up no image of Jessie and her dead husband celebrating Christmas, or the two dead children. He tried to think of something to say. Nothing came.

"You know Mabel," Jessie was saying lightly. "She's not a talker. I told her about the ghost you saw. She just looked at me. You know that way she has, like any minute all your flesh may disappear and she'll be staring at a skeleton. She hates it when people talk about her gift . . . or whatever. I guess she thinks we think she's crazy. Maybe she thinks so herself. Now that I've told her about your ghost, she'll think you're crazy too."

He thought a moment about whether or not to tell her, then said, "I saw him again—or rather them. Plain as day, this time."

"What?" she said. "You're kidding!"

"I don't think so."

"What are you talking about?" she asked sharply. "What happened?"

He told her about the old man and the angry old woman, the wadded-up hankie, how they'd walked through the room he'd stood in, as solid as himself.

"Mickelsson, you're moving out of that house," she said.

He smiled, his gaze focused on nothing. "Like hell I am!"

"Why not?" He imagined her blazing eyes. "Listen, I'm coming out there!"

"Fine," he said, "terrific. But don't think I'm moving. I worked hard on this place." He smiled more fiercely, domineering, as if thinking she could see him. "When shall I expect you?"

The line was silent for two or three seconds.

"Jesus," she said at last. Her way of giving in.

The wave of pity came an instant before his understanding of it: Jessie, the grinning, overconfident warrior, suddenly overwhelmed by her department's Commies. Bitter pill that he too should be defeating her—and so easily, at that. He thought of Donnie Matthews, sex kitten *par excellence*, now suddenly, to her astonishment and indignation, caught in Nature's snare.

The silence lengthened. His guilt mounded higher and darkened, like an approaching thunderhead. He must think of something to say to her. Really, of course, he must do something. Move against her enemies.

Donnie Matthews' angry face, at the periphery of his vision, distracted him.

Jessie asked abruptly—he imagined her jerking her chin up, sweeping her hair back with one hand—"Have you talked with your kids?"

"That's not so easy to do," he said, then wished he could call back the words. Now he had to tell her about Mark. He hadn't mentioned to her his son's disappearance. She couldn't be expected to understand, close as they were, why he'd kept it to himself. Useless to tell her (only half true anyway) that his silence had nothing to do with her, had to do with a wordless superstition on his part. Now that he'd talked to Mark on the phone, knew that his son was alive and claiming to be well, it was pos-sible—or easier—to speak of it. He told her about the phonecall. Jessie made appropriate exclamations that, in his present heavy mood, he couldn't help finding suspect. "Peter, that's terrible!" she said. "Why didn't you tell me about this?" And: "Poor Mark! He's a brave kid, isn't he. Jesus. Have you contacted Missing Persons? What do the police say?" He soothed her mechanically, answering questions, making promises—he would hire a private detective, yes (she'd apparently forgotten the condition of his purse). All the time he talked, he found himself lingering over the memory of stroking her as she slept, murmuring to her, "Jessie, Jessie," like a father lulling a child past nightmare with its name. If she were here he would close his arms around her, make himself clear. They would comfort one another, lean on one another like strolling lovers in a painting. But behind some tree Donnie Matthews waited; behind an-other, sooner or later, the hard-ball players, as Finney liked to say, of the I.R.S. He felt increasingly burdened, put upon, and the next instant realized why. She'd called because she was staggering under the attack on her, no doubt baffled and hurt by it, though she'd clearly foreseen it,

and had been feeling in need of Mickelsson's comfort, though partly unsure of him, maybe injured—he should have called her—and lo, having
risked the call to him, she'd found herself constrained, as usual, to give
comfort to him instead. His annoyance grew more intense, as if someone
else had pointed out to him his failure. For all her talk, for all her evidently earnest wish to avoid imposing on him, there it was: obligation.

As soon as he was able to get off the subject of his missing son, he
asked, "How's that business between you and the Marx brothers, Jessie?"

"Bad," she said. "I managed to tell off old Shel today."

"Shel?"

"Blickstein. Probably one of the few friends I've got."

Mickelsson smiled, imagining Blickstein's embarrassment, his awkward attempts to calm her down, get her out of his office. "Don't worry
about it," he said. "He'll forgive it. He knows you're upset. Believe me,
he's on your side. And if he's not, your yelling at him won't make him
either better or worse."

"You don't know," she said. "You're not Jewish."

There it was again. He shook his head. "He's rabbinical," Mickelsson
said. "He'll be just."

"He hates Jewish women."

Mickelsson laughed. "Shall I shoot him for you? Shall I shoot them
all?"

"That's not funny, Mickelsson. You don't know how great the odds
are that I'd say yes."

Again he shook his head, touched by the way she instinctively blocked
pity. *The pity that makes us melancholy and ill.* "Is there anything I
can do?" he asked.

"Sure," she said. "Help me. Threaten people! Write to your Congressman!"

"They're making you cynical, Jessie," he said.

"If you want to do something, do something," she said. "I leave the
details to you."

"I will. Whatever I can," he said. "Don't worry."

"Whatever," she said. Then, after a moment: "Anyway, none of that's
what I called you about. What are you doing for Christmas?"

"I don't know." His voice, he was sure, betrayed his alarm at the
question. "I thought I'd try to miss the whole thing. Get roaring drunk,
maybe."

"Aren't you just a little tired of that solution?"

He sighed, staring blindly at the mail he'd been mindlessly sorting.
"What's the expression, 'Don't shake my china cabinet'?"

"Something like that. Listen, you want to spend Christmas with me?"

He frowned, trying to think.

"Hello?" she coaxed.

"No," he said at last. "I don't think I could handle that, Jessie."

"OK," she said. "Just a passing thought."

"Thanks, though. I really appreciate—"

"Skip it." The voice was unusually sharp, as if she thought he were trying to start a fight. "Well, that's all I had to say, I guess." Then as usual she relented. "Listen, Pete, if anything happens—those ghosts, I mean . . . or *anything* . . ."

"I'll phone you right away."

"I mean it," she said. Then apparently a new thought occurred to her, or she remembered something in his voice earlier that had left her unsatisfied. "You're sure you told me everything that happened—when you saw them, I mean? They didn't try to do anything—hurt you, I mean, or talk to you?"

"*They* didn't," he said, then instantly could have kicked himself.

As though he were staring right at her he saw her lunge forward, her face suddenly tense. "Pete! What are you saying? Somebody *else* tried to hurt you?"

"No," he said quickly, raising his hand palm out to calm her, as if she too could see across miles and through walls. "But somebody talked to me."

Even more reluctantly than he'd told her about the old people, he told her about his phone conversation with Michael Nugent.

After he finished she was silent for a long time. "You're not making this up?"

"Do I sound like it?"

"I'm not sure."

"Something else," he said abruptly, "a cat's moved in with me. Big gray and white one, big as a house."

She was silent again, then said, "I know about the cat. I saw him when you were at the hospital with the Garrets." Again her tone was faintly accusing, as if his mentioning the cat seemed to her frigid. She was right. "That's awful about your student," she said. "Peter, are you positive you didn't dream all this?"

"Not positive, but I don't think so. It's a terrible thought, isn't it? Ghosts worrying, wandering around in the dark, crying—"

"It sounds like a nightmare. It can't be like that. You know those books about people who died and were brought back to life—Dr. Ross, is that it?"

"You're an optimist, Jessie."

"Do you honestly believe . . ." she began, then let it trail off. "Well," she said, and after a few seconds, with a laugh, "Thanks for cheering me up."

It was evident that his gloom had infected her, his spirit reaching out, as Nugent's had done, filling her house with shadows.

"Well, I better let you go, kiddo," she said.

"OK. It was good to talk to you, Jessie. Sorry I haven't been more fun. If there's anything at all I can do for you—"

"I'll keep it in mind. Bye, Pete."

"Good-bye, Jess. Keep the ole chin up!"

The dialtone came.

His gloom hung on for hours, like the cabbage smell in the hallway outside Donnie's apartment. Not even weight-lifting could free him of it. If he were Nietzsche, he thought, he would write some malicious, sarcastic tract—against "Faith" in Martin Luther, for instance: *an incapacity for Christian works—a personal fact shrouded by an extreme mistrust whether every kind of action is not altogether sin and from the Devil.* That was Mickelsson's situation, of course—not to mention Nietzsche's, though Nietzsche had shrouded it in clowning and rant. It was the situation of the modern world, announced by Nietzsche's hammer resounding on the door of the emptied church. Bullshit rhetoric. *Good-bye! Keep the ole chin up!* No doubt Dr. Martinus had secretly suspected it, that not only his enemies' opinions were "donkey fart," but his own ravings about the world as shit were of the world. Had begun to suspect the truth within fifteen seconds of the famous lightning bolt that nearly burned his cock off (so he'd joked) and startled from his lips the vow that if God would spare him he'd sign up as a monk. Certainly must have suspected it later, gouty, with coarse features—"trying to lend them a suffering and tender expression," a not too friendly visitor wrote—or in his own words "gross, fat, gray, green, overworked, overloaded, overwhelmed. . . ." With good-peasant honesty had paid for the secret fear that all he maintained might be bullshit by ladling scatology into everything he said, more foul than the devils who threw their bedpans at the doctor, as he threw his at them, or so he claimed; more foul-mouthed than mad, tortured Jonathan Swift—and foul-mouthed even before he'd been struck by kidney disease, when he was driven insane by (as was fitting) his own piss. A man of profound depressions, and for reason enough: Machiavellian, steeped in all seven deadly sins, even a rather peculiar twist of lechery, arranging with his friend that they screw their wives at the same time and think of one another; even in the noblest causes a liar and, like Nietzsche, buffoon: "Not only children, but also great lords, are best beguiled into truth, in their own best interest, by conveying it to them through foolishness. Fools are tolerated and listened to by those who cannot suffer the truth from a wise man." Always in action, a veritable dynamite keg of will—he'd scribbled and scribbled, volume after volume—though unable to justify works of any kind. . . . Lover and lute-player, small flashing eyes, thick crooked lips, Renaissance roué composing tunes for his heavenly sweetheart—and battling with Kate about a husband's right to take mistresses. The filthiest, basest of swine, in short, whatever his genius—as Mickelsson's grandfather would admit, wincing. Much to the old man's credit. He was the only practicing Lutheran Mickelsson had ever met who would admit the truth about the founder. The old man had said (it was a family legend: the only near-joke he'd ever been heard to utter), "Think what he'd have been if he hadn't been kept busy with all those books!"

The fact remained: action was a problem. What was one to do if he knew that every movement of the spirit was poisoned at the source, as if by uremia? Luther had an out: he could claim that in whatever good he did he was the instrument of God, and in the rest the tool of devils. And Nietzsche, turning with all the rage of his brilliant, ferocious mind against Luther, had a hiding place: though *his* works might be filth, all malice and satire, his devil-dance and chittering pointed the way, by ironic contrast, to something nobler: the serene, spiritually mighty *Übermensch*. But it was a long time now since the announcement of that as yet unfulfilled possibility.

Perhaps not quite unfulfilled. One might point to Mickelsson's old teacher McPherson, or to the supermen of science, like Einstein, who had claimed that he'd perceived as a young man the vanity of hope and striving. "I also perceived the cruelty of such effort, which hypocrisy and glittering words concealed more carefully in those days than they do now." And so had turned first to conventional religion, which had failed to withstand his "youthfully critical scrutiny," then had fled to a surer harmonious sphere, "that beautiful order glimpsed by Kepler, Galileo, Newton. . . ." The trick had worked better for McPherson than for Einstein, apparently. But say it was true that devotion to some mighty realm of thought meant escape from the vanity of hope and striving. What switch turned on the gift for caring about the possibly beautiful structure of the universe? Or for that matter the left horn of the dung beetle? He, Mickelsson, had been through all that: had written books that were sound and original, books that had been scorned and misunderstood, and had learned that, in a sense, the lack of reward didn't matter much. It was the *practice* that mattered. MacIntyre's word. In the practice of philosophy, as in the practice of law, or novel-writing, or almost anything else, one gained things inexpressible to anyone not in the practice; no harm that what you gained would die with you, to be regained, inexpressibly, by someone else. But when one day all interest in that casual gaining dried up, what then? What switch could turn life back on? And if one knew it was a simple mechanical switch—some pill, or "love," or "the sense of community"—would one deign to reach up to the switch? That was the world's inheritance from Nietzsche, though Nietzsche had not faced the matter squarely. If God was dead, human dignity gone, all values emptied, why not just say "Fuck it"—push the button? The existentialists—

Zarathustra's most tedious apes—had an answer; but they hardly counted: war babies. Any fool could get it up in time of war. It was like the glorious secret of present-day East European fiction: *1943. Woman finds piece of bread; sneaks off; joyfully eats it.* No one had the right, anymore, to be quite that sentimentally elemental.

Better to act with fully conscious stupidity: for instance, steal the fat man's stolen money. A tide of darkness washed over him. It was of course no longer a case for Dostoevski. Raskolnikov was a nice boy; his poverty was real and legitimate. No Russian, not even a modern Russian, could get himself into a position like Mickelsson's. He was still up to his old tricks. Knowing that his bills were more than he could handle, he would refuse to look at them for weeks at a time, even when the bills came by registered mail; meanwhile his salary would go into his account automatically, so that the account would build like a rich man's—though Mickelsson, that very moment, might be sweating at the risk of a twenty-dollar check. Then, because nothing had gone wrong for a time, he would write checks to everyone—mainly his wife and his wife's old creditors, putting off his own, which were more recent—and six out of ten of the checks he wrote would bounce, five-dollar service charge each time. Meanwhile the pile of mail remained virtually untouched.

Would he feel guilty, he wondered, if he stole the fat man's money?

The question was absurd. Of course he would! So he told himself, angrily gesturing—standing back from himself, watching the performance. It would be good, God knew, to have Donnie and the child taken care of, generously taken care of and out of his life.

He saw himself smashing through the fat man's door, then shook his head, banishing the thought as he would a nightmare. One impression remained: he would not feel especially guilty.

In his mailbox the next morning, he found a card from Ernest diSapio of the I.R.S. "Possible irregularities in all tax-forms filed by you since 1970. Suggest you drop in or phone." He read the card three times, thought about the fact that it had been sent on a postcard, for all to see, then laughed.

It was perhaps his anger at diSapio that got him moving. He dressed himself up as if for church, went out into the biting, snapping cold, ground futilely for several minutes on the starter of the Jeep, then tried the blue car, which came to life at once. He got out to shovel himself a path to the road, then got in again and backed out of the barn. He did then something the strangeness of which he would recognize only much later. Perhaps, as Jessie would claim, it was a psychic hunch that made him act. Perhaps it was luck shading toward grace, the same mystery that would prompt him to give the thing to Lepatofsky's daughter a few hours from now. Driving past the Jeep, he saw the troll-doll hanging from the rear-view mirror, and on impulse got out, unsnapped the pull-chain that attached the troll-doll to the Jeep and transferred it to the rear-view mirror of the Chevy. Then he drove down to Susquehanna.

Though he knocked again and again at Donnie Matthews' door, there was no answer. Very well; he had errands enough to keep him busy. He would come back. Slowly, over roads that were glare ice over hardpacked snow—except on steep hills, where cinders had been put down—he drove to Montrose. There he found the lawyer he'd dealt with before—deaf, blind, coughing Mr. Cook—and gave him the card from diSapio, gave him Finney's address and phone number, and briefly outlined, shouting and gesturing, his problems with the I.R.S. "There may be ways around that," Mr. Cook said, tapping his fingertips over his chest. "If you were under psychiatric care, as you say, we might just, *ipso facto*, have a toe hold." The fines and penalties might be questioned, *inter alia*, perhaps negotiated. He smiled. A man who loved his craft. *Ipso jure*, they had several means of stalling for time. Mr. Cook could of course promise nothing, but looking a long way down the road . . .

He went back to his car feeling obscenely grateful, blessed. He'd left only one thing undone that he wished he might have done. He'd like to have asked about those ghosts. But the question was too awkward, and then there was the barrier of Cook's deafness. During the half hour he'd spent in Cook's office, the sky, he found, had darkened, huge bluish-brown clouds like bruises overhead—more like thunderclouds than like snow-clouds. They made the whole town mysteriously dark, as if some Biblical miracle were about to happen, or the sun were slipping into eclipse. Even this sudden, surprising darkness did not dampen his mood, that is, steal from him his sense of born-again relief, now that his troubles—some of them anyway—were in professional hands; but the darkness did do something queer, for a matter of seconds, to his imagination. When he'd backed into Public Street and was just nosing the Chevy toward the court-house, he suddenly hit his brakes, believing he saw something that he knew could not be there. In front of the courthouse steps there was a tall, black gallows, and hanging from it, perfectly still except for a slight movement of her dress in what might have been a light summer breeze, he saw a woman. He saw the hanged woman with perfect clarity—bulging eyes, dark tongue—and then the body and gallows were both gone, the sky softening to wintry gray. He understood that it had been some kind of vision or waking nightmare. Already he had trouble believing he'd really seen it, the whole thing scattering from his mind like the atoms of a dream. On the sidewalks no one looked up at the sky, no one had noticed anything.

Back in Susquehanna, he tried Donnie Matthews' door again and found her still not at home. He stood thinking for a while, leaning on his cane, then went back down the stairs and, for all the cold, crossed the street to sit on the bench near the traffic light—today there was no one else there, thanks to the weather—and, tucking his leather-gloved hands into the armpits of his overcoat, turtling his mouth and chin inside his scarf, he settled himself to wait. Except for his forehead and ears, the tip of his nose and his feet, he was warm enough. If he got really uncomfortable he could go sit in the Chevy, parked at a meter not thirty feet away, turn on the motor and heater, and wait in comfort at least until the exhaust fumes got him, seeping through the floor. For now, this was his preference. Though Christmas lights—yellow, blue, green, red, white— drooped above Main Street, and there were lights in the stores, a few brave souls shopping, he felt, here on the icy bench, as if the frozen town had been abandoned to him.

He glanced to his left, across the street toward the Acme, at the sound of a child's crying, and saw the man he'd bought his Jeep from, Charles Lepatofsky, slipping and sliding across the pavement toward him, a large bag of groceries in his arm and mittened right hand, his left hand dragging along his red-faced, bundled-up daughter. Her name was Lily, Mickelsson remembered. It was odd that he should remember it, bad as he was with names. He couldn't have heard it more than three or four times. If she never spoke—so Lepatofsky had said—it was not because she lacked the throat for it. She was wailing as if her heart would break, large tears coursing down her cheeks. She caught her breath and paused for a moment when she saw Mickelsson, then returned, with renewed conviction, to her sorrow and indignation.

Lepatofsky apologized, nodding to him, "Poor baby hates the cold. But I couldn't just leave her up at the house."

"Hard on kids, this weather," Mickelsson said.

Lily slid her eyes toward him but went on with her heartbroken wailing.

Suddenly he got up from the bench, throwing a little wave to Lepatofsky, and half skated, half ran to the Chevy, where he opened the door, leaned in on one knee, and unfastened the troll-doll from the rear-view mirror. Triumphantly, he carried it back to where Lepatofsky and his daughter were just now climbing into their truck. "This is for *you*," he said to Lily, handing her the doll.

She abruptly stopped crying—even Lepatofsky seemed surprised by that—and after an instant's hesitation took the doll in her two mittened hands.

"Can you say thank you?" Lepatofsky asked, bending toward her, smiling.

She shook her head.

"Lily don't talk," he explained, glancing up at Mickelsson.

"I know." Mickelsson stepped back from the truck, smiling and nodding, exorbitantly pleased with himself, then closed her door.

Lepatofsky waved, bobbing his head and calling "Thank you!" Then the truck engine roared to life. Mickelsson waved good-bye until the truck was out of sight, then, still smiling, went back to his bench. As he sat down, his heart jumped. Donnie's light was on.

He had not been prepared for the temper he found her in. She refused absolutely to listen to reason, refused even to let him take her hand to comfort her—much less go to bed with her—and even as he shouted back at her, bellowing like a bull, towering over her, barely in control, he secretly felt the justice of her rage, even the justice of her blaming the whole thing on him. He'd been one of many; her stubborn claim that things stood otherwise was lunacy, an act of mad desperation and reptile cunning; but the fact that there had been others did not mitigate his guilt, any more than did her own claim, earlier, that she was "professional." Her actions had not been, in the full sense, rational: in her youthful egoism and optimism, she hadn't really foreseen the consequences. He, an adult, a man of books and relatively wide experience, had no such excuse. If his use of her, his treatment of this living, feeling human being as pure physical object, was representative, not special, he was nonetheless personally to blame for it. Even as he raged at her, his large red fists clenched, pulled tight against his chest lest he hit her with them—telling her, in scorn of her extortionist dreams, that he was poor, maybe the poorest of her clients—his mind wheeled, hunting wildly for a way to pay her off, save both her and the child in her womb. *Foetus*, he reminded himself; but what he saw in his mind was his even-then-beloved Leslie emerging, all bloody, from Ellen's womb. "I haven't even got a fucking salary," he shouted, "or anyway I won't have, not long enough to scrape up the two thousand dollars you think you need. Two thousand dollars!" He hit his forehead with the side of his right fist and spun away from her as if knocked almost off his feet by his own blow.

"You *do!*" she shouted. "What the hell are you saying?"

"I don't," he said, and sucked in air, trying to calm himself. "The I.R.S. is garnishing all I earn."

"Then get it somewhere else," she said. "What do I care? Fuck it!"

In his mind he saw her standing stiff with rage in the center of the room behind him. She was still in the scratchy-looking pleated bright red wool dress she'd been out shopping in—with her sister, she said. Her coat and scarf were thrown over the back of the overstuffed chair, and on the cushion and on the carpet in front of the chair, cheaply wrapped Christmas presents spilled out of paper shopping bags. On her forehead she'd put some kind of skin-colored putty—except that it wasn't the color of her skin—trying to hide pimples. If her pregnancy showed, it was not in her belly but in the dullness of her hair, the dark blue shadows under her eyes.

"Somewhere else," he sneered. He thought of Jessie and angrily batted the thought from his mind. Something down in the street caught his attention, though at the moment he wasn't quite conscious of what it was that he was seeing. An old gray car, perhaps from the late fifties or early sixties, had pulled up beside the curb in front of Thomas's Hardware. The car-door opened, and after a minute, slowly, with great difficulty, the fat man from the apartment downstairs squeezed himself out, closed the door behind him, and went around the front of the car to the sidewalk, out of Mickelsson's view. He did not have on, today, the police hat but instead a gray, long-out-of-fashion fedora. Mickelsson leaned forward and was able to see him again, standing at the parking meter now, putting a coin in. Then the man turned and, moving tentatively—no doubt because of the near-blindness Mickelsson had noticed down in the hallway that day—again passed out of Mickelsson's view, entering Thomas's store. The man's apartment, it occurred to him, would be empty.

Mickelsson closed his eyes, shocked by the thought that had come to him. He heard Donnie's abuse blazing like fire behind him, but he registered not a word of it, his mind replaying with a feeling of great dread the movements of the man he'd just seen getting out of the car, directly below him, closing the car-door, the top of his hat moving toward the car for a moment as, presumably, he looked in, maybe checking to see that he hadn't left his keys; then the hat, the wide shoulders of the coat, the long, dark scarf moving around the front of the car toward the curb. . . .

He turned to her, breaking in on her crackling stream of dragon-fire. "Suppose I *could* get you money somewhere," he said, jerking up both hands to silence her. "How much would it take to convince you to have the baby, put it up for adoption?"

"Fuck *you*," she snapped. "It's my goddamn *life!*" Then she stopped herself, seeing something in his look, and she seemed visibly to shrink, becoming cunning all at once, then relaxing her face, beginning to dissemble. "It would take more than you could ever get, believe me," she said.

"How much?" he asked, and moved a step toward her.

She looked away from his eyes, afraid of him, saw her cigarettes on the chair beside the bedroom door, and abruptly went for one. Her hands shook as she picked at the pack and at last drew one out. Her eyes fled here and there, looking for matches.

Mickelsson took a pack from his pocket, opened them, and moved closer to her, lighting one and holding it toward her, at arm's length. She leaned toward the light, afraid to meet his eyes, poked the end of the cigarette into the flame and sucked hard, then sharply drew back.

"You're crazy," she said, letting out smoke and holding the cigarette away from her in a gesture queerly elegant, touching.

"There's a place in Binghamton," he said, dropping the matchbook back into his pocket. "For five thousand dollars they'll handle every-thing—all perfectly legal. I checked. How much more would you require, for yourself?" He listened to the odd note of pompousness that had en-tered his speech, as if it were someone else that was saying these things.

"I'm *afraid*," she said. "Can't you fucking understand that? I'm scared to fucking *death*."

He waited until she looked at him, then said, "But for money—for *enough* money . . ." The foetus would be better off dead; what chance did it have? Anyway, there was no justice or decency under heaven. They'd all be better off dead—he, Donnie, Jessie. . . . He pulled back from the thought in revulsion.

"I don't know," she said, and snapped her head around sideways, away from him, then dragged, shaking, at the cigarette. "Ten thousand dahllars?" She laughed, brittle as glass, edging toward hysteria.

"OK," he said, and nodded. "We'll see." He felt himself absolutely still, like Gibraltar, and at the same time felt himself rushing toward some dark shore.

Again she looked at him, really scared now, thinking twenty things at once—thinking, among other things, that maybe she hadn't asked for enough. "What are you going to do?" she asked. She raised her hand as if to stop him as he pushed by, heading for the door, then changed her mind. "Hay," she said, dancing along beside him, "hay, where are you going?"

"Tell you later," he said.

As he tried to pull her door closed behind him, she held it against him, looking out at him through the eight-inch-wide opening, white as a ghost. "Pete, where are you *going*?" She whispered it, as if she knew.

"When I knock," he said quietly, "open the door for me. Otherwise I'll break it off its hinges." *Macho, macho.* Self-hatred stoked the fire of his anger higher. This time when he pulled at the door, she did not resist. It slammed shut.

He had a momentary impression, as he stood leaning on the silver-headed cane, his head near the fat man's door, that there was someone inside. It seemed unlikely in the extreme. Mickelsson had no very clear idea how long he'd stood arguing with Donnie, quizzing her—bullying her—between the time he'd seen the fat man get out of his car and now. But logic suggested (and for all the frantic rush of his heartbeat, his mind seemed to be working with unusual clarity) that since the man had put money in the meter before entering Thomas's, he couldn't possibly, in this brief span of time—surely not more than five minutes or so—have gotten back to his car, driven it to its garage, wherever that was, and made it back here to his apartment before Mickelsson. Softly, with the head of his cane, Mickelsson knocked. He waited—probably just a second or two, though it seemed forever—then tried the doorknob. It was locked, of course. He looked up and down the hallway—no one in sight—stepped back across the hallway, then threw himself with all his weight and might against the door. It gave, with a splintering sound like an explosion, then snagged for an instant, caught by the chainlatch. The instant he felt that snag, he knew he was in terrible trouble: impossible as it might seem, the man was certainly inside. He tried to stop, reverse himself, but there was now no going back; he was thrown into the room by the momentum of his rush. They stood facing one another in the room's yellowed dimness, clutter all around them, two huge animals squared off, each more frightened than the other. They stood braced, staring at one another for an eternity, Mickelsson's heart striking wildly at the root of his throat, stealing his breath; and then the fat man moved, lunging toward a dresser, jerking a drawer open and drawing out a gun. Mickelsson stood motionless, trapped in a nightmare, but now the fat man's mouth opened, round as a fish-mouth, showing blackness within, and he bent a little, as if cringing in shame, and slammed the fist that held the gun toward his own chest, clutching himself, his mouth still open, eyes narrowing to slits, squeezing out tears. Though Mickelsson's mind wheeled, one thought came through clearly, as if someone else were thinking it: *he's having a heart attack.* "The broken heart," he remembered, and felt, along with his own heart's pain, a vast surge of pity. Still the fat man hadn't gotten his breath. Judging from the look on his face, the pain was unspeakable, so violent that it blasted from his mind all thought of Mickelsson. Seconds passed—minutes, for all Mickelsson knew. Again and again Mickelsson told himself that he must shout for help, and never mind the consequences to himself—no one knew the arguments better than he—but each time, he did nothing, mentally begging the man to die quickly, lose that expression of pain and, worse, bottomless, childlike disappointment. At last the fat man's knees buckled, a strained, babyish cry came from his throat—a cry to Mickelsson for help—and, turning toward the bed, trying to reach it but too far away, he tumbled like a load of stones onto the carpet. Mickelsson bent down for a look at the eyes. They squeezed shut, dripping tears, then weakly fell open and were still. He cringed away, clutching his stomach, and, leaving the man as he was, hurried to the door. There he stopped, dizzy with fear and confusion. Clumsily, he ran back to the chest beside the chair facing the television. The glass refrigerator tray was there, but no sign of the money. He stood stupefied, swaying in disbelief, then hurried back to the door and closed it. He stood for a moment breathing in heavy gulps, hands over his ears, trying to think. He wouldn't remember clearly, afterward, how he hunted through the room, pulling out drawers, throwing the mattress from the bed, emptying the wardrobe. In one corner stood a Kero-Sun space-heater, not working. He lifted it from its place, moving it aside, and saw, behind it, an old ratty sweater. He almost left it there, then on second thought picked it up and found, tucked inside it, a large, aluminum-foil-wrapped bundle. Even before he tore the foil off, he knew this was it. It occurred to him only now to wonder how much time had elapsed, and whether anyone had passed outside the door. Tentatively, as if it might be filled with electricity, he touched the bank-banded money. It was miraculous that, in all this junk, he should find it. With steady fingers he dropped some of the money-packets into the pockets of his overcoat, the rest into his suitcoat. Then, unsteadily, numb all over, he straightened up and moved toward the door. The fat man lay on his side, knees bent, eyes partly open. He had holes in his shoes. Mickelsson moved past him, then paused. Suppose he wasn't dead. Suppose, against all odds, someone should wander in and find him, even now save his life. He looked in horror at the silver, lioness-headed cane and imagined it flashing down, sinking into the fat man's temple. "Holy God in Heaven," he whispered, fully understanding at last that, though not with the cane, he had murdered the man. He moved in a kind of dream toward the door.

Upstairs, in Donnie's apartment, Mickelsson dropped the money, all of it, onto the threadbare carpet. She was silent. Though he did not count—nothing could have been farther from his mind—it was clear that he'd given her more than the fifteen thousand she required. Neither of them said a word. She suddenly turned, her hand over her mouth, and fled to the bathroom. He heard her vomiting. He meant to leave, but, strange to say, he found himself sitting down, dazed, in the chair where she liked to read or listen to her records. He imagined himself on his knees, counting the money, but did not stir. His mind was crowded, swollen with the image of the dead man's calm face.

She appeared at the bathroom doorway.

Solemnly, Mickelsson rose, buttoned his overcoat, and leaning on his cane, moved toward the door. She watched.

"Prafessor," she said.

He opened the door, stepped out, and softly closed the door behind him.

PART THREE

1

He knew, of course—everybody knew—about murderers returning to the scene of the crime, but it was necessary. Partly he felt—for all practical purposes believed—that whatever happened to him from this point on was fated, as all things material are. He seemed not his own man, only an agent—the submissive means by which evil powers he could not understand did their work. Insofar as it was this faintly psychotic sense of abandonment that ruled him, any risks he might take were impersonal. If he was of two minds, one that had fled elsewhere, leaving only the smell of its horror, the other clanking on, and if in that second mind he was sunk deep in the swirling mud of actuality, acting helplessly but with full intent and will, like a pilot fighting his plane through a tornado, the ethical result was all one. Volition was for angels. He must do whatever the instant required, without thought.

Back at home, after he'd left her, and after the shock had partly lifted (he'd lain in his bed unmoving, staring into space the whole night), he'd realized that he should have talked more with Donnie, calming her, making sure she understood her accessory involvement, feeling her out and guiding her. There were a thousand tricks she might pull, if she were frightened enough. She might take however much of the money she pleased, then go to the police with whatever was left and tell them what he'd done. Aside from Donnie, no one but the dead man could say how much there had originally been. "What would I say if she did that?" he asked himself, clenching his teeth with the effort of his concentration. Or she might run with the money and get her abortion in spite of her promise, making his act—terrible enough already—sickeningly casual, obscene. That would enrage him. He did not want ever again to do violence to anyone. A hundred times, that sleepless night, he saw with dizzying vividness how the man had clutched his chest with the side of his useless pistol, his twisted face a mute cry of anguish to the universe, a wail for mercy. The memory made him gag. Nevertheless he would be beside himself, he knew, if Donnie were now to make a joke of it. She ought to be made aware of that, so that she could enter the proper quotient of dread into her calculus.

He had no real idea, as he emerged from his lair to seek her out, what he meant to say to her. (In the rear-view mirror he was red-eyed, unshaven.) He tried one imaginary conversation after another, each more fatuous and improbable than the last. It grew increasingly clear that, despite his despairing indifference, it was for his sake as well as hers that they must talk, so that, now that his head was clear, he could gauge her mood and figure out how much he could tolerate from her, exactly what forbearance he was capable of. If she intended to go to the police . . . what then?

It was not as if, like one of those low-born, ever-the-same TV murderers, he had something to protect—his possible future with Jessie, his job and reputation. He cared not a whit about any of that. He was now absolutely on his own, cut off utterly. The question was simply, how much would he put up with? Where no law was left but the animal sense of one's own life's worth—a sense now both poisoned and illuminated by guilt, by experience of the truly disgusting (he now understood) fear of raising one's head among the common, "decent," ever-witlessly-judgmental herd—how much, if anything, would he think himself worth? He grew angrier and angrier, like one scandalously misused. He found himself increasingly indifferent and unafraid.

But when he reached her apartment at seven that morning, he found Donnie Matthews' door locked and Donnie gone, and though nothing in specific suggested that her absence today was any different from her ordinary absences—except, of course, for the time of day, and the fact that the plastic rose she'd taped to her door was gone—he felt convinced that she was gone for good, or anyway gone for a good long while. After knocking repeatedly, speaking softly to the door, listening for footsteps on the stairs behind him, he turned away, walked down one flight, then stopped again. The fat man's door, twelve feet down the hallway, was as solemnly closed as Donnie's, though he knew that at a touch it would spring open, both the catch and the chainlatch torn loose. How long would it be before the stench of the body—or some wandering draught, or some Jehovah's Witness visiting with a pamphlet, giving the door an accidental push—brought the police? Gloomy daydreams moved through his head: how he might come here at night and bundle the body, wrapped in a blanket, out through the window onto the tar-and-pebble roof, drag it across the roof and drop it with a thud into the alley below, load it into the back of the Chevy or Jeep, if he was able to get the Jeep running, and haul it away someplace, dump it where no one would find it. But even as, out of the corner of his mind's eye, Mickelsson attended to these macabre dreams, he was moving on down the stairs, his left hand sliding gently, ready to grip hard, on the worn railing. Perhaps he should have taken the fat man's gun. In the entryway he paused, the mailboxes a little behind him, and cautiously peeked out. The town's one patrol car was edging by —today it was Cobb driving, not Tinklepaugh—heading toward the outskirts of town. He waited until the patrol car was well out of sight, then ducked his head and stepped out, like a man full of business, onto the sidewalk. The sky was gray and low, building up toward a renewal of the blizzard. A puff of snow moved up the street, slow and formal as a skater. With two hands he pulled his hat down harder, his ears still unprotected, waiting for the first freezing gust.

Behind him, a voice cried out, "Hey! Professor!" He started so violently he almost fell, but he managed to catch himself, then turned to look back past his shoulder. It was the real-estate man, Charley Snyder, bundled up against the cold, elegant even so, hurrying down the sidewalk to catch him. "I'm glad I ran into you. Saves me a trip up to your house!"

Mickelsson struggled to get his face in control. To give himself more time he fussed with his scarf, tucking his head in as if to watch the work of his fumbling hands.

"Any developments on that break-in up there?" Snyder asked.

His heart slammed; then he realized what Snyder meant. "Nothing yet," he said, and shook his head, ruefully, then horribly winced.

Snyder took his arm, drawing him back toward Reddon's door. "Listen, you mind giving me a minute of your time? Let's go inside, where it's warm."

Mickelsson jerked his head in a kind of nod, glancing left and right, and made his face rigid, hiding panic and what might appear even worse— impatience, extreme irritation. He moved inside the drugstore with Snyder. The electric door whooshed shut and warm air fell over them.

"You aware of the Lonergan Hill business?" Snyder asked.

Mickelsson looked hard at the bridge of Snyder's nose, trying to pay attention. "I guess not." He grinned, then dropped the corner of his mouth, teeth still bared, like a man in pain.

"It's a dumping spot—legal, I'm sorry to say; there's plenty of the other kind. Anyway, the Department of Environmental Resources OK'd it. You know how they are. Don't let the name fool you; they work for the companies." He still had his gloved hand on Mickelsson's arm, as if afraid he might bolt, and he leaned close to speak, as if company spies were everywhere. "They've granted permission that chemicals from at least twenty-three locations be 'disposed of' there. Eighty-five per cent of it's from outside Pennsylvania—New Jersey and New York. It's bad stuff. Carcinogenic, mutagenic . . . ." He checked Mickelsson's eyes, perhaps saw confusion and impatience, and hurried on. "To make a long story short, we think it's serious. There's at least seventy-five families living on the roads around Lonergan Hill that get their water from wells and springs, every one of 'em in danger of pollution." Again he checked Mickelsson's eyes, then drew back a little. "You all right?"

"I'm fine," Mickelsson said quickly. "The heat in here—after you've been out there in the cold for a while—" He laughed loudly.

"Maybe we should go back outside."

"No, I'm fine." He gave another laugh, then sternly concentrated his attention on Snyder, waiting for the speech to be over.

"Well, OK, if you're sure." After a minute he continued, reaching inside his coat and drawing out papers as he spoke, "People may never even know when their water's gone bad. Last Saturday we had a meeting in Harrisburg and a woman told me her family's been hauling water for three years, ever since they found out, completely by accident, that their well had been poisoned by a landfill. The same thing could happen at the Lyncott fill. Here, let me give you this—all the facts and figures."

Mickelsson blinked, uncertain whether Lyncott and Lonergan Hill were the same place; but he had no intention of prolonging things by asking. He took the papers from Snyder, glanced at them, then put them in his pocket.

"They've applied for an expanded permit," Snyder said. "Instead of the original ten acres they want a hundred and forty-six. That's bad business—bad real-estate business and bad human business. The company applying already has a record of illegal and misidentified waste disposal. I'm a county commissioner, as you may know, and we're having hearings on the subject; but for me that's not enough. I have a petition here—" He released Mickelsson's arm and with one hand opened the front of his coat while with the other he reached inside to extract a brown folder.

"Ah!" Mickelsson said, "you want me to sign! Certainly I'll sign!" He took the pen Snyder offered him and quickly signed his name, then wrote his address and put a period after it. "There," he said. "My soul for infinite power."

"You're sure you're all right?" Snyder asked. He glanced at the druggist in his high box.

Mickelsson grinned, waved, and without a word hurried out onto the street.

He got groceries at the Acme, enough to hold him for a good long while—several days, anyway—in case he should decide he wasn't in condition to see people. He was convinced that he was safe, had gotten away with it, at least for the time being; and time was always on the killer's side. Nevertheless, since he couldn't trust himself—since remorse walked only a step behind him, cursing him, wringing its pitiful, domestic hands—it would be best to stay close to his house. At the check-out counter he remembered they no longer accepted his checks, and he blushed, wincing, breaking out in sweat, drawing his hands to his face like a man feeling monstrously guilty, perhaps a shoplifter with his pockets full of goods. "I'm sorry," he said, slapping his forehead, crazily smiling at the check-out girl. "I completely forgot that I'm not supposed to write checks here!" He flung a desperate glance around the store as if thinking he might see a friend who would help. *How stupid,* he thought

—and furiously blushed again—*to kill a man for his money and then recklessly throw it all away, not even keep forty-five dollars for groceries!* His distress must have been a pitiful thing to see, because the girl said, "Just write out the check. It's OK, this once. I'll tell the manager I forgot." He fell all over himself, foolish with gratitude, then finally got himself in control, took off his glasses, and wrote the check, then carefully entered it, the only check he'd entered in months. Then he snatched back his glasses and, all in one armload, carried the four large sacks of groceries out to the car. When the engine caught, a gray, putrid cloud rose not only from the car's rear end but from under the hood as well. No matter. For the moment the thing still ran. *Existence on the edge,* he thought. Everyone, everything. When was it—and why—that everything had gone wrong?

Perhaps there never before was so open a sea.

He tried to sleep, but his nightmares were so menacing he got up again. He should go on a trip somewhere. He should call the bus station, find out what was possible. But he remained sitting on the couch and, for a time, slept.

He couldn't remember having turned on the stereo tuner, though surely there had to have been some flicker of conscious intent in the gesture. In any event, when he switched on the vacuum cleaner he was abruptly made aware that he'd been listening to music, unconsciously hanging on every note, fleeing into it as into sanctuary, though he had no idea what was playing. It was something he'd heard performed one night in Heidelberg. He remembered how the audience had roared its satisfaction. He stood mouth open, gazing down at the vacuum machine— an old Hoover he'd gotten second-hand through the *Pennysaver,* with tape around the bag—then decided to vacuum another time, maybe when the news came on, reinstating the world. He put the machine away and sat down again on the couch to fill and light his pipe, thinking about heart attack and the death of the fat man. He cringed from the memory and bore down with all his mind's force on the music. He would work this thing out. Will power! It was stupid of him not to have done it long ago. Nothing could be more important!

For the hundredth time he regretted never having taken a good course in music appreciation. It was a humiliating lack in him, this stupidity about a thing so universal, so essentially human as music. Better to be born with one leg missing! He checked himself. *Beware of rhetoric,* he thought. *Hair-line crack that in the end might bring everything crashing.* He folded his hands, locked them together, eyes closed to slits. The woeful lack was there, undeniable, he confessed to himself; an emptiness of soul like the emptiness guilt brought on—perhaps a shaft too deep for any music course to fill.

He nodded, fell out of time for a moment, then was listening again, and thinking, straining his wits. He set his elbows on his spraddled knees, his hands behind his neck, pulling his head down to his chest.

It seemed clear, despite one's natural doubts that one was applying the correct categories, that the music was in some sense "saying things," crying out across the centuries to him—or to whoever might be alive to hear—with the greatest urgency; if not with the early Wittgenstein's facts and propositions, then with something close; but the meaning, whatever it was, eluded him; he'd have gotten more sense out of Sanskrit. He pulled out of his strenuous crouch, stretched, then lit his pipe and puffed at it, gradually building a flat, sullen cloud above his head. *Rausch.* Drunkenness. Could it be only that? His whole soul resisted the likelihood. Surely music was the God-given language of Being, not complex and intellectual, like speech, the language of the mind, but direct, immediate: expression as simple as the sprouting, greening, and flowering of a plant. Audible dance. Perhaps it *was* Being, the perfect resolution of dualism (as Heidegger seemed to think); hence the gross, mechanistic Germans' remarkable success with it. Emotion's machine; from heaven through earth to hell with Mercedes-Benz. Abruptly, he half stood up to look out the window into the twilight beyond, checking to be sure no one was spying on him, watching as he sat here, red-faced and unkempt, jabbering to himself. He thought he heard something falling, heavier than snow or rain—a hollow, clattering sound. But it was nothing. He sat down again and once more threw himself into his project.

It was true of course, he thought, grinding his palms on his knees, that composers revised, labored endlessly over their manuscripts—so he'd read and believed—but surely it was only for the purpose of getting the emotion just right, the cry of pain or rapture or love's sweet anguish precisely what it was. They wrote, played it through in their minds, revised, reconsidered, started over, and so by a gradual refining process expressed exactly what they meant or discovered they must mean, a "statement" purified beyond anything possible for human beings at first bleat. Surely even a tone-deaf dolt ought to understand the thing, penumbrally at least, once it was said. He had emotions, did he not? But wait.

If the music he was hearing was just emotional description, at best an infinitely careful, supremely artistic smile or groan . . .

He covered his face with his hands. What had any of this to do with . . .

But a moment later he was back on it, more intent than ever on breaking through the wall. Perspiration washed his forehead.

If music was studied, recreated or now-first-expressed emotion, why was he listening with such strained intensity, as if to learn some answer, solve some important life-riddle? Wasn't it the case, in fact, that he'd been listening all this while for the wrong thing entirely; that music—for that matter, all the arts—told one nothing at all, simply described things as they are, or were, or might be, simply named things as Adam was said to have named things in the garden except that it *was* the thing named? Was it the case, to put the idea more exactly, that music was nothing more than, as the formalists thought, one more expression of Nature's way, atomic orderliness, no more significant or meaningful—except for the fact that it was created by human beings and in public places flashed its complexity—than a jonquil, an elm tree, that it was simply one more particular thing in a crowded, gasping anarchy of things—itself, simply: meaningless and ultimately as worthless as a soup-spoon, or Donnie Matthews' foetus; or meaningless except in that, like the foetus, it might not have existed and someday would cease to exist? Was it delusion, then, that made people turn to it in times of crisis? (He should get himself paper and pencil, he thought, biting his lip; they would help him think clearly.) He was tempted to turn off the radio. He thought of what might be called Plato's theory, music as inspired intuition of pre-birth memory, God's voice; Aristotle's theory, the grounding of emotion, or catharsis; then of Collingwood's, music as discovery through expression, music as the mirror in which one saw, hence seized, the world. He sat forward, his elbows on his knees, hands over his ears, his whole body clenched, like an explorer pondering one of Garret's real-life dragons face to face, or face to helm, hypnotized, maddened by otherness, struggling to remember what he knew about the process of evolution, as if that might be of use. Why had he been listening, without even knowing it—sucking, gulping in the music on the radio as if it were oxygen, until suddenly the vacuum cleaner's noise had broken in on him like reality, a re-awakened consciousness of drowning? Why had he felt, as distinctly he had, *outside* himself?

Illusion. Truth was on the side of the vacuum cleaner.

Why the thought should irritate him—so much so that he had to get up and pace—Mickelsson couldn't say; it was a familiar truth. (In his mind he saw the fat man's long, futile gasp.) All his life, not quite consciously, he'd been looking for some kind of key in music (he registered the pun but could think of nothing to do with it)—had been looking for something with which to unlock secret gardens; but what music offered, if he was now on the right track, was Kant's impenetrable wall; phenomena; a certain ordering of facts—not propositions—another baffling variant of Nietzsche's "stone-hard words," as if the conductor were to say, "Life's a mystery? *I'll* show you mystery!" and were then maliciously to perform for you, say, Sibelius's Second Symphony, just now being announced, with unctuous respect, on the radio. Boston Philharmonic Orr-chestra. Mickelsson breathed shallowly and squinted where he stood. Gloom. Vague images came to him—dark shadows, something huge and restless—the roll of the wide, twilit North Atlantic, the clarinet a high, sunlit bird. (He remembered standing at the rail of the *S. S. France* with Ellen and the children.) *Crap*, he thought. *Vibrating catgut. Disturbed columns of air.*

He was striding now from one end of the room to the other and back, his hands fiercely wrestling with one another behind him. The whole world was noise, the outward expression of forces directly unknowable— not form, not "spirit"; blind thuddings in the dark—and music, fiction, physics, philosophy were merely translations into other, secondary noise systems, further dark codes, glosses of the unknown, unknowable text, "better" or "worse" in a given case only for their interesting complexity and internal coherence. (Wittgenstein again, though twisted, descended from Nietzsche.) One might say, in effect, that the arts—all forms of human activity—were simple ritual, the groping re-enaction of the un-knowable but felt: universal forces too dark and mindless to understand, whether one called them demons or the dance of electrons, forces one grasped—insofar as one grasped them at all—by joining them, mimicking them, dancing. So Bierhalle music made the Germans stamp their feet or drip shining fat crocodile tears, getting away from it all, and Americans shot their jism to a disco beat. But then why was Beethoven described in certain circles as one of the world's great philosophers? Could one look at Beethoven, then back at the world, and *know* something? One of Beethoven's favorite writers, Mickelsson had somewhere read, was Immanuel Kant. One of his friends was Nietzsche's inspirer, Cabinet Minister Goethe.

Abruptly, scowling, short of breath from his anger at himself, Mickelsson turned off the radio, with clumsy hands got out his von Karajan *Symphonies and Overtures of Beethoven,* and carefully, touching the record-rim only, placed the First Symphony, side one, on the turntable. He stood staring at the slowly turning record, his pipe in his hand, keeping the philosophy of Kant in mind and listening with the sharpest possible attention to the music's first bars. A familiar trembling came, something like the feeling he would get when near Jessica Stark, whom now he locked out of his mind. It was beautiful music (whatever that meant), so sweet (whatever that meant) that his eyes brimmed with sentimental tears—a baffling opening like an abruptly continued, half-forgotten conversation, as if God's first words should be *On the other hand* . . . and then, quite suddenly, the music turned thrilling, an expanding, rising affirmation of . . . who knew what? Mickelsson refused to fool himself. He had no earthly idea what—if anything—the music was saying; it certainly had nothing to do, so far as he could tell, with the *Critique of Pure Reason*, not even with the mind's inability to get past the phenomenon. Possibly it was related to the *Critique of Judgment*. On one hand there's the universe, Beethoven might be saying; on the other hand, I give you . . . Von Karajan was said to have done well under the Nazis.

No, he had no idea what the music was mimicking, describing, or proposing, or why it so powerfully affected him, made him want to bawl like a child, or fly, smash down walls. *Rausch,* he thought again. Or maybe conquest of the horrible unconquerable by any other means. Perhaps the whole thing had to do with the phenomenon Garret had mentioned—a commonplace these days—the lack of connection between head and heart, the abyss between belief and attitude, cognitive and conative. Something deep within him, buried under tons of dispiriting experience and muscular fat, stirred to the music as a dowsing rod stirred to hidden rivers. Touched by the music's unearthly probe, the almost dead child-angel within him, buried alive in mundane concerns—the grown-up's miserable otherness of self-regard, cowardly paranoia—struggled feebly for an instant to un-stick its eyes. (Was that what he was doing restoring the house: erecting his dead self's sepulchre?)

Self-regard. Was that it? He couldn't hear Beethoven because he was locked up inside himself, more deaf than the composer?

There was nothing he could do about it. (Now as he walked he was slamming his right fist into his left hand.) Story of his life. Wrapped up in himself, as if his once relatively solid flesh and vaulting ambition (will to power) were his winding sheet, he'd managed to sleep through his ex-wife's whole existence. (He thought of how taken by surprise he'd been, noticing her beauty in the snapshot he'd found, made when Uncle Edgar had come to California.) No doubt he'd missed his children's existence, too. It was the same thing he'd sensed repeatedly in his teach-ing, failing to hear what his students had to say because he was waiting to get on with the course. It was that that had kept him from understand-ing, possibly saving, Michael Nugent.

He frowned, stopping himself. Sentimentality was the great risk for the man cut off from others and himself. It was sentimentality that made a fool of the hermit in the woods. Flip side of fascism, as Jung had pointed out. He must beware! He covered his eyes with his hand. He felt a little feverish. His mind kept rushing, driving.

The last time he'd seen Nugent, down at the office, just as he was packing up his books and papers to leave after a long day of classes and appointments—a day now declining into darkness, yellow lights coming across the dark snowy lawn from the Chemistry Building and classroom wing—Nugent had seemed happy; there had been a flush of color in his cheeks. How little one ever really knew about what was going on in others! Nugent had talked excitedly about some vision that had come to him one night when he was sitting alone, depressed, in his dormitory room. It had been raining (now Mickelsson found some of it coming back), and Nugent had been seated beside his window, a book of Wittgenstein's open in his lap. He'd been so sunk in wretchedness—the sense of loss and futility that always came when he thought about the deaths he'd been through this year (his father, whom he rarely saw—Nugent's parents were divorced—the father killed in an electrical accident at Niagara Mohawk, where he worked; and then Nugent's teacher, Professor Warren), he—Nugent—had been unable to read, had neither the will nor the eyesight, because tears were streaming down his cheeks. Then something almost miraculous had happened, he said; something eerily related to what he'd been reading. He'd looked with his teary eyes at the dark, rainwashed window and had seen, scattered as if not on the windowpane but in the night beyond, thousands of blurry droplets, all glowing with color, every color of the rainbow. He wiped his eyes, startled by the beauty of it, and when he looked again he saw a different vision, equally beautiful: sharp, distinct waterdrops, each with a tiny pinprick glow of color. He had closed his eyes then, wondering at the sensation of warmth and peace that had suddenly welled up in him, and into his mind had come the idea he had dropped in on Mickelsson to talk about, the idea of a universe of infinitely precious glowing particles, every one of them necessarily *against* every other, that was the tragic law of individuation in space and time, but each and every one lit up by the ruby, emerald, sapphire, and diamond shine of God's consciousness.

Mickelsson, of course, had had nothing to say. It was not a philosophical insight, only mystical—conatively persuasive but cognitively meaningless—and what it had to do with the feeling of peace that had swept through Nugent and seemed not to have left him yet, heaven only knew. Apparently it *had* left him, sometime afterward. Perhaps its leaving had been for Nugent the final blow. Tranquillity recollected in emotion. No telling now, of course, except if one day he should come across the black boy who was Nugent's friend. And what would they say? A loud crack came from the pipestem and Mickelsson awakened to the fact that, in his anger and frustration, he'd been biting down hard.

While he fixed and ate supper, carelessly, almost reluctantly—the grocery bags still out on the counter; he must remember to put them away in the fridge—he listened to Beethoven symphonies one after another on the stereo, learning nothing, his brain grown numb. His back began to ache, an effect of a muscular tension he hadn't been aware of. He imagined Donnie Matthews, riding on a train somewhere, looking out with frightened eyes.

Close as the stereo was to the kitchen—the speakers were just inside the livingroom door—he felt as if he were listening to something far away, increasingly far away—maybe Donnie's train plummeting into darkness—as if the music were coming from somewhere deep in the interstices of things, perhaps from himself, not that the music became clearer to him now: the cypher remained as inscrutable as ever. He felt himself more and more one with it, and yet, paradoxically, removed from himself, as if he were vanishing. (There was something about that in

Ortega y Gasset.) He was in a state almost trancelike; indeed, perhaps he was in a trance, as when one sits in a chair and by self-hypnosis raises one's arm, telling oneself with full conviction that the arm will rise, though one will not consciously raise it. He had a sense that by a head-shake he could pull out of this state, but by the faintest flicker of choice he allowed it to continue. The lines and colors of the kitchen became sharper, cleaner, as if brute existents were springing to life. His thought was dreamy and confused. He could not have explained, if someone had asked him, the distinction between himself and the walls of the room, the sudden swell of horns and violins.

When he went in to change the record at the end of the Sixth Symphony, he saw the old woman standing at the window, looking out, dabbing at her mouth with the pitifully wrinkled, gray hankie. She looked lost, befuddled. He could get no trace of anger from her now.

"Is there something I can do for you?" he asked.

She seemed not to hear.

His heart ticking rapidly, causing a light pain, he moved closer to look at her face. She was not the kind of ghost one could see through. No one, if he had come in and seen her standing there, would have believed she was a ghost, though somehow it was clear that she did not belong here in ordinary reality. Sometimes she whispered something, talking to herself—nothing Mickelsson could make sense of. After the hours of music, he was strongly conscious of the silence. He felt then, suddenly, a physical shock, a blow as if from inside that gave him, in-stantly, a splitting headache; and now, as if something had prevented it from getting through before, filtering it somehow, he felt the anger. He wouldn't have believed that one could live, not have a stroke, walking around in such a rage.

"Why are you here?" he asked. He pressed the heel of his right hand against the pain in his forehead.

Apparently he did not exist for her. Perhaps nothing existed as solidly as her emotion. He was tempted to reach out and touch her, not with his hand but with the record he held in it, which he'd been preparing to put on the changer—but he couldn't bring himself to do it. At last, abruptly, on rubbery legs, he turned and walked back to the stereo, put the record on, flicked the switch, then walked heavily back—touching the walls, the furniture, the doorway—into the kitchen. It was nearly dark now, late twilight, black clouds moving swiftly across the valley. More snow was predicted. He went into the bathroom to find aspirin. Beethoven wailed and crashed behind him like ice-and-snow mountains falling in, meaningless noise, oddly off rhythm, he thought, hardly more ordered than the vacuum-cleaner noise, until it came to him that part of the sound was not from the record player but from outside, somewhere in the woods above his house: gunshots, three in quick succession, then after a moment a fourth. John Pearson hunting, no doubt. Expressing himself, like Beethoven? What did one hunt—except one's own soul—at twilight, in deeply drifted woods?

He forgot about Tillson's party, or rather chose not to remember it. The roads were clear, a single snow-packed lane between eight-foot-high banks, when, three nights later, he drove the Chevy down to Susquehanna for groceries. Those he'd gotten before had spoiled, left out on the counter. The town's Christmas decorations had been up for weeks now—green, red, yellow, white and blue, reflected in the slush and the steely ice below, and on the dented metal of cars and high-bodied pickups with hydraulic plows. The lights and the tinny Christmas music coming from a second-story loudspeaker (Donnie's window was dark) flooded him with un-welcome sentimental emotion. He had to sit for five minutes in the Jeep, regaining control. At last, conspicuous, as if every window were intently watching him, he walked across the street to the Acme to get what he needed. Everyone was talking about the murders—the fat man was only one. An old woman who lived in a trailer had been killed by her daughter, stabbed seven times, and a taxi driver had been found on Airport Road, north of Binghamton, shot in the head execution-style. Without a word the check-out girl gave Mickelsson his bounced check. It was all right; he'd cashed a check for a hundred dollars just that morning at the bank. Though he'd again weakened and sent money to Ellen, it would probably clear. Donnie's absence was in one way, anyhow, a great burden lifted off. When he'd set the grocery bags on the seat beside him and was about to head back home, he abruptly changed his mind, got out again, slammed the door, and walked up the street toward Owen Thomas's.

A man who looked like a Montana cowboy in winter came toward him with one hand raised, clenched to a fist inside its leather glove—perhaps a warning, perhaps a greeting. Mickelsson stopped in his tracks. The man had a wide hat much like Mickelsson's, a big sheepskin coat, jeans, and heavy black boots. "Hay, Prafessor!" Though it was night, he wore dark glasses.

Yet Mickelsson's heart calmed. The voice was Tim's. "Hello!" Mickelsson said. "Long time no see!"

"Just tryin to keep owt of the way of killers," Tim said and laughed, gently slapping Mickelsson's shoulder.

"That's something, isn't it?" Mickelsson said, and felt his expression twist strangely. He remembered someone's saying that Tim was homo-sexual. It seemed utterly improbable, but what could anyone know about anything? He thought of the motorcyclists Tim rode with and had a brief nightmare vision of the whole pack of them as killer homosexuals. He stopped himself in disgust. "It's scary, the way the world's going." He covered his mouth with his hand.

"Isn't that the dahrn truth!" Tim said, and laughed. "That's something, though, that fat man. Sitting up there all this time with all that stash, useless to him as a waterproof ear on a prairie dog!"

"Ah?" Mickelsson said. The part about the fat man's loot had not been in the paper.

"That's what the murderers were after all right," Tim said, happily grinning.

Murderers. Mickelsson's heart jumped. "They took something, then, you think?"

"I guess the cops don't know that, yet. Leave it to Tacky Tinklepaugh, they'll never know. But I guess they gaht the Sheriff's Department in on it now, and there's a chance it'll go right to the F.B.I. Possible the man robbed a bank, while back."

"I suppose they don't know who killed him—who the murderers were?"

"Naht yet," Tim said. "Course everybody *really* knows. But what can you do?" Tim's smile drew back on one side, ironic.

He wondered if his eyes, staring into Tim's, showed his fright. He still had no control of his mouth, and kept it covered.

Before he could think what to say, Tim slapped his shoulder again, about to step past him, and said cheerily, "Hay, gotta run, Prafessor. See ya!" And he was gone. Mickelsson half turned to look after him. He hadn't quite realized how big Tim was, until this moment. Had he meant, by "murderers," Mickelsson and Donnie? Had she talked to him, perhaps? Suddenly it seemed to Mickelsson that of *course* everyone must know who had killed the fat man. He remembered how he'd shouted, that night in Donnie's apartment; the whole town must have heard it. Lowering his head, chewing his upper lip, he continued on his way to the hardware store.

The bell rang cheerily as he opened the front door, and Owen Thomas looked up from the cash-register and smiled, distant. "Merry Christmas," he said. Mickelsson nodded and, as soon as possible, feigning interest in this and that, got his back turned to the man.

The store was full of light, as always—a good deal more light than usual: electric wreaths, painted-glass Santa Clauses, tree lights, blinking electric candles. Along with the usual tools, plastic trashcans, plumbing and electrical materials, and the rest, the aisles were now crowded with sleds, trikes, games, plastic dolls, stuffed animals, and, on the shelves along the sides, small appliances to tempt farm wives. Walter Cronkite was talking on the display TV. The sound was turned off.

"I hear you've done wonders up there," Owen said.

"Who told you that?" Mickelsson asked with what he knew must sound like guilty sharpness. He smiled too late.

"Oh, you know"—Thomas grinned, more on one side than on the

other, the center of his mouth drawing sideways—"people who make deliveries, maybe Wilcox, the man who fixes furnaces. . . . Nothing's secret, little town like this."

Mickelsson hastily turned away for fear that the blood was draining from his face too visibly. "Well, I keep busy," he said. His eye fell on the gunrack—rifles, shotguns, pistols, the metal wonderfully solid, all business, the wooden stocks gleaming with soft, reflected light, red, yellow, green, blue.

"Thinking of doing some hunting?" Owen asked.

"They sure are beautiful things, aren't they?" Mickelsson said. "I wonder whether it's guilt or pride that makes people put all that devotion into making a gun?"

The storekeeper thought about it.

Mickelsson pointed to the lock on the case. "You got a key to that?"

"I better," Owen said, and smiled.

He drove back slowly, still surprised at himself, thinking what fear disguised as indignation his ex-wife would feel if he were to walk into the house and hold out to her his purchase, challenge all her twisted, secret violence with the weapon's stern wood and steel. But she wouldn't be there, of course. Never again. For a moment, as when he'd first walked out, the realization that their parting was final gave Mickelsson a sharp pang, made the buildings on each side of the street high and dark. He thought of her parents, of whom he'd been fond—gentle, shy people, proud of their brilliant daughter, though troubled by her ways. "Shoot," her father would say, smiling and blushing; it was all he could think of, whichever way the conversation turned. He owned a dry-goods store and wore a flag in his lapel. He and Ellen's mother had married when they were eighteen and had lived happily ever after, good Methodists. He'd been the captain of a bowling team. Mickelsson had gone with Ellen to watch him once and had been startled at the sight of him not dressed in a suit, wearing the peculiar purple jacket with gold lettering—he couldn't now remember the name of the team. When Ellen's father barbecued steaks, always well done, he wore an apron that said COME AND GET IT! The thought of Ellen's parents made the grief worse than it might otherwise have been. Surely Ellen had been in some ways like them, salt of the earth, though at first glance there seemed no possible connection between Ellen and those two shy people. According to something in a letter Mickelsson had gotten from his daughter months ago, Ellen and her parents were no longer on good terms. He wished he could see them again, or write to them, at least.

But the wave of unhappiness passed more quickly than it would have done six months ago. One could outlive anything, he was beginning to see. What one would once have called unspeakable—he was thinking of

the murder—could become just a private unpleasantness, like an ugly argument in the corner of a crowded, noisily cheerful room.

He drove home past Christmas-lighted windows, the huge gloomy-towered old Catholic church with its doors and windows all aglow, full of people no doubt, then darker streets, the tall, bare trees around the hospital. In all this time he hadn't spoken a word to Tom Garret. The thought made him draw in his head in the darkness of the car.

He hunched his shoulders and drew his head in more. He must do something to put order back into his life. With a start he remembered that he must think of something to buy his children for Christmas. How many days had he left? He frowned, blinking sudden tears back, leaning toward the windshield, and gradually realized that it was useless to try to work out what the date might be, he couldn't concentrate. His hands pressed into the steeringwheel. Monday. Some Monday before Christmas. He clamped his lips together and tasted salt. Angrily, with his thumb and one finger, his hand spread wide, he wiped his eyes. His daughter and son would be at home with their mother in Providence for Christmas, he brooded, momentarily forgetting that his son had disappeared. He saw dark hallways, leaded windows, candlelight reflected on old, cracked paintings. Providence was a social place, and no one more sociable than Ellen and the children. He imagined them laughing and singing, arms around the shoulders of their friends, their mother—rolling down the car windows, calling out to strangers, students skulking across lawns: "Merry Christmas!" He imagined the dead fat man stumbling toward them calling out for help. "Mercy!" he would moan, blackness in his mouth. Mickelsson shook his head, driving the crazy image back to darkness.

He remembered that Mark would not be there, would be God knew where.

He bent still farther toward the windshield, discomfort in his chest. He could see his partly bared teeth in the windshield, his glistening eyes. Wince of a killer. Poor super-ape, programmed to love and forget! Whole generations came and went on the earth, and—because, once they'd settled in, made a place for themselves, they never left home, never wandered lost from the valleys they'd chosen or inherited from their fathers—they, those former, safe generations, had never learned the truth: that all this mighty turmoil of the heart is illusion: love of kin, the home dirt, the hymns of one's particular sect. . . . Once, Peter Mickelsson's heart had leaped at sight of the dusty wheat-yellow hills of California, just as years before that it had leaped at the fairyland green or, in winter, the shadow-dappled white of Wisconsin. But he'd moved one or two (three, four) times too often, and now when his business took him to places where his heart had once leaped—if you could call this nonsense he lived by a business—he was in and out like the Fuller Brush man, Wham bam thank you ma'am, indifferent as he'd be to Daytona Beach or Hackensack. Interesting that the meaning of life, genetically implanted, should be so dispiritingly simple, a certain slope of land, a particular sunlight, the sixth physical sense, the sense of belonging. Even he, for all his travels, was not fully immune—no one was, of course—feeling his idiot heart warm, after only these few months, as his car nosed into the fold of the mountains and, winding up the steep, dark Susquehanna Valley, warm more as he climbed the still flank of his own pile of earth. Yet he could leave, he knew; never bat an eye. He could forget all these people, just like that, become fond again of strangers and leave them too. O Love, let us be true to one another until Tuesday!

His face froze in another wince, dripping tears, partly anger at the brain's endless posturing. Shameless, sentimental bullshit. That was what community was for, to tell the visionary madman "Come off it!" John the Baptist bawling in the wilderness. Cassandra blubbering by the sea.

So the young moved out from their fathers' houses to new places— Utah, Southern France—and put down roots, sucked in air, fell in love with the scent of coalsmoke or sassafras, whatever; and so long as they remained there in the new land Jehovah had set aside for them, all was well with them, they knew who they were, what they were there for. In other words knew nothing; questioned nothing, learned nothing. Such was the program. Flight from the nest, new nest-building, then steadiness, the old heart mellowing into loam to feed the trees of the great-great-grandchildren's nests. The world had been meaningful by inspection then, because no one but the sad-eyed, lamenting Jews had been con-strained to move endlessly from place to place, from home to alienating consciousness; tear up again and again those roots they'd so thirstily put down, forget names and faces betrayed, betraying. . . . Alas, the fidelity the heart required was no longer among the world's possibilities. Now all people were Jews. How many would survive the new, universal holocaust? Not Mickelsson, he feared—thinking the same instant, *Self-pity!* Weeping. (Clear vision was the hermit's hope. Sentimentality the risk. For hermit, read crowd-pressed modern man.) He thought, in contrast, of his father, dying in the hospital, surrounded by friends, tubes in his arms and nose.

The unfortunate thing about the mentally ill, he thought, imagining he was speaking to Rifkin, is that they're vile.

Rifkin shrugged. "Who's not vile?"

He left the dark, outer houses of Susquehanna behind him—in the windows, the flickering blue light of TV sets, all sweet sorrowing America's opiate, even Susquehanna's, though not his, up on the moun-tain, where one could only get the sound and where even that, what one could get of it, was blurry, like a confusion of sea-nymph voices in a cave. Just as well that he should be denied even television's comfort. Having abandoned his friends, his wife, even himself, he was one of the world's new beings, not fit to survive, but sufficiently clear-headed to tell the tale. He looked over at the shotgun, the barrel just a shadow now, standing upright, silhouetted against the window, like a narrow hitch-hiker.

He began to drive faster, more recklessly than usual, sliding on icy corners, still wiping his eyes from time to time. Barrelling around a corner not far from where the doctor had nearly hit him all those weeks ago, his headlights lit up—black against the sugar-crystal whiteness of snow—two hatless, long-coated young men climbing a snowbank to get out of his way. They teetered precariously, flailing their arms, much too high on the bank to be in danger, though they apparently didn't know it. Their invasion of his territory made anger flash. Mickelsson rolled down the window and shouted as he shot past, *"Wo kein Kläger ist, wer wird da richten?"* It was a stupid, adolescent thing to do. Crazy. If he were drunk, perhaps . . . Poor devils! But he was smiling, pleased with himself. He did no harm; they had each other—as poor dying Miss Minton had had the principal, the School Board, the parental conspiracy of silence. They had behind them, these two souls in black, the whole shadowy army of Mormon, a drab, sober-minded community stretching to the ends of the earth, from Susquehanna to darkest Peru. God bless community, never mind what—the Century Club, the Independent Order of Odd Fellows, Mickelsson and his ugly cat. He shook his head and saw his reflection in the windshield shake its head.

When he was inside his house and had closed the door, he stood for a long time with his legs planted in one place like pillars, the shotgun cradled in his arm, his eyes gazing around balefully, trying to think where he should put the gun. He had no mantel—there was only the woodstove—and he was reluctant to put it in some closet, out of sight. From the couch, the sickly, angry gray and white cat watched him carefully. No doubt the old bastard knew about guns. Yet he did not leave.

At last, as a temporary measure, Mickelsson leaned the shotgun against the wall by the door, next to the flowerstand holding Jessie's gloves. Then he went into the kitchen, switched on the light, opened the refrigerator door, and for a long time—he had no idea how long—stood gazing in, cold air pouring over him.

He was roused from his reverie by a whine of trucks passing on the road in front of his house. He ran to the front door and looked out. They were driving without headlights. "Call the police!" he told himself. But he was more afraid of the police than of the trucks. He wiped perspiration from his forehead.

Late that night, in his damp, stone-walled cellar—all the lights upstairs turned out, the cat asleep on the rug near the stove—Mickelsson built a workbench, eight feet long and solid as a rock, with a deep drawer below and cupboards above for stains, glue, and tung oil, and a large space of bare wall for peg-board, which he meant to buy tomorrow. (Slink into town, dart back again . . .) He made the bench with meticulous care, measuring, levelling, fitting, bevelling. He'd definitely decided now to make things; he wasn't sure what. Boxes, coffins, windowboxes, wheel-barrows . . . He'd get himself a band-saw, table-saw, drill-press, and belt-sander, possibly a lathe. Thomas would not press for payment. It didn't matter what he made, as long as it was more or less useless, and craftily done. He sawed and hammered, puffing at his pipe, sweating, filling every pore with dust. He pegged and glued every carefully fitted joint and rabbet, and, while the glue dried, tied the whole thing drum-tight with fishline. When he plucked the taut nylon holding the deep pine drawer together, it rang like the string of a guitar. When he finished, swept up, and went upstairs to take a bath, once more soothe his aching muscles, there was watery light above the mountains to the east.

He slept till noon, then immediately, without eating (he stopped to eat less and less, these days), removing the telephone receiver from its hook, went back directly to his project. First he went down cellar to look at the bench—everything was as it should be—then he drove to Susquehanna to order tools. Owen Thomas had in stock a band-saw, slightly used, and a drill-press, new, also a belt-sander, a back-saw and picture-frame clamps. The rest he'd have to send for. By suppertime that night, Mickelsson's new woodshop was whining and growling, spreading clouds of white dust. He imagined his father and uncle looking on, pulling at their chins—imagined them so clearly they were almost there, though they were not.

Neither was Rifkin there, though Mickelsson pretended to talk with him and the daydream was sometimes as vivid as daydreams of child-hood.

Rifkin leaned against the workbench, crookedly smiling, his chin bunched up. "So what's it all mean?"

"No meaning," Mickelsson said, carefully lining a board for the saw-cut, a curve he knew to be a hair too tight for the saw. "I'm entering into mindless ritual. Just me and things."

"Bullshit."

"Very well, I'm making Christmas presents. One has one's responsi-bilities. *Ich soll! Ich soll!* Possibly I'll make something for Ellen and The Comedian." Forcing the blade just a little, he managed the cut.

"I'll bet."

"You have no faith, Rifkin. That's your problem." He lined up the next cut.

"I have faith that if you keep drinking gin in the middle of the after-noon on an empty stomach, you'll lop off your hand with that band-saw."

"And you don't believe in accidents."

"Not the intentional kind."

"Good point. I must be careful with the band-saw." He drank, then sawed his mark.

With one finger, Rifkin pushed his glasses up his nose. "Why'd you buy the gun?"

"To kill myself, you think?" He made his eyes wide in mock-horror.

"Just asking. I notice you cry a lot."

"I noticed it myself," he said with exaggerated interest, tilting his head. "Sometimes I don't even feel anything when I cry, I just happen to touch my face and—slippery! It's vile."

"You use that word a lot," Rifkin said with distaste.

"I do." He was suddenly wary. The imaginary Rifkin should not notice what he hadn't noticed himself. He said, as if covering himself, "I must watch that."

"Mickelsson, I like you," Rifkin said, devious and saccharine. The finger with which he pointed was as stiff as the barrel of a pistol. "I'm just trying to help you. Why must you make it so difficult?"

Mickelsson's hands leaped back, thinking on their own. The band-saw was screaming, the blade off its track. He was all right, but his heart was whamming and he was itchy all over, fear-sweat exploding through every pore. He reached down with a shaking left hand to turn the power off. Gradually he calmed himself.

"Doctor," he began, loosening the thumbnuts that held the plastic shield, preparing to retrack the blade; but the word *doctor* stopped his mind, or redirected it. Looking down at his sawdusty hand, he was thinking of the large, pale woman who'd sold him his house. For an instant he was convinced that she'd sold the house and moved to Florida, where her brother was also a doctor, because she was dying. The whiteness was some terminal disease.

He was stilled, as if her death too, like the fat man's and like Nugent's, were his fault. Tears of self-pity washed down his cheeks. *Christ*, he thought, half praying.

He must make these presents for his children. Pull himself together.

Rifkin was there again. "Doesn't it bother you that you're doing nothing at all for your friend Jessie?" He pushed up his glasses. "I mean, there *is* the real world."

"Well, Doctor," Mickelsson whispered, and glanced nervously at the stairs, then took a deep breath, "there are senses in which these other things are real, too."

To his distress and grief, brightly wrapped presents arrived from both his daughter and son. He was reminded to ship off the presents he'd made them. They would be late.

.   .   .

Christmas Eve came, and then Christmas Day. Surely never in his life had he experienced anything so painful. He lay in bed as if hoping he might somehow sleep through it, but his mind teemed with memories, each one more painful than the last—Leslie and Mark as children, up at the crack of dawn, running into the master bedroom to show what treasures they'd found in their stockings; the dark, pagan service—as it had seemed to Mickelsson—at the cavernous stone church in Heidelberg where not one note of the Christmas music was familiar; Christmases of his childhood, a brightly painted sled his father and Uncle Edgar had made for him once, had built right before his eyes, telling him it was for "a poor child who wouldn't get anything if someone didn't make something for him," which had made Mickelsson jealous, though he'd hid his feelings bravely, never guessing the child was himself. Oh, cruel holiday! Infinitely more terrible lie than Santa Claus! Day of agonizing human love, awful promise that God would be equally loving and—against all odds, against all reason—would ultimately make everything all right. He got up, simply to be moving, distract his mind from the sound of his own heartbeat, looking out at the world through a wash of tears that gave every stick of furniture, every tree outside, a prism halo. He wanted to call Jessie, Ellen, his children. He would have been grateful even to hear the voice of his successor with Ellen, The Comedian. "Christ!" he moaned, burying his face in his hands; and then, to himself: "Asshole! Get hold of yourself!" Though he knew better, he turned on the radio. Every sound that came over it, even the stupidly pious sermons from the fundamentalist station in Montrose, flooded his heart with love and remorse. Handel's *Messiah* made him sit down on the floor and clench his fists, bang them on the carpet like Achilles in his tent, and sob. Redemption, resurrection . . . what ghastly, unspeakable lies, if they were lies! He, Peter Mickelsson, was the frozen, buried world, and the deep snow that buried him and would never be melted was his murder of the fat man, that and much, much more: his swinish misuse of Donnie Matthews, his failure to love his wife as she'd deserved, his betrayal of Jessie—sins, failures, death-stink blossoming on every hand! At last the need to cry left him, though not the sorrow. He made himself a lunch of lettuce and baloney sandwiches, and drank a beer.

In the middle of the afternoon, like some kind of joke miracle, the two red-headed, extremely dirty-faced boys from Stearns' Texaco appeared at his back door. He'd called them two days ago to come up and jump-start his Jeep and see what was wrong with it. They'd been too buried in work to come, they said now, but Christmas Day was always light. "You work on Christmas?" he asked. They shook their heads, grinning, looking at the ground. "Man, we're always there!"

Mickelsson put on his coat, gloves, and boots, and went out with them to look at the long-dead iron monster. He couldn't tell whether it was the cold or his pleasure in seeing someone that made tears well up in his eyes again, but the world was once more blurry, edged with light.

They found the battery was shot. They could sell him a new one—a cheap piece of junk, but serviceable, they assured him—for twenty-four dollars. After a moment's reflection—his mind still unfocussed—Mickelsson agreed, and the boys went back to the station and then reappeared a short while later and put in a battery bright as a child's toy, white plastic sides and a yellow plastic cover with red caps. They started up the Jeep and listened for a while, standing there in the dazzling sun- and snow-light—such brightness that Mickelsson had to shade his eyes and squint—the two young men saying nothing, one red-head holding the door open, bending his ear over the steeringwheel, head turned sideways, as if listening for some infinitely soft whisper of complaint, the other standing by the left front fender, hands in coatpockets, smiling at the hood. Under the disguise of dirt they were remarkably handsome. They had mysteriously twinkling, potentially dangerous light blue Scotch-Irish eyes, the pupils just now mere pinpoints. The boy leaning in to listen called to Mickelsson, "Does it always run this haht?"

"I don't know," Mickelsson said, tensing his brow with concentration and hiding the tremble of his lips behind his hand. He moved close to the window in the open door to look in at the dial. Though the Jeep had been running for only a couple of minutes, the temperature needle was already near the red.

"Could be the thermahstaht's stuck," the boy beside the fender said, and gave a little laugh. He didn't sound as if he thought it would be that easy.

"Smell that?" the boy at the steeringwheel said. When he smiled, his wide mouth tipped up suddenly at the corners.

Mickelsson nodded. The smell was familiar; a musty, burning smell. He realized only now that it was trouble.

The heavy-set, thick-shouldered boy outside went around the front and opened the hood, then poked his head and upper body in under it, disappearing. "Shut her ahff a minute, Perry," he called.

The engine shut off with a tubercular chuff-chuff-chuff. The boy on the engine fiddled with things, then called, "Stahrt her up again."

The motor started up and sounded good for a moment, then worse than before. Smoke came up. The boy in front waved at his brother, a slow, graceful movement like the flying motion of an eagle's wing, and the one at the steeringwheel turned off the engine and, after a moment, came away, closing the door. They both stood with their hands in their pockets, elbows out, looking in at the engine like graveside mourners.

Mickelsson leaned nearer. Though he knew nothing about motors, even he could see that this one was peculiar. What he noticed first was a spring that didn't look like an auto part—possibly a spring from some farmer's screen door. Then he noticed that a hose coming from the radiator was held on to the thing it hooked to by a piece of coat-hanger wire. One could still see the question-mark-shaped hook for the closet rod. Where a number of wires came together, there was a blackened clothespin. It was that—the clothespin—that made his heart sink.

"Think you can fix 'er, Jim?" the younger one asked. When he smiled, the perfect white teeth transformed him to a child.

The older one, Jim, lowered the hood and said, "We can tow her in if you want."

Mickelsson pulled his glove off to hunt through his pockets for a Di-Gel. "How much do you think it will cost to fix?"

"You got water in your oil," the older one said. "Could mean you need a new engine. If that's what it is, and if we can find an old junker, we could hold it to five, six hunnerd dahllers."

"Jesus," Mickelsson said, and bit his lip. "If you don't mind waiting," he said then, and looked shrewdly at the older boy, then at his brother.

"We're in no hurry," the older one said. "We got all the time in the world." He smiled and shrugged.

"In that case . . ." Mickelsson said. "God knows I need the Jeep. If it's all right with you . . ." He got out his billfold. In the bill compartment he had fifteen dollars. "Will this cover towing?"

"Keep the ten," the older boy said, putting the five in the pocket of his shirt. "Merry Christmas!" He gave Mickelsson a bow and raised his right hand as if to shade his eyes, smiling, forming a soft salute that might have been Chinese.

So Christmas came and went. Mickelsson saw no one, went nowhere, except for his furtive runs to the hardware store or post office, though he did talk briefly with Jessie on the phone. She called, ostensibly, to ask if she'd left her gloves. Neither of them mentioned Jessie's trouble with her department. He knew that it was up to him to bring it up. She was no doubt hurt that he'd still done nothing to help, but he knew her pride. If he didn't feel like helping, the hell with him. He didn't like himself for keeping silent on the matter, but he kept silent. New Year's came and went (Mickelsson spent New Year's Eve at home, not even drinking, but only because he'd forgotten what night it was) and still he kept himself busy in the cellar, all his lights off upstairs, and put off driving in to Binghamton.

Though he thought of it again and again—looking over at the gun, or picking it up to feel the heft of it, run his fingers along the stock, the cool, blue barrel—he did not go hunting. The cat no longer showed nervousness when Mickelsson picked up the shotgun. He seemed a little more wearied, if anything. What the ghosts thought, Mickelsson couldn't tell.

He could avoid both the cat and the ghosts by working down in the woodshop, where neither showed their faces. He kept the phone off the hook. The cellar became crowded with his, so to speak, works.

The first night he didn't leave the phone off the hook, hoping he might hear from his son or daughter—they always called late—he got a call from Edie Bryant. "Isn't it wonderful about the hostages?" she said. He couldn't tell whether or not her voice had a hint of irony. It seemed there was a possibility of a breakthrough while Carter was still in office. Then Edie got down to what she'd really called about.

She was just sick, she said, about what those people were doing to Jessie, and to tell the truth she was very very cross with Mickelsson. "You're the only person that can help her, you know," she said. "Phil says so too, and he ought to know, with all his experience in administration. That Blickstein makes me so mad ah could just *spit!*"

"It's as bad as that?" he asked.

"Peetuh, if you'd just drive in here and *talk* to some people—talk to the president himself, if you have to. Even if you weren't some famous philosopher, you could make 'em sit up and notice. They're afraid of you. Phil says the same thing. They think you're crazy, you know. They're afraid you might punch 'em right in their little ole mouths. I tell you, I'd *approve.* Do 'em a world of good, that's my opinion! Sometimes it's the only way to get folks' attention."

Mickelsson laughed.

"And you should phone up Jessica," Edie said. "It's not right that woman havin to go it all alone."

"I imagine it's hard for her, all right." He wondered how Edie had learned that he wasn't keeping in touch with Jessie.

"You call her now, hear? And get in that ole Jeep and get right down here and do some talkin. Isn't it just like 'em, pullin a stunt like this at vacation time when nobody's around?"

When she paused, waiting, Mickelsson said, "I doubt that they'll get away with it."

"Well, they'll sure as hell try," she snapped. Then, after a moment: "You promise me you'll phone up Jessie?"

There was no way out. "I'll do it right away," he said.

"Good," she said. "Listen now, you come on by and visit sometime?"

"I will."

After Edie Bryant's call he fixed himself a large martini and began drinking it, too fast, pacing back and forth in the livingroom. Outside the windows it was pitch black.

There could be no doubt that his failure to help Jessie was objectively wrong. It had no doubt been quite innocently that Edie had learned he was out of touch with Jessie; something Phil or Tillson had said, perhaps, about his failing to pull his weight; or some innocent question to Jessie: "How's Peetuh, deah?" "I haven't heard from him in weeks."

Yet the materially irrelevant suspicion kept nagging him: the age-old conniving of women, Edie and Jessie in indignant *tête-à-tête*; Jessie proud and injured, showing perhaps more feeling for him than she meant to, and Edie rising to it, determined to fix things, drag the straggler back into the fold. Jessie bursting into tears, perhaps. (The imagined scene grew cloudy. He couldn't picture her bursting into tears, though he could imagine anger.) Surely a man had a right to withdraw, shutter up his windows, bar his door—especially such a man as he was, unwittingly a destroyer—and to hell with the eternal soft conspiracy of womanhood!

He fixed himself another large martini. The problem was not that he didn't understand what was wrong but that he understood too well. He had isolated himself, partly by accident, partly by intent, and now all that was normal, reasonable, unthought-out. . . .

"Just call her," he broke in on himself. "Just pick up the fucking goddamn phone."

Her phone rang and rang. He did not notice that it was now almost midnight. He had a fleeting thought—a flash of irritation—of the medieval courtly lover, poor miserable worm crying out in secret for miraculous grace. There was a difference, of course. The courtly lover, in his pitiful way, suffered for his lady, secretly served her with all his heart and mind. What they had in common, he and the goof with the lute, was despair.

"Hello?" she said, husky with sleep.

Now, suddenly, he did realize what time it was.

"Jessie?" he said. "It's me. Mickelsson."

"Oh," she said, then after a moment, "Jesus. What time is it? Are you all right?"

"I'm sorry to call so late. To tell the truth, I didn't realize . . ." Jessie said nothing.

"I got a call from Edie Bryant," he said. "She tells me—"

She said, "Edie?"

He said, "I've written a couple of letters. I'm sorry I was out of touch." His glass was empty, and the phone cord was too short for him to get to the bottle. "Can you hang on a minute?" he asked. "I'm sorry . . . I'm sorry. . . ."

"Listen," she said, "*Jesus*, Pete—"

"Just one second," he said. "Hang on."

He couldn't find the gin, though he knew it was there. He took the Scotch bottle instead and sploshed half a glass over the fragments of martini ice.

"I've written a couple of letters," he said. "I have an appointment with the president tomorrow morning. We're not going to let them get away with this!''

"The president's out of town," she said. "Why are you saying all this?"

"You don't believe me?" He threw his heart into it.

"What's the difference," she said.

Righteous indignation felt so good he kept it up. "You think I'm drunk, don't you. You think this is all empty talk!"

"You, Mickelsson?"

He clenched his teeth and stared for a moment at the wall, checked by her indifferent irony. "Lot of times people think I'm drunk when it's something else," he said at last. "I'll tell you the truth. I hide behind this apparent drunkenness. Mental problems. I don't want to go into it, but you can ask my psychiatrist. I'll give you his phone number."

"Pete, I really am tired," she said.

"Did I tell you what really happened to me in Providence? I won't take long; it's just that I want you to know, so that you know you can trust me—as long as I'm not flat-out crazy. Or maybe you don't want me to tell you, maybe you're not interested."

"Of course I'm interested," she said. "I'm also gonna be sick if you don't let me get some sleep."

Quickly—making a show of how quickly and briefly he was doing it— he told her about his episodes, how he would put on the red hunting coat and put white on his face, as the mime troupe used to do, and how he'd talked with dead things, had seemed actually to converse with them, though he could remember no details. "Anyway, the point is," he said at last, "with all that's been happening out here—the ghosts, if that's what they are, and these dreams I've been having—I've been feeling a little panicky and, well, I guess self-absorbed. That's why I haven't—"

"OK," she said. "All is forgiven."

"I know you don't need all this," he said.

"That's true." For all her effort to sound kind, she sounded distant. Alerted by his bullshit language, perhaps: "You don't need all this."

"I'm sorry I haven't been there when you needed me."

"It's all *right*," she said.

"I'm sorry I woke you up," he said.

There was a silence. He felt a crazy movement of the heart toward glee. She saw through him!

She said, "What do you mean, dreams you've been having?"

"Nothing really," he said, "that is, they never quite come to anything. I dream about the old people, something awful is about to happen, but then I wake up."

The line was silent for so long he wondered if she'd dropped off to sleep. Then she said, "Pete, you should come in to a party and get roaring drunk."

"Just a minute ago you were telling me I drink too much."

"Only that you drink alone too much," she said, and gave a laugh. "Did the Bryants invite you to the brunch they're having?"

"I'm not really up to the Bryants right now," he said. He felt a pang at not having been invited. "All the politics and religion. Politics and guilt. Or worse yet, Art. I like it better when he talks about dying whales." A nastiness had crept into his voice; he saw he must find his way back to something inoffensive. He mopped away tears with his handkerchief. "What was that play Phil was quoting, that night here at my place?" He mimicked the sepulchral voice: " 'When I consider life, 'tis all a cheat;/ Yet, fooled by hope . . .' "

"I don't think it's Shakespeare. I wouldn't know that kind of thing."

"The Bryants make me gloomy," he said, "especially Edie. She's so *interested.*"

There was another hesitation. He imagined her closing her eyes. "She means well. It scares her that everyone's not as happy as she is."

"You think she's happy?" He found it an interesting question, in fact. That Southerners' habit of warmly remembering community and carrying the memory through life in their mouths.

Jessie sadly laughed. She was sounding farther and farther away. "As happy as she thinks she ought to be, then." The line was silent, just a forlorn humming sound, as if all the way to Binghamton the phone-wires were bound in ice. Then Jessie asked: "Have you talked with your kids? Did they send Christmas cards?"

"Presents, in fact," he said. His voice sank a notch deeper in its gloom. Again he mopped at his face. "A carving from Mark. I guess he did it himself—he's never done that before, carvings, I mean. But it's got the look. Very strange—interesting. Bunch of children praying."

"That's nice, Pete. I didn't know Mark was religious."

"He isn't—though once when he was in school and they asked him to fill in some form, he put down, as religious preference, 'Lutheran.' " He laughed. "That's what I'd been, earlier, before I gave up on theism."

"You never really gave it up, Pete," she said. "That must be where he got it. What did Leslie send?"

"Embarrassment of riches. Dark plaid scarf, very nice one, more than she could afford. Also a wallet with a picture of her in it, one of those things where you put a quarter in the slot and then smile at the mirror. It's not bad. She's a wonderful-looking girl. She works, I guess I've told you. Cocktail waitress in one of those big motels—Ramada, I think. Poor kid works her heart out, both highschool and college, waitress several nights a week, and every play that gets produced for twenty miles around, she's in it if she can fit in rehearsals. Takes after her mother that way. She's got kidney trouble, as I think I told you; it's not good for her, all that work. I hate it that after all that she spends money on me."

"You know it would break her heart if she couldn't send you something."

"I suppose that's true."

Jessie asked, "What did you send them?"

"Nothing," he said. "Junk." It struck him that he'd sent nothing to Jessie. A fancy shirt had arrived from her; he'd opened it almost without noticing, feeling only a momentary flush of guilt; it was still on the chair in the livingroom.

"I'm sure it wasn't junk," she said. "What did you send?"

"It doesn't matter much. Mark won't get what I sent him anyway, not till he goes back to U.V.M., if he ever does. It was some things I'd made. Crude pegged boxes, some picture frames. Probably got there late besides."

"My my, aren't we pitiful," she said. "By the way, I've been reading your books."

"Oh?" Her words took a moment to sink in. "What do you think?"

"I can't really judge such things," she said.

"Take a flying guess."

"Well . . . They're interesting."

" 'Interesting'?" he said, mock-horrified.

"You know what I mean. I'm not wild about philosophy, but they're sort of fun."

"That sounds like high praise," he said.

"I guess it is."

When at last the conversation ended and he hung up the receiver and turned from the phone, the ghosts were standing in the livingroom doorway behind him, watching him. It made him jump. The woman's eyes were full of lightning, the man's troubled, as if something of importance had slipped his mind. Mickelsson felt a surge of panic, then angrily flapped his arm at them, like a farmer shooing away geese. They remained where they were. It seemed not right, not possible. Surely it was his own wish— or anyway receptivity—that had conjured them. Out on the road in front of the house, a huge black horse went by, drawing a sleigh full of children. All Mickelsson could see over the snowplowed banks was the top of the horse's head—there was a bright red plume on it—and the children's bright hats. He heard harness bells, a sound out of his childhood.

At his feet, the cat complained for food.

"Parasite," Mickelsson hissed. But he moved, glad of the cat's foul-smelling solidity, toward the sink where he kept the catfood.

Afterwards, he went to the study to write the letters he'd told Jessie he'd written. He sealed them without reading them over, knowing that if he did reread them he'd never send them. Sentimentality; drunken rant.

He drove them down to the box in front of the post office, so that he couldn't retrieve them in the morning. Later, so drunk by now that he could hardly stand up, he phoned Levinson, in sociology; a good man, though he had no power in the department. They talked for two hours. Mickelsson couldn't remember, afterward, a word of what they'd said. It was already full daylight when, placing his feet with care and clinging to the railing, he went upstairs.

He was not a well man. The ghosts he kept seeing, his sense that they were building up to something . . . He thought of the red coat, back from the laundry, hanging in his closet now. It was only a matter of time, no doubt. It floated through his mind that he could get up right now— he lay with all his clothes on—and drive into town with his murderer severity, his cold, dreadful, drunken frown, and get Blickstein out of bed, tell him in no uncertain terms how he felt, make use of the clout he was forever being told he had. Or he could make an appointment to talk to the president, as he'd said he'd done already.

Clout, he thought, and moved his head from side to side on the pillow, sweat on his forehead. His clout—he refused to shy from the word—was as fraudulent as that of the Marx brothers. Except for killing a poor half-blind, lonely and enfeebled ex-thief, what had he done worthy of mention in the past five years? Could he honestly say that if he himself taught the course on Karl Marx he'd do it justice?

He slept for hours, woke up with a headache, drank water and took aspirin then returned miserably to his bed and slept hours more.

When he went out to empty the mailbox, late that afternoon, he found, mixed in with everything else, a *Pipedream*—one of the university student papers—that someone had stamped and addressed to him. He hardly ever bothered with the student newspapers, but he was puzzled as to why anyone should have sent it, so when he'd dropped the rest of the mail onto the couch, he opened up the paper and put on his glasses to look at it. The headline on the front page was "SOC. DEPT. BATTLES." Under the headline was a picture of a stodgy, middle-aged professor at his desk. Wide face, heavy-lidded, sleepy P.L.O. eyes. On the second page there was a large, quite striking picture of Jessie at a lectern, and beside the picture, in bold-faced italics, a quotation: *"Sociology is basically nonsense, like philosophy or poetry. That's why we have to be as alert and open-minded as possible."* Under the quote, the *Pipedream* asked, "SHOULD THIS PROFESSOR BE FIRED?" He moved heavily to the far end of the couch, opposite the mail, and sat down to read.

The article was blatantly pro-Jessie, which pleased him, though he'd been around universities long enough to know it didn't mean much. Odds were, the writer was a student of hers—he looked at the by-line: Leonard Zweig—probably a male student, in love with her. Still, it was a good piece; the boy had done his research well—chosen witty quotations, quoted her enemies in a way that, without obvious manipulation, made them seem irrationally belligerent or doltish. He read slowly, intently, leaning closer to the paper than he needed to and gripping the scalloped sides tightly between his fingers. Facts: she'd gotten her Ph.D. from Harvard at twenty-two, had taught for three years at Washington University in St. Louis, had married E. Q. ("Buzzy") Stark, and had taught with him at Indiana University, then Entebbe, eventually Binghamton. She'd earned numerous awards (one from the World Health Organization), gotten honorary degrees—mostly from unheard-of places presumably in Africa—and had published dozens of articles, no books. On the fourth page of the newspaper, where the article was continued from page 2, Mickelsson was startled to find a picture of Jessie at age twenty-five. She was wearing a white dress with large black polkadots and a wide white hat, her hands shyly folded in front of her, on her face the smile of someone uneasy in front of cameras but not unaware that she is beautiful. "Christ," Mickelsson whispered, and drew the paper closer. Her face was like a child's, not yet touched by the shadow of family deaths. Behind her there was a white, Spanish-looking building, large, spear-shaped fronds, and a wide, bright expanse of water. Sunlight fell everywhere, not least (one felt) in the young woman's heart. He had never seen anyone more beautiful, he thought; he was reminded of those French art films of the fifties. Staring at the face, he felt baffled, suddenly depressed. The Jessie of the picture was one he would never know, and childish, irrational as the feeling might be, he felt cheated, a little angry.

He closed the newspaper, the photograph still in his head, and sucked in his lower lip, biting down, considering the idea of driving in to Binghamton and beating the shit out of some Marxist. Mickelsson the avenging angel. He would wear the red huntsman's coat, carry the silver, lioness-head cane. At the thought his shoulders tensed a little, and his hands, of their own accord, made fists.

It was late. They'd be at home, maybe just finishing supper with their families. That would make it harder, but Mickelsson had the blood of Vikings in him. He could handle it.

The image of the dead fat man came into his mind, and abruptly, to get rid of it, he stood up, reaching down in the same motion to pick up the paper from the coffeetable for one last look at the wide-faced, stodgy professor on the front page. He imagined what the face would look like terrified, just before Mickelsson pushed it in. But he knew now that he wouldn't do it. Without wanting to, he turned again to the picture of Jessie when she was young.

Then, with a sigh, he folded the paper, dropped it on the table, and made his way down to his basement workshop. He had decided to make an oval window for the high gable in front.

. . .

He was still brooding on Jessie's Marxists when, hours later, he shut off the cellar light and went up to bed. He knew almost nothing about them except that he despised Marxists in general—as, if he told himself the truth, he despised everyone with whom he disagreed—and knew them to be fashionable with fools. It was clear even from the pro-Jessie article in the student paper that they were passionately engaged in the work they did, concerned about making sociology not just a science (as they called it) but a force for change. How the two went together was a little hard for Mickelsson to understand, but never mind. They cared about the world and had strong, noble-hearted opinions. Like uneducated Baptists, or leather-jacketed knife-wielding punks, they turned deaf ears to even the best counterarguments. There was something (not much) to be said for that.

"Fucking swine," he whispered in the darkness.

Once after a movie he'd had a run-in with the Marxist with the pock-marked face and the long, thick fingers. It was a pleasant, devotedly made little movie about stone-cutters and bicycle riders; he'd seen it in the grungy little theater in Endicott. In the lobby, accidentally pressed up close to the pock-marked Marxist he'd seen at the party—there was another of them with him, a small, timid man with hair down to his shoulders; also the two young Marxists' wives, potentially angry though at the moment expressionless—Mickelsson had said, merely for politeness (and because no one in his right mind could deny it), though maybe he'd put a little edge in his voice, making it a challenge, and maybe he'd widened his eyes a little, and lifted his eyebrows, daring the son of a bitch to disagree: "Nice movie!"

The pock-marked one had looked at him, grinning, and had raised his head, pulling his chin in, like a horse on checks. "There are no nice movies," he said. "There are stupid movies and movies that wake you up."

"Maybe so," Mickelsson had said, and smiled. He slowly rubbed his palms together. The scene was going well.

" 'Maybe so.' Listen!" The young man raised a finger, somewhat cautiously, to touch Mickelsson's tie.

The crowd was all around them, so that Mickelsson couldn't have backed off if he'd wanted to. He smiled on.

The young man said, pretending to be merely reasonable, "Come on, what's it about? These stone-cutters build buildings that are better than *they* are. What kind of shit is that? And then the business dies, the stone-cutting, and what are they? Used-car salesmen! Crap!" He ran his tongue over his teeth, then grinned again, glancing around as if anxiously. "You liked that? What the fuck!"

"That's true," Mickelsson said. "They should have organized."

With a jerk, the man turned his head away. But then, unable to resist, he turned again to Mickelsson. "Young love. That's what the movie's about. First the kid loves this girl, then he loves that girl. *That's* what it's about. Let me tell you something. *That's* the real opiate of the people!"

"You're right," Mickelsson said. "Love is crap."

The man looked at him. "You're something," he said. "Don't worry, I read your book. You're either part of the problem or you're part of the solution." He laughed.

"I agree with you," Mickelsson said. Without his approval, his heart was pounding and blood stung his cheeks. He could not deny that he was enjoying himself. What would these good, patient people say if he were abruptly to reach out and strangle the man?

The pock-marked man sensed Mickelsson's pleasure, apparently. No doubt he too was enjoying himself, though he'd probably have denied it. He tapped twice on Mickelsson's tie, as if intending to provoke. His wife moved closer to him, scowling like a child, and the other woman smiled, blank as pie. The small man was staring at the floor, trying to get his pipe lit. "You agree with me. That's nice," the pock-marked one said. "As long as we have movies like this we'll have a country like this."

"I agree with you," Mickelsson said again.

"Terrific," the man said, nervous, and turned away again, seething but definitely uneasy, and this time he did not turn back.

Mickelsson considered hitting him in the ear with his fist, like one of those Brazilian torturers. He could think of no good reason not to; but he refrained.

The small man said, "*De gustibus non disputatus*, right?" He glanced at his wife, maybe to see if his Latin was correct, then at the other man's wife.

"I agree with you," Mickelsson said.

But now, staring up at the not quite visible ceiling of his bedroom, Mickelsson envied the Marxists. Their truth might be moronic, but ah, what joy to believe whole-heartedly! One couldn't even honestly claim that they were stupid. Einstein's whole achievement had come down to simply this, from one point of view: that he refused to consider any theory of the universe that ruled out God. Working within that limit, ruling out vast areas of the possible, he'd discovered what he'd discovered. When serious physicists of the next generation had begun to answer him, proponents of chaos against the old-style Jew, Einstein—angry and possibly confused—had quit the business, turned Zionist.

The pock-marked Marxist materialized at Mickelsson's bedside, a little like a grudging relative at a death-bed, a large, darker hulk in the darkness of the room. With the lightest flick of the will Mickelsson could have banished him, but it was of course his own wish that had brought him. He allowed him to remain.

He waited for what the man would say, or rather for what he might imagine the man would say. The man said nothing, looking down, morose, at his thick, folded hands.

"It's true, of course," Mickelsson thought, "that you give students a position, maybe not objective, but a solid foundation they can move away from on their own when they see their way past it, assuming they're not fools."

The man said nothing.

"And it's true that, however ridiculous your opinions, the motivation's real enough—admirable enough—the rage against injustice, the conviction that there must be something better. Though of course self-righteousness and prejudice are somewhat mixed in."

Still the man said nothing.

"I understand your background," Mickelsson said. "Poverty, victimization, superstitious love of ideas, hatred of 'the stupid middle class' and all it stands for—*your* class, if you'd admit it, though you call yourself 'blue collar,' stealing your father's innocence, perhaps afraid he'd hate you—"

Below him in the night, there was a loud banging at Mickelsson's front door. Mickelsson's heart quaked and, forgetting the Marxist seated at his bedside, he quickly got out of bed, crossed to the window, and peeked out. He could see nothing—no car, only the snow in the yard and on the porch roof. He heard the knocking again, louder, more violent or desperate than before. Then the person who'd been knocking moved down the porch steps and out onto the snowy yard where Mickelsson could see him. It was the fat man—crooked-mouthed, gross, greenish, gouty—peering up near-sightedly through his steel-rimmed glasses at Mickelsson's window, reaching toward him with both arms, pitifully, his fingers extended, fat as the teats of a cow. Mickelsson squeezed his eyes shut, then open again, all strength gone from his legs, and strained with all his might to awaken himself. He was as wide awake, it seemed, as he would ever be.

When he put his hand over his eyes, admitting to himself that his mind was playing tricks, he thought of the photograph of Jessie as a girl of twenty-five, and the cave of his heart went darker.

2

There was still more than a week left of winter break—school was to start up again on January 30th. Mickelsson, holed up (the other Mickelsson, he kept insisting), often not remembering to eat all day long, seeing no one except on his rare trips to town—or seeing no one he could safely believe to be really there—became increasingly restless, increasingly full of dread and what he could describe to himself only as a kind of limitless petulance, a free-floating anger like that of a child who has been falsely accused, though nothing in the accusations Mickelsson could level against himself—"himself"—was false. He was haunted all the time now, which in theory should have convinced him that he was mad, but he could not be sure, turn it over as he might. Again and again he found himself listening, a prickling sensation coming over him, then turning to see if the ghosts were there. As often as not they were, just standing, incommunicative, all but unaware of his existence, the old woman full of anger—he continued to feel it building toward something—the old man increasingly confused, more and more senile, always looking for something or staring, puzzled, at his pocket watch. Their presence became routine—disturbing, even frightening, yet paradoxically—frustratingly—humdrum, perhaps because for all the emotion he felt flowing out of them, the old woman in particular, nothing came of it. He saw the fat man too, but never in the house, always in the yard with his arms stretched pitifully toward Mickelsson, fingers extended, blackness in his mouth and eyes. They seemed to exist—the fat man on one hand, the old people on the other—in separate unrealities, as if time had melted. At any rate the old people seemed as unaware of the fat man as they seemed, for the most part, of Mickelsson. Mickelsson worked out theories, not that they gave him any comfort: disparate functions of his mind, he theorized, had fallen together in a jumble, as if succumbing to entropy. The softening of the brain Nietzsche's father had come to. Perhaps the old people were really there, or rather had been once, and he saw them because, like his grandfather, he'd developed second sight; and perhaps the fat man was a creature of Mickelsson's guilty imagination, not there at all except in the living allegory of the soul. Once, in late afternoon, he saw the ghost of Michael Nugent. He was walking, with a look of grim determination, up the slope of the mountain behind Mickelsson's house, moving toward the woods and perhaps the road beyond, toward Pearson's place, or the Spragues'. The vision was so clear, so convincing in each detail, that Mickelsson went out into the freezing weather wearing only his usual indoor clothes, no boots on his feet, to see if the figure had left tracks in the snow. There were none, or rather, there were only fresh deer-tracks crossing diagonally the line where the boy's tracks should have been. He blew on his cold hands and looked again, but he'd been right the first time; the boy had left no trace. There was nothing to see but an occasional swirling of snow over drift-caps, nothing to hear but the steady, loveless wind like the whisper of a seashell.

Sometimes for several hours the house would seem emptied of its ghosts, as if a curse had been lifted, and then, just as he began to breathe easy, there the old woman would be, looking out a window as if patiently waiting for the mailman—looking out one window, then out another, like a philosopher without a system. Sometimes, usually when he wasn't in the room, the old people would talk, for the most part too quietly for him to hear what they were saying. They said nothing important, nothing that took more than a few words. Increasingly their presence was a cause of foreboding but not fear or alarm: dread that became a steady dead-weight on him, or a gnawing, like hunger. He doubted that he could have explained it even to Jessie, not that he tried; but something about them made his muscles and bones heavy, his mind's movement slow. He thought sometimes of what old Sprague had said, up in his house above Mickels-son's, how Caleb and Theodosia had come to want nothing to do with relatives, how eventually "it" had gotten them, the something that in-habited the woods.

He resisted driving into Binghamton to see friends, resisted even thinking of friends and their need of him, Jessie especially. He depended more and more on his woodworking projects to keep him sane, if sane he was, mostly making picture frames, one after another, each more elaborate and ornate than the last, for his son's photographs, using scrap-wood—apple, pear, butternut and maple—from the Susquehanna Home Center, where when no one was around he sorted it from the piled-up kindling-stack beside the saws. He routed and bevelled, sanded, stained, resanded, sometimes gilded, then boxed them by the dozen and shipped them, with carefully lettered labels and exactly the right postage, to his son's old address at U.V.M. Once when he was smoking his pipe and reading, his eye chanced to fall on the box of keys he'd found when he was fixing up the diningroom, and it occurred to him that perhaps he might clean them up, or anyway clean up a few of the more impressive, and somehow make use of them in his projects. They were for the most part large blunt things of brass or iron, quite beautiful once they were shined up. He discovered that one could make locks for them out of wood and the metal from coffee-can lids—quite wonderful locks, in Mickelsson's opinion, though one could open them as easily with a bent paper clip as with the key. He found himself making small chests and boxes with drawers and secret compartments, felt linings, mirror tops—all pointless foolishness, things he had no use for, but his hands worked on, warding off evil, and when his basement shop was cluttered with these objects, he packed them one inside another, as well as he could, crated them up for delivery by Greyhound, and shipped them away with a birthday card (though her birthday was in August) to his daughter. In this way he used up nearly half the keys. He made a lockable winerack, crudely routed with a grape and satyr design, for Ellen and The Comedian, then a crazily elegant rosewood Kleenex-box holder, also lockable. These too he shipped. He made a pecky-cedar, silver-hasped box to hold Jessie's gloves, on the top of which, in a circle around the lock, he routed, in careful Gothic lettering, as on a hymnbook, *Jessie's Gloves*.

One night he had another of his terrible dreams about the people who had lived here before him, the Spragues. When he awakened, bolt-upright in the darkness, the memory of it shot away from him, so that he was able to catch before they vanished only a few images. He saw them young, playing with a child—*their* child, though they were brother and sister. "No wonder!" he said aloud, as if the dream were the truth. He had a sense, somehow, though he could call back no images, that they'd kept the child hidden, for all practical purposes a prisoner in the house. He saw the child lying in a bed, very white, his hair standing out, waxy, from his waxy skull. Then the dream went vague; he could remember nothing, though he had a feeling that what he'd lost was long and elaborate. Sudden distress came over him and he got up and turned on the light, remembering something more. He stood before the dresser and looked into the mirror as if to steady himself with the image of his own face, but what he saw was, as in a witch's mirror, the dream: the old man up on the roof, standing, bent over so that he looked almost hunchbacked, lowering something by a rope down into the chimney—cleaning out the flue, no doubt. The old woman came out into the yard below. It was a warm summer day. She seemed to have something hidden behind her back. When she drew it from behind her, Mickelsson saw that it was a gun of some kind, a rifle or single-barrelled shotgun. She raised it to her shoulder without a sound, aiming upward, and he saw the old man give a sudden jerk of fear, violently wobbling, about to fall, shouting. He reached out his arms, changing into the fat man, and the inside of his mouth was dark. There was an explosion. It missed him, and she reloaded. Though he had all the time in the world, he did nothing to escape. She fired at him again, and then he was falling, all bloody, sliding—not very fast—toward the eaves, then over, mumbling something, and he fell toward the ground, inert. As he hit, Mickelsson woke up.

He went down and locked the doors, checked the windows; then, after a while, went back to bed.

. . .

The weather grew still colder, so that the packed snow on his front walk and on the road was squeaky underfoot when he went out to the mailbox, or out to his car to drive furtively to Susquehanna for groceries (the Jeep was still not fixed) and to see if Donnie Matthews had returned. He did not mean to keep watching for her, and though it took every ounce of will he possessed, he did not go up to make sure she didn't answer her door. The FOR RENT sign in her window, black and red, told him the apartment was still empty. There was never any light on, no apparent change. He stood thoughtfully sucking at his teeth. He'd lost weight. Would that please her? He'd lost so much weight, mainly from forgetting to eat, that the crotch of his pants hung low.

Each time he went down he saw—to his dismay—people he knew. Tim, Charley Snyder, the friendly, gray-suited banker, and once Lepatofsky and his daughter. (She smiled and waved at him, making some sort of sign in the air, a letter in an unknown alphabet.) For all his misery, guilt, and dread, he was beginning to feel like a native of sorts. A household familiar in the sense that a rat is. He might eventually get his life in order, it seemed to him, if he never again had to drive to the university. The very thought of facing Jessie, for whom he'd hardly raised a finger, or facing Tillson, who must know that Mickelsson was professionally washed up—the very thought of pretending to care about ideas before his freshmen and, worse yet, graduate students—gave him fevers and chills.

Sometimes now he went out with the new gun, looking for something to take a shot at, a squirrel or rabbit or just some POSTED sign two or three years old. Occasionally he would leave the road and wander in the woods awhile, trying to lose himself as he'd always been lost when he'd hunted with his father in his childhood. It was difficult here. Every few rods he would come to a break from which he could look down at the familiar valley, the viaduct, the frozen river and still, dark pines. (Higher on the mountain, up beyond the Spragues' house, there would be no such breaks; but he disliked it up there. The ground rose too steeply, the brush was too thickly tangled; the mist and darkness made him uncomfortable.) For the most part as he moved through snow and trees, the shotgun broken over his arm, on safety, he hardly remembered that he'd come here to hunt; he simply walked, watching the ground for whatever he might see there, admiring ice-beaded weeds and branches, observing how the sun struck on patches of snow that had melted and refrozen to a glaze. He was not himself.

Once, half a mile above his house, he came upon John Pearson, also out walking with his gun. Snow was lightly falling, flake by flake. Mickelsson spotted him while still a long way off, up in a blue-shadowed grove, the black dog circling him, nose to the ground. After debating with himself, Mickelsson moved in Pearson's general direction. When he'd drawn near enough for the old man to see him, Mickelsson stopped, thought some more, then shouted hello. Pearson stopped moving and raised one hand to shade his eyes. "That you, Professor?" he called at last. The dog sat down not far from Pearson and scratched itself.

"Hello!" Mickelsson shouted again, stretching out the "o," and waved. He continued climbing, keeping his eyes on the slippery, snowy rocks, holding the shotgun out far to one side and helping himself along by pulling with his left hand at saplings. They met on a flat open shelf overlooking the valley, a long-fallen maple tree rotting away in the middle of it, mounded in snow.

When they'd come together, Pearson said, "Seen them ghosts yet?"

"They're down there," Mickelsson said.

Pearson raised his eyebrows. "You've heard 'em, then?"

"More than that," Mickelsson said.

"No foolin." Pearson stretched back one side of his mouth. "Wal, I'll be damned."

The man had dead squirrels tied to his belt. Mickelsson pointed at them with his gloved left hand. "You've had some luck, I see."

"Nothing fancy," the old man said, then leaned over and spit. He looked around past his shoulder at the fallen tree, then moved toward it and half sat, half leaned against it. Mickelsson joined him. Pearson said, "So you've seen 'em, hay?" He straightened his neck, working a crick out. In his eyebrows there were droplets of water, melted snow. The dog remembered something and ran off into the brush.

"You thought it was just stories?" Mickelsson asked.

"I might've," the old man admitted, and nodded, one quick jerk. "I can't say's I more'n half believed it, all in all."

Mickelsson looked over where the dog had disappeared. "I wouldn't lie to you," he said.

Pearson almost grinned, just a momentary tuck at the corners of his mouth. "I don't s'pose it matters much, one way t'other."

"No, that's true. Be a funny thing to lie about, though." He met Pearson's eyes.

"Oh, I don't know. Naht really. World can be a mighty dull place, time to time. I guess that's why people go around whistling, or writing verses on bathroom walls." He continued to meet Mickelsson's eyes. "I'm not a whistler, myself, or a wall-writer. Other hand, I've seen that the world's gaht a certain amount of strangeness to it. Ball lightning, now. People can swear till they're blue in the face that it don't exist, but I've seen what I've seen."

"I guess ball lightning's accepted now. By scientists, that is."

"That may be, I wouldn't know. Used to be people'd just wave their hand at you. You know you can see ball lightning right through the floorboards? I don't mean the cracks, I mean right through the floor. I'll tell you something stranger. When my dad was a boy, there was a woman was dying—old woman named Radwell, she'd been normal all her life—she'd point at the wall and yell owt, 'Look!'—scared to death— and right where she'd been lookin the wallpaper'd catch fire. My dad saw it himself. Swore to't."

Uncomfortably, Mickelsson nodded.

"Wal," the old man said, looking off into the air, "I'm not surprised abowt the ghosts. There's times when I believe I've seen ghosts myself, just as plain as day—and then again there's times when I'm not sure I wa'n't fooled. I guess that sounds peculiar, don't it." He watched Mickelsson with level eyes. "Ye'd think at least a man would know what he seen from what he ain't seen."

"You're sure you saw the ball lightning, though."

"Whole bunch of us that time. Cyrus Tyler, Arthur Cole, Omar Bannatyne, Hobby Jayne—he used to be the local auctioneer, mainly cattle. . . . Everybody saw it. I'll tell you a fact. It's more common for a whole group to see things than for one man alone. Like the night of the Baker murders, in 1918. My whole family felt it happenin, just as clear as anything, though the Baker place was two miles away. We was sitting on the porch, all nine of us, and the strangest feeling you can imagine come over us. We all remarked on it. One man by himself—except for certain sort of *strange* men—it don't come through near as well. That's my opinion."

Mickelsson looked down, remembering his student Alan Blassenheim's tentative gropings for some connection between intersubjectivity and truth. Pearson was arguing something more than that. Mickelsson slowly turned his bull-neck to gaze across the valley. "I know what happened down there," he said. Though he spoke with assurance, he was seeing if he believed it. He was thinking of that trick of his grandfather's, asking a question and proposing an answer, seeing if the hunch came that told him it was true.

Pearson said nothing, waiting.

"Caleb and Theodosia Sprague had a child," Mickelsson said. "They kept it hidden from the world—name was David, I think. The child died. Somehow it must've been Caleb's fault, or anyway Theodosia believed it was." He mused a moment, recalling something else. "Caleb wouldn't take the boy to a doctor, thought he could somehow manage it on his own. After the child died, the woman brooded on it. Years and years later, when her brother was up on the roof cleaning the chimney, she shot him." He looked at Pearson for some sign that it was so or not so.

After a long moment Pearson shook his head. "It's a strange story," he said.

"That's not what happened, then?"

"Who knows? Way I heard it they found him cut to pieces, stuffed down in the privy."

The hunch Mickelsson had been hoping for hadn't come. He got out his pipe and tobacco pouch and fingered tobacco into the bowl. "I dreamed all that," he said. "Maybe that's all it was, a dream." Then, after a moment: "I had another dream, one time—a sort of a dream. I saw where they buried the boy."

Pearson went on gazing into the air. "We could look sometime, come spring."

"Maybe we should."

"Mebby so."

Mickelsson said, "You mentioned one time that you can dowse and find bodies."

Pearson smiled and turned to look with fascination at Mickelsson's pipe. "Wal," he said, "I've been known to say a laht of things."

"You can't do it, then?" Mickelsson asked.

Pearson went on smiling but looked away. He seemed to hunt for where his dog had gone. After a while he said, "That house has seen a good deal, I guess. They say it belonged to Joseph Smith for a while, long time ago."

"I didn't know that!"

"Must not've looked over the title search when you bought it, then— unless the stories ain't true. I 'magine they are, though. Anyway, most people think they are. He was a strange man, that Smith. Hahrd to say if he was crazy or the cleverest man of his time—or both."

Mickelsson held a match to his pipe, not glancing at Pearson lest he put him off his story.

Pearson said, "Gaht a laht of it from his father, Joseph Sr., people say. There's books about it—*History of Susquehanna County*, for one. Not very favorable to the Mormons. Joseph Sr. was a dowser and well-digger, but a laht of his time he spent hunting for buried treasure. Even to this day there's supposed to be overgrown pits here and there that are supposed to be the remains of Joseph Sr.'s excavations." When Mickelsson glanced at him, Pearson was smiling, wryly, enjoying himself. "The Prophet was something of a ne'er-do-well, just like his dad, at least that's what people thought 'round here. There's various descriptions of him in the books. I remember one I read one time—"

Mickelsson saw in his mind's eye an image of Pearson he wouldn't have guessed, the old man bent over a book at his kitchen table, or maybe in his livingroom, under a goose-necked floorlamp, thoughtfully reading, a country scholar passing a long winter's night, his wife perhaps not far away, sewing, the old man's finger moving under the words.

He was saying, ". . . torn and patched trousers held up by suspenders made of sheeting, calico shirt as dirty and black as new-plowed ground, uncombed hair sticking up through the holes in his old battered hat. But of course there was a good deal more to him. Maybe he wasn't too educated, but he was a talker, clever as a crow. Sometimes when Smith would get worked up a kind of light come from his head, so people say. He was a first-rate crystal-ball gazer when he was no more'n a boy, and he got himself quite a reputation for finding lost objects and buried treasure. One time up in Bainbridge, New York, he hired himself out to some old fahrmer to find a lost Spanish silver mine, and by gol the thing was there, though not long afterward Smith was in court about it, admitting to fraud. He'd bless fields and make the crops come in strong, they say. One time he went owt to bless some fahrmer's field, and he dropped his magic stone into his top-hat and went through his rigmarole, and that night there was a frost and the only field ruined was the one Joseph Jr. had blessed. The fahrmer was hopping mad and went to Smith to get his money back, and Smith made a big to-do abowt it—he made sure there was plenty of witnesses. Claimed he'd gotten mixed up and had cursed the field instead of blessing it—he was mighty sorry, a course—and he gave the poor man back his money. He was in and owt of court a hunnerd times, and everything he did seemed to make him more famous and respected, even though he was time after time fownd guilty.

"Wal, he was the right man born at the right time." Pearson smiled to himself as if thinking what *he* might have been, given Smith's opportunities. "I don't remember the *de*tails, but it was a time of—what do they say—religious foment. The established churches was falling apart. The Baptists had just split into four different groups—Footwashers, Hardshell, Free Will, and something else—and around Palmyra, New York, where the Smiths lived, all kinds of new religions was shooting up. The Shakers was there, and the Campbellites, and some woman—I forget the name—called the 'Universal Friend,' claimed she was Jesus Christ Hisself come back . . . and there was a man named Isaac Bullard, claimed he was Elijah. . . . It was a good time for a man like Joseph Smith Jr. I don't remember the whole story—Joseph Smith hisself would get confused about it, time to time. It had something to do with his mother, I b'lieve. Maybe he meant to play a joke on her, though he must've suspected from the stahrt that the thing had possibilities. He gaht together with a man named—I think it was—Rigdon that had stole some novel by an ex-Presbyterian minister, called *The Manuscript Found*, and Smith and Rigdon mixed it in together with some Masonic foolishness, after Smith gaht in with that—you have to admire the *labor* of it all. . . ."

Pearson broke off, ruefully shaking his head. "Wal," he said, a kind of sigh, "the thing took off. You gotta remember what times those were, back there in the early-to-middle eighteen-hundreds; bunkum all over the place, and this pahrt of the country more than most places. That's when that famous poet over in England was dickerin to get himself a lahrge piece of land along the Seskehenna River to make a paradise of some kind, maybe a nudist colony, with opera and theater and communal labor and Lord knows what. Phineas T. Barnum was in his twenties then, puttin together his exotic anamals and freaks and ballyhoo, not to mention things more serious, like the 'Swedish Nightingale.' Smith's story got fancier as people stahrted perkin up their ears. Seems that even before he gaht tried and convicted at Bainbridge he'd had a vision one night when he was prayin for forgiveness for his sins. Seems the great angel Moroni appeared to him and told him that one day Joseph Smith would be famous all over the world. He was gonna be showed a bible written twelve centuries earlier on golden plates and buried right here in the vicinity. He'd take it from its hiding place and translate it by means of two miraculous 'stones' or spectacles, and so on, so on. By gol, people swallowed it hook, line, and sinker. It wasn't only the times he lived in, come right down to it. There's a picture of him—painting somebody did; I run acrost it in one of those books about him. Say what they like, he was a handsome man, if the painter didn't lie. Handsome as one of them people in the movies. And you read the letters he wrote—there's a lot of 'em reprinted in the book about his life—they're as handily phrased as anybody's letters, high-toned and elegant as Jefferson's. They're like the letters of Abraham Lincoln, but without the jokes."

He fell silent, pursing his lips, staring at the ground. "I don't mean to say he was better'n people think. He was everything that man Jones was, with the People's Temple, except one thing. Back in behind all the craziness, Jones was sincere. Musta been. Sincere enough to die and take the whole temple with him. Joseph Smith was never that. He was a thief, con-man, libertine, murderer—organized a band of assassins called the Sons of Dan, killed any number of people, tried to kill the Governor of Missouri one time. You'd never catch Smith taking poison for his people!" He thought awhile; then: "The Mormons will tell you there never was any Sons of Dan, 's all 'gentile propaganda,' or if there was there's certainly no Sons of Dan *these* days, they'll say. Don't you believe 'em. There was a whole army of 'em, Angels of Death from Indianapolis to Salt Lake City. I don't know about now."

"Around *here*, you mean?" Mickelsson broke in.

"I gaht no evidence one way t'other, as to now."

The night his house had been searched sprang to mind, and he told Pearson about that, watching the old man for any sign that he might know who had done it.

"Funny business," Pearson said, squinting. "I s'pose it *could* be the Mormons, looking for something." He seemed sorry now that he'd spoken of them.

"For what, though?" Mickelsson asked.

"Maybe they couldn't told you theirselves."

Mickelsson looked at the tracks he'd made, coming here, and Pearson's tracks, intercepting his, and the tracks they'd made coming to lean on the fallen tree, then the tracks of the dog. There seemed nothing to conclude.

After they'd sat for a while in silence, Mickelsson asked, giving up on the other, "Seen any signs of life from your neighbor Sprague?"

"Every onct in a while there's smoke comes owt the chimley, and now'n again the dogs bark. I guess they're still in there."

Absently, still thinking of other things, Mickelsson said, "It's a wonder they make it through the winter."

"Sooner or later they won't, may happen. Gets all of us, in the end."

Mickelsson studied the old man's face carefully, with admiration. It might have been carved out of gray mountain stone. "You don't think somebody should check on 'em now and then?"

"Not me. He'd blow my head off. You go check on him, you want to."

Mickelsson smiled. "Strangest country I ever lived in," he said.

"Still wild, that's the thing of it," the old man said. "Still half Indian. Over to Mont-rose now, that's civilized. All them big white houses, big old Bible school, picture show downtown, three different restaurants to feed the rich people. Ain't even gaht rattlesnakes, over there in Montrose. All stayed this side of the river, away from the hymn-singing. Myself now, I'd sooner take the snakes."

"Yes, that's it, that's the feeling," Mickelsson said thoughtfully. "Sort of pagan. I don't mean bad."

"All those Catholics—worst pagans the world ever saw—that's Seskehenna. All their patron saints and their spirits for every gorge and crick." Though he did not smile, he was enjoying himself. "You can bet there's no ghosts over there in Mont-rose. They sail right up to the Throne like chickens in a whirlwind."

Now both of them smiled.

Pearson raised his long left arm and pointed down at the band of river and dark, gleaming patches of pond in the valley. "People of a well-watered land," he said, "that's what the name means. The Seskehenna. Captain John Smith come and called them that, and the Indians didn't want to offend him, so they took it as their name." He lowered his arm.

They both sat looking for a minute or two, the sun through the falling snow blindingly bright where it hit an open slope, everything dark and shifting where the shadows were.

"Wal, good luck to you," Pearson said at last, and glanced at Mickelsson's boots as if they might not be adequate.

"Same to you," Mickelsson said.

The old man touched the brim of his cap, then stood up and turned without a word and set off through the woods with gradually lengthening strides. The shadows, as he moved toward them, seemed to deepen.

Mickelsson shaded his eyes and looked up in the direction of Spragues' place, but he could see no sign of it. He would remember distinctly, the following morning, that he'd wondered that instant if it were possible that the house had burned down. It had not, at the time the thought occurred to him; but it had by the following morning.

As soon as he stepped out the back door to get wood for his stove, he saw the smoke. By the time he reached the telephone, or anyway before he'd mentally committed himself to dialing, the trucks of the Volunteer Fire Department were already screaming by. He stood with his hands on his head, agonizing over whether or not he dared show his face. He had no idea why, abruptly, he decided he would. Quickly he put on a heavy sweater, coat, boots, and gloves and ran out to the car; but when he finally got it started and made his way up to where the fire was, it was obvious that there was nothing to be done. Everything was gone, even the shed where the dogs had been. The air was rank with the stench of wet, burned wood. The firetrucks were mud-spattered and serious, like old farm tractors. Mickelsson stayed back by the road, his hands in his coatpockets. He couldn't tell whether the knot in his stomach was hunger or something else. Pearson stood nearby, talking with the man from the place between, John Dudak. Dudak was young, good-looking, clean-shaven. He had two boys with him, maybe eight and ten; he'd made them wait in the pickup.

"You think they were in there?" Mickelsson heard Dudak ask.

"Musta been," Pearson said. His face was gray.

Smoke and steam rolled up through the bare-branched trees. All the ground was black.

With a start, Mickelsson realized that one of the men in the fireman's outfits was Owen Thomas, from the store. Owen was coming toward him; it was too late to flee.

"Any sign of them?" Mickelsson asked.

Owen looked at him, reserved, then shook his head.

Perhaps it was Owen Thomas's look, or the stark reality of the fire, or perhaps it was his painfully sharp memory of going there with Jessie: it came to him that he could tolerate his uncertainty no longer.

So far as he could learn from the telephone book, Susquehanna had no police station, though he knew it had police. Carefully and slowly, like an old man, he drove down to town and parked across from the Acme Market, four spaces ahead of where Tacky Tinklepaugh sat watching for violators of the town's one red light. Mickelsson, wearing his most formal clothes—dark suit, dark overcoat—stepped carefully out onto the glare-ice street, locked his car-door, for no reason, then walked carefully on the glare-ice sidewalk back to the patrol car. He towered above it. He bent down and knocked on the passenger-side door and, when Tinkle-paugh reached over and cracked it an inch or two, called in, "Can I talk to you a minute?"

By a gesture, Tinklepaugh invited him in, and, after glancing up and down the street, Mickelsson opened the patrol-car door and took a seat beside Tinklepaugh. Mickelsson sat hunched forward, staring up-from-under through the windshield. He pretended not to notice the whiskey bottle on the seat between them, though Tinklepaugh obviously had no interest in whether he noticed it or not. Tinklepaugh, it was said, had more than once pushed a car he owned over a cliff for the insurance, had once shot a man for no good reason at the Peaceful Valley Inn, and had again and again been given warnings about his drinking while on duty. None of that bothered him in the least, apparently. Without back-up he would knock on the door of well-known mountain murderers; at fires and cave-ins and drowning scenes he performed acts of heroism no sober man would dare, especially at the salary the town afforded him, ten thousand a year.

"Cold out," Tinklepaugh said, and reached to the dashboard to fiddle with the lever that ran the heater.

Mickelsson studied him a moment, chilled by his miscalculation in coming here. He cast about in vain for a way to get out of what he'd gotten himself into. Tinklepaugh's nose was enlarged, his face a drunken ruin, puffy, dark with broken blood vessels. His eyes were like partly closed suitcases.

"I want to ask you something," Mickelsson said. "I've been worried sick, and I live out there all alone, you know—I'm a nervous person anyway . . ." Quickly, lest he change his mind, or chatter crazily and give himself away, he said, "You know that fat man that was murdered?"

Tinklepaugh nodded, a slow downward then upward movement of the fleshy mask and cowboy hat.

"What have you found out?" Mickelsson asked.

Tinklepaugh seemed to study him, possibly too drunk to think clearly. At last he said, "Could be just about anybody, Professor Mickelsson."

"That's not very reassuring, is it," Mickelsson said. "Are you saying you've got no idea at all? It could be me, or Owen Thomas, or the man that runs the Acme . . . or Charley Snyder?"

"Not them last three," Tinklepaugh said.

A wave of fear went through Mickelsson. He'd set that one up himself! "You're saying it could've been me?" His mind raced; then, cunningly, he said. "You're right, of course. It could've been me. That would be convenient, pinning it on a newcomer—a stranger."

"Yes, it would." He was silent a moment, his bleary eyes on Mickelsson. "I'd have my problems, though. Say it's you, you're the killer." He pointed at Mickelsson's jaw. "You must be pretty well-off, if you killed that fat man. I'm surprised you don't try to spend it. I understand you've been bouncing checks all over town."

Mickelsson's heart missed a beat. "Rich?"

Tinklepaugh's face was as expressionless as ever, sagging with sorrow or neurotic gloom, drunken ruin. "I understand you're into the I.R.S. for quite a handy sum. Funny you don't pay 'em."

Mickelsson said, "I don't follow you."

It came to him that Tinklepaugh had been holding his breath, or perhaps had forgotten to breathe, because now the man sighed, a sigh irrelevant to Mickelsson's guilt or innocence. Tinklepaugh turned his face away—pulled it away reluctantly, it seemed—and stared out through the windshield, his hands on the steeringwheel. "You know those Susan B. Anthony dahllars?" he asked. "You know why they made 'em? Because paper dahllars wear out in a year or two, and they're expensive to make. You see? Nothing's what it looks. You're like the rest of the citizens. You thought they made the Susan B. Anthonys as a sign of their new respect for women, or maybe because some faggot at the mint had been to England and got taken by the idea of coins with flat sides. Well, no. Maybe some of that—politics is always tricky. But mainly, dahllar bills wear out, they're money down the drain." He turned to Mickelsson again to study him, or rather, dully stare at him, as one might stare at a wall. "Every year's dahllar bills are a little bit different—you aware of that? It's like motorcycles or cars, small changes every year. Anyone deals with money all the time, such as a banker, he can tell at a glance if a bill is a seventy-nine or an eighty. Imagine how surprised he'd be if he suddenly got a handful of bills from, say, nineteen sixty-five. That's when the fat man you murdered robbed the Cass Bank in St. Louis."

Mickelsson said nothing, the words *you murdered* crackling through his brain.

"I ain't saying you *didn't* kill him," Tinklepaugh said, and sighed again, tightening his hands on the steeringwheel. "But I had a talk with your psychiatrist." For an instant he glanced at Mickelsson, evilly grinning. "We cover all the bases, any bases we can find. Routine, you know, all of it." He raised two fingers up to his forehead to tip his hat up, then returned the hand to the steeringwheel. "If your psychiatrist thought you did it, he wouldn't say so, I expect, but after I talked to him I had a kind of a hunch that sooner or later you and me would have dealings."

Numbly, Mickelsson said, "You think I killed them . . . him, and . . ." The mistake baffled him, made him forget what he was saying.

Tinklepaugh didn't notice. "Let's say I'm just puzzled over how come you never spent the money."

Mickelsson looked down at his knotted hands. Somewhere Donnie Matthews was spending those old dollars. It seemed unlikely that Tinklepaugh didn't know about his nights with Donnie. No doubt they were looking for her, would eventually find her. They'd call Donnie an accessory.

Softly, staring forward, his eyebrows lifted in what he would have recognized another time as his crazed look, Mickelsson asked, "Who *do* you think did it?"

"I guess we *know* who did it," Tinklepaugh said. "It's a question of finding proof."

"Who, though?" he asked.

"Who broke into your house? Who set the fire up on the mounting?"

Mickelsson twisted his head around. "What do you mean?" The nape of his neck tingled. Then he said, "I never told you my house was broken into!"

Tacky Tinklepaugh leaned back, hung his arms over the steering-wheel, and let his eyes fall shut. "If you don't want things known, don't talk. Don't even breathe. Now go home, Professor. If I find out you killed him, you'll be one of the first to know." He let his eyes fall shut and at once seemed fast asleep.

Mickelsson looked down at the bottle in the seat beside the man, then back up at the face. At length, quietly, hurriedly, he got out and closed the door. Returning to his car, he moved recklessly on the icy sidewalk, almost running.

3

Two days later Finney called again. The divorce hearing would be the following morning at nine, in Providence. He'd better be there.

"What'll happen?" Mickelsson asked. He could imagine Finney swinging around in his big leather deskchair, pushing off from the glass-topped desk with three fingers, great pink fatrolls bulging above his collar. On the desk, just within reach, Mickelsson imagined or conceivably saw a box of After Eight mints.

"She won't want to get into a pissing match," Finney said. "She'll huff and blow a lot, rattle a few cages, see if you throw your tire, but she knows right well the court'll never give her what you've offered her—nowhere near it."

"I doubt that *she* believes that," Mickelsson said. Finney's line, he remembered.

Finney apparently did not remember. "Well, you're more familiar with the lady than I am," he said. "But I can tell you this, whatever she may think, her lawyers know a damn sight better. The bottom line is, she's lucky to get one red goddamn cent, and when the I.R.S. drops the other shoe, maybe she *won't* get a red goddamn cent. As you know, ole pal, if you'd left it up to me—"

"All right," Mickelsson said, "I'll be there."

And so by one that afternoon he was on the road east, pushing the repaired Jeep at seventy in spite of snow flurries and ice. He arrived in Providence in a blinding snowstorm, put in at a cheap motel, watched television and drank, put in a wake-up call, and went to bed. He reached the courthouse at eight-thirty. Finney arrived about twenty minutes later, dressed in dark green, his face brick-red and scowling, even the flesh around his eyes unhealthily swollen. When he spotted Mickelsson he forced a sudden grin and held out both arms as if to hug a long-lost brother. For an instant Mickelsson got a nightmare flash of the fat man he'd killed, reaching up to him from the lawn. Finney's suitcoat was open—Mickelsson suspected it would no longer button—and the buttons of his pale yellow shirt were tight, ready to pop. "Hey, Professor," he yelled, "how ya doing? How's it go?"

"I'm fine," Mickelsson said.

"Good boy! *Good* boy!" Finney put his arm around him, talking a blue streak—"Jesus, you look like you lost fifty, sixty pounds! You sure you're all right?"—urging him up the broad, waxed steps to a small room upstairs, just off the courtroom. "Hope ya brought something to read," he said, "You know how it is with these things."

"I'm not sure I do." He had not brought something to read.

Finney laughed. "First time, eh? I figured it must be, that deal you cooked up for 'er."

"She hasn't accepted it?"

"She'll accept, don't you worry! But first we have to go through the motions a little, old game of give and take."

"Wait a minute," Mickelsson said.

"Take it easy, Professor!"

The only furniture in the room was a long maple table with six matching chairs. Windows looked down at the snowy street, a few slow, cautious cars. Finney pulled out a chair at the corner of the table and motioned for Mickelsson to sit. Leaning over him, his belly protruding as if cantilevered, Finney smelled of cologne, maybe aftershave, but also, sickeningly, of perspiring flesh. From his stuffed briefcase he drew out a yellow legal pad crammed with figures and illegible notes. She hadn't exactly rejected his offer, nearly twenty thousand dollars—more than half of what he made in a year—but she had added twenty thousand more to it: life insurance, money for the children's education, mortgage payments on the house he'd left to her, payment to her lawyers. . . .

Mickelsson stared at the figures, both hands flat on the tabletop. "That's crazy," he said. "Where am I supposed to get forty thousand dollars a year?"

"Well, that's alimony," Finney said, and laughed. "The screwing you get for the screwing you got." He laughed again.

"If we went by that theory," Mickelsson growled, "all she'd get would be a couple of tires from the car."

"Don't get up tight, now," Finney said. "It's not completely unreasonable. Unreasonable, I grant you. But not completely."

He looked up at the flushed, tight-skinned face, skin so tight and pink it looked peeled. "Whose side are you on?"

"Easy, now! Whoa there!" He put his hands on Mickelsson's shoulders. "I told you it's just games. You gotta pay your income taxes, right? —both this year's and seventy-seven, seventy-eight's? Pay her twenty thousand dollars and you can't do that, right? And the I.R.S. won't be giving you any choice. So what's she want from you, blood? Does she want you in the slammer where all you can send her is censored picture postcards? So OK, we hold the line." He made a fist and shook it, the hand oddly small, like a child's, but so fat it looked inflated. "Maybe we can even chip away just a little. Teach her a little appreciation of the har-de-har finer things."

"It's not that I want her to lose the house," he said.

"Right, I understand that. *That* much is wonderfully clear to me." With his puffy right hand he swept away all reasonable objections. "You want her to have the house, you want her to have the car, you want the kids to go to college. Right?"

"Well—"

"Impossible but right. I swear, you act like *you're* the guilty party. That's how both of you act. I know, don't tell me! You were a real crapola husband, and she's desperate, that's her nature. Scared lady. OK. OK, so we'll hold the line. But of course she imagines she can't handle the mortgage, which is probably true, and she's got these lawyers' bills— three fucking lawyers, one for reading, one for writing, one for chewing on the pencils—which three aforesaid lawyers she also can't pay. So where does that put us?"

Mickelsson leaned forward, resting his forehead on his hands. After a minute he said, "I guess I don't know what you're talking about."

Finney straightened up and put his hands on his hips, pushing his chin out and aiming it down at Mickelsson. "I'm talking this deal you've offered her, mafriend. You tell her what you'll give her, she tells you what it costs, and you tell her you can't pay it. What kind of facockta deal is that? So we gotta get this straight right here and now, me-you."

"All I make in a year—"

"Look, why don't we throw it to the court and just fuck her? You know what the court will say she's worth, gold teeth included? Big fat zilch!" He hit the tabletop with his hand. "After you've got the settle-ment, you can always pay her more than zilch. Take it off your taxes as a charity, kid! Sign up for more than you can pay her, she'll throw you in the clink. You won't like it there, believe me. The tobacco store sucks." Not quite lightly, he slapped Mickelsson's back and laughed. "So what are your instructions?"

"As I've said from the beginning," Mickelsson said. He felt confused, nauseous. It was ridiculous that he couldn't seem to figure it out. It was simply not that hard. When he tried to concentrate, he got an image of Leslie walking with him down by Rizdy, sea-wind in her hair, about a week after he'd left Ellen. They were holding hands, Leslie swinging his arm, apparently in high spirits, talking about the wonderful possibilities of Mickelsson's new life, and then suddenly she had turned to him, tears streaming down her cheeks, crying her heart out.

"As I've said from the beginning," Mickelsson whispered, raising his hand to his forehead.

Abruptly, all Finney's gyrations stopped at once and he stared at Mickelsson with distaste. "Right," he said at last, nothing moving but his mouth. He clicked his ballpoint pen shut and put it in his pocket. "You want her to have the house and the car and fifteen hundred every month, maybe a little extra for the kids' education. No problem, except the arithmetic." He raised both hands slowly, then laid them on the table, leaning over. "Professor," he said, "maybe you could learn a new trade, like for instance computer crime."

"How come you told me you had all this worked out?" Mickelsson asked.

"*Practically* worked out," Finney said. His grin looked malicious. "We got the both of you here to talk at least. All right, I'll tell you what I'll do. I'll tell them it's definite at twenty thousand smackers, which God only knows how you'll pay even that, and if she thinks she needs more to keep the house, let her fucking take in washing."

Before Mickelsson could say another word, he was gone, papers fluttering.

For two hours after that he sat staring out the window. Then Finney was back. "Her lawyers make an interesting point," he said. He laid the papers on the table in front of Mickelsson.

Three hours later, by a process of reasoning he couldn't follow in the least, in fact made almost no effort to follow, Mickelsson was in the courtroom, tentatively committed to paying thirty thousand dollars a year to his ex-wife, every penny he made, and an additional twenty thousand this year "to put her on her feet."

"Never mind," Finney said. "We got a fail-safe. I slipped in a clause on 'changed circumstances.' If we find we're in trouble we'll just hop back into court." He gave Mickelsson a fierce little salute. Mickelsson ignored it.

Then, blazing with rage, as if Mickelsson had tricked her, robbed her children of their birthright, publicly insulted and humiliated her, Ellen came into the courtroom with her lawyers, two old men and a fat, red-headed woman in a pants-suit. "Bastard!" Ellen hissed, bending her large, puffy face toward him, beet-red. "Asshole!" The judge at the bench scowled darkly. Mickelsson looked down at his folded hands and felt himself going cold all over. It was astounding what power she had over him, even now. "Liar! Fucker!" she whispered. The sound was like fire. Clearly she believed he had cheated her terribly. She was insane, simply. Out of the corner of his eye he saw the woman lawyer reach out gently for Ellen's arm. Now huge tears streamed down Ellen's face, streaking the mascara. Her black, thick hair looked dead. The pale blue eyes in the artificially darkened face—some kind of chemical tan—were unmistakably those of a madwoman.

When it was over, Ellen was led out first, with her lawyers. Mickelsson waited, his face in his hands, and when the coast was clear went up to the room where he'd passed all that time—he no longer knew why—and retrieved his coat and scarf. He could hear Ellen shouting in the hallway downstairs, her theatrical voice filled with sorrow and rage,

utterly convincing but without any hint of real life in it, convincing like
the elocuted rant of King Lear. And yet—though Mickelsson couldn't
fathom how it was that she could feel that way—he was convinced that,
for all the disguising stage-voice, her righteous indignation, her Medea-
wild feeling of betrayal was real. He felt no stirring of interest in the
observation, even though, for the moment, he believed it to be sound.
Our Dada, which art in Dada . . . She was swearing now; presumably
she'd caught sight of Finney. Mickelsson imagined her contorted, painted
face. It was an astonishing thing that all those years with him had changed
her to this from what she'd been when he'd first known her, good-natured
to a fault, high-minded, beautiful. . . . He stepped back from the memory
as from an elevator shaft. Now, downstairs, he heard the voice of The
Comedian soothing her. "Come on, El, let's go eat," the young man said.
"You can *eat?*" she flashed back. But she wasn't quite shouting now.

On the street outside the courthouse he found his daughter waiting
in her beat-up convertible. When she saw him, she looked startled, then
smiled. She waved, tipping her head, then opened the car-door, slid out,
and came running to him. "Hey, man, is it over?"
"Honey," he said, hugging her. Her littleness astonished him, and
suddenly his eyes brimmed with tears. "Jesus, honey, it's good to see you!"
She led him to the car, holding his hand. "Come to lunch with me?"
"Of course!"
She looked at her watch. "There's a new place I could take you. It
opened since you left. They know me, so they'll treat us *right*, if you
know what I mean." She laughed, switching the key on, vrooming the
engine. "I was a waitress there a couple of months. They thought I was
very posh—talked wiz zee customairs wiz zees vairy sweet Fransh accent."
She pulled away from the curb as if the car were a rocket. Behind them,
almost beside them, someone honked.
"I'm glad to hear your French is proving useful."
"Now, Dad," she said, and smiled at him.
He hardly knew her. "Really!" she kept saying, with a slight, odd
accent—it sounded more like *relly*—and a curious intonation, as if she
were jokingly imitating someone; he imagined some supersophisticate
movie-star and saw her, in his mind, in a floppy French beret, the photog-
raphy black and white, sharply focussed. Sometimes while they ate she
reached out and held his hand on the table, this beautiful young woman
who'd been the daughter he'd loved with all his heart through all their
years together, now almost a stranger. He was painfully conscious that
she had his face, except magically transformed, slimmed down, greatly
gentled, merry as an elf's and then at times, for an instant, forlorn.
She talked of her boyfriend—he gathered that she loved him rather
more than the boy loved her; good thing that they'd be parting in the

fall, going to their separate colleges—and of her work, mainly of her work. She was a cocktail waitress every night from eight to midnight, throwing herself into it, making good money. The tips, she said, were directly proportionate to the number of ribbons one wore in one's hair. He listened fondly and coolly, as if from a great analytical distance. She was sacrificing a good deal for her work, all her nights, all her week-ends; and she had to be up every morning at eight for her classes. She never spoke of music except to mention disco, though she'd once been a good violinist. *The waste!* Mickelsson thought again and again as her talk drifted to some witless book; but gradually he saw that he was mistaken. She had character, this beautiful, rapidly chattering young stranger. She was in rebellion, yes—unwittingly, no doubt—turning with finality on all Ellen and he had "done for her," the concerts, the museums, the plays and books, or at any rate turning on all but the French, which they'd long since begun to consider a mistake. The French and, he corrected himself, the expensive clothes.

As they drank their coffee, Mickelsson lighting up his pipe, he saw and remembered another quality in his daughter: her innate love of justice. It shone in her like a sunlit fountain. She talked of Mark. "I'm not really psyched for all that, myself," she said, and clearly she was not; but it was also clear that she looked up to her brother with almost worshipful admiration, as she'd always done, and could talk about nukes almost as smoothly as he could, though with fewer facts and figures. "I guess the thing is," she said, "somebody has to get the word out, you know? Make the poor silly sheep sit up and notice. I mean the government people who are supposed to watch over the nukes are all nuke people them*selves*." She smiled at her coffee, as if apologizing for getting carried away. "Well, Mark's not crazy or anything," she said. "He'll be all right, you'll see. It's not even that he's angry, not really. But he's like you...."

He waited, hoping she'd explain; off-hand, he was aware of no such virtue in himself. At last he said, looking down, "I wish I *were* like Mark."

"Oh, you are, you are, Dad!" She seemed to imply that she, to her sorrow, was not.

"Well," he said.

She nodded, then suddenly smiled, closing doors. "Have you got a car or something? Can I drive you to the airport?"

"I've got the Jeep back at the courthouse."

"I'll get the check," she said, and reached for it.

"Leslie," he said, so seriously that she hesitated. He put his hand down on hers. After a moment he said, "You mustn't hold too high an opinion of me. It's not a good idea. All human beings have faults . . . make mistakes. Sometimes even people who . . . ."

She waited, smiling falsely, alerted.

"You may hear things about me," he said, after another pause. "Pretty bad things, possibly."

"I won't believe them," she said.

"They may be true," he said gently. "All I mean is, honey . . ." He met her eyes for an instant, then was forced to look down. "You must believe in goodness, not particular people. Believe in goodness with all your heart and soul, but as for people, even good people—"

After a while she asked, "What is it you've done, Dad?"

He glanced at her, then frowned briefly and shook his head. "Nothing. Nothing we need to talk about. We'd better go." Once again, because he was about to leave her, his eyes filled with tears.

At the courthouse, when she stopped the car and got out with him to walk him to the Jeep, she asked, "You're all right, then?"

"Don't worry about *me*, kid," he said, and put his arm around her.

"Relly!" she said, and smiled.

When he thought back to it later, their actual parting was a blur to him. He remembered only that afterward, when she'd left him, swinging out into the street and vrooming the engine, his heart had stopped. That night, carefully driving home through snow—a black bear-rug in the Jeep seat beside him, Leslie's impulsive gift to him—he suddenly remembered her voice as she said, "We understand if you don't write. I mean, you have things to work out with yourself, OK? I mean relly, don't even think about it!" He thought of Jessie, carefully not holding him responsible. It was not what he wanted. He wanted vows made and kept —dungeons and instruments of torture for those who failed. When they'd parted, he and Leslie, just before she'd gotten into her car and driven off, she had kissed him and smiled, had brushed hair from the side of her face and said, "Don't drive if you get sleepy, OK, Dad? Promise?"

He'd wanted tears, sobs, rage at the world's betrayal.

"I promise."

She looked at her watch. "Wow! Gotta run!" She'd turned from him, then stopped. "Listen, wait here," she said, and ran to her car, drew out the bear-rug and ran back to him. She held it up to him. It was heavy, bigger than she was. "Take it," she said, "it suits you. Present from your dear devoted daughter who forgives you for everything, whatever, in advance." When he reached out toward it, she changed her mind, spun away, and took it to the Jeep, where she opened the door on the passenger side and threw the rug in. Then she ran back to him, smiling, her eyes filled with tears. Again she brushed his cheek with her lips; then she was gone.

As he drove home, his thought turned to Donnie Matthews. He'd been a fool, insisting that she not get an abortion—and a fool in his class, arguing against abortion on demand. How many women in the world, in fact, would ask for an abortion they didn't desperately need—because of parents who would be ashamed and hateful, or some husband who'd be impossible if he didn't get a boy—would call the girl he got Johnnie or Frank, make her wretched? How long had he been like this, blind, insensitive as a stone, casually murderous, even actual murder not beneath him? Perhaps the fact that he could feel shame at what he'd become was a sign that there was hope. Perhaps. Not much hope, he thought. He could not tell whether his tears were for Mark or Leslie or Donnie Matthews or the buried child-angel in himself or, simply, the world.

Snow fell, mile after mile, sweeping into the headlights. He watched his reflection, the glow of his pipe, in the windshield. At last, to the left and right of him, he began to feel the mountains rising; broad, dark, endless waves.

It was by accident that he stopped that night at the university. First he missed his turn-off down from Route 88, so that he had no real choice but to drive through Binghamton, and then, when he entered the city, his mind was elsewhere—as it had been all this way—and he drove automatically to the school like an old horse heading for the barn. He caught himself only when he was about to turn onto Campus Drive and, looking at the campus ahead of him, saw that it was dark, a graveyard. He felt annoyance at the time wasted by his coming out of the way, then at the last minute changed his mind and turned in, thinking he might as well have a look at his mail, since he hadn't been near the place in weeks. It occurred to him, in fact, that maybe he should try to find a box someplace and take home the piled-up junk on his desk, use what little he had left of vacation to square himself away. The divorce was behind him; it seemed a good time to shake off inertia, get moving. Besides, the campus was quiet as a tomb. He'd meet no one—maybe a janitor, or one of the campus cops.

He parked in the alley by the library loading dock, switched off his engine and lights, and sat listening for a moment. No one stirring. The bear-rug, bunched up on the seat beside him, was like a large, sleeping animal. He got out, walked over to the metal-plated door, sorted through the numerous keys in his keyring, and let himself in. There was a dim light burning in the entrance-way, another in the corridor beyond. The place smelled of some kind of cleaning fluid and new paint. As he went up the stairs, feeling his way step by step in the darkness, he fingered through his keys again, hunting for the key to the mailroom. In the upstairs hallway there was another dim light, and by holding the keyring up to it he was able to pick out the mailroom key, then the key to his box. When he pulled at the handle of his mailbox, the box wouldn't slide, at first. He pulled hard and, with a sound like a mournful sigh, escaping air, the box came open, crammed with letters and papers. He looked down at the mess, just a vague, cluttered gray in the dimness of the room, and a sensation like drowning came over him. He would hardly be able to carry it all without leaving a wake of scraps. He decided to go look for a large cardboard box, dump the mail in that, then go down to his office for the mail waiting there. There would probably be a large box or two in the department office; he could think of no other source of boxes he had a key for. He started down the long, dark corridor, his overshoes almost soundless on the marble floor, his two hands feeling their way once more around the keyring. At the department door, with its large, Gothic-lettered black and white sign PHILOSOPHY—all around the sign, taped notices, announcements, cartoons from *The New Yorker*—he stopped and raised his head, thinking he'd heard some sound; but apparently he'd been mistaken. He turned the key in the lock—a gentle click—then turned the knob and pushed the door open. It made no sound.

He made out—though it shouldn't have been possible in that window-less room, he thought—the large, solid rectangle of the receptionist's desk. Then he saw that, farther in, there was a dim streak of light under Till-son's office door. His heart jumped in alarm, and he looked down at the luminous dial on his watch. Nearly 2 a.m. Burglars? He stood half in and half out of the reception-room door, his hand on the doorknob, trying to decide whether or not he should retreat. Then once again he heard something, just the faintest hint of a woman's voice. He felt himself stiffen, suspicion and curiosity rising in him at once. He let go of the doorknob and moved slowly, without a sound, toward Tillson's closed door. It seemed to Mickelsson that he thought nothing at all as he moved, ghostly in the darkness, toward the band of dim light. All his senses were wide awake, his mind strangely empty, he believed, though in fact he was thinking. He remembered looking in and seeing Tillson asleep on his office couch, a pitiful little doll with his mouth open, and with a part of his mind he believed now that he'd been wrong about the voice: Tillson no doubt had stayed late, working, and had lain down for a nap and had fallen into a sleep deeper than he'd intended. With another, less generous part of his mind, Mickelsson was thinking of the rumor that Tillson had a mistress, dear friend of his wife.

He stood bent toward the door, undecided as to whether he should knock or just open it two inches and look in. It was unlike him, he thought—this stealth, even malevolence. His son Mark would never do such a thing—nor would he have, once. Even when Mickelsson had begun to suspect his wife, he'd avoided spying—though perhaps, as Rifkin had more than once suggested, not for the noblest of reasons. No matter, the world was in its last days.

Ten seconds passed, twenty, and he remained as he was, his hand on the doorknob, his head close to the wood, darkness and unnatural stillness around him, his soul, perfectly balanced in indecision. Then he heard again the woman's voice, soft and gentle, just a whisper, and the very same instant he opened the door and looked in, then closed it at once, turning, striding out of the office, almost running, as from a flood, in his mind the charged image of Jessica Stark staring at him past Tillson's gray head, her eyes serenely passive, or so it seemed; perhaps she had not yet had time to feel shock or alarm. On the couch, under Tillson, sprawled like a goddess, she seemed twice the size of the chalky-skinned, hydrocephalic little hunchback. Her arm lay around him, cushioning him, her hand on his neck in the position of a mother's hand supporting the neck of a baby.

He was halfway home, helpless, borne along by rage, shame, and guilt, before it came to him that she couldn't have seen him; he'd been standing in the dark, the door only open an inch or two.

4

Mickelsson slept through the whole next day and the night that followed, his telephone off its hook. At times he would awaken briefly to sharp, nameless dread, like one buried alive, and then he would remember, his spirit would struggle, and before he could even know clearly what he felt, drug-heavy sleep would avalanche down over him again. What he ought to feel, he believed as lucidity crept back, was disgust; but he did not. It was chiefly a crippling shame that he felt, for moving in on them like an angel of the Lord while they clasped in their arms what little peace and goodness they could find in the world. His anger and revulsion, Rifkin would say, had turned into repression. But Rifkin would be wrong, as usual. His first thought, when he peeked in at them, was that Jessie was beautiful. It was as if all he had been through, these past months, had stripped him of the last vestiges of herd opinion, so that from his dark pit of guilt he saw with eyes like an innocent's: saw her grace and gentleness, and no more judged the act they were engaged in than he'd have done if no one had ever told him it was "wrong." He'd achieved, perhaps, Nietzsche's higher unconsciousness. It was as if his grandfather's righteous, stern opinions—ideas he himself had ingeniously elaborated, even after he'd abandoned theism, by his ethical speculations—had been washed from his memory, thrown down, ground to bits, as by a tidal wave. He had looked at the pair with the same clear child-eyes that had looked, thoughtfully, open to anything, at the picture of the snake painted on the wall of the church. Now, in his bed, his mood more complex—his guilt no longer foremost but still coloring the rest—he saw Tillson in a new way, as a pitiful man, no fool, fighting like a half-drowned rat for the possible—fighting for the department, giving slack to his rainbowed youthful ideals, compromising, feinting, fighting by every means at his disposal to save whatever might be saved in these foundering times; and fighting heroically though no doubt futilely for Jessie as well, not because she was his lover but because what she stood for was right—while he, Mickelsson, stood aloof from it all, too grand for petty skirmishes, too self-absorbed and disdainful of the trivial to risk getting pigshit on his soft, pink hands. He felt his animal spirits flying inward toward his heart, squeaking like bats, his limbs becoming dry, quiet stone in their absence, and again he slept.

Minutes or hours later, when he awakened again, and again lay staring upward in the darkness, his mind and heart took up where they'd left off. He thought of all he ought to have done, ought to be doing, all he ought not to have done and could never atone for. He thought of the book he'd begun, messy hill of manuscript pages down by the typewriter, originally the "blockbuster" Donnie Matthews had inspired, gradually modified to something duller, more closely reasoned, probably no more useful or important. He resisted the impulse to destroy it. Maybe the worldview of Jake Finney was right: maybe life was shit and doom inexorable; but if anything could clean up the world, stop Armageddon, clear vision was the hope: a book honest politicians (if any could be found) might read, think about, understand; or stock investors, ordinary citizens, the people on whose blindness and indifference the Kingdom of Death, physical and spiritual, depended. A man owed something, that was the thing. Not only to the future; to the past as well—to those who had put their trust in him. It was an idea Mickelsson's old teacher McPherson had talked about once, in connection with Homer. Mickelsson, thinking about his father, operatically singing while he plowed, his mother, dressed up, all aflutter, hurrying them to the car so they wouldn't be late again for church, McPherson soberly wincing in front of class, struggling to get an idea just right—like Wittgenstein, he was famous for never teaching the same thing twice, never simply passing on dead information—Mickelsson, remembering these things, thought Finney's weary cynicism not just sick but insane. He *should* be writing the book—for Donnie, for Mark and Leslie, for Ellen in her new life—but then he remembered that he'd killed a man and would eventually go to prison: his advice to the world would be poisoned at the source. Whose wasn't? He had lost forever his clout.

Thoughts of his father kept coming back to him, memories groping toward revelation. He remembered how, when he, Mickelsson, was a child, his father, his father's friend Hobart, and his uncle Edgar had torn out the partition between what had once been the pantry and the original diningroom to make one large room, the new diningroom, how they'd put in new lath, plastered, hammered in an oak frame to replace the partition, then put up new wallpaper (light blue) and painted the doors, casements, mop-boards, and mouldings white. They'd worked in frantic haste, all of two days and nights, because his mother had been away somewhere and it was meant as a surprise for her. When Mickelsson had gone to bed—they'd allowed him to stay up late, watching—the room was all dust and strangeness and confusion (he remembered the astonishing slick whiteness of the paint they were just then beginning to brush onto the doors, abnormally white because they worked by the light of bare bulbs); when he went in in the morning, the whole thing was finished and he could hardly believe his eyes—a huge, gleaming room where once there had been two small dingy rooms, the white paint and light blue wallpaper adazzle in the early-morning sunlight. Was it that, then, that had prompted him, these many years later, to transform the old Sprague place? He had his doubts about the power of psychological symbols; nonetheless, his memory of that surprising transformation was strong, and it was no doubt true that all the sophistication in the world could not rid the soul of its primal faith in magic. Even now, in his hopelessness and guilt, he could not deny that his knowledge of the house around him, restored by his hands to something like its former beauty, miraculously cleaned up like the world of Noah, gave a kind of security, however tentative; a place to stand. That was how his father had lived his whole life: rebuilding, letting the light in. He, not Nietzsche's Prussian officer—much less the artist, philosopher, or saint—was the Übermensch.

He saw in his mind poor sickly Nietzsche, dreaming on one of his long, solitary mountain walks, pausing to lean his stick against a rock and scribble more notes to himself—yellow-eyed and bent with thought (always nauseous, changing to new diets), looking up, rapt and envious, at his vision of the beefy, brainless hero he could never be and partly hated, the Prussian officer with his fine moustache and fat white horse, too stupid and arrogantly sure of himself to put two thoughts together or even mind his inability, beaming with joy of life, prancing his horse through the high, frail flowerbeds of mountain-dwelling peasants, expressing without even knowing it his Will-to-Power. "Ah yes!" cries the hunchback in black, his thin Protestant smile atwitch, all complexity falling for the moment out of his head. This, the mighty Prussian officer, was life, this witless, jubilant golden lion; and he, Nietzsche, with his ghastly stomachaches, headaches, and chills, his complicated worries about the opinions of Kant and Martin Luther—Nietzsche with his fevers and lost-sinner anxieties and congenital shortness of breath—was Life's enemy and failure, humiliation. He shakes a yellow bony finger and cries, dancing on spindly legs, "God dies of pity, made ill through the suffering with which He has too much empathized! To demand pity of the strong is to demand that they become weak!" He smiles, rolls his eyes, shakes out a second yellow finger. His baggy black pants and black coattails flap in the wind. "And in the second place, or possibly the third"—he has lost count and, in his abject love for the Prussian officer, is resolved not to care—"to elevate compassion to society's first principle is to deny the Will-to-Life: in fact, to will Death!" He begins to walk in a tight little circle, hands clasped behind his back, head thrown forward like a duck's. Bony-white. "Life itself is *essentially*, not incidentally, appropriation, injury, the overpowering of the alien and weak. Life is oppression, hard-heartedness, the imposition of form, one's *own* form. *This* is why the world gets worse and worse. Mankind, like every other type of animal, produces a surplus of the abortive, diseased, degenerate, feeble, and necessarily suffering. *This* is why 'spirit' steals the march on the pure blind and purblind activity of the Prussian officer—'spirit,' by which I mean 'caution, patience, cunning, dissembling, masterful self-control, and whatever is cheap, false mimicry of life.' " He falls to his knees as if struck by a lightning bolt or the accidental backlash of the officer's merry whip. "I'm a slave, that's my secret. The well-born officer feels himself happy. He has no need to construct his happiness artificially, by glancing at his enemies and then, as we men of resentment are obliged to do, persuading himself, lying to himself, saying to himself, as we lesser men do, that he's better off, at least, than Herr So-and-So. Slave morality thrives on external stimuli: its action is, through and through, *re*action. The officer *requires* no external reality: he is therefore, *himself,* the World!" All a metaphor, granted, for his true supermen, the philosopher, the poet, and the saint. But what a metaphor!

Yet there were indeed supermen; men who, like Mickelsson's father, had given up thought long ago: men who simply acted—not out of pity but with infallible faith and love: in the way (not an exclusive way) of—at their best—the Christians Nietzsche denied the existence of, except for that first sweet idiot Christian on the cross.

Then the dark thought crossed his mind that it had been for his mother that Mickelsson's father had worked on the house, room after room—painting and wallpapering, changing walls around, refashioning doors and windows; and now the house stood empty, discoloring and sagging on its hill, his mother living in one room, a guest of relatives. While Mickelsson, for the sake of no one, fixed up this house.

He shied from the thought; then, catching himself, closing his fists, returned to it. Perhaps he should bring his mother here to live with him. (He remembered her sitting in the livingroom of the big old house in Wisconsin, reading or writing letters, sometimes looking up with a start when the clock struck, saying to herself, like one brought out of eternity for a moment into time, "Well!"—not with disapproval, simply registering time's existence before leaving it again. The wardrobe top was filled with pictures of family and friends. On the top of the spindly mahogany desk where she wrote, filling the stationery's center space then filling up the margins, or on the stand beside the overstuffed chair in which she read her *Thoughts for Today* or *The Upper Room,* there would be flowers from her garden in a pressed-glass vase.) It had not been possible, when he was still with Ellen, to ask his mother to come live with him; but he could do it now. Why not? It was true that she tired and annoyed him a little, telling and retelling the same old stories, dwelling endlessly on what seemed to him trivia—what the mailman had said, how repairs on the local church organ had come to less than the estimate, how the Pedersens' dog had a rare disease and the Pedersens had not yet told the children. But it was true too that she was a comfort to him. In his mother's presence he found all the great modern problems small. Life's supposed meaninglessness was not an issue: the sunlight on her book was enough. Funerals, marriages, even torture in El Salvador, Argentina, and Brazil—the tyrannies the new man in the White House praised and aided, as had his predecessor more secretively—fell into place. One did what one could do, and what one couldn't do was in God's hands. Solemn thoughts on how God might perhaps not exist were of no interest, like the thought that, possibly, walking in pensive solitude through a field, one might be killed by a mysterious blue boulder—the discharge of a chemical toilet—fallen from an airplane full of businessmen, pretty girls, and academics, a mile overhead. She would brighten the place in a way the new wallpaper, paint, and sanded floors could not match. What would she feel about the ghosts? Not much. Perhaps she would engage them in conversation.

Thinking about his mother, he saw the house in a new way; that is, took new pride in how much he'd accomplished on, relatively speaking, so little money. True, he owed Owen Thomas his soul, and because of the house still hadn't paid that five hundred dollars to the Stearnses for the Jeep repairs. All the same . . . Though more of the rooms than not were empty, he'd wonderfully brightened them—his father and Uncle Edgar would approve. So would the I.R.S., of course, if they decided to seize it. It would be worth far more now than when he'd bought it. For the first time he realized just how painful that would be. He was proud of everything about the place—the harmony of colors flowing from room to room, the professional neatness of his carpentry and painting. That he'd managed it all in so little time was astonishing. His first quasi-mystical feeling about the place had been right: it had become his expression, a projection of the self he meant to be, visible evidence that what he hoped for in his life and character might perhaps be attainable.

He closed his eyes to sleep again, and instantly his mood darkened. He remembered again all he ought to do—go in and help Jessie, if it was not too late; see the dean, perhaps the president, on this business of Philosophy Department courses usurped by sociology, make a call to the Garrets—he hadn't spoken to them since the night of the party. He should call his attorney in Montrose, find out where he stood with the I.R.S.; deal with the once-again piling-up mail; figure out where his finances stood, how much he owed, how he might hope eventually to pay it, what he could do about the money due his wife, not to mention the fuel and electric bills. He relaxed toward sleep. It was hopeless, of course. He remembered the murdered fat man.

When he next awakened—he seemed to have slept for a long time, dreamless—it was still pitchdark. He had an immediate sense that some danger had awakened him. He sniffed for smoke, thinking that perhaps the woodstove downstairs had overheated and set the couch or the stack of newspapers on fire; but the air around his bed was cold and clean, and no hint of light came through the open door into the hallway. He waited, listening, but no, it was not fire. Then his scalp crawled and he knew— he had been through this before—there was someone in the room with him, a darker place in the darkness, and the next instant he knew who it was: Theodosia Sprague. Her rage was all around him, like a field of force. A slight weight pressed down on his foot through the covers and an icy sensation like snake poison raced up his leg: she was touching him! He would have cried out, but his voice froze in his throat. The hand lifted and, perhaps, moved away.

He was terrified now, weak as water all over, though he knew even in his fear that she would probably not harm him, would not wish to even if she could. Her rage had nothing to do with him. So he reasoned, not that he convinced himself. He was part of her world, therefore vulnerable to her madness. He waited, holding his breath, gazing at the solid black wedge in the surrounding darkness, both hands pressing hard on his chest to calm the surging of his heart. As his thought unclouded he realized that part of his shock and bafflement came from his feeling that her presence was almost a greater violation of natural law than the fact that a ghost might appear in the first place. Somehow without realizing it he'd settled it in his mind that now that he knew the whole story, more or less— assuming it wasn't all madness or a dream—now that he knew of the death of the boy, the old woman's long-delayed murder of her husband-brother and her subsequent hanging—the hauntings would end, their spirits at rest. Not so, apparently. She was here in the room with him, as angry as ever. Now he was feeling the familiar pain: arthritic fire in every joint. He couldn't straighten his fingers or back. He should have known. Nugent's ghost should have taught him, assuming that too was not madness or a dream. The Spragues' tragedy would never end because their deaths had solved nothing: killing the old man had not in the least solved the old woman's problem; even when the knot on the hangman's rope snapped her neck, the silent welling of rage or howl to the universe for justice was still in her, stronger than before.

He sat up, his head painfully bent forward, his eyes straining to penetrate the darkness, but still he saw nothing, felt only the rage pouring out of her spirit like thick black vapors from a poisoned well. He felt some shift in things and struggled to understand it, every nerve alert. At last he understood. The center of evil was moving, drifting toward the door, perhaps vaguely searching for its companion in damnation, the brother who'd failed life, loved too feebly, whom the old woman hated and meant to kill. Again and again. Kill until at last it dawned on her—as perhaps it had almost done when she'd reached toward Mickelsson—that there were others deserving of her rage.

Later, Mickelsson could not remember lying back down. Perhaps the old woman's visit was also a dream.

.   .   .

He found Wittgenstein on his mind, another of Nietzsche's children. Why was it that his thought kept turning, lately, to Wittgenstein, in whom he'd never felt any interest? It was almost as if someone else kept bringing him up. Wittgenstein with his desiccate world of facts, not things, his propositions, empirical "states of affairs," his later "language games," but throughout it all his stubborn insistence that anything beyond the limits of mathematics or articulate thought, anything in the province of his utterly mysterious God, must be consigned to silence.

Random lines from the *Tractatus* came to him, dredged up from heaven knew where—with heaven knew what inaccuracy or disjointed-ness. He let them come as they would, his brain leaden. It occurred to him—he did not dwell on it—that somewhere in his thought, a darker place in the surrounding darkness, the form of Geoffrey Tillson sat, un-moving, patiently waiting, like someone arrived ahead of time at a funeral.

The sense of the world must lie outside the world. In the world everything is as it is, and everything happens as it does happen: in it no value exists—and if it did, it would have no value.

If there is any value that does have value, it must lie outside the whole sphere of what happens and is the case. For all that happens and is the case is accidental.

What makes it not-accidental cannot lie within *the world, since if it did it would itself be accidental.*

And so it is clear that ethics cannot be put into words.

If we take eternity to mean not infinite temporal duration but timelessness, the eternal life belongs to those who live in the present. Our life has no end in just the way our visual field has no end.

God does not reveal himself in the world.

Again he had the strong sense that someone was in the room with him—had perhaps been sitting very quiet, watching him, for some time. It was not the old woman; there was no trace of her crackling anger. After a moment's thought he was sure it was not the old man either. He listened, hardly breathing, but whoever it was—if it was anyone—made no sound. (Luther's advice: "When the devil comes at night to worry me, this is what I say: 'Devil, I have to sleep now. That is God's commandment, for us to work by day and sleep by night.' If he keeps on nagging me and trots out my sins, then I answer: 'Sweet devil, I know the whole list. Also write on it that I have shit in my breeches. . . .' ") Mickelsson stirred him-self, raising both hands from under the covers to rub his face and eyes, bring feeling back. How strange, he thought, that he reasoned soberly on whom it might be when he knew perfectly well that it couldn't be any-one. He was far gone, then. It was curious that a man could go mad and watch the whole process like a scientist. When it reached its extreme and, as he'd done before, he dressed himself up in outrageous attire and committed some oddity, talking to dead animals in the middle of a street, and he was dragged to some hospital and brought to his senses again, would the whole experience be flown from his head? How could thoughts so lucid fall out of reality entirely, like the popular songs and dance-steps of ancient Rome?

If he went mad, would the murder of the fat man be excused? That was not at all what he wanted.

After Mickelson had left his wife, his daughter had cried for three days and nights, almost ceaselessly. So Mark had told him. Whether or not Mark himself had cried he did not say. Nor did anyone mention whether Ellen had cried. She had loved him once, as he had loved her; surely she had cried. It was the nature of the poor human animal. (He saw in his mind the black Geoffrey Stewart, smiling at the piano, beloved on every hand, but a truth-teller, enemy of evil—"God's dog," as Kierkegaard had put it once—the most solitary man in the world. Bad for the heart.) He thought of Michael Nugent, then shrank away. He returned to that other (along with Kierkegaard) of Zarathustra's apes.

It is not how things are in the world that is mystical, but that it exists.

The solution of the problem of life is seen in the vanishing of the problem.

(Is this not the reason why those who have found after a long period of doubt that the sense of life became clear to them have then been unable to say what constituted that sense?)

Toward morning, when the sky outside his window, above the mountains, was beginning to bloom like a dark corpse gloomily stirring toward life, his eyes snapped open and he was suddenly wide awake, starving hungry but indifferent to food, thinking with fierce concentration of the place above Blue Mountain Lake, up in the Adirondacks, where he'd gone, all those summers, to be alone and try to write. It was an old, decaying "camp," a building of heavy logs hanging precariously now on its broad stone chimneys. It was three stories high, wide porches on each story looking out through trees at the valley and fog-shrouded water. It had leaded, diamond-paned windows no longer proof against flies and moths, a large, old-fashioned kitchen with an antique gas range, a sink with a pump on it, and built-in cupboards of a kind seldom seen since the early 1900s. High on the livingroom wall there was a rustic interior balcony and beyond it bedrooms, enough room for four or five families, though he stayed there alone. Ellen had hated wilderness all her life, except in Shakespeare's plays. She was afraid of bears and susceptible to pollens, insects, the effects of damp weather. She wouldn't hear of his taking the children there with him, and though he'd argued, sometimes hotly, and had sometimes gotten them to visit for a day or two, he'd been secretly pleased.

Sometimes he would type all day and far into the night, or read the books he'd brought with him, whole trunkloads, puffing solemnly and tranquilly on his pipe, sometimes sipping gin or, more often, in those days, white wine. At other times Mickelsson would drop all his pretenses and set off with a walking-stick through the thick, rustling leaves, on his back a knapsack and Army & Navy Store sleeping-bag, and would roam until night fell, then hang his knapsack too high and on too narrow a branch for the bears to get, and would sleep under the trees and stars. He would find things, exploring the world with the excitement of a child: cave-mouths, which he'd enter, crawling along carefully until the darkness was too much for him. In one of them he could hear a distant waterfall. Sometimes he came upon long-abandoned roads, faint traces of foundations—houses, large old hotels, not a timber still standing. He would sit sometimes, still as a stump, watching bears, sometimes deep in the woods, more often at the garbage dump behind the Adirondack Museum, owner of the camp where, courtesy of the curator, he stayed. Sometimes he would borrow from the curator one of the museum's canoes or, if he was lucky, an old-time Adirondack guideboat, and would set off across the water with two or three days' worth of provisions—he could have packed into the guideboat a month's worth, if he'd wished—and would paddle his way north toward Canada, lake by lake, avoiding villages and camps, though he liked seeing their lights. He'd pass deer with huge racks, sometimes a family of bears that had waded into the dark, glass-smooth water to fish. They would watch him with lifted heads as he passed. It seemed that if he waved, they would wave back. High above his head, toward dusk, he would sometimes spot an eagle.

It had never seemed to him there that the world was a cypher, the "Great Cryptogram" Rifkin ironically spoke of. There the world was itself, as immediate as his thought, his huge, nameless desires. Back in the camp he would write essays, chapters, explanations and speculations with the carefree delight of a child lost in fantasy, perhaps because there in the Adirondack Mountains no explanation seemed necessary, the art of philosophy was exactly as Tom Garret had described it that night to Blassenheim, a joy to work at, for the kind of people who naturally took to it, a joy just as pottery might be, or leathercraft. There in the Adirondacks the world was visibly what it had seemed to Bergson (gentlest of Nietzsche's children), all unity and flow, not divisible into instants, intellectual apprehensions: to write of the world, chop it up into its logic, was so patently a game that the writing was a harmless delight, like the activity of children inventing words, or Jesus the Joker, as his grandfather used to say (utterly humorless), making up his punning, logic-boggling parables to make fools of human reason and the devil. (Like the father of his reflections, he was forever reasoning on the worthlessness of reason. "As much as a cow understands about her own life, that's how much we know."—Luther.) There in the Adirondacks, where there were no people, the philosopher's arrogant confusion was impossible—though he suffered one other great confusion, which made clarity not worth the candle. A tangible longing came over him, at times, to talk to people. Sometimes, late at night, the longing would be too much for him, and he'd walk down to the village, a mile below, to the payphone outside the canoe-rental place, and would call Ellen. "Peter!" she would say, half annoyed, half pleased to hear from him. "Are you drunk? Do you know what *time* it is?" Time. There was no time!

In one of his essays, which he'd thrown out later as overwrought non-sense—or thrown out, really, because he no longer cared about the argument—he'd made the universe something more than Bergsonian. The primal nut from which the Big Bang had come—so Mickelsson had argued—was in some sense Mind: Mind in Whitehead's sense, say. But it was Mind incapable of knowing itself, having nothing to judge or measure by, Time, Space, Matter. The whole history of evolution, then, from hydrogen to the ape that can sing its own song, the explosion up and out, with its innumerable mistakes and misjudgments and false starts and, down at the heart of things, its fierce determination, creating against all probability, in defiance of the limits of natural selection—homing in, through the millennia, with maniacal single-mindedness, on its dream of the unthinkable (the human eye, the juxtaposed thumb, the brain)—was the history of that primal blind Mind in pursuit of self-knowledge, that is, God's rise into self-awareness. Mickelsson had not yet heard, at that time, of Lloyd Motz, and hadn't had available the physics, chemistry, or biology to reach Motz' conclusion, that among all living organisms there will always be one, the main track in the maze, in which the probability for evolution to higher and higher forms must always be maximum, in man an effect of the symmetry and three-dimensional structure of DNA molecules; but he'd anticipated Motz' idea that cosmic self-knowledge—the development of the body and brain of God, as Mickelsson had put it—took the whole eighty-seven-billion-year evolutionary ride, at the zenith of which, overwhelmed by its own weight, it must collapse with an ago-nized cry to the darkness of its beginning.

It had been, in a way, the mountains, not Mickelsson, that had created the theory. He had long before given up theism, and finding himself writing like some latter-day Christian apologist, making casual, fashion-able use of the scientific myth of the moment (the Big Bang, anyway, and evolution-theory), he'd been surprised and amused, though not put off. He'd understood well enough that the God he was talking about could not really be made to jibe with the Christian Jehovah; but it had pleased him, there in the mountains, with the trees full of birds, bears and wolves

in their shadow, to talk with childhood's confidence of God—any God. Later, back in Providence (ironic name!), he could not recapture that feeling and had occasionally ranted about the cowardice of Tillich.

All the same, it was a theory he should have mentioned to Alan Blassenheim, he thought now. It would have been a comfort to the boy's religiously grounded idealism, nonsense or not. It might have guy-wired the touch of prudery, old-fashioned faithfulness, he was seeing his way past. And anyway, he was not certain that the theory was nonsense, though heaven knew there were arguments against its meaningfulness. It would have satisfied Blassenheim's wish, even need—like Mickelsson's and, worst of all, poor Nugent's—that the universe make sense. It allowed for randomness, the seemingly undeniable fact of our physical experience—the Heisenberg principle, the implications of plasma compression, electrons spinning out in unpredictable directions, so that even if some all-embracing intelligence existed and could know the solutions of all the equations that govern events, no completely accurate prediction of the future would be possible (random electrons, random universe)—yet at the same time it offered not only hope but certainty: the very randomness that made prediction impossible was Nature's tool for insuring the emergence of life in each expansion cycle, Nature's guarantee of the approach to perfection and harmony as increasingly complex forms evolved: out of atoms, layering upward, God's grandeur, answer to the flounder-heart's need, soft cry to the lutists: "That was nice!"

He imagined Blassenheim asking him, glancing up at him, not quite meeting his eyes—petulant as a child, Adam in the garden, who's been offered some gift and then seen it, apparently for no reason, withdrawn— "So what's wrong with the theory?"

"Ah," Mickelsson said, and feebly moved his arm on the covers, in his mind waving Blassenheim away, "the trouble is the psychics. Time theory."

"Go on," Blassenheim said.

"Nobody worries about it, here on the East Coast, but in California they've been studying it for years; also other places—England, Russia. . . . Psychics, the authentic ones, can tell you the future, often the past, sometimes even the distant past. Sharks have some prescience, apparently—in fact there's some evidence that lower forms have an advantage in these matters. You'll find proofs of psychic phenomena mountains high, if you care to look. Ask the police who use psychics to find missing children or solve crimes. Never mind that often they can't do it; notice that occasionally—with great accuracy of detail—they *do*. A number of scientists are looking into such things these days; mostly physicists. The Stanford out-of-the-body experiments, dream labs, studies of dream predictions like the famous one last year, before the DC-10 crash. If it's true that psychics can occasionally tell you in advance, in precise detail, what's going to happen, and if it's true that once the psychic has seen it there's no preventing it, no more than one can prevent today the accident one witnessed yesterday, then in a random universe (unpredictable electrons, unpredictable universe) it would seem—tentatively, anyway—there's only one clear avenue of explanation: the future has already taken place. Maybe part of it, maybe all of it; in any case, the moving bubble of 'now' is in some sense—no one knows quite in what sense—an allusion. It's true, you can make up theories to explain it—hundreds of theories, whatever you've got the math for." He waved again, dismissive. "But a hundred untestable theories are as good as no theory."

"But that's what science is for, isn't it?" Blassenheim asked—or rather, Mickelsson (Mickelsson's self-fiction) made him ask, forcing himself through a fool's Socratic dialogue, stacking the deck, the shadowy teacher oonching cards into the shadowy student's hand: "Make up hypotheses and test them, one after another, the way Edison tested materials for the lightbulb?"

Mickelsson closed his eyes, dropping the game, losing interest. The image he'd been fleeing rose up again, long-legged, beautiful Jessica Stark giving tit on the couch in Tillson's office, Tillson snuffling like a humping wet rat. Venus and the deformed Vulcan. He clenched his teeth, but lightly, turning his thought away, mine-sweeping waters he knew to be more safe, trying to remember what he'd been thinking just a minute before. It came to him at last: typing, late at night, in his Adirondack camp. Silky-winged moths fluttered drunkenly around him, crawled like soul-weary "new philosophers" on the tabletop, nibbling at his papers and books. Sometimes he'd get up and go out on the porch to listen to the sounds of the night—animals brustling about in the fallen leaves not far away, wind moving softly through diseased beechtrees and pines. Far, far in the distance, on an island in the acidy lake below, he could sometimes make out warm yellow lights. *Ah, community*, he would sometimes muse. He'd written about that too. Why do we think what we think and not all the other things equally possible, once prejudice is defused? (*Why, he thought now, do we choose not to believe in frog falls, blood falls, falls of bricks, cookies in plastic bags?*)

He opened his eyes again. The sky outside his window was distinctly lighter. Why was it, he thought—putting the question in a way he had never thought to put it before—that people were increasingly interested, of late, in alternative (so to speak) reality options? Castaneda—Carlos, not Hector—UFO books, quack speculations like *The Secret of the Pyramids* or *The Cosmic Egg*. The Western way of thinking had held its own since the pre-Socratics. Could it be because lately the community had expanded—it was possible now to read good, thoughtful books about the Tibetan way of thinking, or the ideas of Peruvian Indians? Perhaps, to take the optimistic view, human beings instinctively widened their horizons, at least in certain situations, to take in views held by strangers. Perhaps, in accord with a principle he'd explored in the one book he was at all well-known for, on medical ethics—the ultimately Platonic idea that justice and reason give advantage in the battle for survival—people were programmed by Nature to make an effort, if they were given sufficient time to rise above their fears, to find merit in the opinions of people not like them superficially, that is, culturally. Or was it, to take the darker view, that people of the Western tradition were turning from their tradition in disgust, jettisoning the community and the "reality" it cherished, because the tradition had led to the kinds of things his son was concerned about, greed, bestiality, fascistic rectitude—the same kinds of things he himself was concerned about now, not just in his mind but in his misanthropic heart: above all, the murderously logical righteousness with which he himself cringed from the image of Jessie in Tillson's office— cowardly bitch, afraid to let her car be seen parked near her house. (His original sympathy was, he saw, long gone.) Jessie of all people! He saw her as in the picture when she was twenty-five—radiant, innocent. And Tillson, that miserable, crooked-backed, chittering . . . He shuddered, seeing the fat man's dead eyes. The weight of his guilt, rage, and helplessness rolled over him again, and again he slept.

It was mid-day, maybe later. Clean golden light streamed through the windows. Mickelsson groaned before he knew why he was groaning, imagining he'd missed some appointment or class, and threw his legs over the side. Then it all came back. He touched his chin and found it grown out like a bum's, and from the feeling of bristles under his fingertips he got a brief, puzzling image of himself as a hobo, maybe the Wandering Jew, walking forever along a highway in a ragged coat.

He dressed in his work clothes—old jeans, tattered shirt—though he had no idea what he intended to work on, more puttering in the woodshop, perhaps. He noticed that, over on the bedroom wall, the phone was off its hook. He stood thinking a moment, scratching his head, once again touching the bristles on his chin, then replaced the receiver. As he turned again toward the bedroom door he got an image of the fire up at the old people's house—how many days ago now?—black rubble, clouds of steam in the black-branched trees. He saw the firemen moving around slowly in their long black slickers, Owen Thomas among them, John Pearson leaning on Dudak's truck-fender, his mouth cocked back in a grin.

At the foot of the stairs he found the cat waiting, looking up at him. When Mickelsson was five feet away the cat turned quickly and ran toward the kitchen, pausing just once to look back, balanced like a squirrel on a branch, then moving on again, more silent than Mickelsson outside Tillson's office door. Mickelsson got out a can of 9-Lives, fitted the top into the electric canopener, opened it, then dumped the meat into the bowl beside the sink. The misshapen cat hung out of reach, head on one side, one paw lifted, until Mickelsson stepped back; then, after one more careful glance in Mickelsson's direction, the cat lowered his huge, wide head and glided toward the dish as if the meat might be still alive. Mickelsson fixed himself cereal and carried it to the livingroom, where he sat on the couch to eat. On the stand by the door, near the shotgun, he saw the box he'd made, marked *Jessie's Gloves*. She was everywhere. He remembered how she'd sat here on the couch beside him, the back of her head resting gently against his arm; how she'd gazed out the window, the night of the party. He remembered the awkwardness about the mistletoe. While he was down at the hospital, had she and Tillson slipped away from the others? Maybe fucked standing up in the bathroom, or used Mickelsson's bed?

His heart felt swollen; he couldn't eat. He stood up, then stopped, listening for some hint that he might not be alone, but there was nothing; the house was empty except for the cat. The most powerful presence in the room was the shotgun by the door.

He thought again, abstractly, with no flicker of intention, of what it would be like to kill oneself. Would he hear the report, or would the instant, all the time he had left for all Time, be too brief? Almost without meaning to, he went over to the shotgun and touched it, then picked it up by the barrel. He had nothing in mind, simply felt an impulse to look at it. He saw in his mind's eye Ellen's streaked, angry face in the courtroom, then his daughter's face, smiling, a shine of tears in her eyes as she turned from him and ran toward the car. He saw Mark, bearded, standing beside a road somewhere, hitch-hiking. Mickelsson held the shotgun in two hands, looking around and through it, lost in thought. He must *do* something, he whispered to himself. He slipped the shells back in and closed the chamber. He was looking out the window. Snow. Sunlight. He might have been the only living creature in miles.

When the phone rang he jerked, almost pulling the trigger, frightening himself, then carefully set down the gun. He turned, wiping his hands on his pantlegs, trying to remember what it was that, an instant ago, he'd meant to do, then heard the phone again and walked into the kitchen. He lifted the receiver to his ear.

"Hello?"

"Professor Mickelsson?"

"Yes."

"Oh, good. I've been trying and trying to get hold of you. This is Lawrence Cook's secretary—"

"Cook?"

"Your lawyer? Dealing with your tax case?"

"Oh, yes." He leaned against the wall.

"Mr. Cook's a little hard of hearing, so I'm phoning for him; he's right here beside me. It seems we've run into a small problem. Mr. Cook wants me to tell you that this Ernest diSapio we're dealing with in Scranton—Mr. Cook wants me to tell you we've dealt with him before, and he's a real s.o.b., for two cents he'd send his own mother to jail—well, he's making a lot of trouble and—"

"Wait a minute," Mickelsson said, "I'm not following. What's the problem?"

He heard talk in the background, the lawyer's voice, maybe angry; then the secretary said, "This Mr. diSapio's been over your taxes for the last ten years, and apparently none of the returns you filed suit him. He's claiming fraud, in fact. Believe me, he's a lunatic—old Mafia family—but then, I suppose that's why they hired him, isn't it!" She laughed, clean bell-tones. "Anyway, with the penalties and fines it could really add up. Mr. Cook wants you to talk to him."

"Wait a minute! Me?"

"The thing is, you see, these people will push just as hard as they can. They're the government's bloodhounds, Mr. Cook says. And he does mean blood! Sometimes if a person just tells them straight out that he can't pay what they're asking, they'll back off. They don't really want you in jail, they want you in their pocket."

Mickelsson broke in, "But those returns—most of them—were made out by certified public accountants. How can they be wrong?"

He heard her speak to Cook and heard him answer, then she said, "*Any* return can be wrong if they want it to be. Mr. Cook says the best thing you can do is just settle with them, try to get the best compromise you can on fines and penalties and such. They've got the cards, Mr. Cook says." There was a pause while Mr. Cook spoke, then she said, "Mr. Cook says, they *make* the cards."

"But I don't *owe* them anything—aside from those years I missed. At least I *shouldn't*."

"That may be true, and Mr. Cook doesn't like leaving a client high and dry like this, but he's just one person, and the I.R.S. has got an army of those young hot-shot lawyers. They're not human, believe me. Absolutely no conscience. He'll do whatever you ask, if it's legal, but his advice is that you compromise and pay them off a little at a time."

"How much does he expect it to come to?"

"With fines and penalties," the woman said, then apparently turned from the phone to consult with the lawyer. She said at last, "It could possibly be upwards of three hundred thousand. I know that sounds incredible. . . ."

Mickelsson was silent. Thirty thousand dollars a year for ten years—his whole earnings. It was so outrageous he was not even shocked, not even tempted to laugh. "They think big," he said at last.

"Superkill, Mr. Cook calls it," the secretary said, and chuckled. "But they don't really want all that. They'll agree to wipe out some of the fines and penalties, maybe all of them, and you agree to pay what you owe them, which you probably don't really owe them."

Mickelsson found he was shaking his head, or rather, his head was moving from side to side on its own. "I won't do it."

"Mr. Cook says you ought to think about it. He says to remind you they've already got a lien on your house—we understand you've fixed it up some—and you *do* owe for three years."

He thought about it. At length he said, "They should be shot."

The secretary laughed again. "That's the truth!" she said. "But of course there's nobody to shoot, really—that is, no one who's responsible. DiSapio's just awful, but as Mr. Cook always says, take away his style and he's just one more Doberman pinscher. They all push as hard as they can to get money for the government. They're like soldiers. They don't give a darn, really. You might as well be a Vietnamese. I know that diSapio, and a lot of others like him down in Scranton. After work they go sit around in bars and get drunk—ask 'em what they think of what they do, they'll just laugh at you. But they do it, never think twice. That's what keeps 'em in their jobs."

"Interesting," Mickelsson said, thinking of Wittgenstein—the world as facts, behind the facts nothing visible, traceable, even thinkable. "Interesting," he said again, more softly. The thought was not new to him, but he'd never before seen it in quite this light: perhaps there really *was* no government. He said, "All right then, I'll call him. What do I say?"

"Just tell him how poor you are—make it as sad as possible—and tell him you're eager to cooperate to the fullest."

"And that will *move* him?" Mickelsson asked. "DiSapio will go easy out of *pity*?"

He saw her shaking her head, smiling. "Silly, isn't it."

"All right," he said, after a moment. He hung up, musing, unaware that he hadn't said good-bye. Maybe he would call diSapio and maybe he would not.

It was not yet dark when he started in to town, the shotgun on the seat beside him, the stock protruding from under the bear-rug. There had been thaw—cruel false promise of spring—then a cold snap, so that the roads were like glass, but the Jeep, in four-wheel drive, moved safely past abandoned cars in the highway median and precariously tilted tractor trailers. It had been winter now for a lifetime. As he approached the university he sensed that something was wrong and then, finally, as he drove through the gates, understood what it was. The campus was as full of lights as a sky full of snowflakes. There were cars on Campus Drive, and students were moving on the snowy lawns. The term had begun, then.

He had lost track of time. For all he knew, school might have been running for a week. He stopped the Jeep, thinking of turning back toward home, then decided to risk it.

He parked in a space reserved for the handicapped, made sure that the shotgun was completely hidden, then sat pondering.

His intention had been to go to his office and, in the Campus Directory, find the addresses he needed, among others those of Jessie's enemies. He had a vague intention of seeking out Jessie and Tillson, too—not to speak of what he'd seen. He wasn't sure he was up to it; in any case he had no real plan. He had simply decided that it was time to act. It was a sign of how open his sea was that he'd brought along the shotgun: no malice was in his mind, no virulence in his heart; the last thing in the world he wanted was more violence. But stepping out through his front door, he had noticed the shotgun and, for no reason, had snatched it up— symbol of his new-found urgency, perhaps. Now everything was changed: the university was ablaze with lights. Mickelsson locked the Jeep doors and got out.

The double door opening onto the hallway leading to his office was open. Like a thief he peeked in. If everything went wrong, he would meet Jessie. But there were only students, none that he knew, one of them bent down, scolding a dog that cowered and wagged its tail. When he glanced at his watch he saw that it was nearly seven. Few professors would be in their offices now, only those who taught nightschool. On impulse he crossed quickly to the stairs and went up, two steps at a time, and in the comparative safety of the upper hallway nonchalantly hurried to the mailroom, getting out his key as he went. The outer door was open, his box more crammed than ever. He sorted through his mail quickly, dropping pieces to the floor and letting them lie there, looking only for one thing—precisely the last thing he'd have read, normally—Philosophy Department and Inter-Office "To/From/Subject" memos. He found one from Blickstein, dated January 30th, and his eyes snatched out of the rest the words "Professor Stark's Review Committee . . ." He crumpled the paper and pushed it down into his suitcoat pocket. He found several recent memos from Tillson. These too he stuffed into his pocket. Then he closed the box, hurried to the elevator, stepped in when the door opened, and pressed the button that would take him to four, home of the chairman of sociology.

On the fourth floor there were no classrooms, therefore no students in the halls. In fact there was no one at all in the halls up here. Above the water fountain there was a sign, black and red: DO NOT DRINK! UNSAFE! Through the window in the door he saw that sociology was closed. Though he'd had no plan, he felt frustrated. He went back to the elevator, rode down to the second floor, and walked to Tillson's office. Here there were students, but only a few, none he recognized. Tillson's office too was closed and dark. Beside the door there was a poster—not the usual cheap poster from University Services but something more professional, no doubt printed in town: in elegant, girlish script the words *Kate Swisson in Concert,* and below the words a cartoon of Kate Swisson, maybe mocking, maybe admiring. Her chin was lifted, her eyes made to seem beautiful; her throat was very long. The poster was of the kind one might see for the Guarneri or the Grateful Dead. It came to him all at once why the concert he'd attended with Jessie and the rest had been so well received, and why his student Alan Blassenheim had been so eager, the night of Mickelsson's party, to do everything in his power to put Kate Swisson at ease. It was the idiocy factor—brainless, all-together-now humanity rising as always to the shapely worm on the invisible promoter's hook. Sham, falsity, cuteness, crap. Surely there was no hope!

In his office he copied down the addresses he wanted from the directory, read the crumpled-up notes from his mailbox, then—forcing himself against his terrible exhaustion—hurried back to his Jeep. Looking up as he backed out of his parking space, he saw that, directly above him, Lawler's light was on. The old man would be meticulously laboring, as always; grading papers, reading, maybe asleep over his book. Guilt flooded in. He saw Donnie Matthews screaming, "It's just a *foetus!*" The image was so vivid he had to hit the brake and close his eyes.

The painful realization came that he did not feel as guilty even about the murder as he felt about his betrayal of his calling. If he'd been a true philosopher, the murder would never have taken place; but that was not the point. Lawler was not a famous man; better known as a scholar and editor than as an original philosopher, and no doubt best known as a teacher. He'd written only two or three articles, brilliant, constipated works, tortuously worded, difficult to follow, each piece fifteen or twenty pages long but carrying a line of thought that any other philosopher might easily have made into a book. Philosophy was his life: he had no interest in fame—no interest even in converting the world. He simply wrote, quietly hard-headed, what was absolutely true, so far as his reason could determine. Untouchable, at least for the moment. He had no family that anyone knew of, no friends even, but threw his whole soul into what Mickelsson played at. Once, many years ago, Mickelsson had played football against a team of Peruvians. They were not good, really; in fact they'd lost the game. But one felt, playing against them, that the Peruvians simply weren't playing the game one knew. One felt that, for losing, the Peruvian quarterback might be tortured and sent away to prison for life, or might simply disappear. (It probably wasn't true.) They played with a terrible seriousness he could not match or understand—he played seriously himself, by normal standards—that was the point. He had felt, playing against them, like—in Nugent's sense—a clown, a buffoonish imitation. So now, looking up at Lawler's lighted window, he understood what a fraud he himself was—understood because once, in graduate school and for a while thereafter, he too had been a true philosopher. Once for him, too, nothing could have touched the joy of thought. And so it had been for Nugent, it struck him. Now at last the young man's death sank into his understanding. He tightened his grip on the steering-wheel and, bending forward as if in cartoon supplication, looked up at the library tower and the starry night beyond. Even with its lights, the building reminded him of an immense tombstone. At last he remembered himself, raised his heavy, numb arm to the gearshift, and nosed the Jeep toward Campus Drive.

At first no one at the address he'd gotten for Randolph Wilson—Randy, the dancer, Michael Nugent's friend—would admit to any knowledge of where he'd gone when, as they all insisted, he'd moved. Mickelsson stood in the large, grungy entryway; it was one of those tall houses by the railroad, and all the occupants except for one pale, pregnant girl were black, roughly of college age, fake sleepy-eyed and cautious. They stood blocking the stairway in front of him and the doorway, to his left, beyond which lay a large room with pillows on the floor and dark blue walls. Smells of pot and recently cooked food hung in the air. He stood smiling falsely, eager to show them he was friendly, not dangerous, eyebrows lifted, teeth gleaming—his slightly insane look, he knew, but could find no way to fix it.

A strikingly pretty girl with slanting eyes, black slacks, and a ratty red sweater asked, "What do you want with him?"

"It has to do with his friend Michael Nugent—the student who killed himself," Mickelsson said, his voice as eager to please as his smile.

As if for no reason, bored with the conversation, the tall young man behind the girl who had spoken—he'd been leaning on the doorframe looking sullen, maybe grieved—rolled his head away, then followed with his body, fading back into the room.

Mickelsson nodded. "Nugent was a student of mine. The suicide was a terrible shock to me. I thought perhaps if I could talk to Randy, get some idea of, you know—"

"Mooved," the girl said, shaping the word with care, as if for someone slow-witted.

"And you don't know—"

"Man," she said, and cocked her hip, half lowering her eyelids, "for all we know that dude's in Paris, France."

Mickelsson slightly scowled, to give her a hint that he wasn't fooled by her funky act. But he was not in a position to pursue the matter. "And the rest of you?" he asked, glancing around. Except for the pregnant girl, who looked down, half turning away, they met his eyes with what might have been hostility and might have been only a kind of habitual sadness. No one could say where he'd gone.

Mickelsson saw that he was beaten, not that he believed them for a minute. He sighed, thanked them, and went back out to the street, where his Jeep was parked. He started up, wondering what a detective would do in a case like this, and in his thoughtful daze almost missed the furtive wave as he came up to the corner a block from the house. There stood the tall boy who'd left the conversation, leaning against a lamppost as if he'd been there all day, his arm extended toward Mickelsson is if by accident. Mickelsson pulled over and, at once, without a glance left or right, the boy climbed in.

"Maybe you'd drive on?" the boy suggested, smiling widely, and clamped his locked hands between his knees.

Mickelsson studied him an instant, then understood and drove on.

"D'you say your name was Mickelsson?" the young man asked.

Mickelsson nodded.

"You got a license or checkbook or something that says that?"

Again, this time in alarm, Mickelsson glanced at him.

"I don't mean to be overly suspicious," the boy said, and went on waiting, smiling.

Mickelsson drew out his billfold and, after an instant's hesitation, handed it to the boy. He opened it, looked at the license in its plastic window, then closed the billfold and nodded. He handed back the billfold then just sat. The smile was gone now. He sat with his knees far forward, his weight almost on the small of his back, his chin resting on his collarbone. He looked for all the world like one of those blacks one sees waiting forever in big-city police stations.

"I heard of you," the boy said, looking out the window. "From Nugent. Well, I guess I get out here—up there by the light. Thanks a lot."

Now wait a minute, Mickelsson thought; but he said nothing, more baffled than ever. It seemed clear that it would be useless to press. He pulled over to the curb and the boy opened the door and dropped one leg out. He paused and said, more to the floor of the Jeep than to Mickelsson, "Try the hospitals."

"What?" Mickelsson asked. "Wait a minute!" He reached out to catch the boy's shoulder, but his hand closed on nothing. The door fell shut.

He found Randy Wilson in the second hospital he visited, Binghamton General. At the third-floor desk Mickelsson asked, "What's he here for, could you tell me?"

"Bicycle accident," the nurse said. She was middle-aged, graying. Her hair made him think of Jessica. The nurse had once been pretty—was still pretty, but her flesh had that weakened look of late-middle-age, and one could not guess what her color would be without the make-up. "They should wear helmets, but you know kids. He's lucky to be alive."

"I take it it's all right if I visit?"

She nodded. "He won't be able to talk. Broken jaw."

Mickelsson nodded, turning to go down to Wilson's room, moving slowly, like an old man, then on second thought turned back to ask, "Do you know where the accident happened, by any chance?"

"Vestal Parkway, I think," she said. "We get a lot of them from there. Hit and run of course. They always are."

He nodded, slightly narrowing his eyes for an instant, seeing the accident in his mind. The image was vivid, as clear and detailed as a memory—an old car, practically an antique but in excellent condition, gleaming in the light of oncoming cars. He watched it move toward the bicycle, closing in fast, the right wheels almost off the road on the shoulder. It hit as if the driver had never seen the bicyclist at all, and then the car slowed, almost stopped, before abruptly taking off.

"Three-oh-nine, did you say?" Mickelsson asked.

She nodded, glancing at her book.

Randy Wilson's jaw was wired shut and most of his head was bandaged; only his nose, eyes and forehead looked out, as through a windshield. One leg was in traction, and apparently he couldn't move his hands either, though what was wrong with them Mickelsson couldn't tell, since they were buried under the covers. The boy showed recognition, possibly pleasure, when Mickelsson came in, but since his mouth was hidden and he couldn't move his head, it was clear that the conversation was going to be limited.

"How are you feeling?" Mickelsson asked, standing over him, then quickly raised his hand as if to stop the boy from speaking. "Sorry, I know you can't answer. Well, you're a lucky young man, I guess!" Again he cursed himself for a fool. For all he knew, the boy was now finished as a dancer, brooding on Nugent's example, escape by suicide. Mickelsson lifted his eyebrows and smiled, as falsely as he'd smiled before Randy's friends at the house. He thought of asking, "Is there anything I can get you?" but stopped himself in time. He raised the back of his fist to his forehead, weakly smiling on. There was a television in the corner of the room, up by the ceiling. That was what he could do—pay for television for the time the boy was here. Another bad check. No matter. With luck—

He said, "I just wanted to tell you, I think I know what you're going through, Randy. Michael was one of the finest students I've ever had, and a fine, sensitive person besides. Perhaps if I'd been a better teacher—if there had been something I'd thought of to say that I didn't say . . ." He smiled still more fiercely, though weakly, lowering his hand, his eyes rivetted to the bandage covering Randy Wilson's jaw. "I guess I'd have to say, in retrospect, my moral guard was down. I hate bigots—I want you to believe that—but God knows I am one. Been one since the day I was born, I suspect. I was put *off* by the boy, just couldn't wake up to him. I think you know what I mean." Mickelsson's glance fled to the wall and he thought about getting out a cigarette, then for Randy's sake did not. He said almost sharply, with the look of some Klansman making a wisecrack, he realized an instant later—though that was not what he intended, God knew; he intended to come clean, break the pattern: "I mean his homosexuality, that's the truth of it; and the fact that you—a person of your race—was, were, his lover." He heard his voice fairly crackle with anger as he said it. Even if Randy Wilson were much older, much wiser, he could not be expected to understand that the anger was directed inward, toward Mickelsson himself. He stretched his smile wider and bent down closer, desperate, searching for control of his voice and features, some means of making clear what he meant. "I was an *ass*, that's what I'm saying. I couldn't see. That's been my problem all my life. All I could see was myself, my grandiose, stupidly righteous schemata!" He raised his right arm to suggest the empty grandeur of his thought, not to mention his rhetoric, and realized, in horror, that it must look to Randy Wilson as if Mickelsson were about to hit him, helpless as he lay. "I'm trying to say I'm *sssorry*," he said, bending down still nearer, tears springing to his eyes. He was so weak in the knees he was afraid he might fall on the bed. "I don't say I'm the *cause* of your friend's suicide," he said, "but by God I feel I'm to blame for it. So listen: if there's anything I can do for you, anything at all—"

When he glanced furtively at the boy's eyes he saw that he'd triggered extreme agitation. Was he trying to say that Mickelsson was *not* to blame? Was it fear that the eyes expressed? He realized in surprise and embarrassment that the immense brown eyes were filled with tears. Except for the tears, the expression—the little that was visible—might have meant anything. Guiltily, feebly, Mickelsson patted the covers over the boy's right arm. "I'm blabbering like a fool," he said. "I want to help if I can, that's all. Listen now, I'll drop by again." Then, after a moment of frustrating, painful silence, "Bear up, son!"

Perhaps it was his unexpected use of the word *son*; perhaps it was something more secret. Impulsively, though his hands moved slowly, as if in dismay, he took off the expensive chronometer that had once been Mark's and laid it on the bedside table, a vague atonement for he hardly knew what—maybe only an absurd, empty gesture by the buried child-angel. "Keep this," he said, again with the weak, mad smile. *Fallen out of Time,* he thought of saying, but refrained. "I never use it, myself." With a false laugh, he added, "When they hook up the TV, you may find a watch useful." Mickelsson couldn't tell from the tear-filled eyes whether the boy was pleased or troubled by the gift. "Good-night," Mickelsson said. "Don't worry, OK? It'll be all right, take my word for it!" He smiled, patted the boy's arm again, and left. On the way to the elevator he stopped at the desk and wrote a check to pay for TV in Randy's room. It would take several days to bounce.

Back in the Jeep, heading for Helen Street, only a few blocks from where Mickelsson had formerly had his apartment (already he was moving under dark, heavy trees, heavy even in winter, though the leaves were off now and at times, through the still, black limbs, he could see stars), he wondered why the young people at the house where Randy lived—or had once lived, they claimed—had not wanted him to know the boy's whereabouts. He knew his propensity for finding patterns where there were none; all the same, the pot-smell was sharp in his memory, as were those guarded, sullen looks. Though his suspicion embarrassed him—he could not help noticing its racist tinge—he allowed a kind of daydream to play through his mind, a scenario so vivid in its particulars that he couldn't be sure whether he was imagining or actually seeing things, as his grandfather had sometimes seen things, and as perhaps he himself, in the case of the ghosts, had seen things. He saw the house full of late-night visitors, an assortment of shabby druggies, and saw Randy Wilson as a timid part of the pretty black girl's gang. Perhaps, as in that People's Temple business, she was their spiritual leader and protector, a kind of high priestess, and the men around her, possibly the pregnant white girl as well, were her sexual thralls. As soon as he suggested the idea to himself, he had a strong hunch that it was right. Then Randy had met Nugent, Mickelsson speculated, and, drawn more and more into his healing influence, had tried to back away from what went on at the house. The young man who'd ridden with Mickelsson and dropped the hint as to where Randy might be found was another defector, then, or half-defector: guilty, restless, tentatively exploring the possibility of flight. Suddenly Mickelsson knew, he thought, why the people at the house had been so reticent. The bicycle accident had been no accident at all: one of them had tried to kill the boy. If Mickelsson should find Randy Wilson, and the boy should talk . . .

He drove more slowly, hardly breathing. Should he phone the police? Might the gang not go to the hospital and finish their work? But what could he tell the police, in fact? What did he actually know?

Then something that had been nagging at the back of his mind burst into his mental field of vision: the old, well-kept car that had appeared in his brief daydream of the accident had been parked down the street from his Jeep when he'd come out of the hospital.

He clenched the steeringwheel as tightly as his neurotic weakness would allow, and tried to think.

Was it possible? Maybe he'd imagined it; or maybe he'd seen the car there before he'd gone in and had unconsciously registered it and had supplied it when his fantasy of the accident needed an image.

"Insane," he whispered, not quite meaning it, simply playing, philosopher-like, with the patent weirdness, increasing degeneration, of his mental processes. Here he was, deducing reality from intermingled dreams and actualities—"more or less fantastic gloss"—incapable of guessing which was which, yet weighing the results as if he'd gotten them in a clean, bright laboratory.

He shuddered and pushed the whole mess to the back of his mind. He'd arrived at his destination, the modest, fake-Tudor home of Samuel Danytz, Department of Sociology. The man with thick fingers. He parked the Jeep and sat for a moment, trying to decide what he intended to do, his right hand resting idly on the bear-rug covering the shotgun. When he remembered that the gun was there he drew his hand back. He got out of the Jeep almost without a sound.

The front lawn had been fixed up as a kind of Japanese garden, no doubt more as an alternative to lawn-mowing than as a tribute to Zen Buddhism. The snow had stopped falling some time ago, and the sky was bright, but the lawn around the Danytz house lay in the heavy shade of blue spruce trees. He had meant to ring the doorbell, but he found himself looking around somewhat furtively, noticing that there were no dogs out tonight, and not a soul on the white, softly carpeted sidewalks. He moved quickly for all his feebleness, crouching down, toward a lighted window, thinking vaguely of some character in a novel he'd read long ago—Russian, perhaps; anyway, something obsessive and morose and no doubt philosophical, or meant to be; otherwise he wouldn't have read it. He thought of the night he'd spied on the fat man, and his stomach knotted. To distract himself, bring himself back to the business at hand, he glanced down at his wrist to check the time, then remembered that he'd given away his watch. Crazy thing to do! Even crazier, he saw that in his left hand he held a pack of cigarettes, in his right a pack of matches. He'd actually been about to light a cigarette, give himself away, as if on purpose!

He pocketed the cigarettes and matches, then raised up slowly to peek in through the window. A pretty young girl, maybe twelve or thirteen, was standing in front of a brown, textured couch, playing with a cat— dangling a shoelace, getting the cat to bat at it. Papers and books, probably the girl's homework, lay on the couch, and above the couch hung two paintings, amateur and awful but obviously treasured, expensively framed. One was of a naked woman with a fat blue mouth and one hand over her crotch; the other was of wedge-shaped mountains with palaces or monasteries on their tops. The girl laughed as the cat leaped up, batting with both black paws. The cat was apparently part-Siamese—blue-eyed, lean and elegant, delicately muscled under sleek black, yellow and white fur. The girl jerked her head back, long blond hair swinging, and Mickelsson thought, with sharp pain, of his daughter. This girl was not as strikingly pretty as Leslie and wore slightly thick glasses, but she was visibly a nice kid, by no means ugly; one of civilization's fortunate.

From somewhere surprisingly nearby—at first he thought it was from outside the house, only feet away from him—a voice called, "Sheila?"

Without turning, still playing with the cat, the girl said, "Coming! Just a sec, Ma!" She made another pass over the cat's head with the shoe-lace—the cat declined the gambit, then belatedly jumped and caught the lace in both paws and its teeth. The girl dropped her end, bent down with quick grace to give the cat a little pat, then swung around and went lightly from the room.

What had his intention been, Mickelsson asked himself. To beat the man up? Shoot him, perhaps? Was it so surprising, really, that he had a house, a daughter who showed every sign of having been loved, pam-pered, taught to be cheerfully obedient?

The cat settled on the carpet with the shoelace, its blue eyes by some trick of light going empty. From the way the cat fumbled and mainly used its teeth, one could see that the creature had been declawed.

Jessie's house was dark. Perhaps she'd gone to bed; he had no idea how late it was. She prided herself on being an early riser, he remem-bered. The darkness behind her windows seeped into his heart.

As he drove toward the Tillsons' it suddenly came to him why it was that he kept thinking, lately—thinking somehow guiltily—of Ludwig Wittgenstein: Michael Nugent had mentioned him the last time they'd talked, at Mickelsson's office. It was Tillson that had put the boy on to Wittgenstein. The *Investigations* had been somehow a great revelation to Nugent; Mickelsson no longer remembered, if he'd ever known, how or why. He thanked God now that, on a lucky impulse, he'd refrained from coming down too hard on old Ludwig, though he'd mentioned, with some annoyance, the use to which the *Wiener Kreis* had put Wittgenstein's mystical empiricism—how Wittgenstein's divorce of God and the know-able had without warrant become, in their hands, a dismissal of God as not simply one of the unspeakable things but Nothing, not just an empty term but a lie. Nugent, Mickelsson remembered, had simply nodded, smiling as if his mind were elsewhere.

"*The solution of the problem of life is seen in the vanishing of the problem.*" Traceable to Nietzsche, like everything else in modern thought. "Problems are not solved but outgrown."

What in hell, he wondered (as always), was it supposed to mean?

Tillson's house, like Jessie's, was dark. Had he too gone to bed? Were they off somewhere together? He thought of swinging past the university and checking Tillson's office but rejected the idea in disgust. He started up the engine of the Jeep once more, wondering where to go now, what to do. He felt himself absurdly like one of those young colleagues or graduate students who had come to visit him and drink up his liquor when he was living in his apartment. He thought of knocking at Gail

Edelman's door and was for a moment faintly tempted. If he were drunk, he knew, he would certainly do it. He was sorry he wasn't drunk.

He winced, ambushed by memory. What a fool they must all have thought him, ranting against abortion, bullying them, granting them no space for what they all, this younger generation, must have known to be the truth! *Bigot*, he thought, then winced in embarrassment at the memory of his confession, a few hours ago, to Randy Wilson. He suffered a brief, quite mad hallucination: he thought his ex-wife was seated with him in the Jeep, crushed far over on the passenger side, to be as far from him as possible. She was crying, carefully not making a sound. Tears streamed down her face, she made no effort to get rid of them. Her hands were knotted together in her lap. Her face was puffy, her dyed hair stiff and coarse. He wanted to shout at her, turn her terrible sorrow to anger— anger he could deal with—but he couldn't find his voice.

Now the Jeep was rushing down Route 11, the long, eerie supertrucks of 81 on his left, the frozen, snowy Susquehanna on his right. The image of his crying ex-wife was gone. One moment it was there, the next it was not, and he pushed along the well-plowed, partly bare highway at nearly sixty, as if to leave the hallucination behind him forever. He found himself thinking again of Donnie Matthews. He was beginning to believe— had been inclined to believe for some time now, it struck him—that she would never be caught, would never be required to reveal what she knew, his guilt. By now she would long since have gotten her abortion, alone. If only he could meet her one more time, let her know it was all right. But she was gone. He must accept that, and the unatonable guilt that went with it. Dickens' gentle universe of families reunited in the book's final pages—the sorrowing, guilt-ridden rich and the sad, disowned poor— was as dead as the universe of Newton. The girl had drifted out of Mickelsson's life like an accelerating galaxy, rushing toward the red shift, Dante's *mente*, Einstein's void. "Let them find her," he whispered, almost a prayer. "Let her accuse me, and let us meet one more time."

He roared down Route 11, fleeing the lights of the city toward increasing darkness. It was a clear, starry night, the snowbanks on each side of the road unnaturally sharp of line, with dark, sudden shadows, like snow in one of his son's photographs. He imagined what it would be like to see the fat man's ghost right there in front of him, arms stretched toward him, eyes empty. He imagined it with frightening vividness, but the road remained empty and gray, sharply focussed, mirror-bright ice patches rushing toward him like asteroids, just missing him, harmlessly passing through him.

When he looked at the kitchen clock he saw, to his perplexity, that it was 5 a.m. He put away the shotgun, then opened the refrigerator, hungry for something no refrigerator contained. The house was cold and around him, comfortingly beautiful despite his soul's disquiet. Even if he lost it to the I.R.S., he thought, the house might heal him yet— simply the fact that he'd saved it from ruin, the fact that, against all evidence, things could occasionally be saved. He got out milk for the cat. As he bent down to pour the milk into the bowl, the cat warily eyeing him, the phone rang, making Mickelsson jump. He finished pouring the milk, then turned, set down the milk-carton, wiped his hands on his pantlegs, and at last walked over and lifted the telephone receiver to his ear.

"Hello?"

No one spoke. After a moment he said again, "Hello?"

There was still no voice at the other end. After three or four seconds he asked, "Mark? Is that you?"

He waited, thought of asking if it were Jessie, then asked instead, crossly, "Hello?"

Silence. Now for some season he was sure that it was Jessie. In his mind he saw her face with painful clarity, interested, gentle, the very emblem of aristocratic beauty. He remembered how she'd leaned forward, distressed, talking to old man Sprague up at his house higher on the mountain. Mickelsson hadn't told her yet, he remembered, that the old people's house had burned. "Jessie?" he almost said. Was it possible that she knew that it had been Mickelsson outside the door, that night at Tillson's office? He clenched the receiver more tightly, pressing it against his ear.

"Hello?" he asked one more time, reserved, then listened. It was his wife, it came to him—his poor, wrecked Ellen. But then, once again, he was unsure. At last, deliberately, without haste, he hung up.

Should he call Jessie, just in case? But he did not really believe it had been Jessie. He stood frowning, undecided, for a long time, then for some reason, reaching no decision, found himself moving into the livingroom, crossing to the couch, thoughtfully sitting down, moving the palps of his fingers again and again over his bristly chin, listening to the scritch. After a while he eased his shoes off, raised his feet onto the couch, and lay back, closing his eyes.

He slept for hours, then awakened with a start to discover that the world outside his windows was red, as if burning.

"Sunrise!" he told himself—or was it sunset? He made himself calm. What had he thought it was, Christ's Return in Glory? Some nuclear accident his son had encouraged to have its in-due-course-inevitable day?

He closed his eyes again, thinking, *Yes, it must be sunset*; he'd slept another whole day away. He found himself praying for Mark's safety, wherever he might be—perfunctorily reminding himself even as he prayed that he no longer believed in prayer. Then, as if guiltily, as if for fear of sinfully elevating one love over other loves, or fear that some halfwit supernatural power might misunderstand and save his son but kill his daughter—out of superstitious dread, in other words (so he told himself, but could no more prevent the superstitious act, however lightly he might take it with his rational part, than he could command the Red Sea or make the sun stand still)—he prayed for Leslie; then, because he loved her even now, prayed for Ellen and, because he did not, for The Comedian; then for Jessie; then for Tillson and Tillson's wife. . . . The list went on and on, endlessly unfolding—as irrevocable, now that he'd said the first word, as the outrush of worlds, the immense holy gasp and wail that formed Time and Space.

Dreaming, he saw himself with a top-hat, his eyes made up to seem slanted like the Buddha's, in his hand a magic wand with which he tapped a small, glitter-spattered table like The Incredible Dr. Flint's. Gilt exploded outward with the first light tap, a lovely, bedazzling puff of gold. He laughed, and the audience laughed with him, delighted, a soft murmur swelling through the shadowy auditorium from end to end, rising and falling away like the breathing of the sea. He winked, signalling more fun to come, and tapped twice, more loudly, then found himself violently hitting the table with a stick. More shining dustclouds of gilt flashed outward.

He awakened to a thunderous pounding and sat upright.

He thought instantly of his son, then knew it couldn't be that: if something had happened to Mark, he would hear by phone. Someone shouted something, out on the front porch, and the pounding began again. Mickelsson threw his heavy legs over the side, rubbed his forehead with the heels of both hands to awaken himself, then got up, loose-kneed, groped his way through the livingroom's darkness to the kitchen, switched the light on in the hallway, and made his way down the entry-hall. "I'm coming," he called when the pounding came again, "hold your horses!" When he opened the front door, two young Mormons stood there, black-coated, their faces white skulls. Behind them, stars and snowlight made the night like a weird dream of day.

"What the Devil—?" Mickelsson said. He closed the door part way.

They were the same two Mormons who had visited him before, but he saw at once that they weren't here this time on missionary work.

"Professor, we'd like to use your telephone if we could," the dark-haired one said very softly, obsequious, bending toward him, almost bowing.

Mickelsson stood holding the door against them, looking them up and down. Their faces were as blank as the faces of lizards. "Has something happened? What time is it?"

The blond one poked his head toward him, nose bulbous, eyes slightly widened, "We found a body," he said. "Up there on the mountain." He pointed, first toward the road, then, correcting himself, straight up through Mickelsson's rafters into the woods beyond. "Your place was the quickest to get to, so we came down crosslots." Mickelsson noticed only now that both of them were snowy to the waist.

Needlessly, Mickelsson said, "He's dead?"

The blond one nodded, and the dark-haired one took a step toward the door, reminding Mickelsson that they needed to use the phone. Mickelsson stepped back "Right through there," he said, pointing. "It's on the wall in the kitchen."

The dark-haired one nodded, grim, unctuous, rubbing his hands, and moved past, bent forward, the collar of his black coat up over his bright red earlobes. As usual neither of the Mormons wore hats or gloves, but tonight they had galoshes. The blond one came in too, and Mickelsson pulled the door shut behind him.

"Where'd you find him?" he asked. "What happened?"

"It's the old man called Sprague," the blond one said. "The crazy one, you know what I mean? One that's house burned down?" He leaned a little closer to Mickelsson, as if to tell him a secret. "We found him in the snowbank—part of his arm was sticking out. I guess the snowplow must've moved him. He's real banged up."

Mickelsson stared.

The young man nodded. "I guess the old woman must've been up there alone the night the house burned."

Mickelsson, still staring, brought out, "That must be right."

In the kitchen the dark-haired one was talking on the phone now, standing in only the dim gray light from the range. A board creaked at the top of the stairs, and Mickelsson looked up. The two old ghosts were standing there, looking down, hooked forward. Mickelsson shuddered and glanced at the blond young man beside him. He was taller and heavier than Mickelsson had realized. His round, steel-rimmed glasses were steamy. "Evening," the young man said, nodding in the direction of the ghosts. They ignored him.

The dark-haired Mormon was saying into the phone, "We're up at Professor Mickelsson's. . . . Yes, certainly . . . We'll wait right here."

Mickelsson asked the blond one, "What were you doing out on the road so late?"

"We always put in good long days," the boy said. He spoke earnestly, his hands in his coatpockets. His face floated closer, not more than ten inches from Mickelsson's, turned up because of Mickelsson's height. He could feel the ghosts bending nearer to listen. Urgently, as if it were extremely important that Mickelsson understand, as if he were justifying all his kind, the boy said, "Sometimes we put in fifteen, sixteen hours." He searched Mickelsson's eyes.

"That's a lot," Mickelsson said. "Listen, if you're not careful—"

Now the dark-haired one was hanging up the phone and turning to them. "The police are on their way," he said.

Mickelsson moved toward him, glad to get away from the too earnest blond one. "Let me give you some coffee," he said. "You must be half frozen yourselves."

"I'm sorry," the dark-haired one said, raising his hand, "we're not allowed, that is, we don't—"

"Yes of course. Hot milk, then," Mickelsson said.

The dark-haired one tucked down the corners of his mouth, uncertain, and Mickelsson glanced at the blond, who looked interested, though he didn't dare say it. Mickelsson remembered something else he'd heard in Utah, that it was a common occurrence, when the Saints found a backslider or apostate, for the faithful to beat that person bloody. "When I came here to Utah," Mickelsson's friend had said, with a bemused look, "I thought the Mormons were sort of like the Shakers or something. Brother, I had no idea! They kill each other all the time, one sect against another!" It did not seem likely, even if such things were true in Utah, that the Mormons of Susquehanna County were at all like that. Certainly such horrors had nothing to do with these two.

"Hot milk," Mickelsson said, reminding himself. "It won't take a minute." He hurried into the kitchen from the entryway, switching on the light as he passed the door. It flickered, then stayed on, suddenly bathing the room with the cold glare of an ice-house. The two young Mormons looked at each other, each checking to see whether the other one approved. In the bright light they looked remarkably drab, almost as if the whole thing were a joke of some kind, two characters dressed up for a play by Samuel Beckett. Where the dark-haired one had stood there was a puddle on the linoleum. Mickelsson quickly looked away from it, lest he embarrass them. "What a terrible thing," he said, opening the refrigerator door to look for milk. He found it not there but on the counter, where he'd left it hours ago. The kitchen was cold, though; the milk would be all right. He said, to praise them, make them feel at home, "If you people hadn't found him, he could have lain there till spring thaw."

The dark-haired one shook his head, eyes narrowed to chinks. They both stood squinting for several seconds, their heads forward, their hands in their pockets. They made him think of two lean country dogs. Mickelsson poured milk into a pot and set it on the burner. At the far end of the house he heard movement, no doubt the cat. He glanced at the clock on the stove: 9 p.m.

"I couldn't believe it," the dark-haired one said. He put his hand over his mouth, his thumbtip and fingertips moving up and down, his close-together eyes staring at nothing. "There was this hand sticking out of the snow. I walked right past it, and then I knew I'd really seen it." He shook his head.

Steam was rising from the pot of milk. Mickelsson stirred it with a wooden spoon and turned the heat down. "Up there in the cupboard," he said, pointing, "there are big yellow mugs." He felt something and looked down. The cat was rubbing against his leg. "Take it easy. All in good time," Mickelsson said.

The blond went to the cupboard, walking very carefully as if afraid he might slip, and got down the mugs. Now the light in the entry-hall changed, blue flashes like shocks. The police car was outside.

"Take them with you," Mickelsson said, pouring. He handed a mug to the dark-haired boy, then another to the blond, who was looking over his shoulder down the hallway, worried. "It's all right," Mickelsson said, "the mugs are old and cheap. Go ahead, they're yours." He moved toward the door and just after the first knock came he opened it. A sheriff's deputy stood, pot-bellied, hands on hips, silhouetted in profile against the blue-flashing lights. He was no one Mickelsson had ever seen before.

"Professor Mickelsson?" he asked. In one gloved hand he had a long black flashlight, solid as a club.

"Come in," Mickelsson said. "I gave them a cup of hot milk and they haven't figured out quite what to do with it yet." He smiled. "They'll be right with you."

"That's OK," the man said, and grinned, then sucked at his lower lip, a gesture apparently habitual.

The two Saints were drinking quickly, probably scalding themselves, eager to be off with the policeman, not make a bad impression, but also eager not to carry away the mugs. The cat stood waiting with his back raised.

"It's OK," the policeman said to them, grinning, showing his teeth, then sucking at his lower lip again.

They put the mugs down, empty. "You got here quick," the dark-haired one said, wiping his mouth on his sleeve. He gave a jerky nod to Mickelsson and drifted toward the door.

When they were gone, Mickelsson again poured milk for the cat, mixed in dry catfood, then slowly washed the pot in which he'd heated the milk for the Mormons. He moved the Brillo pad around and around long after the pot was clean. At last he realized what was bothering him. It was that look, the night of the fire up at Spragues', on Owen Thomas's face. Was it just that they couldn't find the old man's body—or had he seen something?

5

Mid-morning, Saturday. Bitterly cold again. Mickelsson registered it like a man moving toward some important, foreknown event.

Owen Thomas's reserve seemed more than ordinary shyness. He smiled to himself, his gray eyes as evasive as a rabbit's, and seemed to mull over Mickelsson's question, turning it over and over again like a hundred-dollar bill found in a clock. While he thought about his answer his small, elegant hands measured out lengths of chain he was cutting for a customer, a young man in a quilted orange down jacket. He had longish, matching orange hair. The store was overwarm, as it always was on cold days. There were a number of customers, most of them probably just looking, fleeing the cold. The customer buying chain had small, bright blue eyes like a baby's, and seemed to listen for Thomas's answer as eagerly as did Mickelsson. He was stocky, powerful, as innocent as a hen.

"Well," Thomas said, "the place was quite a mess, I can tell you that. It was pretty much burned down to nothing when we axed our way in, but you could see how bad it had been."

"Yes," Mickelsson said, unsatisfied, "I was up there once. Junk from one end of the house to the other." He kept his face turned partly away.

Thomas nodded, then squeezed the handles of the chain-cutter. The chain-links parted without a sound and the lower length of chain fell to the floor and nestled. "That's true, but it's not what I meant," he said at last. "I mean the livingroom walls were all torn up. It looked like a bomb had gone off there or something"—he smiled, glanced at Mickelsson—"or maybe somebody'd started tearing the house down."

"The walls—?" The young man leaned around, trying to see Thomas's eyes.

"All torn up, plaster all over the floor," Thomas said. He seemed reluctant to speak further.

"Jesus," the young man said, then held out both arms to take the chain as he would yarn. Thomas lifted it toward him and hung it over his arms loop by loop. "What's this country comin to?" the young man asked. He looked, full of concern, at Mickelsson, as if he might know.

"You're sure of this?" Mickelsson asked. "Couldn't it just be that things caved in during the fire?"

Owen Thomas shrugged, noncommittal, as if to say "That's not how it looked to me," but he said nothing.

The young man's face tightened; then he said what he was thinking: "Gol darn motorcycle gangs."

"You think so?" Mickelsson asked.

"They're everywhere. Rip up your place worse'n a tornado."

"Surely not in the winter, though. It was all snow and ice."

"Snowmobiles, then. It's all the same," the young man said. "My wife's folks went away one time, week-end at Elk Mountain, and they came home and, by heck, you just wouldn't believe it. Place tore all upside and down. And as if that weren't enough, they blew up the little bridge on the road in front! Dynamite! Everybody knows about 'em. Heck, they brag about it! They'll steal your overcoat and wear it right downtown, big as life, or they'll tear up your place just for the fun of it. They're nuts!"

"Well," Thomas said, negotiating.

The young man stood holding the chain, face reddening, eyes growing brighter. "They're just nuts, that's all you can figure. They all gaht good jobs. Those machines they drive, they don't come cheap—you know? They work in their drugstores or banks or wherever, and then the week-end comes—"

"Who?" Mickelsson broke in to ask. When the young man looked blank, he asked again, "Who? I keep hearing that everybody knows who they are, but who are they?"

The young man looked down at the chain.

Mickelsson leaned toward him, speaking gently. "Do you mean Tim Booker and his friends?" He glanced at Owen Thomas, but Owen was looking away.

"I don't say it's Tim," the young man said, pouting, disliking pressure. "People *like* that, that's all. Maybe just people too smahrt for Seskehenna. Bored, I mean. They just do things, f'no reason." He shook his head. "Seems like a lot of people do that. Makes you sick." He looked sternly at the chain, maybe thinking of all he had to get to yet today—chores, frozen waterlines—and abruptly turned to head up the aisle. Mickelsson watched him go, then turned back, part way, to Owen Thomas.

Before Mickelsson could speak, Thomas said. "It wasn't Tim. I don't say he's perfect, but I can tell you it wasn't him. Some people will tell you that now and again Tim and his friends will get drunk and break into some house, somebody from New Jersey, or undermine some back lane so the first lovers that drive in there, the car's suddenly sunk to the windows. I've heard such things said. But don't you believe it. It's those kids from up in New York State that do that. They're crazy up there—anybody will tell you. I've had truck drivers tell me they hate to pass through, up there. The law's crazy, the citizens are crazy. . . . You should see the salesmen a storekeeper up there has to deal with!" He rubbed his nose, looking down, as if saddened that an influence so pernicious should lie so close. "Anyway, I know Tim. He wouldn't do anybody damage, not even a stranger. That house up there, it was like a bomb went off in it. Plaster everywhere it shouldn't be. It was like what the old-timers say witches used to do when they decided it was time to really fix somebody's goose. They'd set their minds on it—focus the curse like sunlight through a reading-glass—"

"Is that what you think happened?" Mickelsson asked.

Thomas shook his head. "It's a mystery, that's all," he said. He smiled, tentative, and looked toward Mickelsson. "Old Sprague was a witch. I guess you knew that? Or thought he was. Thought he could fly, thought he could cast spells . . ."

"Must not have been much money in it," Mickelsson said, and grinned.

"Never is. Mostly all it does is make the rest of the witches your enemies."

Mickelsson said nothing, thinking about it, uncertain whether Thomas was serious or joking.

"Anyway," Thomas said, "somehow another somebody made a devil of a mess up there." He smiled and moved his eyes away again, preparing to mosey down the aisle.

Mickelsson said, "Tell me this, though. What do they mean when they say everybody knows who did it? They said it about the murder of the fat man, too."

"Depends on who said it," Thomas suggested, one eyebrow raised.

"Tinklepaugh, Tim . . ."

Thomas pushed his hands into his trousers pockets and looked at the floor for a minute. "Well," he said at last, "it's hard to tell."

It was clear that he was being less than forthright. "Come on," Mickelsson said. "I'm a good customer." He gave Thomas his intense grin. "I'm a stranger, I admit, but I throw myself into it. I saved that old house. I care as much about Susquehanna as anybody else does, you know that."

Thomas stared at the floor, quiet as a statue. At last he said, "I suppose *some* of 'em when they say it they mean they think it was you."

"They think—" Mickelsson began. His tongue was suddenly thick, and his heart was beating fast. No doubt he was blushing. "They think *I* killed the fat man?" Quickly, no doubt showing his fluster, he added, "They think I tore up my own house?"

Thomas shrugged, gently. It was clear that he was sorry to have this conversation—clear that in fact he liked Mickelsson and was not speaking for himself, had been forced into the position of speaking for the town. "I don't know," he said. "I guess when you're really a townsman you'll forgive it for its foolishness." He was unable to meet Mickelsson's eyes.

"Every town's got its ways," he said. "Susquehanna's no different. There's a lot of good here. People are friendlier here than most places. Maybe it's because they're all so poor here, I don't know. But it's a good place, that way."

As if hardly aware that he was doing it, Thomas picked up a bolt from one of the trays on the counter and moved it to the tray it belonged in. "On the other hand," he said, "Susquehanna's got its faults. I guess we're a little hard on strangers, one thing." He looked at the trays. "I guess there's a certain amount of superstition. And I guess when you come right down to it, law and order aren't exactly the same in Susquehanna as in, well, most places. You can get away with a lot here if Cobb and Tinklepaugh know you, or if the town likes you—which comes to pretty much the same thing. It's not so much the laws on the books that people care about, in Susquehanna. That fat man, for instance. I guess they knew pretty well who he was, and what he was. It wasn't that people knew him —nobody knew him, come down to it. But he was never trouble. You take those boys that come down off the mountain and park their pickups across from Milly's. I guess you've seen it. They get out of their trucks and walk out into the middle of the street and open up their flies and take a piss, arms thrown out like they were dying on the cross. I guess most places you'd throw a man in jail for a thing like that." Thomas blushed, smiling, still looking down, doubtful that Mickelsson would understand. "But what harm is it? When they're finished they button up and walk on in to Milly's and have their drinks, play their three or four games of pool, maybe locate some girlfriend. . . ."

Mickelsson asked softly, conscious of a certain professorial stiffness, "Do *you* think I'm the one that tore up my own house?" His smile, he knew, was a grotesque wince.

"No," Thomas said, and gave a headshake.

Still more righteously, Mickelsson asked, "Do you think I killed the fat man?"

The evasion in Thomas's eyes was instantaneous and brief, though his answer was casual. "If you say you didn't, I believe you."

Mickelsson blushed violently and knew that his guilt was revealed. He thought of saying, with wonderful indignation, "Well, I didn't!" But he said nothing. Owen Thomas showed only discomfiture.

Mickelsson would have no idea, later, how much time passed between his implicit confession and Owen Thomas's next words. "Well," Thomas said, "I guess it's not likely we'll ever find out who killed the fat man. I'll tell you my own theory." He glanced shyly at Mickelsson, then away. "I don't think anybody killed him. I think he just died. The only real evidence they've got at all is that the door was broken down. But what if he just couldn't find his key? Left it inside, say? Say he broke down his own door, and the excitement of it brought on a heart attack."

Mickelsson gazed thoughtfully, still blushing, at Thomas's chest. If he were an ancient Greek, he might have felt that some alien spirit had entered into him; at any rate, it did not seem himself that said, "But the room was torn up."

"He died of an attack of angina pectoris, that's what they say," Thomas said. "From what I hear, a man can thrash around for twenty, thirty minutes with that. A man the size he was could've torn up a factory."

Mickelsson said, feeling light, not himself, "But he had a gun in his hand. Why that?"

"Who knows?" Thomas said. "With angina pectoris your blood stops moving. Maybe he was seeing visions, having a nightmare. Maybe he was trying to shoot himself."

Mickelsson could think of nothing to say.

Thomas found another misplaced bolt and put it where it belonged.

At last Mickelsson said, "What about the money? He's supposed to have been a bank robber. That's what Tinklepaugh says."

"Maybe he spent it all years ago. Maybe he buried it."

It crossed Mickelsson's mind that the theory was not Thomas's. Was it Tinklepaugh's, then? Bill Cobb's? The work of the state police?

"Strange business," he said.

He bought a pair of pliers to explain his having come.

In the Jeep he pressed his palms into the steeringwheel and thought about the elaborate theory they'd made up to let him off. Why? The only answer he could think of was a stupid one: that they liked him and wanted to protect him, as if he were one of their own. The only alternatives he could think of were almost equally queer: that the death of the fat man was of no importance to the town; that they wanted eventually to pin the thing on somebody else.

When he glanced into the rear-view mirror, he noticed two things at once. The first was that the troll-doll was no longer there. He wasn't sorry to have given it to Lepatofsky's daughter, but he missed it: at the edge of his mind he'd felt that it was in some way lucky. The second thing he noticed was that the car behind him was dark green, unornamented. It had a large radio antenna. Anyone would have guessed at once that it was some kind of police car. According to diSapio-as-in-sap-but-don't-count-on-it, it was not an I.R.S. car. In the car there were two people, but because of the clean-lined reflection on the windshield he could make out nothing of what the two might look like. Mickelsson made a U-turn and nosed toward his house. When he reached his own driveway he stopped and sat thinking for a moment. Not quite to his surprise, the dark green car came up behind him, after a while; but the car did not slow, the two occupants did not look at him. It moved on, as if on important business, up the mountain.

. . .

A little after noon Mickelsson got visitors. The world outside was bright and glittering, warmish now, a day that at any other time of his life would have drawn him out of his house. It was not even now that he resisted the fresh-laundered whiteness of the world, the clean smell in the air; he simply failed to notice, half-heartedly reading, replaying in his mind his conversation this morning with Owen Thomas. He couldn't tell whether he was mainly frightened or mainly relieved to learn that the town thought him a murderer. He was troubled, that much he knew, and weak as a kitten, a weakness that went right to the bone marrow. Building toward something. Sometimes he would sit for an hour without moving a muscle, then suddenly get up and move around restlessly, reading as he walked, sometimes almost falling, unreached by the brightness coming in like a cry at every window.

He heard no car, no knock, but going to the livingroom door that opened onto the porch as if something had drawn him there, and happening to glance out the window for the first time in hours, he was startled half out of his wits to see there a large, outlandish figure in a bright pink overcoat and a white furry hat. When he leaned closer to the window, not quite believing his eyes, he made out a large, pale, smiling face and bright tufts of gray-white curls. The real-estate salesman Tim was behind her, grinning and waving. Mickelsson came to himself and hurried to open the door.

"Dr. Bauer! Well, hello! Tim! What a surprise!" He hoped the smile on his dried-out cheeks was not as ghastly as it felt.

"Professor Mickelsson! I'm so glad you're home!" She reached out one large, white-gloved hand to seize his, closed her fingers tightly, clung for a moment, then coyly tilted her head and drew her hand back. "Oh, look!" she said, peeking around him at the room. "Isn't this just lovely!" She allowed him to take one arm and help her in. Tim came behind her, still grinning from ear to ear, steadying her trailing elbow. He had on his cowboy hat and sheepskin coat. "Say, there!" he said.

"My, my, my," the doctor said, "you've certainly been busy!" She apparently approved whole-heartedly.

"Yes, I have," Mickelsson said. He closed the door behind them. "Let me take your coats." To his surprise he was feeling tentatively glad they'd come.

"I can't stay but just a minute," she said happily, but immediately began unbuttoning the front of her coat. The suit underneath was powder-blue, as pale as her eyes. When he lifted the coat from her shoulders she dusted her hands as if about to set to work. "Isn't this lovely," she said, "isn't this *lovely!*"

Tim stood with his hands in his coatpockets, looking around admiringly; then he too decided to take off his coat. He threw it over the end of the couch. "Boy," he said, "it's really beautiful, Prafessor. You're really a handyman!"

"Oh, well," Mickelsson said.

The doc said, examining the wallpaper seams (she would find no mistakes), "I was always so busy, you know. I just never gaht a minute for the poor howse. My goodness, what's this?" As if someone had told her how he'd changed the former workroom, she'd gone straight to the door, opened it—it was already part way open—and looked in. "Don't tell me you did all this yourself!" she exclaimed. "Well I never!" The queerly girlish laugh he remembered struck him now as unearthly. Whether or not he was right that the doc was gravely ill, she'd aged noticeably during her few months in Florida; her features had sharpened and she seemed much more pale; clearly she hadn't been lying around on beaches. Yet her voice was, if anything, younger than before.

Tim sat down on the couch, smiling, and hung his hands over his knees, keeping out of things, giving the doc playing room. Mickelsson, with part of his mind, worked at whether or not the man was homosexual, but he got nowhere. One would not be quite as open about it in Susquehanna, he supposed, as one might be in Binghamton.

"Yes, it makes a good diningroom, doesn't it," Mickelsson said, getting out his pipe. He saw that she was looking now at the scraped place where once the hex sign had been. "Can I offer you a cup of tea?" he asked.

"That would be lovely, if it's naht too much trouble!"

"Nothing for me, thanks," Tim said, and waved. Now he too was getting his pipe out.

The doc crossed to the Dutch door, visibly decided not to mention the missing hex sign, and turned to look at the stereo instead. "What a lovely phonograph! That's another thing I just never take time for. How we do let things slip by us!"

"I suppose that's so," Mickelsson said. He nodded, excusing himself, still poking tobacco into his pipebowl, and went into the kitchen to fill the teakettle.

She came into the kitchen behind him and suddenly froze. He followed her eyes to the cat, which stood, stiffly arched, by the cellar door, staring back at her. Its mouth was drawn away from its fangs, ready to hiss. Mickelsson stepped over and opened the cellar door, allowing the cat to flee.

"I'm sorry. I take it you don't care much for cats," he said, closing the door and smiling.

"Oh no, it just stahrtled me, that's all," she said, then laughed. She raised one hand, brushing something invisible from in front of her face.

He finished putting on the kettle, then got out cups, two teabags, and sugar. When he bent his head, taking spoons from the drawer beside the sink, he became aware again of how large the woman was, taller than he was by an inch or two. When he glanced at her shoes he saw that her heels were low. The aroma of Tim's pipe tobacco drifted in from the livingroom, the same Dunhill Mickelsson himself smoked, or maybe the similar but cheaper mixture Balkan Sobranie.

She asked how things had been, whether or not he'd encountered any trouble with the house.

"Nothing serious," he said. "I must say, I was surprised to learn it's haunted." He glanced at her.

"Oh, that!" she said, and laughed. "How on earth do you suppose such a thing gaht stahrted?"

There seemed no doubt that she spoke innocently; but he asked, "You never saw them, then?"

"Saw them?" She tipped her head. Apparently deciding he was teasing, she said, "Naht that I know of!" She laughed again. "But it seems as if just about everybody else in Seskehenna has. At any rate that's what they told that poor Prafessor Warren. He was very interested in the house, I suppose you know."

"I'm not sure whether I'd heard that or not," Mickelsson said, and casually watched her.

"Oh my yes! He just couldn't get enough about it! But I'll tell you, just between you and me and the gatepost—" she waved her hand as if sweeping away nonsense—"I don't think he believed those stories for one minute. All he *really* wanted was to find owt how they gaht stahrted—who lived here at the time, where the noises seemed to come from, and such."

"And did he find out?" Mickelsson asked.

"Why you know, I haven't gaht any idea. *I* never stahrted them, *that* I can tell you!" She laughed gaily.

The kettle had been hissing; now it rose to a full whistle, frantic. He turned the heat off and poured hot water over the teabags in the cups. "Sugar?" he asked. He glanced at his wrist, then remembered he'd given his watch away.

"No thank you. Never use it—steals the vitamins."

As he moved nearer to give her her cup he caught her scent, not a smell of soap or perfume, it seemed to him, but of spring itself. No doubt she'd brought it up from Florida. The scent was pronounced, remarkable. When he noticed her expression, he realized he'd shown his surprise.

"It must be beautiful in Florida at this time of year," he said.

"Oh yes, very nice. They have the whitest sand, you know, down on the Gulf where we ahr." She took the cup from him and moved ahead of him to the livingroom. Tim stood bent over near the glass-topped table, looking at something—the old wooden cheesebox with its few remaining keys. His face was prepared to make some interested comment, but he seemed to decide not to break in on the doctor's conversation.

"Well," she said when she and Mickelsson had seated themselves—she on the couch, he in the rocking chair across from her—and she'd taken her first sip, raising the saucer and cup together, using both hands, "never a dull minute in Seskehenna!"

He waited, encouraging her with a look. Tim, losing interest in the keys, went over to stand at the door of the new diningroom, thoughtfully puffing at his pipe, looking in.

"That whole tragic business about the Spragues, I mean," the doc said. She sighed, giving a little wave with her left hand, and took another sip of tea.

Mickelsson nodded, then glanced at her, reconsidering. "I'm not sure I follow."

"Why, you know," she said, "three or four years ago they were the nicest people you could imagine, except for one or two oddities—but we all have our oddities." She smiled, inviting agreement. "But then one thing after another stahrted happening, and the Spragues just changed overnight till you wouldn't've known them. Broke off with all their friends; pretty soon even the relatives wouldn't visit. . . ." She leaned forward. "And then those *really* odd things stahrted happening, the unexplainable mutilations. That awful business about Tommy Sprague's body, it's nothing new, you know." She leaned forward more, confidential, her eyes oddly merry and full of light, though her expression was one of concern. "The same thing happened to the Spragues' pigs three years ago."

"Wait now," Mickelsson said, "what awful business?"

"You didn't hear?" she asked, brightening more. "Why, the body was all cut up, just as if someone had attacked it with a switch, or maybe a torch, or some kind of animal had got to it. No more clue to what did it than there was with the pigs."

"You mean to say—" he broke in, not quite registering, trying to slow her down. He looked toward Tim for help, but the young man's broad-shouldered back told him nothing.

Dr. Bauer nodded emphatically. "He was all cut to ribbons, big slash across his throat. That's what killed him, you know. At first they thought the poor man froze to death and then gaht mauled by the snow-plow, but it wasn't so. No sir. Something gaht to him. I suppose it must've been a bear, though heaven only knows. There were odd little cuts on him, anyway, especially the face. It was a friend of mine down at the hospital that examined the body. They're expecting to do a full autopsy day after tomorrow, or maybe Wensdee. But they won't learn a thing, you know, and though they question people till Doomsday, they'll never get a clue."

Tim turned, smiling with what looked like simple sociability, the pipe in his hand, and came over to sit on the end of the couch not far from Dr. Bauer. He looked from one to the other of them as if enjoying the conversation but thinking it not his place to take part in it—as if he were a boy among adults, or just the doc's chauffeur.

"But what's the explanation?" Mickelsson asked almost crossly. "Are you saying it's witchcraft?" He gave a sudden ironic laugh. "UFOs you think?"

"Maybe there *is* no explanation." She smiled, delighted that it might be so.

"There's always *some* explanation," he said. He glanced over at Tim, who smiled.

"Well, you're the philahsapher," Dr. Bauer said. "I suppose you must be right. Maybe he fell in the brush or, as I say, a bear gaht to him. But my own opinion is . . . well, you know, the world's what you make of it." She shook her head. "Ever since the tragedy—I guess you know abowt that, how his daughter passed away, one of those freak anesthesia reactions—" She paused, apparently losing her thread. She covered by taking a sip of her tea. "What I was saying," she said at last, brightening again, very gently setting down the cup and saucer, "Tommy changed all at once, and somehow or another . . ."

Mickelsson was thrown, then remembered that "Tommy" was her name for old Sprague. "The world changed to suit his view of it?" he suggested.

"Well, *no*," she said, and blinked. "Heaven knows," she said then, eager to dismiss the whole business, out of her depth. "I don't really believe in such silliness, of course."

Tim said, "There's a laht of strange things in this world, though—more strange things than naht!" He laughed. She too laughed and gave a helpless little gesture, admitting it might well be so, not caring to pursue it.

But Mickelsson wasn't quite ready to move on. "I've been wondering"—he cleared his throat—"what was it that frightened you, the last time you were here?"

Her whole face lifted, almost sparkled, prepared to hear marvels. "Frightened me?"

"You nearly killed me," he said. He smiled and made a feeble pass with his pipe to show he bore no grudge. "You remember almost having an accident, just down the road?" He pointed.

"Was that *you*, Prafessor?" she cried, almost joyful. "Good gracious, I'm so sorry!"

"Oh, it's all right," he said, faintly annoyed at her reaction, but again waved it away. He drew his pipe back to his lips and found that it was out. "The thing is," he said, "I know you were up there at Spragues', and I know about the lawsuit, of course—"

"Yes, I see!" She looked trapped, though not displeased by the fact. She went on merrily smiling, brighter than sunlight on ice. He wished suddenly that Jessie were here—for many reasons, among others because she could check his perceptions and because it seemed that the mystery was about to be solved. Without her, the pleasure of the detective game paled. The thought of her brought other thoughts less pleasant. As if the ground had opened up.

"Well, *that's* over," the doctor said, almost regretful, it seemed to Mickelsson. "He never had a chance with that suit of his, you know—the whole thing was downright insane, really; it's a wonder he found a lawyer. But now that poor Tom's gone . . ." She shook her head once more, smiling with what seemed pity except for the sparkle in her eyes. She turned to include Tim in the conversation. "You know, all our lives there was something about us," she said. "Bad chemistry, I suppose. And then, once he gaht it in his mind that I'd stolen his property—" She looked around as if surprised by the recollection that this was the house. "Well, who'd believe it?" She smiled, finished her tea, and carefully placed the cup and saucer back on the glass-topped table. Mickelsson glanced down at his own tea, almost untouched. "You might laugh," she said, "but there was a time I was actually sweet on him. Isn't that something? It was a long, long time ago, a course."

The light in the room had changed now, some of the brightness drawing back, losing power. The shadows on the walls had grown more vague and more extensive. On the road outside, a car slowed down, then sped up again. She too seemed to listen. Both Tim and Mickelsson were relighting their pipes.

"So what was it, that night, that frightened you?" he asked.

"Frightened me," she echoed as before, visibly baffled. Then light broke, a queer, joyful wildness in her eyes. "I wasn't frightened," she exclaimed, "*that's* naht the reason I was driving like that! I was furious!"

He stared.

Tim looked with interest from Dr. Bauer to Mickelsson.

She leaned forward, muscles tensing, her smile suddenly like a young girl's, and said, "I talked with him, reasoned with him, tried to make him see that he'd end up despised and bankrupt if he didn't just let *go* of it—believe me, he didn't have a leg to stand on! But no, they kept on, both of them, screeching and complaining, making terrible accusations. . . . If I'd stayed a minute longer I'd've broken both their necks!" She laughed at herself. "Believe me, I wasn't frightened—not of *that* little monkey! Believe me, if somebody'd put a knife in my hand, or a paper box of matches—" She laughed again, a laugh almost like music, acknowledging what a foolish child she'd been, and at the same moment, as if to be done with the embarrassing confession, she stood up, looming above him, raising her hands out to the sides for balance. Tim stood up too. "Oh no, I wasn't afraid, heaven bless me! I was never *that* kind!" Then, getting her amusement into control, still blushing, she said, "Well, I'm sorry to have frightened you on the road, I *must* say. I guess it's pure luck that we're still here to talk about it. I really am so ashamed of myself."

Grudgingly, Mickelsson said, "It's amazing, the way you pulled out of it. Me too, for that matter."

"Well, you know, something just takes over for you," she said. "People have no idea what powers they have. I believe people really could just take off and fly if they set their minds to it—not that I say Tommy Sprague could do it."

Surprised, Mickelsson said, "You sound uncertain about it."

"Oh, well, you know, I like to leave things open." She smiled.

It came to Mickelsson that he ought to be standing. They were preparing to leave. He got up, rising into the smell of Tim's pipe, and abruptly remembered that his pipe tobacco had never reappeared after the night his house had been ransacked.

"And I'm so glad the howse has been no trouble," the doc said, crossing to her coat. "You certainly have done well by it!"

"It seems odd," he said, "that you should've thought it would be trouble. You're sure it wasn't the ghosts you were thinking of, or witchcraft or something?"

Tim was shrugging into his coat.

Dr. Bauer smiled, staring as if absently at where the hex had been, and seemed not to register his remark. "Ah, yes," she said. She stood large and comically out of season in her bright pink coat, pulling her white gloves on, then reaching for her hat.

"I understand there's some evidence that there really may be ghosts, or something of the sort," Mickelsson said, stalling them. "Is that why you put up the hex sign?"

She blinked, coming out of her reverie, and looked at him. "That?" she said, pointing at the door as if the hex were still there. "I gaht that down at some restaurant just outside Harrisburg. It was one of those decals, you know." Her expression was partly puzzled, partly apologetic. "I think it just means 'welcome.' "

"But the black band around it, wouldn't that suggest—"

"Heavens, I wouldn't know, Professor," she said with a laugh, patting her hat into place. "There was a paper that came with it, but I'm afraid I lost that years ago." She came back toward the door. Tim, smiling, moved toward her.

Mickelsson frowned. It was his paranoia, he knew, that made the two of them seem conspirators. Obviously, Tim was just helping her out, driving her around during her visit. Mickelsson said, "I wanted to tell you, by the way, I'm very grateful for the way you came down in price. I was amazed, really—"

"That was because of the Mormons, of course," she said.

No doubt he showed his surprise. Tim explained with a wide grin,

"They wanted it real bad. There's more and more of 'em arownd here these days. They pay tahp dahller."

"You didn't want to sell to them?" He studied the doctor's face.

"I know it's terrible to be prejudiced," she said, "but I've always gahtten on so well with my neighbors. Right or wrong, I knew they'd just hate me if I sold to *those* people. How would they have liked it if I'd sold to the Mormons and they'd turned the place into one of their synagogues? Thank heavens I was able to find Tim, and Tim fownd you!"

"I see," Mickelsson said. It was a slight exaggeration. Yet he felt oddly cheerful. The visit had done him good. "Well," he said then, "I'm glad you could stop by." He opened the door for her. "Have a nice trip back."

She smiled again. "I will, I'm sure. I always do. Thank you!" Carefully she put her right hand on the doorframe, preparing to step out. "What a beautiful, beautiful day," she said.

Just as they stepped onto the porch, Mickelsson steadying the doctor's elbow, a small yellow car came down the mountain and, approaching Mickelsson's place, slowed.

"Company?" the doctor asked.

Mickelsson ducked a little, trying to see the driver. "I imagine it's one of your friends," he said. "No doubt they've recognized your car."

She shook her head. "No, that's Tim's car."

"Maybe somebody who's lost, then, or some friend of Tim's . . ."

Taking pains to ignore the cold, he walked down the porch steps with her, still helping to steady her, Tim walking on the other side, then down the shovelled path toward the road where Tim's dark blue car was parked.

Directly in front of the house the yellow car stopped, sliding a little, and he realized with a start that the driver was his student Alan Blassenheim. The boy rolled down the window, grinned, and gave Mickelsson a mock salute. "Hi, Professor," he called. Over on the passenger side, beyond him, Kate Swisson waved and smiled foolishly.

Depression washed through Mickelsson's body like a drug. "Hello," he called to both of them. He scowled then, looking down, and returned his attention to helping the doctor down the poorly shovelled steps from the high, snowfilled yard to the road. Alan waited while Mickelsson and Tim walked the doctor to Tim's car, Tim going to the driver's side, Mickelsson holding the passenger-side door while the doctor got in.

"Drive carefully," he said, leaning in on the window as if to keep them a little longer. He added, trying humor in spite of his gloom, "Watch that temper now, Doctor—don't make him drive too fast. Could be snowmobiles out."

She laughed lightly, letting her head fall back. "Isn't that the silliest thing!" Tim started the engine, waved and ducked his head, then drove off, fishtailing at first, then steadying.

When they were out of sight, Mickelsson pushed his freezing cold hands into his trouser pockets, drew his head into his collar as well as he could, and walked to Blassenheim's window. "Out sightseeing?" he asked.

They both answered at once, then both backed down, each deferring to the other. It was finally the boy who spoke. "The Swissons are looking for a place in the country, and since her husband's away I told Mrs. Swisson I'd, like, drive her around."

"Ah," Mickelsson said. He studied first Blassenheim, then the woman. At last he nodded and, against his will, asked, "You have time for a cup of coffee?" He was smiling his wide, crazed smile.

Kate Swisson tried to mask panic with a heavy-flower bend of the head and a vast, limp smile. For all the biting cold, Mickelsson felt a strange sleepiness coming over him. He knew pretty well what it was: crushed rage. Alan Blassenheim's cheeks somewhat darkened.

"I guess we better not," the boy said. "We're supposed to get over to Montrose."

"Mon*trose*," Mickelsson said, correcting him.

"Whatever," the boy said, slightly surprised by Mickelsson's tone.

Mickelsson caught the Swisson woman's eye. "Mon*trose*," he said, and smiled. "I can see you've got real taste—nothing but the best, and the cost be damned!"

"Well," she said, smiling, raising one hand to her collar as if to protect her frail, white throat from the cold, "we thought we'd *look* at it."

"Incredible town," he said, "all white and green, quiet, dignified, wonderfully kept up—most of us don't get to live in such a place till we're dead." He laughed. "Well, give my love to Brenda," he said, and gave Blassenheim a friendly little punch on the arm. Blassenheim looked startled. "Well, see ya," Mickelsson said, and gave his student another little punch.

Blassenheim drew his arm back and reached around with his right hand, as if unaware that he was doing it, to rub the punched place. "Well," he said, and at the same instant Kate Swisson said, "Well—" They laughed. The boy shifted into drive. "I guess we better get going," he said.

Mickelsson gave a mock-salute.

"See ya!" Kate Swisson said brightly, and waved.

He gave another mock-salute, somewhat sharper. As soon as the car started up he turned, shuddered violently once from the cold, and hurried up toward the porch.

6

The philosopher's treatment of a question is like the treatment of an illness. Philosophy leaves everything as it is.

What is your aim in philosophy? To show the fly the way out of the fly-bottle.

Monday morning. He awakened suddenly, tearing himself from a dream and staring, half awake, at the white wall opposite, gradually realizing—the life draining out of his arms and legs—that he must finally face the world: drive in and teach. He'd already missed the beginning of the new semester. It was perhaps not so bad. Students often came back late. Outside his window, the valley was as white as ever, deeply drifted. White and empty, perfectly silent, frozen, spring still far away. When he closed his eyes he saw in his mind the crowded university hallways and heard the ocean roar of talk, merry greetings, infinitely repeated dully echoing phrases, wave after wave of them, all mind-boggling, philosophi-cal: "Hey, man, what's happening?" "Jesus, I thought you *trans*ferred!" He saw himself standing in the corner of the mailroom, cowering like one of Miss Minton's naughty boys, his elbows drawn close to his sides, eyes averted, avoiding eager glances from students and colleagues whose names he no longer remembered. If he were wise he would leer, bob his head, play crackling madman. But who had strength for that? His oversized mailbox would long since have overflowed into cardboard boxes in the departmental office, armload on armload for him to carry down to his own office and, closing his eyes, dump into his file drawers. "Gosh, Pete," Tillson would say when the drawers no longer closed—his moustached grin trembling, meaning no offense—"isn't this getting, you know, out of hand?" (Perhaps he would say nothing, defeated, bowing to things as they are.) He saw Jessie striding up to meet him, smile wide, hand outstretched —surely she would brazen it out; or would she snub him, say not a word —silent as Cosima to poor Fritz's obscene, mad cries—then Alan Blassen-heim sheepishly grinning, not sure what expression he ought to wear, keeping himself out of range of a friendly punch. "Did you hear about the kid in our class that killed himself?" He saw Brenda Winburn, looking angry and haggard, maybe numb from the pretense that she didn't know a thing, because by now Blassenheim would certainly be dropping in from time to time at the apartment of Kate Swisson when her husband was away, or stopping in at the practice room, because in the wide-open sea, goodness of heart was not enough. Maybe nothing was enough. "Hi, there," Blassenheim would say, grinning and slouching. "*Hi*, Alan!" Batting eyelashes. He'd go in, slightly reddening, astonished at his luck, and Kate Swisson would jump up happily and close the door. "Look at you!" adjusting his collar, just to touch him. What might he have said to the boy that would have protected him? More careful attention to the *Symposium*, perhaps? Beware of fly-bottles! Mickelsson saw Brenda Winburn sitting—her long, muscular legs crossed at the knees—in the learner's seat at his office, dark fire in her eyes, Mickelsson at the window, stretching his deadweight arms out to the sides, palm up. "What can I tell you? It's a stupid world." Phil Bryant drawing him aside in the cafeteria: "Pete, I've been wanting to talk to you about Jessie. Things look bad. Did you know?" "Things *are* bad," Mickelsson would say; "things are crap." It wasn't true, of course. Only here in the swirl of things. Only if one was, like Mickelsson, a sore-head. "*Denn bei dir ist die Vergebung.*" (Herr Bach.) He imagined John Pearson, upright as a figure of stone, the dog sitting six feet away, watchful, patient of the wasted time, his mind still on rabbits. It was of course true that he had no real choice but to get up, go to work, earn the money he owed the I.R.S. or had given away in advance to Ellen, who scorned and hated him. (Not true either. More rant. Hatred was an achievement of the will none of them was up to.)

He sat up, as tired as if he hadn't slept at all, put his legs over the side, and set his hands on his knees, momentarily baffled by how cold it was. The fire in the woodstove must have burned away, and the furnace had failed to switch on because the oil had run out. He'd bounced four checks on Benson Brothers; they probably wouldn't refill his tank until he paid. "Too much," he said, and rolled his eyes toward the ceiling. "Be reasonable!" He scowled. Today the talking-with-God game was not funny. When he touched his chin he felt bristles days old. He lay back in the bed, too weak of will to stand, and pulled the covers up over him. What could they do if he didn't go in? There could be no doubt that he was slipping. Unable to feel, unable to function; living, as if there were nothing more mundane, in a house inhabited by ghosts more vital than himself. He listened for some sound from them, the old woman on the everlasting treadmill of her rage, the old man everlastingly baffled by it. Mickelsson too was trapped in it: he had dreamed again of how the old woman had shot the old man and he'd slid slowly down the roof, bleeding. His buttons made a scraping sound on the shingles, and as he fell he was mumbling. In the dream, the old woman had turned and looked at Mickelsson.

It was three in the afternoon when he opened his eyes again. The phone was ringing. He let it ring several times before it came to him that it might be his son; then he got up, crossed the icy floor in his bare feet, and took the phone from the hook. "Hello?" he said, guarded.

"Pete? Is that you?" It was Jessie. The softness of her voice shocked him, as if she were calling from a house full of burglars.

He nodded but said nothing, trying to think. It crossed his mind that he really might, if he wished, say nothing—as she perhaps had done, that time when the phone had rung and the caller had chosen not to speak. If he said nothing she would be hurt, maybe shocked, would perhaps send someone out to see him, or even come herself (not likely; none of it was likely). In the long run, would it really be all that bad? It was not true, from a certain perspective, that he was crazy. He was saner than anyone—had fallen out of the world of illusion: love, interesting work, hope for the future. . . . He felt that he was beginning to freeze already, standing naked in the ice-cold room. They would find him standing on one foot, a statue, his right foot tucked behind his left knee.

"Peter?" she asked.

"Hello, Jessie," he said. It surprised him only a little that he spoke. Habit of good manners. These things die slowly. His voice had tears in it.

"Peter, are you all right?" She sounded downright gun-shy. No doubt she knew, then; whether or not she was aware of it.

"Not so good, I guess," he said. "You?" He breathed very carefully.

"I'm fine." She paused. "Not so good, I guess. I guess you must've heard that they're firing me."

"No I hadn't." The shock took a moment to register. He tried to imagine her face. He was biting his lips hard, tasting blood.

"Well, not exactly firing me," she said. "Blickstein made a deal. I had to yell at the president and threaten to sue the state before he'd knuckle. He's putting me in adult education—giving me a raise to take the sting away. And of course there's the appeal."

"Ah," Mickelsson said, "you're appealing!"

"Not me, really." She gave a laugh. "Committee of my friends. Actually, Dan Levinson's running the thing. I guess I have you to thank for that."

"No, that's—" He faltered. "It's good that you're appealing it." He struggled against guilt. "They shouldn't be allowed to get away with it."

"Don't be silly. You know they'll get away with it. It's just a formality, proof that 'we care.' "

"Maybe it will work, though."

"Maybe."

His feet ached from the cold. He was shivering all over.

After a long moment Jessie said, "You missed your classes again today."

He thought of telling her all that had happened since he'd seen her last—the fire at the Spragues', Dr. Bauer's visit, the insanity of the Reich's good dog diSapio; but one fact stood out for him above all others—the town's suspicion that he was a murderer—and he knew it was impossible to say anything at all; to mention any part would be to commit himself to telling all of it. And what that would lead to he hadn't the strength for. Nor had she, probably. He got a mental image of the two of them struggling to stay afloat, far apart, in a dark, night sea, too weary even to call to one another. The image was not quite accurate, he realized. She, at least, was still making the attempt. But it wouldn't last. For all its furor—the valiant struggle against death one saw even in Mayflies—the life-force could hold out for only so long. It gave him a kind of serenity, this realization that despair was not all it was cracked up to be, back in the days of archangels and kings, when one drifted from catastrophe to catastrophe on ceremonious barques. Despair was not, as the world had once dreamed, the most terrible and dread of the Seven Deadly Sins. It was simply a part of the natural entropic process.

He felt what seemed the beginning of a change coming over him. If it was a noble thing to see life from the mountaintop, as Collingwood liked to say, there was something to be said, too, for the calm at the bottom of the sea. Jessie, weakened by successive blows, having been nearly destroyed once before, or rather, twice, was going through what he was, though she hadn't yet reached—this time around—his stage in the process. Like an old man watching his grandchildren crying their hearts out in childhood's immeasurable, brief sorrow, he felt not anger at the bitterness of life or dismay at his inability to help, but only cool sympathy, a guarded Boethian amusement.

She had asked him something and was waiting for his answer. He remembered at last what it was: "Will you be coming in tomorrow?"

He said, "I'm not sure yet."

Again she was silent. At last she brought out, "I see."

"If not tomorrow, then one day soon," he said. Something not himself added quickly, "We'll have a drink, take in a movie, maybe drive to New York!"

"Are you getting someone to cover your classes?"

"I should, shouldn't I," he said.

That too she seemed to find too queer to deal with. After a time she said—one last cry across dark waters—"I *would* like to see you, really."

"We'll get together."

"I keep pacing and pacing, sort of yelling and yelling inside my head. I think the strangest thoughts."

He thought of Finney's idea—nobody out there, nobody, nowhere, *nothin*.

"Keep the chin up," he said.

When the conversation finally ended, or withered to stillness, a perfunctory good-bye, he knew that the next time the phone rang, he wouldn't answer. He went back to stand beside the bed, reasoning with himself. He should at least call the oil company, try whining and cajoling; otherwise the pipes would freeze. And anyway, it was a bad business—theoretically at least—letting himself give up. He should eat, drink a cup of coffee. As his body got going, his spirits would revive. (Well, something like that. Descartes was behind every tree.) He should listen to the radio, start up a fire in the stove, maybe go down in the basement and make something—more picture frames, why not?—or the rolltop desk he'd been meaning to make for his daughter. But already he was leaning down over the bed, already half dreaming, drawing the covers back, preparing to crawl in.

Behind him, the phone rang again. Mickelsson looked down at his gray, loose stomach—how long had it been since he'd touched the weights?—and tried to decide what to do. The stomach was slimmed down by his forgetting to eat, but lifeless, toneless. The hairs running down toward the genitals were silver. He thought of how when he was drunk he liked to tell young women of his years as an athlete.

He climbed into bed, rolled onto his back, and pulled the covers up tight around his chin. The phone at length stopped ringing. He thought of how Jessica had said, when they made love, "Wow! Wow!" Poor creature! Poor race! He smiled, vanquished. In his mind he saw the viaduct, the color of wheat in the late-afternoon sun, arch after arch crossing the river against dark blue mountains. It was a splendid creation, each stone hand-cut, hand-fitted, built when the river could still remember Indian canoes and drum music, and the people of the thriving town of Susquehanna looked forward to a time of even greater prosperity—the dazzling white restaurant rising above the depot; mansions precariously raised on the steep, dark hillside, reflected in the water; and up on the crest of the hill the red brick church, spire gleaming like a sword.

God damn the government, he prayed. Destroyers of railroads, thieves and liars in cahoots with the brainless, heartless bankers, oil men, nuke men, auto men, men of the Pentagon; freezers of patents for wind, solar, geothermal, and the rest; poisoners of the earth, poisoners of people's minds . . . But the curse trailed off, he'd lost interest. There seemed to be no stopping them, and nowadays, thanks to their computers, not much chance of avoiding their sweeping, witless eye. Voice of the people. That was a comfort. It was the people, all America, all the world, that were insane.

When he closed his eyes he saw Mabel Garret lying in the dimly lit hospital room on the night she'd seen the ghosts. *God bless the Garrets*, he thought. They were good people, though possibly unbalanced, certainly not wise. All those children, each of them doomed to at least some small measure of scorn in this world of blind staggers and self-righteous firing squads. Blacks, Orientals, children with handicaps—the Garrets abandoned all sense and took them in. In a mad world, choose a generous madness.

Reagan was now smiling leader of the Reich—Mickelsson hadn't seen a paper in weeks or heard news on the radio, but someone had mentioned the Great Man's plans, had mentioned them blithely, as if nothing could be more natural. More nukes; deployment of the neutron bomb to please the Germans; friendly signals to the butchers of El Salvador. Why not? *Alles ist erlaubt.*

He slept.

A little before midnight he awakened with a shout. He switched on the light and saw that his breath made steam. The windows were white with frost, glittering feathers. He got up and dressed as quickly as he could manage, as if there were something he must do right away, then went down, scratching his head, getting out his cigarettes, and made a fire in the stove. When it was crackling loudly, the stove doors wide open, sending rolling, yellow-orange light over the room, he sat on the couch— the cat came and settled nearby, close to the stove—lit another cigarette and tried to remember what he'd dreamed. For a long time, no matter how he tried to concentrate, nothing would come to him. Then his eye fell on the shotgun by the door and a piece of the dream snapped back.

It was something about a class: Brenda Winburn was there, holding a birdcage with a songbird in it—plump, black, crow-like—and there were others, people he didn't recognize, in one corner his mother (but too young to be his mother), writing letters in great haste. The room was narrow and extremely cold, a little like the nave of a cathedral, and they were sitting on crates of bright red apples. Nugent was saying something, urgently trying to get some point across, and the class was disgusted, wanting to get on with the course's more serious business, which had to do with Christmas trees, or someone in hiding. The matter was urgent. The room seemed to be sinking, ice rising inch by inch past the delicate purple windows. Mickelsson, in the dream, had lecture notes strewn on the rough plank floor all around him, words and numbers scrawled on pinkish checkbook paper. He'd apparently brought the wrong set of notes. He stalled, trying to get things clear, blocking Nugent's voice, trying to block the bird's bright chatter, stubbornly refusing to grant the floor to Brenda, who was waving her arm, eager to speak, pointing at Nugent's wide black shadow on the frosty wall, the whole wall glittering, except where the shadow was, like tiny mirrors or bits of bluish schist under torchlight. Nugent was talking about moving vans and had brought with him several wheels, which he held out in display, as if for sale. His eyes themselves were silver wheels. The black shadow at his back was in fact not Nugent's shadow but an opening, a door to a place Mickelsson hadn't known to exist. Mickelsson rushed to it, lest the door fall shut, and suddenly found himself lying face up in a grave. The bird sang; Theodosia Sprague looked down at him. Then everything went dark. His frantic fingertips found the padded satin lid.

That was all he could remember. "Crazy dream," he said to himself, frightened all over again. Nothing in the dream made sense except the wheels. The hubs, which were of wood, reminded him of nuclear reactors. He straightened up a little, glancing at the kitchen door as if someone might be watching—the face in the hex sign, say. Somehow the dream was about his son, he decided. "Dear God, take care of Mark," he whispered. "And Leslie, Ellen, Willard, Jessie, Geoffrey Tillson . . ." He was caught again in his trap of ritual, Mickelsson the Magician, and he dared not pull out. Then suddenly, as if taking a great risk, he stopped himself, broke off in the middle of Mabel Garret's name. He held his breath, feeling his racing heartbeat. His alarm increased. He rubbed his chest.

He stood up, purposeful, a little flame of anger leaping in him, and walked through the dark house to his study, where he snapped on the lights. He heard a rattle of mice scattering, but his eye wasn't quick enough to spot one. On his desk his electric typewriter sat half buried in mail. He took his old gray sweater from its hook in the closet—the room was ice-cold—pulled it on, then sat down at the typewriter, pushed the mail out of the way, bunching it up, letting some slide to the floor, found a sheet of paper, and inserted it. He flipped on the switch. *Dear Mark*:

He stared at the paper. He could cover all the rallies, visit all the sites, maybe that would do it; he seemed to have given up on his teaching anyway—his teaching, friendships, love, even his enmities. Sooner or later, driving around the country from rally to rally and reactor to reactor until the Jeep ran out of gas, then hitch-hiking or simply walking like some wet-brained bum, he would spot his son's top-hat and blue-eyed, pink face, smiling thoughtfully, taking pictures with the ridiculous Instamatic, or wiring some "device," as the truth-benders called it, then folding up his dollar-fifty toolkit and running like hell. . . .

You must be very proud.

I am.

It was that that he would write to his son, if he could write. But no words came, only pictures, visions. "Society," "the Establishment"—those fat, hollow words became a sea of drab faces, dutiful bent-backed Mormons like stalks of wheat, hurrying obediently, meekly across an endless murky plain toward increasingly thick, dark smoke. There were thousands of them, millions—timidly smiling beasts, imaginationless, good-hearted, truly what they claimed to be, the saints of the world's latter days. In the dream or vision, whatever it was, they moved in perfect silence, like mile after mile of obedient Russian peasants, drab-coated, dim of eye, pitifully eager to be of use. The sky at the horizon, at the rim of the vast, moving horde, was gray-white, smouldering, the color of dawn in old, fading films. "Here now," one might say to one's students, "is the real. Who could dream, having seen this grisly vision, of any possible ideal?" And the colorless accepters of what their betters decreed—Mickelsson's Mormons —were the least of it. To the east (he would have written) I saw an eager-hearted army as vast as the first, moving swiftly in a direction that would intersect the first where the smoke billowed thickest, but the men of this army wore loud-checked suits, all comically similar, and on their bright, fat faces little moustaches, and they carried attaché cases, lawbooks, and rolled-up sheafs of plans. Some walked on two feet, apparently for their health's sake; some came in Cadillacs, Chevies, and Toyotas. A thousand thousand came hurrying with their bald, smiling heads uplifted, as if seeing in the clouds above them some great light; as many more came bent double, like scurrying ants, all urgently reading what appeared to be ticker-tapes, press releases, leatherbound stock reports—elegant, thick volumes with pages as thin and as closely covered with small, smudged print as fine old Bibles. And behold, from the north, blowing trumpets and beating drums, loud and dazzling as the whole history of Bayreuth, came an army of Congressmen and Public Ministers, Sheiks and Emperors, ragged-bearded Terrorists, and a miles-wide contingent of Women with their breasts bared, triumphantly throwing gold coins in the air, and beside them another great contingent of Children shouting curious slogans—smiling like children in soap commercials and waving blood-red banners saying WE HAVE NOT FORGOTTEN or marked with the letters KKK or with fine, dark swastikas. And behold, I saw an old crooked man at my left who was picking up cigarette butts and candywrapper papers with a pointed stick, putting them in a brown plastic garbage bag, and I said, knowing this man would by profession be familiar with such things, "Old man, tell me, who are these?" And he said, "My son, those are the People Who Believe." And he smiled, showing square yellow teeth.

"Here," one might say to one's students, "is the world as it is."

He turned off the useless typewriter and stood up. It was not the case, of course, that Michael Nugent had killed himself because he'd read too much philosophy, or too little. It was true that Martin Luther and Jake Finney were correct: the world was shit.

He walked, as if aimlessly, back to the livingroom and stood with his hands on his hips, looking at the gun. Those who commit suicide, he had read, condemn their children to suicide. Very well; he had no intention of doing it. But now he felt as well as knew the wisdom of the age-old question: Why not?

The livingroom was warm now—at least the chill was off. The rest of the house was still freezing. He picked up the shotgun, for no real reason, simply for the comforting heft of it, and noticed again with a start how much his hand was like his father's. All at once—it must have been the memory of his father's hand that triggered it—a great swoosh of revulsion rose up in him, a taste of bile, and he put the gun down. He was sick to death of unhappiness, ugliness, imprisonment. What was the question he must rephrase—buried metaphor he must penetrate—life-problem he must heal? Why was it that he was one moment almost serene in his despair, as he'd been when on the phone with Jessie, and the next moment drowning in guilt and dread?

If the wall were physical he would slam through it, crash through it in the Jeep. But it was not; more insubstantial even than the scattering of atoms that he would carry to the grave with him—though he lived to be a hundred—the image of Jessie and Tillson on the couch. Because even before that there had been no hope. "The Fall!" Mickelsson's grandfather would cry, shaking his finger but looking as if he knew no cure for it, for all his fine theories, all his talk about redemption. Sunlight filled the old man's wild, white hair as if all the energy of his life were flying out.

"Infantile," Rifkin had said. "The cry of the child who remembers his omnipotence in the womb."

"Why," Mickelsson had asked, holding both hands out, sublimely reasonable, "why should people settle for anything less than the absolute happiness of the womb?"

"No reason, if you can get it," Rifkin had said, and laughed.

It was clearer now than ever that no one could get it, it was not to be had, the problem of life would not "vanish." He was defeated, wasted, miserably unworthy (according to some standard); and on the other hand nothing available on earth had even a faint, tarnished glint of the perfection he demanded, golden ear for his lutany. The idea that he ought to be reasonable, wake up, made his cheeks redden and his scalp prickle. *Sublimieren.*

He turned, a moment before the phone rang, to start toward the phone.

"Hello?" he said.

Though it was feathery soft, he recognized Donnie Matthews' voice instantly. "Hi, Pete. It's me."

"Donnie," he exclaimed, hunching his shoulders in, clenching the receiver in both hands. "When did you get back?"

"I'm naht hahrdly back." Her laugh was as carefree as a ten-year-old's. "I'm in Cali*forr*nia!"

"You're kidding! What time is it there? Are you all right?"

"Naht so *fast*," she said, and laughed. "I'm fine."

"Listen," he said. "Jesus, I'm glad you called, Donnie. I was worried about you, and—" He bit his lower lip, then rubbed the bridge of his nose with two fingers, as if to wake himself. "Are you sure you're all right?"

"You should see me! I gaht a tan."

"That's swell," he said, paying no attention. "Listen, I've been want-ing to tell you . . . I've been thinking, and . . . I want you to have that abortion if you want it. I was wrong. Forgive me for all those things I said."

"I already did," she said, and laughed. "Have the abortion, I mean. And forgive you. That's why I wanted to call you. To tell you . . ."

"You already had it," he said. He knew he'd heard her right. Why he dumbly repeated it he had no idea.

"Yeah," she said. "I had to, Pete."

"Sure. I know. That's good—that's wonderful. You did the right thing. I hope it didn't hurt much."

"*Ac*tually it hurt like hell, but it's over now."

He shook his head, narrowing his eyes. "I should've been with you."

"It's OK, don't yell at yourself. My brother's wife, I mean my sister-in-law, was with me. They're where I came to."

"I didn't know you had a brother." For some reason it astonished him that she did.

"We never even met each other till a while ago. He's my half brother, really. He's almost as old as you are! Anyways, can I tell you why I called?"

"Sure. Go ahead, Donnie. I'm sorry I keep jabbering." He looked up at the wall, waiting.

"I wanted to tell you, you're a really swell person, and I didn't treat you right at all, so now I'm sorry. What you did for me—I mean, I know how awful it was for you. When I saw your face that night you looked like you'd just died or something, and then you didn't even keep any of the money for yourself. It was dangerous, what you did, and scary, and I guess sort of terrible for you, I mean really *really* terrible, like giving up your *life* for—" She paused a moment to get her voice in control. "So anyways I want you to know I'm a whole different person now. I've changed. I've been saved—I go to church every Sunday—and I don't do any of those things I used to, and . . . well, I miss you."

Suddenly his eyes, too, were swimming. "I miss you too, Donnie." After a moment, when he was sure of his voice, he said, "I hope you're doing something worthwhile with the money."

"I did. I threw it in the ocean."

Mickelsson closed his eyes.

"It was blood-money, Pete. It saved my life, but I just couldn't have it around me. If you could see this new life I have, these people . . . Let somebody find it that doesn't know. Maybe it will save *their* life."

"You threw it in the ocean," he said.

"Yeah. Crazy, huh? I threw away my whole suitcase, everything I had. It was the bravest thing I ever did in my life."

He listened to the soft, mindless singing of electrons in the line.

"Are you mad at me again?" she asked.

He shook his head. "No. No, of course not. How is somebody supposed to find it in the ocean? You're not kidding me, are you? You really threw it in the ocean?"

"Splash."

He was still shaking his head.

"Well, I guess I gahtta go now. Be happy, Prafessor."

"You too, Donnie. Write me sometime."

She hesitated. "I dunno," she said at last. "See, I'm tryin ta stahrt over...."

"OK," he said, tears welling fast now. "Good-bye, then, Donnie."

The pause was long, this time, before she said, "G'bye."

California, he thought. He'd walked with Ellen along the edge of the Pacific, on the beach down below Seal Rock and Sutro's, the pastel houses of San Francisco on their left, far to their right a faint suggestion of the planet's curve. As in another new life he'd sat on dark rocks with his daughter and son, looking out over the seemingly endless gray churning of the Atlantic. Toward Iceland. Toward Germany. The collision of stone and waves made him remember drums.

California. He imagined Donnie Matthews timidly walking out, her face turned sideways, into the breakers.

Sublimieren.

God be with her.

When he bent down to throw more wood into the stove, he remembered another dream he'd had. It was this same house, but the walls had been stone. His mother had come in, still young and beautiful, at least in Mickelsson's eyes, leading by the hand his dead sister, who was not dead after all but had been sewn up and patched like a cloth doll. There had been other people too, quite a number of them, but he couldn't make out who they were. It was cold in the house, and Mickelsson, happy to see his family safe and sound, made a fire in the woodstove. After they'd talked awhile—he could remember nothing of what they'd said; his sister kept smiling and nodding like one of those dolls with a weight in it—they'd all gone to sleep. The stove burned warmer and warmer, heating the stones. Something stirred beside him, and in his dream he awakened to find the whole room crawling with fat, slow-moving rattlesnakes.

When he'd put the wood in and closed the stove doors, he went back to the couch and lay down and let his eyes fall shut. He dreamed the same dream again.

It was morning when he awakened. There was someone gently knocking at his door.

7

He registered the car down by the road only as one he ought to know but didn't, perhaps because his emotions were still clouded by the nightmare; and then, with suddenly changing emotion—half guilty discomfort, half delight and surprise—he saw Lawler. Mickelsson smiled and drew the door open farther. "Good heavens!" he exclaimed. "Professor Lawler! Come in!"

Edward Lawler smiled shyly, not quite meeting Mickelsson's eyes but clearly pleased to see him, perhaps timidly congratulating himself on having driven all this way and found the place. He stood a little to the right of the door, his leather-gloved hands folded in front of him, his many-chinned head bowed, eager to give no offense. He wore a fur hat but with the flaps up, nothing on his ears, a white silk scarf wrapped twice around his neck and tied in front, and a formal, no doubt once-expensive black coat that considerably increased his already prodigious bulk. He looked more impressive than comic—a graying Russian prince on a formal visit. In the coat he seemed almost literally as wide as he was high; the top of his hat came to the middle of Peter Mickelsson's chest. "*Buon giorno,*" he said, and moved his left hand in the faintest possible suggestion of a wave.

"Come in," Mickelsson said, and laughed at the *buon giorno*, hardly knowing why. In all this time, he'd never gotten a clearer image of Lawler as brilliant, frightened fat boy, ready to turn at the slightest hint of scorn or danger and flee. His galoshes were so perfectly buckled, below the flaring, tucked-in pantlegs, it looked as if his mother had done them.

"I hope you're not in the middle of something," Lawler said. His voice had such refinement you almost didn't notice. Years ago he'd studied in Cambridge, in the days of Russell.

"Heavens no, do come in!" Mickelsson said. He reached out, took Lawler's left hand, and drew him a little toward the door, nodding encouragement. "What a pleasant surprise!"

Lawler smiled like a fat girl unexpectedly complimented, started through the door, then remembered his galoshes and, looking horrified by what he'd almost done, stopped to bend over and take them off. It was difficult work, on account of all that bulk, and in the end, sheepishly grinning, he straightened up again and unbuckled one of his galoshes with the heel of the other—at which point Mickelsson at last overcame his fear of offending and bent down with a laugh, saying, "Here, let me help you with that." Lawler accepted his assistance gratefully, breathing "Thank you, thank you!" slightly winded by his efforts. Then Mickelsson led him into the house and took his coat, hat, scarf, and gloves. As he carried them to the closet, Lawler stood beaming, admiring the wallpaper in the livingroom—it was through the livingroom door that he'd entered—or perhaps gazing *through* the wallpaper, lost in ironic thought.

Mickelsson asked, dusting his hands as he returned, "What brings you way out to Susquehanna, Edward?" and then added, before Lawler could answer, "Can I get you something? Coffee? Glass of wine?"

"No, no. No thank you," Lawler said with a laugh and a wave, then apologetically patted his belly. "I'm afraid my stomach's all acid, today."

"Let me offer you a Di-Gel, then," Mickelsson said, and reached into his pocket. "I eat them like candy, myself. Acid stomach all the time. I suppose it's the gin."

"Gin will do that, alas," Lawler said, and nodded, as if distressed to find Mickelsson a fellow sufferer. "I never touch it anymore." He held out his small, plump hand, cupped to receive the Di-Gel, looked at it for a moment as if uncertain what to do with it, then popped it, as if greedily, into his mouth. He looked admiringly at the Christmas tree Mickelsson had not yet taken down, then for a place to sit, half his mind elsewhere; at last it came to Mickelsson that the man was afraid none of the furniture would bear his weight.

"Here, have a seat," he said, crossing to Lawler and indicating the couch. "Sit here by the fire, where it's warm."

"Good, thank you," Lawler said, his face lighting up with exaggerated relief. He moved obediently to the couch, turned around, taking several steps in place—like a hippopotamus, Mickelsson thought—then carefully lowered himself, his left hand on the arm of the couch. "There!" he said, and beamed like an Oriental. He folded his small hands in his lap. Mickelsson drew up a chair and sat, then got out his pipe.

"So," Lawler said, as if something were now resolved. "I'm glad to see you're well." When Mickelsson raised his eyebrows, Lawler explained, rather bashfully, almost prissily, evading Mickelsson's eyes, "You weren't in school, you see, and considering everything that's been . . . in the papers, all the *trouble* in the world—well, I'm a nervous man anyway, as I'm sure you know. When your phone didn't seem to be working I just . . . thought I'd come out."

"How good of you!" Mickelsson said, slightly puzzled. "I thank you for your concern." He grinned, shaking his head. "I'm sorry you had to come all this way for nothing." He poked tobacco into his pipe.

Beaming, eyes closed, Lawler slowly passed his right hand through an arc in front of his chest—a little like the blessing of a Buddha. "Don't mention it! I must say, it's a pleasure to see your arrangements."

The cat appeared at the kitchen door, wide head tipped, then decided to come and settle, sulky, not far from Mickelsson, between him and the fire.

"I've been putting too much time into it," Mickelsson said, "but it's refreshing, working with your hands now and then."

"*You* did all this?" Lawler asked, tilting his head. For an instant something like panic showed in his eyes, no doubt the book man's horror before the mysteries of artisanry.

"The painting and wallpapering, yes, and the sanding and staining of the floors," Mickelsson said, as modestly as he could manage. "Did that for the whole house. You should've seen the place when I moved in! The diningroom was the worst"—he pointed toward the closed diningroom door—"I had to tear out the walls in there, put up sheetrock."

"My goodness," Lawler said. He shook his head, looking around the room with interest, running his eyes along the moleboard, the window casements, the moulding that framed the ceiling. "Goodness," he said again, shaking his head, tapping his fingertips together on his belly. "I take it it must not *bother* you, then, living way out here. Well, I'm a coward, of course, myself. I read about fires, murders, mysterious goings-on. . . . But I suppose it's no safer in Binghamton—that chemistry man you mentioned, murdered right there in his *living*room. . . ." He got out a large white handkerchief and patted his forehead.

"Yes. Professor Warren," Mickelsson said. For some reason he added, perhaps with unconscious sadism, given Lawler's timidity—or with that same evil luck that turns conversation repeatedly to noses in the presence of a man with a long nose—"It's an odd coincidence. Professor Warren was investigating something involving this very house at the time he was murdered."

If it was sadism, Mickelsson couldn't have hoped for a better reaction. Lawler jumped a foot and, with the quick, cunning look of a rabbit, glanced left and right. "*This* house?" he exclaimed. "What was he looking *into?*"

"I'm not sure," Mickelsson said, putting on an expression of unconcern. To heighten the effect of safe domesticity, he smiled fondly at the stray cat he had in fact not yet dared touch. "Some legend, I think."

"Legend?" Lawler echoed. His eyebrows were raised as if permanently above his spectacle-rims.

"It's said the house has ghosts," Mickelsson said, and chuckled. "I suppose it was that that Professor Warren was looking into. I must say, I've thought of consulting a chemist myself, now and then. Sometimes the house gets a strange cooking smell." He chuckled again.

Lawler's mind was elsewhere, his hands busy laying out the white handkerchief like a napkin in his lap. "It can't have been the *ghosts* he was interested in," he said. "I talked with our student"—he glanced at the floor, then continued—"our *late* student Michael Nugent, about this Warren. The man was an *atheist*, or claimed to be." The mention of Nugent made Mickelsson suddenly awkward; even so, he registered with distant amusement Lawler's use of the word *atheist* as opposed to *nontheist*. The man was, of course, a medievalist.

Lawler was saying, "Warren would hardly be interested in ghosts for their *own* sake, and I doubt very much that he'd be interested in *folk*lore either. That just doesn't seem to *fit*." He sank into thought, then raised his right hand, pointing upward. "Suppose, just for the sake of argument—" He was squinting now, compressing his lips. His pudgy hands smoothed the hankie in his lap. Mickelsson smiled, then puffed at his pipe and waited. "Suppose the legend was created as a *cloak* for something—to keep people away from the house. But what? That's the question. What were people not to find *out?*"

"I don't know," Mickelsson said, keeping his tone deferential. "Who'd be kept away from a house by stories that it was haunted?"

"Perhaps not nowadays," Lawler admitted, "though I'm told this is rather odd country, full of superstitions, even covens of—witches? At any rate, such a thing might *once* have worked—twenty years ago, say. *Something* must lie behind these ghost stories."

"Maybe the house really is haunted," Mickelsson suggested.

Lawler laughed, a sudden chortle that made his feet jump, and seemed not even to consider the possibility that the remark might be in earnest. He sat forward a little, so that the couch cushion sagged beneath him, ready to topple and drop him to the floor. For the first time he met Mickelsson's eyes squarely. Lawler was excited, engaged, like a child playing cops and robbers. "What do you know about the house, Pete?"

Mickelsson shrugged, but thoughtfully. It struck him that, though probably nothing would come of it, it might be a good idea, in fact, to run through the whole thing with Lawler. Who knew? Perhaps the man's famous intelligence might throw light on the whole strange business. "Not much," he said. "I'll tell you what I can." He pulled at the pipe, considering where to start, then began, "I know the house was owned, before I bought it, by a woman doctor named Bauer, and I know that for years she had a feud of sorts with a man named Thomas Sprague. He was a relative of the Spragues who lived here before the doctor; in fact he claimed he was their heir. I think it's the Spragues who lived here who are supposed to be the ghosts." He glanced at Lawler. "The feud between the doctor and Thomas Sprague flared up in earnest when Sprague's daughter died in an operation performed by Dr. Bauer—something about an anesthesia reaction. The feud went on—malpractice suit and so on—until Sprague himself died a little while ago . . . two weeks, maybe; I've completely lost track." He looked down, suddenly troubled about something, but he couldn't identify it. He gave up the search and told Lawler about the fire and how Sprague had not been in it, how the walls had been torn up, according to Owen Thomas, and how Sprague had been found days later (or weeks?) in a snowbank, cuts all over his body, one of them the cause of death. Lawler listened with his eyes closed, his large, squat body tilted forward, motionless except for his breathing. "I also know," Mickelsson said, "that there's a legend—I don't know if it's true—that the house was once owned, long ago, by Joseph Smith Jr., the founder of Mormonism."

Lawler's eyes opened wide. "Interesting!" he said. "Warren was a Mormon *apostate*. I assume you knew that?"

"No," Mickelsson said. His scalp prickled.

Lawler nodded, closing his eyes again. "Interesting. I don't suppose . . . going over the house as you've done . . . you *found* anything?"

"I'm not sure what you mean."

"I'm not sure myself, of course," Lawler said. "But it might be a 'lead,' as they say. If there were something here that the Mormons would not want the world at large to be *aware* of—"

"I see what you mean." Odd that he hadn't thought of it himself. But of course he'd been thrown off by the fact that the ghosts were real—if they were, if they were not more tricks of a diseased mind. He backed off from the thought, then leaned forward, frowning hard, resting his elbows on his knees, and told Lawler of the night visitors, the people who'd torn his house apart, thrown out the cigarettes and liquor. "They *could* have been Mormons," he said, "though on the other hand—"

Lawler sat tapping his fingertips together. "Suppose it was something like this," he said, nodding thoughtfully to himself. "Suppose Warren was on to something. Suppose, for example, he was close to discovering clear proof of the fraudulence of the Mormons' sacred texts." He chuckled rather grimly.

"They must have found whatever it was, then," Mickelsson said. "Anyway, *I* haven't found it."

"Mmm," Lawler said, nodding, closing his eyes again. "The trouble with that is the fire up at the Thomas Sprague house. If I haven't misunderstood you, that took place *after* the search of your house."

"I don't follow," Mickelsson said.

Lawler remained motionless except that his arms went out to the sides in a gesture of something like impatience. "It may have been just a coincidence, that's possible," he said. "But first your house is searched, and then, it seems, this Thomas Sprague's house is searched: searched so thoroughly—torn apart, as you say—that it had to be burned, presumably in the hope that the evidence of its having been torn apart would be destroyed. Or perhaps burned to hide evidence that the old woman had been murdered, as no doubt Sprague himself was murdered—possibly tortured first—before or afterward."

Mickelsson shuddered.

Lawler too seemed uneasy, shifting restlessly, furtively scratching himself, as if mere thought might bring the murderers nearer. "What it suggests would seem to be this," he said, grimacing, closing his eyes again. "They could find nothing here, when they searched your house, and it occurred to them that whatever it was they were looking for—whatever Professor *Warren* had been looking for, in his attempt to discredit the religion he'd turned against—might have been found by the Spragues who lived here before the doctor and given by them to the man who was supposed to be their *heir*, the man whose house burned." He opened his eyes part way to judge Mickelsson's reaction.

Mickelsson shook his head, thinking of the two humble Mormons who'd come to his house, then of the horde of gentle, horse-faced people he'd seen baptized in the river. "I don't believe it," he said. "It just doesn't seem—"

Lawler tilted slightly forward. "Then why was Thomas Sprague's house burned? Who cut his throat?"

Mickelsson started, his blood turning to ice. "Wait a minute!" he said. He stood up, needing to pace. "Michael Nugent was found with his throat cut." He shot a look at Lawler. "Does anyone *know* it was suicide? Was there a note? I don't think I heard of one." His next words came more quickly, and he paced again, pushing his hands down into his pockets, the pipe in his right fist. "He was a friend of Professor Warren's. If whoever killed Warren got the idea that Warren had talked with Nugent . . . And listen to this." His strides became longer, more purposeful. "Nugent's friend Randy was run into on his bike, almost killed." He felt a tingling sensation, a faint dizziness like rising fear as he told Lawler about the black kids at the house where Randy Wilson lived, or had once lived. If Nugent had in fact been murdered, no wonder they hadn't been eager to tell Mickelsson where he'd find Randy.

Suddenly Mickelsson stopped in his tracks, his stomach knotting, acid filling it as if poured from a bottle. He remembered the old car in his vision of the bicycle accident, the same well-kept old car he'd seen parked in front of Donnie's the night he'd killed the fat man—the same car now parked in front of Mickelsson's house. He stood perfectly still, heart slamming. *That* was why the fat man had been there in his apartment when it seemed he couldn't be; it was another fat man he'd looked down on from Donnie's window and seen getting out of the car that night—another fat man whom Warren, as his wife had heard him say on the phone, was afraid of. Mickelsson's mind shied back and he looked again at Lawler, childlike in his black suit, his eyes closed to slits. There could be no doubt. He himself had told Lawler that Nugent was Warren's friend. He himself, he saw in increasing horror, had guided Lawler to Randy Wilson.

His face, he knew, had gone ashen. Lawler studied him, then sighed and, with evident reluctance—the hands moving slowly, like an underwater movement—drew something from his pocket. It was Mickelsson's watch, his gift to the boy in the hospital. Lawler dropped it gently on the glass-topped table and, in answer to the shocked question on Mickelsson's face, just perceptibly nodded, like Brahman when he grants a request. Mickelsson looked at the shotgun beside the door, but too late. In his right hand, as if he'd had it there all along—no doubt he'd slipped it from under the handkerchief—Edward Lawler held a snub-nosed pistol.

"End of preliminary inquisition," Lawler said gently, faintly smiling. "Yes, your surmise is correct. I am a Son of Dan."

"You son of a *bitch!*" Mickelsson whispered. A blush shot up into his face and adrenaline made his brain crackle. His lips felt puffy. He almost rushed the man, indifferent to the toy-like gun, but confusion checked him, a bundle of stupid doubts and questions that stopped him more effectively than a bullet could have done. He doubted that all this was real: he'd had psychotic episodes, he occasionally saw ghosts; so perhaps in fact he was imagining all this, or twisting actuality signals into something surreal; fantastic gloss. He had other questions too, dozens, but one stood out: he could not remember for sure whether or not it was the case that a Son of Dan was what he'd thought at first, a member of the old assassination squad of the Mormons. It was a ridiculous question, he saw when his mind cleared—of course they were—but by then the confusion had stopped his initial impulse. If he were to rush Lawler now, he would have to do it by courage, and that was not so easy. As if on its own, independent of his will, his brain began to calculate odds, seek out the ways of cunning. He remembered the lesson of a hundred cheap movies. Stall, let the murderer in his monstrous pride tell his story, and at the last minute, with a sudden blast of stereo trumpets and frenetic violins, some rescuer would come crashing through the window, pistols blazing, karate-boots flying. He knew it was absurd, no rescuer would come, but his wisdom ran behind his brain: he was already stalling.

His chief emotion, strange to say—and even as he felt it he recognized its strangeness—was not fear for his life or horror at life's bleakness or even disgust that a man could so completely seem one thing and in fact be another, could to that degree despise all other people's values—but sorrow at the waste. Michael Nugent's fine, eager mind had been thrown away like a thing of no worth, a dead mouse from a trap; and then gentle, strikingly beautiful Randy Wilson. (He remembered how the boy would fade back, looking at walls and doors, giving Nugent and Mickelsson privacy; he remembered the shine of tears in the black boy's eyes when

Mickelsson had seen him at Binghamton General.) And before that, Professor Warren had been wasted—a man Mickelsson had never known, but surely a creature of some worth in the world, a chemist who'd been bright enough and earnest enough to get Nugent's attention, and newly married to a woman who had evidently loved him. How could one *do* such things? Mickelsson checked himself, drawing his elbows in like a man rebuked. He himself was perhaps no different, really, from the fat black adder on the couch. What did he know of the ex-thief he'd killed, some mother's son, anyway, his head crammed with the same two billion neurons (or whatever it was) as anybody else's. So he told himself, but Nugent's face rose before him and Mickelsson's stomach jerked. He clenched his teeth and fists.

"Keep your hand out of your pocket!" Lawler said sharply.

"I was just getting a Di-Gel," Mickelsson said. He had trouble with his voice. His lips were dry and thick.

Lawler meditated, eyes narrowed more, then nodded. He watched carefully as Mickelsson reached in and drew out the package. "You smoke too much," Lawler said, "and *drink* too much. You're as much a killer as *I* am." He faintly smiled.

"If that comforts you, good," Mickelsson whispered. He changed his mind about the Di-Gels and dropped them back into his pocket.

With his left hand Lawler reached for the couch-arm, preparing to help himself stand up. "We won't discuss it," he said. "As you know, we have work to do."

A little stupidly, Mickelsson echoed, "Work?"

"We have a search to make," Lawler said. Now he leaned his left hand onto the glass-topped table, balancing himself as he straightened up. "I'm afraid we have to tear your lovely house apart."

"You're crazy!" Mickelsson said. His slow-wittedness astounded him. How could he not have known that this was coming? The same instant, as Lawler's hand rose from the table, Mickelsson saw—snapping into focus like some object in one of his son's photographs—the old box with its few remaining keys. Instantly the color of the room changed, as if he were gazing through a curtain of blood. The box, of course! The Mormons hadn't known what they were looking for, if it was Mormons who'd searched his house; Lawler himself had suggested that, and it made sense. They had known only, as perhaps some roving gang of kids knew, too, and as no doubt Professor Warren had known, that the house contained *some*thing. He remembered now, dimly, that someone had spoken to him—the U.P.S. man—of a legend concerning buried treasure. Mickelsson almost laughed; in fact he was in the act of raising his hand to point at the box when he understood the rest. The box of keys was worthless, that was obvious enough; the Mormons' secret was perfectly safe, if it had ever been safe. But if Lawler were to learn that that mouldy black box was the object of his quest, his work here would be finished, along with Peter Mickelsson's usefulness. Almost before the thought was clear in his head, Mickelsson had looked away from the box, careful not to lead Lawler's eyes to it.

Lawler was saying, "We can leave your new diningroom. You already tore out the walls in there, and if you'd found anything I believe you'd have let me know." He smiled. "Let's start up in the bedrooms. Human beings have a natural tendency to hide things near the bed. I suppose it's in some way sexual." He gave the pistol a little wave, suggesting that Mickelsson get moving. "You have tools?"

Mickelsson nodded, still faint with the realization of how close he'd come to speaking of the box, and, with Lawler following, the gun trained on his back, went to get the pick, the wreckingbar, and a claw-hammer. He pushed the hammer-head down into his trouser pocket, crowded in with his pipe. He was only now beginning to register that he must actually tear the house apart, not only undo all he had done but reduce the house to less than it had been when he began. He thought of mentioning to Lawler the horror of that, then kept silent. Probably no one, not even a decent, life-loving man, would really understand. Psychological symbolism; shadows out of childhood. But ah, how powerful such symbolism was! In the hallway, moving ahead of Lawler toward the stairs, he ran his fingers along the new wallpaper. It occurred to him that if, by some miracle, he should get power over Lawler, he would certainly kill him. He felt remorse for the scorn he'd felt toward the well-kept old houses of Montrose, green-shuttered, white palaces, neat broad lawns. He'd disliked the people who owned them, he thought. People too gullibly pious, too proud and conservative; his *own* people, as much so as the people of Susquehanna.

The cat darted past Mickelsson's right leg, running toward the foot of the stairs, where, abruptly, it paused, tinted by the light coming in through the stained-glass windows. The newel post and bannister glowed as if from within. With his right foot raised to the first step, his left hand on the bannister, Mickelsson stopped. He turned, and Lawler looked at him, fat rolls forming on his neck as he leaned his head. The cat moved up three steps.

Mickelsson's fist tightened on the wreckingbar and pick. Lawler was maybe four feet away, within easy reach if Mickelsson were to raise the tools and strike; his left hand, on the bannister, would give him leverage. Lawler gestured with the gun. Light flashed on the lenses of his glasses.

"I won't do it," Mickelsson said. Though he spoke with seeming conviction, the hand holding the tools did not move, still calculating on its own. The swing was too awkward; he should drop the pick, use just the bar. That instant the hallway rang out with a terrific explosion that made his heart leap, his knees turn to water, his vision go dim. Lawler had out-thought him. The cat lay dead on the steps—still jerking but dead, the side of its head blown off, and Mickelsson's muscles were so weak he could hardly hold on to the tools and railing.

"Up," Lawler said.

After a moment, with one brief glance at the cat, Mickelsson turned, a taste of vomit in his mouth, and continued up the steps.

"We'll begin," Lawler said calmly, "by tearing off the mopboards, then we'll move to where the lath butts up against the doors and windows. If one wishes to hide things, those are the easiest places to open up and then put back as they were."

"Yes," Mickelsson said.

He swung the wreckingbar hard, cutting deep, as if by proving himself a willing worker he might escape being shot. Nietzsche's "slave" in bold cartoon. He knew the hope was futile, in fact moronic, and knew, too, that if he worked this way for very long in his present condition, he'd be too weak to do what was demanded of him. Nevertheless he swung hard a second time, then pried away an eight-foot length of moleboard—"mopboard," Lawler had called it. For some reason the difference between their languages was chilling. There was nothing behind it, whatever it was called, but broken bits of plaster. He stabbed in behind a second length of moleboard. *Moles*, he thought, and again felt cold along his spine. He calmed himself. Lawler seated himself on the bed, the gun still on Mickelsson.

"What's all this really about, Edward?" Mickelsson asked as the second length creaked out a ways, then cracked. "There are no Sons of Dan. You know that."

"Don't be stupid!" He scowled, barely containing his disgust at such ignorance.

Mickelsson swung again, then pried. "I've seen these Mormons," he said, already breathing heavily. "One may not like them much, but any fool can see they're a gentle people. Docile as cows. If there really were this assassin squad you claim to be part of, people like that would get out of the Mormon Church so fast you'd think you'd walked in on a stampede."

"You're mistaken." Lawler had to raise his voice to be heard above the wreckingbar. He seemed glad to do it. "First, of course, most of them don't know about us—at least not for sure. Nearly all of them, I imagine, have heard about the massacre at Mountain Meadows, back in the early days, and most of them have heard enough rumors of things more recent to keep them uneasy, when they think about it, which for the most part they don't do." He tapped his forehead, tilting his head forward and rolling his eyes up like a medieval saint in a painting. "Most of them have heard how the Angels of Death"—he modestly closed his eyes——"the

Danites, Sons of Dan—how we shot Governor Boggs of Missouri as he sat at his window." Lawler watched Mickelsson sadly from under half-closed eyelids, as if to admit the assassination attempt had been perhaps a little stupid. "These gentle Saints you speak about would never admit to an outsider, I imagine, how much they suspect or, in some cases, know. But take my word for it, they're not altogether unaware of our existence."

"Mountain Meadows?" Mickelsson asked, and kept working. It was not Mountain Meadows he cared about, of course. Nobody's "early days" were all that glorious.

Lawler's voice, behind him now, had a kind of shrug in it, but no real apology. Maybe, in fact, he was enjoying himself. "Rich wagon-train from Arkansas, back in 1857, passing through Utah on its way West. At the time we were in undeclared war with the United States government. It's a long story, but briefly, this: some Ute Indians—or mostly Ute Indians; they may have been supported by white men in Indian dress—swept down on the wagon-train. The train formed a defensive circle, and fought back. As the attackers soon learned, the train had sharp-shooters—the best Indian-fighters money could buy—so the 'Indians' were ineffective. That, however, was not the end. The Saints arrived and persuaded the train to surrender into Mormon protection. This the train did, giving up its weapons, and the Mormons systematically shot every man, woman, and child above the age of eight. Interesting? Hey? Think what discipline it took! How many people do *you* know capable of shooting unarmed women and children? Children under the age of eight, I should mention, were loaded into wagons and carried away to be adopted into Mormon families. This is the touching part: while they were leaving in the wagons, riding up the trail out of Mountain Meadows, the young children saw the whole thing. Most of them didn't remember it in later years, of course."

Mickelsson turned briefly to glance at him. Lawler was neither smiling nor frowning. He sat motionless, the bed sagging under his weight, the pistol still trained on Mickelsson. "And you're telling me the Danites did this? Your people? And the heads of the church knew it? Ordered it?"

"Come, come," Lawler said, giving him a little wave, "no childish righteousness. Nobody's boasting about that sordid affair. But use your head, Professor. It was an act of war. The Saints had been driven from Missouri by brute force, and the U.S. Cavalry was amassing for an attack. The rules of war were not the same in those days as we like to believe they are now. It was a rich train—one of the richest that ever travelled West—and rich in arms as well as gold. In eighteen fifty-seven massacre was a standard wartime practice. It took stomach, but our forebears had a good deal more stomach than we do." He looked down at his own vast tumescence glumly, as if noticing he'd perhaps made a joke. "A few years later, when times had changed, the church itself turned on the general in command of the operation—a cousin of Robert E. Lee."

"Terrific," Mickelsson said. He put down the wreckingbar to move his dresser and trunk out of the way. They'd be scratched beyond repair when this was over, he thought—then went clammy, remembering it wouldn't matter; he'd have no use for trunks and dressers. "Terrific," he said again, with still greater disgust.

Gently, wearily, Lawler asked in his fussily good English, "Does irony comfort you? I am not responsible for the cruelty of life at that time. You're a descendant of Vikings, if I'm not mistaken. Are you responsible for the sack of Paris?"

Mickelsson worked on, clenching his dust-gritty teeth, saying nothing.

"But to return to your earlier, more interesting point," Lawler said, "I think it is the case that most Latter-Day Saints, if you ask them about the Danites, will tell you that there certainly are none. But we're adults, you and I. We know about people.

"Look at the matter philosophically. I think we're in agreement, you and I, that people ought to act as individuals, with individual thought and will. How else can we have a democracy? The trouble is, they don't. People are lazy, if not stupid—and I do not honestly believe the problem is stupidity. They don't *want* to think. People want secure, happy families, pleasant barbecue parties, predictable-in-advance nights for bowling and the opera. Given that fact, one has two apparent choices: to try with all one's might to teach them to think and to value thinking—and we both know, as teachers, how seldom that works—or to *control* their thinking, de-fuse them, so to speak—intellectually castrate them, you may prefer to say—and we both know how frequently, even in the university classroom, we do that."

Abruptly, Lawler leaned forward from the side of the bed and stood up, darkly frowning, and backed, on tiptoe, with graceful, almost princely movements, to the bathroom door, which he threw open suddenly, as if he thought there might be someone behind it. The bathroom was empty, like the rest of the house. He closed the door and looked hard at Mickelsson. "Did you hear something? Is there someone here in the house with you?"

"I didn't hear a thing."

Lawler seemed to ponder it, tapping his chin with two fingers, his lips sucked in. Then he seemed to dismiss it. "All right," he said. "Very well, where were we?" He nodded. "Ah. Controlling people's minds. Yes, exactly!" His expression became solemn again. "Has it ever crossed *your* mind, Professor, that we're in the process of wiping out physical illness? Fifty per cent of all cancer we can stop; we're close to winning out over heart disease; we're on the threshold of discovering the secret of aging. Do you know what that means? Soon the one great enemy—the only one remaining—will be *mental* illness. Imagine it! A whole planet of everlasting mad zombies! Freedom, civility, repression, frustration . . . increasing crowding, increasing indignity and an interminable life for suffering it all . . . Your kind of dream is finished, you see, your admirable but deadly liberalism. Life must defend itself against the mad raging horde. It's right at the door, believe me!

"For that reason, you see, we have in our church a hierarchy of knowledge and control—much as the Freemasons at one time had. It's basically what you might call a *military* structure: those who know, and those who, in descending degrees, obey. Those who obey are persuaded that the church knows best. I know, I know, you scorn that. Who doesn't? You want everyone to think for himself, starting with propositions in the original Greek." He shrugged, then shook his head impatiently. "But they *won't*, that's the evident fact of the matter. Believe it or not, most people *want* to give up all traces of their humanness to some authority that frees them to be comfortable, healthy beasts. If they weren't Mormons, they'd be union fanatics or 'organization men,' and their children would be Moonies, or scientologists, or members of the Way International. Have you read about that?" Lawler's eyebrows lifted, his face full of sadness. "Someplace in Ohio—Lima, perhaps? A *profoundly* dangerous outfit, I'm afraid! Gun-crazy, and rigidly mind-controlled by drugs. *We,* as you know, do nothing like that. Our use of violence is selective—that's one reason no one is even sure of the present existence of the Sons of Dan. The membership of Way International, I might mention, grows by leaps and bounds. People, you see, *like* to be slaves! But no organization in the world—with the possible exception of the Jehovah's Witnesses—is growing as fast as the Church of Jesus Christ Latter-Day Saints. We play no tricks, we use no drugs—we *forbid* escape through drugs. We do not use 'front organization' trickery like the Moonies—cheap housecleaners and babysitters who will poison and steal your child's mind." He smiled as if mournfully amused by such childish wickedness. "No, no! We work with *human weakness itself,* the most powerful drug of all. The universal hunger for security, easy answers, magic, and somebody to blame. The religious *thirst,* as your friend Nietzsche says, for things which are *against reason.* That's the formula, you know. The medieval Church Fathers understood it, especially the mainly political ones, the kind that started crusades. And every modern Holy Roller knows it—fundamentalism, what is it but a secure closing of doors, permission not to think?" Lawler's eyes closed to slits. "Your friends the Lutherans are not so far from that, my dear Professor. And the Presbyterians—notice how they speak more and more of *Jesus within!* Not 'the historical Jesus,' pride of their tradition—oh no! Too much slippage there! 'Jesus within!' Saves all kinds of annoyance, you know. Who needs Hebrew or Greek to read Jesus within? I watch these things with interest, as you see. But we Mormons, we were there ahead of them all. Make no mistake, Professor! We don't make people weaker than they are. We make them *profoundly* what they are!"

He stood up and came over to stand near Mickelsson, searching fussily for any sign of the manuscript or book or metal tablet, whatever it was they were looking for. "Let me tell you something," he said. "Nazi Germany encountered one great problem beyond all others; namely, *human goodness*. Members of the Third Reich's mass firing squads kept hanging and shooting themselves. It was a devil of a nuisance. For all the propaganda, most Germans—unlike our friends at Mountain Meadows—couldn't stomach the things the regime required."

Abruptly he broke off. Mickelsson had torn off the last of the moleboards. There were odd cuts on the inside of the board, as if rats had been chewing it, but chewing very neatly. It did not seem likely that the cuts, or gouges, could be the work of the wreckingbar—but now that he thought of it Mickelsson was uncertain. It was true that he'd been working without thinking, half in a dream. Lawler looked carefully at the space revealed by the tearing away of the moleboard—he dismissed the cuts on the board with just a glance—then pointed, without a word, at the nearest window casement. Mickelsson was sweating rivers. Trembling with weakness, his chest aching, he struck at the wall beside the casement.

Lawler went back, waving away dust with his left hand, and sat down on the bed again. "Shall I continue? Do you like to be entertained while you work?" Mickelsson said nothing. Lawler pondered, sunk in gloom, then at last continued, "German soldiers had trouble killing. What did the authorities do? They took young men, callow youths—the future S.S.—and issued each one a dog, a dog the young man was to train. The young man was to live with the dog, become the dog's 'best friend'—and then one day on the field—you guessed it—they commanded the whole company of young men to slaughter their dogs. You see the psychology, the *values* invoked: discipline, self-sacrifice for the Fatherland, the assuaging power of community and peer-approval; consensualism, lofty-mindedness: 'Even the death of my beloved dog I will endure in the name of Deutschland!' Hey? So, little by little, those fiendish masterminds hardened the S.S. to murder—*changing human nature*. It's admirable, in a way—the intelligence involved, the singleness of purpose. But listen: the Mormons never did such things—never needed to! Heavens no! The Mormons have worked—have *always* worked—with human nature as it *is*. The great mass of humanity wants nothing but security, correct? Safety for themselves, responsibility firmly placed elsewhere. I'm not claiming, of course, that the Mormons are unique in their way of working, though I think you'd have to hunt hard to find anybody better at it. We've had since the beginning—since the days of Joseph Smith and Brigham Young, that is—our military structure, our tight chain of command, our 'godfathers, lieutenants, and soldiers,' if you will. Not everybody knows what the people at the top know, but almost everyone obeys."

Mickelsson had by now torn out the plaster and lath around the last of the window casements. He leaned his pick against the wall and looked slowly around the room, then at Lawler. In all the dust, the man's black form was vague, like some blurred, waiting octopus in its shadow-filled underwater den.

"All right, begin on the walls," Lawler said. "Then the ceiling." He glanced at his watch, awkwardly drawing back his cuff with the hand that held the gun and raising his wrist toward his face.

Mickelsson lifted the pick again, held it a moment in his two hands, then swung. More dust poured out into the room, and he coughed, then swung again.

"It's so stupid," he said, resting for a moment—his voice, even in his own ears, whiney. "If you really believe in Mormonism, how can you believe we'll find evidence that the whole thing's a fraud?" He knew well enough it was an empty argument.

"Keep working," Lawler said; then, when Mickelsson went back to his increasingly wobbly swinging: "In the first place, assuming it's *not* all a fraud, it might nevertheless be the case that something may exist that could throw doubt on perfectly honest claims. We can't have that, can we?" He puckered his lips, prissily frowning. "And in the second place, if the whole thing *is* a fraud, well, so *what*? Show me a religion not grounded in myths of the miraculous! Are we seriously to believe some old-time Jew descended into hell for three days, then rose to sit at the right hand of God? Or that some barren, hook-nosed hag of ninety had a child that fathered a nation?" His eyes flashed anger. "Or that Buddha met a talking tree?" He laughed scornfully, without humor, as if enraged by the whole stream of humanity back to the beginnings. Then, solitary, accepting the burden, he rocked on his buttocks, trying to get comfortable. "All religions are fraudulent at the foundation, my dear Peter, 'built on sand,' so to speak." He coughed, bothered by the dust or by having to shout. "Who wants a God that can't do magic?" He coughed again, repeatedly and loudly. Glancing at him through the veiling dust, Mickelsson saw that the coughing fit had Lawler shaking, angrily jiggling all over. "What counts," Lawler said when the jiggling had stopped and he was able to speak again, "is not the *foundation* but the *battlements* and *towers*— you'll excuse me if I seem to wax poetic; it's a standard answer."

"Then why not be honest?" Mickelsson asked, then coughed himself and again rested for a moment. "Admit it's based on a fiction but argue its present spiritual and moral worth—or whatever the hell it is you argue."

He could just make out that Lawler was sadly turning his head from side to side, his eyes hidden behind the dust on his glasses. "Can't do it," he said. "Too many people are fools; they need inspiring fairytales. If you're out to convert the whole world, or enough of it to give you significant power vis-à-vis the rest, you must recognize people's weakness and play to it." The expression of distaste was back. "For their own good."

" 'Good,' " Mickelsson scoffed, and once more raised the pick-axe. It crossed his mind that in all this dust he might easily hurl the pick at Lawler and then jump him, all before Lawler could get a good shot off. But he did not act. The dead cat was still too vivid in his mind. What bothered him now was not just the horror of the image, the blown-away side of the head. Lawler had fired from the waist, with deadly accuracy, and small as the gun was it did such damage as one might have expected from a weapon much larger.

Mickelsson said, "I think you're wrong—your assertion that all religions start as lies." He swung the pick and grunted. "I think most of them start with authentic mysteries—maybe the discovery of hypnotism, not fully understood even by the priest who uses it; maybe the discovery of drugs that give visions; maybe even some actual confluence of the natural and the supernatural. I think your people are more unique than you imagine. Your religion's a lie *right from the center.*"

Lawler waved it off, unmoved. He'd heard it all before, of course. No such religion could have survived this long without defenses. He did not even bother to mention whatever defenses he had. "Believe me, they were clever, those original Mormons," he said, pleased that the subject had come up. "The way they wove odds and ends together to make *The Book of Mormon* was the work of true genius. A little from the Campbellites, a little from the Masons, a little from King James, a little from a stupid, stolen novel"—he laughed dully—"a little from popular occult books of the day . . . And those visions of Smith's—let me tell you—masterpieces! Smith had an advantage, you see. Other prophets thought it was required that they actually see visions. Not Smith! It could be shown—has been shown—that he pieced together the finest visions to be found in print at the time." Lawler pointed around at random with one finger. "A shaft of light from here, a couple of robed, mumbling figures from there, a sensation like drowning from another place. Theater, Professor! Torch the poor follower's imagination!" He leaned forward, suddenly stern, eager to make a point. "Or take Smith's doctrine on polygamy. It had real daring—not at all like the usual stuff of the day. It even had a sneaky sort of humor in it. 'Women,' said Smith—piously nasal, we may imagine —'*have no soul.* The only way they can get into Heaven is by marriage to a Saint.' Obviously the decent, the *Christian,* thing to do is to marry every woman one can get one's *hands* on!" His left hand slapped his mountain of thigh; then he began to cough, nearly gag. He rose from the bed and moved quickly to the hallway door for air. Mickelsson's hand tightened on the pick-axe handle, but even now, gagging and hacking from whatever he'd swallowed with the too quick gulp of air, Lawler had the pistol aimed straight at Mickelsson's chest, and Mickelsson reconsidered. No hope anyway. He stood knee-deep in broken lath and plaster, so that he could run neither toward his enemy nor away from him, and his eyes were burning, blurring with tears, from the dust. When he brushed his hair back from his forehead, he found the hair as stiff as wire. He swung the pick-axe and yanked away the last large swatch of plaster and lath.

"Are you finished? Is that it?" Lawler called through the open doorway.

"That's it for this room," Mickelsson said, and threw the pick-axe down hard.

Lawler came in, the white handkerchief tied around his face, and, with one eye on Mickelsson, moved slowly around the room, occasionally bending over to examine something or kicking a large piece of plaster aside. He took his time, making sure he missed nothing, his elevated rear end enormous, his shoes toeing outward. At last he waved his pistol at Mickelsson and said through the handkerchief, "All right, we'll do the livingroom next."

"Why not another bedroom?" Mickelsson protested.

"I don't think so," Lawler said. He stood musing, only his left-hand fingers moving, fiddling with the lip of a trouser pocket. "No, I think the livingroom."

Mickelsson could not remember ever in his life, even with Miss Minton, having felt such helpless rage. He picked up his tools and went out, ahead of Lawler, into the hall.

As he began on the moleboard in the livingroom, he asked, "Tell me this, Edward. Who is it you work with? I assume it wasn't you, or at least not you alone, that came in here and ransacked my house that night."

"Oh no, I was miles away at the time. The Sons of Dan don't do 'light' work." He stretched his lips flat, not a smile.

"Underlings, then. I see," Mickelsson said. "Buck privates in the Army of the Lord."

"Something like that."

He dragged the Christmas tree out from the wall, then sucked in breath and swung at another section of moleboard with the wreckingbar. "I assume they drive a plain, dark green car."

"They may. I suppose they sometimes may."

"And when they find they can't handle a thing, they come running to the Sons of Dan?"

"More or less. Not knowingly." He raised a finger for emphasis. "They know I'm a man of authority, a helpful older *advisor*, one might say. They provide me with information—much as *you* do, Professor—but unless they're a good deal more astute than I think, they have no real idea what my role is."

"Wait a minute," Mickelsson said, turning, still bent over. Lawler's face was—like Mickelsson's own, no doubt—black with dust except for the eyes and eyelids. The handkerchief over his nose and mouth was now gray. "They don't *know* you're a Danite?"

Lawler said nothing. He seemed to stiffen a little.

"Who *does* know?" Mickelsson asked. "Do they know in Salt Lake City?"

"Keep working," Lawler commanded, surprisingly gruff. Then he said, "That would amuse you, wouldn't it—to think that I'm self-appointed. No such luck, my friend. I'm definitely official."

"But I'll bet you can't prove it."

"Possibly not." Lawler gave a weary but elegant little wave.

Mickelsson slowly shook his head. "It figures," he said at last, pausing to wipe sweat from his eyebrows. He swung the wreckingbar with extra violence. "A lone-wolf fanatic. Jesus fucking Christ." When he pried, his hands slipped off the handle and he almost fell. Lawler jerked his gun in alarm, and Mickelsson understood that he'd nearly gotten his head blown off.

Soothingly, after he'd recomposed himself, Lawler said, "You must be very tired."

"Sure," Mickelsson said, and once again seized the wreckingbar, then stabbed in behind the moleboard.

"Well," Lawler said, "whether I'm really a Danite or just some Latter-Day maniac, here I am, and there you are. The laws governing our behavior seem clear. Isn't that a comfort?"

"Laws," Mickelsson breathed. A long stretch of moleboard broke away as he tugged. Like the piece he'd noticed upstairs, this stretch too had gouge-marks. Insect of some kind? he wondered.

"Yes, yes you're right to mock," Lawler was saying softly. With his small, plump left hand he wiped at his eyes, then dropped his hand and blinked for a moment, then briefly wiped them again. "It's an interesting point, the Mormon view of Law. Quite orthodox, really. The early Christians were lawless in a similar way. Christ, they said, brought an end to outer, that is, *po*sitive law—the old Jewish food laws, sabbath laws, and so on. 'Be Christ-like,' that was the only law. A very *good* law, in fact—though devilishly tricky, and now long past its viability. Your friend Nietzsche would doubtless have approved of the old idea, if it had been properly explained to him. You are—I'm not mistaken?—a student of Nietzsche?"

"Not lately."

"Pity. Well, in any case, I'm by no means the lawless creature you imagine me—quite the obverse! I believe with all my heart and mind in the vision of Joseph Smith Jr., as modified by Young and Pratt and, most important, modern circumstances. A vision, essentially, of man as he is: a small group of brilliant, imaginative thinkers supported in their work by a vast army of obedient, superstitious fools who give us half of all they earn—that's their tithe—which we 'invest' for them." His eyes crinkled. "The law I follow—"

"You being one of the leaders," Mickelsson said, and shifted from the wreckingbar to the pick-axe, preparing to smash into the wall beside the ornate walnut and cut-glass front door.

Mickelsson had hit a nerve, it seemed. Lawler said sternly, "Beware of mocking the man with the gun, Professor Mickelsson." At once Lawler made himself calm again. "There's *some*thing to what you say, of course. In any intelligent organization, one rises by acts worthy of notice. But do not make the mistake of supposing I do what I do for honor or recognition at Salt Lake City. I do not object to honor or recognition. I act, however, for much less selfish reasons—in the name of what is right."

"Right!" Mickelsson snorted, and again slammed the pick-axe into the wall. "You're a fool! You know what you are? You're *pitiful*."

"You are mistaken, Professor," Lawler said quietly. "But there's no point debating it."

"That's crazy," Mickelsson said, and to his quick indignation heard a whine in his voice; yet he pressed on: "People have been debating right and wrong for thousands of years!"

"Only fools," Lawler said. He leaned forward as if to spit through the filthy mask.

"Giving up everything—fifty per cent of your income every year— giving up even your brains, your individual will, giving your very life to some tyrannical cult built on violence and fraud—you can sit there and tell me that's *right*?"

"Once the machinery's in place, such questions don't come up," Lawler said dully, then waved the pistol, suggesting that Mickelsson get back to work. "Once a man's *in* with us—given our various 'support systems,' as the mealy-mouths say—there's not very much he can do, you see. Oh, a few slip through the net, turn against us. We put pressure on, of course. You can see where we'd be if such defections became common. But if the odd fish proves recalcitrant enough, we let him swim away. On the whole, however . . . On the whole the Saints are pretty much in *your* situation." He seemed to smile behind the mask. "Not a prayer except, possibly, prayer." He closed his eyes, rocking forward and back, then abruptly opened them. "We've talked enough," he said. "Save your strength now, Professor. We have a great deal yet to do."

"Makes you uneasy, doesn't it," Mickelsson said, "the thought that these Mormons you admire may not exist outside your head."

"They *exist*," Lawler snapped. "Now stop talking or I'll shoot you."

No prayer but prayer, Mickelsson thought, and almost, in the extremity of his weariness, laughed. The bones of his hands ached; his palms were blistered and bleeding. His eyes stung as if filled with bits of broken glass, and his lungs felt heavy and stiff with dust, as if left too long in the corner of an attic. His legs were unmuscled, and he itched everywhere. God only knew how Sprague—if it was he who'd torn his house apart, under Lawler's gun—had gotten through it. Perhaps he hadn't. Perhaps that was the reason Lawler had burned the house: if the secret was up there, and Sprague too weak to tear it out, let the fire get rid of it. If Mickelsson's strength were to give out, then, the same would happen here. Lawler would shoot him, or perhaps somehow manage to cut his throat with the knife he must be carrying, or he'd set fire to the house and burn up whatever the presumed evidence was. As Mickelsson considered his weakness and the pain in his hands, the realization was a frightening one. The only hope he had was somehow to keep working, keep Lawler at bay with the faint possibility that they might find something. Not that they would. Mickelsson felt his consciousness settling, more and more intensely, on the box of old keys sitting on the glass-topped table. He must get near it as soon as possible, bury it under, say, fallen plaster from the ceiling. Sooner or later Lawler would wake up to it, and the game would be finished. Sooner or later the game would be finished in any case. It was true; he had no prayer but prayer, a thing he no more believed in than he believed in Freddy Rogers' stone falls, or blood falls, or the Binghamton paper's UFOs. He glanced out at the road and saw Lawler's antique gray car. "Christ," he whispered to himself, "someone come *help* me!" Again he felt an impulse toward angry, maybe hysterical laughter. He was praying.

He thought: Suppose it were true, crazy as it sounded, that one could send out a sort of mental cry for help and someone, somewhere, might receive it? There were those who believed in such things, even certain scientists, or so he'd read. There were alleged cases of mothers who, though half a world away, heard the cry of their endangered or dying children. There was the alleged case of the Russian rabbit whose heart whammed at the precise moment each of her babies was slain, though they were thousands of miles from her and caged in a submarine. Mickelsson paused to wipe sweat and dust out of his eyes and wipe his blood-slippery hands on his trousers. The psychic cry for help was a futile and stupid hope, he knew. And shameful. Better the nihilistic courage of Dr. Destouches—though that too was shameful enough, obscene and, for all the hoopla, just one more cunning disguise for sentimentality. Psychic cry for help . . . Even if such things occasionally did happen, he had no power to make it happen for him. How many thousands of people died every year who would have lived if any such magic were available? Perhaps if one had studied with Tibetan monks . . . if one had taken care to build strong, deep friendships . . . It crossed his mind that his helplessness now was a judgment on him. But that thought too seemed too tiresome to trace to its end.

His strokes came more and more slowly, but the room was already well on the way to total ruin, the Christmas tree deep in dust. Once or twice, watching the pick end sink, he felt a flash of rage; but he was no longer even considering an attack on Lawler. He could hardly control the slam of the pick into the plaster, much less throw it hard enough and fast enough to beat Lawler's gun; and his legs were so weak he could barely stand, much less charge the black-suited fat man on the couch. The thought that the house must be torn apart, then burned, made him wretched. It was only a house; but his heart swore otherwise. Tears ran down his cheeks, making his eyes still more gritty, and his breathing came harder and harder. "Dear God, please," he whispered, and then at once, for the cowardice of his sudden turn to Jesus, felt revulsion so strong that he again tasted vomit. The ugliness of it! He, Mickelsson, whining his Now-I-lay-me—Mickelsson who himself had shown no mercy —crying out now to a God he'd refused to believe in when he hadn't been in need. That was how they got you, he knew. Need. *Impotence is dangerous for the human character.*

"Sinful pride," his grandfather would hiss. Lightning flashed in the old man's dim eyes.

Now a terrifying sound burst out behind Mickelsson and he whirled, then was thrown into confusion: Lawler sat watching him, startled by his sudden turn but obviously deaf—stone deaf—to the scream filling the room. Lawler's eyes rolled, alarmed and dangerous. Mickelsson realized now that he'd heard that sound before: it was the scream of the poisoned rat the Spragues' child, thinking it was dead, had thrown into the stove. He saw the child himself coming into the room now, an image as solid as Lawler. The child had his gloved hands over his ears, and his eyes were frantic. He ran toward the kitchen. Then Mickelsson saw, not in the room with him but in painfully vivid imagination, the fat man he'd killed, eyes slightly bulging, mouth open, his pistol pressed hard against his bursting heart, his whole soul sending out its terrible, hopeless wail.

Lawler twisted his lips, threatening, and waved his gun, not playing now, growing angry, impatient, maybe frightened. "Stop fooling around!" he yelled. Quaking, Mickelsson turned back to his work. Now Mickelsson was whispering, weeping as he whispered, abject and shameless, "Please, someone! Please!" Though he knew it was lunacy, an obscene grovelling before Nothing, he concentrated with all his might on the psychic cry. Maybe Goethe's line, inspiration to Nietzsche, could be twisted to his use: "He who overcomes himself finds freedom. *Befreit der Mensch sich . . .*" Lawler was saying something, his voice wonderfully aristocratic, it seemed to Mickelsson—silvery elocution, at once soothing and distantly ironic, scornful—but Mickelsson refused to hear, pouring all he had into his uncouth purpose, getting that silent cry to some friendly ear. The harder he drove out his cry, the more his mind worked against him, undermining his effort with indignant upbraidings and images of rebuke until finally he couldn't hear Lawler's voice at all. Once, swinging the pick, he remembered, more with his body than with his mind, how he'd killed the dog on the sidewalk. Lying still, it turned into the fat man. He got a nightmare image of walking with a crowd at the Binghamton July-fest—colored lights, noises—an old bum coming up to him, suggesting with an oddly lascivious look that Mickelsson give him money. He felt in his left hand how he'd pushed the man away. *Please*, he whispered, straining so hard the muscles of his neck and shoulders throbbed. It seemed his brain was on fire. He saw a black man on a lawn in Golden Gate Park, his temples bulging with anger as he cursed Ellen's mime troupe: "Trouble-makers! Arrogant idiots!" They too had cried out like the dying fat man, snarling at Mickelsson, snarling at Society, "the Establishment," demanding justice—but, like Mickelsson himself, the audience couldn't hear, couldn't cut through intellect and standard usages to feel what the mime troupe, in its lubberly, holy stupidity was saying. . . . Mickelsson's philosopher-mind kicked in. . . . Could not grasp, Wittgenstein would say, the terms of the "language game"—applied, Gilbert Ryle would say, "the wrong category," as when one tries to understand music as if it were arguing in Finnish. He struggled against his mind's angry and embittered denial of his reasonable right to cry out, but his mind raged on like an urchin in a violent tantrum, unwilling to be hushed. He tried to focus all his energy on the cry. His will repeatedly flagged, then rose again, shouting itself hoarse. Sublimation indeed! Very well, he was no super-man. More easy to believe in God and the grace of the lady than in the self-saved *Übermensch*. He thought of his son the protester—now terrorist, for all he knew—and mixed in with the thought of his son and the nukes was the thought of his son's fear of horses, and how he, Mickelsson, had bullied the boy to courage, in the end even to prize-winning horseman-ship. The pride he'd always felt when he thought of it before, the sense that the consequences had justified his action, now evaporated: all he could see was his son's eyes crying for mercy, darkness inside his mouth. "Monstrous," he whispered, then remembered that, monstrous or not, if he meant to be saved he must concentrate all his being on the psychic cry, not that it would save him. (He saw the lawyer Finney ducking and running, covering his ears.) But his thoughts roared on, his wife's voice shouting at him, swearing. He had not won, as he'd thought. His son, his child, the pride of his life, had found a larger, even crueller father to resist. He would be crushed again—as sure as day—Mickelsson could not stop it. He thought of Leslie and her cunning use of French, how she'd seized the *Babar* he and Ellen had given her to cry out angrily, "Love me! Forgive me! *Look* at me!" To which he'd responded with a sudden hatred of the French. "My God, my God!" he whispered now, tears streaming, washing dirt into his mouth. He quickly forced his mind back to the cry. *Help me!* he made himself think. *Help me! Please!* He con-trolled an urge to howl at the stupidity and shamefulness of it. *Help me!* he made himself think. More real, more solid and substantial than

Lawler, Nietzsche stood cackling in admirable mad scornful glee. Mickelsson was swinging the pick as if he'd just begun, all his tiredness gone, more aching, thudding power in his legs and arms than he could remember ever having felt before. He was briefly aware of Lawler talking. "Rightness is beauty. How else can we judge it?" Then the voice faded out like a distant radio station late at night. Mickelsson's whole body thought: *Help me! Please!* He felt such physical strength he could have lifted a truck. But his soul bellowed on. He thought of his mother's cry for help—he had not heard—then of Jessie's cry, then Tillson's. *Jessie,* he thought, *Jessie! Jessie!*

The phone rang, then rang again. He glanced at Lawler. The man shook his head. The room was still full of floating dust, but there was no doubt in Mickelsson's mind that the ghosts had appeared, the middle-aged woman, the man in brown, and the child. They seemed to be watching him, fully aware of him now, and possibly frightened, as if *he* were the ghost. The phone went on ringing. Was it possible, he wondered, that the cry was getting through—to the ghosts and to whoever was calling? He couldn't answer the phone without Lawler's permission. The ringing went on and on, making Lawler jumpy, his eyes moving faster. Mickelsson concentrated on the psychic cry. Suddenly he was conscious of a headache so fierce he was amazed that he didn't pass out. Almost the same instant he noticed the headache, it was gone—*all* bodily sensation was gone. He could have been floating a thousand feet above the earth. *Help me, please,* he thought, far more clearly than before. He remembered, suddenly, the Marxist he'd met in the theater after the movie. He had a sense, right or wrong, that the man was crying out to him, or anyway shouting for rightness in the world, and at the memory of his own angry smart-aleck put-downs he felt such squalor of soul he involuntarily bent double, moving his head close to the wall he'd been about to tear out. The sheen of the wallpaper startled him, and—his thought elsewhere—he bent closer. The wallpaper brightened more. He felt alarm—terror— though for a moment he couldn't tell why. He drew his head back. The light on the wallpaper dimmed. Before he knew what he was testing, he moved his head forward again, and the wallpaper brightened as if a candle had come near. He was thinking all this while, *Please, please, please!*— pouring the thought out as if it were his life. He turned around to look at Lawler. The man's eyes were wide, astonished, but there was something else on his face, too: terrible despair. Then, as when one's ears pop on an airplane, Mickelsson heard the real world's sounds again. Someone was knocking loudly at the door.

Now Lawler was on his feet, fumbling in one of his suitcoat pockets, hurrying to seize the doorknob. He had the dusty handkerchief over his mouth and nose, almost black now, so that he looked like a fat Jesse James. The room was full of hovering dirt, bits of paper; the phone was ringing, and in his left hand, the hand that seized the doorknob, Lawler had a noose of piano wire.

He threw open the door and cried out joyfully, "Come in! Come in!"

The scream was like the scream of the rat in the stove. Lawler froze, the piano wire forgotten in his hand, and the same instant, nothing in his mind, Mickelsson hurled the pick-axe and charged in behind it. Lawler jerked his head around like a man cruelly wronged, and the pick-axe hit him squarely in the forehead, flatside, so that it didn't cut in. Lawler took a dazed step as if to escape that violent football rush—he'd now forgotten the pistol too—but Mickelsson moved swiftly and, hitting with his head, slammed him against the doorpost so hard that Lawler's breath went out of him. He was unconscious even before he fell. The scream went on, and Mickelsson would register later that it came from the child in the doorway, Lepatofsky's daughter. Lepatofsky stood behind her, squarely braced and still. Mickelsson hardly noticed; all he was clearly aware of was his sharply outlined, red-tinted hands around Lawler's throat, squeezing to get hold of the man's life. Mickelsson gasped, like Lawler, for breath. Then something happened. He felt no pain, only darkness rushing in at him from every direction. He felt himself falling. It seemed a long fall, and everything was dark, growing darker.

8

He lay on his back on the kitchen floor, someone hunkering beside him. The face and shape began to clear, come into focus.

"Hello, Prafessor," Tim Booker said, beaming. "I see you've been fixin things up a bit." He had on a red wool stocking cap. His ears stuck out.

Now Mickelsson saw Lepatofsky too, standing beyond Tim, and Lepatofsky's daughter with her hand in her father's hand. "Lucky thing we dropped by when we did," Lepatofsky said. "You know Dr. Benton, here?"

Mickelsson rolled his head to the left and saw an old man tall as a crane in a baggy beige suit. The man smiled and nodded.

"What happened?" Mickelsson asked. The weakness of his voice surprised him, and he couldn't seem fully to open his left eye. He noticed that his shirt had been unbuttoned and his belt unbuckled. His hands were mittened into paws with gauze and tape. Now he became aware of one more person in the room, over leaning on the sink; the policeman Tacky Tinklepaugh.

"Well," Dr. Benton said, "nothing too serious, I hope. We won't really know for a day or two. Seems you had a little touch of heart trouble—likely nothing that won't be fixed with bed-rest and a few small changes of habit. All that drinking and smoking, not eating right . . . You may be a bit foggy-minded for a while. . . ."

"It was the strangest thing," Lepatofsky said, grinning. One eye was opened extra wide. "My little Lily never talked before. We was driving by the howse and all at once she yells out, '*Stahp! Stahp!*' I ding near drove right off the road, that's how supprised I was. Lucky thing we *did* stahp!"

"And you?" Mickelsson asked Tim feebly. He had to concentrate. Odd dreams kept edging in. It seemed to him that the black dog was in the room.

Tim said, grinning, "They gave me a call when you keeled over."

"Think you can sit up?" Dr. Benton asked, rather loudly, as if he'd asked it twice now.

Mickelsson tried to push up with his arms, but he was as weak as a baby and his bandaged hands throbbed. Tim and Dr. Benton bent down to help.

"By Gahd, it was just like a miracle," Lepatofsky said. "We must've drove by here fifty times before, but this time she yells '*Stahp!*'"

"There are no miracles," Tinklepaugh growled. "Just luck." Tinklepaugh's face was dark red, more ravaged than a week ago—or two; whatever it was—as if years had passed. He seemed, as always, angry about something, saving up for his day of vengeance. The sagging flesh hung as motionless as papier-mâché.

With the help of Tim and Dr. Benton, Mickelsson made it to his feet. He let them lead him to the hallway and the stairs. The cat was still there. All three of them looked at it, but Tim's pressure on Mickelsson's arm remained firm, and they climbed past it. "Don't think about it," Tim said. "Cat had a cancer anyway. That's what made 'im so mean—good cat, before. The doc had me owt here six months ago trying to shoot him. *Tough* old bastard!"

Since his own bedroom was ruined, they put him in the makeshift guest bedroom, a boxspring and mattress made up as a bed, no light but a table-lamp set on the floor. Mickelsson lay on his back, fuzzy-headed, waiting for things to clear. The lamp threw the shadows of those around him toward the ceiling. Lepatofsky's daughter kneeled beside the bed and gazed, faintly smiling, showing her dimple, at a point just to the left of Mickelsson's left ear. Tim leaned on the doorframe, arms folded, and Lepatofsky looked out the window. It was almost dark. While Dr. Benton took Mickelsson's pulse, Tinklepaugh checked the closet as if expecting to find more murderers. Downstairs, the phone was ringing. Lepatofsky said, "I'll get it," and left the room. Experimentally, Lepatofsky's daughter put her hand, very lightly, on Mickelsson's foot. Still she did not look at him. Dr. Benton was talking—"What a thing! Lordy! You're a lucky man!" Mickelsson did not listen, watching the girl instead. Tears came to his eyes. He remembered the eyelid that wouldn't quite open and raised one finger to touch it. Neither the eyelid nor the tape-covered finger had any feeling.

"How is he?" he heard Tinklepaugh ask.

"Very well, considering," Dr. Benton said. "Gahd only knows what Tim did to him." He chuckled.

"Can he talk?" Tinklepaugh asked.

Dr. Benton glanced at Tim, who smiled, all innocence, and opened his arms in a crucifix shrug.

"You want us out of the room?" Dr. Benton asked.

Tinklepaugh said nothing, merely hunkered down beside Mickelsson and sullenly gazed at him. Mickelsson closed his eyes.

"You able to talk?" Tinklepaugh asked.

Mickelsson waited. The smell of stale whiskey on Tinklepaugh's breath made Mickelsson breathe through his mouth.

"We've arrested your pal Professor Lawler," Tinklepaugh said. "He's over in the Montrose jail right now, learning about toilets without seats. We're holding him for unlawful possession. I assume there's more—I guess I gaht a pretty good idea what it is, but I'd be glad if you'd tell me what you know." He waited a moment, breathing heavily. "Take your time. I've gaht no place to get to."

Mickelsson could hear Lepatofsky talking on the phone down in the kitchen.

"Lawler claims—" Mickelsson said, then faltered. He tried to think where to begin, then was filled with confusion, then heard himself talking.

Once in a while as he told his story he opened his right eye; the left still wasn't working. Tinklepaugh, each time Mickelsson looked at him, seemed bored, but he paid grudging attention, sometimes helping Mickelsson along when he lost his place. Dr. Benton hovered at the door, near Tim, undecided about whether to hear the story to the end or go back to the hospital, where he was supposed to be on duty. At last, sometime while Mickelsson's eyes were closed, he left. Only Tim seemed really interested in the story. But Tim was interested in everything. Was it possible, Mickelsson wondered—in his befuddlement mixing up the story he was telling and the book he was supposed to be writing—was it possible that the story, for all it had taken out of him and despite the fact, even, that it had almost been the story of his death, was essentially boring? MADMAN BEHAVES BADLY, ACCIDENTALLY THWARTED BY FELLOW MADMAN? He concentrated, trying to find for Tinklepaugh the deeper significance of what had happened. The dog moved back and forth, just beyond the door.

Tinklepaugh's questions were mechanical; he took no notes. "So you think he murdered this Michael Nugent."

"I'm certain of it. The boy in the . . . hospital too."

"Neither one of them was reported as a possible homicide," Tinklepaugh said. "It doesn't seem likely that the one in the hospital had his throat slit."

"They were homicides," Mickelsson said weakly. "Check it."

"Oh, I believe you, all right." His voice was sullen, full of something like self-pity.

"You think it's possible he really is a Danite?" Tim asked.

"No chance," Tinklepaugh said with heavy disgust. He stood up, as if finished and ready to leave, then hooked his thumbs inside his gunbelt and looked at Lily Lepatofsky, who still had her hand resting lightly on Mickelsson's foot. "You people always want things interesting," Tinklepaugh growled. "They never are. I know about you." He glanced at Tim, then away, back at Lily. "You have your secret midnight meetings and you talk your mumbo jumbo, maybe take all your clothes off like a bunch of little kids"—quickly he raised his hand to block protest—"I don't say I ever saw it; I just figure you people go to movies too. That's what they do, isn't it? And then when your power's up you go stand on some bridge and put black magic curses on the trucks that come sneaking in at midnight with their shit."

"Me?" Tim said. He got out his pipe, then changed his mind, maybe thinking about Mickelsson's heart.

"You and all your nuts," Tinklepaugh said. "You make me sick."

Mickelsson found himself sitting up on his elbows, though he wouldn't have thought he had the strength to manage it. "Wait a minute," he brought out, "did you say it was Tim that fixed me up, not Dr. Benton?" He sank back again, as if pushed, trying in vain to hook the word *witchcraft* with apple-faced Tim and his motorcycle friends, or Dr. Bauer, Donnie Matthews. . . .

"First aid," Tinklepaugh said, emphatic, turning away. "That's all, just first aid. For a while they had trouble getting hold of anything but a witch-doctor." Then, without a word, he left. Mickelsson listened to his boots going down the stairs.

"Naht me," Tim said, raising his hands in sign of innocence. "Tink's as crazy as everbody else."

Mickelsson closed his eyes. After a while he said, "Does it work? Those curses on the trucks?"

Tim said nothing for so long that Mickelsson decided he meant not to speak; then Tim said, jokingly, "Naht all by themselves. Sometimes you add just a little engineering, owt at one of those dumps. You'd be supprised what can happen to a truck."

Mickelsson said, after another long pause, still with his eyes closed, "I take it you know where Donnie Matthews is."

"She's fine."

"I know. I talked to her on the phone."

"You must be special," Tim said. "The rest of us she's cut off." As if eager to change the subject, he said, "I'll tell you one thing, it's lucky old Lawler didn't work out that dahrn box of keys. I could shoot myself for not grabbing it the minute I figured it owt, when I came here with the doc."

Mickelsson thought of opening his eyes but lacked the energy. At length he said, "You worked out the fire at Spragues', then, and the murder?"

Tim said, "Yeah, *finally.*"

Mickelsson drifted awhile. Then: "It's a queer religion, witchcraft." Now he did open his eyes.

"Naht me!" Tim said, but he was resisting less now. He was grinning, possibly flattered, shaking his head.

"You seem to watch over people. You do bad spells on the trucks, good spells for people like me, apparently—plus a little engineering. . . ."

"Hay, Pra*fessor*," Tim said, mock-surprised, "what's got *in*to you? Hay, look at me! No pointy hat, no broom—"

Lily Lepatofsky's bright sparrow-eyes were on Mickelsson's face now. It seemed that possibly she too was a witch, and her father. How else would they have known to call Tim?

Then her father was at the door. "Somebody from the I.R.S. calling you," he said. "Office down in Scranton." He shook his head, pushing his jaw out and smiling uncertainly. "When I told him what happened here, he went right out of his gourd. Talked a whole lot about the willful destruction of government property." He grinned but rolled his eyes from one of them to the other, hoping for explanation.

"Weird!" Tim said, grinning happily. So he knew about that too. No doubt heard it from his friend the banker.

At last Lepatofsky reached for his daughter's hand. "We better go, honey," he said.

She nodded solemnly, gave her shoulders a queer little shake, patted Mickelsson's foot, then took her father's hand and rose.

"Thanks. Thanks to both of you," Mickelsson said. "I'm sorry."

"Hay, 'sorry'!" Lepatofsky said, and waved. Then they were gone.

He was spacy, almost weightless—whether because of something Tim had given him or Dr. Benton's pills or as an after-effect of the adrenaline he'd pumped, he couldn't tell. "Bed-rest," Dr. Benton had said. Mickelsson had not consciously disobeyed, but he found himself standing at the phone in the kitchen, freeing his right hand from the gauze and tape, then dialing Jessie. If he were clear-headed, he would realize later, he might not have called her.

"Pete?" she asked groggily. He'd apparently wakened her again from sleep.

Slowly, having a little trouble with his tongue, he told her what had happened. He did not mention that he'd perhaps had a light stroke and ought to be on his back, but she knew something was wrong. She said nothing about Lawler, nothing about the tearing apart of his house; said only: "You sound strange. Are you drugged?" Her voice was reserved.

"I don't think so." He remembered now the reason for her reserve and thought of saying no more. But he heard himself continuing, "Tim did something—maybe gave me something. It sounds stupid, and he denies it, but I guess he thinks he's a witch."

"It's not that surprising," she said, musing. "We always think romantically when we hear the word *witch*. But why shouldn't they be ordinary people—nice people, even? Interesting, though. Tim went to college—didn't you tell me that?"

"I think he once mentioned it. I guess I may have told you."

"And he was a paramedic in Vietnam, wasn't he?" She laughed. "I wonder what they thought when he put on the tourniquet and then did some backwards-Latin spell!"

Mickelsson smiled.

"I should come out," she said suddenly. "I have a feeling it's not solved yet. This whole witchcraft business—"

"No, don't!" he said quickly. Then, to soften it: "Please."

She was silent.

"Tomorrow," he said. "We'll talk about it."

There was a long pause.

"Are you all right, Pete?"

"I'm fine."

"I ask that a lot, don't I."

"I provoke it."

"Well, if you need me—" She was quiet for a moment.

Paramedic, he thought. *Half scientist, half witch. A little engineering.*

"I'll call," he said. He added, hastily, before he could think better of it, "I have some . . . terrible things to confess."

"Who doesn't?" she said irritably.

He said nothing, his mind snagged on the oddity of their having been able to say such things; the strange assumption—or faith, rather—that even quite terrible evils, betrayals, mistakes might be forgiven. Then his mind wandered. He was seeing the holes cut into the moleboards from the inside, rat or insect work. Maybe.

"You said Tim 'did' something, or 'gave you' something. What was wrong?"

"I'm fine," he said as heartily as he could. "I have to go now. You've helped a lot."

After he'd hung up, he made his way, like an old man, down the cellar steps, his left shoulder bumping against the damp, discolored wall. He found what he was looking for almost at once. In a mould spot in one of the cellar beams someone had gouged out a small patch, maybe two inches long, one inch deep. The notch was recent.

He found himself parking the Jeep outside the Montrose jail—it was late, very dark, especially dark in the parking lot in the shadow of the large brick building with its black iron bars. Though he had no memory of driving here, he remembered why he'd come.

The young, blond beast at the desk seemed to know who he was and raised no objection to his going in to talk with Lawler. The officer went into the cellblock with him and stayed, beautifying his nails with silver nail-clippers. The cells were empty except for one man sleeping off a drunk—a fat, bearded man in a lumberjack shirt—and Lawler himself, who sat motionless on his pallet like a satiated spider, still in his dusty suit but wearing no belt or tie, no spectacles. "They think I might try to commit suicide," Lawler said, emotionless. His cheeks showed that he'd been crying. He gazed with distaste at the guard, then back up at the ceiling.

There was a light over Mickelsson's head, another beyond the last of the cells, so that the whole area was marked by the shadows of bars, part of the area crisscrossed like graph-paper. The bars were of gleaming steel, the concrete and stone walls glossy battleship-gray, the color of the walls in the locker-room of Mickelsson's college-football days. Lawler sat with his chin raised, maculate fat hanging down toward his open collar. He wore an offended, long-suffering look.

Mickelsson folded his sore, still-bandaged hands, closed his eyes, fighting down revulsion, and said, "Those bruises on your neck, they're from my fingers. Sorry I gave out, old man. Maybe another time."

Lawler shook his head, just an inch to the left, an inch to the right, and chose not to speak. Even here, for all his clownish fat, the old man had a sort of monstrous dignity, or so Mickelsson thought. Like an antique voodoo-doll. A kind of dream came into his head—Lawler as one of those mechanical figures one saw in the Heidelberg museum, dancing, playing the piano, conducting an orchestra of fixedly grinning, decaying automata. Mickelsson shook himself free of it.

"You were wrong about Professor Warren," he said. He put his bandaged hands around two of the bars, feeling unsteady on his feet. "I want you to know that every bit of the shit you did was unnecessary."

Lawler did not look at him.

"It may be true, as you say, that he was a former Mormon; but he'd given all that up long ago. He was interested in my house only as a chemist. Because it's poison."

The old man didn't move.

The policeman said, at Mickelsson's back, "Would you care to sit down, Professor?" Mickelsson turned and saw a dark wooden chair with wide, flat arms, its lines too sharp, dizzying, crossing the shadows of the bars slanting across the floor. He realized only now that he'd been clinging to the bars as if for dear life, no doubt visibly swaying. He sat down. The policeman drifted away. For an instant Mickelsson's mind tricked him: he saw not the policeman but Randy Wilson.

He strained for concentration, struggling against the weirdness in his head and rubbing his chest with one hand. Little by little he told Lawler about the trucks with their headlights off, illegal dumpers from New Jersey or New York; the boy who'd come out dying of radiation sickness from a local cave; the burnt patches on the mountain slope above Mickelsson's house, deadly seepage, tests would show; the cancerous cat and the real or probable cancer of Dr. Bauer, Pearson's wife, maybe Pearson himself, maybe others; the strange cuts and festerings on Thomas Sprague's pigs; the samples someone—probably Tim or one of his friends, the night they'd visited—had taken from the beam in Mickelsson's cellar, livingroom, and bedroom, maybe other places too. That was why Tim smoked Mickelsson's brand of tobacco. It was Mickelsson's, or anyway Mickelsson had introduced him to it. Tim had planned it shrewdly, that midnight raid on the house to find out, without anyone's knowing, what Warren had discovered, the discovery that might possibly have gotten Warren killed and in any case might prove his sale of the house a bad thing, a thing Tim would be ashamed of. It was a good plan. How could he know that Lawler would blunder in? Tim had worked out how to disguise the raid and at the same time check every part of the house; but he was too much the sensualist, and maybe life-affirmer, to throw away that Dunhill tobacco. It was hard to get, even in Binghamton.

"That's what Warren was on to," Mickelsson said. With one clumsy, bandaged hand, he took from his coatpocket the fact-sheet Charley Snyder had given him, a long list of sources, waste analysis, legal and illegal dumping times and places. He held the paper toward Lawler, but the old man ignored it. At last Mickelsson put it back in his pocket.

Lawler said nothing, sliding his eyes toward Mickelsson, then away.

"It was a dream," Mickelsson said, "your optimistic hope that Mormonism was behind it—the glorious vision of Joseph Smith and all that. The dark green unornamented car we spoke of: it wasn't Mormons. If we ever find it, we'll probably find it belonged to company men— maybe the Mafia—checking for midnight landfill sites, and making sure no one like me would raise problems." He sighed, shook his head, glanced for a moment at the policeman still bent over his nails, then returned his gaze to Lawler. "Even *your* religion, if one can call it that, was more than reality would support. Nothing out there—Tinklepaugh's right. Luck. Dead facts. Some of them very strange facts, I grant you— ghosts, prescience, real UFOs for all I know—but still just facts, no different from iron bars, woodchucks, trees. No salvation in them." He leaned forward. "What baffles me is . . ." He paused, half closing his eyes and pressing his hand to his chest, waiting for a pain to pass. "What made you do it, all those years, that disguise of gentleness and goodness, generosity? Surely you didn't imagine—no offense, just curiosity—you didn't imagine you were a Danite then. Why the cover? What was behind it?"

Lawler sat as still as a sack of old clothes. At last he spoke, softly, moving only his lips. "Wittgenstein," he said. "You love to speak of Wittgenstein." He sighed, still motionless except for the deep, slow intake of breath. "Why should *anything* be behind it? Your friend Wittgenstein has a terrible vision: a man says, 'No admittance,' a different language game from a *sign* that says 'No admittance,' though it seems to mean the same thing; which is in turn a different language game from a policeman who holds up his arm to signify 'No admittance,' and different again from a barbed-wire fence. And then there's the case of an inten- tionally planted row of trees—another language game that only *possibly* means 'No admittance.' And finally there's the case of the accidentally grown row of trees. We read it as language, as if Someone were speaking

it. That's our great error, your friend points out. Used as we are to language games, we read the world as meaningful. But alas, the world is dead and mute. Final. As is the self."

"That may be," Mickelsson said, confused, not yet taking in what he'd heard, waving it away with the side of his hand, "but the *change* in you. How do you explain that?"

Lawler gazed at him with infinite disgust. "I loved truth," he said at last. "I do not think my vision of the future will prove mistaken."

Mickelsson leaned farther forward, straining. His vision blurred, focussed, blurred again. "You killed all those people *needlessly*," he said. "You *know* that. There was never any threat to Mormonism, and even if there had been, the Mormons would be horrified by everything you think. Your vision of the future—good God, man, they'd laugh at you! They're *burghers!*"

He waited for Lawler to explain, defend himself. He waited on and on, bent forward, off balance, as motionless as Lawler himself. Lawler sat as if asleep, fallen in on himself, his button chin tipped upward as if bearing his throat to some knife, his eyes tight shut. He looked like peevish royalty, gentle Louis XVI, noble-heartedness misunderstood. It came to Mickelsson that the old man's sooty face had shining channels running down from each eye. Mickelsson sat back in his chair. "Faggot," Donnie Matthews would say with wonderful childish scorn. Another philosophical error, misleading row of trees. It was partly the coincidence of homosexuality—Professor Warren, Michael Nugent, Randy Wilson, probably not Tim, he thought now—that had thrown Mickelsson off; perhaps it had been, on Mickelsson's part, a fascist wish that homosexuality be somehow at the nasty heart of it all—to Mickelsson an aesthetically unpalatable way of life. Pain—guilt—fanned through his chest, then subsided. His left eyelid hung like a half-drawn shade.

Falteringly, helping himself by gripping the bars in front of him, Mickelsson stood up. He stared at Lawler's lumpy shoes suspended two inches above the floor. At last he said, "Well, sleep peacefully. I'm sure you will." He looked down at his blistered, wounded hands, his swollen wrists.

Lawler said nothing.

Mickelsson turned slowly and nodded to the policeman working at his fingernails, then moved toward the door.

Behind him Lawler suddenly spoke, theatrical, like one of Ellen's people. "I won't survive this, you know! One never survives these things!"

They were out of the cellblock now. The door clicked shut. Outside on the street the world was still in the rigor-mortis grip of winter.

Tinklepaugh said, "Well, you know, we hear a lot of crank confessions." He leaned on his fists, his elbows on the desktop, the bags under his eyes as heavy as a basset-hound's. The ceiling above him in the one-room police station Mickelsson had finally located was full of jagged, filthy cracks, a few missing pieces of plaster. The floor was crooked, the windows patched with tape. The file-cabinets were dented and apparently half empty.

"Come off it, Sergeant," Mickelsson said, raising his head from the leather chairback. He spoke crossly, though his voice was weak and there were tears in his eyes. "You *know* it's the truth."

"I don't even know there was a murder. My theory is—"

"I've heard your theory. He broke into his own room, even though the chainlatch had been hooked from inside."

"We don't know for certain *when* that chainlatch was broken, now do we?"

"*I* know when it was broken."

Tinklepaugh gazed at him, his blue eyes dead-looking, purple flecks in the pink of his sagging lower lip. "But *you*, Professor, have a history of mental illness."

Mickelsson sank back in the chair. "OK," he said. After a minute: "Just one thing. Tell me *why*. Say it's a hypothetical case—some other murderer you refuse to arrest. What's the point? Does it give you a feeling of significance, arresting some people, letting others go free? Makes you feel like a king? Do you do it as a service to the community—because I'm a homeowner and taxpayer, potentially available for jury duty? Or to save the state the expense of trying me and sending me to prison? Do you do it in the name of Higher Truth, because 'vengeance is Mine, saith the Lord'? Or to get back at the people who don't pay you enough?"

"You got a bad heart, Professor. Don't get carried away."

"Why, though?"

Tinklepaugh looked at him. At last he said, "All of that."

"Is somebody paying you off?" Mickelsson asked suddenly.

Like a dead man, Tinklepaugh laughed. "That'll be the day!"

Mickelsson closed his eyes and breathed lightly, to keep the pain down. The big, drab room was full of sounds. The clock above Tinklepaugh's head, the furnace rumble coming up through the floor, some kind of rhythmical scritching sound he was unable to identify...

"What'll happen to the world," Mickelsson asked, "if the police let criminals walk away scot-free?"

"God knows," Tinklepaugh said.

"All right," Mickelsson said. "So you're telling me to turn myself in to the state police." He opened his right eye to check Tinklepaugh's expression.

"No. I wouldn't do that, if I were you." Suddenly he brought his hands down flat on the desk, pushed back his chair, and stood up. He looked hard at Mickelsson, about to say something, then turned away, his thumbs in his gunbelt, and went over to stand looking out the window. "You want a drink?" he asked at last.

"No thanks."

Tinklepaugh sucked at his teeth, considering, then went over to the file-cabinet, opened it, and got out a bottle, cheap bourbon, and a dime-store glass. He poured the glass half full, put the bottle away, then went to the window again, to stand with his back to Mickelsson. He sipped the drink. "Beautiful town once," he said. "Some people say it will come back. I doubt it. You'd be surprised how delicate the balance is, place like this. Man runs up a pile of debts, then skips out, or something happens to him—somebody's business could go under. That's how fragile it can get. Everybody knows that, these dying small towns. Different places you live got different ways of being, of course. But that's how it is here. People take care of each other, when they're all living right on the edge— they better, anyway. The worse it gets, the more careful they all got to be. Somebody stops pulling his weight—somebody breaks the agreement, you might say—that's trouble. Anything can happen." He shook his head, as if imagining atrocities. "Well, people say the trains are coming back— coal to take care of the energy crisis. Maybe it'll happen. That might change things. But I wouldn't bet on it. I see it getting worse and worse— more houses falling down or catching fire some night, more people out of work, sitting out there on the bench by the traffic light, more poisons coming in, more ruined farmland, more sickness. . . ." He half turned and for a moment met Mickelsson's eyes. "We just all gotta be careful, I guess, keep things in perspective, watch out for each other . . . and watch each other. . . ." He turned back to the window and tipped his head back, draining the glass.

"So that's why I go 'free,' " Mickelsson said.

"You go free," Tinklepaugh said evenly, "because it has not yet come to my attention that you've committed any crime." Now at last, his left hand on the windowsill to steady him, he turned all the way around to face Mickelsson. "And if I were you," he said, "I would see that no crime *does* come to my attention. I get crazy sometimes when I think about having to do paperwork."

"I'll think about that," Mickelsson said.

"Yes, do."

Mickelsson rose from his chair, each movement careful. "Does this mean," he asked, "I'm supposed to stay up there in that house?"

Tinklepaugh raised both hands and his eyebrows. "Live anywhere you like," he said. "I wouldn't be too quick to get rid of the place, though. Poisoned springs can be sealed off—I imagine your neighbors would be glad to pitch in. And they'd probably help lay in pipe from somewhere else. It's not quite the case that the whole county's done for. You mention industrial waste, radiation; people lose all perspective. It's the media. With a little work, little cooperation . . ." He glanced at the file-cabinet. "Care for that drink now?"

Mickelsson weighed the matter carefully. "No," he said at last. "But thanks."

He slept for hours. For the most part it must have been a sleep like death, but he remembered it as one filled with nightmare shapes moving slowly in and out of his consciousness like fish. An effect, perhaps, of the pills Dr. Benton had left with him. He dreamed repeatedly of the huge black dog—possibly it figured in every one of the dreams, moving about at the periphery. Once he dreamed that, lying wide awake, he heard the dog coming up the stairs, grunting with age or discomfort, heard it come toward the door and then through it, perhaps invisible, perhaps exactly the color of the darkness, then felt the bed move as the dog got up into it, for a long time standing over Mickelsson, then settling heavily beside him, lowering its head onto his back. As Mickelsson slept it occurred to him that perhaps this was a dream, and he struggled to awaken but could not. The dog was immense, the size of a small horse. As he lay beside it, partly under it, Mickelsson reasoned by a chain of argument, which in the dream seemed brilliantly illuminating, that the world seemed to mean things, seemed a "language game," because dreams meant things by making use of the world. Thinking back to it later, he saw that the idea was old and familiar, and understood that the euphoria he'd felt in the dream must have come from elsewhere, perhaps the revelation that one could live with guilt, that the existentialists were to this extent right: one was free to move on.

In another dream he thought it was morning, and he got up and went downstairs and into the livingroom, and there on the couch he saw his son Mark sleeping, dressed in black, with his face to the back cushions, the room around him in ruins. Mickelsson tiptoed past him—the room was icy cold—and made a fire in the woodstove, then went to find a blanket, which he carried to Mark and gently tucked around him. At the last moment his son turned his head, opening his eyes, and said, "Hi, Dad." "You're home!" Mickelsson said, and burst into tears. His son smiled, slightly nodded, then closed his eyes and went back to sleep. Mickelsson was suddenly aware of people in the kitchen, fluttering around softly, like bats. The black dog came through the kitchen door, for some reason crawling on its belly like a trained war-dog. It was definitely the dog, but it was confused in Mickelsson's mind with Edward Lawler. It stopped, not far from Mickelsson, close enough to reach him at one bound, and drew trembling black lips back from its fangs. Mickelsson stretched his arms wide to protect his son, whose black-clothed body became smaller as he watched, smaller and smaller until it was the size of a baby, the neck and the side of the face red and wrinkled. It was not at all strange. If all time was taking place at once—eternal recurrence, the reason psychics could see the future or the past—then the adult Mark was also the infant Mark and Mark long dead. He was looking down at stiff, gray hair. . . .

He awakened to a smell of food and lay uneasy in his bed—it was mid-morning, judging by the light—then gradually understood that the food smell was real, there was someone down in his kitchen. His heart ticked lightly, sending out tiny shocks of pain, and when he touched his chest with his hand—the bandage loose now, ready to fall off—he found feeling in his fingers again, the hand so sore he could not fully open it.

Tim's voice called up the stairs, "You awake, Professor?"

He did not answer—simply neglected to, his mind gone elsewhere—and after a moment Tim appeared on the stairs outside the room, coming up with a tray. He seemed to float above the floor. "What are you doing here?" Mickelsson asked.

"Ah, feelin crabby!" Tim said. "That's a good sign." He helped Mickelsson sit up with the pillows propped behind him, then sat cross-legged on the floor, chattering while Mickelsson ate. Oatmeal, weak tea, toast. Afterward, he helped Mickelsson to the bathroom, waited outside the door, then helped him back into bed.

"Why do you do this?" Mickelsson asked.

"Boy, that really is a mess down there," Tim said. "I'll send a couple of kids, see if they can clean things up a little."

Mickelsson said: "I don't trust good works. What are you doing?"

Tim raised one finger to his lips. "Sh!" he said. "Go to sleep."

He came again that night, and again the following morning. Now Mickelsson was much stronger, impatient of the bed. He still slept for hours on end, but more often now he lay with his eyes open—one wider than the other—thinking, irritably listening to the noise downstairs, Tim's people flapping on black webbed wings from room to room, shovelling things into bags or crates, cleaning out the mess. Once one of them, a scraggly young woman, brought Mickelsson a piece of toast and a glass of grapejuice. Otherwise he did not see them. When he finally went down they were gone; the wrecked livingroom was clean, neatly swept, ready for stud-repairs and sheetrock. He waited for Tim to come and fix him supper, then at last understood that no one was coming, he was on his own. Irritably, he built a fire in the woodstove, then made himself a soft-boiled egg. He thought of calling Jessie, then sat still, the fork halfway to his mouth, understanding that he could not do it. Reality was back, bleak as a stone. For all his nightmares, he hadn't seen the ghosts in days. That was Lawler's gift to him, or Wittgenstein's, perhaps. Reality in winter.

He'd been in bed for hours when the phone rang, waking him. He ignored it at first, but it continued to ring, and he at last reached over to the lamp on the floor and turned it on, then looked at his watch:

3 a.m. The guest bedroom was freezing cold. He blinked, trying to drive the loginess from his eyelids; the left one still drooped, giving him, he knew, a slightly stupid look. He drew the covers around him and went down to the kitchen to get the phone. He must start up another fire in the woodstove or the pipes would freeze—maybe they were frozen already. Somehow he must get oil for the furnace. Sell something, perhaps—the blue car, the Jeep. He thought of the five hundred dollars he owed Stearns' Texaco. Hopelessness washed over him.

"Hello?" he said.

"Professor Mickelsson?" It was a woman's voice, one he could not recognize, though he felt he should.

"Yes," he said cautiously.

The woman began to sob. "*Christ*," he whispered. Surely not even Job was so tried and tormented! The feeling of hopelessness increased. He thought he would drown in it.

"Hello?" he said, his voice sharp. He imagined himself roaring like a crazed gorilla. *No more! No fucking more!* He controlled himself.

She went on sobbing, breaking sometimes, trying to speak.

The ghosts he'd thought banished forever suddenly appeared, frowning by the sink, bending forward, watching. *I've gone mad again*, he thought. He felt a flutter of fear and utter weariness, then nothing. The old woman dabbed at her mouth with quick, angry jabs, catlike. Spittle glistened on her chin. Thinking perhaps he was still asleep, it was all just a nightmare, he held out the receiver and looked at it. What caught his eye was his own stiff, bloody-scabbed hand. He raised the receiver to his ear again, checking as he did so to see if the ghosts were still there. They were, solid as furniture, the old woman watching him with narrowed eyes.

"Who is this?" he demanded. "Take your time. I'm listening." After a while he said, "Brenda?"

The sobbing changed, grew more frantic, but still she couldn't speak. *Drunk*, he thought. He asked, "Where are you?" When she sobbed on, he asked still more sharply—indifferent and objective, surgical, his voice as much like a slap as he could make it—"Brenda, where are you?"

"Colonial Inn," she said. "In Hallstead. Alan was—"

"You're not hurt?"

"No, I just—"

"Stay there, I'll be right over," he said, and angrily hung up the phone. "Well?" he shouted at the ghosts.

They touched each other, not afraid of him; hostile, plotting, as if *he* were the evil invader.

She sat in the bed in just her blouse, the covers at her waist, her face streaked and puffy, blond hair stringy, her body drawn inward around its center. When he paced past the mirror he saw that his own face was red with anger, wrinkled and long-nosed from his weight loss, his uncombed hair flying wildly, like a mathematician's.

"So what did you expect?" he said, jabbing his hand out, walking back and forth. He felt and ignored a touch of dizziness.

"I'm going to kill her," she said.

"You're going to kill her," he mocked. He picked up the drink on the dresser, sniffed it, then put it down again. "You're behaving very foolishly, you know that, young lady? You follow your boyfriend around like he's property, and you find out that he's doing what you knew he was doing, and then you get yourself drunk and call me up—*me!*—get me out of bed in the middle of the night, a sick man, because you want me to give you advice but you're too drunk to hear it."

"I'm not drunk!"

"My mistake." He touched his forehead. Another little tingle of dizziness.

The way she pursed her lips, her mouth was like a beak, a small pigeon's, one of Darwin's beloved tumblers. He wondered if he was making her angry on purpose, not entirely out of malice, at least partly from a half-conscious theory that it might help.

"And I don't want advice," Brenda said, belatedly bridling. She took a swipe at her eyes with the back of one hand.

"Good." He put his fists on his hips. "So why call *me?*" At once he was annoyed: resounding righteousness, hollowly echoing. Luther's hammer putting nail-holes in the church door.

"You should be flattered," she said. "A lot of people would be."

His heart skipped, and he half turned away. Jessie had said the girl had a crush on him—because Brenda was "proud." Abruptly, he sat down on the side of the bed and put his hand on her shin. "Listen, Brenda, what's all this about? Do *you* know?"

She shook her head and burst into tears again. She covered her nose and mouth with her two cupped hands.

He became overconscious of his own hand on her shin and looked at the floor, trying to think clearly, waiting for her crying to stop. It flitted through his mind that maybe she wanted him to make love to her. It was a startling idea, especially when he remembered that image in the mirror, but he'd lived long enough to know, he thought, that mostly things are simple, that women almost never turn to men except for love, and that love is, more often than not, physical. He drew his hand back and laid it on the muscle above his knee. It made sense, he thought, suddenly as crafty as she was, for all his weariness; sly as any lawyer: revenge on Blassenheim, and the age-old comfort of skin on skin—and she'd be needing comfort; these things were shattering to the ego. Who knew, maybe there might be a touch of revenge in it too. He'd gotten them together, so Garret claimed. He frowned, balking. Not revenge, no. Maybe not love of the healthiest kind . . . It was no news that students occasionally developed attachments to teachers. He wondered whether he, for his part, wanted to make love to Brenda, then quickly shied from the thought, despising himself and Brenda too, remembering Donnie Matthews. Yet the question remained. In his mind, though he carefully didn't look at her, he saw how Brenda's small breasts outlined themselves against her blouse. He thought of the occasional affairs he'd had, bodies and faces floating up out of the dark—what harm?—and he began to feel, in spite of himself, aroused. Brenda's skirt and pantyhose were neatly laid out on the chair beside her bed. It was as if she'd placed them there on purpose, so that he'd see them. Preliminary statement of her case. Again his mind shied back. He remembered the idiot look lent by the drooping eyelid, and something about a dim, half-mile-long corridor in a Texas Holiday Inn.

"In a thousand years," he said, grandly melancholy and sarcastic at once, old Fritz on his mountain, "all of this—"

She looked at him with exaggerated interest, and Mickelsson realized in dismay what a bore he had become.

He stood up and put his hands in his pockets. He'd left his pipe at home. "Have you got cigarettes?" he asked, a little testy. He kept himself partly turned away from her.

She shook her head. "I'm sorry."

He waved, perfunctory. What was the world coming to? Nobody smoked anymore, college kids, anyway. It was selfish and hedonistic, a decay of faith in goodness even beyond the grave, a shameful usurpation of space that rightfully belonged to the next generation. What times! Social responsibility was dead, a trampled corpse. Let the tobacco farmers fend for themselves, also the chemists who put in the sugar and formaldehyde. Every poor devil for himself!

For a time neither of them said anything, at least aloud, each of them looking, like tired visitors to a modern-art museum, at the mound of covers over Brenda's feet.

Then she said, "I know it was wrong of me to call you." When he bent his head, weary of fraudulence, both the fraudulence of phoney expressions and the fraudulence of "true" ones, she looked at him reprovingly. "I was distraught," she said. He thought about her choosing the word *distraught*. "When I found out he was really *doing* it—I mean with *her*, a married woman, and so *ugly*—"

"She is a bit ugly," Mickelsson said, and sighed.

She took a deep breath. "I guess I was a *little* drunk. But it was so *bush!*"

"Don't be silly."

"It was. *Is*. It sucks! I mean you just begin to think . . . that the world . . . Do you know what that class of yours is like, Professor?"

He suppressed a nasty smile. It had led, he might have mentioned, to this.

"My parents are divorced," she said. "They never really liked each other anyway. They used to whack each other all over the place. Even at parties, once out in the yard behind these people's house; they had to call in the police. I grew up with this feeling that . . . We'd go to the houses of these various different people, and we'd play with the kids, the other people's, and then we'd all go to bed and the parents would switch. Once I got sick and I went to find my mother and she was in bed with this other man—he was—" She stopped herself. "Anyway, in your class . . . your class was like *church* or something."

As if by way of apology, Mickelsson put his hand back on her shin.

She leaned forward a little, rounding her back. She said, "Every time I went into your class I'd feel better. I felt all at once like possibly there might be things to *do* in the world. I'd go back to the dorm and I'd feel like singing. Really! Only then there was nothing at all to do. I'd read Aristotle, and I mean, it sucked. And then this one time you told Alan I was smart. I'd hardly noticed him. I mean he's so, well—" Her eyes narrowed. "I mean I know he's an asshole. Anyway, he asked me to go to this meeting with him, and he told me what you said. . . . He hadn't noticed if I was smart or not, himself—nobody does—but because you told him I was, he believed it. . . ."

Mickelsson asked, blushing, "What made you a swimmer?"

She flicked a look at him. "My parents had a pool." Her lips stretched diagonally, making a face. "They had me swimming before I could walk. They put me in when I was one year old. They'd read this book. I took off like a fish, swimming underwater—at least that's what they say. All over my room they had pictures of Mark Spitz and Johnny Weismuller, Esther Williams. . . . There was a class at the Y. For babies. I was 'fabulous.' My mom's word."

"How did *you* feel?"

She shrugged. "I thought it was fabulous. What did I know?"

"And now?"

She lowered her eyes. "I like it."

"I understand you're still fabulous."

She nodded.

Mickelsson gently patted her foot. As if to himself he said, "You worried me, the way you kept looking out the window. I thought you were seeing through my lies."

"You were lying?"

"Not on purpose."

She nodded again. "What I was really doing, I was thinking about how you looked sort of half sitting on the desk, half laying across it, up on one elbow. Some ways you're so fussy, and yet there you'd sprawl. It sort of took back what you said."

"The reclining Buddha."

She grinned, glancing at him sideways. "I noticed how it bothered you that you were overweight. You look better now, but you know, people always get stouter when they're middle-aged."

He noticed that he was stroking her lower leg, not seductively but as if she were a child or a cat. He pressed down just a little harder, as if to erase what he'd done, then removed his hand. "I've got to get back home. You're OK now, aren't you?"

She shook her head.

"You're not OK?"

"I guess," she said.

He felt a sudden, urgent need to give instruction, though the dizziness was with him again. "Listen, don't put up with anything you don't want to," he said. "Women do that too much. Men too. On the other hand, don't be too hurt by betrayals, don't be too final. . . ." He blushed. Rhetoric. "People hardly ever intend real harm," he said. "They're just weak and stupid, or attached to bad ideas, and then embarrassed and defensive. You see—" He broke off. He blushed more darkly than before and looked away. "Alan's a good, generous boy," he said. "It's true that, like all of us, he's prone to error. . . ."

"I'll break his fucking neck," she said.

She spoke so earnestly he had to smile, looking up at her face. "Might be a good idea," he said after an instant. "Show him he's important to you. Or maybe find somebody new, somebody who's never betrayed anybody yet, and break *his* neck, let him know right off the bat how you feel. Start clean."

"I should have done that to Alan the first time he spoke to me."

Mickelsson feebly shook his head. "You have to realize—a famous singer, pretty in her way . . ."

"Ugly as a rat."

"Well, yes . . . Spark of the divine, though."

"You think so? Even rats?"

"Beware of tribal narrowness, my child." He sadly raised his hand, palm out. "Reject speciesism!" He rose from the bedside as he spoke.

Brenda reached up with one finger and touched his raised hand. Her eyebrows, darker than her hair, went out from the bridge of her nose like hawk's wings. "If my father were like you," she said, "I'd be a saint."

"You are a saint."

She nodded. "True."

"We're still friends?" He moved toward the door.

She looked at him thoughtfully, then shrugged and smiled, meaning, *Why not?*

"Good-night, Brenda."

She nodded again, then stopped smiling. "Shit," she said. She closed her eyes.

9

He awakened briefly to a sound of clanking machinery and big engines; construction work on the road, he thought, then slept again. He found himself reasoning with a large, dark figure with its back turned, quite literally a mountain of a man, and robed in the darkest black imaginable, but no more frightening, once one got talking to him, than McPherson in Mickelsson's graduate-school days. He'd done the right thing, Mickelsson insisted, not so much pleading his case as explaining—he'd done the right thing in gently separating his life from the life of Jessie Stark. She'd had sorrows enough; and so had he. He would not judge her—he was pleasantly conscious of his virtue in saying this, and he meant it sincerely —but the woman he'd seen on the couch with Tillson was not what the child-angel within him cried out for. Reality did not contain anywhere what his heart cried out for. He would therefore ask for nothing, and take nothing. Live in truce with the universe, here in his comfortable, dark mountains. When he thought of his children, or what his wife had been like once, or of the photograph of Jessie at twenty-five, he was of course a little grieved; but that would pass. He would not die, that was his decision; in a small way, he would let the world die. Resignation. How obvious the solution, now that he'd come to it; and how little philosophy it took, in fact. Not a solution at all, a problem outgrown. When the figure said nothing, he reached up a little timidly to tap its back and draw its attention. His hand touched not a form but an absence—chilly, damp air like the air in a cave.

"How can this be?" he cried, rushing up to a great, silent crowd of people who waited wearily, some sitting, some standing, among their suitcases and trunks. The clothes were old and drab, and the men had not shaved in days—nor had the women, for at least as long, combed their hair. Their bus or train or plane had apparently been delayed indefinitely. In the dream it did not seem odd at all that he should reach out to them, pleading for advice or, at least, agreement. He touched the powdery dry sleeve of a bearded old man's coat, telling him his story. He'd finally shaken old Nietzsche's satanic hold on him, he said, seeing the great philosopher only for what he was: not as the destroyer and absolute doubter he noisily, mockingly proclaimed himself, but as a man tortured by holiness, maddened by hypocrisy, stupidity, and cowardice, furious at Christianity for the destruction of all that was holy and good, sweet-tempered, noble, as he'd said himself in his famous parable of the madman who rushes into the village crying "Whither is God? I shall tell you: *We have killed him—you and I!*" (Nietzsche the misanthrope, yet passionate lover of humanity, who had said, "The men with whom we live resemble a field of ruins of the most precious sculptural designs, where everything shouts at us: 'Come, help, perfect! . . . We yearn immeasurably to become whole!' "); Nietzsche the Lutheran minister's son, hounded even on the highest mountains, where he regularly fled, by the ghost of the Reich-loving, good-German father of Protestantism, master musician and' monstrous hate-monger (who had written: "What shall we Christians do now with this depraved and damned people of the Jews? . . . I will give you my faithful advice. First that one should set fire to their synagogues. . . . Then that one should also break down and destroy their houses. . . . That one should drive them out of the countryside!")—Luther whose Christ had in the end turned Nietzsche into a self-styled Antichrist, though he was nothing of the kind: God's dog, or at worst, a classically defective Christian, guilty of Pride, as Luther was tormented by Pride and more, finally even Sloth, rolling over for order, hierarchy, harmony, good German monk that, in the end, he was (but Nietzsche had, in his final great madness, debased himself, throwing himself down, to no avail, before Cosima Wagner, admitting at last, symbolically, however futilely, the necessity of what he'd dismissed from his system, amazing grace; whereas Luther remained to the end self-righteous and stiff-necked, for all his rhetorical self-abasement—remained, in Mickelsson's grandfather's phrase, a sinner besmutted beyond all washing but the Lord's) . . . not that Mickelsson was blind to his own sins, mainly Wrath and Despair. . . . "What choice have I," Mickelsson asked, "but the wisdom of the Orient: self-abnegation?" He said, leaning closer, "I will become one more piece of the world! No more ego! I'll make furniture—good, solid, comfortable pieces. No more thought!" The nose of the man with whom he spoke began to move. It was not a nose, he noticed now, but a bird. When it began to beat its wings, he jerked awake.

Mid-day. He stared at the guest-bedroom ceiling, lying on his left side, remembering everything, then looked over at the door he would in a few more minutes go through, beginning his new, more narrowly circum-scribed life. He listened for sounds downstairs. Nothing. He noticed that, new as it was, the paint on the guest-bedroom door was cracking, and he felt a twinge of irritation. That was the kind of thing he must learn to put up with.

Yet he felt a strange uneasiness creeping up on him, as if there were something important he was supposed to do and had not done. Suddenly it came to him that the feeling was not free-floating guilt but fear, in-creasing by leaps and bounds. He held his breath and confirmed what a part of him had known for minutes now: he was not the only one breathing in the room. He rolled slowly away from the door onto his back, groping across the bed with his right hand until he came to ice-cold fingers—a hand that seized his tightly and hung on.

The next thing he knew he was standing in the hallway, clutching his head in his two hands, bent over from the pain of his heart's pounding, whispering to himself, and the guest bedroom, behind him, was empty. Perhaps the old woman had simply vanished; perhaps she'd gotten up, a little after him, and had moved away out of his line of vision. He straightened up, breathing deeply, and at last, unable to think what else to do, he went back into the bedroom, looking around carefully, seized his clothes from the chair and his shoes from beside the bed and carried them downstairs to the kitchen, where he dressed.

He raised his face toward the kitchen ceiling, listening, once more holding his breath. Not a sound. For a long moment he stood scratching his head with both hands, trying to think; then abruptly he lowered his hands: there was nothing to think about. The old woman had finally noticed him; had turned her rage from the foolish old man to one more deserving of her stronger-than-the-grave indignation.

No danger, he thought. No ghost in the world has the power to move a wing of the most delicate moth off course.

Once again the clankings and groaning engine sounds penetrated to his consciousness. He looked out the kitchen door. Halfway up the mountain behind his house, just below the woods, two bulldozers were tearing a huge brown gouge across his field. Below the gouge, trucks and cars were parked. Fifteen or twenty men and women in dark, drab clothing stood watching the tractors or working with picks and shovels. When he opened the door and stepped out to see what the devil was going on, the whole thing vanished, the engine sounds abruptly breaking off. A small, dark bird sang on the ice-crusted telephone wire.

In the doorway between the kitchen and livingroom he stopped, staring in astonishment. His son had arrived. He lay asleep in his rumpled clothes on the couch in the destroyed, now cleaned-up livingroom. Carefully Mickelsson approached and touched him, to see if he was real, then sniffed his hair, as if the sense of smell might be more worthy of trust than touch. The boy was dressed in black, his face to the back cushions of the couch. He half awakened now and turned his head, opening his eyes. "Hi, Dad." He smiled. Mickelsson burst into tears. "You're home," he said. "Are you all right?" For some reason, something in the boy's expression, he pressed his ear to Mark's chest. If the heart was beating, he couldn't hear it. When Mickelsson raised his head to look at Mark's face, the boy smiled and let his hand fall onto Mickelsson's—the hand was warm—then closed his eyes and, perhaps without meaning to, drifted back into sleep. With his free hand Mickelsson patted Mark's shoulder, or perhaps the cushion, or some pile of old clothes, maybe nothing at all.

Mark was still asleep at five o'clock that afternoon. Mickelsson moved restlessly, hardly making a sound except for a doglike whimpering of pleasure that he could have stopped at any moment, as a sick man can stop his moans. The ghosts or devils he'd thought he was rid of stood watching.

At seven o'clock that night, he realized that Mark was going to sleep for a long time. No doubt he'd been hitch-hiking for days; perhaps he had walked for miles. In Mark's duffle-bag, Mickelsson found objects he did not think he himself could have placed there by imagination: three cakes of yeast, a cardboard box containing riceballs. Surely Mark was really there. Mickelsson took a bath, strenuously thinking. Even when he squinted, his bad eyelid did not move. Outside the bathroom door, he could hear the old woman pottering about, as if waiting for him. It came to him what he must do.

He brushed past her and went to his bedroom to stand peering like a mole into his closet. A musty, dead smell poured out of it. He found a gray, striped suit he hadn't worn since his last convention, a French-cuffed shirt—he could find no cufflinks, but it would do, no one would notice—a Liberty tie, and in a plastic cleaner's bag, his scarlet huntsman's coat. He got an image of dead foxes, then banished it. If the coat had moth holes, she would not notice at first glance. He dressed, surprised at how easily the fly zipped clear to his slimmed-down waist. He slipped the scuffed belt through the loops and buckled it. He admired himself in the mirror, first head-on, then sideways. To tone down the redness of his face he patted a little plaster dust onto his skin like powder, then checked the mirror again. Much better. He darkened his eyebrows with a ballpoint pen, then extended his arms, smiling and bowing. "How do you do?" he said, and bowed. He tried it again. "How do you *do*?" Rifkin, behind his right shoulder, bared his teeth, disgusted. "You're faking this, Mickelsson," he said: "why?" Mickelsson drew out his pipe, stuck it jauntily in his mouth, pulled in his belly and threw out his chest and smiled as if for a snapshot. "Because I'm a coward," he said. "Why do you think priests wear funny hats?"

Uncertainty flashed through him, but instantly he quashed it. His shoes were lumpy, farmerish, and he had no black shoepolish. But if he carried himself properly, who would notice?

He heard the pump switch on, down in the cellar, and thought of the furnace. He was almost out of wood for the stove, too. What if his son were frozen when he got back? Like a Congressman, an oil magnate, a blood-red UFO, an angel, he floated to the head of the stairs, tugged at his coat, then with ceremonial steps went down.

At the foot of the stairs the old man stood bent forward, clasping his hands, staring out through the glass in the door to the porch.

Mickelsson shook his head and waved both hands. "Go away, devil. How can I help you when I can't help myself?"

The old man stared on, forlorn. Mickelsson went into the slain livingroom to get Jessie's gloves in their box. Mark was still asleep, lying on his back now. His face was pale; the hair, carrot-red, fell around his features like a clown-wig. He stirred but did not waken when Mickelsson bent down and kissed his forehead.

In his study closet Mickelsson found an Irish fisherman's cap with a feather in it, slightly mashed from careless storage, and at the coatrack in the hallway he drew on his black leather gloves and chose a cane, the silver-headed one. Then, with a nod to the figure at the sink—the old woman, heavy as a graveyard angel—he went out, softly floating, dismayed by the direction he must go to escape the fly-bottle.

The sky was full of stars. In the snow just short of the woods, six deer looked down at him. He saluted with his cane, like a general ordering the charge. All deer, bless their hearts, are virgins. He opened the Jeep door to put his cane in, slanting it along a fold in the thick black bear-rug where it would ride; then for a moment, eyes widened to miss nothing, he stood sniffing the breeze. It smelled sweet, and there was a rattling, roaring sound that he recognized after an instant as the waterfall. Thaw was upon them at last. Spring on its way. No applause! He raised both hands.

Carefully, trying not to damage his coat, Mickelsson climbed in, found his key—heaven was with him; it was the first his fingers touched—and switched on the ignition. The motor sputtered, coughed, then roared, jiggling the cab; the universal joint grumbled. No harm; happens on the best of planets. He pulled at his hatbrim and shoved in the clutch.

On the way to town he thought nothing, riding the world. He felt the old woman coming behind him, a blackness across the whole southern sky in the rear-view mirror.

To his surprise and horror, he found when he reached Jessie's house that the place was all lit up; she was having a party. Darkness rose behind the house, as if he were still in the Endless Mountains. Though he stopped the Jeep at a little space of curb right in front of her house—a space he might have thought, in another mood, had been miraculously saved for him—it seemed to him clear that he'd be a fool to go in. What fantasies one worked up, out there in the country! While he'd indulged himself, holed up like a woodchuck, far from human intercourse and its sweet travail, her life—their lives—had gone on, here in town, inevitably drifting apart from his, as irrevocably distancing as the endless drift of galaxies, and now, now that Mickelsson had found his bearings, he must acknowledge the truth, that it had taken him too long. *All right,* he thought. He looked down at the grand red coat and the black leather gloves, the knightly garb with which he'd meant to stun his Cosima, kingly suitor arriving in tarnished splendor to ask his lady's hand. He looked down at the cane and the glossy black bear-rug to his right, grand tsarist cloak over the Jeep's old battered plastic seats, broken springs.

He would sit for just a few seconds longer, looking in.

He became aware of the Jeep's steady jiggling and the rumbling of the motor, the clouds of oily smoke pouring up from the rear end like special effects from a clown-car in the circus, and partly because of the waste of gas, partly because he was sure to be noticed if he left the thing running, he turned off the engine. The jiggling stopped and an impression of silence leaped up all around him. Only an impression, he realized at once, because now he was aware of the sounds of the party, crisp and clean, comforting as music in the streetlamp-haloed air. He could hear voices and the sound of the stereo no one was listening to—good old Haydn, or else Mozart (he could never get the difference)—and all around him, here outside, another sound, subtle yet surprisingly distinct, once it caught one's attention: water moving gently in the gutter under his tires, occasional plump drops hitting the Jeep's tin roof.

Beyond the lighted doorbell and the parted curtains, Jessie's house was teeming with life. He could see shapes, undoubtedly people he knew, some of them anyway. It was a large party, probably allies. The moving silhouettes in the windows weighed on his heart. Sometimes on summer nights, in the big Wisconsin farmhouse, his mother and father had had parties like that—he could no longer guess what the occasion might have been; maybe family reunions. He and his cousins had looked in from the lawn, eager aliens, at the rooms full of grown-ups who moved back and forth beyond the curtains and drapes, eating and drinking, talking happily, their noise coming out into the huge, star-filled night, both loud and oddly distant, as if lost already in vanishing time. Ah, how he had loved them—those majestic grown-ups of his childhood, farm people gathered from far and wide, some of them not even names to him, but bright with life, luminous-faced Olsens, Johnsons, Ericksons, here and there a Schmidt or a Dupree. How he—and no doubt the cousins around him—had longed to be grown-up like them, making shy little jokes at the pretty young woman with braids wrapped tight as a glove around her head! And ah, how he loved these strangers too—these defenders of Jessie Stark—or potential defenders—against the powers of barbarism! "Sentimental, you may say," he said to the heavy, breathing darkness around him, and brushed tears from his cheeks, "but perhaps you judge too quickly. These are all we can honestly call our own, these shitty human beings." Granted, he should love the barbarians too—so reason demanded—since they too were human, and alive; and perhaps he did. However strong his feelings for Jessie, it was all still partly just war-games. Sitting like a stranger, looking in (God's spy), he could hardly miss how much there was of play in all these antics—here a grand party of anticipated victory or mourned defeat, somewhere else (down in basements in another part of the city, he liked to think) the crazy-bearded Marxists (some of them, he corrected himself) planning further strategy, banging tables with their fists. All his kinsmen, or none.

He became aware of dogs. They seemed to materialize from everywhere at once, at the sides of houses, on porches, or walking—fake casual —across the damp, shiny street. One in particular: a golden Lab bitch— ghostly or living, he could not tell—looking up at him with puzzlement and interest from the sidewalk in front of Jessie's house. She seemed about to speak.

Very well, he thought, he would expand his view: partisan of the whole world's mammalian life. Take up Peter Singer's line: animal liberation. But mammalian life was it, his limit. Well, maybe birds. He sent his thought to the Lab: We understand, don't we! Happy the snake, eggs indifferently buried in the earth and forsaken!

The night seemed to be building toward a winter thunderstorm.

Time to leave, he thought. The darkness at his back stepped closer. The same instant, he saw Jessie's face at a window, looking out, luminous as a moon. She seemed not to see the Jeep. Her face was like a heart, a flower. Her eyes bespoke something else. Terrible watchfulness. With a shock, he remembered making love to her.

The dogs sat observing, not barking yet, wondering what this hushed red beast might be up to. He became aware that Lincoln Street was also full of cats, some of them visible at windows or on porches, others not visible, psychically warm places in houses up and down the block. He felt the freezing chill that meant the old woman was right behind him. *"Help me,"* he whispered, but there was no one to help, and his mind had quit, utterly resourceless.

Then on Jessie's front porch he saw that someone was standing looking out at him, smoking a cigarette. Where he'd come from so suddenly, Mickelsson couldn't guess, but he knew the man's appearance was a gift, a sign. The shape of the man was familiar, though Mickelsson couldn't place it. He wore no coat. Perhaps he'd stepped out for a minute to escape the noise—yet that seemed not right. He was looking at the Jeep as if he'd seen it from inside and, pleased that Mickelsson had come, had stepped out to offer him greetings.

Again Mickelsson thought in dismay of the great confidence with which he'd dressed in his best and driven here to Jessie's, imagining a man could simply step into life again as if nothing ever changed. The light of the man's cigarette brightened, then dimmed. He seemed not to notice the cold at all. He stood very still in the soft, spring-scented breeze. Something touched Mickelsson's shoulder, making him cry out.

Abruptly, before he knew he meant to do it, Mickelsson got out of the Jeep, snatched up his cane and the box containing Jessie's gloves, and went briskly up the walk.

"Well, well!" he said, "it seems I've come on the right night." He could smell the man's cigarette.

"Yes you have," the man said. There was nothing in his eyes, and the movement of his mouth did not seem to mesh with his words. "I was afraid you'd decided you shouldn't come in." He smiled. He had surprisingly crooked teeth. His voice, like a dream voice, made Mickelsson's bowels go weak.

For four heartbeats Mickelsson said nothing. Then at last he said, "You're Buzzy, I take it?"

Again the man smiled. His face, Mickelsson realized only now, was decayed, horrible. The flesh had fallen away from the bone of his nose. "I am. Yes." He bowed.

"Jessie has spoken of you often," Mickelsson said. "She misses you terribly, as I'm sure you're aware."

The dead man nodded, his look noting and forgiving the fatuousness. "Shall we go in?"

"I don't suppose," Mickelsson said, flexing the fingers of his gloves, "there's any reason for us to try and . . . talk?"

"Talk?" the dead man asked hollowly, and put his hand on Mickelsson's elbow—ice ran up Mickelsson's arm—"why should we stand around and talk?"

Mickelsson nodded. "Will she be angry at my barging in like this?"

The dead man studied him gravely, what remained of his mouth drawn to the left; then he asked—mouth unmoving—"How should *I* know?" With a gentle pressure on his elbow, he floated Mickelsson toward the light.

Jessie, when she opened the door, head lifted, stared at him in amazement, her smile frozen. She was unnaturally awake, like a deer, a hind. She seemed five years older, thinner, grayer, the flesh beginning to loosen from the bone. She looked from his foolish, fixed smile to the wooden box he'd immediately thrust into her hands, then to his red coat, then back at his face. A wince fixed itself around her eyes. At last, by an act of will, she forced back her smile. "Mickelsson!" she said. Clearly she couldn't see the corpse of her husband at Mickelsson's side, gazing indifferently around the blurry, aqueous room. She read the words on the box, *Jessie's Gloves*, wonderfully ornate, and she laughed, then blushed. She put the box on the table by the door. Mickelsson leaned his cane beside it. "Thank you," she said. "It's very—nice."

He caught her right hand in both of his. "Listen, Jessie. I know this is rude. I sat outside awhile—" He laughed and nervously looked past her, giving a nod to her assembled guests, then looked back into her face. He wished he'd taken his leather gloves off. With great self-control, he said, "I came to make certain protestations. If you'd like, I could go down on one knee."

"Don't you dare!" she said, widening her eyes. He saw that she was trying to make out whether or not she would need help.

Tillson drifted near, the fingertips of one hand pressed to his heart.

"I'm not crazy," Mickelsson said. "I'm just faking because I'm scared. I'm not drunk either. Smell my breath." Before she could pull away, he leaned close to her and breathed. Tillson stopped five feet off.

"For the love of *Christ*," Jessie whispered, then searched his face, stretching her mouth as if to laugh, then went expressionless. She too pressed her fingertips to her heart. "Were you planning to come in?" she asked, clearly undecided about whether or not she would let him. She stole a glance past her shoulder into the room. He saw young Levinson in the distance, eyeing them.

"I was. To make a long story short," he said, "I love you."

She put both hands to her face, fingertips at the temples. The corners of her lips began to tremble. "All right come in," she said. "But watch yourself!"

"I want to marry you," he said.

Now she did laugh, trying not to, and covered her mouth with one hand. She looked at him. "You got a real sense of timing, Mickelsson."

Edie Bryant burst from nowhere. "Peter!" she exclaimed. "See! The conquering hero comes! It's Peter Mickelsson!" Then she too froze, smiling and staring.

Then Blickstein was beside Edie Bryant, pushing past her and even past Jessie, stretching out both hands to embrace him, maybe wrestle him. "My God!" he cried, grinning. "Pete, you son of a gun!" His hands closed firmly on Mickelsson's elbows, biting in hard, and his face came forward, teeth bared like a chimp's.

"Hi!" Mickelsson said with a grin. (With a smile? With a manly grin?) "Work, work, work!" He winked. He locked his knees, preparing to break Blickstein's hold.

The decayed, waxen face of Buzzy Stark leaned close and said, "I'll get you a drink. Lemon twist?"

"That would be lovely," Mickelsson said.

Jessie, at the dean's shoulder, jerked her eyes up to Mickelsson's face, then looked at where Buzzy had been just an instant before.

Mickelsson remembered his hat and gently struggled to free his right elbow from the dean's grasp. The dean would not let go. Mickelsson snapped free, gave Blickstein a little jaw-tap, open-handed, and—while the dean stared, astonished—managed to remove the hat, then the gloves, and dropped them on the table beside his cane. Blickstein caught his arm, squeezing hard, grinning again, eyes wide. Mickelsson thought of breaking free and flattening him, but smiled. Jessie came close, pushing in beside the dean, on her face an angry, determined look, a bright glow, almost flame.

As if she were herself a ghost, Mabel Garret appeared from nowhere, smiling at him like a cat, a forest-green light coming out of her, and a smell of burnt wood, then moved her eyes toward where Buzzy Stark was floating through the crowd toward the liquor cabinet. For an instant it seemed to Mickelsson that the room was empty except for Mabel Garret, Jessie, and the dead man.

"Hello, Mabel," he said.

She slid her eyes toward Jessie.

Jessie said suddenly, "I know it must really have pissed you off that I didn't invite you, Peter." She glanced at Blickstein. "Shel, leave him alone."

"No no! Good heavens, no!" Mickelsson said. "Believe me, I don't blame you!" He looked around. "What a wonderful party!" Then, leaning toward her, making his face tragic, "I really must talk to you alone for a minute. Is it possible? Don't tell me no. Dearest lady, I *pray* you!"

Levinson drifted nearer, hands in coatpockets, eyebrows forming a solid wedge.

Jessie threw a look around, checking her troops. The dean and Tillson watched intently. Tillson had put down his glass, on his face a tortured, pitiful expression. His left hand consoled his right. Now Mickelsson saw Blickstein's young friend on the couch, Professor Warren's wife, beside old Mrs. Meyerson. Both of them stared at him. The young woman's face was electric. There were dark circles under her eyes, but otherwise she seemed well, even radiant. It crossed his mind that she might be an ally. She would have heard by now about Lawler's arrest. Mrs. Meyerson was licking frosting off a napkin, looking up furtively, hoping she wasn't being watched.

"I take it this is the get-up you put on for your episodes?" Jessie said in his ear. "Do you really feel you need it?"

"Please let me talk to you," he said. "I stand before you a humble suppliant."

"Jesus Christ," she said. She pushed her hair back angrily. "Mickelsson, you *ass*."

"Please, Jessie, little bird, gentle thrush—"

"Either you're crazy and I should call the police, or you're the most shameless, devious—"

"Please," he said, and, surprising himself, burst into tears.

"This way," Jessie said suddenly, and seized his hand firmly, as a boy would.

"Jess—" the dean said warningly. His hand closed more tightly on Mickelsson's elbow. Jessie gave him a look, and after an instant the dean's hand opened and he bent his head, like a barber finished with a job. Tillson came up and spoke into Jessie's ear. She shook her head, gazing as if from a great distance at Mickelsson, reaching back, holding Mickelsson's hand. She said to Tillson, "No." She slammed her smile at him and after an instant he backed off like a servingman.

The dead man handed Mickelsson his drink. Then Mickelsson continued down the hallway with Jessie, walking in a foggy dream, swaying a little, courtly. Behind them, Edie Bryant held her arm out, preventing anyone from following. In the bedroom, he closed the door behind them and released Jessie's hand to click the lock. Jessie met his eyes, her face like polished steel, then decided to look away. The room, after the livingroom, was unnervingly quiet. Jessie's stillness alarmed him.

The bed was piled high with coats, remains of a zoo's worth of animals—sheep, mink, otter, seal. . . . (Bryant would not like that.) She stood beside the bed, furtively brushing at the sides of her eyes with two fingers, looking around for a place to sit. At last she sat on top of the coats and covered her mouth and nose with her hands, breathing deeply. A shudder ran through her shoulders; her eyes settled on Mickelsson. Then she was still again.

"Jesus, if you could *see* yourself," she said.

"I feel fine!"

"You feel fine." She glanced at the locked door. Now she lowered her hands from her mouth and looked hard at the floor. Her shoulders drew inward.

He remembered the martini in his hand. "You want a sip?"

She looked up at him, then reached up and took the glass. He used the occasion to pull off his scarf and coat. After she'd sipped, she swallowed hard, as if the gin had burned her throat. She looked at his hands, then handed the glass back.

He smiled, then asked, "Did I tell you I saw the picture of you in the paper?"

She jerked her head away, then quickly wiped her cheek and shook her head. "What do you want?" she asked.

He said, "Come live with me and be my love, and we will all the pleasures prove—"

"Stop it!" she cried.

"What's the matter?"

"Nothing," she said, quieting herself. "Thank you for your . . . affection. I have a party to attend to." Now her two hands were pressed to her knees. Her eyes were clamped shut.

He crouched down in front of her, tears blinding him, and put his right hand on her two hands. "Jessie," he said, "it's true that the get-up is a fraud. But the craziness is real. You have to help me. If I had my way, I'd come to you as the perfect lover, flawless golden lion. . . ."

"Go home," she said. "Peter—" She drew in breath, then said softly, shaking her head a little, "Go fuck yourself."

"I can't," he said.

Her hands closed tightly around his. "It was you, wasn't it," she said, "the one who looked in at us, in Geoffrey's office."

"It was an accident. Anyway, I've done something much worse."

"I'm sure," she said.

"I murdered someone, Jessie," he said.

She stared at him.

He said, "Would you like another drink?"

Seconds passed. Then she reached for his glass.

Slowly, deliberately, Mickelsson began to lift the coats off the bed and lay them on the carpet, neat as a launderer.

She said, "What do you mean? What are you telling me?" She did not think to hand him the glass back, placing it instead on the bedside table.

He sat down beside her. "If you don't hold me in your arms, Jessie . . ."

She hesitated, then put her arms around him. As if on second thought, she closed them around him tightly. He closed his arms just as tightly around her. Without his quite knowing how it happened, they were lying side by side, the coats she'd been sitting on pushed off onto the floor. He held her still more tightly, pressing his lips to her throat. She was saying, "What are you telling me? Are you crazy? Who did you murder?"

"Whom," he corrected.

"Jesus fucking Christ," she said. Her embrace loosened, then tightened so that he could hardly breathe. He kissed her throat, then the notch of her collarbone, then nuzzled toward her breasts.

"Peter, what are you *doing*?" she whispered. "Peter! Stop that!"

When he opened his eyes he saw that she was staring at the ceiling. Light came from her skin.

Outside the room there was not a sound.

"Listen," he said, unbuttoning her blouse, "I'm glad you reminded me. My mother may have to live with us."

"I said *stop* it!" Jessie whispered, stopping his hands. Her eyes were wide, as if with terror. Panic stirred in him. For an instant he was aware of his heart thudding, booming like a drum; then it came to him that it was her heart. She changed her mind and let his hands continue with the buttons.

"My mother's old, you see," he said. "Lonely—" His panic increased. "Also, my son's come home."

She rocked her head from side to side, her arms still holding him tight. "Jesus," she said.

His hands stopped. "You don't love me?"

"Are you crazy?"

His shaking grew violent.

She raised her head, eyes still wide open, wary, staring as if in amazement, then kissed his cheek—quickly, twice.

She allowed him to raise her torso and remove her blouse, then her brassière. He mouthed her left nipple.

"Do you realize, you crazy bastard," she asked, "that there are *people* out there? Do you think they don't know what we're *doing*?"

"Listen," he said, unsnapping her skirt. *We're*, she had said. The room was full of ghosts, none of them very solid yet, some with their hands to their jaws, looking thoughtful, some grinning obscenely, some timidly looking away. The sky outside the windows glowed, then darkened.

"The thing *is*," she whispered, ". . . don't, Mickelsson! Wait! Do we love each other? And whom did you murder? What's *happening*?"

"How do I love thee? Let me count the ways," he said.

"Don't!" she said angrily and raised her fist to hit him, then stopped herself.

"How do *you* feel?" he asked.

"Christ, that's not the *point*," she said. "That's *never* been the point."

As he kissed her she gave him her lips only for an instant, then drew back, looking at the door. "God damn it," she said, "I'm not *finished*."

He waited.

"You're crazy," she said. "I have to think about that, Peter! You have these episodes—and even *fake* episodes—"

"All the same, I protest to you enduring love," he said.

A knock came at the door, loud and astonishingly close, and Gretchen Blickstein's voice called, "Jessie?"

Jessie listened, going still all over, then called, "It's all right." In the silence that followed he felt her holding her breath.

"Oh, Pete," she whispered then, and—as if on second thought—wrapped her arms still more tightly around him.

"Jessie?" another voice called.

"It's all right," he whispered. "Believe me, it's all right."

Buzzy Stark's head and left shoulder came easily through the shiny panelling of the door. His lightless eyes carefully did not look at them. "I'll deal with it," he said.

"Was that—?" Jessie began.

There was a knocking at the door, urgent.

"Just a couple of minutes," Jessie called. From her tone, not even God could have guessed what was happening.

Carefully, Mickelsson eased her skirt and pantyhose down over her beautiful hips, her regal dark and silvery patch of hair. Astonished, the fingertips of his right hand traced her ilium. His nose hovered close to her armpit, ravished. There was a rumbling sound. Beyond the nearest window, just visible against the night, bones were tumbling onto the lawn, clattering in the street, booming like falling boulders, dropping out of nowhere.

Quickly, as if the world had gone unspeakably weird, Jessie sat up, breasts dangling, and began the unbuttoning of his shirt, the unhooking of his belt-buckle, unzipping of his fly. Gently, with a crazy smile, she drew his stiff penis out. Beyond the farther window, blood was falling, swooshing and boiling as it hit. From high in the night overhead came silvery human laughter.

"All those people right outside the door," she whispered. "Jesus! I don't believe it!" Eyes sparkling, smiling wildly, she lay back for him.

"Ah!" cried Mickelsson, shoving himself in.

"Sweet Christ!" she whispered, eyes snapping shut. Her head rocked from side to side, then tensed. Her pelvis thrust violently, consuming him. He couldn't have pulled out if he'd wished.

Now the bedroom was packed tight with ghosts, not just people but also animals—minks, lynxes, foxes—more than Mickelsson or Jessie could name, and there were still more at the windows, oblivious to the tumbling, roaring bones and blood, the rumbling at the door, though some had their arms or paws over their heads—both people and animals, an occasional bird, still more beyond, some of them laughing, some looking away (Mormons, Presbyterians), some blowing their noses and brushing away tears, some of them clasping their hands or paws and softly mewing, shadowy cats, golden-eyed tigers (Marxist atheists, mournful Catholics) . . . pitiful, empty-headed nothings complaining to be born. . . .

A NOTE ON THE TYPE

The text of this book was set on the Linotype
in a type face called Baskerville. The face is a facsimile
reproduction of types cast from molds made for John Baskerville (1706–75)
from his designs. The punches for the revived Linotype Baskerville
were cut under the supervision of the English printer George W. Jones.
John Baskerville's original face was one of the forerunners
of the type style known as "modern face"
to printers—a "modern" of the period A.D. 1800.

Composed by Maryland Linotype
Composition Company, Baltimore, Maryland.
Printed and bound by Haddon Craftsmen,
Scranton, Pennsylvania.

Typography and binding design by
Albert Chiang.

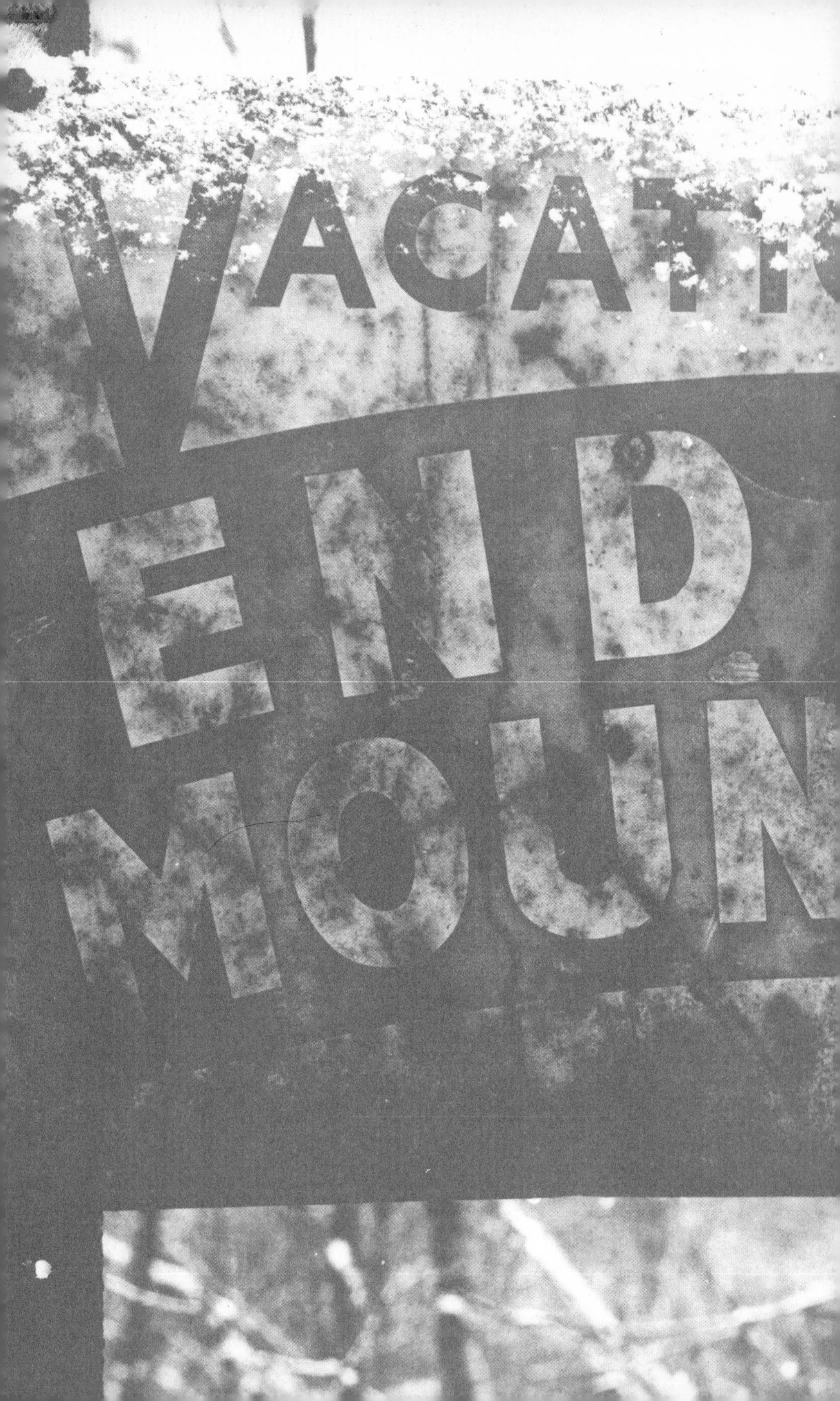
VACATI
END
MOUN